EMPIRE ENDER

EMPIRE ENDER

TORTH BOOK SIX

ABBY GOLDSMITH

Podium

Published in 2025 by Podium Publishing
www.podiumentertainment.com

EMPIRE ENDER

THE NAMELESS LURKER

The nameless lurker traveled in slow space for seven sleep-wake cycles. His late-model luxury streamship vacuumed space dust and random particles out of the way so he could cross parsecs of emptiness at reckless speeds.

He approached the enemy's freehold in stealth mode.

The Giant scanned this reject solar system on a regular basis, which kept most Torth away. The nameless lurker was unafraid. As a Servant of All, he understood the logistical impossibility of scanning vast tracts of space, so he knew the Giant would regularly miss large areas. Besides, the Conqueror had reputedly instructed his oversize minion to welcome any lone singleton vessel, no doubt hoping the boy Twin or some other rogue ally would show up.

The nameless lurker docked in orbit around the gas giant planet. There he waited.

And waited.

At last, an opportune day arrived. The Giant was hit with insanity gas and went missing in action. This was a window of time in which the monster was unable to scan or protect any of his territories.

WE ARE WINNING!

Smash the runaways!

Take back Our cities!

Yay!

The dancing, singing, viciously victorious news feed was mere background noise to the nameless lurker. The Torth Majority was as meaningless as the stars that dotted the cold black sky. He tuned out their blather and piloted his personal streamship toward Reject-20.

He knew better than to land at the crude yet busy spaceport of Freedomland. Slaves were constantly training there. Instead, he aimed for deep wilderness. He flew over the dark side of the planet.

The lack of launchpads meant he had no choice but to crash-land, but he was prepared. He was an expert pilot. He controlled his crash, plowed through a bog, and ended at the base of a hillock.

He left his streamship dead and hiked for several days and nights through uninhabited jungle terrain.

Only his intensive survivalist training as a Servant of All enabled him to thrive in the alien wilderness. He sipped recycled water from his backpack gear. He ate protein bars. He was grateful for his musculoskeletal enhancements, as well as the exercise regimen he had forced himself to keep up with.

He used distraction drones and tranquilizer darts to ward off predators. Those methods only failed once. When a carnivorous megalizard ambushed him, he used his power to twist the beast's mind.

When his digital map showed that he was approaching the outskirts of Freedomland, he ditched his backpack and other gear. He stripped out of his camouflage jumpsuit and donned rags.

And a slave collar. Its shockers and pincers were disabled, but that was normal. Penitents only suffered partial slavery. Their overlords were foolishly merciful.

The nameless lurker tossed away his map, his water, his weapons—everything. Most Torth, even Servants of All, would feel vulnerable without belongings. But deprivation fit in with the lurker's regular habits.

He even considered dosing himself with the inhibitor, in case the enemies decided to search for intense life sparks in the penitent slums. But his raw power had never been quite enough for teleportation. His glow would likely be dismissed as that of an Alashani warrior, or perhaps the Conqueror himself, if anyone happened to search the city in that way. He would keep himself semidepleted just to be on the safe side.

The lurker crept into the penitent slums while the Megacosm frothed with victory celebrations.

Local penitents were too busy eyeing each other askance and worrying about their future to pay much attention to a penitent who seemed rather unfamiliar. No one looked at him twice.

Oh my. The Torth are winning.

Will the Torth (capture Us) set Us free?

Are We going to be Torth (superior and godlike) again?

Is it even possible to return to that life?

The nameless lurker passed work crews and errand runners who were lost in their own thoughts. He was fortunate to appear average in a multitude of ways. He had a gracile body type, which was the second most common type among able-bodied Torth. He was well within the average height range for an adult male raised on one of the major hub planets. He was an average age, not too wrinkled, not too baby-cheeked.

He had already doctored his ocular lenses so he did not have the ominous blank gaze that would mark him as a Servant of All. Instead, he blinked sweet iridescent-yellow irises. Yellow was the most common color. It complemented his sandy blond hair and rugged, slightly sunburned face.

? A penitent woman eyed him, wondering which barracks he slept in.

Then she lost interest. Her mind was full of concerns about her chores. The lurker sensed that if she failed to help her work crew cut enough construction planks, they would lose mealtime privileges, and they would blame her for it.

The nameless lurker knew, from years of experience, that he could make his mind appear bland. It was a talent and a technique. Voters had given him a proper name-title, of course, but he was not that person right now.

He was no one. Just another penitent.

Can I help? He approached a crew of concrete workers, their naked backs glistening with sweat. This crew only had nine laborers, not the usual ten count. They must have lost a member recently.

Please.

Yes. Please.

The laborers made room. They mentally showed him how to mix concrete and how to pour it into casting caulk. The nameless lurker matched their workflow, letting them guide his movements.

Soon he stripped off his ragged shirt. He was just as sweaty as they were.

While the crew built troughs and bollards, they engaged in silent conversation. They introduced themselves. They explained that their missing crewmate had broken her ankle and had thus been transferred to an easier assignment. She was now packaging food items in an assembly line alongside other physically disabled penitents.

So, where did you come from?

Yes, tell Us about yourself.

Who are you?

They didn't really care. They were not truly curious about the newcomer. The nameless lurker understood that they were merely hanging on to a phantom shred of civilized discourse, being polite.

Their lack of interest enabled him to offer shallow replies that aligned with their expectations. He admitted that it was strange, the way he had wandered into the concrete-mixing zone and volunteered to work. He implied that he'd had a problem with a bullying crewmate. That was enough of an explanation as to why he had requested a transfer to another work crew.

Ah.

Your previous labor crew must regret losing you, with your strong back.

Yes. You seem to have quite some energy for manual labor.

He pretended to enjoy their compliments.

It wasn't wholly pretense, of course. Mind readers could not lie to each other. The nameless lurker partitioned his mind. He let his simple enjoyment of physicality fill the forefront of his mind, eclipsing everything else. Let that represent who he was.

I can't wait until the Torth Empire sets Us free, one of the laborers thought.

Yes, another agreed. *In the meantime, at least We are mostly ignored here. We haven't been forced to undergo a mind probe by the Conqueror (yet).*

Yet, another echoed cynically.

Aw, I want that mind probe! another thought. *Then I'd get promoted to live in a household. This sunburn is killing My skin.*

Their silent chatter went on, and the nameless lurker listened.

I want to get promoted so I can live under stairs and perform a bestial act (of sex) with a supergenius.

!?

Yeah, didn't you hear that rumor?

Aw, there's no proof.

Day turned to night.

The nameless lurker accompanied his newfound coworkers to supper in a mess hall, where overseers made sure the hundreds of mind readers kept social distance between each other. Later, he followed them to their barracks. He stood while an ummin clerk noted his existence in a log file. He slept.

The next day, he breakfasted with his coworkers. He went to work again.

He learned.

If he was going to succeed in his covert mission, he could not afford to make even the slightest mistake. This city might seem foolish, dominated by slaves as it was, but it was ruled by Thomas the Conqueror. One did not challenge a renegade supergenius without a lot of preparatory work. And caution. An overabundance of caution.

So the lurker learned everything he could learn about the enemies and their rebel nation.

For seven days and seven nights, he performed manual labor and passively soaked up information.

Much about life in the penitent slums could already be found in the Megacosm. Some penitents secretly leaked their perceptions to inner audiences, so the Torth Empire had a basic concept of how Freedomland functioned and how the city was laid out. The names and faces of Kessa's lieutenants were known.

But there were extra tidbits that the nameless lurker picked up from locals. For instance, he learned potential shortcuts between major boulevards, through shops and over fences. He learned which sewers led where, and which back porches or outdoor stairwells could be used as temporary hiding spots.

He identified fifteen penitents who were ardent, if secret, Torth loyalists. He might seek their help in a crisis.

And he learned of several hundred who were fully devoted to Kessa the Wise. He remained cordial to those penitents, but he would avoid relying on anyone who worshipped the Conqueror and his minions.

The nameless lurker was unable to learn exactly where the rebel leaders slept. Penitents were not privy to war councils or military meetings. But he did learn whose minds might be scanned in order to find out more. He learned that the Conqueror typically worked inside or near the so-called Dragon Tower of the academy. The Giant and the Imposter slept inside that war palace up against the cliff, and the Imposter might use zombification victims as door sentries.

By the end of the seventh day, the nameless lurker solidified a plan.

"Is there any way I can transfer to a hauling crew?" He kept his head bowed, his face meek, as he begged an overseer for a job transfer. He made his voice sound human. "I just want a change in what I see every day. I would love to glimpse the grand buildings raised by Ariock."

The clerk made a note on his file. "We'll see. Next!"

The nameless lurker went back to work, making room for the next penitent in line who had a request.

He was in no hurry. Sooner or later, he knew, he would be allowed into the posh uptown area of the city.

Sooner or later, he would encounter a clerk or a chambermaid who had regular interactions with the enemy leadership.

He didn't need much. Just a small opportunity.

It would come.

PART ONE

I shall withhold judgment.

—Proverb for followers of Gwat

CHAPTER 1

THE GIANT AWAKENS

"You weren't in your right mind."

"The deaths were not your fault."

"You fought the effects of insanity gas."

"You did your best."

Ariock gathered pebbles of truth from the whirlwind of excuses concocted by nussian battle captains. He gathered that a lot of people had tried to stop him.

Like Thomas. He had given the initial warning.

Thomas was the Wisdom of ancient prophecy, yet everyone on the war council had dismissed his misgivings. Ariock remembered that part clearly.

Then Garrett had made multiple attempts to stop Ariock. So had Jinishta. Orla. Shevrael. Vedlor. Fayfer and the pilots of the Cloud Fleet. Garrett again and again. Garrett had nearly died in his failed attempts.

None of them were here. Maybe they were too terrified to face the Giant, after what he had done.

Ariock sat on the hastily carpeted floor of an assembly hall beneath Flawless City, the headquarters for an anti-Torth guerrilla resistance operation. More than half of his territories on the planet Nuss were now occupied by Torth. CloudShadow MetroHub and other cities were badly damaged from his earthquakes and storms.

Battle captains stood between hanging lanterns that made their armored skin shine like beaten gold or bronze. It was stuffy in the room without air-conditioning, but nussians didn't mind heat. Weptolyso crouched nearby. Evenjos had given herself a chair.

She was the one who had finally stopped him.

Evenjos had tended to Ariock like an angel, bringing him water as he woke up, answering his initial questions in a reassuring tone. He'd gotten a brief summary: Evenjos, it seemed, had overcome her fears and risked her very existence in a one-shot gamble with a nussian tranquilizer dart.

He didn't need Garrett to explain that the Transformation of Strength had come to pass. He had seen the prophetic painting.

"You were self-controlled, despite the neurotoxin," Evenjos said, as if she still needed to soothe him. "Instead of causing a planetary apocalypse, you only destroyed a desert. That required valiant self-control."

Valiant. Really?

Ariock pulled away from her. His favorite Alashani premiers and warriors were dead. Thousands of his people were dead or enslaved. It was all his fault, no matter what excuses people made for the Son of Storms.

A nussian captain rumbled, "Well, he also destroyed a few outposts."

"And a city," another one said.

Nussians could be counted on to offer the unvarnished truth. Knowledge was worth pain, as the nussian proverb went.

"Even so," Evenjos said. "That much restraint, under those conditions? It must have required immense inner strength."

The nussian captains exchanged looks to make sure none of them would dare disagree. Then they rumbled their unanimous support.

Ariock did not believe them. How many of their loved ones were dead now because of him? He felt sure that if he could read minds, he would detect seething bitterness beneath their kindness.

He needed frank bluntness. He wanted to nudge their brutal honesty to the surface.

"How many people did I kill?" Ariock asked.

"You should not look at it that way," Evenjos said. "There were deaths. But no one died because of your intent."

"It was the Torth," a captain assured him.

"No one blames you, if they understand what happened," Weptolyso said.

Ariock clenched his fists, frustrated by their forgiveness. It had to be false. Why were they afraid to tell him the plain truth? Did they fear that he would fly into a towering rage?

The nussian captains looked wary, thorns protruding.

Evenjos gripped his arm and gave him a warning look. Ariock followed her glance and saw sand and grit hanging in midair. That was not her doing.

He had subconsciously expanded his awareness.

Abashed, Ariock reeled it in, making himself as small and meek as possible. Control was vital. Control was everything. He must never allow himself to get angry, or the least bit frustrated, ever again. Anger was off-limits from now until the end of time.

He rephrased his question in a reasonable tone. "How many people died?"

Evenjos and Weptolyso exchanged looks.

"We don't know." Evenjos chose her words with care.

"More than a million," Weptolyso said.

The truth was so painful, Ariock flinched. He felt crushed by the weight of it.

But pain was what he deserved.

He braced himself, and then forced out an even more difficult question. "What happened to Jinishta?"

Weptolyso bowed his head in a gesture of mourning. "I am told she did not survive."

Ariock had believed himself ready for bad news, but it hit him harder than he expected. He had taken his albino cousin for granted. They were supposed to have a long future together, with many battles ahead.

Jinishta had befriended Thomas even though her people wanted nothing to do with *rekvehs*. She was a force of nature without being a stormbringer. Her people would follow her anywhere. And she had supported Ariock without ever challenging him. Not even once.

How would Ariock manage the Alashani without her? They wanted no part of this war.

He needed Jinishta.

He absolutely needed her.

How would he cope without her stern advice and that kindhearted nature that she kept so well hidden? She had been like an older sister to him. She had sacrificed more than anyone should.

And for what? She had died violently.

Because of him.

"Orla?" Ariock had to work to keep anxiety out of his tone. "What about Orla?" He really needed to hear something miraculous.

Evenjos shushed Weptolyso before he could rumble a response.

"He should be told," Weptolyso said.

That made the devastation obvious. Ariock curled around the pain. He had murdered some of the best people on his side. How could anyone stand to look at him?

"Fayfer is alive," Weptolyso said.

But much of the Cloud Fleet was a wreck. Pilots were missing. As for the hundred-plus warriors Ariock had brought into that desert? There weren't even any remains to bury. Ariock had folded them into the desert in his mad rage.

"We will discuss this later," Evenjos told Ariock with crisp kindness that he surely did not deserve. Her manner was almost gruff, the way Garrett might sound. "You should rest."

The suggestion was obscene in light of what Ariock had done. "I don't need more rest." Hadn't he already slept for two days while Evenjos healed him?

What he wanted, instead of unearned relaxation, was brutal honesty. He wanted a purely honest reaction to the disaster he had perpetrated.

He knew whom he needed to seek out.

Thomas would not mince words. Thomas must remember how Ariock had ignored his very explicit warning.

And why?

Because of idiocy.

After so many victories, Ariock must have begun to believe his own hype. Deep down, he must have thought he was indestructible. Now Jinishta was dead because of his erroneous pride. A million innocent people were dead. He had ignored advice from the strategic mastermind who'd made every single one of his victories possible. What sort of idiot did that?

Ariock figured he owed more apologies than he could ever give, but at least he knew where to start. He needed to give Thomas the respect he was due.

"I'm going to Reject-20." Ariock stood, avoiding one of the unlit chandeliers.

Evenjos looked more concerned than ever. "As a medical adviser," she said, "I strongly advise that you take some time before you do anything that resembles work."

How diplomatic. She was trying to keep him away from potential rage triggers.

The last anyone had heard from Freedomland, Thomas was warding off an invasion. Supercoms were no longer working, so no one knew how—or if—that battle had ended. The news reports had been chaotic and unbelievable.

For all anyone knew, Vy was a slave. Or dead.

Ariock needed to find out.

He began to put himself into a clairvoyant trance. But before he could loosen his mental tether to his body, he hesitated. Wasn't teleportation the last thing he had attempted to do before . . . ?

It was. He had tried to ghost while on insanity gas.

If it had worked, then Ariock would have lost control of his powers in Cloud-Shadow MetroHub, or even Freedomland. He could easily have destroyed everyone he loved.

Could he trust himself, even now? What if some malignant trace of the gas lingered in his system, like a ticking time bomb, waiting to activate?

"I would like to check on my mate, Yuey." Weptolyso seemed to be wrestling with his own inner worries.

Another captain swung his head in deference to Weptolyso. "We will defend our cities here. The Torth think they have won?" He snorted in disdain. "But we are still free."

That sounded heroic.

And it reminded Ariock that the free universe could not afford multiple days of his absence. During his drugged sleep, while Evenjos healed his brain, many cities under his protection had fallen. Every day he hid would likely entail another victory for the Torth.

Ariock considered combat.

But when he imagined expanding his awareness across miles of broken urban terrain, where enemies roamed . . . and getting angry . . .

There was no way around it. If he meant to rip transports out of the sky, or crush Torth with a telekinetic grip, he would have to feel strong feelings. That was what combat was. It was unrestrained rage.

Too risky. Bad idea.

Were there calmer ways in which he could support the guerrilla fighters? He could mass-teleport supplies to them. He imagined visiting various depots and survivor groups. Ariock could move troops to wherever they were most needed . . .

. . . where Torth pilots might fly overhead and spray him with insanity gas. They'd find it easy while he was in a clairvoyant trance, oblivious to the world around him.

Ariock shuddered. A familiar feeling of helplessness washed over him. He had not felt vulnerable in a long time, but it was a feeling he knew well.

The Torth Empire owned more than 99 percent of the universe. They had multiple supergeniuses. What did Ariock have against all that? What made him audacious enough to try to conquer the entire galaxy? Some crazily ambitious friends? Some ancient prophecies?

"Will you help us fight, Son of Storms?" a battle captain asked.

Ariock really wanted to help. Perhaps he would consider workarounds? Maybe he could carry tranquilizer darts and inject himself if he began to feel the least bit irrationally angry?

But he wanted to discuss any ideas with Thomas first. All plans ought to come from the Wisdom of the prophecies.

"I'm sorry," Ariock said. "I don't think I can be much use to you right now."

The captains looked dismayed and disappointed.

"I will stay and fight the Torth." Weptolyso reached into a pouch slung across his chest plates and handed Ariock a data marble. "Will you please see that this gets to Yuey?"

Ariock recognized the form of a recorded message. "I will." He took the marble and addressed the line of captains. "I'll deliver anything or anyone you want to send with me to Freedomland." It seemed the least he could do.

Evenjos pursed her lips as the captains scrambled to record holographic messages. Perhaps she thought delivery work was beneath his station?

No, that was unfair. She probably just thought Ariock needed more rest.

"Thank you for saving me." Ariock sat so he could face her. "I think you may have saved this planet."

Evenjos looked up at him, her lavender eyes bright with interest. "Are we even? Is all forgiven between us?"

Ariock hesitated.

The problem with Evenjos was that she treated serious matters like they were games. She had mimicked Vy and attempted to rape Ariock. A nonviolent rape, but still, she clearly had no respect for consent. Could he wholeheartedly forgive Evenjos for that? And for stranding Vy in a dangerous mountain wilderness?

Evenjos looked away. "I truly am sorry."

Ariock had a vague memory of Vy appearing to him while he was in the midst of his drug-induced rage.

He knew, without a doubt, that it had been Evenjos in disguise. That false Vy had torn at his armor using powers, then extended an ultralong arm and stabbed him in the throat. The real Vy would not, could not, do that.

Evenjos slumped. "I know I promised to never mimic her again. I swear, it was the only way I could think to get you to let down your power shields, if only for a second. Otherwise I could not have stopped your destruction."

And this planet would be destroyed.

"I can't be angry at you for that." Ariock gave her hands a gentle squeeze, frustrated by his own hypocrisy. Did he need it spelled out? He had murdered his own friends by accident. What gave him any right to be judgmental toward the woman who had saved this planet?

"We're on the same side." Ariock let go of his last shreds of animosity toward Evenjos. She was a friend.

Besides, Evenjos could have molested Ariock while he was on the inhibitor and crazed from insanity gas. They had been alone together inside a cozy glacial cavern. He would have been easy to take advantage of. Instead? Evenjos had fixed his devastating, uncontrolled rage.

"I forgive you for everything," Ariock said. "And I hope you'll forgive me."

There was nothing seductive in her grin. She only looked patient. "Of course."

"Would you like me to take you to Freedomland?" Ariock felt a bit foolish for asking. Lots of people on Nuss would be grateful for healing from the Lady of Sorrow. She would probably want to stay and—

"Take me with you." She held his gaze. "Please. I fear that insanity gas as much as you do."

Ariock saw the depths of her fear.

And her compassion. He saw that, too, for the first time. Evenjos alone understood his planet-size guilt.

Stormbringers were weapons. They could be turned against their own people. Evenjos understood that. Ultrapowerful Yeresunsa were not safe to be around, especially with supergenius enemies involved. That was a fact.

Ariock had apparently needed to learn it the hard way.

"I misjudged you," he confessed. "You're not a coward. You never were a coward."

"I don't know about that." Evenjos looked down. She held his massive hand with both of hers. It seemed a sisterly gesture, the way Jinishta used to be, without any sexual charge to her touch.

What would Jinishta say about all this?

If his albino cousin were here, maybe she would offer stern advice about whether he should dare go into a battle zone ever again. She would probably suggest some way for him to face Vy and Thomas with a tiny shred of self-respect. If she only . . .

Ariock could not hold his tears back any longer. He stifled his sobs, keeping them silent.

He was a screwup. He was worse than Evenjos. He was worse than anyone.

"Shh." Evenjos held him and used a wing to shield him from curious nussians. "Let's get you home. Let's get you to Vy."

CHAPTER 2
SAYS THE UNIVERSE

Vy ordered a dinner that she thought Ariock would like, and she had it preserved under domes so the sauropod steaks would stay hot. She pushed the hovertray up the grand ramp. Dignitaries and clerks eyed her with curiosity. Vy was the Lady of Paradise, not a chambermaid who would be tasked with deliveries.

But some of the dignitaries looked encouraging. Some were even hopeful.

Everyone waited for daylight to pierce the overcast sky. Snow blanketed the rooftops of Freedomland. Crops were frozen. The Bringer of Hope was taking too long to mourn his losses.

How long would he avoid battles?

During the first few days of his return, Vy had not even thought about duties or politics. She had curled up by his side. Ariock did not weep or moan about what he had done, but there was a haunted look in his eyes.

He had attended the stately funeral procession held to honor Jinishta and the other dead war heroes. It had been a miserable day, with cold sleet, and Ariock had not lifted the weather. Nor had he attended the commemorative feast hosted by nussian battle captains.

He was ignoring survivors. His heart seemed to be with the dead more than with the living. People whispered that Ariock was being rude.

Only Vy saw the hollow sadness in his eyes.

Ariock probably didn't trust himself to speak in public about the disaster. He was quietly beating himself up, hating himself, but nobody else saw that side of him. Only Vy.

Oh, and the mind readers, of course.

Garrett visited Ariock every day, sometimes multiple times per day. He gave annoying pep talks that went ignored.

Thomas, on the other hand, had only visited once after Ariock's initial apology to him. Vy had cringed when her foster brother had bluntly reiterated the situation: *"You screwed up."*

Ariock had sat across from Thomas with gratitude, as if he needed to hear it. And then he had leaped into a self-flagellating monologue. He was a murderer. A tyrant. He should not be trusted with power or authority. He dared not go near war zones. He dared not risk flying into a rage. Not ever again. He wanted Thomas and Kessa to take full leadership.

Thomas had looked more and more overwhelmed, until his emotional absorption circuits seemed to hit a critical overload point. He had backed out of the room with excuses. Sorry, he had to get back to work.

He had shot Vy a parting look full of desperation, and she knew, without needing to ask, that he expected her to work miracles on Ariock's psychology.

Vy was supposed to fix the messiah. Somehow.

Maybe she could do it with the aid of telepathy gas? But Ariock refused to sample a Torth weapon, and Vy supposed he had good reasons. Anyway, no one wanted a loved one rooting around inside their brain. She wasn't entirely comfortable with the idea, either. She didn't want Ariock to glimpse every minor little judgment she made about him. That wouldn't be good.

Thomas had said that he would check in on Ariock again. So far, he hadn't.

Garrett, on the other hand . . .

". . . this much guilt isn't healthy." Vy heard Garrett's grandfatherly voice as she pushed the dinner tray into the lobby atrium of Ariock's giant-size suite. "And it isn't right."

Vy slowed. She no longer held any hope that Garrett could succeed where she kept failing, but even so, she didn't want to interrupt a private conversation.

"I understand your fears about insanity gas." Garrett had a long-suffering tone. "But people need you. I can't save two planets by myself. I'm trying, but . . ."

Garrett paused, interrupting himself. He must be listening to Ariock's unspoken thoughts.

"Well, sure," Garrett said after a moment. "You're a big target. But we have to take risks. There's no other . . ."

Another pause.

A heavy sigh. It sounded like Garrett was frustrated.

Vy could commiserate. During those first few days, she had held Ariock. She had been wholly with him, even supportive of his guilt. Never mind the petitioners who cried for the Bringer of Hope to teleport their recaptured loved ones out of danger. Never mind the hundreds of Alashani warriors who were on strike, refusing to fight unless the "alleged messiah" rejoined them in taking deadly risks. Never mind the unseasonable snow, emblematic of Ariock's depression.

But unlike Ariock, Vy left the suite sometimes. She didn't just overhear news. She saw the faces of the people Ariock ruled.

He had built an empire. He held it together. And it was unraveling.

Hordes of people were being reenslaved on Umdalkdul and Nuss. Survivors hid in the ruins of their cities, using guerrilla warfare tactics to fend off Torth raiders. How long could they hold out?

Flen and other self-styled preachers claimed that Ariock was nothing but a puppet dancing on strings held by the *rekveh* Thomas. They outright accused Thomas of having Jinishta murdered.

Vy had cornered Cherise, demanding to know why that toxic lie was spreading. And Cherise had admitted that she had no power over Flen. The truth could not be proven. No one had survived Ariock's rage, except for Garrett and Evenjos and Ariock himself. As far as most albinos were concerned, there were no credible witnesses.

More than anything, people simply needed to see that Ariock was still interested in defending freedom.

Hope would go a long way toward easing tensions in the city. Vy could see that, even if Ariock himself could not.

"We can't win this war without you." Garrett was pleading.

Vy peered around the corner, trying to gauge whether or not to interrupt.

Ariock sat on the giant-size sofa, where she had last left him. Bleak winter light filtered through the keyhole-shaped window. Pedestrians huddled in leather coats or padded robes.

That window framed the city in a picturesque way, lined by sea glass that was reflective enough to ward off enemy teleporters. Ariock gazed outside all day long. It reminded Vy of the way he used to gaze out of his sky-room window, according to his mother.

Now, as then, Ariock was afraid to leave his sanctum. This time, however, he was more afraid of what he would do than what might be done to him.

"You're wrong about that." Garrett sounded gruff. "I understand exactly how it feels to be a danger to the people you love."

He sat on the bench, mostly eclipsed from view. Neither one of the Dovanacks would see Vy unless she rounded the corner.

"I think I need to tell you something about my past." Garrett seemed to gather his composure. "You're not as bad as you think you are. I promise. Let me tell you, and you'll understand."

Ariock looked toward him. Garrett had actually gotten his attention.

Vy quietly sat on a plush chair, out of sight but positioned where she could overhear every word. Sure, it was intrusive to listen in without permission, but . . . well, mind readers listened in all the time, didn't they?

If Garrett could rebuild Ariock's self-confidence, then she wanted to hear how he did it.

"Your great-grandmother . . ." Garrett sounded unusually hesitant. "Julia. I never told you much about her. But she was the love of my life."

Silence.

After a moment, Garrett responded to whatever Ariock had not said. "Well, that's true. We changed our names. When I stopped being Jonathan Stead, she stopped being Julia. But I'd known her as Julia for longer than I knew her as Sarah. Remember, I'd spied on her family. I knew the Steads for years before they met me and adopted me."

Vy frowned. Had old Garrett married his adoptive sister? Had he stalked his future wife? Judging by the casual way he skipped over details, he must have already shared some of his past secrets with Ariock.

"After I escaped the Torth Empire," Garrett went on, "and the Alashani underground, I came home in time to help Julia through the last stages of her pregnancy. I was so happy when our daughter was born. I delivered her myself."

A pause.

"Nah," Garrett said. "This was before I figured out how to avoid Torth spies and agents, so we were living on the run. I wanted to avoid hospitals and official records. Besides, it was the early twentieth century. I think my healing powers were safer for her than a hospital visit would have been."

Vy supposed that might be accurate.

"Sarah recovered beautifully," Garrett said. "And I thought, for sure, we were blessed to have a perfectly normal, happy family, for the rest of our lives."

How normal could a family with superpowers be? Vy wondered.

Ariock must have wondered the same thing.

"Normal is not the same as average," Garrett said. "We could never be an average family. There were always Torth agents on Earth, hunting for anomalies, and I knew I had to avoid those mind readers at all costs. That was why I made it a point to become a multimillionaire. Money can't buy happiness, but it can buy some protective measures."

Vy recalled the Dovanack mansion. It was a fortress. A remote fortress, buried in an obscure forest, off a road that didn't exist on conventional maps.

"I bought paperwork," Garrett said. "Legitimate birth certificates and so forth, to make our false identities real. I wholly became Garrett Olmstead Dovanack."

"God." Ariock sounded judgmental.

"Oh, those initials were a harmless jest," Garrett said. "A token of defiance. I was giving up everything about my former self, and I guess I wanted to retain a little shred of who I used to be. Not just a father and a grandfather, but a hero."

A pause.

"And yes," Garrett added in a tone of admission, "I could walk on water if I wanted to. I had escaped an evil galactic empire. Was it so wrong for me to indulge in a little bit of vanity?"

The pause after that sounded awkward to Vy.

"I'm getting to the point." Garrett sighed. "First, I want you to understand that we had a good marriage. Sarah isn't here to speak for herself, so all I can do is give you my word and try to paint a picture. Neither of us had to work. I collected off-the-books income through poker, bridge, horse races, and high-stakes casino games. Sometimes I played under the Dovanack name; other times I faked a temporary identity. I moved money through proxies. I had a team on Wall Street who would bid on anything I told them to bid on. If it was corn futures or soybeans? Well, I made the weather. I predicted the crops."

He was always bragging.

"The money freed us up to enjoy ourselves," Garrett went on. "We didn't need to endure long journeys on ocean liners or anything like that. I would just take care to fly us over uninhabited oceans or forests instead of towns. The sky wasn't full of airlines, the way it is nowadays. So we left Rose with a full-time nanny for half of every week, and I took Sarah on trips around the world."

Vy wondered what that had done to Rose's early development.

"We joined the most elite clubs you can imagine," Garrett said. "In Antalya, in Singapore, in Calcutta. We mingled with movie stars and kings and queens. We had a villa in Monaco, and another in the Maldives. Sometimes, we just wanted a quiet week to ourselves, and I would find a deserted tropical beach, or a volcanic precipice, and set up a little campsite."

Garrett must be building up to a tragic end. Vy could sense it.

Ariock probably sensed it as well. "What happened?" he asked in a gentle voice.

"Power is a strange thing." Garrett's voice was flat, like something deflated and dead. "We aren't always in control of it. Even when we think we are."

"What do you mean?" Ariock asked.

A pause. Garrett must be collecting his thoughts, or bracing himself. Vy wondered if the old man had ever revealed his secret to anyone before now.

"We were camping on an uninhabited island," Garrett said, "off the Central American coast. It wasn't anything unusual for us. I must have taken Sarah to a hundred remote islands. We'd done trips like that a thousand times before. I imported a five-star meal from Paris, and we picnicked while watching a gorgeous sunset. That night, we made love on the beach."

Vy wondered if Garrett was ever going to get to his point. He seemed to be circling a topic, perhaps afraid to poke it. Perhaps it had lain dormant in his heart for a long time.

Garrett continued in a slow, frayed tone. "As I made love to her, I was oblivious to the ocean waves getting bigger. There was a vicious retreat of the water. I didn't even notice."

An intake of breath from Ariock.

"It was an underwater earthquake," Garrett said, confirming whatever Ariock had not said. "That I caused."

Silence.

Vy clasped her hands over her mouth, stifling her urge to vocalize. She did not picture Ariock's reaction, or Garrett's pained expression, because she was inwardly reeling.

Rage wasn't the only trigger for a loss of control.

All her fears about sex with Ariock were well-founded.

"I don't understand," Ariock said after a moment. "Are you saying you . . . caused . . . an earthquake? That killed her?"

"Yes." Garrett sounded broken. "It was an accident. I accidentally killed the person I loved more than anything, while making love to her."

That confirmed it.

This revelation shouldn't be so shocking, Vy knew. Ariock had a certain lack of control whenever he got excited. How many times had she witnessed that? She was careful not to tease him sexually too much.

"But . . ." Ariock clearly had questions.

"The wave crashed over us," Garrett said. "It ripped us apart. I was shocked, and it took me a second to stop drowning. I was choking on seawater. If I had to guess, it took me fifteen or twenty seconds before I had the mental wherewithal to start searching for her. The problem is that oceans are teeming with life."

Ariock sucked in a breath.

Vy knew, from conversations with Ariock, that life sparks all felt the same, more or less. A nussian, an ummin, and a sky croc would radiate near-identical glows. There were variations—bugs emitted teensy life sparks, and Yeresunsa were more intense. But people and animals of roughly the same size tended to have the same intensity.

"My best explanation for what happened," Garrett said, "is she must have hit her head on a rock. There were a few sharp rocks underwater. If she lived after that, it was maybe for a minute."

"Did you find her . . . her body?" Ariock sounded pained.

"I did." Garrett sounded elderly. "I searched all night, and then all the next day. I searched for three days straight. I didn't sleep. And yes. I found her remains on the third day."

The sorrow in his voice was obvious.

"I had to return to Rose," Garrett said. "I went home to my four-year-old daughter. And I had to tell her that her mommy was gone forever."

Ariock was silent for a while.

"I'm sorry," he said.

But Vy knew he must be struggling with self-recrimination as well as judgment against Garrett. Vy was saddled with a mixed bag of feelings, too, as heavy as cement. Could she ever be truly safe with Ariock? What if he killed her by accident while making love? Even if she decided to throw caution to the wind, would Ariock ever feel okay about doing so?

They hadn't made love yet. Maybe they never would.

"You lost control of your powers?" Ariock said, as if to clarify things. "During sex?"

"Sex is a powerful drug," Garrett said. "It can lead to powerful feelings. And those are the sorts of things that set us off. Rage, as you know. But also pain, and fear, and . . . well, unfortunately, pleasure."

The sofa creaked. Vy could imagine Ariock resting his forehead in his hand.

"We are dangerous." Garrett's voice was heavy with regret. "There is no power in the universe that can change that. At least, not as far as I know. We are elemental. We are forces of nature." His tone softened. "I never wanted to have this talk with you. I would have preferred for you to skate through life in a way I never did."

"Vy." Ariock said her name in a way that wrenched her heart.

He wasn't asking to see her. It was a helpless plea.

Objects in the hall began to levitate. Rugs, vases, trinkets, the dinner.

Vy herself began to levitate.

Ariock wasn't even conscious of it, she knew. He was just devastated. Tendrils of his awareness had leaked out, seizing everything in his suite.

"I never stopped loving Julia," Garrett said. "I want you to understand that. Our love felt predestined, like it was an epic story. There was never a down in our relationship. Only ups. I never got over her death."

That did sound epic.

But love had not saved Julia or Sarah or whatever her name was.

There was a scraping sound, and Vy pictured the old man using his staff to haul himself to his feet. "I just want you to have a greater understanding of what you fear," Garrett said. "Whether it's insanity gas that causes uncontrolled rage, or an orgasm that makes you feel divine . . . what does it matter? We have triggers. We can't avoid it. Because we are, in essence, human."

Garrett must have said that for dramatic effect, unless he thought of himself as human. Vy heard him limping away from Ariock, toward her.

What a pep talk.

But Vy understood it. Garrett had clumsily begged Ariock to embrace his own flawed nature and to settle for eternal atonement. Because that was how Garrett coped with his own terrible misstep. He thought that that was the only way to handle it.

Vy inwardly wondered if she might be able to control the intensity of Ariock's lust. He had triggers embedded in his mind. What if she drugged him before sex? Maybe a tranquility mesh would work?

If not for the war, she would dose him with the inhibitor.

Whenever Ariock lost his powers, that was when Vy could truly focus on their similarities instead of their differences. That was when he was at his most human.

"I really didn't want to have this talk with you." Garrett sounded quietly mournful.

The levitating objects lowered with slow care. Vy settled back onto the plush seat. It seemed Ariock was back in control of his emotions.

"That's why you wanted me to get with Evenjos." Ariock stated it in a flat tone.

A pause. Then Garrett admitted, "Yes."

Vy used to wonder why Garrett Dovanack was such a jerk. Now she understood. He didn't want to risk an accident like the one that had killed his wife. He had no desire to get close to people who were breakable.

And he wanted the same for Ariock.

Old Garrett had set up a divider in his mind. There were people with power. And there was everybody else. As far as Garrett was concerned, the two types of people should never get too fond of each other.

"Don't worry." Garrett sounded resigned. "I've given up on trying to dictate who you love. That was wrong of me."

Silence from Ariock.

But Vy was shocked. Garrett had tried his best to hook Ariock up with Evenjos. The fact that he now recognized it as a lost cause . . . that was a sign that Ariock stubbornly loved Vy, no matter what. He loved her despite the dangers.

"Who knows?" Garrett limped toward the lobby, staff thumping on the stone floor. "Maybe you and Vy will find a way to make it work."

Garrett rounded the corner and saw Vy sitting there. He looked shrewd instead of surprised.

Vy held her breath. Had the old man purposely given that talk when he knew she would overhear? Would he make some rude comment about how inadequate she was for his precious great-grandson?

"I tried." Garrett spoke in a whisper that would not carry into the next room. "If you can get him to face battles again, countless generations of future people will thank you." He thumped past her. "So will I."

CHAPTER 3

DIVINING WILL

Garrett Dovanack hobbled toward the fluted columns that framed the entry to his suite. A clerk passing through the hallway saw him, turned, and fled.

There was a time when such a fearful reaction would have made him feel sad and ashamed. But that had been a different chapter of his life, before the death of his wife. Now? He told himself that he was glad to avoid dealing with people. He would rather be left alone.

He wondered if Ariock was growing as sour and disenchanted with people as he was.

Eh. Did it matter? Garrett reminded himself that he wasn't concerned with Ariock's happiness, or with anyone's happiness, for that matter. Emotional health was not his prerogative or his field of expertise.

Survival was.

The Will was the first and the last hero mentioned in the prophecies of Ah Jun. His role was as an instigator, an ignition key, and an accelerator. Garrett figured that his role was arguably the most important one. His sacred duty was to shepherd the present into the future. He had to guide the heroes and funnel events in a certain order to ensure that the prophecies would continue to unfold the way the ancient oracle had intended.

If he failed? Then everyone failed.

Garrett extended his awareness. He normally posted zombies outside his sleeping quarters, but the local supply of zombie minions had dwindled to just a handful of dying shamblers. He needed to acquire more prisoners.

The heroes desperately needed to get back to winning battles.

Only a Yeresunsa could access the heavy lock bar hidden inside the specially hollowed doors. Garrett used his powers to lift the bar and levered the enormously heavy doors open.

It was a paltry trick, to make his suite inaccessible to anyone who lacked powers. Garrett knew that chambermaids gossiped about his paranoia. They didn't like any part of the palace being off-limits to their vacuum dusters. But, well, so what?

Garrett swung the doors shut once he was inside. He used his powers to lower the lock bar back into its iron cradle. He felt a tiny bit safer, knowing that no one could walk in and disturb him.

He sank into his study chair and lit a pipe. An observer might guess he was simply relaxing. In actuality, Garrett was scanning his suite for life sparks. He was especially wary about the ghostly presence of Evenjos's disembodied mind.

Satisfied that no one was spying on him, he used his powers to open the secret vault in his floor. He used to store his valuables in a titanium-shielded vacuum chamber on an asteroid, but these days, he went into battle too often for galactic teleportation on a whim. He needed to preserve his strength for battles. So he used a local cache.

Garrett pulled out the ancient Book of Prophecies he had compiled and placed it on his huge desk.

He lit the hanging lamps and used his powers to delicately turn pages he intimately recognized. He paused on the two-page spread that depicted Evenjos carrying Ariock to safety.

"The Transformation of Strength," Garrett muttered. He supposed this one made sense in hindsight, like all the other prophecies that had come to pass. Ariock was transformed.

But was it for the better?

It seemed to Garrett that the Strength needed to be visible and heroic, not mopey and self-hating. When would Ariock transform back into being a heroic messiah? Surely that must happen soon? How could they win this war otherwise?

Garrett gently turned the page.

There were lesser prophecies sandwiched between the two-page spreads. Garrett had learned that those were more like suggestions than guidelines. So he tried not to focus overmuch on what looked like a truce between Evenjos and Ariock, or various depictions of ummins in meditative trances, eyeing each other meaningfully. He kept turning pages.

The boy *(the Conqueror) (the Wisdom)* showed up in several minor prophetic images, looking pissed off or commanding zombies.

There were random panels that contained no one he recognized. Nussian freedom fighters. Penitent Torth hard at work. One penitent directing others. Who knew what that meant? Three lone streamships, two together and one passing them, going the other way. What a puzzle.

But those small panels didn't matter. The crucial, vital prophecies were the two-page spreads. Garrett stopped turning pages when he arrived at the next one.

"The Return of Wisdom," he read, translating the ancient glyphs emblazoned along the outer frame of the painting.

This was the prophetic vision that gave him stomach ulcers from stress.

The picture showed the boy standing—standing!—on the far side of a chasm, apart from the other heroes and friends. Why? The boy looked like he was giving the rest of them some kind of ultimatum. And why was his side dotted with planets? The boy seemed to have the entire galaxy behind him, backing him up.

The future version of Garrett looked furious. The future version of Ariock was kneeling, as if in supplication to the Wisdom.

Garrett didn't like the implications.

Apparently, the Wisdom was going to return from somewhere. Where? How long would he be absent? Why would he leave in the first place? And why did his return look so smugly one-sided?

The prophecies did not explicitly state that the Wisdom would betray them, but everyone knew the boy had Torth sympathies. He had forgiven his own monstrous birth mother. He considered himself to be one of the penitents!

This was precisely why Garrett needed to keep a close eye on the so-called Wisdom.

Garrett also knew a few extra things that were not common knowledge. He was aware, for instance, that more than half of the penitent population hero-worshipped the Conqueror. The enslaved mind readers seemed meek and cooperative . . . but they would follow the boy over a cliff, or into space, or anywhere he led them.

All those planets in the painting seemed ominous. They looked like the galactic Torth Empire. They implied a Megacosm.

And if anyone could shove the ancient prophecies aside, it would be that boy.

Supergeniuses were unlike anyone else. Thomas was too monstrous to have such an innocuous human name. He was a bloated colossus of enmeshed personalities, less predictable than the weather. If the Conqueror did decide to split away and start his own breakaway empire . . . well, he could easily found his own new empire with half a billion mind readers.

He could probably figure out a way to lure Servants and Rosies to his side, too. He could surely invent an anti-inhibitor and who knew what else.

The danger zone was coming up.

All Garrett could do was hope The Return of Wisdom was just a metaphorical event. Perhaps the heroes would simply have a heart-to-heart chat and regain some good old-fashioned common sense?

"One could argue that we are somewhat lacking in wisdom right now," Garrett muttered to himself.

He turned more pages, looking for clues farther ahead in the future. The remainder of the prophecies each added their own weight to his burden of misgivings. After The Return of Wisdom, the next two-page spread was The Pact of Strength. Ariock was at the center of that one. But it was just as murky and ominous as any painting that depicted a future that had not yet happened. The future version of Ariock appeared to be giving the rest of them an ultimatum. And the future version of Garrett looked like he was arguing against it.

The small panels after that one were provocative. Vy featured prominently. Cherise showed up, too. And Kessa. Even the Twins. These little paintings were why Garrett could not easily dismiss the importance of those particular individuals. Ah Jun had clearly seen them in her visions. They must be instrumental to the final defeat of the Torth Empire.

Garrett turned the final pages of the huge book. How many times had he pored over these final panels? The imagery was so disturbing.

The final one of the Will was enough to make his innards turn over with fear. Decapitation. What a horrible, violent way to die. Was that really how his life would end?

And the final two-page spread made him—

His wristwatch buzzed. Someone was calling him.

Garrett closed the book, surprised. The incoming call was from Kessa, of all people. She had never contacted him like this.

He used to get regular calls from Jinishta. Poor Jinishta. She never appeared in the Book of Prophecies after a certain point. Garrett had simply not seen any possible benefit to warning her. The prophecies needed to happen in the correct way, in the correct order, or else the Torth Empire would thrive.

"Kessa? How are you?" Garrett took care to always be polite to Kessa. Her role in the prophecies seemed increasingly important, especially toward the end. He doubted that anyone, least of all Kessa herself, would guess her future fate.

"I am outside your door," Kessa said in a pleasant tone, her beak large in the camera feed. "There is a matter I wish to discuss. Will you please let me in?"

Garrett supposed that Kessa's informant network had let her know where to find him. She had loyalists all over the place.

"Of course." Garrett ended the call.

He used his powers to send the book back to its airtight vault. He sank the vault into its secret cradle and slid the floor tile over it, hiding it from sight. At the same time, he telekinetically opened the doors of his suite.

Kessa trotted inside.

She looked quite small, since every room of the war palace was built to Ariock's scale. Doorways and ceilings were towering. Furthermore, Kessa was alone. That was brave of her. It seemed she had left her assistants and clerks and bodyguards elsewhere.

"Peace, elder." Kessa used a respectful greeting in the slave tongue.

Garrett realized that he probably should have greeted her first. "Peace, elder." He wondered if he should offer refreshments. Probably.

He gestured to an armchair that was within his range of telepathy. "Have a seat, if you'd like. I have flavored waters. Or would you like a hot tea?"

"I'll have a water, thank you." Kessa leaned against the far wall, arms folded. She wasn't going to sit within his telepathy range.

Ah well.

Garrett used his powers to pull a hovertray out of his kitchenette. He never received guests in his suite except for Evenjos, so he had to pull beverages out of his minifridge. On Earth, when he'd been a wealthy gambler, he had learned that tycoons, high rollers, and mafia bosses expected to be greeted with a certain flair. It had been a long time since he'd needed to call upon his etiquette.

"I have an important favor to ask," Kessa said.

Garrett did not quite dare to walk over and pluck it out of her mind. He wasn't going to be that rude. "Yes?"

"The labs are able to recreate telepathy gas," Kessa said. "Varktezo and others have reverse engineered the gas emitters, to the point where they can create the stuff. In a closed room, they are able to make it linger in the air. It spreads brain wave patterns, so that even an ummin can read minds."

"Hmm." Garrett hid his disdain. He hoped the boy was devoting attention to more serious projects. Telepathy gas might be a fun party trick for ummins, but it would not win battles.

They needed to inoculate Ariock against the insanity rage gas. Maybe that would be enough for Ariock to feel comfortable going into battle again? The scientists really needed to focus on what was important. Such as immunity to the inhibitor! All the warriors, including Garrett, ought to become invincible in battle.

Garrett snagged a pomegranate water. He parked the tray near Kessa, and she picked up a water with alien cactus fruit flavoring.

"So ummins can read minds now," Kessa said.

Garrett nodded and sipped his water. He hoped she would make a point soon.

"But to us," Kessa said, "telepathy is a confusing jumble of perceptions and thoughts. It has come to my attention that deciphering that jumble is a skill that can be learned." She cocked her head at him. "I think you are the teacher we need."

Garrett swallowed. "Whoa." The conversation had taken an unexpected turn. "What about the penitents?"

Kessa shook her head. "I would be a fool to get within range of a penitent. I know too much."

Garrett should have thought of that himself. Kessa hung out with the boy on a regular basis. She must know some of his dearest secrets as well as about his science projects. Her friendships extended to Varktezo, Weptolyso, Vy, Cherise, and others. She knew all kinds of military secrets.

"Besides," Kessa said, "the penitents are serving penance. That is their purpose. I don't want them in positions of authority over former slaves."

"Fair." Garrett stroked his beard, imagining himself as a teacher. How long would it take for a nontelepath's brain to adjust to a whole different paradigm? Years?

A lifetime?

His imagination wanted to rebel at the concept of learning telepathy as an adult. It seemed absurd, like teaching a pig to fly. Surely his time and energy could be better spent elsewhere?

The Wisdom could probably explain, with eloquent apologies, why it was a bad idea. "Have you asked the boy?" That way, Garrett wouldn't have to tell Kessa no.

"I did." Kessa's tone held a note of aspersion. "And he refused. He said he was too busy, and he suggested that I ask you."

Garrett bit back his urge to swear.

Kessa placed her drink back on the floating tray. She looked earnest. "If we are to face Torth with telepathy gas again, it will be a major benefit if we can surprise them and navigate their traps. And overhear their secrets."

Garrett sat back. "But how long will it take for you to get to that point?"

Kessa spread her hands. "I cannot know. But I may have a guess once I've had a few lessons."

"I'm sorry," Garrett said. "But I'm quite busy."

Kessa gave him a stern look. "I am not asking for much. How about twenty minutes every third day? Would that be a burden?"

Garrett hesitated.

His schedule could accommodate some harmless lessons. Plus, friendly time spent with Kessa might deliver benefits, if not quite what she was expecting. He would get to read her mind. Perhaps he would delve into her inner secrets, with a reciprocal expectation. She was friends with the boy. If anyone could understand why the Wisdom might leave and then return with some sort of ultimatum . . . well, she might contain some buried clues.

"Twenty minutes," Garrett agreed. "I think I can manage that every day, if that works for you."

Kessa beamed.

"We'll just see how it works out," Garrett warned. He would terminate the sessions if they proved arduous or worthless.

"Thank you." Kessa tapped her data pad, sending him her calendar in order to schedule the first lesson. "If a few of us can learn, we will teach others."

Garrett hid his doubts.

"It will help." Kessa bowed in a gesture of gratitude. "I am sorry, but I cannot stay long. I look forward to our first lesson." She moved to leave. "We may learn faster than you think."

CHAPTER 4

A PLETHORA OF SECRETS

Thomas never used to think of himself as secretive. He considered himself open and honest.

But whenever Varktezo asked for his expertise in using telepathy gas . . . ? Thomas found himself inventing excuses. He didn't want his chief assistant—his friend—marveling at his ridiculously complex mind. He had no desire to remind Varktezo, of all people, that he was freakishly alien and impossible to decipher. There was already a gap between him and everybody else. He wasn't going to lever that chasm even wider.

"Not today," he told Varktezo.

"Not today," he told Varktezo every day.

And when Kessa asked Thomas for telepathy lessons? He'd insisted that he was too busy. He had told her to ask Garrett.

Was that rude?

Thomas found reasons within himself, beyond vanity, to avoid the mental scrutiny of his peers. He did have secrets, it turned out.

The way he felt about Cherise, for one thing.

It wouldn't do for people to find out he still cared for her more than casually. Flen's huffiness might transform into ballistic rage—and that was actually a political risk. These days, without Jinishta, a lot more warriors were listening to Flen.

The Pink Screwdriver. She was a big blotch of guilt in Thomas's mind. A hero of prophecy was not supposed to feel gentle and tingly about an enslaved Torth. He should not fraternize with the enemy. He definitely should not devote any brainpower to imagining sneaky methods of bringing her, unseen, into one of his hidden bomb shelters, where he might spend time alone in her company.

He knew better. He really did.

And yet some dumbass, hormone-driven part of his brain would not relent. That teenager part of himself internally screamed, "I'm lonely!" and "She's as hot as Cherise, and she's available, and she secretly worships me!" and "No one important will find out!" and "So what if they do? I'm the Wisdom of prophecy! I'm the Conqueror and I live in a Dragon Tower! I can do what I want!"

That was the sort of overconfidence that could get one killed.

Ariock could attest to that. Ariock had decided to rescue a city's worth of crucified people because he was the messiah and no one dared tell him no. Now he was paying a steep price for thinking of himself as near-invincible. The rest of their forces had to pay that price right alongside him.

The Upward Governess could have attested to the blindness of Thomas's overconfidence, too.

He felt a painful twinge whenever he remembered his utter failure to give his mentor the protection she had needed. He had been too focused on winning. He had made the mistake of underestimating a fellow supergenius, the Death Architect.

Twice now.

That chilly-minded supergenius was sly, unreadable, and impossible to predict. Thomas understood on some instinctual level that if he underestimated the Death Architect a third time, it would mean doom for him and his whole side of the war. He could not afford mistakes. He could not afford to be carefree.

So Thomas ignored his urge to start a tryst with the Pink Screwdriver. He was staunchly holding out.

He had other inadequacies, other secret flaws and weaknesses that he needed to shore up.

Two Alashani eyed him askance. *It's the* rekveh. *Avoid.*

Ugh.

They crossed the street, boots crunching on the layer of frost. Their minds faded from his peripheral perceptions.

Thomas wrapped his emotions in cold logic and pretended that hatred did not affect him at all.

He knew he was attempting to lie to himself, like a Torth. It was shameful. But this was the most densely populated Alashani district, full of albino pedestrians. The fear and hatred aimed toward Thomas was everywhere.

He struggled to focus on mundane things instead of the minds of passersby. Shop signs hung over doorways, painted with mushrooms, cave sheep, fish, stalactites, or loopy icons.

He glanced skyward for a moment, just to give his eyes a break. Unlike a Torth city, the sky here rarely included shuttles taking off or landing. The makeshift Freedomland spaceport was mostly used for pilot training. They only had a small collection of stolen streamships.

Thomas harbored yet another secret.

He hoped to see a landing Torth vessel. Or maybe two vessels? Both Twins had gone rogue.

Thomas had asked his friends to keep silent about the Twins' potential as allies. It was best not to raise everyone's hopes out of proportion to reality. Just because the Twins had exited the Torth Empire did not necessarily mean they would join Thomas's side.

And yet he hoped.

Thomas parked his hoverchair in a garage beneath one of the immense war fortresses. He found a spot between hoverbikes. The Alashani population could not avoid technology entirely. Not if they wanted to do business with the rest of the city.

He used his control sleeve to engage his leg braces. He stood.

It felt dangerous to leave his vehicle, especially in a place where he had no friends. Thomas wasn't exactly swift. He could not run.

Perhaps he should have sent an emissary to arrange a private meeting with the warrior known as Daindlor?

Except Thomas knew such a request would be rejected. What he wanted was best achieved through a face-to-face surprise meeting. Thomas did not want to give the crotchety old warrior any warning. Daindlor should not have time to invent excuses.

Thomas took purposeful, mechanized steps up a ramp.

"*You ought to have zombies to guard you,*" Garrett had growled at Thomas, more than once.

Thomas always dismissed that recommendation. But he felt a certain lack of protection now as he made his way through the fortress. He couldn't even call on Azhdarchidae. The sky croc could not fit through doorways here, and anyway, he was huddled under a huge, knitted blanket, unused to the wintry conditions outside.

Albinos gaped at Thomas in shock. He wasn't reckless enough to attempt an albino disguise here, among albinos, so they recognized him instantly. They glared at his temerity.

Evil. A woman made a sign to ward off demons, then hurried away.

Should be killed. That thought came from a stout warrior, dressed in purple linens with white fur trim. The warrior didn't scurry away. He sized up Thomas as an opponent.

Thomas met the warrior's challenging glare. He didn't show any emotion, but he didn't have to. His purple-eyed gaze was enough. The stout warrior found a reason to hurry down a side hallway, away from the *rekveh.*

There were more albinos. They jumped aside, or they stared as if Thomas carried a plague. He caught whiffs of their terror and disgust.

Untrustworthy.

   What an uppity penitent.

    Hope the undergrounders succeed.

    He never should have been given so much freedom.

Their emotions oozed into Thomas's pores. Before long, he felt grimy and disgusting, as if he needed to take a shower.

Part of him felt as if they were right. He was an unclean thing, unwanted and obscene.

He wanted to go back to places where he had friends. He wasn't even powerful enough to fight his way free if a bunch of warriors decided to gang up against him. He wasn't a stormbringer. What was he doing here?

Lack of power is the reason I'm here, Thomas reminded himself. He had certain weak points that he needed to work on and fix.

So instead of turning around and leaving, he extended his awareness and used his holographic projection power to bend light around himself.

It was not a perfect invisibility cloak. Thomas could not alter or dissipate his own body, like Evenjos. Instead, he distorted the environment around himself in a million ways, frame by frame. There were so many variables to manifest and keep track of— atmospheric distortion, luminosity differentials as he moved, individual variations in perceptiveness, and so forth—that he could not fully erase himself from view.

Alashani were used to low light conditions, so a few of them might have noticed an indistinct shadow that moved.

And they heard him. His leg braces emitted a faint whirring sound that caused people to look around.

Thomas moved as fast as he dared, one foot in front of the other. He remained hyperalert, aware that he was alone in a palatial fortress full of people who might potentially kill him.

At last, he arrived at the correct address.

Many warriors commissioned fancy iron grillwork to decorate their doors, or inlays of smoked glass or reflective tiles. It seemed Daindlor was not showy, despite being a retired premier. The door to his suite was relatively plain.

Thomas raised his fist, feeling like an imposter in his own skin. He had never knocked before. He had never been able to.

What if the old warrior raised an alarm?

Thomas just needed a chance. He would get inside the suite, then explain.

He rapped his knuckles on the wood.

When Thomas heard the door latches being undone, he dived into Daindlor's mind, along channels of expectation. The old warrior was not expecting any visitors. However, Daindlor would be pleased to see his lady friend, or perhaps a neighborly visit from his friend, Premier Boryuchal.

Thomas quickly conjured an illusion of the latter.

Daindlor opened the door. "Boryuchal? What a happy coincidence." He stepped aside, inviting. White whiskers fuzzed his chinless face, and his ears stuck out.

Thomas hated to be deceptive, even if he wasn't actually voicing a lie. It was nearly the same thing.

"Come in, come in," Daindlor said. "I just acquired a fresh bottle of that brandy you recommended."

Thomas walked into the suite. He was a little bit self-conscious about his own ears. He had lost part of his earlobe during a wild zoved attack. The telepathic apes had tried to eat him. Not that Daindlor could see that yet.

Like most rooms in the fortress, this one had slightly rounded walls, narrow windows, and a roaring fireplace. The furnishings were typical Alashani palace pieces—quartz and iron, with spears used as decor.

Daindlor seemed too distracted to shut the front door.

Thomas shut it for him.

"Wait." Daindlor stared and squinted, because Thomas had quit paying much attention to his illusion.

It required a lot of processing to maintain something so lifelike over his own moving body. There were colors to edit, light and shadow to redirect, perspective, dimensionality, and so many other variables. Such an illusion would be impossible for anyone with a normal mind. Even for a supergenius, it was a stretch.

Thomas let go of the effort. He could not have kept it up for more than half a minute longer, anyway.

Daindlor's eyes flew wide-open. He was stooped with age, but he took a few nimble steps backward until he pressed against the wall.

"I'm here to beg for your expert help." Thomas spoke quickly and smoothly, using words he calculated to be the most likely to put the old warrior at ease. "You're the most renowned warrior in existence aside from the Dovanacks. You've trained legends. You were responsible for training Shirm, who trained Jinishta, among others." Thomas struggled out of his coat. "I would like to learn from you."

Daindlor gaped.

"I'll pay you for your time, of course." Thomas's voice broke and dropped in an adolescent way. How embarrassing. He hated puberty.

War credits were derived from the military, which meant Thomas and the other heroes had the equivalent of unlimited funds. But Daindlor didn't seem particularly materialistic.

"You can ask me for favors as payment," Thomas clarified. "I'd be happy to oblige." He scanned the old warrior's hidden desires. "I can, for instance, make sure your friends receive better and more fitting rewards for their heroic acts. They surely deserve it."

Daindlor closed his mouth. Still blinking in shock, he huffed, as if to clear his sinuses of a bad smell. He seized a wooden staff and used it to stabilize himself.

"Leave!" Daindlor pointed to the door. "I don't teach *rekvehs*."

Thomas tried not to roll his eyes in exasperation. "Do you believe in the messiah?"

He already knew the answer. He had researched Daindlor. The old warrior habitually avoided the undergrounders, which meant he was likely a true believer. And Thomas confirmed that with a mind scan. This old warrior trusted in ancient prophecy. He would follow Ariock anywhere. By extension, that meant he should trust those who advised Ariock.

"I believe," Daindlor admitted, sullen. "But that does not mean I will help you. I only train Alashani."

Thomas offered a respectful nod. "That's why I've come to you. I want to be able to fight like an Alashani."

Daindlor made a sour face. "From what I hear, you know everything already."

"I don't." Thomas tapped one of his leg braces. It made a hollow sound. "I'm still learning how to walk."

Daindlor regarded him for a moment, looking frustrated.

He struck at Thomas with lightning speed. His face betrayed no warning. One moment he was standing within Thomas's range of telepathy. The next instant, his staff arced toward Thomas's ankle.

Thomas sensed the move coming. He would have avoided the blow, except Daindlor infused his rickety body with inhuman speed, faster than a decision. Thomas hopped, and one of his legs avoided the staff, but not the other foot.

The shock of his miscalculation ruined his balance, which was always delicate.

He landed hard, one-footed, and he was so unused to that, he stumbled. Only his exosuit kept him from an awkward fall.

"We are nimble." Daindlor danced out of Thomas's telepathy range. "You are not."

Thomas used his remote control to shuffle his legs into their preprogrammed default stance. "I want to learn."

Daindlor raised a hand, and five spears levitated out of the quiver resting against the wall.

Thomas forced himself to look pleasant rather than sweating with fear. Would he be able to dodge in time? No way. Not at this close distance.

He might be able to redirect the spears with heat currents. He might turn the spearheads to plasma and cause them to fall off course. But he would have to make optimal calculations, and Daindlor might prove too fast for him.

The old warrior had purposely chosen five spears. That was the maximum number that an average Torth could subitize.

"We move objects with our minds." Daindlor glared at Thomas without mercy. "From what I hear, you use wildfire and ice. Like the Torth."

"Yes," Thomas admitted. He lacked the common Alashani powers of telekinesis, lightning, and healing. He had tried to infuse his body with extra strength or speed, and it never worked for him.

"We kill Torth." Daindlor lowered the spears with disdain. He had made his point. "I cannot teach one such as you."

Clearly, the warrior expected Thomas to give up and go away.

"I kill Torth, too." Thomas summoned all his courage as well as his focus. He bent light around his form. "And I have other talents that are not common among Torth."

Daindlor saw Thomas become mostly invisible. His eyes widened. There were some Torth who could manipulate water vapor to create the equivalent of strange shadows or cloudlike formations, but none could form holographs or realistic illusions. None could become essentially invisible. They lacked the brain processing capacity.

"I'm not an average Torth," Thomas said.

He let go of his illusion. It was an intense mental workout, like calculating an entry point to a temporal stream for wormhole space travel.

Still, his effect had hit its mark. Daindlor looked contemplative.

"I can manipulate thermal currents to move things, like a telekinetic." Thomas demonstrated, causing a sheet of parchment to waft across the room. "I'm not great at it," he admitted, letting the parchment drift onto a desk. "But I wonder if you can teach me better techniques?"

Daindlor gazed out one of the narrow windows, wintry light illuminating his creased face. Thomas did not need to be within range to guess at the man's concerns.

Daindlor was an upstanding pillar of his community.

And Thomas was a notorious *rekveh*.

Two such as them were not supposed to meet, let alone talk. They were supposed to hate each other. What was this war about, if mind readers could be trusted with Alashani secrets, and vice versa?

"I understand your reluctance," Thomas said, acknowledging the downside. "But will you at least think it over for a few days? And if you're concerned about my skills, you're welcome to test me in whatever ways you see fit."

That should make the unspoken benefit obvious. Daindlor could potentially grill Thomas for information. He could learn all sorts of things about what Torth champions were capable of. Such insights could be distilled and disseminated to all Alashani warriors.

Daindlor growled in frustration and clenched his fists.

Thomas gathered his coat.

"All right," Daindlor snapped, just as Thomas was about to leave. "I'll do it. But we're going to keep this a secret. It can't be public knowledge. Is that all right with you?"

It was just one more secret for Thomas to add to his increasing burden of things he didn't want his friends finding out about.

"Of course." He grinned, tossed his coat aside, and prepared to spar.

CHAPTER 5

TELEPATHY LESSON #1

Kessa ensured that the telepathy training room could comfortably accommodate all kinds of people. An assortment of stools and chairs lined the burnished walls, with enough room left over for nussians or hoverchairs. The space was large enough for half the war council.

But most of the seats were empty.

Varktezo and several lab assistants entered the room, plus a handful of Kessa's lieutenants, including Braglem and Utavlug Hano. Pung and Dyoot were a surprise. Kessa had sent them each a last-minute invitation, but she'd been sure that Dyoot, in particular, would be too independent to take lessons from the very mind reader who used to own him. Here he was, clambering onto a stool.

Weptolyso was busy leading freedom fighters on Nuss, so he could not be here, but Kessa was surprised to see his mate, Yuey. Accepting an invitation to read minds seemed like an especially brave step for an Alashani nussian who had grown up believing that *rekvehs* were vile demons.

All in all, there were thirteen ummins, three govki, and just the one nussian. No Ariock? No Vy or Cherise? Ah well. It seemed that most of Kessa's invitees had declined to show up.

Garrett cleared his throat. He sat in an armchair by the window. "Before we begin," the old Torth hybrid said, "let me tell you about minds."

No doubt Garrett was already absorbing the thoughts of those who sat nearest to him in the circle: Pung, Junwon, Humtut, and Varktezo.

The boxy device on the table next to him must be an emitter. Once Garrett turned it on, everyone in this room would be comparatively helpless. They would be unable to discern reality from imagination.

Kessa pushed down her tingle of unease. She was not a slave trapped with an unfriendly mind reader. She had chosen to be here. She was in control of this situation. Garrett was just grouchy, not dangerous. Not to her.

Varktezo raised his hand.

"Yes, Varktezo?" Garrett looked slightly annoyed at being sidetracked before he had even begun to teach anything.

Varktezo's hand dropped, and he looked gratified to have been called upon. "Will Ariock attend these lessons?"

Garrett hesitated.

It must be a question on a lot of people's minds, judging by the expectant looks around the room. Everyone suspected Ariock was just as vulnerable to psychic confusion as any ummin. A helmet and air tank might not even protect him. The effect was related to waves of dark energy. It could bleed through walls, given enough saturation and enough time.

"Ariock is . . ." Garrett seemed to change his mind about whatever falsehood he had been about to speak, perhaps realizing that the students in this room would soon be absorbing his thoughts. "Ariock will consider taking these lessons at a later date. We'll see how it goes."

That was a diplomatic answer. Kessa could guess the truth. It was rather obvious. Ariock was depressed.

Frost blistered the windowpanes. Snow covered the rooftops of the city. Dead critters, such as lizards and tiny snakes, hinted that the unrelenting grimness outside was supernatural rather than seasonal. Ariock did a few duties, such as mass-teleporting troops and volunteers to places where they were needed. He imported and exported cargo.

Other than that? He was doing far less than usual. He refused to join battles. He refused to even enter a battle zone.

Kessa had confronted Vy, begging to know why Ariock was so withdrawn. Vy had made excuses, but the truth was in her eyes. Not even she could lift Ariock's dark mood.

Garrett stood, drawing the class's attention away from the matter of their despondent Bringer of Hope.

"Firstly," Garrett said, brusque, "let's discuss how minds synthesize information." He began to pace. "There's perceptual data. There are neurochemical reactions, otherwise known as emotions. Perceptions plus emotions combine into abstractions, which—in sapient people and high-level animals—can then be conducted into concretized thoughts and imaginings."

Kessa had chatted with Thomas often enough to get a sense of how he perceived living beings. He said that every sapient mind was like a world unto itself. Thoughts and imaginings could become memories, if conditions were right. An accretion of memories, etched with runnels of individualized thought processes, comprised an individual's personality.

"Now, let's talk about our differences." Garrett paced. "We are not the only sapient species in the galaxy." He gestured around the room. "Besides ummins and govki and nussians and the humanoid species, there are Kemkorcan feather people, Toishifellan cave worms, Soghian water dwellers, and so forth. There's even a sedentary species of intelligent treelike people on Bemelglurd."

Kessa blinked. She used to believe that she knew every sapient species, but nowadays, she knew better.

"The reason you don't know about people who dwell in liquid or gaseous or high-pressure environments," Garrett went on, "is because the Torth rarely give them the major modifications their bodies would need to live full-time in the environments which we find habitable. They're restricted to mining colonies or zoological facilities on their planets of origin."

Kessa recalled the sad-eyed cave worms she had known, and she shivered. They claimed that breathing felt wrong to them. They had spoken of medical facilities and pain. In hindsight, she guessed they must have undergone surgical operations before they were imported to New GoodLife WaterGarden City.

"Our species," Garrett went on, gesturing between himself and the rest of the room, "experienced some convergent evolution. We're all air breathers. We all walk on land." He paced. "We have different nutritional requirements, different reproduction, and different circadian rhythms. But thanks to the sound conductivity in our cradle worlds, we naturally evolved ears. Thanks to the fact that we evolved on planets with sunlight and a spectrum of color, we all evolved eyes."

Kessa made a mental note to learn more about evolution. She might borrow a few books from Cherise, who had access to an Earth library or two. Varktezo also seemed to have access to a lot of books.

"However," Garrett went on, "you will notice that ummins generally have superior eyesight, compared to the rest of us."

The listeners exchanged curious glances.

"And nussians and govki tend to have a far superior sense of smell," Garrett said. "They'll scent things long before I can. Nussians are sensitive to seismic activity. They'll pick up tremors in the floor and determine where and how far away. They also have impressive navigational abilities."

Yuey, the sole nussian in the room, looked proud.

"My point," Garrett said, pacing back and forth in front of the big window, "is that I want you to be prepared to understand each other in new ways. Perceptions will be the most immediately obvious difference between the way you think and the way your friend thinks. You'll soon become aware of differences in cognition, also. Some of us have better short-term memories. Some of us can subitize, or enumerate, more items in a glance than others. Some of us are quicker to recognize and control our emotions. Some of us can intuit things quicker than others. Differences are very varied and individual. No two people think alike."

The three adolescent ummins fidgeted, as if they were considering excuses to leave. Maybe they were ashamed of sharing their personal advantages or flaws with each other?

Garrett stopped and gave the whole room a stern look.

"I don't care what new things you learn about your friends and neighbors. You might learn they have some weird sexual fetish, or a dark secret. I don't care. Try to embrace the ummin philosophy of Gwat and withhold judgment."

It took Kessa a moment to understand why Garrett was concerned. It was natural to measure oneself against others. Everyone in this room was about to gain a vastly different scale of measurement.

Would they gain new justifications for feeling inferior or superior to each other?

"In other words," Garrett said, "please don't turn into a bunch of Torth."

The other students chuckled.

But Kessa didn't think Garrett was joking. She used to assume the Torth were convinced of their own superiority because they wielded so much power. Now she knew that the Torth stole all their advantages through violence. They robbed alien civilizations. What would cause a gang of thugs to feel eternally superior to their victims?

Well, the Torth were constantly reading minds. They measured one's knowledge against another's knowledge. They kept slaves in ignorance. Those were the minds they felt safe in ignoring.

Torth knew each other very well on a day-to-day basis. Why did they arrange themselves in a hierarchy, with the most self-aggrandizing Torth rising to the top, to influence all the rest? Perhaps it was because they could not help but compare their own minds against one another's. They measured each other's social influence.

Torth judged each other incessantly.

We are better than that, Kessa thought uneasily.

But plenty of people judged Thomas and the penitents without getting to know them.

The Code of Gwat was all about ignorance. Its main tenet was that one could not—should not—judge another person without comprehensive and intimate knowledge of their circumstances.

So what happened when one gained godlike knowledge?

Gwat never addressed that possibility.

"All right." Garrett took his seat and rested his hand on the emitter. "Is everyone ready?"

Varktezo gave an eager "Yes!" and everyone else uttered assent.

Garrett pressed a switch on the device. A button glowed, signifying that it was on.

A few people inhaled deeply, as if scenting fresh, home-cooked meals.

Kessa knew, from conversations with Varktezo, that telepathy gas did not work by soaking into people's bodies and penetrating the blood-brain barrier. It was not a neurotransmitter. Instead, it altered energies within the room, causing unnatural conditions that amplified brainwaves. Just as sound could travel farther underwater than through air, thoughts could travel farther through a dark energy matrix than through natural energy conditions. The thoughts grew in amplitude, allowing non-telepaths to perceive them.

Varktezo looked (*Kessa saw herself*) awestruck, beak agape.

People stared at each other (*like broken shards of mirror*) (*kaleidoscopic*) seeing (*her*) themselves (*each other*) so much.

The feeling of too much input quickly escalated.

Kessa was eighteen (*or a thousand?*) people. She had too many limbs, too many tongues. She was afraid to speak, because it would pour forth in a babble out of multiple mouths. Every time someone else (*scratched an itch*) (*imagined a friend*) (*felt nauseous from the invasion of other people's ideas*) her mind echoed theirs. That made her afraid to even attempt to make the smallest of decisions.

She wanted to retract her spikes, but she didn't have spikes. Her fur puffed out, but she didn't have fur.

She regretted inviting so many people to these lessons.

Garrett's mind stood out as the only one who wasn't reeling with shock or confusion. His voice sounded sonorous, laden with an echo as it was perceived through multiple ears.

"Close your eyes."

Kessa closed her eyes.

She knew when everyone else had shut their eyes, because it was a blessed relief. The cacophony was reduced.

"I want you to focus on your right hand," Garrett's voice intoned. "Don't open your eyes. Just enjoy the sensation of having a right hand. Be aware of that hand, which is yours."

At first, Kessa was aware of her own hand plus all the others'. She felt the heft of the massive nussian hand that was Yuey's. She felt the natural dexterity of having two right hands, like Dyoot.

But those hands were clearly not hers.

After a while, Kessa was able to assure herself of which right hand belonged to her. It was the most familiar, the most obvious. She truly enjoyed having that sensation.

"Bodily autonomy is important," Garrett said. "It's probably the first thing a baby mind reader learns."

Kessa remembered Torth sitting in lounges, their gazes faraway, with meshes encircling their brows. Now she understood why Torth liked to sit around doing nothing. It would be overwhelming to focus on someone else's existence while walking or performing daily tasks.

"Familiarize yourself with your bodily boundaries," Garrett suggested. "Just keep your eyes closed and focus on the body that is yours, the only body under your control."

Kessa was amazed by how much the lesson helped. She still perceived alien sensations, but the din was manageable now.

She had her body. Others had theirs.

Is this really how he sees the world? Varktezo's mental voice was obvious. His voice echoed his thoughts, causing an overlap effect. "Is this really how you see things? *(I mean)* All the time?"

"Yes," Garrett said. "Except I'm not used to being in a room with, uh . . ." Kessa sensed him self-edit his thoughts, erasing terms such as *demented* and *fledglings.* "Mind readers I can actually trust," he said. "It's weird."

Kessa sensed the veracity of his words. Garrett truly found it unnerving to be among mind readers who lacked the predictable nature of Torth.

Do you hear an echo? ". . . Echo?" Varktezo said, and then finished in his mind *. . . Every time someone speaks out loud?*

Kessa winced. But she had been wondering the same. How could Garrett and Thomas stand to have conversations in spoken languages? It must be excruciatingly annoying and repetitive for them.

(Varktezo) "Varktezo, it's rude to speak only in your mind." Garrett sounded stern. *(Some)* "Some people missed what you asked. Repeat it out loud so everyone can hear it."

Varktezo reluctantly did so. *(Do you)* "Do you hear an echo whenever people speak out loud?" *(loud?)*

Kessa heard the echo. It synced up closely, giving his words a hollow, sonorous timbre.

(Yes) "Yes," Garrett said, his own voice likewise sonorous. *(And yes)* "And yes, it's annoying, especially when there is a large gap between voice and thought." *(It's just)* "It's just something to get used to."

No wonder the Torth outlawed spoken speech. Now Kessa understood.

Amid the general cacophony of random perceptions and thoughts, Kessa sensed a clear vibe from Varktezo. *With this gas, I can learn so much more and faster! When will the Teacher (Thomas) let me read his mind???*

Never, Garrett thought with a snort of derision.

A second later, Kessa sensed Garrett try to self-edit. But it was too late. Everyone in the room had overheard his opinion.

? Varktezo wanted clarification. In his opinion, mind reading was the fastest way to learn. Surely the Teacher would understand the need?

Garrett hesitated. Kessa sensed his thoughts turning over and stewing. She could not quite grasp what the old mind reader was hiding from the rest of them.

She leaned closer. Garrett's mind had no shape or substance, yet it seemed to have a . . . a surface of some sort. A shield? A carapace? Whatever it was, Kessa sensed its texture, calm and swirling. There were inlets.

What if she chased that swirl of indecision deeper . . . ?

(Stop) "Stop that, Kessa," Garrett said. *We'll save mind probes for a (much later) lesson.*

Braglem stared at Kessa in consternation. And Kessa realized, with a sick sense of shame, that she had been probing like a Torth.

"The boy *(Thomas)* is embarrassed," Garrett said, trying to explain. "Because *(he's such a freak)* he doesn't have a normal mind."

(Duh) "I know," Varktezo said. *(Everyone knows that.)*

Kessa sensed unspoken depths within the exchange. Apparently, Varktezo had actually glimpsed Thomas's mind once. That glimpse had drastically reshaped his conception of the boy whom he had begun to consider a friend. Now, as far as Varktezo was concerned, the Teacher was a god of knowledge.

"Well," Garrett said, "good luck getting him to let you peer into his soul ever again."

The conversation was making everyone else curious. Kessa kept her eyes closed, but she sensed other people glance at Garrett.

????????

"The boy *(Thomas)* presents himself as small and weak," Garrett said, struggling to explain. "He counts on being perceived as *(harmless)* powerless. But . . ."

Kessa felt the anticipation in the room. It was like tremors.

(But) "I don't think words can adequately describe what a supergenius is," Garrett said. "It's the sort of thing you have to experience. There's a reason the Torth Empire put a lot of legal restrictions on people like him. They're freaks."

Garrett's spoken tone was calm, whereas his thoughts writhed with fearful vehemence. Whenever he pictured "the boy," he pictured a towering solar storm of inscrutable and godlike knowledge. Thomas's face was just an incidental attachment to that terrifying galactic deity.

Kessa stared at Garrett. She had suspected he feared Thomas, but now? She knew it. Garrett legitimately had trouble trusting the supergenius.

I need to sense the Teacher's mind again, Varktezo thought with determination. *I could learn so much this way!*

"He won't let you," Garrett said. "He's savvy enough to know that it's a bad idea *(to show)* to show people the truth of what he's capable of."

Varktezo radiated frustration and secret hope. He clearly disagreed with Garrett.

"Sorry." Garrett patted the emitter. "You're stuck with me as your teacher for the foreseeable future. I wouldn't count on the boy for this." *(Or for much of anything.)*

There was that distrust again, strong and pungent.

Kessa considered how easily Thomas exposed his mind to the penitent population as he vetted them. He was willing to share himself with fellow mind readers.

But not with ummins?

That wasn't fair.

Both Varktezo and Garrett might have good points about Thomas. Kessa inwardly vowed to seek clarification with Thomas. As long as mind readers shared secrets with each other, excluding all other species, she would feel dissatisfied and inferior.

"All right," Garrett said, his powerful voice and reassuring mind cutting through a babble of thoughts once again. "Let's practice some more with tactile sensation. Close your eyes . . ."

The lesson resumed.

Kessa was alert and eager throughout the entire class. When it ended, she resolved to practice with a friend or two. She had mastered reading and writing, thanks to daily practice. She would master telepathy.

The chasm between herself and the penitents—and perhaps between herself and Thomas?—was going to close.

CHAPTER 6

AT THE HEART OF IT ALL

Vy awoke weightless.

She was levitating. Again. This was the third time in a week.

"Ariock?" Vy cleared her throat. She must have slipped out of his embrace while they both slept, and now she could not physically reach him, defying gravity as she was.

Ariock lay asleep and dreaming below her. The huge bed, sculpted from meteorite, might be too massive for him to float it on a subconscious whim. Either that, or Ariock automatically anchored whatever furniture he happened to be using.

Curtains floated. Wall decor floated, unmoored from its hooks or shelves.

The sheet twisted and rippled above Vy like a magic carpet possessed by a restless spirit. Orb lights, holographic projectors, data marbles of varying sizes, and other knickknacks bobbed in the air.

"Ariock?" Vy adjusted her billowing nightclothes. Her multiple thin braids coiled like coppery snakes, lifted by unseen tendrils. "Ariock!"

He spasmed awake. Everything crashed to the floor.

Vy flopped onto Ariock's bare chest. The sheet landed on top of her.

She shoved it aside and scooted up so she could meet Ariock face-to-face. She held his scruffy cheeks and stared until he blinked up at her.

He looked amazingly relieved, as if he had expected to see devastation instead of Vy. He enfolded her gently in his arms.

"That must have been one hell of a nightmare," Vy remarked.

"Sorry." Ariock looked ashamed.

"Another nightmare." Vy studied him up close. They could only get face-to-face when he was lying down.

"I'm fine." Ariock stroked her waist, seeming to enjoy her contours.

Vy glanced meaningfully at the mess of shattered baubles and lanterns, overturned pottery, and books on the floor.

"It was just a dream." Ariock spoke lightly. "No big deal. Eh. I guess the stress of the war is getting to me."

He had nightmares every night. Vy knew, because she slept in his arms.

Each day brought a fresh wave of awful news. Rosy Ranks kept appearing unexpectedly in crowded plazas with hand grenades or dirty bombs. Their explosions killed people. Most of the Rosies lacked enough power to teleport away, but that didn't seem to matter to them. They martyred themselves. They were suicide bombers.

It wasn't a problem in Freedomland, or in any of the megalopolises. By now, the major city blocks had enough mirrored surfaces to prevent teleporters from making sudden appearances. Plus, Thomas's team of scientists had reverse engineered the pink inhibitor gas, and they'd set up traps in any location where a Torth might appear.

But it still happened once or twice per week. That was more than enough to unnerve everyone.

And Vy knew that Ariock had unhealed wounds inside his memory, raw and painful. Last week, he had created a crude likeness of Jinishta and the other warriors he had accidentally killed, to commemorate them. He had sculpted the frieze outside the war fortress complex where the warriors lived. But it wasn't enough atonement.

Nothing would ever be enough.

It never mattered how many people forgave him. Vy loved him every day, hugging him, touching him, listening to him. But no one, not even Thomas, could move Ariock. He was as stubborn as a mountain.

That was often a good quality. But now? Not so much.

"I know." Vy stroked Ariock's cheek, enjoying the softness of his scruff. "Hey. I wonder if we could find someone professional to help with your nightmares?"

She understood Ariock's bitter smile. Freedomland had many wondrous things, but there was a notable lack of psychologists.

"I tried talking with Thomas," Ariock said glumly.

"And . . . ?" Vy figured if anyone could bring Ariock out of his depression, it would be her foster brother.

"He advised me," Ariock said with some sarcasm, "to seek an Alashani spiritualist. A dream interpreter."

"Oh." Vy wondered if Thomas had given that suggestion out of desperation. "Well, maybe that's a good idea." She studied Ariock's face, looking for clues. "Have you?"

"I think Thomas is just fed up with me." Ariock sounded despondent. "No. We don't need rumors flying around the city that I'm mentally unstable."

Vy refrained from saying anything. Ariock's effect on the climate was obvious. People must be wondering about his mental state whether he sought help or not.

"They're just nightmares." Ariock sounded defensive. "Everyone has nightmares. Right? It's normal."

Vy felt a foreboding.

Whenever Ariock dismissed his nightmares, they turned out to be prophetic. He didn't seem aware of that particular behavioral pattern.

"Um." Vy caressed Ariock, making her voice casual. "Would you mind sharing what you're dreaming about?" She had assumed he was reliving the catastrophe on Nuss, but what if it wasn't that at all? What if he was glimpsing a future problem?

"It's just stress," Ariock assured her. "Plenty of people have much worse things to worry about right now."

That was true.

And yet it was also true that those people needed Ariock. He was supposed to be the Bringer of Hope. Didn't he care about how his mood affected morale throughout the free cities? Sure, depression was not something that could be easily treated, and maybe winter was his normal mood from now on. But didn't he owe it to his people to keep trying?

"Leave it to me," Vy suggested. "I'll find the right person for you to talk to. I'll make sure it's discreet."

She expected Ariock to brush that off. To her surprise, he actually looked hopeful. The light streaming through the windows became a bit sunnier.

"Really?" he said. "I would appreciate it."

Vy realized Ariock could not entrust a random clerk with his private secrets. Maybe she was actually helpful to him, in a small way?

"Of course. No problem." Vy kissed him.

Moments later, they both went their separate ways, doing their morning routines. Ariock merely propped himself up on the disorganized pillows. He reached for the decanter of water by his bedside, realized that it had fallen and spilled, and used his powers to refill it from the rockfall of pure mineral water.

He took a sip. "I'll be checking our realms." With that, he went statue-still, his eyes unfocused and vacant.

His mind was probably a thousand parsecs away.

Vy sighed and slid off the bed. Unlike Ariock, she could not teleport urine out of her bladder.

After screwing on her prosthetic, she used the bathroom like a normal human being. Then she began to put away the mess of fallen objects.

Ariock would require rest breaks between each five-minute jaunt across the galaxy. Sometimes he stretched or drank water, but he wouldn't bother with conversation unless there was major news. He would just rest for a few seconds and then jaunt off again.

He included Earth in his security sweeps. Vy was grateful for that. Whenever Ariock found the Torth encroaching on their homeworld with an armada, he would vanish for a few minutes. That meant he was hanging out in an air bubble in the void of space. He would use his powers to shove the armada toward the temporal gateway, which was enough of a threat to panic the Torth pilots and navigators.

Thusly, Ariock protected Earth, as well as Umdalkdul and its colonized moons, and Nuss. And if he received any alerts on his supercom wristwatch? He would mass-teleport troops from Point A to Point B.

He did that all day.

The only thing Vy could be sure of was that he would eventually return for breakfast. She bustled about, straightening the bedroom.

She did worry about local space. The nearest temporal stream was far away, and isolated points of life might be easy for Ariock to miss in the vast emptiness between here and there. He had confessed that he might miss a few sneaky shuttles. The Torth would not be able to conceal an armada speeding toward Reject-20— Freedomland—but they might pull off a terrorist attack.

Vy removed freshly squeezed fruit juice from the juicer, preparing breakfast. Maybe she was absorbing too much pessimism from Ariock? Thomas, unlike Ariock and Garrett, wanted to welcome sneaky solo vessels.

"I made a mistake in failing to protect the Upward Governess," Thomas had said. *"We cannot afford to make the same mistake again. That's imperative. If either one of the Twins shows up here—and that is a real possibility—we have to make them feel welcome. It's important. Okay?"*

Ariock had hesitantly agreed. He hated the fact that the Twins had invented insanity gas, but he trusted Thomas's advice, now more than ever. And the spaceport commissioner, a mer nerctan named Gojal, had made the same promise. Any solo ship would be received with a wary welcome instead of with blaster cannons. Unless it shot first, of course.

Vy stepped into the washroom, stripped off her clothes, and walked under the waterfall shower. She soaped up.

There were duties she could take on if she wanted to match Ariock's busy schedule. But she had learned that it was better, and kinder, to allow elected volunteers to step into those roles. Former slaves were ready and eager to make big, important decisions, the kinds of choices that had been denied slaves. Vy didn't need to get in their way.

The only thing people wanted from her, it seemed, was news about the Bringer of Hope.

When would Ariock fight in a battle? When would he make a public appearance? What did he do all day? Why was he in such a relentlessly dreary mood?

Vy wondered how people would react if they learned that Ariock wept in his sleep.

That kind of news would probably incite a mass panic. She wasn't going to say anything.

But she was sick of feeling like a helpless bystander.

Vy toweled off and stepped into a fresh outfit. That left her with nothing else to do except order breakfast for both of them.

When it arrived, Vy bustled around, arranging the table. She set up a vase full of black lilies as a centerpiece. It seemed to match Ariock's snowy mood. Not that he would notice, or if he did, he wouldn't comment.

Vy climbed onto the tall chair, propped her feet up, and scrolled through tasks on her wristwatch. She waited.

"Come back to me," Vy said to Ariock's empty body.

When had he decided to deal with everything alone?

Why did he have to be so unreachable?

Pilots practiced around the Freedomland spaceport every day, preparing for unexpected invasions because they could not rely on their Bringer of Hope. The tropical jungles were blanketed with snow. The sky was perpetually overcast. Yet Ariock pretended that he was just "taking a break."

He said he felt fine.

He wouldn't even tell Vy his dreams.

He had promised to always make an effort to listen to Vy. He had agreed that doing so was important. Instead, he was distancing himself, and Vy had to wonder if it was because of . . . well . . . because of Garrett's damned story.

Was Ariock so afraid that he would kill Vy by accident?

Maybe he should worry about what Vy would do to him for shutting her out.

Ariock joined her eventually. "Thanks for ordering breakfast." He lifted domes off the food plates, revealing French toast and fresh fruits.

Vy lazily moved her feet off the extra chair. She gave Ariock enough time to report any news.

He said nothing. He just began eating.

"So." Vy stirred her bowl of oatmeal. "Anything new in the universe?"

Ariock shrugged. He seemed to think breakfast was more important than confiding in her.

Vy supposed she should be grateful that he enjoyed eating. Otherwise he would skip meals, or just teleport nutrients directly into his stomach.

"I have something to confess," Vy said. "It's embarrassing."

That got his attention.

Vy waited for him to finish chewing, to swallow. Then she went on. "I overheard you and Garrett the other day, when he visited. He told you about how his wife died."

Ariock looked like he wanted to apologize on behalf of his whole family for being too powerful.

"I didn't mean to eavesdrop," Vy said. "It was accidental. But I'm not going to apologize. Because if I hadn't overheard, then I would feel like absolute crap, wondering why you're being extra, extra gentle around me."

Ariock began to say something.

Vy cut him off before he could utter a useless apology. "I can handle words. Your fears and dreams will never shatter me. I can handle anything you tell me. I swear. Just tell me. Stop being strong and silent and be real and human with me."

Ariock looked stunned.

After a second, he looked around the room with mock wariness. "Is there telepathy gas in here?"

Vy laughed. "I don't need to read your mind to make educated guesses. I know you pretty well. Remember?"

His pretense melted into shame.

"You're not as terrible as you think you are," Vy said. "You do a lot of good."

"I am death." He sounded serious.

Vy glared across the table at him. "You are not *death*."

Part of the problem, she knew, was that he had killed his parents. Or he believed he had. That weighed on his soul. The disaster with Jinishta and the other warriors only exacerbated the self-hatred that was already there.

"You're a hero," Vy said. "I'm a nurse. We have certain occupational hazards. People die in our care. If a nurse or a doctor fell apart every time they lost a patient? Then we wouldn't have hospitals. And a lot more people would die."

That gave him something to think about, at least.

"I've thought about giving up on you," Vy confessed.

Ariock studied her, pained.

"I thought that maybe we're too different," Vy went on. "You are dangerous. We're in agreement on that. So I went to Thomas, to get his advice, and you know what he said?"

Ariock looked curious, despite his moroseness.

"He thought I was being stupid." That was not exactly what Thomas had said, but Vy was exaggerating to make her point. "He said we're both overly fixated on our differences instead of our similarities. He said that if he had been that fixated on his differences with Cherise, and vice versa, they never would have had such a strong bond. He wouldn't have had any friends. He never would have considered himself human. He wouldn't be on our side. He wouldn't be a hero."

She could see that she was reaching Ariock, at least a little bit. And she could guess what his self-hatred was whispering now. *"Thomas isn't a killer."*

As if.

"Thomas is just as dangerous as you are." Vy pointed a spoonful of oatmeal toward Ariock. "And you have just as much self-control as he does. Maybe not as much wisdom, but who cares? You're human." Her voice roughened. She was trying so hard to convince him.

Ariock looked chagrined. He slumped, as if conceding a minor defeat. "I guess . . . well. I guess so."

"There's no guessing." Vy felt keyed up. If Ariock was unwilling to admit he was human in every way that mattered, then he might be beyond her reach. She could not reach a man who thought he was a demigod. Even if he had legitimate reasons to believe himself special or divine in some way, he needed to acknowledge the vulnerabilities and flaws that came with being human. He needed to remain human within his heart. Only then could they be more alike than different.

"I'm so afraid of hurting you." Ariock looked defeated. "I couldn't live with myself if I hurt you."

Didn't he realize that being cold and distant, and emotionally withdrawn, hurt her just as much as any physical pain?

"We can face that fear together," Vy said. "Just don't give up?"

He looked miserable in his uncertainty.

"I haven't given up." Vy set aside her spoon. "And I never will, unless you ask me to. Is that what you're asking me to do?"

She waited for him to admit that he needed her, that he wanted her, and that he was glad she was so willing to take the huge risk of loving him. Oh, and also, he should be grateful that someone loved him enough to stick with him, despite his rather severe depression.

Ariock shoved aside his plates and put his elbows on the table, resting his head between his massive fists. He looked too anguished to eat.

Fear gripped Vy's heart. Had she forced him to a breaking point?

"I've been having a recurring nightmare," Ariock confessed. "It's the same dream every night."

Vy blinked. She had not expected this.

"In my dream," Ariock said, "I lose you. Every time."

An icy chill crept up Vy's spine. She tried to ignore it.

"I know it's just a representation of my fears," Ariock was saying. "It's not going to come true. But it's awful. In the nightmare, the Death Architect has some kind of bomb, and I'm not strong enough to stop it from detonating. I'm not fast enough, not smart enough. And I lose you forever."

When he was a child, Ariock had dreamed that his father would burn to death. Then it had actually happened.

His mother, Delia, had shared that secret with Vy in their slave bunk room. Ariock himself had forgotten the trauma. Ariock was clueless about his own tendency to sense disaster. Yet it was obvious to anyone who knew him well.

"Hmm." Vy stirred syrup into her oatmeal. "How long have you been dreaming about my death?" she asked with a casual lack of concern.

"A couple of weeks," Ariock said. "That's one reason I won't go to those telepathy lessons. I don't need people peering into my head. There's nothing good in there. They'd just get worried."

"Yeah. That makes sense." Vy considered how to ask him for details of his recurring dream. If it was prophetic, maybe being forewarned would help her avoid a deadly disaster.

"It's not just the dream that's bothering me," Ariock said. "It's not even my guilt over what happened on Nuss, although that's definitely part of it." He shook his head, as if he had so many things to confess, he didn't know where to begin. "It's the zombies. It's our whole approach to this war. It's the brutality. Doesn't it seem like we're turning into tyrants?"

Vy had never expected to be asked that question.

"We have ninety million planets left to conquer," Ariock said. "And I can barely protect the three that we have. I just don't see any end. There's no good ending. It's a never-ending war. And I'm sick of killing."

Vy heard the sincerity in his voice.

She slid off her tall chair and went to put her arms around his shoulders. She had to stand on tiptoe to do it. She was just so glad that Ariock wasn't like his great-grandfather, who reveled in brutality.

"I don't have answers," she said. "But I trust that answers will come. Thomas will figure something out. Or something good will happen and everything will change."

Ariock seemed uncertain.

"Maybe we'll gain new allies." Vy was careful not to mention the Twins. Enemy supergeniuses were a touchy topic. They had invented the chemical weapons that had gotten so many innocent people killed. She wasn't sure she would be able to trust the Twins, even if they did show up, even if they swore allegiance to the Bringer of Hope.

"For now?" Vy went back to her chair. "Let's take it one day at a time." She picked up her spoon and made a pointed gesture toward Ariock's unfinished plates. "I know that hours of clairvoyant work takes a lot of energy. You should eat."

Ariock looked hesitant.

"And thank you for trusting me." Vy smiled at him. "You haven't chased me away yet. If that's your goal, then you have to try a lot harder."

Ariock's smile was so huge, the sky outside brightened as a sunbeam pierced the clouds. "I love you," he said.

Vy grinned and sprinkled seasoning into her oatmeal. "That's the best thing you've said all week."

CHAPTER 7

TELEPATHIC DEPRAVITY

"Next," Thomas said, while his instructions sank into the exposed soil of the zombie's broken mind.

His mental voice took root and unfurled into a simulacrum of instincts. The hollowed mind now contained something like a shabbily constructed intelligence, which was designed and assembled by Thomas. His will replaced the victim's personality and opinions. It was all that remained.

The newly minted zombie trotted toward the clerk's desk at the far end of the passageway. Clerks would reprogram the zombie's ocular implants to be glaringly white, remove its slave collar, and then send it outdoors to the livestock pen.

Zombies got treated like livestock. Most of them went to specialist handlers among soldiers and warriors.

It was a brutal system. Thomas hated it, despite the fact that he was its chief director and its root cause.

He fiddled with an origami sky croc. Nror had kindly delivered the handwritten letter to him, which he had idly folded.

I understand that you are forced to choose between one morality vs. another, Cherise had written. *You are pressured from many sides. I am sure Garrett is telling you one thing, while Ariock wants you to do another thing, and Jinishta, if she were still here, would ask for a third thing.*

Thomas uncreased and recreased the paper wings. Cherise still understood him, somehow.

"Please have mercy, great Conqueror?" The next prisoner fell to his knees. "Please. I will serve you in any way AHHH—!"

Thomas twisted his mind.

These prisoners were the psychopathic dregs of the penitent population, the ones who genuinely missed being able to torture slaves. Every one of them had gotten caught breaking a law.

They did not deserve mercy.

That was what Thomas told himself.

And in all practicality, he could not afford to be merciful. Zombies were the only force that kept the Torth Empire from sweeping through his conquered lands and reclaiming everything. He could no longer rely on Ariock or the Alashani warriors.

Before Thomas called for his next victim, he imparted his usual packet of baseline knowledge into the fresh zombie. *You may only harm or kill Torth. Do not harm or kill any free citizen. Here is the military hierarchy.*

A normal person would have required hundreds of hours to recite the whole list of baseline instructions, which included thousands of exceptions and important clarifications. Only a telepathic supergenius could deliver so much knowledge within seconds. Only a telepathic zombie could receive and process that much knowledge within seconds.

Thomas instructed the zombie in how to punch, kick, evade blows, and use its body as a shield to protect its masters.

Lastly, he gave it a self-maintenance package. The zombie needed to blink, swallow, lick dry lips, shift its weight, relieve cricks or cramps, and perform basic personal hygiene rituals. It would prioritize defensive battle maneuvers, but otherwise it must survive while also obeying commands from its handlers.

"Next," Thomas said.

The fresh zombie trotted toward the clerk's desk. A team of nussians used chains to drag the next unwilling lawbreaker out from the dank holding cell. It was another man with iridescent red eyes.

"Conqueror." The former Red Rank fell to his knees. "I swear, that govki attacked me. I didn't mean to break its arm. If you show me mercy AAH—!"

Thomas destroyed yet another person's free will.

Kessa's laws were known to all penitents, and Thomas trusted her with law enforcement. If Kessa deemed these prisoners to be beyond any hope of salvation or redemption? It wasn't his job to cross-examine her decisions. She appointed competent judges to evaluate every case. They would not send anyone innocent his way.

He replaced the former Red Rank's personality with his own artificial simulacrum of one.

Without Jinishta, Cherise had written, *the Alashani have lost a crucial voice. She only wanted to protect her people. Is that what you're doing?*

It seemed so.

Thomas twisted another mind.

And another. And another.

The victims begged for mercy. They made all manner of promises to the Conqueror, spoken or silent. They urinated in fear.

If zombies are the only way to protect the free cities, as far as you can see, Cherise had written, *then I trust you to make the hard, yet practical, decision. I have always trusted you to do that. I always will.*

What flattery.

Did Cherise still retain some trace of her old hero worship? Or was she resorting to desperate tactics as a measure to protect the albino warrior she loved? Thomas wished he didn't have to guess.

"Next." Thomas sank into yet another shrieking, crying crevasse of evil and despair. And he twisted it.

"Next."

What sort of creature gobbled up sins all day, rolled in the filth of evil minds, and wrecked personal inner worlds? A hero of prophecy?

A cretinous supergenius who thought of himself as the Conqueror?

Sometimes Thomas suppressed an urge to call Cherise and ask what she really thought. Whenever he visited the Alashani complex of war fortresses where he trained in secret with Daindlor, he considered taking a detour to the apartment that Cherise shared with Flen.

It just wasn't worth the humiliation.

Cherise must have suspected Thomas was growing more monstrous with every enemy consciousness he absorbed. Otherwise she would have visited him in person instead of writing a letter. She wanted nothing to do with the monster he was becoming.

She was wise that way.

"Next," Thomas called.

He zombified another dozen. And another dozen. His soul was filthy from the awfulness he absorbed. But he was finally getting to the end of his workload.

I only wish there was another way, Cherise had written.

She knew that what Thomas was doing was wrong. She wanted him to find a reason to stop.

"Next."

He made another windup toy out of the broken husk of a person's soul.

"Next."

Finally, the last zombie of two hundred and seventy-nine filed toward the livestock pen.

It was fewer than last week's catch. Even so, their terrified stares would haunt Thomas's nightmares. He remembered every single one of the people he ruined.

Thomas floated past the thorny prison guards without a word. They radiated nervousness.

Don't go near him.

. . . say he's tame, but . . .

. . . can't believe the messiah trusts him.

Thomas accidentally floated close enough to absorb some of their thoughts. Oops.

The nussians backed away in a hurry. Unlike his lab assistants, they did not think of him as any sort of Teacher. Military personnel were never sure how to treat the city's supergenius.

None were stupid enough to mistake Thomas for human. They knew better.

And Thomas knew that there was no point in feeding them petty, empty reassurances.

He didn't look at the guards while his subconsciousness mashed through all the lives he had absorbed. He plucked the visor from his hoverchair compartment and placed it over his eyes. He wanted to limit his visual input to dark nothingness. He did not want to pretend to be friendly.

Whole memories were shattered into fragmented flotsam inside his subconscious. His lower mind sorted and compiled and digested it all.

He considered going to an empty room before he returned to the academy research annex, just so he could sit in a fortress of solitude for a few hours and shove down all the excrement he had just absorbed. He needed to hammer it all down into the hard-packed filth at the bottom of his mind. He might be capable of friendliness and warmth in a couple of hours.

"Boy? You've been avoiding me."

Garrett lurked in the prison lobby.

Thomas could have groaned, but such an utterance would not inspire guilt in the old warrior. It would just be a pointless expenditure of energy.

"Go away." Thomas floated toward the exit. Perhaps he should not have ignored so many texted requests for meetings.

"You've been doing a commendable job of creating zombies." Garrett approached, the golden accents on his armor reflecting on the burnished floor. His black cape created a shadow. "But can we talk, please?"

Thomas inwardly growled. Agh. Didn't he owe Garrett obedience? The old man had helped to give him a future.

He flicked his hoverchair controls to glide to a halt.

"What do you want?" Thomas braced himself for unreasonable requests.

Garrett turned to the nearest guard. "Would you mind giving us the room?"

Soon they were alone, two mind readers in the lobby of a prison for mind readers. Garrett stood within inches of Thomas's range. He did not dare step any closer.

Garrett took a deep breath, like he was preparing for a fight. "I need you to step up your work in the lab."

Thomas felt a stab of annoyance. "We're all working overtime."

"I'm sure." Garrett's tone was an accusation. "How long does it take to invent immunity to one of those weaponized gases? Because we needed them, like"—he snapped his fingers—"yesterday."

Thomas struggled to find tranquility within himself. At least Garrett pretended not to be intimidated by him. That was sort of refreshing these days.

"I know you've warned us against engaging in an arms race," Garrett went on. "But come on. The Torth are so far ahead of us, we're losing!"

"Right," Thomas said. "My lab is working full speed ahead on immunity to the various gases. I promise. We're doing everything we can."

"Really?" Garrett glared. "Except I know you're spending time on useless activities. Like exercise. And playing with your sky croc."

Thomas glared back. Garrett had better not order him to quit the few things that kept him sane.

Garrett seemed fully heated up. "And begging the Torth to join us?" he ranted. "They won't. It's time for you to give up. Admit that you were wrong, and stop!"

Thomas removed his dark visor to give Garrett a full view of his frustrated glare.

Join Me, Thomas urged the Torth Empire on a daily basis. *I offer paradise.* He extended mental arms to the enemy masses. *I offer a chance for you to be intellectually and emotionally free.*

There were never any takers.

Yet.

Just one renegade, though, might usher in a flood of allies. Just one or two important renegades might allow Thomas to quit zombifying people.

It was a hope and a prayer. It was a chance that he could not ignore.

"Your forays into the Megacosm are a security risk," Garrett complained.

"I take every precaution." Thomas spread his siren's call only when he was alone and in a safe place. He let the Torth Empire see very little of his daily events, so they should be unable to guess about what vulnerabilities he might have, or how to predict his routine movements.

"The Twins," Garrett said pointedly, "are never going to legitimately join us."

Thomas looked around the lobby, worried there might be eavesdroppers. He didn't see anyone.

"Shh," he told Garrett.

Garrett puffed up. No one else dared to speak to him with condescension. "We can't trust them. Letting enemy supergeniuses in on our military secrets would be complete insanity! You need to let go of that dream."

Thomas tried to dial down his frustration. He really missed tranquility meshes.

He forced his words to come out with measured patience. "I'm aware that the Twins invented the insanity gas," he said.

"And the gaseous inhibitor," Garrett said. "And the telepathy gas. They're mass murderers!"

"They were coerced." Thomas wondered why he was even bothering to argue with an idiot. "If they join us, we absolutely need to find a way to let bygones be bygones."

Garrett folded his arms across his armored chest. His words dripped out. "That's easy for you to say."

His sarcasm might, unfortunately, be warranted. Garrett wasn't the only hero who had reason to hate the enemy scientists. Would Ariock be able to forgive the duo who were ultimately responsible for triggering his murderous rage, the disaster that had killed Jinishta and so many other warriors and innocent people?

Evenjos wouldn't be pleased, either. She despised the gaseous inhibitor more than anything. That gas was the only weapon in existence guaranteed to kill her.

Perhaps that was why the Twins were afraid to show up? Thomas would be hesitant, too, if he were them. Unlike the vast majority of penitents, the Twins were smart enough to have doubts about how much control the Conqueror was able to exert over his close friends. They might suspect he could not fully control Ariock and Evenjos and Garrett.

Yet Thomas yearned for their help. He thought of the Twins often, like a silent prayer.

If his promises in the Megacosm weren't enough to lure the Twins . . . should he send a signal of some sort? An encoded projection that hinted he was fully in control of his friends?

"How can you even think about trusting them?" Garrett seethed. "They might come here as undercover agents. How would you even be able to tell if they're on your side or just faking it?"

Some risks are worth taking.

Thomas wanted to say that, but he swallowed instead. This wasn't worth an argument as long as the Twins remained absent and out of reach.

"You can't!" Garrett threw up his hands. "It's impossible!"

Welcoming the Twins might be the only way for Thomas's side to win.

Instead of retreading that argument, Thomas studied Garrett anew. He suspected the old man's helpless rage had more to do with his great-grandson than anything else. "You're worried about Ariock. Aren't you?"

Garrett chewed on his lip in an almost childlike way. "Maybe."

"Give him time," Thomas suggested. "I'm sure he'll fight again."

Garrett studied Thomas, no doubt seeking reassurance.

"I pointed him in the right direction, I think," Thomas said. "Through a suggestion that will reach Vy. She'll take care of the rest."

Garrett grumbled, not quite trusting Thomas. "Right, right," he muttered.

"I understand you're overworked." Thomas forced himself to sound kind. It was an effort. "While we wait for Ariock to rebuild his confidence, I think we need to get a lot better at patrolling orbital space around our planets. Fayfer is ramping up our space fleet. I'm doing everything I can to help her."

"Is that enough?" Garrett's voice cracked, and Thomas caught a glimpse of how much stress he was under. "I go into battle ten times per day. I patrol the Megacosm fifty times per day."

No wonder Garrett was upset. He wasn't even expending energy for a cigarette.

Thomas was painfully aware of how many cities they had lost, with Garrett acting as their only hero. Dozens. There were guerrilla fighters who were just barely holding on to their freedom. The Torth were growing bolder and more murderous.

"I heal dying warriors," Garrett went on. "I give speeches to the troops, even though they just want to hear from Ariock. I go to sleep near depletion every night, and then I wake up and do it again. I'm not saying this to throw a pity party." His gruff tone precluded any accusations of weakness. "I'm handling it. I don't need sympathy and flowers. But I want you on the same page. I'm working as hard as I can, and it's not enough."

Of course it wasn't enough. They could not defeat the Torth Empire by killing one Torth at a time.

Thomas refrained from saying that out loud.

"I need a little help," Garrett said.

Neither one of the Dovanacks liked to ask for help. Thomas understood that, and he empathized. Admitting to weakness opened one up to being taken advantage of. It made one a target for bullies and enemies.

Thomas supposed he had his own shortcomings that he was reluctant to admit. He was among the eldest supergeniuses in existence, yet his functional knowledge was on par with a younger, unripe supergenius. Most of it consisted of mental excrement. He had not absorbed nearly as much efficacious knowledge as his peers in the Torth Empire.

The Twins and the Death Architect were smarter than he was. Heck, even the Rind Topographer, the Geodesic Flux, and the Spin Overture were ahead of him.

And he would never close that gap. He had a small memory leak.

His loss of data was not enough to cause cognitive impairment, but Thomas knew he was unfit to compete against a supergenius in peak condition, let alone a whole team of them. He worked and he worked, but he still could not quite grasp the principles behind insanity gas and the inhibitor gas. He needed a lot more time.

Or he needed the Twins.

Thomas sighed. "I'll pay more attention to our military projects in the lab." He supposed he could pile even more pressure onto Varktezo and other lab assistants. It would be loads of fun.

"I'd appreciate it." Garrett gave Thomas a stern look. "Also, how about if you quit your, uh, mystery excursions?"

Thomas should have guessed Garrett would spy on him.

He really wanted his sparring sessions with Daindlor to remain a secret, at least until he could hold his ground in a duel. If the old man chose to make a big deal about it . . .

"It's one of those Alashani maidens." Garrett spoke in a dry tone of insinuation. "Isn't it?"

Thomas made himself look innocently polite instead of laughing out loud. What sort of Alashani would flirt with the devil? It was preposterous.

"Look." Garrett dared to lean slightly closer. "I'll be the first to admit, some of those albino lasses are gorgeous, in a delicate, flowery sort of way. But you can't let yourself get distracted. Okay? I need you to stop."

Really?

Logically, Thomas knew, it was in his best interest to let Garrett keep his bad guess and depart without any further arguments.

But what right did the old man have to dictate his personal life? What an arrogant jerk!

"You're playing with dynamite." Garrett placed himself in front of Thomas, arms folded. "The undergrounders will panic if they learn you're messing with a shani woman. That's a no-brainer. Most of our warriors are already on strike. We can't afford more bad PR there. So I need you to quit your shenanigans."

Thomas couldn't quite manage an agreeable look.

What a double standard! Garrett didn't have to pretend to be an asexual scientific hermit. He had the love of a nearly indestructible woman who contained ancient secrets and who had a lot of love to give. People observed mini-whirlwinds outside the old man's apartment, kicked up whenever Evenjos was paying him a visit.

Lucky bastard.

"Look. I was a teenage boy once," Garrett said. "I get it. But just stow your horniness. All right? You need to stay out of trouble until after this crisis is past and we're winning again."

Thomas tried to look bland. But this crossed a boundary.

This was personal.

"I'm giving you an order," Garrett said. "No shenanigans. I want you entirely focused on work."

The old man gave Thomas one more stern glare of warning. Then he seemed to consider the matter settled, and he strode out of the prison lobby.

Thomas floated in precious solitude for a minute, trying to regain his balanced mood.

A seething fury writhed within him.

It must be nice to be able to teleport to a vacation spot on a whim. It must be nice to be friends with benefits with a goddess shapeshifter. Oh, and it must be really nice to be able to walk down city streets without overwhelming waves of hatred aimed one's way.

Garrett had all the power in their working relationship.

Meanwhile, Thomas was a slave. He supposed that obedience to that geriatric jerk counted as true penance.

He knew someone who would understand and empathize.

Thomas raised his wristwatch. His finger hovered over the call button. How many times had he mentally run through scenarios where he might discreetly summon the Pink Screwdriver and . . . well . . .

Screw?

She wouldn't say no.

She wouldn't even think *no*, Thomas felt sure.

Thomas could make it happen with a few strategic calls to various guards and errand runners. None of those assistants would guess the bigger picture. They would not know Thomas meant to arrange a tryst in one of his unused bomb shelters.

He shouldn't do it.

He really, really shouldn't.

Thomas glared at the exit where Garrett had gone and began to make arrangements.

CHAPTER 8

ANGELIC

"Try this." Cherise sliced a piece of fudge and offered a square to Flen. "You might like it."

Flen looked highly doubtful. He accepted the chocolate and nibbled a tiny corner. Cherise watched, delighted, as his expression changed.

"I don't understand," Flen said. "It looks weird. But the smell is good. And the taste? Mmm!" He popped the rest of the fudge into his mouth.

"Yeah, it's a treat on Earth," Cherise said. "Like rock candy." That was what the Alashani called their version of sweets.

"I'm convinced." Flen swept the rest of the imported fudge to one side of their kitchen counter. "Let's serve this at our wedding."

Cherise laughed agreeably. On the inside, she churned with doubts.

Flen had given her a golden hairnet studded with rubies. Those gemstones symbolized love among the Alashani. It was a marriage proposal. Obviously, Flen was eager to wed his angel from paradise.

And why not? Cherise was rich. She was popular. Some foolish albinos even revered her, as if she was in the same league as deities such as the Maiden of Candlelight and the Lady of Sorrow.

Cherise was supposed to be similarly eager to marry a dashing war hero. Flen had recently been elected to serve on the war council. He was a pillar of their community. He was everything that most albino maidens wanted.

"Have you ever tried a curscura truffle?" Flen asked.

"No," Cherise said.

"Try this." Flen dipped a tiny spoon into a tiny jar of chutney and offered it to Cherise.

She tasted the chutney with some apprehension. A sweet and nutty flavor filled her mouth, and her taste buds wanted more of it.

"Mmm." Cherise licked her lips.

"It's even better mixed with ice," Flen said.

"Why haven't I ever tasted this before?" Cherise asked.

"It's extremely expensive and rare." Flen looked glum. "Now that our cave cities are gone."

"It only grows in caves?"

"It comes from a truffle native to our homeworld," Flen said. "But it requires special conditions to grow, and I am not sure anyone has planted a batch."

"We'll have to remedy that," Cherise said. Privately, she wondered if the truffle could be found elsewhere in the galaxy, proliferated by the Torth. She could ask around at the academy. Some students used to be slaves who had specialized in culinary arts that catered to Torth tastes.

"Have you given any more thought to wedding invitations?" Flen turned his back to their haul of unique food gifts.

The food thing had become a tradition in their relationship. They cooked together once per week. They made a habit of teaching each other dishes that were new to the other. Unlike with music and art and TV, Flen was willing to experience new foods. Perhaps that was because Freedomland was a melting pot of cuisines, to such a degree that even the most stubborn Alashani purist could not avoid tasting weird alien dishes every once in a while. Eating fusion cuisine was acceptable in his social circles.

"Uh . . ." Cherise leaned against the counter next to him.

Flen gave her a beseeching, exasperated look.

She and he fit together nicely. They hit all the right checkboxes for romance, according to stories. They found each other attractive. They cared about each other. They got giddy and giggly with each other sometimes. They had great sex. At least, Cherise assumed it was great. It wasn't like she'd ever had any other partner to compare Flen to.

But they fought so often.

Almost every night.

Flen assured Cherise that arguments were a natural part of relationships. Cherise tried to believe him. Everyone knew that romantic dramas and comedies left out the parts where the sweet couple yelled at each other for buying the wrong set of drapes. No one wanted a love story marred by frazzled bed hair and petty arguments. It was like bathroom stuff. Everyone used a toilet, but no one wanted that to be a regular part of stories.

So the stories streamlined everything. Two people met and became friends. Check. They had sex. Check. Next thing? There was a wedding with balloons and cake, and they lived happily ever after.

Wasn't that Cherise and Flen? Wasn't it what they both wanted?

Everyone said relationships required work. Both people had to put in effort. That was common knowledge.

Cherise gave an uncomfortable shrug. "I just feel like I'm too young to get married."

She could barely meet his eyes. Part of her did want the wedding. After Thomas had tortured her, she would have been happy to watch him suffer while she walked down an aisle with Flen.

But Thomas had been coerced, and Cherise had been broken, and that was not who either of them was anymore.

"I . . ." Cherise managed a weak smile. "I'll settle on a wedding date soon. I just need a bit more time."

By now, Flen knew all her excuses. And he seemed painfully aware that they were excuses.

He leaned one elbow on the kitchen island and stared at her with his lovely lavender eyes.

Cherise gave him a warning look. She was so, so, so tired of arguing. Would she have to endure stupid arguments every night for decades to come? The notion made her innards wither.

"I understand why you're reluctant," Flen said.

His kindhearted acceptance was unexpected.

Cherise studied him, disbelieving. Did Flen truly understand how much she hated arguing? If so, then why did he keep picking at the same wounds in their relationship?

"It's because we've been withholding secrets from each other," Flen said.

"Oh?" Cherise tried to sound nonchalant. She was certain Flen had no idea that she had delivered a letter to Thomas. No one in his social circles could even translate written words. Whenever Flen saw Cherise writing instead of drawing, he dismissed it as an alien frivolity.

"Yes." Flen pulled up a stool and straddled it. "You must have noticed that I'm gone a lot."

"I guess." Cherise eyed him with suspicion. She knew he was holding angry rallies. It wasn't exactly a secret.

It was a major point of contention, though.

Cherise never brought it up because she was sick of arguing about Flen's opinion of Thomas. The last thing she wanted to do was start a fight.

"Haven't you wondered where I am?" Flen seemed hopeful.

She gave a noncommittal shrug. "I think you're holding rallies."

"I'm doing a lot more than that." Flen seemed happy to tell her, almost relieved. "I'm part of a secret society. Have you ever heard of the undergrounders?"

The undergrounders. Oh no. If Flen was an Alashani purism extremist . . .

Actually, Cherise felt some relief. It gave her an excellent justification to cool down their relationship. She could not be part of a purist movement. Surely most people would understand that.

"What have you heard?" Flen asked.

"They're Alashani purists," Cherise said. "They want to quit the war and form a breakaway underground society."

Flen took her hands as if she had said something romantic.

When he saw her reluctance, he said, "It's not about species purism. We're happy to accept people of all species, just as Alashani have always done. That is a staple of our way of life."

Cherise gazed down at their intertwined hands, her skin extra dark against his. She believed that Flen believed that. But hadn't he noticed the unspoken policies of Alashani-only establishments? Those places admitted aliens, but only aliens without neck scars. Liberated slaves were frowned upon with contempt.

"You're an angel," Flen said with reverence. "From paradise. No one would have a problem with you."

He brushed a lock of her hair aside, gazing at her the way he sometimes did in bed, as if she truly was an angel.

"Sure. Maybe." Cherise pulled away. "I'm not really worried about that. What I don't like is the idea of abandoning our friends to hide underground while they have to continue fighting the Torth alone."

Anger flickered across Flen's face.

"I had no right to say that," Cherise realized. "Sorry. I'm not the one who has to fight Torth." She hung her head.

"It's no big deal," Flen said in a tight voice. "You care about Vy. I get that." He shrugged uncomfortably. "But even you admit this war is impossible to win. Right?"

"It seems that way," Cherise said, full of misgivings.

She did agree with Flen on certain facts. Thomas had failed to predict the insanity gas disaster. Now he was pitting inexperienced pilots against much more experienced Torth pilots in aerial combat. What was he thinking?

His decisions looked desperate. He seemed rudderless, without a cogent plan.

Like, why did Thomas and Kessa insist on integrating penitent Torth into society? Why waste so many people's time and effort on that?

Cherise kept trying to see things from Thomas's perspective. He wasn't a monster. She was pretty sure of that. But she had to wonder if he cared about the Alashani warriors at all.

He certainly appeared to care about Torth. The penitent program showed them a lot of mercy.

"I enjoy killing Torth," Flen said. "It gives me great satisfaction. But there are certain facts I cannot ignore. My people are being whittled down. We are dying in this war."

"I know." Cherise took Flen's hands. He needed her. He needed her the way Thomas used to need her on Earth. The war kept claiming fresh victims among his friends and colleagues. Without her, Flen would be completely alone.

He clasped her, as if he was drowning and she was his lifeline.

Cherise kissed his forehead. She kissed his nub of a nose.

"Angel," Flen whispered against her forehead. "I think you can save me."

If only she could.

Cherise wondered if her written letter would have any influence whatsoever on Thomas. If not, she figured that Flen and Thomas were on a collision course. There was no doubt about who would win in such a showdown. Flen's self-righteous supporters would never shield him against the galactic supergenius.

Maybe a letter wasn't enough? Maybe Cherise ought to ask Vy to arrange a secret meeting between herself and Thomas?

But Thomas must like to evoke fear and awe. Otherwise he wouldn't have set himself up in a Dragon Tower with a pet sky croc and clandestine meetings with heroes of prophecy. He probably wanted Cherise to come begging to him, like a provincial peasant going to a much-feared sorcerer.

He might just toy with her and dismiss her.

And if anyone learned that Cherise wanted to beg for mercy on behalf of her boyfriend? That would humiliate Flen while enhancing Thomas's powerful reputation. Some Alashani would just assume the mighty *rekveh* had ensorcelled poor, sweet Cherise. Flen himself might jump to that conclusion.

She rubbed her forehead. Oh, how she wanted to trust Thomas the way she used to. She wanted that so much.

"Come." Flen tugged her toward the bedroom.

As he undressed, the wintry light from outside painted him in shades of snow. Cherise lit the brazier while he nuzzled her neck. These days, every room in the fortress needed a crackling hearth to stay warm.

Flen kissed her with passion. When he tried to peel Cherise's remaining clothes away, she decided that her blood was warm enough. She undressed in a few quick movements.

Soon they were cuddling upon layers of soft blankets. In delicious moments such as these, Cherise could envision herself spending the rest of her life with Flen.

"I'm not the only one who's been keeping secrets." Flen's smile was gentle and teasing.

"Oh?" Cherise wondered if she needed to distract him. She guided his hand to her bare breasts.

Flen cupped her breast. "Yes," he said. "I've heard what magic you're capable of."

Cherise giggled, loving the playful side of Flen.

His hand smoothed downward, caressing her abdomen. "Here."

Oh.

Magic? Yeah, right.

Flen refused to use the primitive condoms peddled by Alashani herbalists. Not that Cherise could blame him. The skin bags looked gross and uncomfortable.

So she let Flen believe she was fertile and okay with risking a pregnancy.

In actuality? She had asked Vy for a favor. Every once in a while, Ariock raided supply warehouses on Earth, taking medicines and sending private monetary donations as a roundabout way to pay for the missing supplies. Cherise had secretly obtained a supply of contraceptive pills.

"I haven't missed a period yet." Cherise maneuvered Flen's hand back up to her breasts. He thought the concept of pregnancy was sexy. It didn't do anything for her.

"You can have an augmented baby," Flen whispered, kissing her. "A powerful hybrid baby."

Cherise stopped moving.

"Orla figured out the theory." Flen nuzzled Cherise, as if he could not restrain his love for her. "She told Haz and a bunch of people before she died." He kissed Cherise's cheek. "It's a cute secret. I don't blame you for keeping quiet. It makes men jealous. But now? I know, love."

Cherise lost all her libido.

"Let's try not to be so secretive with each other from now on," Flen said. "All right?"

Cherise felt voiceless and trapped. She didn't want to accidentally confirm the theory, just in case Flen merely suspected that humans could breed powerful hybrids. No one knew for certain.

Well, maybe Thomas knew.

"I won't tell anyone." Flen gently kissed her silent lips. "Your secret is safe with me. Just as I know mine is safe with you."

He was right.

Cherise dared not report Flen as an undergrounder. She didn't want him exiled to some miserable outpost on Jerja.

But all the secrecy felt dangerous. It was like an unstable house of cards, a structure that would collapse at the slightest provocation. Kessa, Pung, Yuey, and Varktezo were all taking telepathy lessons. Cherise had refused to join in, unwilling to lose the mystery component of her friendships, but what if the use of telepathy gas became popular and widespread?

Had Flen even considered that?

Probably not. Flen laughed scornfully at the idea of nussians and ummins reading minds. He didn't believe it was even possible.

Orla had died weeks ago. Her theory must have circulated widely, to have survived her death.

This explained why so many men seemed interested in wooing Cherise and Vy lately.

Cherise hadn't known what to make of all the gifts that appeared outside the door of their suite. She had quit hanging out by herself at cafés in the Alashani district, because local men kept smiling at her and giving her compliments. She had even heard that a few shani were interested in taking her classes at the academy. They would have to wait until the next semester.

Ugh.

Cherise shivered and sat up. She began to pull on her clothes.

"You're beautiful," Flen said, watching her.

Cherise normally enjoyed his yearning gaze. But now? She wondered what Flen saw, exactly. A magically exotic eighteen-year-old? Or a magical baby-bearing vessel?

Did Flen love her? Or did he just love the potential of her womb?

Distrust isn't sexy, Cherise reminded herself. Flen kept telling her that.

She mentally pushed away a memory of the disabled boy who had saved her, and who had made her feel divine and loved for the first time in her life. That boy was history. Thomas didn't even look the same as he used to.

For better or worse, Cherise and Flen belonged to each other.

CHAPTER 9

SPARKLES AND SNOWFLAKES

Thomas checked his messages. A "package" had been delivered, along with a data string that he decrypted as one of his secret bomb shelters scattered throughout the city. This one was near the fishing wharfs.

He exited the research annex and bypassed the hovercart loading zone. Soon he was zigzagging down city streets in his hoverchair, past dirty snowbanks and bundled-up pedestrians.

"Agh!" An Alashani mother grabbed her two young toddlers and urged them into an alleyway full of kiosks and shoppers. "Don't let the *rekveh* see you."

An unfortunately common attitude. But Thomas knew he wasn't exactly giving people reasons to love him. His whole side of the war was floundering. He really shouldn't risk traveling in public.

And he definitely should return the sexy "package" to Lieutenant Yolpeen right now, instead of giving himself until sunrise. He should make wise decisions.

The canal district stank like fish. Certain attributes were common across habitable worlds, and saltwater oceans were one of those things. Most of the aquatic wildlife on Reject-20 was eel-like. The common eel species were popular in a lot of cuisine.

Thomas entered a nondescript alley between adobe buildings. He sped through a doorway before anyone might catch a glimpse of where he went. Down a ramp, through another door, and then there was a dead end.

He peered into a tiny camera lens. His facial recognition software approved his entry.

The vault door slid aside.

Thomas floated down a corridor that was paneled in mirrors. The booby traps were inactive, although anyone inside the bomb shelter could arm the system, which would then automatically kill anyone who resembled a Torth. Thomas was slightly apprehensive. He had installed a master override in the control sleeve he wore, just in case.

He parked his hoverchair at the end of the mirrored hall. For some reason that he did not examine, he wanted to show off his physicality. He wanted to walk into the bomb shelter rather than float.

He tapped his personal military code into the digital lock of the final vault door. It slid aside.

Within the empty underground bunker, the Pink Screwdriver reclined on a nest of blankets and pillows. She was gorgeous, lush, and almost naked.

Penitents were not supposed to know anything about his secret lairs. It was a huge security risk, and possibly a huge mistake, to give one of them military access, plus hints about the hidden booby traps. Thomas barely knew the Pink Screwdriver.

Well, that wasn't true. He had absorbed her entire life history and all her deep secrets.

Not that his knowledge mattered, insofar as security. As a penitent Torth, she might accidentally share the location of this bunker with a penitent whom he didn't know so well. Thomas could not police her day and night for the rest of her life. He could not control who bumped into her, or whom she bumped into. He could control for a lot of variables, but he could not predict everything.

Especially with telepathy gas growing in popularity.

Ah well.

If Kessa found out and didn't like it, if Garrett found out and disapproved . . . screw them. They weren't living his life. Everyone should be allowed a vice or two.

The Pink Screwdriver wore a diaphanous robe. White gauze did not hide her tawny earth tones. She sat up when Thomas entered. A lock of her black hair was loose, and it spilled across a pillow like a ribbon.

Her robe was loose. One of her breasts was half exposed in a tantalizing swell.

Thomas made sure the vault sealed behind him, locking them both inside. Then he whir-stepped onto the blankets. He felt unsteady and unbalanced, especially with so many folds and pillows surrounding his feet. He was likely to trip and fall.

The Pink Screwdriver sensed his unsteadiness. She rose to her knees and helped guide him to a comfortable sitting position. *I am so surprised (honored) that You want to see me again.* Her wordless thoughts came to him in rapid overlaps and overlays—the Torth way of communicating.

Unfettered imagination was so much faster, so much more eloquent, than any spoken language. Thomas felt himself relaxing a tiny bit.

Yes.

They faced each other. She was taller than him, since she had already gone all the way through puberty.

Thomas marveled that she wasn't crying in fear or banging on the vault door in a panic. After all, he had trapped her. She was, essentially, a slave. Terror would be a default reaction for a penitent trapped alone with the Conqueror.

Thomas hated himself. Why did he keep messing with her life? Who would welcome that?

Garrett was right. This was a mistake. Thomas should be focused on science, not on awkward encounters with a beautiful penitent. A supergenius ought to know better.

The Pink Screwdriver reached out with a gentle hand. She touched his shoulder.

Thomas knew she was forcing herself to ignore the thunderhead of his freakishly enormous mind. She caught glimpses of ugly Torth memories churning within. He contained evil.

He was evil.

He seized minds and twisted them. He was a destroyer of souls. There was no way to hide his monstrous deeds from a fellow mind reader.

(Yes) I sense what You have done, the Pink Screwdriver admitted. *But if I am supposed to tremble in fear of You . . . ? Well, let me know.*

She was actually reassuring him.

There was self-loathing within her as well. Thomas sensed it. They were both tainted, albeit to different degrees. They were both sinners. The Pink Screwdriver was not proud of the way she had mistreated her personal slaves. If someone *(the Conqueror)* wished to punish her, well, she would accept it.

Thomas realized he felt safe with her, in a way he felt with no one else in the universe. The Pink Screwdriver would not judge him. She already judged herself more harshly than anyone else, and no one—not even the Conqueror—could compete with her self-hatred.

The Pink Screwdriver unbuttoned his vest.

Thomas held her at arm's length. *I have made enough slaves (zombies) this week. It is not My intention to create yet another mindless slave. This visit is not meant to be (should not be) penance.*

The Pink Screwdriver gently bypassed his grasp and continued to remove his clothing. *I know.*

Thomas sensed that she had been practicing for this very opportunity. She had even practiced on a couple of fellow penitents, in the dark of the night. In secret. The Pink Screwdriver and her bedfellows suspected that sensuality was tied to emotions and self-expression, which was connected to creativity, which, in turn, was connected with invention and all the wondrous things the slave species created.

She was done being a Torth.

She wanted to try something new.

All right. Thomas gave up on trying to hold her back. If she wanted to experiment sexually with a deranged supergenius . . . well, what could he do to stop her? He wasn't exactly in the mood to singe her or torture her with a pain seizure.

The Pink Screwdriver propped him up on pillows. Her touches on his naked skin set off starbursts of tingles throughout his hormone-infused body.

Nobody ever touched him.

The sensation brought back memories of Cherise, and Vy, and Mrs. Hollander. And also Evenjos, when she had healed his neuromuscular disease. Yet the Pink Screwdriver was different from all those touches. She wasn't trying to keep him alive or perform some hygienic task. She wasn't here to feed him or bathe him.

She was here to have her way with him.

Sensuality was a skill, and the Pink Screwdriver had purposely absorbed relevant memories. She had tried to study the sexuality of ummins and nussians and shani. She had reviewed what worked best for them. And she wanted to show off all that she had learned.

You (Conqueror) have actually lived among humans (lucky). She mounted him. *You know so much.* She sank onto him, rubbing her nude body against his. *What is human sensuality like?* she silently inquired.

Thomas swallowed.

He was an expert on many, many things. So he dug into the bedrock of his vast memory banks, searching for relevant experiential memories, for answers to show off.

Most of the adults he had known throughout his life were Torth.

The teenagers who used to live with him in group homes had been maladjusted. Many came from backgrounds of molestation. Thomas had encountered a few healthy sexual relationships . . . but he had been too preoccupied with his own survival to study them at the time. All he had done was absorb them and file them away without any insights. Before puberty, he just hadn't been interested.

He was now.

Um, I've absorbed a few movies? Thomas played sensual scenes from Hollywood films and TV shows in his mind.

The Pink Screwdriver saw him as a god of knowledge. Yet she wasn't impressed.

Porn? He offered her previews of humans pretending to enjoy themselves.

She was even less impressed.

Hm. Thomas didn't blame her. A lot of porn reduced sex to an animal act, and that didn't hold much appeal to Torth, who considered animals far beneath them.

Um. Erotica? He fanned out his collection of sexually charged drawings and prose, absorbed from humans at some long-ago point in his faded childhood.

None of it seemed quite relevant to them. Those were all humans doing human things.

The Pink Screwdriver grinned. She actually giggled. *This godlike mind is even less knowledgeable (!) about this topic than I am!*

She was right. Thomas grinned.

She leaned close to him, her breasts grazing his chest, her fragrantly clean odors filling the air. *Never mind. Stop trying to impress me.*

The way she moved . . . Thomas groaned with pleasure. He could not help it. He was ridiculously hard.

She had been practicing. It was obvious. She moved in ways that actually made it difficult for Thomas to think.

He didn't want to stop thinking. For him, thinking was as necessary and natural as having a heartbeat and a pulse.

Yet she guided him, and her guidance proved to him that high-level thoughts needed to take a back seat for a while. If he was going to fully immerse himself in sensuality, then he needed to quit scheming and worrying, if only for a few seconds.

Be here with me. The Pink Screwdriver engulfed him in wet warmth. *Give me pleasure.*

She slid off him, onto him, off and on, in a rhythm that his body automatically responded to with fervor.

The war would wait.

The lifetimes he'd absorbed would keep.

Thomas surrendered to her meager demand. It was so simple. For this one moment, he was just a person, not a soulless aggregate of other people's life stories. Not a freak who stole other people's free will. Not a breaker of minds, or a terrifying *rekveh*, or a scheming supergenius.

Part of Thomas acknowledged that he was, indeed, still all those things . . . but the Pink Screwdriver did not care that he conquered worlds and destroyed minds. She was not interested in those aspects of him. She reveled in the immensity of his consciousness.

Their bodies moved in a rhythm as natural and traditional as the most ancient rituals of their sapient ancestors.

Their mingled heat and passion had nothing to do with Torth culture. It flouted Torth civilization. It defied everything she had been brought up to believe. It challenged his vaunted ability to think clearly and rationally.

The Pink Screwdriver lost herself inside his mind, even while he lost himself inside her body.

*! * ! * ! * !*

Thomas inhaled her emotions. While he felt everything she felt, he lost his last shred of self-control.

The Pink Screwdriver rocked on him, her body on top, her mind underneath his. She gripped his back, fingers digging into flesh.

He climaxed right along with her in a great and violent release, pressing into her.

*** ! *** ! *** ! ***

Their passion concurred, and they did not use their voices for the mutual crescendo, only their minds.

Afterward, she rolled off him. He sensed her smile at the starbursts and shimmers that were fading away.

!?

Thomas realized that when he'd lost control, he had accidentally caused wildfire sparks, shimmering shurikens of heat, and a few snowflakes.

Like a reckless doofus.

Or like a typical human. Like a Dovanack.

Back to self-chastisement? the Pink Screwdriver thought in a teasing tone. She snuggled up to him with a satisfied smile.

Thomas reeled in his expanded awareness. It was a good thing he hadn't accidentally ignited the blankets. He should keep tighter control of his subconscious. How would a Dovanack handle sex?

Maybe they're no better at self-control during sex, the Pink Screwdriver silently suggested. *And maybe, just maybe, this isn't the best topic for a sexual afterglow.*

Fair enough.

Thomas let himself enjoy the feel of her hand beneath his head, and the flowery scent of her long hair. He basked in a feeling of wholesomeness.

Amazement, even.

He had just done something normal that was entirely new to him.

He had actually managed to shove aside all his galactic concerns. He had never imagined he would be capable of something so intimate. So fun. And so simplistic.

This cozy feeling chased away a lot of the darkness inside him.

Same, the Pink Screwdriver thought with sleepy contentment, holding on to him. *It's like We aren't Torth at all.*

Thomas stroked her raven-black hair. This was all new to him.

The Upward Governess had yearned for this feeling, hadn't she? She had tried to coax Yellow Thomas into transcending Torth-ness. She had done that even when he himself had not believed that escape was possible.

The Upward Governess was the first penitent, the Pink Screwdriver thought.

That was true. She was the first.

That was something.

Thomas gazed at the shiny bronze ceiling, where he had accidentally created snowflake crystals and fiery paths. He smiled at the underlying fractals and cubic splines. His brain was decompressing.

He had plenty to worry about. For now, though?

He and the Pink Screwdriver weren't Torth at all. They were something new.

CHAPTER 10

EMPTY MINDS

Bringing zombies into the war palace made Garrett feel a tad guilty.

They could not be mistaken for penitents, with their foul rags. People leaped aside. Chambermaids pressed against burnished bronze walls, radiating fear.

"They're harmless," Garrett assured clerks and dignitaries of different species.

He silently commanded his four ripe zombies, *Duck your heads when people look at you.* That should allay the fearful reactions, a little.

People were unused to mind readers in these halls. Garrett supposed the milky-white eyes had something to do with inspiring fear. Tall or short, flabby or athletic, zombies all gave the impression of being Servants of All. Altering their eyes was the boy's idea.

A good idea, Garrett had to admit.

Legit Servants of All in the Torth Empire were starting to feel ashamed about the way their eyes looked. Some begged the Majority for an optics change. They had no desire to look like zombification victims—especially when everyone knew that they were the main targets for zombification.

The Majority kept ignoring their whinging complaints. Heh. The political fallout was making for good drama in the Megacosm.

Garrett parked his rental hovercart. Every part of him ached, from his forehead down to his toes. A depletion headache threatened at the edges of his consciousness.

It had been a long day of defending Umdalkdul from a Torth invasion fleet.

Stand guard, Garrett silently commanded his newly purchased acquisitions. *Peer around corners. Watch places where other zombies are not watching as carefully.*

To zombies, all commands and all masters were alike. They had zero curiosity. They filed off the hovercart like bedazzled children following a Pied Piper and assembled themselves according to Garrett's will.

Stop any Torth from entering My suite, Garrett silently reminded them.

Thank goodness the boy had figured out a way to set zombies up with basic directives, including survival and combat skills. That made them easy to handle. Otherwise? They would be impossible.

Garrett limped to his palatial doors, leaning on his silver staff. He had just enough raw power to lift the hidden lock bar and let himself into his apartment.

Whenever he felt vulnerable like this, it was like being a helpless child at the mercy of his monster of a father. He hated being weak. Depletion meant he could not ghost or teleport. He could not leave his body.

He needed to sleep for a while.

Once inside his suite, Garrett shut the heavy doors manually. He removed his cape and hung it on a peg. He limped past the six drooling zombies who stood inside his antechamber, ready to stand guard while he slept. Their minds were as echoey as chasms. They felt no moods. No opinions. They did not register exhaustion or pain. There was no way to tell which ones used to be Yellow Ranks and which ones were former Servants of All. They were all the same now.

Just animated corpses.

Inwardly, Garrett admitted that zombies were a bit creepy.

Everyone understood why they were necessary, of course, now more than ever. Zombies were the sole reason why Ariock still had warriors willing to fight and die for him. Zombies were the reason why Umdalkdul and Nuss remained free.

Garrett used the bathroom, then shuffled toward his bed, rubbing the small of his back. The ache in his lower spine returned every night, no matter how often Evenjos healed it.

"I can give you rejuvenation healing," Evenjos had offered as they lay in each other's arms. *"You don't need to suffer with arthritis and slipped discs."*

Sweet.

And silly. Rejuvenation healing was an enormous energy sink that neither of them could afford. How could Garrett possibly take a week off? And Evenjos needed to avail herself in field hospitals. Warriors and soldiers relied on her to fix critical injuries, now that most of the healer Yeresunsa were dead.

Ariock continued to refuse to go near war zones. What a stubborn and self-absorbed idiot.

Garrett sank onto his bed, too exhausted for any of his evening routines. He wanted to smoke some premium tobacco for an hour or so, but he couldn't waste that much time. He hadn't slept for more than a couple of hours in the last three days.

He set his alarm clock for six hours hence. It wasn't enough sleep, but a lot of desperate fighters needed a hero.

Garrett snuggled under his covers. With zombies on guard, no one was likely to knock on his door. And no Torth could appear inside his suite due to all the mirrored surfaces. The six zombies inside his apartment rounded out his defensive measures. He was safe.

He closed his eyes, and saw death, death, and more bloody death.

His merciless imagination replayed every Torth he had slaughtered today. There was the one whose spine he had broken. And the one he had burned to death. Oh, and the Rosy Rank who had tried to spray him with insanity gas. Garrett had disemboweled that trickster. Good riddance.

He yawned.

Perhaps he should attempt to train the boy in fighting techniques? Mental advantages might make up for shortcomings in strength and athleticism. Perhaps the Wisdom of prophecy could actually become a halfway decent warrior? With some expert training, of course.

And a lot of moral guidance.

Garrett's drifting subconsciousness continued to fight various threats even as sleepiness overtook him. He was Jonathan. And he was never any good. Just the outcast son of a monster.

He certainly wasn't the one that all the albinos waited for. He wasn't the messiah.

He was supposed to have saved her. Sarah. Julie. His wife. His one and only. A true hero would save her, because she was all that mattered. Why did he keep lying to himself, telling himself that he was a hero?

He was just a ghost.

A pathetic, unwanted, unloved piece of crap who did not belong in any world.

He was not human.

Not Alashani.

Not even a demonic monster, like the creature who had raised him. He had no voice, no body, no nothing.

He'd tried to save his wife. But the ocean was stronger than he was. It was dark and brutal and unrelenting. He swam. But he was unable to breathe.

He gasped. Or he tried to.

Something was tight around his throat.

Something smothered his face.

A knife plunged into his stomach.

Garrett woke to blackness and pain. He struggled to scream, but a pillow was pressed hard against his face, blocking his access to air.

Someone was stabbing him in the gut.

It felt like knives shredding his intestines. The pain was indescribable. Garrett had no chance to draw breath. Mental fog rushed inward. He was losing consciousness. Someone's hand leaned on his throat.

This was wrong.

This was not how the book of prophecies depicted his death!

Garrett expanded his awareness. He tried to use his powers to hurl away his attackers. But he was inhibited! An attacker had injected him, possibly using his own glove, which lay on the nightstand.

Meanwhile, a pillow covered his face. His throat was broken. The pain. His gut, and his head.

He was not going to make it.

His attackers had minds, sort of, but they seemed broken. There were four of them. Or six? Their minds were nothing but a hollow roar.

Zombies?

Garrett ascended into the Megacosm without making any conscious decision to do so. It was a reflex. He floundered for an audience in the same way that someone drowning would reach for help, no matter what, at any cost.

Help. Help. Help. He sought someone, anyone, to acknowledge his death throes.
???

Curiosity seekers gathered around his desperation. As soon as they identified who he was, the festivities began.

It's the Imposter!

   He is dying!!!

Torth roared with triumph.

Some brave champion must have stabbed him!

   Who?

     Who cares? Death to the Imposter!

Torth do-si-doed with each other's minds, sharing the good news. *DEATH TO THE IMPOSTER!!!!!*

Had Garrett expected that his plea might actually reach someone heroic? Who? Like, the boy? The Wisdom of prophecy only checked the Megacosm rarely. At this hour, he was likely sound asleep.

Blackness engulfed *(Garrett)* Jonathan Stead.

Had he just been decapitated, the way he was painted in the final round of Ah Jun's prophecies? Ah well. Death embraced him, as kind and gentle as he had always imagined his mother to be. If only she hadn't been murdered by the monster who was his father.

He fell into her.

"Garrett?"

The voice of Evenjos was distant. Meaningless.

"Garrett!"

Healing power coursed through him, as inescapable as an ocean. Power thundered through every one of his veins. It fought the agony. Power crashed through every part of him, from his cells on up to his brain.

He was raised off the bed, floating upon waves of power. His eyes fell open. He was surrounded by white starbursts and ripples of unseen energy flowing around him and into him. He was utterly at the mercy of the Lady of Sorrow.

Excess force eddied around her, lifting her hair in tendrils. The bladelike edges of her wings fanned out. Her face was godlike with concentration.

The healing continued even after Garrett regained his ability to breathe and to think.

He could hardly believe that he was alive.

His guts knitted back into a semblance of wholeness. Garrett felt the repairs. His tunic and bedcovers were splashed with blood, much of it still warm and wet.

He should be dead.

He was dimly aware of unmoving bodies in the corners of his bedroom. Evenjos had killed the six zombies with her powers.

Zombies?

Someone had dared to use his own zombies as murder weapons against him.

The boy *(Thomas)* loaded every zombie with baseline instructions, ensuring they would never attack a hero or an ally. They were supposed to be incapable of harming anyone except enemy Torth. Their basic directives were so complex, it would take weeks for anyone to untangle those instructions, let alone reprogram them.

Unless the boy reprogrammed them.

Would he dare?

I don't believe Thomas would attack us, Evenjos thought. She showed Garrett her recent memories. The city was buzzing with news about simultaneous attacks. Other victims were dead, killed by traitorous murder-zombies.

Chaizatel. Orlon.

They were premier warriors. Assassinated.

Garrett's wristwatch buzzed with notifications. It looked like he had missed at least a dozen emergency alerts while he was being murdered.

Too bad you cannot question zombies, Evenjos thought.

Garrett sensed her fatigue. She had healed people all day, as usual, and then she had killed a bunch of murderous zombies and also healed Garrett from near-death. This close call taxed her emotional stamina, if not her raw power.

"Sorry," she said. "For lurking."

Ah. So she had floated inside his suite as air molecules, crawling along his ceiling. She must have heard the news and gotten worried Garrett would be a target. That was how she had known to save him.

Garrett would normally chastise her for invading his privacy, but he felt like a pile of vomit. He was nauseous and ravenous from the intensive healing.

And he was alive.

He wrapped his arms around the true hero and brought her onto the bed with him.

They lay in each other's embraces. Neither of them would be any good in battle for a few days.

Garrett stroked her metallic feathers. "You saved me."

CHAPTER 11

AMELIORATION

Ariock had read enough books and seen enough TV to know that good leaders cared about their people. And he did care.

So why was he so reluctant to face the war council?

Vy gave him one of her encouraging looks from the sideline colonnade. It was endearing, how she treated Ariock as if he was the one who needed protecting.

He braced himself for hatred and stepped into the public spotlight.

No one yelled that he was a bad messiah. No one screamed that he had let premiers get murdered last night, or that his warriors were losing battles thanks to his lack of support, or that the horrible weather was his fault. No one mentioned that he had slain one hundred and four of his own warriors in an uncontrolled rage fueled by insanity gas. No one mentioned Jinishta's death. There was no spoken blame.

Just a thunderous silence.

Ariock walked past Garrett, who looked grateful to see him. He passed Evenjos. Kessa and Thomas sat on the far side of the plaza stage. Some of the outrage was aimed at the boy.

That anger should all be aimed at Ariock. It was a wonder anyone could stand to look at him.

He took his seat in his mica-flecked meteorite chair.

His throne.

Because who was he kidding, really? Kessa and Garrett had each called assemblies and press conferences in recent weeks, but neither of them used his extra-huge chair. It was a backdrop, a reminder to the galaxy that Ariock should stop moping and return to his obligations as the ultimate leader of their military society.

He was supposed to protect everyone. All the time.

People called him a hero, a king, a messiah. Every one of those titles was a euphemism for the same thing. It meant protector.

It meant he should never fail.

"Zombies attacked me in the middle of the night!" A premier warrior jumped out of her seat, apparently too upset to wait for an official statement. "I almost died!"

She peeled back her sleeve. Apparently, she had left some injuries unhealed in order to provide evidence. Ariock winced. He believed her. He just . . . Well, he didn't understand the calamitous reports.

"I didn't do it." Thomas made that a clear, unambiguous statement.

Thomas had said the same thing on another planet, in another year. The prophet Migyatel had silently read his future and then dropped dead of a stroke. The Alashani populace had accused Thomas of murdering her. They were wrong then, and Ariock figured their rage was similarly misplaced now.

"The same thing happened to me," Garrett said.

Ariock turned to his great-grandfather, shocked. This was somewhat harder to believe. Garrett took a lot of paranoid precautions, with a lock bar on his suite and an unpredictable schedule, plus his zombified sentries. He would not make for an easy target.

"It is true," Evenjos said. "If I had not showed up, Garrett Dovanack would be dead."

"She healed me." Garrett held up his hands in a gesture of helplessness. "The zombies shot me with the inhibitor, so I'm afraid I'm out of commission for a few days."

Ariock spread his awareness a bit. Sure enough, Garrett's life spark was subdued enough so that he would be lost in a crowd. He had no powers.

"They smothered me," Garrett said, "choked me, and stabbed me repeatedly. It was a near-death experience for sure." He leaned forward on his chair, gazing around Ariock to stare directly at Thomas. "I would really like to know who ordered my own zombies to murder me in my sleep."

All eyes focused on Thomas.

The boy dry-washed his hands. "Someone else. A hidden lurker."

The shock of that statement hit Ariock like a cannon blast.

"Probably a Rosy or a Servant of All," Thomas said, "hiding in plain sight among our penitent population."

"Jumping Jehoshaphat," Garrett muttered, not in the slave tongue.

The murmurs erupted into outrage. Many councilors remained seated, but the albinos leaped to their feet as if they wished to hurl spears.

"What are you saying? Someone *else* is making zombies?!"

"Someone who isn't you?"

"Targeting our war heroes? How can we stop them?"

One premier—Flen—leaped onto his chair and shouted, his voice shrill with outrage. "Are we just going to sit here and believe that *rekveh*?"

Flen wore a purple mantle and council finery, but he still looked immature to Ariock, barely eighteen years old.

"Thomas would never hurt people on our side." Ariock used a bit of power to amplify his voice. It rumbled over the plaza, overriding the outrage.

The assembly quieted.

"If there's a Torth with powers hidden among our penitents," Ariock said, "I'll find who it is." He closed his eyes and let his awareness creep outward.

It always felt dangerous to expand like this. He might accidentally hurt people. But he should be able to control himself long enough to find an incandescent life spark out in the slums where penitents lived.

"You won't find them that way," Garrett said. "Not today."

Ariock needed to know what that meant. He collected himself, growing smaller.

"I mean," Garrett said, "whoever it is will be wiped out right now, near depletion. Zombification or rezombification takes raw power."

Ariock returned to his normal human—sort of—stature.

"You can try in a few days," Garrett suggested. "They might be at the same raw power as our warriors, but they won't be in the Alashani quarter, I'm sure."

"You should try," Thomas said, "but I suspect this hidden lurker is smart enough to purposely keep themselves in a state of partial depletion. They know how you scan for life sparks."

Of course.

The lurker had managed to infiltrate the private suites of top military leaders, including Garrett. That wasn't easy. Their skills leaned toward stealth rather than raw strength. Either they were a clever rogue Torth, or they were managed by a supergenius.

And Ariock was outmatched.

"It's possible they don't have a ton of raw power to begin with," Thomas said. "They seem to have used gentle influence rather than blunt-force mind control."

"You mean . . ." Ariock figured he had missed a power lesson. "There's a magnitude of power below zombification?"

"Correct." Evenjos's tone was full of dismay. "The assassin used our own zombies against us. It would not have taken much power to tweak a mind that is already broken." She shuddered. "A person with fourth-magnitude telepathy can go undetected very easily. They can make people doubt their own memories, or forget the passerby they just saw. Their power does not cause permanent damage. It is temporary brainwashing."

Thomas was nodding.

He knew about the mental-influence power. Had he ever wielded it himself?

Ariock wanted to crumple beneath the revelation and this new threat. Everyone looked toward him, expecting the great messiah to solve the new problem. But he had no ideas. All he could think about was his recurring nightmare. What if the brainwasher got to Vy?

Or worse—what if the brainwasher casually ambled within range of Ariock? They could turn him into a murder machine.

"I'm sorry this attack took us by surprise," Thomas was saying. "I've long theorized that I'm not the only telepath with a power to twist minds."

Great.

"I think we're mostly safe," Garrett said, seeing the rising agitation in the audience. "I spy on the Torth Empire every day, and the Majority wasn't even aware of what happened here. They're not buzzing about brainwashers. I strongly suspect it's just the one."

Thomas gave him a sidelong look.

The unspoken criticism was obvious to Ariock. Brainwashers could twist the minds of fellow Torth. There might be hundreds of them. They might go unnoticed for years, even in the Megacosm.

Ariock rubbed a huge hand across his face. He hated feeling so outmatched. They could force him to kill people he loved. It would be like the insanity gas, except worse.

"We have enough problems," one of the councilors said. "This is . . ." She shook her head, at a loss for words. "It is too much."

People murmured in agreement. They could not sleep soundly with an enemy mind twister on the loose. Anyone might be the next victim.

"We should get rid of all the penitents!" a premier suggested.

"We should definitely kill all the zombies," another said.

In better days, Ariock would have told them to stop making such brutal suggestions. Now he let them speak. His side of the war had to get rid of the brainwasher, no matter the cost. Ariock could not allow himself to become weaponized ever again.

He turned to Thomas, pleading. "Is there a better way to handle this?"

"There is," Thomas said, placating.

That was encouraging. Ariock focused on his friend. He desperately needed hope.

"Telepathy gas," Thomas said, "diffuses thoughts and spreads them around, which causes problems for brainwashers. It's actually a dark energy matrix that reflects any mind-twisting back on the perpetrator. So they can't twist minds while they're in a telepathy gas zone."

Ariock recalled that the Torth Empire had nearly defeated Thomas that way.

"Go on," Garrett said.

"We'd create a telepathy gas zone," Thomas said, "in a large room, and systematically parade penitents through that room. With all those thoughts floating around? The penitents will be unable to avoid treading on each other's secrets."

It sounded toxic.

"One or two of the penitents might suspect who the culprit is," Thomas went on. "And once a few know it in the telepathy gas zone? They'll all know it." He gestured to the heroes. "We can handle it from there."

On the surface, it was a good idea.

But Ariock could think of ways it could go wrong. Should they really expose all the penitents in the city to each other's thoughts? Wasn't that equivalent to letting the captive Torth have their own version of the Megacosm? The penitents would gain an instant ability to coordinate attacks against their overseers.

And also . . .

"What if the brainwasher can teleport?" Ariock asked.

Silence from the assembly. No one wanted to hear that possibility.

"They can fool Kessa's lieutenants." Garrett stood, leaning on his staff. "We are talking about someone who can brainwash anyone into doing anything. Once they figure that we're trying to root them out, they'll brainwash a clerk into thinking they were already exposed to telepathy gas in a previous group. They'll evade detection."

Thomas looked uncomfortable.

"This is your domain." Garrett pointed a gnarled finger at the boy. "You're the one who can absorb thoughts faster than breathing. There's no need put Ariock or Kessa's lieutenants at risk. You can visit the penitent barracks and scan them, before the assassin has a chance to recover their powers and strike again."

Thomas's jaw tightened.

"Use telepathy gas if you have to," Garrett said, "but this should be one hundred percent your job."

It was an unfair ask. Yet Ariock found himself remaining silent. He understood Garrett was being noble in his own way, doing his best to ensure that his ultrapowerful great-grandson wasn't prone to the nefarious brainwasher.

Thomas looked profoundly unhappy. "There are millions of penitents in the city. You want me to scan them all? Within a few days?"

Garrett puffed up. "You're capable."

"I can try." Thomas dragged the words out. "But it means halting all my other work." He gave Ariock a pleading look. "And it will have a negative impact on my mental health."

Ariock hesitated. He didn't want Thomas to be psychologically unhealthy. That sounded . . . well, frankly, that sounded dangerous.

Yet the assassin—or assassins?—must have blended in with ordinary penitents. No one had suspected. Even now, there was not a hint. Not a clue. They were still lurking in his city.

"This takes priority over all your other tasks," Garrett said. "I am ordering you to take this on, boy."

The low-key tension between Thomas and Garrett never went away, but this seemed like the makings of an explosive argument. Ariock figured they were both under far too much stress. Garrett took daily risks in battle—and now he was inhibited—while Thomas was putting in overtime hours at the lab. Add in a stealth assassin who was capable of appropriating zombies, and of course everyone was on edge.

A premier warrior stood. "Jonathan Stead is correct," she said. "We need to be able to sleep safely in this city." She glared at Thomas. "If the genius *rekveh* thinks his own health takes priority over ours, where does that leave us?"

Thomas could have reiterated that he felt overworked, but he seemed to realize how crucial this task was. Evil was running amok in their city. It must be rooted out and destroyed. The enemy brainwasher could end freedom throughout the galaxy.

Besides, Thomas was supposed to obey direct orders from Garrett.

Only Ariock had the authority to veto this decision.

He took in the hundreds of expectant expressions. They trusted him to make the threat go away. Ariock glanced toward Vy, who sat outside the main assembly, on the sidelines between pillars. Her gaze was full of compassion and worry.

He could not allow anything bad to happen to her. He could not let himself be used as a weapon by the Torth ever again.

"If Thomas agrees to do this," Ariock said carefully, "then he needs protectors. I want warriors by his side."

That left an opening for Thomas to back out. It also ensured some proper respect. If Thomas was going to absorb the minds of millions of penitents, then everyone ought to acknowledge the baggage and the risks he was taking on.

The audience shifted their gazes toward Thomas, who floated in his smoke-colored hoverchair.

There was an unreadable fierceness in his eyes. Ariock hoped it was fury aimed toward the unknown lurker.

He nodded, shoulders hunched. He would do it.

Ariock gave him a nod of gratitude. Then he faced the assembly. "I want volunteer squads of warriors. Thomas needs round-the-clock protection while he scans penitent minds."

Mutterings. Albinos shifted their feet or adjusted their mantles.

"Why can't he use zombies?" a premier warrior shouted.

Garrett fielded that question. "No one can reprogram minds while they're in a telepathy gas zone. If the zombies are pawns of the enemy, then the boy would be an easy target. I think we need to back off on using zombies as long as this enemy brainwasher is on the loose."

"Well, surely nussians could protect him?" another warrior suggested.

"And snipers?" someone else said. "From afar?"

"Those might help," Ariock acknowledged. "But he needs warriors." Bodyguards and snipers might not react fast enough if the culprit could teleport, or if the culprit sent zombified people to make unexpected attacks. Warriors were better equipped to deal with this kind of threat.

"It's okay." Thomas began to float toward the exit. "Whatever. I can rely on nussians."

Ariock considered ways to force the warriors to reconsider their hatred. Thomas had designed their fireproof armor. His communications technology made it possible for loved ones to communicate across the galaxy. His laboratories ensured a standard of living that nearly rivaled that of the Torth Empire. His zombies and battle tactics ensured that the largest free cities remained free.

Why were so few Alashani cognizant of all the things Thomas did for them?

Thomas was the reason their people still existed at all. If not for his ability to absorb blueprints for a colony starship, the Alashani would have perished along with the Torth Homeworld.

An old, bald-headed premier warrior stood. "I'll protect the *rekveh*."

Thomas glided to a stop. He looked disbelieving, but there was also wary gratitude in his expression.

"Thomas is offering to risk his life for us." The bald premier glared around the assembly plaza. "It seems the least we can do is show him the same respect. It is what Jinishta would have wanted."

"Or he's tricking us," Flen said.

"Don't be stupid," the bald premier snapped. "If Thomas wanted us dead? We would be dead."

Ariock struggled to remember the name of the dignified bald premier. It came to him after a moment. "Thank you, Boryuchal. You have honor and integrity, like Jinishta."

Boryuchal accepted that with a simple nod. "Well?" He seemed to be daring his fellow premiers. "I have fifty warriors under my command. Are you telling me that mine, and only mine, should take on this life-or-death duty?" He folded his arms. "I thought you all cared about saving Alashani lives."

Stillness.

And then, incredibly, another premier warrior stood up and said, "I will join you, Boryuchal. I have sixty-two under my command."

Another stood, looking chagrined. "You can add my fifty-eight."

It was not easy for Alashani to overcome their loathing of mind readers. Ariock was impressed. Somehow, while he was on hiatus, it seemed Thomas had earned a little bit of credibility among the Alashani.

Even Thomas looked stunned. When he spoke, he sounded heartfelt. "Thank you."

CHAPTER 12

OVERLOAD

Torth, in aggregate, were banal.

They watched each other for cues on how to act and what to think. None hid unique ideas. Their secrets, if they had any, were petty and tasteless. Their crude concerns were as basic as a herd of animals'.

Was this the alleged master race? These were the superior, godlike beings who had appointed themselves to rule over everybody else?

Huh.

Thomas probed each and every penitent without moving. Mind readers shuffled past his chair, one by one, under threat from the Yeresunsa warriors who stood on the wraparound balcony above. At least none worried about getting zombified. Telepathy gas filled the hall, causing thoughts to echo and spread like underwater music, reducing the chances of any sort of attack. Stranger Danger would be unable to use their power here.

Where are you, Stranger Danger? Thomas wondered between mind probes. *I know you're in My city.*

The mind controller did not reveal themselves.

On it went. Penitents entered through one huge door and exited through another. The warriors above looked hellishly bored. Since the balcony was above the telepathy gas zone, they were not inundated with *(blah) (blah) (blah) Oh Great Mind!* or *(blah) (blah) (blah) I miss fashion shopping.* All they heard was blessed silence.

Morning passed. Then lunchtime.

Everyone had a bit of excitement when one moron decided to attack the Conqueror. Thomas detected the upcoming malice. He scooted backward, although the four-yard range was distorted and augmented, thanks to telepathy gas.

The pain seizure never hit him. Instead, it reflected back upon the attacker. It also scattered into several other penitents who were standing too close. They winced, but the pain was much less severe than it would have been had it been focused upon a single target. The effect was shared around and thus lessened.

The attacker writhed for a second, full of *???*, before he figured out that he had accidentally attacked himself.

So he quit the pain seizure and lunged. He intended to strangle the Conqueror to death like a savage.

"Kill." Thomas pointed.

Spears hit the attacker at bullet speeds. He died a gruesome death, impaled by a dozen projectiles.

Thomas had a moment of regret. Perhaps he should have asked the warriors to drag the attacker away, for later use as a zombie? That would have been a more economical use of resources.

Nearby penitents exchanged fearful glances. *Oh Great Conqueror!* They scrambled to worship him, terrified of being mistaken for enemies.

Thomas decided that instant death was plenty of punishment.

"That wasn't the mind controller." He figured that his saviors up on the balcony would want to know. So saying, he got back to work.

Another hundred.

Another thousand.

Another fifty thousand.

More and more and more.

Cringing, whinging thoughts saturated the hall, scattered farther than usual because of telepathy gas. It felt like soaking in a cesspit. Thomas wanted to vomit. But he kept working.

"*Rekveh.*" The premier warrior on the balcony had a kind voice, despite his use of the insulting word for telepaths. "Would you like to take a break? We can give you a meal."

Oh. Right. It was growing dark outside.

Thomas hardly felt his own body. He was an amalgamation. He had nearly forgotten that some people had to speak out loud like animals.

"Silence," Thomas said in a robotic tone.

The premier looked offended.

Thomas belatedly realized he was expected to behave more like an angel from paradise than a Torth. After all, he was from the same homeworld as the messiah. He had grown up in the same household as Cherise and Vy.

Well. The process of calculating a proper apology seemed more complex than quaternion geometry. Thomas wasn't going to even attempt it right now. Sure, he was a half angel, but all the minds he'd absorbed told him he was actually the sum total of six hundred thousand wretches from a cesspit.

His human self was a long ways away.

The warriors could go ahead and hate him. Whatever. Some of them would hate him no matter what he did or said.

By the time Thomas had thoroughly probed seven hundred thousand minds, he questioned the wisdom of continuing. He could hardly separate his own opinions from the morass. Was he supposed to think critically? He barely remembered how.

He thought of Azhdarchidae, soaring free. Lucky sky croc.

Azhdarchidae had learned how to fend for himself, especially during Thomas's long work hours, but he returned to his roost atop the Dragon Tower every night. Thomas tried to visit him every morning. Ironically, his pet yielded more fruitful information than many hundreds of thousands of penitents. The sky croc's keen observation skills gave Thomas a daily overview of what was happening around his city. He saw the fishing boats and the harbor, the teleportation flats, the rural spaceport with its makeshift launchpads, agricultural fields, the zombie pens, soldier training grounds, and the dumps where most penitents lived.

Dinnertime passed. Thomas hardly noticed.

Nror, his assistant, placed a protein shake in his cupholder. Thomas took small sips as he worked. He had to forgo his daily physical therapy regimen. He needed to find Stranger Danger before the villain could strike again.

Ariock was depending on his success.

The whole city was depending on him. Plus all his territories. His people.

Besides, he *(was a penitent)* had promised to obey Garrett Dovanack. He had duties. He dared not shrug them off. He would not make himself into a liar.

Another ten thousand. Another twenty thousand.

Thomas felt his own personality losing coherence, subsumed by hundreds of thousands of others. His mental capacity seemed infinite in comparison to the capacity of ordinary minds, but perhaps it was not infinite. He might actually have a limit.

A warrior leader spoke. Nror said something. Thomas could not even spare the bandwidth to translate their sounds.

Another five hundred hyperalert telepaths. Another five hundred.

Deep down, Thomas knew that stopping would be the wise decision. The healthy choice.

Were some of these former Torth a little bit different than others? Was he imagining it?

The subtly different ones would have escaped his notice under normal circumstances. They would not have stood out in the Megacosm. Thomas could hardly even pinpoint what made the different ones different.

He pondered that question in the tiny corner of his mind that was still sane.

The penitents were too terrified to dig into his private musings. They were unaware that he had picked up something unusual.

The rarities stood out in a room full of telepathy gas, where thoughts bounced around, diffuse. Their thoughts stuck to other minds. They seemed more influential than others, in a weird, subtle way.

Only a supergenius would have noticed such a subtle distinction, and only one who was saturated with data and still paying attention.

Thomas paused on the next rarity he came across.

She stared back at him with wide-set yellow eyes. *Please, great Conqueror, I swear, I am innocent.* She quivered with typical fear and standard thoughts. *I will obey You in all things! I promise!*

Sincerity emanated from her. It echoed in the telepathy gas zone, as moods tended to do. Her sincerity bounced off other minds.

But her influence was strange. Nearby penitents felt more sincere, more scared. Just like her.

It was not a power. But it might be a . . . well, a something.

A potentiality?

Thomas flicked his fingers, dismissing the terrified penitent. She slunk away, allowing the next penitent to step into her place.

Thomas took the precaution of screening his inner thoughts with tornado-like flurries of data. What made the influential ones different? Could they be Yeresunsa?

Well, all Torth were Yeresunsa, technically.

Third-magnitude telepathy was a somatic power, which meant one did not need an outsize sphere of influence or extra raw strength in order to use it. Telepathy was as intrinsic as breathing. Telepaths used their ability no matter what, whether they were on the inhibitor or not, whether they were depleted or not.

The ones with extra influence . . . perhaps they were stronger telepaths?

Their extra influence was only detectable with telepathy gas, echoing and reflecting off other minds. It was the same way Thomas's mind control power would echo and reflect upon him, should he be suicidal enough to use it within an artificial telepathy zone.

Fourth-magnitude telepaths, Thomas realized with a chill.

Their memories held no trace of recognition that they were capable of subtly brainwashing people.

Of course not. They had never been traumatized enough to snap into survival mode, the way Thomas had when his abusive foster father assaulted him in a burning house. Most of their lives were spent in luxury.

Now?

They were a gigantic bomb just waiting for a trauma trigger.

Thomas backed away from the endless chain of penitents, feeling overwhelmed. Eight hundred thousand minds in one sitting was too much, even for him. He could not go on. He needed fresh air.

Especially now that he knew he was outmatched.

The clueless brainwashers were fewer than one in a thousand. Thomas never would have noticed them if he had stopped after a thousand minds, the way he usually did. But after a hundred thousand . . . after eight hundred thousand . . .

Statistically, they seemed to comprise about 0.10 percent of the ordinary Torth population.

If they were, indeed, fourth-magnitude telepaths, they would naturally be more common among Rosy Ranks and Servants of All.

Altogether, there must be billions of them in the Torth Empire.

Billions.

Thomas sped into the cold night air, hyperventilating. The Torth Empire had thirty-eight billion latent brainwashers.

In the wrong hands, that resource could be transformed into a universe-ending calamity. Once the Death Architect realized what a gold mine she was sitting on . . .

Oh, but she probably realized it already.

She just needed to unearth it.

Everyone knew, by now, that trauma was the key to unlocking powers. The Death Architect must yearn to torture Servants or Rosies, to traumatize them in order to spark their buried, latent brainwashing powers. What held her back?

Just popular opinion.

She probably felt a bit too insecure on her metaphorical galactic throne to torture her most powerful underlings. Maybe she was engineering a reason to do so?

All she needed was an excuse.

Thomas closed his eyes and tried to slow his breathing. He felt defeated. Even with all his brains, he could never outfox more than thirty-eight billion brainwashers. Especially when they could be led by an enemy supergenius.

Unless . . .

Holy crap.

Unless Thomas flipped the potentiality to his own advantage.

"Are you okay, *rekveh*?" a kindly premier warrior called to him.

Thomas reexamined his idea.

He tested out mad hypotheses and extrapolated possibilities. He gawked at ramifications. This was incredible.

It could blow up in his face and doom the universe.

His timing would need to be perfect, if he decided to do it. This was not something to try casually. He would need to do a lot more scheming, to shore up holes, and to seal away flaws. All his friends would need to be on board. And if the Death Architect anticipated his plan? Even at the last microsecond?

It was an enormous risk.

The whole mad idea should be a last-resort solution. But if it worked . . .

The Torth Empire would become history.

"*Rekveh?*" The premier, Boryuchal, sounded concerned. "Do you need a nurse? I am calling for help."

Thomas tried to reply. All that came out was an embarrassing squeak.

"Nope." He cleared his throat to reestablish his speaking voice. "I'm fine. I'm done for tonight."

With that, Thomas floated down the road, leaving a retinue of warriors to scramble after him. At a respectful distance, of course.

Soldiers would clear out the assembly hall and prepare it for Thomas's next visit tomorrow morning.

He buried his idea beneath the many layers of his consciousness. After all, one never knew when Garrett or some other mind reader would show up.

He would sleep alone, as usual.

Alone except for the multitudes of screaming memories weighing upon his soul. And an unfurling map of future possibilities, as complex as the neural pathways in his brain.

CHAPTER 13

THE DEATH OF TRUST

All hail the Death Architect!
  The best Commander ever!
    Worship Her!
      She is amazing!

The Death Architect gazed at the mica-flecked meteorite walls of her cogitation chamber. She would not impede the prideful boasts of her orbiters. Let the fools revel. They had valid reasons to celebrate, as the military arms of the Torth Empire continued to hammer enemy garrisons on Nuss.

But Torth victories would not last.

She foresaw the future, even if no one else did.

The Death Architect descended from the Megacosm in order to think freely. Her orbiters had become more numerous than the stars beyond her frozen asteroid. Their insipid celebrations went on, wake cycle after wake cycle. How many of them acknowledged that the trio of newly invented weaponized gases had not actually destroyed the Conqueror or his most powerful minions?

The problem with precognitive visions was their open-endedness. The future did not have a conclusion. Centillions of possibilities were more than anyone, even she, could compute.

But her careful plans had not yielded the predicted, desirable outcome.

She had failed.

The Conqueror was alive and free to continue his schemes. And that was not the worst of it. Ummins and other slave species were not supposed to be able to read minds. If they learned to master telepathy . . . ? Her dreams showed her that the absurdity could become reality.

A future where even animals could read minds was not a future she wanted to live in.

The escape of the Twins had seemed trivial at the time, just an annoyance. But after the Conqueror had expelled all Torth troops from his city, the Death Architect had taken a nap—and she had suffered disturbing dreams.

All future possibilities were now flipped in the Conqueror's favor.

If the Twins reunited? That was catastrophic. Together, they could introduce a slew of unforeseen ripples into the matrix of future possibilities. They might cause the end of the Megacosm. If they joined the Conqueror, there was a strong possibility they would help him end Torth civilization.

They should have been killed.

That was obvious in hindsight. Supergeniuses should never be given any leeway, no matter how small. They should have been executed as soon as their military inventions transitioned from the ideation phase to the manufacturing phase.

After a few seconds of deep pondering, the Death Architect concluded that she had, indeed, been wrong to place any trust in her colleagues.

Never mind how smart the Lone Twin was. Never mind how loyally she had acted.

It was not the first time the Death Architect had made this grave error.

She used to admire the Upward Governess in her younger years. She used to look up to the older girl.

And she had misjudged Yellow Thomas as well, dismissing him as a loser. She had failed to even dream of him as formidable, even when he'd rescued the Giant and gone renegade. She had not foreseen that he would become the ultimate nemesis of civilization.

She used to esteem both of the Twins. They were older than herself, more knowledgeable, and they had signaled that they valued civilization by working hard to complete new weapons.

Her mistake with the Lone Twin was technically the fourth time she had misjudged a fellow supergenius.

The Death Architect had no choice but to acknowledge the uncomfortable truth. Despite her total rationality—despite her near perfection—she did have a mental weakness.

She wasn't a very good judge of character.

Well, no more mistakes like that. She would never rely on anyone else ever again. She must work alone from now on.

Satisfied that she had shored up her own flaw, she shifted her attention to the webwork of future possibilities.

She crawled up one thread and down another. Her perfect trap for the Conqueror was in ruins. Her web was full of rotten crevices and hidden sinkholes.

She attempted to spin fresh ideas. Unfortunately, she had already analyzed the most plausible futures. Every time she managed to think of something new, the possibilities exploded in complexity by a factor of millions. She had to test every one of those and extrapolate new theories, then test every branch of a branch.

It was all up to her. At least nobody dared question her. At least she was the unchallenged ruler of the Torth Empire.

One branch was interesting.

According to the rare penitents who dared visit the Megacosm, an actual rogue mind controller was hiding in the Conqueror's city. *Stranger Danger.* That was how the Conqueror referred to this slippery entity.

Might Stranger Danger become a useful tool?

Whoever it *(he)* was, he was operating on his own. Her shadowy glimpses revealed that Stranger Danger was a Servant of All, and he seemed loyal to the Torth Empire.

But he was too independent. He was unlikely to take advice. And even if he conceded to obey her? Well. She had that flaw, that inability to judge a person's character.

She dared not partner with anyone.

Especially someone with that power.

If only she possessed the power to twist minds herself. She would use it without hesitation or mercy. She would transform her champions into corporeal extensions of herself and bend them toward the great purpose of saving civilization.

If only.

She gazed at her own indistinct reflection in the polished wall. Her frail size and her skeletal hoverchair were irrelevant. Only her huge consciousness mattered.

Dark, quiet solitude enabled her thoughts to float, abstracted.

Colored lights beaded the upper molding of her cogitation chamber. The beads had a rhythm, correlating with radiation from the nearest heavenly bodies. Anything that interrupted the spectral patterns would change the beads, which would alert the Death Architect. That was how she knew whenever guests approached her lair.

Lesser minds figured that her light strips were just random prettiness.

Some Torth never forgot she was a child. Most Torth lacked curiosity.

Really, lesser minds were useless.

People had value only in aggregate, not as individuals. They were like atoms or molecules. Only somebody with a great mind—a ripened supergenius, old enough to have developed a sure sense of self—could be a worthwhile individual.

And even supergeniuses were worthless if they valued emotional incivility over civilization.

Great or small, Torth or not, all sapient beings overvalued their own worth while contributing next to nothing. Other people's stupid ideas were obstacles in the way of achievement. People in general were too unpredictable to work comfortably with. People were frustratingly independent. If only . . .

Her breath caught. Her toes twitched as she began to germinate a solution to all her problems.

The root of all problems, really, was free will.

Every time a person made a choice, the future erupted with a fractal of unfurling possibilities. Each personal decision was yet another twig in an endless forest of brambles. The Death Architect kept trying to scramble and hack her way through those obstacles—other people's decisions—seeking a route toward a desirable future.

The path was so overgrown, the galaxy so stuffed with people, she could no longer even glimpse a decent future.

What if she simply destroyed the obstacle generators?

Get rid of the brambles. Destroy the whole morass.

It would be difficult to destroy free will throughout the known universe. It would require brilliance. Elegance. Vast cosmic knowledge. Absolute authority, unchecked by the stupid Majority. Utter freedom. A perfect sense of timing. And ruthless logic, unmarred by primitive qualms.

These were all qualities that she did, indeed, possess.

The Death Architect began a promising new brainstorm.

CHAPTER 14

CARNIVAL

Ariock hesitated as Vy tugged him toward the fairground. It sounded like an actual nighttime festival was underway. With crowds.

"Come on!" Vy said.

Ariock was sure that once he ducked beneath the entrance archway, everyone would stare. Some fair-goers would fall to their knees in worship. They'd shout, "Messiah!" and draw an unending, relentless mob.

And there would be haters. Albinos would probably spit at Ariock and turn away in disgust, blaming him for getting their loved ones killed.

He couldn't go to a carnival. He would be the biggest freak in sight.

Nope.

He turned to head back home.

"Ariock!" Vy sounded exasperated. "The seer won't make appointments outside the fairgrounds. He won't see anyone except on this one night, the Festival of Lights. It's holy to the Alashani." She gripped his hand. "Please?"

Her eyes were so pretty.

Ariock wondered what sort of seer refused to see the messiah except on his own terms. A carnival huckster? This would likely just be a humiliating waste of time, unlike his encounter with the prophet Migyatel. Prophets were so rare as to be once in a generation.

Anyway, the whole concept of talking to a spiritualist was an exercise in futility, Ariock thought. His problems were galactic in scale. Talk therapy wouldn't fix them. Why had he agreed to this nonsensical outing?

He opened his mouth to excuse himself.

"If you buy me flowers," Vy said, "then we won't stand out so much."

Her cheeks were pink, and not just from the chilly nighttime weather.

Oh. Wait.

Was this a date?

Ariock had never imagined he would have an actual girlfriend. It seemed absurd. Did Vy really want to be seen with the freakish giant around the general population? This wasn't the war council. How would she feel once everyone started pointing and staring?

How could she be so brave?

"Come on," Vy said. "I don't think anyone will yell at you for showing me a good time."

Ariock allowed her to pull him toward the archway. Vy had never pressured him into a decision that he'd later regretted. Maybe he should trust her?

They entered a wonderland.

They passed albino fire dancers. Vendors sold concessions and toys. There were games with prizes. Ice sculptures. A shop with rainbow-scaled dresses and tunics. Street performers in outlandish costumes, reenacting tales of heroism. A petting zoo with children cuddling alien wildlife.

Ariock couldn't see inside the warmly lit kiosks unless he bent down. To him, the festival was mostly canopies and crowds.

People gawped at him. A handful of passersby did look sour when they saw Ariock, but in those cases, a companion said something that lightened their expression, and they moved on.

The worshippers were actually polite. A few did bow to Ariock, but they didn't block his way or mob him. Most of them wished him well and moved on.

It seemed people were too wrapped up in enjoying themselves to give Ariock more than half a minute's worth of reaction.

Sure, he was excessively tall. But was he really more eye-catching than a multi-species acrobatics performance?

Ariock clapped in appreciation of the acrobats, along with Vy and the rest of the impromptu street audience. He felt foolish for his narcissistic assumption that he would be the most fascinating attraction at the fair.

"Weren't they talented? That was amazing!" Vy looked happier than Ariock had seen her in a long time. "How could they somersault like that?"

Her eyes sparkled. As she tugged Ariock by the hand, her exuberance was infectious. Ariock couldn't help but smile back.

There was a difference between bringing hope and bringing joy. He was no good at the latter. The real experts were here.

"Want to go to the salted truffle kiosk?" Vy looked immensely pleased. "Oh! Look over there. Are those children Yeresunsa? Oh, we have to see what they can do."

Ariock had expected to get his talk therapy session over with as early as possible. Instead? He found himself following Vy here, there, and everywhere. He watched her play a seashell-themed game. She donated credits to a booth full of cute ummin children who were selling handcrafted gadgets. When Ariock saw a vendor selling tiaras made of flowers, he bought a garland for Vy and placed it on her head. She giggled, looking like a fairy princess.

"Okay, there's Mystic Avenue." Vy pointed. "That's where your appointment is."

Ariock followed Vy down the subdued street. His size still attracted stares, but at least the pedestrians here looked preoccupied with their own thoughts. Some were deep in serious chitchat.

He passed bejeweled yurts. All the tents were sized for shani. It was like the underground cities, where most ceilings were too low for him.

Vy stopped at a yurt festooned with black velvet drapes and purple glass lanterns. "This must be it."

Ariock knelt, searching for a doorway. The wall was all curtains.

"Wait here," Vy said. "I'll see if he's ready."

She nearly bumped into a bejeweled man who emerged from the yurt. Although the albino was small and perfumed, an enormous cushioned hat plumped up his head. His elaborate robes also added to his size. Artful fabric flowers, metallic lace, and gemstones adorned every inch of the costume.

"Peaceful and joyous greetings!" The albino was as flamboyant as his costume, his gestures large and animated. "Where is my next client?"

"I'm looking for the Great Mwagru?" Vy said.

"Then look no further. You have found him!" The Great Mwagru did a double take and stared at Vy with surprised reverence. "Oh my, my. Am I to interpret the mystical dreams of a most lovely angel from paradise?" He crossed his bejeweled hands over his heart. "I am honored."

"Sorry, no." Vy offered an apologetic smile. "The appointment is not for me."

"Then who?"

"It's for him." Vy aimed a thumb at Ariock.

The seer's teasing manner drained away as his gaze followed Vy's gesture. He had to crane his head back to find Ariock's face, which was probably lost in shadows, silhouetted against the overcast night sky. "Oh!" He squeaked, then cleared his throat. "Oh, the holy messiah? Bringer of Storms? Son of Hope? Oh my. Are you truly here for my services?"

Ariock nodded.

"We booked this appointment through Nezertorl," Vy said, as if that would clarify things.

"Ah, okay," the seer said. "Nezertorl told me to expect an illustrious client tonight, but I expected a war hero, or a military mayor, or, you know. I did not expect . . ." He chuckled, perhaps realizing that he was nattering on. "You are most welcome, Ariock Dovanack. This is too great an honor."

The Great Mwagru did not look like someone who would comfortably bow. Nevertheless, he made an attempt.

Vy seemed to remember Ariock's reluctance. She leaned close, shielded her mouth, and whispered, "A lot of people recommended this guy. Not just shani."

"Come in! Come in!" The seer swept a gesture toward the door flap.

Ariock had plenty of experience with places that were not sized for him. He spread his awareness and estimated the interior space of the yurt. Satisfied that it was large enough, he used his powers to push the drapes aside. He awkwardly crawled into a curtained, candlelit, and perfumed interior.

He settled cross-legged on the ornate carpet. He had to hunch to keep his head from poking the low ceiling.

Vy sat on a cushion close by.

The seer scampered inside. "I apologize, great messiah. My services may be too meager for you. Are you seeking a horoscope? Or a dream interpretation?"

Vy gave Ariock an encouraging look.

"Dream interpretation." Ariock inwardly braced for embarrassment. This was going to be such a humiliating waste of time.

"Excellent." The seer tapped a display of mirrored crystals, causing them to chime. Candle flames reflected off their vibrating surfaces, making the whole room shimmer. "Oh. Uh . . ." He gave Vy an apologetic look. "Dream interpretations can get personal. Would you like your lady angel to wait outside?"

Ariock hesitated. He didn't want to make a habit of keeping secrets from Vy.

On the other hand, if the seer did happen to dig into his recurring nightmare, Vy might take it personally. Would she fear that Ariock was subconsciously willing her to die? He really didn't want Vy to overhear any of the disturbing details.

Vy seemed to catch a hint in Ariock's gaze. She stood and squeezed his shoulder in reassurance. "I'll go for a walk."

"You don't have to," Ariock said, knowing he sounded unpersuasive. Maybe he should beg her to stay? Wasn't that what boyfriends were supposed to do?

"No, it's okay. This session is for you." Vy grinned. "Just tell me about it afterward."

She bounced onto her tiptoes and kissed him. Then she exited.

Ariock gazed at the swinging drapery where she had gone. Vy was his bedrock, his perfect reminder of why the war needed to be won. Little moments with her were enough to get him through any number of violent events and sad reports. He almost begged her to stay.

He just didn't know what to expect from the albino stranger.

Probably nothing bad. There was no reason to be nervous. The Great Mwagru was probably a charlatan.

Probably.

"All righty." The seer ignored a cushioned chair that was studded with gems and plopped onto the tasseled carpet. "This works by touch."

He reached for Ariock's hand.

Ariock jerked away, remembering blind Migyatel and her gnarled little hands. She had touched him and foreseen quite a lot.

"Oh, I am not a prophet," the seer said with kindness, perhaps realizing what Ariock was afraid of. "I will not glimpse your future. The touch is just an aid, to help me visualize . . ." He seemed to give up. "If you'd rather not?" He held up his hands in a gesture of harmlessness. "You can just tell me your dream. We don't have to touch."

Ariock felt foolish. He was being paranoid.

"It's fine." Ariock relented, offering his hand. "If it helps, go ahead."

The seer delicately grasped Ariock's hand with his albino digits. He closed his eyes, as if entering a trance. "Tell me your dream."

"It's a recurring nightmare."

The seer looked politely interested. "Tell me about it," he said in an encouraging tone.

"I'm trying to stop a weapon that will destroy the universe." Ariock saw a menacing, overly complex holographic display in his mind's eye. "It was invented by an enemy supergenius. I'm the only one who can stop it from happening."

The seer was clearly trying to look nonchalant, but his lavender eyes widened beneath his plump hat. "Ooh," he said. "Um, where does this dream take place?"

"The details are vague." Ariock wished he knew. "I think it's an asteroid."

The seer nodded for him to go on. He was probably imagining some sort of stalactite in the sky. Alashani tended to have a shaky grasp of astronomy.

"So anyway," Ariock said, "I'm using all my strength. I mean, all of it." His voice broke. He hadn't realized this would be so hard to talk about. "And some kind of secondary bomb goes off. I don't detect it in time. And I realize that everyone I care about . . ." He lowered his voice, as if speaking quietly would reduce the risk of some aspect of the dream coming true. "Everyone. Everyone is dead or dying."

The seer let go of Ariock's hand. He must have a lot of practice as a professional listener, yet even so, his look of disturbance was so great, it might be theatrical.

Ariock expected some profound comment.

But the seer only said, "Go on. Is there more to your dream?"

"Yes." Ariock wanted to make sure that his emotional devastation was plain. As long as he was sitting across from a professional dream interpreter, he might as well see if he could gain any semblance of sagacious advice. "Vy is tumbling away from me, through space, without a spacesuit. And I'm too weak to save her."

Ariock stretched for Vy's diminutive body in the dark vastness of space.

But she was flying away at a rapid pace, and no matter how far he stretched his awareness, it wasn't enough. The air was leaving her lungs. Frost formed on her lips and eyes. Her life spark was indistinguishable from radiation and space dust. It was a guttering ember. She was dying.

"I'm not fast enough," Ariock explained with a shiver. "Not strong enough. And I fail."

All his power was worthless. It didn't matter that he had the power of a god. It wasn't enough.

"And everything ends."

He fumbled and failed to protect Vy, and he could never catch up to her, or find her, or save her. He was bereft.

The devastation was so total, he knew only darkness afterward. Nothing existed anymore. Death was all there was.

"Half the time, when I wake up, I'm causing bedroom furniture to float." Ariock figured the seer must be familiar with Yeresunsa clients. Just in case, though, he added, "That's a sign of emotional disturbance in Yeresunsa."

The seer appeared to be deep in thought.

Ariock waited for advice.

They gazed at each other.

"Uh, that's it," Ariock said. "That's my dream. I fail and the universe ends and everyone dies."

CHAPTER 15

A FOREVER WAR

"Well, well." The Great Mwagru stood. "Would you like a pot of tea?"

Ariock wondered if the seer was making fun of the serious subject matter.

"I promise, I heard the gravity of your dream." The seer bustled about his tiny kitchenette. "But I need a moment to begin my interpretation. Let's get comfortable. I have honeyed spice, a mushroom blend, or an herbal zest." He used a flash boiler.

"The nightmare probably comes from my big failure on Nuss," Ariock admitted. "I guess I don't need professional advice to understand that. I'm sorry to have wasted your—"

"Your visit is not any sort of waste of time." The seer's tone was urgent. "Please, Bringer of Hope. Stay. I really wish to discuss this."

Ariock settled back. He had a strangely vulnerable feeling, as if he was a kid.

The seer set a teacup next to his own cushiony chair and poured a few ounces for himself. "Honeyed spice," he announced and set the steaming pot next to Ariock. He must realize it was pointless to offer tiny porcelain tableware to a giant.

"It's just from leftover anxiety, probably," Ariock guessed. "It will go away in time. Right?"

The seer sat on the chair and adjusted his robes, making himself comfortable. When he finally faced Ariock, his lavender eyes were intensely curious. "Have you ever had prophetic dreams? Do your dreams ever come true?"

What a weird question.

"No . . ." Ariock trailed off as he thought about it. Hadn't he dreamed of his mother impaled on a piece of metal shrapnel, weeks before it happened?

But he had been under a huge amount of stress at the time. He'd battled in an arena for a silent audience of Torth, forced to endure amped-up emotions due to the helmet they'd made him wear. That nightmare about his mother must have just been a grim coincidence.

And he had dreamed about Jinishta dying in a raging storm.

But that was also due to stress, most likely. His dreams were full of violence and killing.

"No," Ariock decided. "If I had prophetic dreams, I'm sure I would know." Thomas would have told him, at the very least.

The seer looked immensely relieved. "When did you begin to experience this dream?" he asked.

Ariock thought back. Jinishta had still been alive, the first time he'd woken to find objects floating from his distress. "I guess since before the catastrophe on Nuss."

"Ah." The seer crossed his legs and adjusted his glittering robes. "You've been plagued by this disturbing dream for many pendulum swings. And . . ." He sipped with delicate finesse. "It has not come true yet."

Ariock actually felt reassured. That was an excellent point. His recurring nightmare held no truth whatsoever.

"What do you fear?" the seer asked.

Ariock hesitated.

"Never mind." The seer put aside his tea. "I realize that you don't want to blather all your vulnerabilities to a lovely stranger." He gestured to himself. "I respect that. So I hope you will allow me to deduce the obvious? We can use that as a starting point."

Ariock wasn't sure what the seer meant. He raised an inquiring eyebrow.

"I am guessing that this is your first visit to a spiritualist?" The seer's tone was as warm and reassuring as honey. "People generally come to me for one of two reasons. Either they want assurance that their beautiful dream will come true, or they want to make the nightmares stop."

"Oh." Ariock perked up. He did want to make the nightmares stop. He really wanted that. "You can do that?"

"I won't overpromise," the seer said. "But I believe I can help."

Ariock leaned on his knees. He was ready for help.

"Obviously, you fear losing your lovely angel from paradise," the seer said.

Ariock nodded.

"Have you always feared being unable to hold on to the people you love?" The seer gave Ariock a kindly look.

A memory of smoke and flames flashed through Ariock's mind. "Ever since I lost my father," he admitted. "When I was a child."

The seer nodded in acknowledgment. "Yet you were not plagued with a recurring nightmare until recently. Your fear has grown, hasn't it?"

Ariock slumped. He didn't need a professional to tell him why he kept dreaming about being a colossal failure. It must be obvious to everyone in the galaxy.

He confessed it out loud, anyway. "I failed the warriors who were relying on me. I failed to save Jinishta. And Orla."

"But that isn't it," the seer said.

Ariock looked at him, confused.

"You said the nightmare began before that," the seer said.

That was a valid point. Ariock frowned, trying to figure out what might have triggered his anxiety, if not the disastrous trap he had blundered into.

"I know the stories of your great deeds, messiah," the seer said. "You are a hero for a reason."

Was this professional just going to offer empty flattery? Ariock could get that anywhere, and he certainly didn't need more of it.

"You are renowned as a fighter," the seer continued. "When the Torth beat you, you spat out the blood and got back up. When they robbed you of your powers? You used your fists. You shoved them off a tower top in the dead city. When they pitted you against angry beasts in an arena? You discovered your powers. When the Torth had you cornered in the borderlands? You revealed the Servants of All for the Yeresunsa they were."

Ariock wondered if the seer wanted a private worship session. How useless. He searched for a way to make a polite exit.

"My point," the seer said, "is that something changed." He folded his hands over his heart. "Inside you."

Perhaps that was valid. In his darkest moments, Ariock feared that the insanity gas, or perhaps Evenjos's healing, had damaged him in some permanent, fundamental way.

"It sounds as if you are willing to let the Torth defeat you," the seer said.

Ariock sat up straighter, although his head poked the canvas ceiling. "No." He was offended. "It's not that I'm willing. It's that I feel helpless to stop them."

"You?" The seer gestured, indicating the width of Ariock's shoulders. "You feel helpless?"

Ariock knew it must seem absurd to someone who lacked big muscles or big powers. "Yes," he admitted. "I was outwitted by an enemy supergenius. That can happen again. I'm not . . ." He stammered to a stop, unsure if he should admit his vulnerabilities.

But his frustration was too great.

"I'm at the mercy of supergeniuses," Ariock said. "You think I'm a great leader? Well, leaders rely on advisers. I'm only as good as the people who help me make plans."

"Ah." The seer studied him. "So you are having trouble trusting your supergenius friend."

"No. It's not that." Ariock was tired of correcting Alashani who detested *rekvehs*. "Thomas is the reason any of us survived. He warned me about that trap. And anyway, I trust him with my life on a regular basis. The people in this city have no idea how much they owe their freedom to Thomas."

The seer crossed his legs the other way. He looked intrigued. "So," he said, "it sounds like you worry that the enemy supergeniuses are collectively smarter than Thomas?"

Ariock nearly denied it. But he stopped.

Maybe there was some truth to that.

"You are a symbol of faith," the seer said. "But you have lost your own faith?"

Ariock didn't think religion had much to do with his worries. Still, in an abstract way, he supposed he had lost some faith. "I guess so."

"What decision has Thomas made lately," the seer said, "that you question?"

Ariock wished he had not complained. This was certainly not a topic he ought to discuss with a stranger. Even so, as he considered the question, he realized that the seer had struck a nerve.

There were things Thomas did, lately, that made him uneasy.

Thomas had become withdrawn. He was ill-tempered. He refused to help out with telepathy lessons. He refused private council meetings. Whenever Ariock asked to hang out, he was busy. He seemed to have a simmering anger just beneath his surface.

And there were all the zombies.

Ariock tried to approve of the army that Thomas was single-handedly building with the power of his mind. But deep down, he remembered Thomas refusing based on moral reasons.

Thomas no longer spoke of morality.

Ariock remembered the story of Audavian and Unyat. Anyone with an ordinary mind—including Ariock himself—was vulnerable to that particular power. With every increase in the numbers of zombies, Ariock felt as if his side of the war was sliding down a dark path.

It was dishonorable, to rob people of their free will.

It was cruel, even when the victims were the worst sorts of Torth.

"I can't point to any one decision," Ariock said. "Every decision we've made together seems good. But . . ." He hesitated.

Well, a professional dream interpreter probably knew better than to blab secrets of the messiah all over the city. Right?

Ariock leaned his forehead into his hands and took a plunge. "I'm climbing an endless mountain of corpses. That was a dream I had, when I was a gladiator in an arena for Torth pleasure. I dreamed that I caused endless amounts of deaths. Mostly Torth, but there were others. My mother included. She was dead. And then it turned out that . . . yeah, that dream came true. I killed her by accident."

The seer looked deeply disturbed and sympathetic. He set aside his teacup.

"I'm a slaughter machine," Ariock said. "I told Evenjos that this is an age of war. And maybe someday we'll have an age of peace, but I don't see it happening anytime soon."

He covered his eyes with his hands. If only he could cancel out the horrors he caused.

"Killing disturbs you." The seer's voice was gentle.

It felt strange to Ariock to admit how much he disliked killing, even when it was justified. His guilt was unheroic. Garrett must see it as a gross sign of weakness. Thomas, too, probably thought Ariock was being pathetic. And Vy. Everyone must think so.

And they were right.

The situation on Nuss was untenable. The Torth had reinforced their garrisons there, and Ariock's people were afraid to venture beyond city walls. Anyone who soared too far got shot down. If his people dared to ride a hovercart, or go for a hike, they were likely to get snatched and collared.

His fault. Because he wasn't there. Ariock was supposed to bring hope and justice. What good was he if he failed?

"What would happen if you no longer felt guilt?" the seer asked.

Ariock struggled with that question. "I guess I wouldn't be me." He would become something soulless and Torth-like. "I guess the Torth would win," he admitted.

Perhaps some guilt was good. It kept him human.

"But I shouldn't feel so much guilt," Ariock amended. "It's stopping me."

"Is it?" the seer asked.

"Yes. I'm burdened by guilt. Mostly because I keep destroying people I love. And I can't just downplay that, or forget what I've done. I know everyone wants me to. But it doesn't feel right, to cast aside all my morals so I can be the supposed hero that everyone looks up to."

He wasn't a hero. That was the problem. Heroes were not mass murderers. They were not butchers.

Thomas was the hero. His plan to recruit Torth instead of murder them—that was heroic.

"Your morals make you a hero." The seer made it a statement.

Ariock began to argue. But then he realized the seer had restated what he himself had implied.

It wasn't the way Ariock would have phrased things. If someone had asked him what made a hero heroic, he would have talked about duty and delivering justice. He would have cited the ability to be tough and determined in any bad situation.

But it was morals.

"I'm not moral." Ariock hunched. It made him feel so small, to blatantly confess his own monstrosity. "I do terrible things."

And not just once or twice.

Ariock thought of all the people he had slaughtered, on purpose or by accident. There was a mountain of corpses in his past and in his future. It seemed endless. The Torth Empire had thirty-eight trillion individual Torth. Ninety million urbanized planets. Was he supposed to kill or enslave every single one of them?

It would take centuries.

Millennia.

Ariock suspected old age would not slow him down much. Not with longevity pills plus Evenjos's regeneration healing, plus his own quick self-healing. Thomas might die of old age, and his hope of freeing all Torth would die with him. There would be no more penitents. And after a thousand more years of nonstop war, would Ariock be more callous than Garrett?

He didn't see any way to hold on to his humanity.

If he had to mete out death every single day for a thousand years . . . he would become the equivalent of a grim reaper. He would grow inured to it. There was no way around that.

"I know of the terrible things you have done by accident," the seer said. "Those were things that Torth forced you to do. But are there any terrible things you have done on purpose?" He emphasized the last two words.

Ariock prepared to list a litany.

Then he hesitated. Would an Alashani consider Torth to be victims at all? The seer probably believed that all Torth should be decapitated, with their heads displayed on spikes.

"The ummins of Umdalkdul have a philosophy," the seer said. "Gwat. It is easy to judge that which we do not know, but followers of Gwat take the hard path. They endeavor not to judge. I adhere to that philosophy for myself." He pinwheeled his hand, indicating that Ariock should go on. "If you believe you have done injustice against certain, uh . . ." He hesitated, clearly avoiding the offensive term. ". . . mind readers, then I respect your guilt, and your sense of responsibility. I have never met a Torth. Nor have I met a penitent. I cannot fully judge what sort of people they are."

There was no sarcasm or irony in the seer's tone. He seemed truly receptive.

"Have you done harm to innocent people?" the seer asked.

Ariock thought of Rosy Ranks and Servants of All, begging.

Crying.

Losing all their hard-won dignity in a last-ditch, futile effort to retain their free will.

"I don't know how innocent or guilty they are," Ariock admitted. "But their fate is worse than death."

He felt like a traitor, voicing that out loud. Garrett wouldn't approve. Thomas would probably give him a hurt look. Yet still . . .

"No one deserves what we are doing to them," Ariock said.

"Ah," the seer said. "Now it is very clear, to me, why you have not jumped back into fighting. It is a great mystery to the rest of the galaxy. But I no longer have to wonder."

The seer made it sound self-evident. He drank from his porcelain teacup.

"Do you think I'm right?" Ariock felt like a child begging for approval. The greatest minds in the galaxy believed he was too softhearted. Thomas had agreed to zombify hordes of enemy Torth. Although he clearly hated doing it, he claimed that it was necessary "for now." He received power boosts by linking with Ariock. And he had abdicated any responsibility for making military decisions.

Ariock alone had the final say.

And everyone else, from Weptolyso to Kessa, seemed to approve of the zombifying. Even the enemy Torth knew it was effective. The threat of zombification was the only thing holding them at bay. No doubt all those people thought Ariock was an idiot for dragging his heels and being weighed down by guilt.

"I believe that your recurring dream is a message." The seer seemed very professional. "The dream shows you failing to be a hero by the definition of your friends. Instead of being a hero in the way you know it is defined—by your morals—you are trying to please your friends, to be a hero by their standards. And that is a dangerous path. It leads to turmoil, and possibly to calamity."

Ariock wondered if he dared ignore a friend like Thomas. The last time he'd ignored Thomas, a whole lot of Alashani warriors had died.

"You look conflicted," the seer observed.

"You've given me a lot to think about." As Ariock considered the seer's interpretation, his concern for Thomas grew.

Because Thomas also found the zombification effort to be morally repulsive.

In private, away from listening ears, Thomas insisted that renegade Torth were the key to everything. But he had been saying that for nearly a year.

There were no Torth jumping to join the good guys. There were only prisoners who could not be trusted. In many ways, the penitents were just . . . well, Ariock hated to think of people as worthless. But they were baggage.

Did Thomas secretly hate himself for being wrong about the Torth?

Had anyone addressed the guilt Thomas might secretly be coping with? Did Kessa dare discuss it with him? Or Varktezo? Probably not. Thomas hardly talked to anyone anymore. He was distant. He was brusque, even rude, perhaps oversaturated with Torth life histories.

And lately he was hellishly overworked, now that Garrett—and Ariock—had bullied him into absorbing the minds of every single penitent in Freedomland.

I need to check with him, Ariock realized.

"I hope I have not given you more cause for stress?" The seer laughed in a delicate way. "I regret that my skills are less than what you may be accustomed to."

"You've been very helpful," Ariock said.

The seer seemed overcome with embarrassment, as if he had just remembered that he was sitting across from a celebrity. "You walk a hard path, messiah. It is like Gwat. Brutality is easy for those born with power. I hear warriors brag about how many Torth they have killed. Mercy is not in their vocabulary. But I hear it in yours." He looked at Ariock with admiration. "Restraint and mercy are very difficult for those with power, especially for those who have been wronged. Yet this is what you have chosen. That is a point of pride, not a point of shame. I see it as proof that you are far stronger than people give you credit for."

"Thank you." A weight lifted from Ariock's shoulders. This mystical seer judged him kindly, in a way that few people did. Certainly not Garrett.

"I know what warriors say about your reluctance to fight." The seer blinked, as if to flick away annoyances with his eyelashes. "They are wrong. Compassion, even for enemies, is never a weakness."

For once, Ariock did not want to escape. He felt seen.

"If you'd like to try the tea?" the seer said. "Let me know what you think."

The teapot was sized for an Alashani, so it was tiny in Ariock's hand. He drank everything in the pot within three swallows. It had a soothing taste, as light and delicate as the seer's mannerisms.

Perhaps he could relearn how to be a Bringer of Hope instead of a bringer of death?

"I am honored that you came to me." The seer slid off his chair. "If I can be of service again, please let me know. And everything we discussed is private." He swirled his cape. "The Great Mwagru never tells."

CHAPTER 16

FREE-FLOATING DANGER

Another day, another eight hundred thousand lifetimes dumped into Thomas's brain.

And he had managed to absorb them all before nightfall.

He was angry all the time. He hated sunlight. He detested people. He was pretty sure he was developing stomach ulcers from the stress of processing too many lifetimes too rapidly. And he still had not unmasked Stranger Danger.

You'll never find the culprit, his inner critic taunted him. *This is the Torth Empire outsmarting you.*

Thomas told his inner critic to shut up. He was full of the collated opinions of a whole lot of stupid, fearful, self-absorbed mind readers. He wasn't going to let them dominate his personality.

He floated uphill, toward the academy. He had neglected Azhdarchidae for a week. The sky croc could take care of himself, but Thomas really wanted to share in some innocent and pleasant memories right now.

Plus, his exercise equipment was inside his tower. Physical therapy was never fun, but if he let the habit slip away entirely, the results were predictable. He was a growing fourteen-year-old. He ought to go through daily exercise routines so he would be able to resume his sparring sessions with Daindlor once he had enough free time.

Maybe, someday, he would run and jump without the aid of mechanized leg braces? That was something to look forward to.

He needed dinner. He needed a bath. And then?

Ugh. He supposed he would return to the putrid barracks and choke down another hundred thousand minds, searching for the sinister interloper.

What fun.

His wristwatch pinged with a notification. Thomas glanced at it. Kessa had invited him to dinner later in the week.

Too bad. He deleted the invitation, just like he had deleted five previous invites. Kessa would just try to get motherly, asking how he was doing and expecting him to answer any question she asked. Thomas could guess what she would try to dig out of him. Humanness.

Well, he was saturated with Torth-ness.

That didn't make him damaged or messed up in the head, despite what his friends might think. His life was a bit rough at the moment, but what else was new? He was doing all right. He was surviving.

But people had better leave him alone.

Thomas paused under a shady tree and deleted half a dozen concerned messages from Varktezo. Sure, he missed leisurely chats with his chief lab assistant—

but Varktezo's new favorite hobby was telepathy gas. The adolescent ummin was obsessed with the practice of reading minds. Thomas had no desire to hear about that. Or deal with it.

Oh, and a message from Ariock, too? Hm. Did the depressed hero want some extra therapy? No thanks. Thomas deleted the invitation to "talk." If Ariock simply wanted a friendly visit, too bad. He could try again next month.

Having cleared his inbox, Thomas floated across the garden park that everyone called Reflections Plaza. Students strolled over bridges, crossing interconnected ponds that were rife with alien waterfowl.

(Yikes.)

(Steer clear.)

Thomas did the pedestrians a favor and swerved wide around them. He just did not belong in a place where innocent adolescents were going to school. Everyone knew it. He belonged with zombies and animals.

He was so sick of people.

Thomas closed his eyes and conjured a vivid simulation of his ideal retirement. Wide-open skies. Distant snowcapped mountains. A wilderness with plenty of animals and no people whatsoever.

He wanted it so badly.

But then the Torth Empire would win and all his friends would die. Solitude and quiescence weren't quite worth that cost.

As Thomas approached the huge archway that delineated the academy grounds, an instinct made him pause.

Maybe it was a shadow in the wrong place.

Maybe it was a scent that didn't belong.

Thomas contained a million lifetimes' worth of life experience, and some of it came from Servants of All, nussian fighters, ummin military pilots, Alashani warriors, heroes of prophecy, and more. Whatever caused his sudden paranoia, he trusted those instincts. He overclocked his perceptual intake.

The flagstones ahead of him erupted.

Thomas, registering every microsecond, calculated that the explosion would rip through him unless he moved away at superhuman speed. He flicked his hoverchair controls and connected to the air with thermal thrust. He used heat to propel himself violently backward.

But the shock wave overtook his reaction. His hoverchair flipped over.

Thomas should have rolled into a somersault and landed on his feet, the way Daindlor was training him to do. But it all happened too fast. He'd had to pour his focus into thermokinetic propulsion, which left him with nothing for superhuman speed.

He landed on the flagstones headfirst, hard enough to rattle his jaw and stun him.

His hoverchair banged onto the ground nearby. The impact shattered its delicate hoverdisk. It bounced and rolled to a stop, useless. It was just junk now.

Distant screams.

Thomas pushed himself to sit up. He was strong enough to do that.

His forehead felt bruised, and he figured he would have a lump there. The impact could have been much worse. His hoverchair might have smashed into his neck or head.

The bomb could have splattered him all over the pavement.

He forced himself to zero in on the threat. Smoke and debris. Nothing else.

Thomas scanned the park, searching for danger. He needed to identify the saboteurs who had nearly succeeded in murdering him.

People were running to safety. A few people stared and pointed or looked astonished, but nobody looked gleeful or unsurprised.

Whoever had planted this trap must have presupposed which route Thomas would take to get home. An easy guess. There were only so many ingress and egress points to the academy. As for Thomas's schedule? It was public knowledge these days.

He had made it easy for them.

The saboteurs had probably dug beneath the pathway at night, when no one was around. They'd been technologically savvy enough to include a remotely controlled detonator with their explosive. If it was the undergrounders, they must have recruited someone who enjoyed technology. A student at the academy? Or one of the lab technicians?

Or this could be the handiwork of Stranger Danger.

The unknown mind controller could have turned anyone into unwitting helpers.

A lookout had probably been watching the traffic from a distance, finger on the remote control, ready to trigger the bomb when Thomas showed up. If they were still watching . . .

There might be a second bomb.

Thomas crawled off the flagstones, pushing his brain into hyperalert mode again. He scanned the plaza with methodical care. In hindsight, he thought it had been a sound that triggered his instinct, a tiny electronic sound that did not belong in this setting. He listened.

Nothing.

Just wind and the distant exclamations of people who had seen the explosion.

Thomas pulled himself onto a hill of cultivated wildflowers. He knew he ought to stand up. He should begin the arduous journey of walking toward safety. He would have to walk, with his awkward, unbalanced lack of grace, on grass and flower beds.

He really should get going.

Instead, Thomas drew up his knees and laid his forehead against them.

He felt shaky and cold, and he didn't trust his legs to hold him upright at this particular moment. He wanted just a few seconds.

Bystanders craned to get a look at him. Thomas nearly snarled at them to go away.

Lots of people in this plaza probably wished the bomb had done its job. More than half the city would celebrate his death. Alashani undergrounders. Torth prisoners. Penitents. The secret mind controller, Stranger Danger. Ordinary free aliens. Students.

The bomb could have been planted by anyone.

And perhaps Thomas deserved all the hate.

Clearly, mistakes had been made. Otherwise Jinishta wouldn't be dead. Otherwise the Twins and other renegade Torth would show up, happy to join the good guys. Otherwise the Upward Governess would be working with Thomas instead of reduced to a mere memory in the Megacosm.

Thousands of freed slaves were currently suffering the indignity and horror of wearing slave collars again. The freedom fighters on Nuss were losing ground to the Torth Empire.

Ultimately, whose fault was that?

It was easy to blame mistakes on the big guy. Ariock was the military leader . . . but only because Thomas had put him in that role.

Ariock relied on Thomas's strategies and battle tactics. He acted on Thomas's recommendations.

So whose fault were all the mistakes? Thomas could not blame anyone but himself.

"Are you all right?"

The speaker was a kindly looking govki. She must recognize Thomas as the dreadful *rekveh*, yet she extended two of her four hands to help him up.

Thomas detected her goodwill as she entered his telepathy range. This was an aerospace engineer, not an assassin. She respected the Teacher.

Unless a mind controller had subtly brainwashed her into lulling Thomas into a false sense of security?

Stranger Danger could almost certainly perform subtle brainwashing. That was the fourth magnitude of telepathy, a magnitude below full zombification. Stranger Danger might have implanted a hypnotic suggestion in this engineer. She might do something unexpected, sudden, and deadly. And sure, Thomas could preemptively brainwash her to be harmless . . .

But that crossed a line.

He wasn't going to reprogram the minds of innocent people. If he dominated his own people like that, removing their freedom of choice, then how was he any better than Stranger Danger or the Death Architect?

He wasn't a Torth.

He was a monster, but not the inhumane type that the undergrounders believed he was. He was not going to reduce his own people to disposable pawns.

"Go away." Thomas leaned his head against his knee braces.

He could imagine the Death Architect's covert instructions to Stranger Danger. She would command the brainwasher to send waves of nested assassins. If one assassination attempt failed? There would be a succession of fallbacks. That would keep the Conqueror off-balance and increase the likelihood of him making a fatal perceptual error.

If he was the Death Architect, that was how he would win.

Thomas waved the helpful govki away. "Leave me alone."

CHAPTER 17

OVERSHARING

Varktezo felt guilty, placing telepathy gas emitters in the back room above the Leaven Street Brewery. He shouldn't smuggle such valuable devices outside the lab.

There was a bar. Some students were already getting drunk or snacking. The brewery owner was friendly with a popular student who was friends with one of Varktezo's most creative lab assistants, and she'd been excited to host this semisecret party.

The promise of telepathy gas seemed to excite a lot of people. Varktezo could hardly believe how crowded the room was growing.

A band of impromptu musicians arrived. They claimed Varktezo's colleague had invited them, and even though he suspected they were lying, he agreed to let them stay. It should be fine as long as he liked their music.

"Are you the chief scientist? Varktezo?" A cute female ummin actually sounded happy to talk to him, not judgmental.

"I am." Varktezo checked to make sure the third emitter was stable.

"Are you the one who set up this party?"

"Yes," he admitted.

"Ooh, I've heard a lot about you." She riffled the flaps of her head cover, making sure it was pretty. "I'm Ounzong."

Varktezo grinned at her. "Um, hi." He wasn't sure how to greet a friendly stranger. Her lack of a collar scar hinted that she probably came from a slave farm, like him. Or maybe she was shani? He didn't want to be rude with personal questions. "Ounzong? That's a pretty name."

Ounzong looked happily around the crowded room. "This is going to be miraculous. Truly. Are we really going to read minds? Have you actually done it?"

"Yup!" Varktezo stepped back from his handiwork. He eyed the emitters, making sure they were roughly equidistant.

He had told the Teacher he was experimenting with free radicals and ionic polymerization the last time they'd spoken. Instead . . . ?

Well, he hadn't lied. He had finished his experiments, and then he'd decided to reverse engineer and duplicate telepathy gas emitters. Why not? Was Varktezo supposed to just dismiss the intellectual curiosity of his fellow lab assistants? It seemed harmless to invite loads of people to practice telepathy.

It would even be beneficial. People ought to be prepared for the next Torth invasion. If people grew familiar with telepathy gas, they were more likely to survive.

The band began to play music. The combination of their drums and stringed instruments added to the festive atmosphere. One of them grabbed a microphone and began to croon into it.

Voices got louder to compensate. A few people began dancing in place. Ounzong bounced to the rhythm.

Was she giving Varktezo a flirty look? He must be misinterpreting it.

"When do we get started?" Ounzong asked.

"Um . . ." Varktezo looked around the room.

"Let's read minds!" someone shouted.

Cheers.

Varktezo grinned at all the enthusiasm. People shouted his name. They yelled for the party to get started. Ounzong whooped, clearly ready.

"All right!" Varktezo twisted the knob on the nearest emitter, and the crowd roared in approval. They cheered for Varktezo as he ran from one emitter to the next, turning them on.

Varktezo raised his hands for attention. "Let's get this party started!"

. . . Started!

. . . Started!

His own words silently echoed with unique enhancements, augmented by the varied perceptions he picked up. Varktezo felt incredible. He was at the center of a vortex of attention.

People saw him.

They saw him from a variety of angles, through different eyesight and height levels, colored by different emotions and opinions of geeky ummins like him. They weren't all friendly. They did not all follow the code of Gwat. But just about everyone thought he was worth knowing, because he had put this awesome party together.

He could get used to this feeling.

"Yes. I'm pretty awesome, aren't I?" he admitted.

People cheered.

They actually agreed! That seemed miraculous.

The musicians tentatively experimented with their song. As soon as they sensed how well it was received, they gained confidence, the same way Varktezo felt. They seemed to thrive on the energy of the crowd.

As more and more people enjoyed their melody and rhythm, their music changed, reflecting the overall mood in the room. It grew more energetic and joyous.

Ounzong was thinking, *He looks so happy. I wonder if he would like me if I bought him a drink?*

Varktezo laughed at the absurdity of someone wanting to impress him. Usually it was the other way around. He just wanted to dance with her!

Ounzong laughed in astonishment. She grabbed his hands and pulled him into a dance.

Soon they were bouncing to the rhythm, neither needing to speak. Thoughts reached them no matter how loud the music was. When Ounzong became confused, inundated by too many alien perceptions, Varktezo shared the focus techniques he had learned from *(a grizzled old mind reader)* Garrett. He led by example. He led the dance.

Can I take telepathy lessons from you? Ounzong gripped his arm, enchanted by the idea.

!

!!

!!!

Half the room seemed to echo her sentiment. People mobbed Varktezo, not physically, but mentally. Their minds swept around him like orbital satellites around a planet. He wasn't an expert, but he was the closest thing to an expert who was not a full-time mind reader.

Oooh.

I want lessons!

Invite me?

Varktezo eyed the eager crowd, surprised. Garrett's private lessons had a limited invitee list, but only a fraction of the official list ever attended. Plenty of dignitaries, including Ariock and Vy, never showed up. So it had not occurred to Varktezo that a lot of people would want to experience telepathy on a regular basis.

Cravings surrounded him. He had underestimated public interest.

All right. Varktezo spontaneously decided that yes, he could become a teacher. Why not?

!!!

!!!YAY!!!

(Party!!!)

People whooped. They jumped and danced, happy to celebrate. They wanted to become telepaths.

Ounzong danced with Varktezo, filled with joyous hope. Every idea sparked a reaction in the other. Their thoughts bumped together like cloacae during a mating dance.

It was unlike anything Varktezo had ever experienced.

Thoughts surrounded him and Ounzong, but most of those thoughts were dull, just not worth exploring. He and his newfound partner were creating their own symphony. They ignored everyone else in the room. They built upon each other's imaginations, making each other giggle, creating a covalent bond. They were diatomic.

Later in the evening, some outside thoughts did intrude.

!

!!!

Really?

An Alashani came here?

I (we) don't believe it.

There were enough silent exclamations for Varktezo to look toward the door, along with the majority of partygoers. They wanted to verify that this new arrival was real.

Everyone perceived her. She had the dimensions of an Alashani maiden, although her face was hidden by a hood and a sun hat. But why would a shani attend a student party? Very few albino people took classes at the academy. They preferred their own schools, where they learned their own things.

Also, the albinos detested telepathy. Everyone knew how they felt about *rekvehs*.

As Varktezo watched, the maiden removed her hat and shook out her long black hair.

Not an Alashani at all. He knew who this was.

? ? ?

     (Cherise) right, it's the angel.

"Cherise?" *(Cherise?)* Varktezo's voice resounded, bolstered and verified by other people's affirmations. The music faltered. Everyone was surprised to see someone famous show up at a student party.

Cherise looked unnerved. She eyed the doorway, and Varktezo sensed her inner doubts.

"Stay!" He tried to make his voice inviting. "You're welcome here."

The music found a confident rhythm. Varktezo wound through the dancing crowd with Ounzong by his side. The closer they got to Cherise, the easier it would be to pick up her thoughts.

Cherise waited politely. But her fear was as stark as a color. *I shouldn't be here.* She eyed the door. *How many people will Varktezo tell? Will Flen find out? (Or Thomas?)*

Varktezo blew breath out through his beak. These days, the Teacher *(Thomas)* never visited. He was too busy mind probing penitents. It might take him a whole week to find out about this party.

Oh. Cherise marveled at the thoughts she had just overheard from Varktezo. *Oh my.*

Indeed. Thanks to telepathy gas, nontelepaths sometimes knew more than the Teacher. It was incredibly amazing.

Varktezo swept a bow.

Next to him, Ounzong offered to guide Cherise around the party. *Do you (Cherise) take telepathy lessons with Garrett?* she wondered, polite and curious.

Cherise looked away. *No.* Her mind glowed with sublime interest in telepathy lessons, yet Varktezo could actually see her reasons for avoiding the lessons. Her boyfriend *(fiancé) (Flen)* would not approve of Cherise doing *rekveh* things. Her fear was as vibrant as the banded sky. Cherise did not want Flen enraged at her.

Varktezo gawked.

Then why . . . ? He stared at Cherise, curious, soaking up her reasons for showing up at his party.

"I shouldn't be here." Cherise hunched her shoulders defensively, her thoughts spilling and overlapping. *Gosh, this is embarrassing. They're overhearing my thoughts!*

But she had been curious.

Cherise was in the habit of staying late at the academy to chat with students or to draw in her sketchbook. She had figured she could get away with a few minutes at this semisecret party. Students and Alashani did not share social circles. Clearly, Cherise had figured that a party full of random students would be too obscure for Flen to learn about.

She had not expected to run into someone she knew. Varktezo's presence made her nervous.

Ounzong radiated an opinion. *Well, I can understand Flen's point of view,* she thought. *(I am sorry but) Cherise looks like a Torth. If she learns to read minds . . . ? Humph. Then what will separate her from Torth?*

That concern seemed ignorant to Varktezo. He did not conflate friends with enemies. Even Thomas, who was a half-Torth hybrid, was in a league of his own. No one should equate the Teacher with a Torth—let alone Vy or Cherise. That seemed ridiculous.

Cherise's iridescent-amber gaze bounced from the colorful lights to the musicians to the various people dancing and laughing. *Looks fun. (All alien crowd, no humanoids.) How can I leave politely?*

Her discomfort made everyone nearby feel discomforted. People shot her annoyed glances.

Why doesn't that human leave?

Yeah.

The unfriendly chorus gained traction.

Varktezo wanted no part of the common sentiment, so he made an effort to reject it. "Please." He clasped Cherise's hand with deliberation. "Stay for a few minutes?"

The alarm in Cherise's mind was louder than the music. She felt the hostility, and she expected jokes made at her expense. Perhaps an attack or two?

Varktezo was amazed to learn that the human adolescent shared his own social fears.

They were from different worlds. He was an ummin, she was a human, he was a scientist, she was an artist, and yet they both had trouble fitting in with a crowd. For each of them, friendship was a complicated dance that required too many steps. As for dating . . . ? Ha. That was harder than rocket science.

Oh? A teasing spike of humor came from Ounzong.

I'm fine. Cherise stepped back. *I don't have trouble dating. I love Flen.*

But that was a lie. Varktezo sensed Cherise's inner doubts as clearly as if she had advertised them. She regretted losing Thomas. She missed him.

I get that, Varktezo silently admitted. Lately, he feared that his friendship with the Teacher was slipping away.

Cherise blinked at Varktezo, shocked by his understanding.

Ounzong took one step back and shifted her mind to orbit others, which made her fade to the periphery of Varktezo's telepathic perception.

I don't have to intrude. Cherise began to step away, to retrieve her hat and cloak.

Varktezo did feel a special closeness with Ounzong, but he dared not claim a relationship with the pretty ummin. Ounzong had probably only gotten intimate with him thanks to the telepathy gas. Would she even want to speak to him after tonight?

I will definitely speak to you again, Varktezo. Ounzong waved with a casual smile. For a wonder, she glowed with acceptance and patience. She understood Varktezo wanted an opportunity to discuss the Teacher with someone who used to know him well. *You're darn cute, even if you are a science geek.*

Varktezo gaped.

Cherise chuckled, radiating an artistic array of emotions.

If you two need fresh air, there's a nice view from the rooftop. Ounzong pointed, then vanished into the crowd.

Other partygoers had also picked up on Varktezo's quiet invitation to Cherise, and many quit their hostility. They returned to experimenting with shared perceptions. It seemed that a number of people here actually respected Varktezo's wishes.

How marvelous.

You came here to learn about Thomas, Varktezo silently observed.

Cherise hesitated. It was true. She wanted to gain some perspective on how Thomas used to perceive her.

And she also sought secrets.

She had doubts about where her relationship with Flen was headed, and she wanted to learn if the general population knew about the Alashani undergrounder movement. Was Flen dangerous? Did people perceive him as being dangerous?

"Let's talk for a bit." Varktezo actually wanted to converse, he realized. Mind sharing was too intense. It got rude fast.

Cherise silently agreed. They found the rooftop balcony above the brewery.

Varktezo inhaled the night air, making sure all traces of telepathy were gone. Cherise seemed to do the same.

"It is too much," Varktezo admitted. "When we're friends, I mean. I think telepathy is better for strangers."

Cherise nodded. "Thomas used to tell me that. I think he felt guilty for absorbing all my secrets." She hesitated. "He used to, anyway. I guess."

"The Torth may have trained him to stop feeling guilt about it." Varktezo could not imagine the slave masters feeling guilty about anything.

"Yeah." Cherise made a face. "The way they think . . . ? It's more obvious now. Isn't it?" She shivered, drawing her knitted cardigan around her shoulders. "It was weird. Like being part of a swarm of insects."

Varktezo supposed she had a point. Telepathy could be uplifting and amazing. It empowered mass coordination.

Yet there was a dark side to sharing every mood and erasing every secret. Disagreements became dangerous. Mental gulfs became treacherous. Hostility could build up with savage speed. Varktezo thought of how swiftly the crowd had turned against Cherise, and he shuddered. The moods of crowds were frightening.

The early Torth had experienced that. Mass joy, but also mass hatred. Mass outrage. Mass fear.

They had collectively voted to get rid of emotions.

It must have seemed like a wise choice at the time. A kindness. But one bad vote led to another, and over time, perhaps within just two or three generations, the collective of destitute peasants had transformed into tyrants who owned slaves. Their cooperation was glorious. It gave them immense power. But the price of that power . . .

The Torth had collectively given up their morals and their human kindness in exchange for power.

No wonder the Teacher had wanted to escape.

"Thomas doesn't go with crowds," Varktezo said. "He's not interested in capitulating to other people's emotions and opinions. Not at any price. I think that may be why he left the Torth Empire."

He considered other supergeniuses, such as the Upward Governess, and the Twins, and all the generations that had come before them. And he grew more certain. The others were certainly smart enough to identify the negatives of oversharing, yet they had stayed. Perhaps they were too self-doubting to disagree with their orbiters?

Or they were beholden to the masses in some way. They were addicted to other people's knowledge. They wanted to please crowds. They wanted to be liked.

Thomas, raised on Earth instead of on a baby farm, had felt unique and different from the start. He'd grown inured to the feeling. He was used to being an outcast, and he had embraced uniqueness as his core identity.

"Otherwise?" Varktezo concluded, "he would have stayed."

Cherise leaned on the railing, thoughtful.

Varktezo did not ask what was going through her mind. That was private and personal, and it would be rude to intrude.

He was content to admire the view.

Maybe he shouldn't try so hard to join a swarm, no matter how glorious and almighty it was.

Maybe it was good to be different.

SHEPHERDS OR SHEEP

Penitents could sense malice or impending attacks aimed toward them, if the attacker was close enough.

So Flen kept his distance. He used his powers.

He stayed well away from the line of penitents who were winding toward the assessment facility, and from a safe distance, he shoved an elderly female who wasn't scurrying fast enough.

Another penitent caught her and helped her to limp along. Ugh. Both penitents shot wary looks toward Flen. These mind readers probably knew what had become of Flen's sister and mother. They were probably laughing like demons inside their minds.

"Go easy on them, will you?" Anchet offered a strained smile. "We are not in a war zone. These are just prisoners. We are merely shepherding them."

Flen shot his second-in-command a withering look. More than a tenth of all the Alashani warriors in existence were dead, yet some idiots—like Anchet, for example—still trusted the alleged messiah and his *rekveh* puppet master. It was unbelievable.

Flen gestured at the seemingly endless line of *rekvehs* who were pretending to be as docile as cave sheep. "I have not forgotten what these things are."

Some of the penitents looked like mockeries of Alashani. The ones with white hair, for instance. That was offensive. Someone ought to outlaw that. *Rekvehs* should not have anything in common with albinos.

"I believe we can handle this duty on our own, Premier." Anchet clasped her gloved hands behind her back, respectful. "You can go home to your fiancée, if you wish."

How kind.

Did the warriors honestly favor the company of penitent Torth over that of their appointed premier? Flen couldn't quite believe that.

"Right, Premier," another warrior called from the opposite side of the street. "We'll keep the penitents in line." He chuckled. "At least we're out in fresh air. Better than being in one of those *rekveh* indoor cities."

Flen hated the immense sky. Right now it was colored by the sunset plus that banded planet and far too many scudding clouds. He distrusted every chilly breeze. He would have preferred unchanging stalactites. Even so, he inwardly admitted that guarding this boulevard was preferable to standing inside a gigantic facility pumped full of telepathy gas and mind readers. What a nightmare.

He was grateful that no one had insisted he go near the *rekveh* Thomas or the telepathy gas zone.

"Did you hear about the telepathy gas party last night?" another warrior called, apparently making conversation to relieve the boredom of guard duty.

"What?" Anchet asked.

"Yeah, it was in a brewery on Leaven Street. Apparently a bunch of those academy students think they can become *rekvehs*."

Anchet tittered. She apparently thought that recreational telepathy was funny instead of absolutely horrific. "I'm curious to try telepathy. My ummin friend said—"

"Hush," Flen snapped. "This is not a discussion we should be having in front of mind readers."

That shut them up.

Too many people were losing fear of *rekvehs*, thanks to ludicrously lenient policies. Some foolhardy aliens actually allowed penitents to prepare their family meals.

Flen found the implications darkly disturbing. Chambermaids could earn their way out of slums, if they were fortunate in family or friends. Might penitents rise out of the slums like that?

The boulevard was full of penitents trudging out of their barracks right now. The line zigzagged across multiple intersections, bridges, and market squares. Flen was tasked with keeping the *rekvehs* apart from ordinary pedestrians. He also had to make sure none of the vile creatures tried to bolt away before their turn to stand in front of the *rekveh* Thomas. It was demeaning—

Distant screams broke Flen's musings.

Penitents scattered in all directions.

"Anchet! Baysuch!" Flen drew his spears and shouted directions to his warriors.

Corralling penitents was unlike the battles Flen was used to. These Torth were unarmed, unarmored, and extremely easy to kill. A few dozen spears stopped them. Penitents sprawled, their backs or sides pierced with iron projectiles. The rest of the Torth cringed together.

"Stranger Danger!" one screamed.

"There are brainwashed nussians!" another yelled.

One penitent shouted directly at Flen. "You have to stop them!"

It might be a Torth trick, an escape attempt. But those screams were coming closer.

And was the ground trembling?

Flen wondered if Ariock was causing an earthquake. Was this the end? Was extinction the fate of the Alashani? Was he helpless despite his powers?

The penitents hurled themselves to the ground, cowering and pleading for Flen to take action. That was when he saw the rockslide of red and orange storming downhill toward him.

Nussians.

They galloped on all fours, snarling, making the ground tremble. Pedestrians leaped aside, screaming with terror. Any who were too slow got trampled. The nussians were in berserker mode.

Flen whirled around to see what the nussians were rushing to confront, half expecting a horde of Red Ranks. Nussians would not behave like this without a good reason.

But there was no army. No enemies.

Were the nussians zombified?

Were these penitents actually telling the truth?

"Stop them!" Anchet called from a distance. She had somersaulted out of harm's way, up on top of a portico. Four of her spears hit one target, and that nussian sprawled and slammed against her perch. The jarring impact caused a pillar to crack. The portico collapsed, spilling downward.

Anchet shielded herself with wreckage. The other nussians flew past their fallen peer and his slayer.

Their small red eyes were utterly vacant. They did not even react to the people they trampled or spiked out of their way.

Flen readied his spears.

He wasn't fast enough.

Suddenly Flen was amid overwhelming violence. The penitents bolted, but many were spiked or crushed. The thorny nussians were as merciless as transports speeding downhill. There wasn't enough room to throw spears.

Flen infused his body with extra strength and speed. That empowered him to leap high. He bounced off one thorny spinal ridge, then another. He pushed with his feet, somersaulting in midair. Another kickoff. He spun and landed hard on a steep slope. The sewage canal.

Flen saw what was coming, but there wasn't time to stop it. A zombified nussian whacked him aside. He was airborne, and before he knew it, he fell into unutterable filth with a splash.

He spewed sewage out of his mouth as he struggled to stand. The stench was overpowering. He had to infuse his body with power just to eject the stuff.

Even his quiver was waterlogged. Disgusting.

And why was it foggy? Was the fog pink?

He was not the only victim staggering around in the sewage canal. Other people had fallen in. A child wept.

Flen drew four spears. Perhaps there really was a second brainwasher in the city? No doubt the unholy *rekveh* would blame this calamity on Stranger Danger, whether that was true or not.

Those poor nussians used to be people with hopes and dreams. They probably had families. Some of them might have been shani nussians. But now? They were nothing but weaponized corpses. They would have to be slaughtered like dangerous beasts.

Someone screamed.

Another panic started. Filth-covered aliens floundered, mobbing away from a group of figures in the twilight gloom.

Penitents.

Ten of them. A work crew.

They looked sinister in the blackness beneath a stone bridge. Their slave collars glowed like evil grins inside their cowls, illuminating nothing above their chins. Just flesh. Flen certainly did not want to get near them.

He infused his spear-throwing arm with extra strength—or he tried to. Suddenly he could not expand his awareness.

His powers were gone.

Pink gas, Flen realized. Someone must have thrown inhibitor gas off the bridge.

This was a clever attack. Someone had orchestrated it.

The work crew of penitents moved with coordinated speed, wading toward Flen. Perhaps they knew he was a premier?

He tried to run, but it was like a nightmare. He was too slow in the sewage. They were gaining on him.

This wasn't fair! He shouldn't die easily, the way his father had, the way his mother and sister had gone. This surely wasn't what a war hero like Flen deserved. He had earned a better ending than this.

The wind picked up, blowing the stench away. It became a blast that cleared away the pink miasma.

Watery lights appeared, bioluminescent eels that shimmered beneath the filthy water. They gathered into tendrils that broke the surface and rose higher. Those tendrils gathered into strands of cloth and hair and wings.

The Lady of Sorrow glowed with terrifying beauty.

Flen whimpered. Glowing like that, she was the embodiment of the tales his mother used to tell. She looked like a goddess of life and death, a being who straddled the river and controlled its vital blessings. She reached out a hand, and that hand stretched into a glowing white fire.

The cloaked penitents scattered like rats fleeing a torch.

The Lady of Sorrow morphed into a writhing mass of glowing serpents. She tried to follow each and every one of the scattering figures. But they blended into the gloom. Flen could not tell if they splashed farther up the sewer or if they climbed a ladder or ducked into a side tunnel.

The goddess's power must have limits. The farther apart her serpentine forms traveled, the less cohesive they became. They broke apart.

"Ugh," the Lady of Sorrow said. "I cannot track them all."

Her glowing serpents wheeled apart and came back together as a single feminine form. Her hair and gown rippled in an unseen breeze. She was pristine and glowing, and sewer filth did not touch her.

Yet Flen did not want the Lady of Sorrow to come any closer to him. She was a mind reader. A goddess, perhaps, but a *rekveh* as well. He didn't know whether to worship her or revile her.

"Are you all right, Premier Flen?" The Lady of Sorrow used her powers to wash the filth out of his hair and off his skin and his ruined armor.

Flen shivered.

"You are safe," she said.

To his relief, the Lady of Sorrow moved on, rescuing victims and healing injuries. She floated bodies onto dry ground.

Safe?

Flen sloshed to the embankment and climbed onto the boulevard. This monstrous attack should have clarified what evil *rekvehs* were capable of, if anyone had doubts. He would not regain his powers for several days. He wasn't safe.

Nobody in Freedomland would be safe until they got rid of all the mind readers.

CHAPTER 19

FACE-TO-FACE

An oiled sound.

Thomas was instantly wide-awake. All the dreck he'd absorbed from penitents made him restless at night, and an unexpected noise in his bedroom reminded him of his worst years in foster care. Sneaky footsteps used to signify a malicious foster sibling or two. Thomas used to be the victim of lots of cruel pranks.

The vault door rolled ajar. Shadowy figures crept toward him in the dimness.

Five of them. Too big to be shani.

Few people could even guess where Thomas slept on a nightly basis. He used an unpredictable schedule of sleeping vaults, all fortified, shielded, and secret. He always posted minions—well, zombies—in the outer vault.

This attacker had learned where he slept. They had co-opted Thomas's own zombies and bypassed his pressure plates and motion detectors.

They were being orchestrated by someone smart. Not undergrounders. Definitely Torth.

Thomas forced himself not to move except for one eye, which he cracked open. He remained outwardly motionless and watched the mirrored wall next to his bed.

A brazen attack from Stranger Danger was not entirely unexpected. Thomas had absorbed most of the penitent souls in the city, which left the unknown culprit with limited resources. Indeed, the lurker had begun to take major risks, having attacked shani warriors and other innocent people. They must feel strategically cornered. So here they were.

ATTACK! Thomas mentally commanded the reserve zombies in the secret compartment behind his bed.

Thomas's extra zombies busted out. They leaped high or somersaulted sideways, moving in unpredictable ways so as not to become immediate victims.

The enemy squad met their attacks with martial precision.

The zombies fought hand-to-hand, moving with such fluid grace they almost seemed to be dancing. Hands met fists. Kicks met torsos. Zombies whirled and ducked and struck.

"You need more protection," Garrett had told Thomas after the second attempt on his life. *"Especially when you sleep."*

Thomas had bristled at the implication that he needed babysitters. He no longer relied on caretakers for daily needs, and he valued that independence. The last thing he wanted was people shadowing him everywhere he went.

"I don't mean nussian bodyguards," Garrett had growled. *"You need living shields. Zombies, I mean."*

Thomas had refused. Weren't personal slaves or minions a sign of major insecurity? He wasn't the Death Architect. He was a good guy.

Or so he told himself.

"Your life matters more than your popularity," Garrett had insisted. *"This is non-negotiable. You will zombify a squad of personal bodyguards. I command it."*

It seemed Garrett had actually been right.

Thomas took full control of the five proxy bodies that belonged to him. He lay in bed, but he was also in motion, blocking the five minions controlled by Stranger Danger.

The enemy bodies fought with mechanical expertise. They simply weren't as good as Thomas in direct control. Thomas knew every military campaign the Torth Empire had ever fought. He knew every martial arts technique in known history. He imbued his extra bodies with all that, plus his overclocked perceptions.

His proxy bodies were faster than the enemy zombies. Smarter.

His bodies snapped fingers. Poked out eyes. Kicked and stomped and won.

Thomas sat up straighter in his bed, worried that he might accidentally miss some extra threat. Stranger Danger had nearly murdered Garrett and gotten away with it. They had managed to remain hidden in a city under investigation by a supergenius. Whoever they were, they were judicious. It could be deadly to underestimate them even by a smidge.

Should he summon Ariock?

Thomas hesitated with his finger over the emergency alert button on his control sleeve. The problem was, Ariock was vulnerable to mind control. That was scary. Besides, Ariock might require minutes to locate Thomas, which was too slow.

It wasn't worth the risk of bringing the big guy near a battle with an enemy brainwasher involved.

Thomas figured he was suited to handle this danger on his own.

He used the mirrored walls as visual aids. Bones cracked. Bodies fell in broken heaps.

Thomas had not wanted to feed and care for a plethora of extra flesh, but now he was grateful for Garrett's insistence that he make his own bodyguards. The five zombies that had guarded Thomas's bed could not have been accessed by anyone except him. Stranger Danger had not had a chance to repurpose them. At least, not yet . . .

A cloaked figure darted into Thomas's bedchamber.

It could have been another zombie. But when it raised a hand, the air shimmered with heat. A fireball coalesced.

Thomas inwardly swore. Naturally, this cloaked assassin had avoided being processed and vetted like a normal penitent. Stranger Danger was a fully capable Yeresunsa, probably a Rosy or a Servant of All. The rags and slave collar were a sham.

Thomas reached for his blaster glove, but he already knew he couldn't move fast enough. His mind was quick but his body simply lacked that capability.

The fireball flew at his head.

Thomas used two proxy bodies to intercept it. The zombies fell on Thomas's bed, sizzling. A sickening stench of burned clothing plus bacon filled the air.

The final two enemy zombies lunged at Thomas. They had broken fingers and dislocated shoulders, but they also had unspoken instructions.

Thomas blocked like an expert, his muscles trained from his secret sparring sessions with Daindlor. He summoned his three remaining proxy bodies. They were all swift-moving elbows and knees, and they bought Thomas enough of a respite so that he could quickly twist the already broken mind of one of the enemy zombies, bringing it onto his team.

Stranger Danger aimed a gloved hand at Thomas's head.

He wore a blaster glove.

Thomas had not expected a penitent, even a false one, to be armed. He should have known better. This assassin must have a whole network of lightly brainwashed victims to draw from. After all, the stranger had learned where the Conqueror slept, which implied he had eyes and ears all over the city.

Thomas threw a zombified proxy to block the blast. He infused his body with superhuman speed, Alashani style, and rolled.

An enemy zombie seized him. His own zombies tossed the attacker away, leaving Thomas with scratches and a bruise.

Thomas grabbed his own blaster glove from the nightstand. He jammed the weapon onto his hand before his opponent could whisk it away with telekinesis or thermal currents.

Stranger Danger dropped into a somersault to avoid Thomas's spray of microdarts. When he stood, his hood fell back, revealing sandy blond hair and a weathered face.

Thomas recognized this famous Servant of All. No wonder he had hidden so well. The Somehow Nexus (*formerly known as Stranger Danger*) looked unremarkable. His eyes gleamed yellow in the dim room, a common color among penitents. He must have altered his irises.

Thomas hissed in agony as his body turned to ice.

The surface of his control sleeve cracked. Its battery died, and it became useless junk.

So much for the option to call Ariock. Thomas briefly wondered if he should have programmed the thing to automatically send an alert if it got wrecked, but it was a moot point. He truly did not want to bring Ariock into a battle where the giant might get brainwashed.

Thomas had to expend energy to thaw himself. Tingling sensations ran through his limbs.

Meanwhile, the Somehow Nexus aimed at Thomas's head and triggered a blast.

Thomas commanded a proxy body to take the hit. That zombie fell in a heap of gore, and Thomas commanded the other bodies to shove the Servant of All into his telepathy range.

Another blast went astray, shattering the mirrored wall. Shards rained down on the bed.

Die, Conqueror (abomination that is My fault). The Somehow Nexus dived into Thomas's consciousness and burrowed into his core.

They would have been evenly matched if Thomas was not a supergenius. This assassin had a slippery mind. A powerful mind.

But he was slowed by the sheer mass of Thomas's memories. He had to dig through a galaxy.

Meanwhile, Thomas drilled past a labyrinth of mental firewalls, marveling that the Somehow Nexus had managed to sneak into this secured vault of a bedchamber, surprise the Conqueror, and nearly kill him. Whoever had sent this savvy champion was an impressive tactician. Had the Death Architect leveled up? Or was this the handiwork of the Twins?

Die, Conqueror (My son). The Somehow Nexus radiated guilt. *I never should have had a son. I am sorry.*

Son?

Thomas tried to ignore the guilty assertion. He could not ignore the blaster glove aimed at his face by the assassin. Anyone could make an analogy. Maybe the Somehow Nexus saw the Conqueror as the unwanted son of the Torth Empire?

Except his guilt felt personal.

The Somehow Nexus offered a thin, bitter smile that looked an awful lot like the way Thomas smiled.

That was too much. Thomas could no longer overlook the truth. Now that he was suspicious, he saw physical similarities between himself and this assassin. He was locked in deadly combat against his own biological father—not a human, but a Torth!—in a room full of broken corpses, shattered mirrors, and damaged zombies.

Thomas had to defend himself. But as he burrowed into the assassin's primal core, ready to brainwash him, the Somehow Nexus lowered his gloved hand.

Thomas hesitated.

I cannot keep this secret any longer, the assassin inwardly moaned. *The Majority deserves to know how this war (this disaster) truly began.*

He ascended.

At this close range, Thomas could not help but overhear the immense audience coalescing around his biological father's mind. *! ? ! ? ! ? ! ?* Millions of distant Torth demanded answers as soon as the truth struck them. Like Thomas, they had believed the Conqueror was birthed from a renegade female Servant of All who had illegally bedded a human man.

Except she clearly had not.

She must have had a dalliance with a fellow Servant of All. This one.

HOW IS THIS POSSIBLE??? millions of minds thundered.

What illegal perversion occurred?

How was he (the Conqueror) not born on a baby farm?

How can both of his gamete donors have been Servants of All?

!? !? !?

Although Thomas was below the Megacosm, he was one of the questioners. He stared at his biological father with silent expectation.

The Somehow Nexus still wore that bitter smile. He had never imagined his dalliance would have such far-reaching repercussions. He had never imagined that the whole galaxy would someday find out.

It was supposed to have remained a secret forever.

Now he finally confessed. He'd had sex with a lot of Servants of All. Yes. He had brainwashed them into forgetting afterward.

He replayed old memories, showing his audience—and the Conqueror—that he had, indeed, been a rogue Torth who messed around in ways he should not have.

He figured a lot of Servants of All got up to similar mischief.

His favorite plaything had been the blond clone sister to the Swift Killer, the Lone Assassin. She'd been willing. Heartbreakingly gorgeous and eager to experiment while they both playacted as humans on Earth. They would meet in hotel rooms in different guises. Afterward? He had wiped her memories and left her with the vague impression that she'd had sex with random human men.

It was safer for both of them that way.

The Somehow Nexus always made sure other people took the blame for his many illicit acts. Since his sexual partners lacked the power to brainwash, the one who was caught in a web of suspicion was unable to defend herself.

Thomas stared at his biological father.

Instead of zombifying this assassin, instead of attacking, Thomas paused. Everything he had known about his own identity was either questionable or wrong. He was mentally cartwheeling over the edge of an abyss.

Thomas Hill was not a human hybrid.

Thomas wasn't human at all.

Never mind his supposed "human side." He did not have an intrinsically kind-hearted nature, like Vy and Kessa and Ariock and other friends believed. Not at all. Instead, he was the spawn of monsters.

"*The boy's barely human,*" Garrett had said to Ariock once.

Garrett was right more often than Thomas wanted to credit. It turned out he was not a half angel from paradise. Thomas Hill was nothing but a terrible mistake—a Mistake—who never should have been born. And now everyone in the galaxy knew it, except for his ignorant friends.

We cannot trust Servants of All. The chorus began as a whisper, but it quickly picked up steam.

(Never trust them.)
   Especially the Somehow Nexus.
     Strip away his name-title.
      Strip him of all rank.
       Strip away his possessions and wealth.
        He's the worst (Servant of All) criminal ever.
         (. . . and Earth is a hotbed of criminal activity. We ought to enslave
           that planet NOW.)

Thomas sensed the entire Torth population reeling as the news continued to spread from mind to mind. Billions were drawn in by the dramatic confession. Trillions. They gaped and gawked.

KILL THE CONQUEROR! they urged the assassin.
   YOU OWE IT TO US!
    YOU OWE US FOR YOUR MISTAKE!

Thomas prepared to twist the assassin's mind to defend himself. He just . . .

Well. He just couldn't decide what to do with his now-exiled biological father. Zombify him? Imprison him?

Talk to him?

I made such an awful Mistake, the Somehow Nexus moaned inside his head. *This war. This boy. It's all My fault.*

The whole galaxy listened and agreed.

The Somehow Nexus stared at his biological son and felt solely responsible for the rise of the Conqueror.

He felt even more remorseful about the woman whom he had bedded. The Lone Assassin haunted his memories and his dreams. *Guilty.* She was a phantom who agreed with the Majority. *Guilty.*

In life, she had never pointed an accusatory finger at the Somehow Nexus. She could not. When she'd gotten caught for the crime of having sex, the Somehow Nexus had not taken any of the blame. Silence had seemed pragmatic.

And later? When everyone in the Megacosm learned that she had given birth like a primitive savage, the Somehow Nexus had stayed silent. That had seemed prudent.

But his criminal behavior had turned out to have major consequences.

I created a monster (unwittingly) by accident (I didn't mean to). The Somehow Nexus rotated his gloved hand. *Millions enslaved.* He thought of the penitents. *Billions may yet die.* He thought of the beleaguered Torth Empire. *IT IS ALL MY FAULT.*

The Torth Majority agreed. They were fed up with criminals who hid in plain sight.

The criminal formerly known as the Somehow Nexus has reaped DEATH! orbiters chorused. Their opinions coalesced into a Majority opinion.

Guilty.

He should die.

KILL THE CONQUEROR AND THEN KILL YOURSELF!!!!!! they urged.

Thomas shielded himself with thermal currents. He braced himself for an attack, summoning the remaining zombies to intervene.

But he wasn't the one in danger.

A concussive sound shook the corpses and injured zombies in the room. Unceremonious gouts of blood painted the walls red. Blood mist vaporized in Thomas's heat shield.

His biological father was headless. In the end, he had disobeyed the Majority one last time.

His decapitated body toppled sideways off the bed.

Thomas continued to breathe, disbelieving that his would-be assassin had pointed the blaster glove at his own face instead of at the abomination he had unwittingly sired. The Somehow Nexus could have—should have—made another attempt to assassinate the Conqueror. He might have actually succeeded.

But he had not.

Instead, he had remained a rogue, but he'd buckled under the relentless pressures of secret self-loathing and self-recrimination.

He had been burdened for many years. All of Thomas's life.

So he had obeyed the Majority and executed himself.

So Thomas had survived.

That should be a good thing. Thomas the Conqueror ought to bask in blessed relief that the fight was over and triumph in his superiority. Now was the time to milk the Majority's attention.

Thomas ascended, showing off his survival.

Countless billions slammed into orbit around his colossus of a mind. They foamed with fear and envy and secrets. They marveled at his vitality, his intellect, his triumph.

Feel free to join Me.

That was all the Conqueror managed before he fled back to solitude.

CHAPTER 20

RENEGADE

Ramifications played through Thomas's imagination as he stared at the headless corpse of the biological father who had abandoned him.

This scene would not remain a secret. The whole Megacosm had seen it. Trillions of Torth knew. Ergo, it would be a short time—maybe a few hours, maybe a couple of days—before Garrett checked the galactic news and soaked up the indisputable fact that Thomas Hill was a full-blooded Torth.

The repulsive reality of Thomas's parentage would spread throughout the free realms like a plague. There was no way to stop the news.

Thomas felt feverish as he struggled to stand up. His eyes burned with unshed tears. He wasn't sure why his innards were such a knotted mess of emotions.

He managed to keep his balance as he made his way toward the outer vault, where he had parked his borrowed hoverchair. Cherise was going to find out. She would realize that she used to be friends with a full-blooded Torth. No doubt she would be disgusted with herself for that.

And Vy? Vy would realize that her foster brother was not only an emotionless, robotic boy, but an actual alien. The worst kind of alien.

Ariock would look at him in a new light. An ugly new light.

Kessa. Varktezo. Nror. Pung. Weptolyso. How could any of them stand to be around him? Their supposed Teacher was a Torth.

His friendship with Evenjos would dissipate like dust. Evenjos only tolerated him because she liked human hybrids. Her traumatic memories gave her every reason to fear and hate a full-blooded Torth.

The Alashani? Thomas didn't have to exercise his imagination to guess how they'd react. Flen, Deschuba, Guradjur . . . they already thought of him as a monstrous *rekveh*. This news would only confirm their beliefs. Would Daindlor continue to mentor him? No way.

Hatred aimed at Thomas would multiply. The undergrounders would gain traction.

And why not? They were right to despise Thomas as an overprivileged penitent. That was exactly what he was. He was no different from the Pink Screwdriver and her ilk, except he'd gotten lucky enough to make the right friends.

"I'm no different from your kind," Thomas told the filthy, burned, and blasted Torth zombies in his bedchamber. "I am you."

It was nothing but the truth. Thomas specifically aimed to zombify only Torth with Yeresunsa powers. That was exactly what he was.

Why was he destroying them by the thousands? What made him act so superior to them? His father had been one of them. His mother had been one of them.

And they had both died so that he might live.

They had sacrificed everything. For him.

And he used the gifts they had blessed him with—freedom, life, and a future—to desecrate and murder their own kind of people.

Was there any justice in the universe?

Thomas plopped into his hoverchair and struggled to make sense of his roiling emotions. If not for the illegal sexual union of two morally shady Servants of All, he never would have been conceived or born. He was a literal Mistake. All the million-plus penitent minds he had soaked up within the past couple of days concurred. Their gestalt told him that he belonged in the Mirror Prison as much as any Servant of All.

What made him so certain he should mastermind a hostile takeover of his own people's empire?

He had been wrong about millions of Torth willingly joining him in going renegade.

He had been wrong about his own humanity.

What else was he wrong about? How many of his own plans should he reexamine? Could he even trust himself to make decisions?

As Thomas surveyed the carnage in his room, he knew that he wasn't going to ask Nror or Ariock to clean this up. He could not face any of his friends as a full-blooded Torth.

Not anyone.

He could not possibly report what had just happened while pretending to be stoic and emotionally strong. He felt damaged. Something inside him was shattered. His dearest beliefs, perhaps.

He could not simply return to life as usual and pretend that he was okay. He wasn't going to become a liar.

And he was never going to obey any more damned commands to twist minds and destroy lives.

No more. He could not destroy people like his mother and father. He would not violate the minds of penitents as he'd been doing. He wasn't sure he could ever look at a Torth prisoner again, let alone rob them of freedom.

He didn't want to be part of this war.

He didn't want to destroy one problematic civilization only to replace it with another problematic civilization.

Thomas felt cosmically trapped. He struggled to breathe, grappling with a sickened feeling of self-hatred, discarding all the awful choices he faced. Until a decision clicked into place.

He needed time to think.

He needed to escape. He needed a safe place, away from the wrongful obligations he had taken on and the messes he had caused and the horrors he had wrought.

He was going to stop being the Conqueror.

Thomas rotated his hoverchair to face the carnage one last time.

He did not want anyone to examine the headless corpse and make conjectures about what this fight had been like. So he channeled heat into the corpse of his father, superheating it until it combusted. The body incinerated in a white-hot flash.

All that remained were smoldering, body-shaped cinders.

Thomas considered sweeping the cremation ashes into a portable container. But his own infallible memory had enfolded the Somehow Nexus, and that was a better consecration than any sentimental funeral. Thomas wasn't going to honor the father who had abandoned him.

He used thermal currents to disperse the ashes.

Gone.

He turned his hoverchair and floated out of the bunker. He unlocked his broken control sleeve—he had to bang the frozen piece of junk until it fell open—and he dropped it in the hallway. The numbed, frostbitten feeling began to ebb.

Once Thomas emerged into the slumbering city aboveground, he donned his floppy-brimmed hat. There. He could pass as a shani from a distance. Most of his bruises from the enemy zombies were hidden by his clothes.

Not that he had to worry much about being seen. The city remained fearful of the rogue brainwasher, so there were few pedestrians outside at this hour. Thomas avoided streetlamps and moved swiftly toward the spaceport.

If only he had time to visit Azhdarchidae.

His sky croc might feel abandoned, but Thomas dared not detour to the Dragon Tower. Azhdarchidae was a resourceful monster. He would be fine on his own.

A glowing streak lit the dark sky as a jumper shuttle landed in the distance. The city's makeshift spaceport was busy at all hours, even on a quiet night like this. Military pilots logged a lot of practice hours. Most of them had learned the basics of how to operate small shuttles or even streamships, but training was important. Maintenance protocols and military maneuvers were a work in progress.

Thomas took a casual path uphill. He parked his borrowed hoverchair amid a cargo lot with preloaded hovercarts, ready with supplies for the upcoming morning work shift.

He checked the power charge on his leg braces. Satisfied that it was good enough, he climbed into a nondescript delivery vehicle. The dashboard was easy for him to unlock. He had memorized override codes for almost every machine in Freedomland.

Soon he was steering past hulking aircrafts and sleek jumper shuttles.

"Hey." A sleepy govki waved to Thomas, mistaking him for a fellow maintenance worker. "What brings you here at this quiet hour, good shani?"

Thomas steered close enough to the govki worker for a mental scan, although he took care not to reveal his own face. "I'm helping to repair a thruster," he mumbled in a terse voice, impersonating the mushy accent of an Alashani.

He soaked up the worker's thoughts. That gave him a rough idea of which streamships were in decently flightworthy condition. He even learned which ones were preloaded with enough drinking water and nonperishables for a voyage.

"Oh, is it an emergency that can't wait until morning?" the govki asked, interested. "Which ship?"

Thomas sensed what the govki needed to hear in order to update the maintenance logs. He called out an acceptable answer without slowing down.

It was easy for him to choose an optimal streamship. He didn't need to run through a long checklist of criteria or look up access codes. He already knew those things. All he needed to do was abandon the hovercart and walk up the ramp into the ship.

Walking was not easy for him. But as long as he used his exosuit regularly, the braces should continue to aid him. Kinetic energy caused the battery to recharge.

Thomas entered the ship.

He checked to make sure he was alone. There were no accidental stowaways. He checked the ship's supplies.

As Thomas sank into the command chair, he asked himself if he was doing the right thing.

One domineering part of his brain reasoned that fleeing his own city was an overreaction. He had designed and founded Freedomland. So what if the locals tried to murder him for being a full-blooded Torth? People were stupid. He was a rational, logical, smart, and magnificent being. Wasn't he capable of handling any fallout from the revelation of who his biological father was? Couldn't he weather whatever storm Garrett wanted to hit him with? Did he actually care about an up-tick of hatred aimed his way?

Why did he even need friends? Or emotions?

Thomas slammed his head down into his hands.

His Torth brain was stoic and calculating and undeniably dominant. He could not rid himself of his Torth qualities. He was a *rekveh*.

Yet it seemed he had absorbed enough humanity to feel things deeply, despite his cursed genetics. This pseudohuman aspect of his consciousness wanted to curl up and swallow toxins until he could no longer think.

When he urged himself to go to his Dragon Tower, to work on suppressing his mess of fear and anger and behave like a hero again, tears leaked from his eyes.

Running away was bad. It might be yet another evil act, another terrible decision made by the traitorous Conqueror. It was stupid, primitive behavior.

Even so.

Thomas could not bear to soak up another penitent's soul. He could not twist another prisoner's mind. Those acts were destroying him.

And he could not bear the judgment of a friend or ally right now. Those judgments would break him.

Running away was wrong, but it was the right choice for his mental health.

Thomas fired up the engines and prepared for liftoff.

PART TWO

*Four shall counter many. All four heroes must be present and willing,
else the many will tear the universe asunder and take all with them unto death.*

—Ah Jun's prophecies

CHAPTER 1

VICARIOUS

For Kessa, each day was better than the previous day.

She started her morning with a healthy breakfast of butterseed blooms, plus a strongly flavored brew that gave her an extra bit of energy. While she ate at her leisure, she received missives from spies who were stuck in Torth lands, pretending to be slaves.

She transmitted a response across the galaxy to give a spy more information. They needed to know which launchpads to sabotage, and which high-ranked Torth ought to be distracted during a critical time window. Only a handful of planets had supercom access. Kessa knew which and when. She orchestrated dozens of covert operations to undermine the Torth Empire.

Few people gave the spies credit for the huge differences they made. Kessa never forgot them. If a spy retired, she ensured that they received parcels of land, military credits, or other substantial rewards.

After breakfast, Kessa invited her executive secretary to deliver a summary of important news. Instead of launching into a list of which cities were struggling or which territories were lost, Yanyashta had local news to report.

"Thomas failed to show up for his morning absorption of minds," the pink-cheeked albino maiden reported. "Some of the overseers and premiers are upset about his absence."

"Give me a moment." Kessa used her wristwatch supercom to call Thomas.

He did not answer.

Kessa decided not to let that bother her overmuch. Whenever she saw Thomas, he looked more sallow and exhausted. Maybe he was sleeping in? He had definitely earned some time off once he rooted out the so-called Stranger Danger.

She recorded a brief message expressing concern and sent it to his inbox.

"What else?" she asked her secretary.

"A few lieutenants say their penitents are acting oddly this morning," Yanyashta said.

Kessa stood, alarmed. Penitents tended to react to events in the Torth Empire. None would ever admit to ascending into the Megacosm, since it was against the rules, but they were a conduit to the enemy empire.

"What are they saying?" Kessa asked. "Do they warn of an impending Torth attack?"

"Not that anyone has reported to me," Yanyashta said. "The lieutenants just say that they seem distracted."

"Distracted in what way?"

Yanyashta made a face. "Penitents are secretive. They won't say."

At least some penitents would say something out loud, if danger was coming. Kessa relaxed. Perhaps they were just reacting to unimportant gossip?

The behavior of condemned Torth might be more telling. A backlog of prisoners awaited zombification. If any of them seemed hopeful, or furtive, or anything unusual . . .

"Are there any reports from the Mirror Prison?" Kessa asked.

"No," Yanyashta said. "Want me to ask?"

"Please."

Kessa chatted with her secretary a bit more, but there was no more news, and nothing actionable. Soon she wrapped up the meeting. As she sped toward the palace on her hovercart, she made calls, suggesting elevated security measures.

Telepathy lessons were the highlight of Kessa's daily morning schedule. She arrived late and hurried to a leftover seat near the door. Class was already in session.

How many fingers am I holding up? Garrett silently asked the class.

Kessa sensed his trickery right away. Garrett was not holding up any hands or fingers, yet he imagined himself to be holding up three fingers. Exercises like this helped to train Kessa and other students to separate fact from fiction, and fantasy from reality.

Answers bounced around the room. The emitters were pumping, filling the classroom with telepathy gas. After forty wake cycles of regular lessons, Kessa no longer struggled just to make sense of perceptual overload. She could separate who was who and where each thought originated.

Garrett confirmed that Kessa and other top students were correct—no fingers—and he moved onto another thought exercise. Telepathy lessons were rapid. Thought was much faster than speech, once one got used to it.

How many game pieces? Garrett tossed tiny spiky things onto the floor, where everyone could see them.

Kessa saw forty-three at a glance. She sensed two other students come up with the sum right away, like she did. Others echoed the ones with a sum in mind. Still others counted the pieces, one cluster after another. They also came up with a sum of forty-three, but it took them longer.

Varktezo met Kessa's gaze from across the room. He had seen the sum right away, like her.

One of the counters, a govki, glared at them.

Peace. Garrett mentally acknowledged the feelings of inferiority and superiority swirling throughout the room. *Cognitive differences are no big deal. Everyone has strengths that outweigh other people's weaknesses and vice versa . . .*

Kessa lost track of the lesson as a new presence entered her awareness. Whoever he was, he radiated a ludicrous amount of certainty. This was a person who believed that he could literally lift mountains.

Yet he was trying to talk himself into opening the door to the classroom.

He worried about Thomas, who had not responded to his latest messages and was not answering calls. He was willing to learn a useful new skill, telepathy. Maybe that would motivate him to face battles again? Maybe it would help him connect with Thomas? Except . . .

. . . Don't want Vy reading my mind, he fretted. *Don't want my innermost fears made public.*

"Oof." Kessa slid off her chair. She had never read Ariock's mind, but she felt quite sure that he was nearby. Who else would contain that mixture of immense strength and self-doubt?

She opened the door. Sure enough, there he was.

Kessa tilted her head back to give him a welcoming look. "Your inner doubts are driving us all crazy. Come in!"

Ariock flushed.

"Yes, we overheard your thoughts," Kessa confirmed for him. The students nearest to the door had overheard his surface thoughts, anyway, and everyone else had overheard them. "We'd be happy to have you join us for lessons." She took her seat again.

Yes!

Please!

The rest of the class heartily agreed without speaking a word. Garrett had been most interesting during the one time he had expanded his awareness during a lesson. The Bringer of Hope was on another level. What would it feel like to vicariously experience his raw cosmic power?

Ariock's face remained red. He ducked through the doorway, and Kessa sensed him compare the staring faces here to an unhappy memory. Other kids *(humans) (fifth graders)* had watched him slouch toward a desk that was too small for him. Those kids had smirked. And stared.

A bunch of boys had thrown trash at him after school.

Kessa exchanged glances of disbelief with other telepathy students. A powerful miracle worker such as Ariock could not possibly fear ridicule. Could he?

It's about time you (Ariock) joined My lessons, Garrett thought.

Despite the criticism, Garrett's mind bubbled with happiness. He was genuinely glad that Ariock wanted to learn.

Great-grandfather. Ariock silently acknowledged his telepathic relative, but he seemed overwhelmed. He was clearly struggling with the overload of perceptions.

Kessa understood what he was going through. As a beginner, she had also felt pummeled by outside thoughts. Ariock must feel as light as an ummin and as heavy as a nussian, at the same time. His vision must look fragmented, torn into multiple perceptions.

"Sit," Kessa urged him.

Yes, other students agreed.

Sit.

Join us, Bringer of Hope!

Kessa sensed a focal point, guided by Garrett. Her classmates showed Ariock the sturdy bench where he would likely be most comfortable.

Ariock sat.

He continued to agonize over a plethora of inner doubts. Kessa overheard every worry in Ariock's head. He wished he had asked Garrett for private lessons. He regretted coming here, because he had not expected this class to be so far ahead of his skill level. He felt boggled!

Kessa scrutinized Ariock. Had he honestly expected to outdo students who'd had months of daily practice already? He was a complete beginner. How could he expect to master a difficult skill within seconds?

Oh.

As Kessa thought about it, she realized that of course Ariock assumed that he was better than everyone else. He built cities and starships. He singlehandedly slew armies. Whenever people complained that a task was monumentally difficult, Ariock got it done. He was the messiah. He performed miracles on a regular basis.

Ariock hunched his shoulders and guiltily acknowledged that Kessa's assessment was true. He was aware of the common complaints about telepathy being a difficult skill to master, but in his experience, hard tasks were only difficult for other people. Not for him.

You see? Garrett thought to the class. *Even the messiah (even a hero) can make a simple cognitive error. We all have strengths and weaknesses.*

The class considered that.

Here's another object lesson in cognitive differences. Garrett used his powers to gather the game pieces, then tossed a bunch of them onto the floor again. *How many are on the floor?*

Kessa saw the sum right away, effortlessly, in a glance. Thirty.

But she sensed Ariock counting the pieces in clusters. He felt overwhelmed and bombarded by extraneous thoughts, and that slowed him down, yet even so, Kessa realized that he did not see the sum. He had to count.

It didn't come naturally to him. Not the way it was for Kessa and Varktezo.

Yup. Ariock and I are morons, Garrett thought with sarcastic good humor, demonstrating that he also needed to count. *Just like the Torth.*

The implication was plain. The Torth were not nearly as wise or clever as Kessa used to believe. Someone could rule cities or planets and yet be unable to count items in a glance.

The Torth believe that they are superior beings, Garrett thought as he used his powers to gather up the game pieces. *Because of telepathy. But this power only enables a person (a mind reader) to borrow the wits, the knowledge, and the perceptions of (slaves) other people. It empowers one to be mentally lazy. Most Torth have flabby minds.*

Kessa thought about her blue-haired owner. Sometimes that vain creature had commanded Kessa to do mysterious things. She would toss pins on the floor and demand that Kessa pick them up. She used to bring Kessa on shopping excursions for no apparent reason.

Had she borrowed Kessa's ability to do sums? To see things the way Kessa saw things?

Let's loosen things up with a perceptual exercise, Garrett thought. *This half of the room should look through that window.* He indicated. *And the other half—*

An alert pinged.

Ariock looked sheepish. He glanced at his wristwatch and Kessa sensed his concern. The local garrison commander would not call unless there was a security or military problem.

Perhaps the hidden mind controller had attacked again?

Whatever was happening, it was not public knowledge. It wasn't news. Kessa could see a plaza outside the windows, and a shopping bazaar beyond that. If there was an emergency situation, people would be running to the nearest shelter. Instead, pedestrians were strolling or shopping. There were no klaxons.

Ariock stood, preparing to leave the classroom. Kessa sensed his intention to call the garrison commander in private.

? Garrett emanated concern, and Kessa felt the same way. Was the call related to Thomas's absence from his duties this morning? Or maybe it had something to do with the reported unease among the penitent population?

Other students stared at her. Even Garrett and Ariock were alarmed.

Thomas is missing?

What do you mean, he's absent?

He missed work?!

Penitents are uneasy? Why?

Garrett's wristwatch pinged.

So did Kessa's. Her secretary, Yanyashta, wanted a callback.

All right, class adjourned, Garrett thought. He used his powers to shut off the emitters.

Students emanated dismay as the telepathy gas died. Kessa overheard *(oh no)* *(please don't turn it off!)* unrequited curiosity and unspoken pleas.

Kessa was not the only student who eyed the telepathy gas emitters with longing. Varktezo looked crazed by curiosity. The emitters were so easy to turn on. All that was required was a flick of a switch.

But she understood why telepathy might be problematic in an emergency. It was best not to exacerbate a panic by telepathically linking to twenty other people.

Perhaps this was why the Torth frowned upon intense emotions? No one wanted to be bombarded by panic.

"What's wrong?" Ariock put on his earpiece, listening. No one was likely to overhear the other side of the conversation while he was standing.

Kessa clipped her own earpiece to one flap of her headdress. Unlike humans, she did not have an external ear, but head covers were useful that way.

She hurried to a corner of the room for privacy and called her secretary.

"Kessa," Yanyashta said. "I wanted to let you know, there's a, um, rumor going around about Thomas."

Kessa's skin prickled as if the room was too humid. This must be something worse than the usual whispers about puppeteering the messiah or spying through the perceptions of lizards. "What rumor?"

Yanyashta hesitated.

The sky outside darkened. Clouds gathered over the mountains and rolled over the ocean horizon as well.

"Thomas is missing," Yanyashta said carefully. "And, um, it looks like there was an altercation in the bunker where he slept last night."

"An altercation?" Kessa glanced toward Ariock and Garrett. Their faces were as grim as the stormy sky. She halfway wished the telepathy gas was on, so she could read their minds as they spoke to their own military agents. "What do you mean?"

Yanyashta relented, reverting to plain language. "Dead zombies were found. And injured ones, as well as a lot of blood and some char and shattered mirrors. It looks like a battle took place there."

Kessa's throat felt stiff. She should have raised an alert the instant Thomas failed to answer his supercom.

Except he was hard to communicate with lately. He rejected meetings. He never answered messages or calls.

What, exactly, were the implications?

"The city is being searched," Yanyashta was saying. "Discreetly. Obviously we don't want any penitents to learn that he's missing."

Obviously.

The Torth Empire might launch a wave of attacks if they believed Thomas had been abducted. Or if he'd been . . .

Killed.

No. Thomas could not be dead in any obvious way. His adolescence and his leg braces made his body recognizable, and surely the whole city would know if one of those corpses had been him. Kessa remembered to breathe.

But what if he'd been put under mind control?

What had the rogue brainwasher done to him?

"Wait." Kessa managed to speak. "What about his hoverchair? Has anyone found that?" She wanted a clue.

"No," Yanyashta replied. "But he was using a borrowed, generic hoverchair, so it will take a while to track it down. It could be any hoverchair in the city."

Kessa nodded, speechless. She had nearly forgotten that the most recent attempt to assassinate Thomas had resulted in damage. His signature smoky hoverchair was broken.

Just how many people wanted to murder Thomas?

Kessa never should have believed that he would ignore his many duties. Would he luxuriate in the Dragon Tower while people waited for him to show up for work? No. That wasn't Thomas.

He should not have been sleeping alone.

He should not have been coerced into confronting the lurking brainwasher alone. That wasn't right. Thomas was a capable hero, but he was not all-powerful or superstrong, and he'd been forced to take on too much alone. He needed friends! Kessa wished she had insisted on prying into his private life. Could she have persuaded him to accept a friendly visit or two?

"I'll let you know if there are any updates, all right?" Yanyashta said.

Kessa wasn't sure what to say. "Thank you."

She gave her secretary a few seconds to volunteer more information. When none came, she ended the call.

Outside, canvas stall dividers billowed in a gale.

Kessa hoped the Dovanacks would get their emotions under control. A violent storm might clue the Torth Empire into realizing that something was amiss in Freedomland. That might be disastrous . . .

Unless the Torth already knew.

Penitents were acting distracted.

"I'll check the Megacosm," Garrett said, making Kessa glad the telepathy gas was switched off.

"No," Ariock said. "Don't."

"It's a risk," Garrett acknowledged. "I get it. We don't want to accidentally tell the Torth Empire that our one and only supergenius is, uh, missing. But we have to—"

"The Torth aren't his only enemies," Ariock pointed out. "He might have been abducted by Alashani undergrounders."

Or he might have been brainwashed by a rogue Torth. Nobody guessed that out loud, but Kessa figured she was not the only person with that terrifying thought. She saw the wariness in Garrett's eyes. Varktezo looked grave, too. They both probably regretted allowing Thomas to deal with the brainwasher alone.

"Once the Torth Empire knows," Kessa said, mostly for the benefit of her fellow classmates, "there is no turning back. They consider Thomas to be their main enemy. He's their Conqueror. If they think he's gone? They will feel emboldened."

"They'd hammer us," Garrett said, morose. "Relentlessly."

It would be worse than ever. The Torth Empire was already emboldened because Ariock, the Giant, refused to go into battle zones anymore. Kessa did not say that. She was glad that no one could overhear her thoughts right now.

"Let me search for him." Ariock sat back on the bench seat, which creaked under his weight. "Maybe he escaped and is hiding in the city? He could be injured."

"Right." Garrett made a cigarette appear. Smoke trailed him as he paced. "Good idea."

Kessa tried to imagine Thomas locked in some basement in the Alashani quarter. It was remotely possible, wasn't it?

Ariock closed his eyes. Students watched him with expectation.

No doubt Ariock was expanding his awareness across Freedomland. Any life spark that seemed strong enough to be Thomas would warrant a clairvoyant inspection.

What did it feel like, to encompass the city?

More than a few students flicked their gazes toward the emitters. Telepathy students were, by definition, overly curious. But all they could do was wait. Kessa checked her messages and considered how she might help.

Ariock roused himself after a minute. "I don't think he's in the city."

"Are you sure?" Garrett demanded.

"Not one hundred percent," Ariock admitted, frustrated. "He could have gotten hit with the inhibitor. Or he might be drained."

Garrett swore. "He could be anywhere. What if some Torth figured out how to teleport with a passenger?"

Students exchanged fearful looks.

"For all we know," Garrett said, "the Torth could have figured out how to boost their powers by linking." He threw his hands in the air. "We don't know!" He paced so furiously, he was wreathed in smoke. "I should check the Megacosm," he concluded.

"Not yet," Ariock said firmly. "Find out if any spaceships are missing." He closed his eyes. "I'll scan local space."

What if Thomas was trapped and terrified in some cage?

As Kessa surveyed her fellow classmates, she knew it was only a matter of time before the news trickled through the city and into the ears of penitents.

They had to find Thomas soon.

CHAPTER 2

STORM OF REACTION

By the second day into the search for Thomas, Ariock was numb from ghosting so often. He was frozen dust and cosmic radiation. He was a vast nothingness.

He lost access to his other powers whenever he was disembodied, as well as his senses of smell and touch and taste. Colors were desaturated. It was like floating in a desensitization chamber. Except it was worse, because he had trouble holding on to his emotions and his train of thought.

His only breaks were to nap, to snack, and to take care of bodily needs. An average clairvoyant might manage five minutes per day. Ariock had superhuman endurance plus a nearly infinite reservoir of power, which empowered him to do ten-minute stints again and again, for hours and hours and hours.

He began to fully recognize the torment Evenjos had suffered.

He had not anticipated so much mental confusion and exhaustion from repeatedly maintaining a metaphysical, disembodied state. Even when he teleported in order to inspect strange things—asteroids, space junk, objects shaped like asteroids—all he heard was his own breathing inside his helmet. All he saw lacked color.

By his fourth day as a space ghost, Ariock began to doubt his own existence.

Was he really alive? Had his whole rise to power been nothing but a hallucinatory dream, or a fictional story in some ridiculous book?

After nightfall on the fifth day, Ariock snapped back to his body, as he automatically had to do every few minutes. Instead of casting himself out yet again, he removed his layers of armor until he wore nothing but underclothes. Then he lay on his bed like an invalid. He folded his hands on his chest.

He stared at shadows patterning the brushed quartz-and-bronze ceiling.

When he spent so much time in the void of deep space beyond the solar system of Reject-20, inspecting the parsecs around the nearest temporal stream gateway . . . a long, cold distance away . . . he tended to forget what he was searching for. That happened more and more often. Only when he returned to his body for a refreshing nap could he shake off the mental fog.

What if he forgot that he had a body waiting for him?

The tug of his mortal coil might just snap and break. Then he would be a disembodied ghost forever, unable to remember his own name, or whom he used to be.

He was so exhausted, he did not even dream. There were no nightmares. His life had begun to resemble a nightmare.

He awoke gradually to delicious smells coming from the kitchen. Someone was cooking pancakes and toast.

Unfortunately, it wasn't Vy. This chef hummed a pop song from Earth in a baritone voice.

Ariock rubbed sleep from his eyes. He got up, padded to the kitchen, and leaned in the archway with his arms folded.

Garrett was flipping a hearty omelet. His sleeves were rolled up, and he moved from one pan to another with practiced ease.

"Breakfast is almost served," Garrett said.

Somehow, Ariock found it comforting to see his great-grandfather in a domestic setting. It reminded him that Garrett used to be a dad.

"Need any help?" Ariock asked.

"Nah, I've got it." Garrett seemed to enjoy the act of cooking. He could have ordered a meal delivery, but instead, he was here, doing everything manually. He wasn't even using his powers.

Well, except for a few things. Some ingredients poured themselves.

Soon they were seated across from each other, bathed in morning light that filtered through the keyhole-shaped window. The kitchen table was already set with utensils and plates.

"Mmm." Garrett took a bite of the omelet. "Those farmed avians lay tasty eggs."

Ariock sampled a piece of omelet and nodded in approval.

"Have the rest." Garrett gestured. "Ghosting drains you."

That was true. Ariock was actually gaunt, and he now realized that he was famished. He ate the rest of the omelet, then pulled a stack of pancakes onto his plate.

"It's all locally sourced." Garrett sounded proud.

"Thanks for the meal." Ariock poured syrup onto the pancakes. He didn't need to read Garrett's mind to understand why he merited a serious visit. Thomas's absence was escalating into something worse than a temporary crisis. It meant the end of the war—and not in a good way.

Ariock wasn't keeping up with the news, but he understood that the Torth were collectively growing bolder in their attacks, taunting the heroes, daring them to use some brilliant strategy. Hadn't the Torth fully sacked and reconquered Tempest Arena? They kept bombing CloudShadow MetroHub and other liberated cities on Nuss.

They were winning.

But this meal was a kindness. Ariock tried to enjoy it. The food tasted wonderful, the banded planet filled the sky, and sunlight danced on the ocean. He liked being alive and in his body.

"So." Garrett blotted his mouth with a napkin, apparently done eating. "We can't put it off any longer."

The Megacosm.

Ariock imagined Garrett scanning for news—and the Torth Majority learning just how vulnerable Ariock was.

It was easy to imagine. Celebrations would break out in Torth-ruled cities across the galaxy. The enemy supergeniuses were probably just waiting for confirmation that Thomas was being delivered into their custody. As soon as they knew for sure? They would slam all of Ariock's cities with insanity and telepathy gas.

It would be the end of freedom.

"Not yet," Ariock said.

"The Torth must know by now." Garrett simultaneously rolled his eyes and thumped the table. "Think about it from their perspective. They know you've stopped mass-teleporting. They can guess that I've stopped spying in the Megacosm, since they were able to recapture an entire city. You can be sure they've scanned minds and learned what's new on our side. It all adds up to the boy missing."

That might be so.

Garrett had become a lone bulwark against full-scale invasions on Umdalkdul and Nuss and even Earth. And without using the Megacosm, Garrett might as well be blind.

None of the penitents offered so much as a guess as to who had taken their Conqueror. A few told wild tales. They claimed that Thomas was fully Torth. They said he had gone rogue, or that he was rejoining the Torth Empire. But those claims were plain nonsense. They had to be.

"The fastest streamship travels at half the speed of light," Garrett growled. "If the boy is trapped aboard that stolen ship, they'll be at the temporal stream any day now. Any hour. From there, they can go anywhere in the known universe!"

Ariock did not need the reminder. Someone had stolen a streamship from the Freedomland spaceport on the night of Thomas's mysterious battle and disappearance. The lurking brainwasher had not struck since then. It all amounted to dark implications. Had the brainwasher absconded with Thomas in that stolen ship?

Or worse. What if there was a grain of truth in what the penitents said? Thomas might be acting under nefarious orders, no longer in control of his own destiny. He might have gotten brainwashed. What if he'd been forced to unwittingly fly straight into the open arms of the Torth Empire?

"Torth are definitely waiting for him," Garrett said darkly. "They've got clusters of ships camped out near the temporal stream. I know you've noticed."

Ariock reached for a generous helping of French toast. "There are lone Torth in shuttles all over our solar system."

Garrett's jaw dropped.

"They're not a threat." Ariock tensed up, aware that Garrett tended to overreact. "I'm worried that Thomas could be in any one of them. I keep checking."

"Agh!" Garrett jumped off the stool, too outraged to sit still. "Are you saying we have an invasion fleet on our doorstep? Why the devil haven't you told me?"

Ariock shrugged and went back to eating. "They're not an invasion fleet."

"They're gunships!" Garrett began to argue.

"They're tiny vessels." Ariock knew what a space threat looked like. He had once hurled the largest tower in the known universe at a Torth armada. "There are no dreadnoughts or battleships. They're minimally armed. They could be mistaken for rocks."

"Well, you've got to kill them." Garrett made it sound like an obvious conclusion. "Make sure they're not the boy. Then teleport and destroy them, one by one."

"No," Ariock said.

Garrett's eye twitched.

"It's possible they're renegades seeking our protection," Ariock explained tiredly.

Garrett looked as if he was sizing up an insane opponent. "Renegades?"

"Yes," Ariock said. "A couple of those vessels look scientific. There are slaves inside. I think they might be the Twins, coming here to take Thomas's offer and join us."

Garrett looked pained.

"I'm not going to murder possible allies," Ariock said. "Thomas wouldn't want that."

He made himself sound certain, but inwardly, he feared Garrett was right. Garrett kept being right. After all this time, Ariock had yet to see a renegade other than the Upward Governess.

Most of those lone shuttles were stocked with food and potable water, and they were cloaked or disguised as asteroids. Each contained a single Torth. They were likely just waiting for Ariock to fail so they could attack Freedomland like a bunch of sharks.

He didn't like it.

But he wasn't going to start an unnecessary battle, especially right now. The Torth Empire loomed like a storm on the horizon. Any one of the Torth militarized fleets could swarm through the temporal stream network and then crush the nascent space fleet captained by Fayfer.

"If the Torth get the boy," Garrett said, "then all your stupid kindness won't matter. If they take him into that temporal stream, they can take him literally anywhere. And then we're screwed!"

Ariock nodded. That was the deadline. They needed to find Thomas before he could vanish forever.

He just didn't want to admit that he felt worn-down.

Or that the search seemed futile.

"The problem is," Ariock said, "I have a nearly infinite area to search." He held his hands apart to demonstrate, still holding a fork in one hand. "It's two parsecs from here to the temporal stream. I've searched that distance in a straight line, no problem. But I didn't see any ships along that route. They're not traveling in a straight line."

"Of course not." Garrett climbed back onto one of the tall stools Ariock kept for guests. The old man had probably ghosted through the same area, although clairvoyance was far more draining for him than it was for Ariock. He did not have nearly as much raw power.

"They might be here, here, here, or here." Ariock indicated by moving his oversize fork all around the imaginary fixed path. "They might be way out here." He held his opposite hand beneath the temporal stream gate, then behind it. "Or here." He held the fork in the opposite direction, far from the gate.

"I get what you're saying." Garrett gazed out the window, at colorful rooftop canopies and herb gardens. "Every minute the boy is gone, the area we have to search expands exponentially."

Ariock nodded. He might be powerful enough to destroy a planet, but even his sphere of influence had limits. On a galactic scale, even when he went fully titanic, he was actually quite small.

"And all those little ships out there are dark," Ariock explained. "They look like rocks at a distance. Once I found one that had a life spark inside?" He laughed without humor. "I realized I would have to investigate every single asteroid in order to determine if it's a ship or not."

"Oh." Garrett sounded sympathetic at last. "Crap. You are really doing a lot of work."

"I am," Ariock acknowledged. "I've been teleporting. With space armor. With air tanks." He drank juice from a decanter. "That's the only way I can detect them."

"You're searching for a needle in a haystack," Garrett said in a tone of realization. "Except it's a haystack larger than a solar system."

"Much larger," Ariock said.

"Well, the boy has to be somewhere." Garrett flung a hand skyward, indicating space.

Ariock agreed. But what more could he do? If Thomas was in that stolen ship, it must be cloaked and floating in some unpredictable place. Ariock had already investigated thousands of random asteroids. He might be too exhausted to even recognize Thomas if he ever found him.

"Let me check the Megacosm." Garrett looked beseeching. "It's possible they know something we haven't even guessed at."

Ariock felt constricted. He had so few options.

Garrett clasped Ariock's hand. "We cannot win if the boy shows up on the Torth side. If they get him, then it's game over."

That was undeniable.

"Besides," Garrett said, "what if he's critically injured? What if he needs immediate help? We have to take the risk."

Ariock had seen footage of the carnage found in Thomas's bunker. Thomas had taken a lot of precautions simply to sleep, yet even so, an attacker had tried hard to kill him. For all anyone knew, the attacker had succeeded.

"I'll be stealthy." Garrett folded his hands on the table, earnest. "I can pop in and out without sharing much of what we know."

Ariock glanced at his wealth of furnishings. He slept fearlessly in a palace. He lived well. Meanwhile, what was Thomas enduring right now?

If Thomas was free to return, he would have done so. Everyone knew that.

Was Ariock just finding yet another excuse to avoid battle and responsibility?

"All right."

The go-ahead spilled out of Ariock. He wasn't sure he was ready. But when he imagined Thomas alone and scared, and possibly injured or brainwashed . . . well, wasn't any risk worth taking?

He would just have to prepare for Armageddon while he was at it.

"Thank you." Garrett closed his eyes.

Ariock sat back and watched the old man's face. He yearned for good advice. Garrett could not offer advice on Thomas's level, but maybe he would be able to provide a useful hint? A direction in which to search?

The tranquil morning sky blackened with sudden clouds.

Hailstones began to pummel rooftops and plazas in a furious staccato. Lightning flashed. The storm came so fast, goose bumps broke out over Ariock's skin. He would have involuntarily popped out his spikes if he were a nussian.

"TRAITOR!" Garrett leaped to his feet. "HE'S A TRAITOR!"

Ariock got up and seized his great-grandfather, trying to slow him down and make him explain. Thomas was too good for the Torth Empire. He would never join them.

"He IS a Torth!" Garrett met Ariock's gaze. "He's a full-blooded damned Torth! He's the real deal!"

"Slow down, please." Ariock made his deep voice reassuringly gentle. "What did you hear?"

"Agh!" Steam rose off Garrett's skin. He was so furious, he was fluctuating the air temperature around his body. "Both of the boy's parents were Torth!" He slammed his fist into his palm repeatedly, emphasizing each statement. "His mother? Was a Servant of All. And his father? Was also a damned Servant of All!"

Thomas had a father? Ariock stared at Garrett, perplexed.

Anyway, since when did the Torth Majority concern themselves with family gossip? This didn't sound like typical Torth news. Garrett must have misinterpreted the mental chatter.

Or . . . could it be a deliberate lie? Was that possible?

Either way, there was a miscommunication.

Garrett rose in the air, lifted on a wave of power. Plates and cups floated.

"HE! IS! A! TORTH!" Garrett screamed in Ariock's face.

Ariock jerked back, but Garrett seized him.

"It's not a lie, and it's not a mistake." Garrett drew breath, obviously struggling to regain control of his emotions. Tableware clattered down. The hailstorm outside became a flood-like downpour. "The lurking brainwasher," Garrett said, "was the boy's biological father. Never mind that for now! The point is that he betrayed us!"

"Who?" Ariock felt as if he was struggling to keep up with a madman.

"The boy!" Garrett said explosively. "He left us! He deliberately ran away and left us!"

"What?" Ariock couldn't believe that.

"Believe it!" Garrett snapped. "There's no other logical explanation! He stole that streamship on his own and left us!"

"I don't—"

"He gave up on us!" Garrett yelled. "He's GONE. He ABANDONED US."

Ariock tried to prioritize his questions. Very little of Garrett's ravings made sense to him. Had Thomas discovered his biological father? Okay, but if so, why would that cause Thomas to flee the safe haven he'd made for himself here? Why would Thomas purposely hurtle into the dangers of the Torth-ruled galaxy?

Could Thomas really be a fully biological Torth?

Ariock tried to swat away that painful question as unimportant and inconsequential, but it reeled through his mind like a wrecking ball. Certain details about Thomas began to jell and to make sense in a more coherent way.

Thomas lacked the titanic power of a human hybrid. Because he wasn't actually a human hybrid.

The Torth Empire had originally welcomed Thomas with open arms. Their eldest supergenius, the Upward Governess, had vouched for him. So had the Torth Majority. All the smartest and savviest mind readers in the galaxy had conferred and unanimously agreed that Thomas had exemplary Torth qualities.

Thomas had always been unapologetic about his Torth tendencies.

He had a way of going emotionless and knowing everything. He even considered himself to be one of the penitents.

"He's a Torth." Ariock spoke softly, trying to get used to the disturbing idea.

He hoped it wasn't true. He wasn't sure why. Couldn't he handle a minor adjustment to the identity of his friend? A little factoid didn't really change anything. Did it?

It changed everything.

Many liberated slaves respected humans, and they considered Thomas to be an honorary human. Once they found out Thomas had unshakable familial ties to the hated mind readers who used to rule them . . . there would be a lot more assassination attempts.

Many Alashani barely tolerated the *rekveh* strategist who advised the war council. Premiers and councilors would take this as proof that Thomas had turned traitor. They would react like Garrett.

Evenjos? She would equate Thomas with Unyat. She would never trust a full-blooded Torth.

As for Ariock himself . . .

He's still the same person he always was, Ariock assured himself. That had to be true.

But then, why had Thomas run away?

Why would he voluntarily abandon the good guys?

"I'll show you the whole thing." Garrett was still fuming. "Come with me to the telepathy gas classroom. I'll show you exactly what happened."

Ariock hesitated.

He needed to experience whatever had triggered Garrett. He needed enlightenment. Yet at the same time, he worried that enlightenment would cause something like a storm surge in himself and his friends.

And what had the news done to the Torth Empire?

Whether Thomas had been kidnapped or had actually run away, wouldn't the Torth rally a massive manhunt? They would surely try to grab the wayward supergenius before Ariock and his friends could do so.

Thomas was likely in more trouble than he'd ever been in. Everyone in the known universe would want to capture or kill him.

"All right, all right." Ariock fended off Garrett's tugs. "You can show me."

Garrett was full of grim triumph. "You'll see why we can't trust him. He's running to the Torth Empire right now!"

Ariock doubted that. Thomas might have run away. That was crazy and hard to believe, but if that really was the case, well . . . then maybe . . .

"Maybe he didn't feel safe here," Ariock said with dawning realization.

CHAPTER 3

TO STAND UP

Vy laid a washcloth over her eyes and instructed herself to banish stressful thoughts. Forget news. Forget consequences. Forget the trauma she'd absorbed thirdhand from Garrett's stress-crazed mind via telepathy gas.

She inhaled the fragrance of essential oils and bath salts.

She slid deeper into the bathing pool, using her hair as a pillow. She had a lot of hair, and it was twisted into a loose knot. The water was warm and soothing.

The seventh day.

She tried to push that alarmed thought out of her mind. But everyone knew the significance. Thomas was gone.

Her foster brother was gone, possibly forever.

The zombie stock was depleted. The war council was a screaming mess of despair. It was painfully obvious that Ariock's defensive tactics actually came from Thomas. Weptolyso and his forces were barely holding on to their territories. Ariock wouldn't even enter a battle zone. Meanwhile, the Torth military never made the same mistake twice.

The entire galaxy knew Thomas was missing.

People blamed Thomas for every loss, and he wasn't here to defend himself. He wasn't mitigating any of the disasters.

He was an alien.

A full-blooded Torth.

Vy still wanted time to process that. On one level, she knew that it didn't—it shouldn't—matter. Thomas would always be a member of her family. She had taken care of him, and lived with him, for years. His biological parentage did not erase their sibling relationship.

But she, of all people, knew that bad parents, even absentee parents, inflicted emotional damage on their children.

How many of her foster siblings woke from night terrors? How many of them dealt with phobias and depression and psychological disorders and scars?

One of Thomas's biological parents had abandoned him as a helpless infant in a freezing winter forest. The other . . .

Vy had spent an actual moment inside a memory of the Somehow Nexus's perspective. He'd genuinely believed that he had created an apocalypse-bringer. The Conqueror. His opinion about his own biological son, who was right in front of him, in telepathy range, was nothing short of monstrous.

And then an overwhelming blame chant from the Majority had induced him to aim a blaster glove at his own head and thumb the trigger.

! ( )!

Vy flinched.

It was such a visceral memory. She felt as if she had committed suicide herself, even though the mnemonic replay had been filtered through the Megacosm and Garrett's mind. She had only experienced it thirdhand, through telepathy gas.

Thomas had felt that self-execution up close and personal.

He had actually listened to his biological father announce that his own son was a major Mistake and then end his own life out of shame. That was enough to screw up anyone, Vy felt sure.

A knocking sound interrupted her thoughts.

Vy splashed upright. She didn't need the security system to identify her visitor, because the knocks were even higher up than Garrett could comfortably manage.

She reached for her wristwatch and buzzed Ariock in.

"I'll be out in a moment!" she called.

As she selected clothes, she considered reasons why Ariock might take a break just to visit her. His schedule was packed. On top of all the ghosting he'd been doing, he was under massive political pressure. The war council demanded that he find Thomas, teleport the space fleet, bolster defenses, reconsider the penitent population, plus a million other things.

Instead, he was here.

At times like this, she yearned for Yeresunsa powers. Her prosthetic was a wonderful gift—a miracle from Thomas, like so many of the things he had done—but it was still a process to put on. She hopped out of the bath and dried herself with a towel fresh from the warmer bin. She toweled off her stump. Then there were straps, and cinching. She screwed the bionic leg into place.

"What's up?" Vy called around the corner.

"Uh, sorry to interrupt your bath," Ariock said.

"I'm always glad when you visit." Vy twisted her hair to squeeze out the last drops of water. "So, did you give up on trying to find the needle in the haystack?"

"That's one way to put it."

Vy rolled her eyes. "I can hear you beating yourself up needlessly. You're not a failure. You've been doing way too much. Honestly, it's smart of you to quit exhausting yourself."

Teleportation was the biggest drain a Yeresunsa could endure. Very few activities dented Ariock's energy levels, but the one time he had nearly died from a depletion coma, it was because he'd been ghosting and teleporting too much.

"Right." Ariock sounded dejected. "There's no way I can outwit a supergenius. It's time to give up."

"Is that what you think?" Vy wriggled into a light tunic.

"Armageddon has started," Ariock stated.

The first concern that popped into Vy's mind was not safety for herself. She thought of Thomas and Cherise. Soon she was thinking of everyone she'd ever known closely. Like her mother.

Vy didn't quite dare to ask if Earth was all right. Ariock would tell her, surely?

"We're not in immediate danger," Ariock said. "Yet."

Vy walked into the sitting room. Ariock awaited her on the beanbag cushion sized for him, slumped. His mood brightened when he saw Vy. He looked relieved and a little bit disappointed that she was clothed.

"Tell me about it." Vy plopped onto Ariock's lap without permission. They knew each other's boundaries after so many late-night chats and time spent together. "What's happening?"

"There's a vicious battle at the temporal stream gateway," Ariock said. "Right now."

"In space?"

Ariock nodded. "It's chaos. Some Torth camped out there and Garrett decided to wipe them out. So he roped Evenjos into linking with him to boost his power. They got our space fleet involved. So yeah, now it's a full-on space battle."

That sounded dire.

"And it's completely stupid!" Ariock thumped a fist on the floor, expressing frustration. "They're so busy killing each other, they won't even notice if Thomas slips through. He can think faster than anyone. And he's more creative than a computer."

"Isn't it possible to blockade the gate?" Vy asked, wishing she understood more about how those wormholes worked.

"No one can see a temporal stream," Ariock explained. "Or predict their exact location. They're like . . ." He shrugged, possibly because he didn't understand the wormholes himself. "Garrett explained it to me. They're like a rippling ribbon that doesn't show up on sensor equipment in any useful way. There are multiple entry points that are in constant motion. Our galaxy itself is moving. That's why entering temporal streams requires precise calculations."

"Ah." Vy imagined her foster brother in a cloaked streamship, hurtling faster than a bullet toward some entry point along an invisible aurora while evading space mines and warheads. "I guess if anyone could sneak past a war zone in space . . ." she admitted. "It would be him."

"Exactly." Ariock sagged. "I've spent most of this week out of my body, examining every space rock within a parsec of the stream. What makes anyone think we have a chance? He's gone." Ariock bowed his head. "He's gone forever."

"I don't believe that." Vy clung to Ariock, seeking strength. "I'm sure he'll return."

Ariock searched her face, no doubt looking for a reason to hope.

Vy thought of Azhdarchidae, perched atop the Dragon Tower. Waiting.

And Kessa, protecting the penitent slums with rotations of armed guards. And Varktezo, in charge of the research annex, where a lot of junior scientists expected their Teacher to return. Wouldn't Thomas miss them?

He might even miss Cherise. He was a good person.

Vy trusted that about him, even if no one else did.

"I'm sure." Vy made herself more comfortable in Ariock's lap. "I know him. He'll make things right."

She had her own guesses about where her foster brother might go. Thomas used to appreciate day trips to alpine lakes and valleys. He had chosen a mountainous region in which to found Freedomland. He used to speak wistfully of retiring in remote meadowlands surrounded by mountains.

Hadn't the planet Reject-81 had some gorgeous mountains?

No doubt there were other reject planets with similar landscapes.

"Well," Ariock said, "we need him soon. Garrett is out there slaughtering Torth with power boosts from Evenjos, but they're exhausting themselves in the process.

Meanwhile? The Torth Empire is gearing up for something awful. They're amassing an armada ready to enter the temporal stream network."

"Oh." Vy leaned her head against Ariock's chest, unmindful of making his shirt damp with her hair. Perhaps he wanted reassurance, but so did she.

He hugged her gently. "I don't know what they'll target."

He did not say that he felt overwhelmed, but he didn't have to. Nor did he need to outline his fears. Without the Wisdom, were the heroes still on track to fulfill the prophecies of Ah Jun?

They were up against the Death Architect and other Torth masterminds. Heroes such as Ariock were vulnerable to insanity gas and other airborne weapons. Weptolyso's guerrilla soldiers might fend off Torth for a while, and Fayfer's space fleet might kill a bunch of Torth as well. But without supergenius plans, they would eventually fail.

And once Freedomland fell?

So would Earth.

"There's no way he's gone forever," Vy said, trying to force herself to believe it. "He's probably just taking a vacation."

"A vacation?" Ariock echoed in a deadpan tone, and Vy realized how absurd that sounded.

Thomas had left for good reasons. It wasn't a whim. The whole city believed he was biologically their enemy. He could no longer claim the privileges of being a human hybrid. Or a hero.

Technically, he was no different from the cowering prisoners slated for zombification. He might as well be one of those wretches.

"A lot of people are screaming that his head belongs on a spike." Vy hesitated, not wanting to imply that Ariock had missed something painfully obvious. "I know you've been mostly off planet. But I think Thomas needs a public image upgrade."

That was a dreadful understatement.

Vy had tried, and failed, herself. In private, she had confronted Cherise. Her foster sister admitted that the undergrounder movement was out of control, but she couldn't persuade Flen to stop preaching against *rekvehs*.

He was Premier Flen now. His lack of respect for Thomas made Vy furious. But what could she do about it?

Her own failure was somehow too hard to confess to. She was the equivalent of a queen here in Freedomland. Why couldn't she sway public opinion? Was she just not trying hard enough? Or smart enough?

Ariock leaned back on the extra-large beanbag chair. "You know what?" he said.

"What?"

"It never occurred to me that Thomas would feel unsafe here." Ariock looked embarrassed. "Until this week. I'm the worst friend ever."

"No." Vy nestled on top of Ariock, aware that he must be beating himself up on the inside.

"He's so capable," Ariock said. "He's the smartest person in the universe. I just assumed . . ." He shook his head, disgusted with himself. "I assumed he has mental armor that's a million times stronger than mine."

Vy leaned against Ariock. "No one is stronger than you."

But on the inside, she acknowledged that there were different kinds of strength. Not even Ariock could salvage Thomas's reputation, it seemed. Ariock had loudly proclaimed Thomas to be a hero more than once. Those proclamations only exacerbated the divide between people who trusted the messiah and those who saw Ariock as the *rekveh*'s brainwashed mouthpiece.

"I didn't think bullies would faze him," Ariock confessed. "He seemed to just shrug and dismiss them as a nonthreat. In fact, he even told me not to hunt down the undergrounders, or imprison any of them."

"Because every war hero is valuable," Vy said with bitterness.

Some of the so-called war heroes held up placards showing Thomas's bloodied, decapitated head. Like Flen. Were people like that really so crucial as to be above justice?

"When he said he was fine, I just assumed . . ." Ariock looked ashamed. ". . . that he was."

Vy felt oddly guilty herself, as if she had personally driven Thomas away. She wondered why. She certainly hadn't planted bombs or tried to murder him.

Was she blameless, though?

She and Ariock probably should not have witnessed the self-execution of Thomas's biological father. That was an intensely personal traumatic shock. It wasn't something that ought to be shared and reshared with the entire galaxy.

Not that Thomas would complain.

He would just shrug and pretend like it was no big deal.

The way he did for just about every personal problem.

"Thomas is really good at giving the impression that he's completely self-reliant," Vy realized. "Even when he's dying. He's always been that way."

Ariock massaged his forehead, like he wanted to rearrange some ideas inside his head. "It's an act?"

"I don't think it's on purpose," Vy said. "Maybe he's fooling himself? But yeah, he pretends like he's just fine even when he's not." She wished she had discussed Thomas in depth with Ariock earlier. "I thought you knew that about him?"

"I should have," Ariock said.

They sat in silence for a moment.

Ariock leaned all the way back, inviting Vy to lie on his chest. "Can I tell you something personal? Something I've never told anyone?"

Vy snuggled close. She rested her chin on her arms. "Please."

Ariock hesitated. Vy didn't pressure him. She let him gather his thoughts.

"I'm a lot like Thomas," Ariock said. "I had a similar problem, even though it was much smaller scale. I avoided school because of the way people reacted to me." He gestured to himself. "I never told you exactly what happened."

"You told me people stared at you." Clearly, he did not fear Vy's stares. At least, not anymore.

"There was a group of boys," Ariock said. "After school, they'd throw things at me. Trash. Things like that."

Vy winced. "I'm sorry."

"It happened two or three times," Ariock said. "I pretended that it didn't affect me." He avoided her gaze. "I didn't tell my mom, or anyone. I convinced myself that it was no big deal. See? I can't even remember how many times it happened."

Vy heard buried pain in his tone. She nearly asked him why he'd kept silent, but she wanted to let him explain at his own pace.

"The way they treated me . . ." Ariock paused, then seemed to force himself to go on. "They made it clear that I was a freak. And a target. They weren't the only ones, of course, but they sort of paved the way. Other kids saw that it was all right to punish me for being different. So they went ahead. Before I knew it, everyone in the school figured it was all right to use me as their punching bag."

"I'm sorry." Vy could imagine smug classmates making rude remarks. All that negative attention must have been excruciating for him.

"That's why I stopped going outside," Ariock said. "Every incident where people stared at me became an instance where I was singled out. To me, being singled out meant I was a target."

People would have done double takes at young Ariock, staring at his gangly height combined with his prepubescent face. It must have happened not just in school, but anywhere in public.

"But it started with those bullies, throwing trash," Ariock said. "It's easy to pretend those little incidents don't matter. But they really do. Those incidents erased all the potential I had. You remember who I used to be?"

Vy took a moment to remember Ariock the way he had been when she'd first met him. He had seemed afraid to move. He'd hidden in the shadows beneath a balcony, petrified in fear of her.

"I could heal fatal illnesses," Ariock said. "I could fly, and I could control the weather. But I would have been stunned to learn any of that. I didn't believe I was anyone special." He shrugged uncomfortably. "I would have shriveled up and died like that if the Torth hadn't ripped me out of my safe place."

Slave legends had transformed Ariock into the Bringer of Hope.

But human bullies had transformed Ariock into the reverse of that. They had wiped out his potential.

When worshippers said that Ariock was their messiah, he had become that. But when bullies said that Ariock was a loser freak? He had become that.

Vy thought of Thomas. He had begun to seem like . . . well . . . like what the bullies accused him of being. Emotionless. Withdrawn. Cold. Dangerous.

"So I get why Thomas pretended the bullies are nothing," Ariock said. "It's easy to accept praise, but admitting that mere words are deeply wounding? I'm not even strong enough to admit that. It's humiliating." He swallowed. "During the one telepathy class I attended, the other students were shocked to learn that the Bringer of Hope used to feel bullied. People can't imagine it because I never talk about it. It's too shameful. And now I don't ever want to attend another telepathy lesson."

Vy wrapped her arms around Ariock's shoulders. She couldn't reach all the way around him, but she wanted to let him know that she admired who he was, even with his vulnerabilities.

Especially with his vulnerabilities.

"Thomas has been enduring the equivalent of kids throwing trash at him," Ariock said.

"And assassins throwing bombs," Vy said. They never should have ignored the problem.

"Where have I been, while he dealt with that?" Ariock said mournfully.

"Well, to be fair," Vy said, "you've been busy liberating the galaxy from slavery."

"Thomas did that," Ariock said. "He planned every successful battle. It's obvious to everyone on the war council. Anyone in the military can see it."

Vy wasn't sure she entirely agreed with Ariock's dark self-assessment.

Ariock wrapped his big hands around her waist. He smoothed her tunic, tracing her contours. "I think I need to quit hiding."

Vy sat up on Ariock's torso, straddling him. "What are you going to do?"

"What do heroes do?" Ariock said. "They stand up for the meek. They protect deserving people who can't or who won't defend themselves."

Vy liked the sound of that.

"It's time for me to be a hero," Ariock said. "For real."

CHAPTER 4

STRENGTH REFORGED

Ariock reforged the metallic infusions in his armor. He made the purple bright with dichroic crystal, contrasted against black chromium. Spikes jagged upward from his shoulders. The spiral arms of the galactic disk swirled on his chest, biceps, and back, depicted with embedded mica and diamonds.

Instead of teleporting to a war zone, he flew over the crowded boulevard that overlooked the penitent slums.

Here, Alashani faced off against each other. Half of them blocked the alleyways that led into the slums, standing shoulder to shoulder with nussians and other armed soldiers. These were the defenders.

The other half—the more outraged ones—shouted that all *rekvehs* should die. This impassioned mob consisted of civilian agitators. They carried placards with crudely gruesome paintings of decapitated heads. The war heroes among them, such as Flen, wore wide-brimmed hats and embroidered vests instead of armor. They were differentiating themselves from the military.

"The Torth," Ariock said, "are murdering our people."

His deep voice rolled like thunder, amplified on air currents.

Both the defenders and the agitators gawked as Ariock levitated between them.

"They are stealing back the lands we won with our blood and lives." Ariock clenched his armored fists. That made the spikes on his forearms jag outward, adding to the spiky size of his silhouette. "They think they can enslave everyone." He flung a hand toward the penitent slums. "And *this* is what you're worried about? Harmless street sweepers and janitors?"

The agitators shrank back from his fury.

Ariock descended out of the sky in a light whirlwind. He sent enough of a breeze to blow back people's hats and bonnets and to make their signs flutter. As an additional touch, he stirred distant clouds, causing thunder. A storm was approaching.

It got people's attention.

"I'm done letting the Torth Empire celebrate victories while I hide." Ariock stood tall. "It's time to show them justice." He purposely eyed the agitators who wore rich purple mantles. Flen. Byursaffur. Emstachor. Their black-and-purple armor was probably collecting dust in their apartments. "Who's with me?"

A few of their civilian supporters dropped their placards and fled.

The rest stood their ground, although they looked uncertain. There were children and elders among the agitators, and Ariock knew these were not homicidal brutes. If a mother shouted, "Off with their heads!" it wasn't about violence for her. Not really. It was about safety and justice.

So they believed.

"*Rekvehs* do not belong among good people!" one of the agitators shouted.

"Wake up!" One of the war heroes stepped forward and confronted Ariock with a desperate shout. "The *rekveh* who was controlling you is gone!"

Brave words to say to a stormbringer.

Ariock wanted to argue, but these were not supposed to be his enemies. He wanted to show that he was listening. So he stood his ground and let the agitators shout their grievances.

"We're done being used as pawns!"

"We've lost too much!"

"We need a home apart from Torth!"

"You're fighting a battle that cannot be won!" Flen called.

"Yeah!"

"You keep asking us to sacrifice our lives. For what?"

They had legitimate complaints. Ariock felt that, and he was ashamed for his role in their ruination. Jinishta had not deserved to die. Nor had Orla, or so many others. The destruction of the Alashani underground was, ultimately, his fault. He could not blame them for being devastated. He knew what it was like to lose one's family.

At last, their anger began to die down.

Ariock amplified his own voice using his power. "You're not the only people who have suffered from Torth injustice." He paused, letting that message sink in. "But you are some of the only warriors in existence who have the power to deliver justice. As am I." He thumped his armored chest, implying how meaningful that was. "When I led you away from your dying world, Jinishta had me swear the War-rior's Pact."

They went silent.

Every albino knew what that vow meant. Warriors carried poison in case they were captured. It was better to die than to endanger the civilization that they safe-guarded.

"I swore it," Ariock said, "willingly, because I want to protect the Alashani. You are my people."

Some of the albinos looked grateful. Others were chagrined.

"As are the nussians," Ariock said. "And the ummins. And the govki. And all the other innocent victims of Torth evils." He glanced toward the slums. "The mind readers who are brave enough to defy their oppressive kin are on our side. They have thrown themselves on our mercy. They have nowhere else to go. The Torth Empire robbed them of their humanity. They are victims, like us."

The rows of defenders looked vindicated and exhausted. No doubt they were tired of fighting people who were supposed to be their allies.

"Thank you for remembering your duty." Ariock gave the defenders a nod of respect. These were people who must care deeply about liberty and equality and justice as universal principles, rather than as principles that applied only to the Alashani. "You're more honorable than most of us. Including me."

The defenders looked proud. They must have struggled the entire week to pro-tect penitents.

"They're fools!" Flen looked as if he had holy wisdom.

"I've heard about your undergrounder movement." Ariock eyed Flen and his fellows. "You want to flee and hide, the way you used to? I'm sure that sounds noble. That's what I've been doing." He flung a hand toward his war palace.

A few of them shifted, perhaps embarrassed.

"I came up with all sorts of excuses," Ariock admitted. "Like, I don't want to get more warriors killed." His voice broke. "I led Jinishta and so many others on a mission that was actually a Torth trap. That was my fault. My idiocy got Jinishta and over a hundred other warriors killed."

The agitators looked more uncertain than ever. It seemed they had stopped expecting an apology.

"I'm sorry." Ariock bowed his head.

They exchanged looks. Perhaps the apology meant something to a few of them, but Ariock knew it was inadequate.

"Do you know what my mistake was?" Ariock asked the mob.

Most of them remained quiet. They had waited a long time for Ariock to take responsibility, apologize, and explain what, exactly, had gone wrong.

"You listened to a *rekveh*!" someone shouted.

"Just the opposite," Ariock said. "Every battle we won was because of Thomas. He is a strategic mastermind. My big failure was the one time I ignored his advice."

They looked stunned.

Agitators exchanged glances, gauging each other's reactions. Some might consider Ariock's words to be an engineered and rehearsed speech, masterminded by the *rekveh*. But Thomas had been missing for a week. If he was behind this presentation, he would have had to preplan it well in advance.

At least a few of them seemed to be reevaluating their life choices.

"I owe every success I've had to Thomas," Ariock said. "I'm not saying that because anyone forced me to. I'm saying it honestly, as a soldier and a warrior. And I'm embarrassed to admit how much I rely on Thomas. But I have to say it. We cannot win battles if we refuse to look at hard truths and hard facts."

Any military veteran would agree with that last statement. Mistakes that seemed acceptable in civilian life were unacceptable in war zones. Battle captains or premiers who ignored facts got their troops killed.

Ariock paced, his heavy footfalls emphasizing the weight of his armor and his words. "We cannot win this war without allies who are mind readers. That's not just advice that comes from Thomas and Kessa. That's my own conclusion, as well."

Everyone within earshot was probably shocked to hear that.

"Then where is your mind reader?" someone shouted. "Did he abandon us?"

People on both sides grumbled in agreement.

"I trust Thomas to return," Ariock said.

The defenders looked heartened. They stood taller. A few exchanged looks of hope.

"In the meantime?" Ariock took a deep breath. He faced the agitators, then the defenders, then anyone else who was listening in the distance. "I'm done hiding like a coward. I will face battle again."

They cheered.

Defenders and agitators alike looked amazed. A few of them dropped their placards or their weapons. Others jumped in celebration.

"I don't know if I can win battle after battle," Ariock confessed. "We need Thomas for that. But I'm going to take risks again. I'll wear air tanks if I have to. But I'm done letting the Torth have an easy time. I will do my best to save the lives of people who need protection, for as long as I can."

People cheered.

"I will follow you anywhere, Bringer of Hope!" one of the defenders called.

Others voiced their resolve.

"Let's drive away the Torth!"

"Liberate more cities!"

Ariock nodded toward the Freedomland spaceport. "Some battles will be fought in space, or in the air, by pilots. We'll keep gaining ships. I know that we can damage the Torth Empire with the valor of our pilots and those who maintain their machines. We don't need zombies."

More cheering! A few of Flen's colleagues even dared to talk with their armored counterparts among the defenders.

Ariock began to ask warriors and battle squads to meet him at the teleportation flats in one hour. He didn't care if he only managed to gather a small fighting force. There would be more volunteers if he could win a skirmish or two.

Garrett popped out of the air in a crackle of lightning and a smell of ozone. He dropped to the ground, bulky in his space armor. Sweat matted his white hair.

"What are you doing?" Garrett demanded. "I need your help at the temporal stream!"

"That's not our battlefront," Ariock said bluntly.

"There's still a chance we might catch the traitor!" Garrett's eyes were wild.

"You're wrong about Thomas," Ariock said. "He will return on his own, but only if we show him that it's safe. We need to prove that he can trust us."

Garrett sounded like he was strangling on his own outrage. He spluttered, then spat out his opinion. "The boy's a traitor!"

"Thomas." Ariock emphasized the name. "Would never betray us."

Garrett bared his teeth, as if he wanted to bite something. "Let me refresh you on a few facts. First of all, he promised to obey me. I told him to zombify prisoners on a regular basis."

Ariock began to defend Thomas, but his great-grandfather steamrolled on.

"His abandonment of his duties constitutes a failure to obey. Ergo, when he told me he would be my slave? He lied. What does that tell you about our ability to trust him? The boy's a liar. He's a lying supergenius mind twister!"

There was a little bit of pragmatism buried in that accusation, Ariock thought. But only a bit.

Ariock stared down at his great-grandfather and wondered how he had missed the obvious insecurity. Garrett was terrified of Thomas. He equated "the boy" with his long-dead, abusive father. He saw abusive tendencies in every mind reader he encountered.

Just like the undergrounders.

"How is he any better than Unyat?" Garrett demanded.

"He's afraid of you," Ariock said.

"What?" Garrett went back to spluttering in wordless shock.

"Thomas is just as afraid of you as you are of him," Ariock said. "Why do you think he ran away? He could guess how you would react."

"Well, anyone sane would be angry at betrayal!" Garrett said. "He—"

Ariock used his deep voice to steamroll over his great-grandfather. "You and a lot of other people here have been abusive toward him."

"I have not!" Garrett drew himself up, indignant. "I never threatened him."

"You bullied him," Ariock said.

Garrett threw up his hands in outrage. "What, did you expect me to coddle him? He's not a child. I mean, technically, sure, he has the age of a child, but that doesn't matter next to . . . agh, never mind, this is beside the point! Do I need to remind you of what's at stake? The universe! Our future!" He emphasized every word. "The boy isn't coming back on his own. He betrayed us and switched sides. Don't you see that? Open your eyes! We need to grab him before the Torth Empire welcomes him home!"

Ariock knew his great-grandfather was a flawed individual, but he had failed to realize just how pathological his hatred was.

"Thomas isn't joining the Torth." Ariock made it a statement of fact.

Garrett began to argue. "The prophecies—"

Ariock found that he didn't care what nonsense Garrett had glimpsed in the prophecies. Whatever it was, he was sure to have misinterpreted it.

He overrode the old man. "I'm not draining my powers for a pointless melee in the middle of nowhere. We have people who genuinely need our protection. They're on planets we rightfully conquered—and every one of our conquests was led by Thomas. Now we have citizens waiting for our aid. And if we ignore them? Then we're the traitors."

There were voices of solidarity.

Garrett glared at Ariock from beneath his bushy eyebrows. "If we lose the boy? We lose the war."

"We didn't lose him," Ariock said.

"He betrayed us! He's—"

"This is my army." Ariock put a heavy hand on Garrett's shoulder, encompassing the whole area, despite Garrett's bulky space armor. "I will decide what regions we protect. And who our enemies are."

Garrett closed his mouth. Mind readers were hard to surprise, but he looked shocked.

Well, Ariock was done taking criticism in public. If he was going to be an effective leader, then he needed respect.

"Take time to replenish your powers," Ariock said. "Then prepare to fight where I tell you to." He studied his great-grandfather. "Unless you want to betray me?"

There was a look in Garrett's eyes that was difficult to define. Maybe he was outraged, but he also seemed almost, well, respectful.

"Tell Evenjos," Ariock ordered. "I won't force anyone to fight, but I'm not letting anyone go rogue. Not while the Torth raid our lands." He gave Garrett a meaningful glare. "And I'm done tolerating disrespect toward the Wisdom who built Freedomland and helped us win every battle until recently. Either you remember what Thomas did for us, or I don't have any use for you." He strode away. "Anyone in fighting shape who wants to kill Torth? Meet me at the teleportation flats in one hour."

CHAPTER 5

UNEXPECTED TIMES THREE

Kessa sat blearily at her workstation, jotting notes as she played voicemail after voicemail. Most former slaves were in the process of learning how to read and write, so reports tended to be audio recordings. Fayfer's fleet had won a victory. But according to Kessa's lieutenants on Nuss, a mess of penitents could no longer be trusted, because—

"Wise one?" Yanyashta rapped on the door frame of Kessa's spacious office.

"What is it?" Kessa barely glanced up.

"Commissioner Gojal wants you at the spaceport," Yanyashta said. "Immediately."

Kessa yawned. Didn't anyone realize how late at night it was? Whatever this was, it wasn't Thomas. Kessa expected jubilant celebrations and rage-fueled riots when he returned. This was probably a nonemergency that could wait until morning.

"What does the commissioner want?" she asked.

"Two unknown streamships have landed." Yanyashta looked unnerved. Her albino cheeks were pinker than usual. "He says there are slaves aboard, and three Torth who want to claim our amnesty."

Amnesty?

Kessa needed a moment to remember the standing orders she had issued to spaceport officials. Any Torth who showed up and willingly surrendered—who gave up their weapons and asked to join Thomas—was to be held for questioning rather than killed.

It had never happened before.

Kessa blinked her sleepiness away. A lot of questions materialized inside her mind.

"The arrivals want to meet Thomas," Yanyashta said. "They don't appear to know that he's, uh, missing."

"Tell me about these newly arrived Torth." Kessa grabbed a coat to wear over her tunic. "We can talk on the way." She hurried toward the front door.

Yanyashta trotted to keep up. "I don't think you should go. It might be dangerous! The three Torth were dosed with inhibitor darts, but even so, they might have tricks planned."

The spaceport did not have enough mirrored surfaces to keep teleporters away. It was too vast and open. So it was possible that the Torth Empire might try to lure someone important—like Kessa, the face of the war—to a place where Torth champions could teleport in and bomb her to death.

"If this is a trap," Kessa said, "then three Torth are acting as bait. Not just one. All three are taking a risk of dying in crossfire. That seems foolhardy for a trap."

"Maybe." Yanyashta hesitated, perhaps unsure how to explain the threat. "But you're a valuable target."

Kessa understood. Torth might send multiple suicide bombers just to get rid of her. Still. Three kamikaze emissaries seemed excessive when one would work just as well.

"How many soldiers are watching them?" Kessa asked.

"An army." Yanyashta made that sound obvious. "And Ariock is probably on his way, if he isn't there already."

"Have these Torth done anything to prove their goodwill?" Kessa asked. "What are their claims? How many slaves did they bring with them?"

Yanyashta explained as they went to the curbside pickup zone, where Kessa signaled for a valet to bring her personal hovercart. "Their slaves vouch for them. There are at least twenty, all ummins and govki. They say these Torth are truly unique, and kindhearted, and so forth. But . . ." The shani shrugged. "Slaves will say anything they're commanded to say."

Kessa ignored the unintentional insult. Many people, Yanyashta included, overlooked the collar scar around Kessa's neck. They forgot that she had suffered most of her life as a slave.

Unlike people born in freedom, Kessa knew that slaves were not all automatons. Sure, a handful of slaves might obey evil commands. Some slaves might deliberately feed deadly misinformation to friendly soldiers. But a group of twenty?

It was hard to imagine that a group of slaves—twenty who had traveled together for a while—would be uniformly depraved enough to tell deadly lies that would get innocent people killed. Being called a liar was one of the worst insults a slave could hurl at a fellow slave. Some of them would stick to moral principles, even under torture and threats and death.

Kessa's long-dead mate had been like that.

She jumped behind the control panel of her hovercart, more curious than ever. Yanyashta reluctantly joined her. Soon they peeled away from the war palace and sped uphill toward the spaceport.

"What else can you tell me?" Kessa shouted over the wind. "Do any of those recently arrived slaves make unusual claims about their owners?"

"I'd say so." Yanyashta leaned on the railing, close to Kessa. Her tone became disparaging. "They gush about how lenient their owners are."

Kessa steered up a major boulevard, past boutique shops and apartments. "What are their owners like? Can you describe them?"

"I did not see them," Yanyashta admitted. "I learned about this through a call with Gojal."

"That's all right." Kessa figured she would see the alleged supplicants soon enough.

"But they were described to me. One is athletic, and she has purple eyes." Yanyashta blinked her own eyes, as if to hide her own purple color.

"She removed her optical implants," Kessa guessed. "Or had them removed. She wants to prove that she is a renegade." Thomas had done something similar, although not on purpose. His eyes had lost the iridescent yellow lenses and been restored to their natural violet hue during his regeneration healing.

"The other two are Blue Ranks," Yanyashta went on. "They're extremely sickly, small and disabled."

Kessa gaped.

"They float in hoverchairs," Yanyashta went on, oblivious. "Their slaves say they are very smart. They claim to be a pair of supergeniuses known as the Twins, even though they do not look even remotely related to each other." She noticed Kessa's wide-eyed stare and said, "What?"

"The Twins?" Kessa wondered if her secretary ever bothered to learn anything about Torth culture. "The Twins are actually here? This is real?" Maybe there had been a misunderstanding. "Are you sure?"

"I am just telling you what I heard," Yanyashta said. "Does it matter? Isn't one Torth the same as another?"

Kessa figured there was no point in arguing with her secretary. She focused on driving. "Call Gojal," she ordered. "Right now. Tell him not to kill the Twins unless they make a majorly threatening move. They should be protected. Have him station a perimeter of soldiers. It is vital that the Twins are defended from threats."

Yanyashta looked as if she thought Kessa had lost her mind. She had not seen the Upward Governess get assassinated.

But she pulled out her tablet and made the call.

As Kessa steered past launchpads, she saw other people rushing toward the cordon of soldiers. News spread fast.

Kessa had to park along with other hovercarts and scooters. She allowed soldiers to escort her down a hill, beneath levitating rings of light. Messengers rushed up and down a makeshift pathway between soldiers. Beyond all the bustle and lights, two unfamiliar space vessels loomed against the night sky.

Scrawny ummins sat amid the hubbub, sipping hot beverages or soup. Their collar scars looked freshly exposed.

"Kessa the Wise!" an official greeted her. "Thank goodness you're here."

Kessa looked past him, toward the brightly lit, cleared area in front of the space vessels. Sure enough, three Torth faced the crowd. Their huddled isolation reminded Kessa of her first encounter with humans.

Vy, Cherise, and Delia had grouped together like that.

These three looked nothing like those three, of course. The Twins floated in ornate hoverchairs. Other than their rumpled robes, they looked just like the holographs Thomas had projected in order to distribute illustrations of them. The girl Twin was particularly malformed and pallid. The boy Twin was fat, with very dark coloring.

A third Torth stood behind their chairs, her athletic poise hinting that she used to be a military rank, either a Red or a Servant of All. There was no way to judge by her eyes. A streak of white in her black hair made her distinctive.

"What have they said?" Kessa inquired.

"Not much," the official said. "Only one of the three has spoken, uh, out loud. He requested that we dose him and his companions with inhibitor. He also asked to see the, uh . . ." The official reconsidered whatever he had almost said. "The, uh, Thomas. But obviously, we don't want to give any hints that the, uh, Thomas is gone."

"Good thinking." Kessa patted the official's arm reassuringly.

The officials must be shaken up, terrified of making a mistake that might condemn Freedomland. Commissioner Gojal and everyone who sat on the war council must suspect what the Twins were capable of. They would be wary about holding any sort of dialogue with supergeniuses. Clearly, nobody was allowed to go any-where near their range of telepathy.

"May I please speak with Kessa?"

Kessa turned, startled to hear her name from the distant clearing. The speaker was the fat Torth, the boy Twin. He looked and sounded deferential.

But Kessa wondered about the timing of his arrival. These three supplicants had shown up only when Thomas was missing. Was that a strategic move? Might the Twins have something to do with Thomas's recent hardships and disappear-ance?

In any case, Kessa was not obedient to Torth. She wanted to make that clear. She turned her back on the Twins.

"Let them wait," she told the official. "First, I wish to speak with their slaves."

"Very good." The official seemed happy to let Kessa take charge of the situation. He ushered her toward crates and trunks, makeshift benches where the newly re-leased slaves sat.

Kessa sat in their midst.

The ragged ummins and govki gawked at her in awe.

"Kessa the Wise?" an ummin asked, eyeing her neck scar. "The runaway who enslaves Torth? I thought you were a myth."

"I am sure you've heard plenty about me," Kessa said gently. Her spies purpose-ly spread tales throughout Torth-ruled cities. "I would like to hear about you. Will you be so kind as to tell me about your journey here? Was it a hardship?"

"No, not at all," the ummin said. "But it was very strange for us."

He explained that he and his companions had been cooped up inside a labora-tory vessel. Their environment had been unpleasant, and they had all felt bored and depressed at first—until their owner broke away from his guardians.

After his escape from the gunship and military ranks, the boy Twin had begun to get talkative, even chatty.

"He says he is not a Torth," one ummin said with wonder. "I know it sounds incredible. But I actually believe him!" His gaze begged for Kessa to believe.

"He told us all kinds of things," a govki said. "Not just the legends. He told us how to pilot a space vessel!"

"And all kinds of things about how the Torth function," an ummin said, leaning into the conversation. "He described their Megacosm."

"Really?" Another ummin was wide-eyed. "Your owner told you all that? Our owner said not a word."

"He said there is an academy here!" another ummin said with fervent yearning. "A place for former slaves to learn the knowledge of the gods?"

"That is correct," Kessa affirmed.

"Wow!" Several of the liberated slaves exchanged wide-eyed glances of awe. "So this is Freedomland? It's real?"

"What's Freedomland?"

Kessa realized that one contingent of liberated slaves was puzzled. They stared at the spaceport in wonder, eyeing streamships stolen from Torth cities and the crowd of well-dressed aliens. Since they were so enthralled, they did less talking.

"He gave us high-quality food," one of the talkative govki was saying. "Torth feasting food. He allowed us to eat from his own rations."

"That's right." Others joined in, all striving to assure Kessa that the boy Twin was friendly.

"He has a name," an ummin said. "Mondoyo."

Kessa raised her brow ridges. Some penitents did adopt spoken names, when urged repeatedly, but she had never heard of a Torth who preemptively chose a name before even meeting one of her lieutenants.

"What about your journey?" Kessa focused on the quieter contingent. "What is the girl Twin like?"

"You mean the tall Torth with a streak in her hair?" a chatty ummin said. "She traveled with the boy and us, but she hardly ever speaks."

"What about the girl who uses a hoverchair?" Kessa said pointedly. "What is she like?"

The liberated slaves exchanged glances.

"I've never heard her say a word."

"She's scary." One govki shivered.

Kessa kept probing. The ones who had traveled in the girl Twin's vessel said she was unfriendly. She had not punished anyone with a pain seizure, but people feared her. They could not articulate why.

"But Mondoyo is talkative?" Kessa circled back to the topic of the one renegade who sounded promising. "What do you think of him? What sort of person is he?"

The former slaves considered her questions with gravitas.

"It's hard to trust a mind reader," one finally admitted. "But I would trust this one."

CHAPTER 6

FREEDOM TO BE

Ariock folded his arms, ignoring the pitted dents in his armor. He had been battered by a recent tussle with nuclear missiles. Too bad his faceplate was broken. His lack of a helmet might seal his doom if the Twins hid a secret superweapon.

At least there was a row of soldiers between him and the supergeniuses.

The young duo looked disarmingly weak.

Ariock narrowed his eyes and wondered if the Twins were here to win accolades from trillions of adoring fans. Did they plan to bring victory to the Torth Empire? Or did they truly want to do penance for all the lives their insanity gas had wrecked?

"Hold up," a gruff voice called.

Garrett made his way through the crowd, leaning on his silver staff. He had been taking a sleep break, so his armor looked fresh.

"Are we sure these, uh, supplicants are really who they claim to be?" Garrett said. "I wouldn't put it past the Torth Empire to send decoys."

One of the Twins frowned at Garrett, as if he could not quite believe the reception he was getting. That was the entitled look of a pampered Torth.

"Let me just . . ." Garrett blinked out of existence.

Ariock looked around and gawked in shock when he saw that his great-grandfather had appeared between the Twins.

Within their telepathy ranges.

What an idiot! Why allow unaffiliated supergeniuses to read his mind? What if the Torth Empire was waiting for one of the heroes to get within targeting range?

Ariock began to spread his awareness, to shield Garrett, but the old man moved too swiftly. He infused his old body with superhuman speed and returned to Ariock's side.

"Yup." Garrett skidded to a halt, hair windblown, wide-eyed and chastened. "They're supergeniuses."

Ariock huffed at his recklessness. Someone smarter than Garrett ought to decide what risks were worth taking.

Garrett shot him a look full of wounded pride. "Hey now. Since the boy isn't here, someone had to make sure—"

He interrupted himself as the night air crackled with sparks of lightning.

Soldiers readied their blaster gloves, glancing around with unease. This might be some sort of surprise attack.

The Lady of Sorrow coalesced amid a web of lightning. She looked like Judgment personified, floating high above the Twins, hair lifted on tendrils of excess power. She raised her arms.

Ariock sent his own awareness into the air between the Twins and everyone else. He solidified air into a forceful pyramid of pressure.

Evenjos's lightning superbolt slammed into his barrier. The impact caused soldiers to jump. The Twins and their companion looked rattled. Lightning parted and zigzagged down the sides of Ariock's invisible pyramid of protection, then fizzled out.

Evenjos whirled to glare at Ariock with glowing eyes.

"No," Ariock told her.

"They invented insanity gas," Evenjos said, her voice strong enough to be heard across the spaceport. "They invented the gaseous inhibitor." Her gaze was godlike and merciless. "They are responsible for the deaths of millions."

Soldiers muttered in solidarity. Many whispered that such villains deserved death. Every soldier had at least one friend or family member who had been re-enslaved because of Ariock's folly. They blamed the insanity gas.

"They are children." Evenjos's tone dripped with disparagement as she glared at the Twins below her. "But they can slay us, Ariock."

"They're on the inhibitor," Ariock pointed out.

One of the Twins looked impartially curious. The other one, though? The terror and guilt on his face looked like genuine emotions.

"They came to us," Ariock said. "Unarmed."

He hoped they were unarmed, anyway. The soldiers had supposedly searched their hoverchairs and bodies.

"The risks are too great." Evenjos's tone was as final as death. "If they were ordinary Torth, we could give them a chance. But a mistake with these two?" Her voice held implications. "It would be the end."

The end of freedom. The end of hope. Ariock understood.

He felt as if judgmental ghosts perched on his shoulders, agreeing with Evenjos. Jinishta. And Orla.

Well, they could pipe down. He wasn't going to kill disabled children without a qualm. He wanted to at least hear what the Twins had to say for themselves.

If only Thomas were here.

"Pardon me." Kessa stepped out of the crowd. She looked regal in a brocaded outfit. "I believe that you all entrusted me with the duty of judging penitents and supplicants from the Torth Empire?"

Although she sounded humble, as always, she aimed a challenging look toward Evenjos, Garrett, and Ariock.

Evenjos looked affronted.

Garrett looked incredulous.

Ariock, however, took a step away from the clearing where the Twins waited. He would not snatch away Kessa's authority. He publicly supported her role. Besides, Ariock had actually glimpsed Kessa's mind during the one telepathy class he'd shown up for, so he knew that she was far more comfortable with mind reading than he would ever be.

"Will you allow me to do my job?" Kessa asked politely.

Ariock nodded.

"No one goes within their range," Garrett ordered.

Kessa clicked her fingers in annoyance. "Obviously."

"All right." Garrett stepped back and beckoned to Evenjos. "Go ahead, Kessa." He narrowed his eyes at the three supplicants. "If their answers are a problem? Then we'll decide what to do with them."

The boy Twin looked nervous. So did the standing supplicant.

The girl Twin continued to look impassive.

Kessa turned to the captain of the soldiers. "Make sure the supplicants remain safe. Their slaves were treated kindly. I believe that is a sign of goodwill. Do not harm them unless I ask you to do so, please."

The captain relayed commands to his troops. Soon a ring of armed soldiers stood at attention, blocking the supplicants from harm. Ariock was tall enough to see over the heads of the armed guards, but no one else was. There would be no faraway snipers.

Evenjos flew down and landed next to Garrett. She continued to glare at the Twins as if their existence offended her. Ariock suspected she would restrain herself, if only to impress Garrett. She did seem to love the old man, in her weird, twisted way.

Ariock remained tense. He would create a barrier shield at a moment's notice.

"Torth supplicants." Kessa's voice carried in air that had gone still and silent. "Thank you for bringing your slaves to liberty."

The three Torth focused on Kessa.

"We have questions," Kessa went on, "before we can welcome you to Freedomland."

The boy Twin offered an encouraging nod.

"First," Kessa said, "I want to know why you took so long to show up."

It was a weighty question. Ariock scrutinized the Twins, and he saw Evenjos do the same. No doubt she was ready to kill them for a wrong answer.

"It wasn't easy," the boy Twin said, "to escape the Torth Empire." Unlike most penitents, he spoke with ease. His voice carried, perhaps amplified by power from Garrett. "I know the Conqueror—Thomas—made it look easy. But we aren't him."

Kessa's gaze flicked to the other Twin, and to the woman who stood between the two. Neither spoke.

"We had to evade warships," the boy Twin went on. "The whole empire was hunting us with all their resources. We dared not use temporal streams unless the Torth Majority got distracted. We had to be opportunistic and wait for the right moments."

Ariock recalled Thomas saying something similar about his escape from New GoodLife WaterGarden City.

"That's plausible." Garrett sounded begrudging. "But you took an awfully long time."

The boy Twin nodded in acknowledgment. "I dared not come here without my partner." He aimed a fond look of warmth toward the girl Twin. "She needed time to escape on her own."

The pallid girl Twin didn't so much as glance at him. Her misaligned features were icy.

"If I'd shown up here without her," the boy Twin said, "news would have hit the Megacosm, and that would make it impossible for my partner to escape. The Torth would have killed her rather than take the risk that she might flee."

Ariock considered that and inwardly admitted that it was likely. The Torth Majority had threatened all their supergeniuses. They had aimed nuclear warheads at their secluded labs.

"We expected to meet Thomas once we got here." The boy Twin searched the crowd, no doubt seeking a boy in a hoverchair. The artificial cerulean color of his eyes glowed in contrast against his dark skin. "Is he okay?"

Everyone knew that Thomas would have been the first in line to greet his long-anticipated brethren. Thomas was the only hero who could properly evaluate supergeniuses. His absence was a big, gaping hole.

Was the boy Twin genuinely concerned? Or was he feigning it in order to lull the Conqueror's friends into trusting him? Supergeniuses had the mental tools to fool anyone.

Kessa must share these worries, because her beak was tight. "Why are you the only one speaking?" she demanded.

"Oh." The boy Twin gestured to his partner. "Serette was born without a tongue."

Ariock blinked at the girl Twin. He had not expected that.

Kessa scrutinized the girl from afar. Her brow ridges knitted with sympathy. "She has a name? Serette?"

The girl Twin nodded.

"We all chose names," the boy Twin said cheerfully. He swung his legs like a child. "I'm Mondoyo." He gestured to the standing woman. "This is Zai."

Zai bowed her head in supplication.

"Zai can speak," Mondoyo said.

"I can speak." Zai's voice was a hoarse whisper. She sounded like a typical penitent, although she wore a formfitting bodysuit instead of rags and a slave collar. She had striking features.

Ariock felt uneasy about her. Zai must have removed her ocular implants, because her eyes were naked purple, like his own. Her former rank was obfuscated. Still, Ariock had fought and killed enough military ranks to notice her powerful stance and strong physique. She had bodily enhancements. He would have bet on it.

"Zai," Ariock said. "Are you a Servant of All?"

He expected her to deny it. Torth champions never got a chance to be enslaved as penitents. Servants of All went straight to the Mirror Prison, where they languished in dungeon cells until Thomas got a chance to zombify them.

"... Yes."

Her reply was barely audible.

Ariock's eyes widened.

Troops stirred, checking their weapons as if Zai had access to her powers. This was a military concern.

"She doesn't belong among penitents." Garrett's voice was a low growl. "We have to kill her."

Ariock held up his hand, signaling a stop to the brewing violence. He was curious about Zai. A renegade Servant of All? Was that even possible?

"Zai is on the inhibitor." The boy Twin, Mondoyo, spoke in a voice that was loud despite his childish timbre. "She took the risk of coming here, helpless and on bended knee, to beg for a chance to help you slay Torth." His cerulean gaze fixed on the heroes, especially Ariock. "I thought that's what you wanted?"

Ariock swallowed. This was, indeed, the sort of warrior he had daydreamed about, back when Thomas had first mentioned Servants of All as allies.

But . . .

"Zai," Ariock said. "What if I commanded you to shoot a Torth Servant of All in the back of the head? What if it was someone you knew?"

Zai's raspy voice was strong with emotion. "I am here because I want the freedom to make my own decisions." She clenched her fists—a human gesture. "Mondoyo showed me what freedom is. It is plain to me that no Torth have this freedom. I will do anything to have it. I will die for it, or kill for it. I will be your slave for it."

Strong words.

Zai's voice had a firm authority, even though it was broken and weak from disuse.

Ariock allowed himself to imagine going into battle with this renegade by his side. Unlike his usual warriors, Zai would actually be a match for enemy champions. She likely had powers that the shani warriors lacked.

And if she truly valued freedom? She would be ruthless against the Torth.

"I would like to know more about why you decided to rebel against your empire, Zai," Kessa broke in. She shot Ariock a look, and he offered a shrug in apology. He shouldn't have taken over the questioning.

Zai hesitated.

"Why did you go renegade?" Kessa prompted.

Zai spoke in a low, husky voice. "I was chosen to guard the boy Twin. I was proud to be elected for such an important duty. But a part of me, in here"—she touched her breast—"knew that I had not made the decision. I had never made a decision in my life."

Ariock remembered the Swift Killer. Hadn't she also chafed at serving the Majority? It seemed this Servant, Zai, had a similar outlook.

"When Mondoyo offered me a chance to break away from the Majority," Zai went on, "I sneered. But only because everyone else would have sneered. You understand?"

Ariock supposed that he might understand. Telepathy facilitated peer pressure. He remembered his one lesson with telepathy gas, and he hoped he would never have to endure the stuff in a group ever again.

"Mondoyo helped me to realize," Zai said, "that every path I took was at the urging of my betters and my peers." She looked regretful. "Choosing to go renegade was the first decision I ever made for just myself."

She sounded like that meant something to her.

Kessa nodded in appreciation. "Zai," she said. "What does your name mean? Where does it come from?"

Zai cleared her throat, perhaps trying to make her vocal cords work better. "A slave took care of me when I was young. I would like to honor my caretaker by commemorating his sister's name."

She sounded emotionless. Yet her words could have come from a human.

"Well." Kessa turned to Ariock. "Would you be willing to have Zai evaluated as a possible warrior?"

Ariock understood. Kessa's authority ended where the military began. She wasn't going to take responsibility for the threat named Zai. Nor should she.

"Zai," Ariock called to the former Servant of All. "What powers do you normally have when you're not on the inhibitor?" He paused, and dared to ask, "Can you teleport?"

Everyone seemed to hold their breath.

"Yes." Zai spoke like a Torth, emotionless. She seemed oblivious to the ripples of unease and excitement that her answer stirred up.

Ariock and Garrett were the only heroes who could teleport. A third person with their rare power could make a huge difference in winning battles. Ghosting and teleportation were enormous advantages.

"What about mind control?" Ariock asked it with wariness. He inwardly wasn't sure if he could tolerate someone else like that on his side, no matter how loyal she claimed to be.

"I am not aware of any mind control or brainwashing power that I may have," Zai said.

Ariock hid his relief.

"I can throw wildfire," Zai said. "And ice."

Standard powers for a Servant of All. Ariock reimagined his future battles. The Torth would be quite unsettled.

He couldn't help but shift his gaze to the Twins. Although Zai might be useful, a pair of renegade supergeniuses was something else altogether. He really needed to learn whether or not he could trust the Twins.

"Shashet?" Ariock turned to the nearest Alashani warrior. "Will you please ask Premier Efvaltel to make room for Zai in one of the war fortresses?"

Shashet looked daunted. The warriors might object to training someone who could replace them. And the whole shani population would hate having a *rekveh* in their midst.

Well, that was too bad. The common penitent barracks were not the right place for a renegade Servant of All. Zai was too potentially powerful to be let loose among hordes of disgruntled mind readers. She needed to be among warriors.

Kessa turned to Shashet with a gentle look. "I have met more than a few penitents who genuinely want to redeem themselves," she said. "I believe that Zai is worthy of a chance."

Shashet looked skeptical.

"I expect you to keep Zai safe," Ariock added. "I'll evaluate her once she recovers her powers."

That should make the stakes clear.

Shashet gulped. She didn't dare argue with her messiah, but Ariock could tell that she wanted to.

"If anyone bullies her, I will find out." Ariock gave Shashet a stern look. "I expect warriors to value a potential renegade Servant as much as I do. I won't tolerate unprovoked threats to Zai." He waved his hand in dismissal. "Please assign a protective escort for her."

Shashet bowed and hurried away. No doubt she would spread word and find a place for Zai. Otherwise she would face the wrath of the messiah.

Soon an armed escort of guards invited Zai onto a cargo hovercart.

The renegade, Zai, seemed amazed. As she stepped onto the hovercart, she gazed at Ariock as if he was a miracle worker. There was no smile, but her violet eyes seemed to brim with gratitude.

Ariock might be able to trust the former Servant of All—if only Thomas would evaluate her mind.

Someone smart did need to evaluate Zai, he supposed, and it wouldn't be Thomas, or Garrett, or Kessa, or any of the higher-up military officials. They should not accidentally share military secrets with Zai. It would have to be some third party, preferably one of Kessa's lieutenants. They would need to use telepathy gas.

And if the lieutenant declared Zai to be trustworthy?

Well, then Ariock would try to integrate her with the rest of his warriors. He would worry about crossing that bridge later.

Zai knelt on the hovercart and prostrated herself toward Ariock. "Thank you, Bringer of Hope." She raised her gaze to his. "Freedom. There are Torth who yearn for it, too."

CHAPTER 7

THE CHEAT

Two Torth supplicants remained in the spotlights, surrounded by soldiers. Kessa studied Mondoyo and Serette. One looked amiable, one looked severely somber. One was as dark as night, the other as pale as sand. One was fat, one bony. They were visual opposites. Neither one looked dangerous. They lacked powers.

Yet Thomas had said they were formidable.

The Twins hovered next to each other, so close that Kessa knew they were basking in each other's thoughts. She recalled what Garrett had said about their identical minds. These two supergeniuses mentally siphoned off each other.

"Move apart, please." Kessa gestured. "I wish to question each of you, and I don't want you to coordinate your answers."

The Twins hesitated. Either they did not trust her, or they were unused to obeying an ummin.

"Serette is unable to speak out loud," Mondoyo said. "I can serve as her voice, if you will allow it?"

"That will be expedient," Kessa allowed. It would be easier than having Serette type on a tablet, anyway. Few people could read. "But I will question you without her aid. Move apart."

She hoped she would not have to repeat herself a third time. She should not need to explain that she was in charge here.

The unsmiling girl glided apart from the reluctant boy. He likewise moved his hoverchair. Soon each floated within their own bubble of space. They would not be able to read anyone's minds.

"Mondoyo." Kessa focused on the boy Twin. "Tell me, why did you and Serette leave the Torth Empire?"

Mondoyo glanced toward his partner, as if seeking affirmation. He looked more uncertain now that she was beyond telepathy range. "Um, we each have different reasons."

That was interesting. Kessa had half expected a breezy and bland answer.

"Tell me your reason, then," Kessa invited.

"I never wanted to be a Torth." Mondoyo spoke with plain simplicity. "All my life, I yearned to be someone better. I just needed the right opportunity."

"All your life?" Kessa was skeptical. She saw Garrett, Ariock, and Evenjos tense up, suspicious. "You wanted to escape even before Thomas invited you to join him?"

"Yes." Mondoyo spoke with an earnestness that seemed far more human than penitent. "I've always had a full range of emotions. I did my best to suppress it, but it was an awful struggle."

"Nope." Garrett made a noise of disgust. "I'm calling bull crap." He turned to Kessa. "This kid passed his Adulthood Exam. That means he literally witnessed slaves being tortured to death, and he did not react. No matter what he says, he is a Torth citizen who attained Blue Rank. He is a master at suppressing his emotions."

"I cheated on the Adulthood Exam," Mondoyo said.

"That's impossible!" Garrett sounded incensed. "You can't deceive Torth or cheat on that test. He's got to be lying to us."

Kessa had heard about the horrific exam directly from Thomas. Eight adult Torth surrounded a teenager—a victim—and forced them to wear a specialized mesh that amplified their own emotions. The testers then collectively imagined visceral scenarios, indistinguishable from reality, designed to elicit slavish emotional reactions.

Only 40 percent of Torth children passed the Adulthood Exam.

Those who failed were sentenced to death. Their bodily organs were harvested for scientific research and medical purposes.

Kessa was highly interested in meeting underaged Torth who had yet to encounter their Adulthood Exam, given the implication that 60 percent of them had a full range of human emotions. Torth children might be easily rehabilitated. They might be able to skip the penitent stage and become full-fledged members of society, just like humans and Alashani.

But so far, Ariock's forces had yet to liberate a baby farm. The Torth Empire always evacuated any baby farms on an at-risk planet, and they were good at obscuring and defending their locations.

Garrett spoke to the whole crowd. "I met a Torth boy who believed he was an Athpinari slave in the skin of a Torth. Believe me, he would have *loved* a way to cheat on his Adulthood Exam. He did have emotions. And he had to run away before they could test him—because he knew he wouldn't pass."

Kessa recalled Garrett's first retelling of that event. In public, in front of all the battle leaders, Thomas had forced the old man to admit a shameful secret: Garrett had purposely missed opportunities to save the renegade boy and the slave village that had sheltered him.

Because the Majority made the rules.

Garrett could not subvert them.

Thomas could not change their minds.

Any individual or minority group within the Torth collective had no choice but to follow the will of the Majority.

Kessa spoke, letting the Twins know she would not be easily fooled. She was far from being an ignorant slave. "Not even Thomas was able to deceive his testers."

"Well." Mondoyo sounded like he was confessing to a shameful crime. "I figured out a way."

"How?" Kessa asked.

Mondoyo seemed to realize he needed to prove his extraordinary claim. "Well, first," he said, "I was able to arrange for my testers to be visually blind." He indicated his eyes. "I orchestrated special interest groups, so that certain Brown Ranks would be available during my testing. There were two with vision, but I arranged for them to, uh, accidentally ingest a toxin that impaired their vision on the day of my exam."

Garrett spoke to Kessa, his tone scathing. "Even if he did that, it wouldn't matter. Torth don't rely on eyesight."

Kessa knew the truth of that from firsthand experience. She took daily lessons with telepathy gas.

"The blind testers would sense if anything was amiss," Garrett said huffily. "He's lying. There's no way he could fool them, or get an imposter to—"

"My partner can pass as me," Mondoyo cut in. "Her mind is identical to mine." Garrett gaped.

Every mind was indelibly unique, Kessa knew. Was it possible that the Twins were that much alike, mentally? It was hard to believe.

"Serette had already passed her Adulthood Exam," Mondoyo said. "And we both knew she could pass as me."

"But!" Garrett spluttered. "Wasn't she on another planet at the time? You two didn't move in together until years later. You had never even met each other in person!" He gave Mondoyo a hard look. "Jeez, you were only—what?—seven?"

"She lobbied for a right to visit my city," Mondoyo said. "Since she had recently gotten promoted, her orbiters granted her that right. She persuaded the exam committee that she should physically be in the audience when I was raised to Yellow."

Garrett gawked as if Mondoyo was a strange new exotic alien.

"I enlisted help from slaves on my baby farm," Mondoyo went on. "Even though I had never spoken to them before, I knew what would motivate them to help. I knew them well. The trick was to swap me for her, right before the exam began."

Kessa found herself gawking, too. She had learned how secure baby farm facilities were. They were probably the hardest places to infiltrate in the Torth-ruled galaxy.

"I also had to make sure I was drugged," Mondoyo added. "I couldn't let anyone walk by and accidentally sense my mind. So I had to be asleep during the exam."

Garrett looked flabbergasted. "And then you would need to wake up right afterward, right? So the audience could see you when you got awarded with new optical implants?"

"Yes." Mondoyo dipped his head in acknowledgment. "It was a logistical nightmare. It took a lot of preplanning." He nodded toward Serette. "She secretly invented a sleeping potion. It was similar to what Thomas invented when he went renegade. That's how I stayed asleep, behind the curtain, so to speak. I was in an elevator, and I asked a slave to jam it, so that it wouldn't return me to the baby farm."

"And . . ." Kessa marveled at the Twins' level of subterfuge. "Serette took your exam for you?"

Mondoyo nodded with pride. "She passed."

Supergenius minds would be particularly hard to probe, if not impossible. Kessa supposed it was possible for the exam committee to be fooled by an incomprehensible storm of data. Perhaps the Twins were enough alike for that.

"While the testing chamber morphed from night to day," Mondoyo went on, "a slave woke me up. I hurried out of the elevator to claim my place as a citizen. My partner hurried into the audience, and she used a prearranged excuse to prove that she'd gotten delayed, to explain why she wasn't waiting with the rest of them earlier."

If only Thomas were here. He might have been able to verify the story.

Instead, Kessa had to check on Garrett's reaction. Everyone looked toward Garrett.

"It's remotely plausible," Garrett admitted with gruffness.

If the old man was willing to admit the possibility . . . Kessa studied Mondoyo anew. Perhaps he really was everything she and Thomas hoped for?

"So you faked your way through the Adulthood Exam." Kessa conceded that Mondoyo might be telling the truth. "And then you pretended to be an adult Torth. But why didn't you join Thomas as soon as he called for fellow renegades to join him?"

"I wasn't sure about Thomas at first," Mondoyo admitted. "I kept expecting him to get killed."

Kessa accepted that. She, too, had been unsure about Thomas at first.

"Instead, he survived." Mondoyo gestured at the urban lights of Freedomland. "And then he thrived."

Perhaps Thomas had thrived due to a mighty advantage: Ariock. Without the Bringer of Hope, where would the Conqueror be?

A strong female voice rang out across the spaceport. "None of this is an excuse."

Kessa realized that Evenjos had made a very incisive point. No matter how human Mondoyo was, he had continued to work for the Torth Majority when he should have been on Thomas's side.

"Normally," Evenjos said, "I would have sympathy for this child. But I cannot forgive him and his partner. These two children destroyed millions of lives. People are dead or reenslaved because of the chemical weapons they invented."

The girl Twin remained stony-faced. She didn't seem to care.

The boy Twin, Mondoyo, looked contrite. "I'm sorry."

As if a mere apology was enough.

Kessa saw opinions shift throughout the troops. Gazes hardened. Gloved hands flexed. Too many people had lost loved ones thanks to telepathy gas, insanity gas, or the gaseous inhibitor. Everyone had a reason to hate these particular military scientists.

Mondoyo seemed to shrink. "Those projects began before Thomas gained regenerative healing. At the time, it wasn't clear to anyone that you had a chance of winning."

A poor excuse.

Ariock looked forbidding. Thunder rumbled in the distance.

"Even if we had quit," Mondoyo said, "the terrible weapons would still have gotten invented. Our supergenius peers are capable. Telepathy gas was already close to completion when we first received the project notes from the lab of the Upward Governess. We stalled its release for as long as we could."

Perhaps that was true. The Torth Empire was capable of atrocities, even without help from the Twins or the Upward Governess.

"We couldn't sabotage our own work too much, or too obviously," Mondoyo said. "If we were to do so, the Death Architect would have noticed. She would have insinuated it to the Majority, and they would have had us executed."

Kessa wondered how many Torth did awful deeds solely out of fear of the Majority. Was the Death Architect also a secret renegade?

"So you invented insanity gas." Ariock's tone was dark. Clouds covered the banded planet in the sky. "Because you were obedient to the Majority."

"We did stall its release," Mondoyo said. "And of course, we secretly laid some groundwork to invent the antidotes."

Antidotes?

That put a stop to any brewing violence. Ariock, Evenjos, and Garrett all exchanged looks of suppressed hope.

"Are you saying," Garrett said with slow deliberateness, "that you secretly invented immunity to the inhibitor?"

Amid the troops, the albinos in black armor stared at Mondoyo just as fervently as Garrett, Evenjos, and Ariock. Immunity could potentially turn the war around. Instead of losing ground, they could get back to conquering Torth cities and winning.

Mondoyo looked uncomfortable at all the attention focused on him. "Uh, we laid the groundwork. We still need to run some experiments."

Garrett looked like he wanted to squeeze a better answer out of the boy Twin.

"Obviously, we couldn't even think about immunity." Mondoyo spoke quickly, as if eager to appease his audience. "Not in public. Otherwise the Torth Majority would pressure us to invent it. But Serette and I did think about it, and we swapped ideas via encrypted messages. We've built up a lot of solid hypotheses that ought to be tested."

Serette nodded.

"We wanted to be able to offer Thomas a gift," Mondoyo went on, "to prove our goodwill."

That was a nice gift, Kessa thought.

"We can never make up for the atrocities our inventions have caused." Mondoyo bowed his head. "I will spend the rest of my life atoning. That's why I'm here. But I—we—both want to do anything we can, in order to help you replace the Torth Empire with something better."

Ariock beckoned to Garrett and Evenjos. The heroes huddled, with Ariock kneeling. Soldiers stayed a respectful distance away. No one wanted to be caught eavesdropping.

Kessa joined the heroes. After all, she was in charge of penitent Torth.

Ariock spoke in a low voice. "If we accept the Twins, we would have to give them access to Thomas's lab."

Kessa nodded.

"They would have access to his research," Ariock said. "Is that wise? Is there any way we can do that without a huge risk?"

It was a good question. Could the Twins be trusted with military secrets?

"Ugh. Maybe." Garrett looked frustrated. "I suppose I could keep an eye on them."

As if Kessa didn't matter. As if her job was nothing.

Kessa straightened. Someone would need to oversee the Twins, to coach them toward humanity and redemption, but Garrett was the least qualified to do that. His management style had probably driven Thomas away.

"You appointed me to evaluate any Torth who is willing to work toward redemption," Kessa reminded her friends. "I would like to finish evaluating the Twins. *If* I deem them safe to work with"—she emphasized the fact that Ariock had interrupted her evaluation—"then I will fully take charge of them."

Ariock, Garrett, and Evenjos exchanged glances.

Kessa was aware of her lack of intrinsic power. All her authority had been given to her.

But was earned authority really worse than inherited power? Did it make her inferior? Or just different?

"This is the job that Thomas gave me," she explained. "And it is a job that I respect."

"They ought to be handled with care," Garrett said, as if Kessa was a fool.

"You are all bigger targets than I am." Kessa met the gazes of the heroes of prophecy, defiant of their power. "Let me buffer you from the danger. I will handle this."

She might put Varktezo through the steps to become one of her lieutenants. Not that she wished to dump a huge burden onto the shoulders of a busy adolescent, but she might need his help.

Garrett opened his mouth. He seemed to search for more arguments.

Kessa did not give him time to find any. "You agreed to let me do this," she reminded him. "I assume those were not just empty words you threw out to humor Thomas?"

She had backed Garrett into a corner. Ariock looked impressed. Even Evenjos looked reluctantly admiring.

"All right. Fine." Garrett made a cigarette appear. He stuck it in his mouth, ashamed. "They're all yours. But if they get to be too much for you to handle? Call me."

"I will make them my priority," Kessa said.

Ariock, Evenjos, and even Garrett looked appeased. They wanted immunity to the inhibitor. They might not embrace the Twins, but they were not going to assassinate them, either.

Mondoyo scanned the crowd, his gaze searching. "I guess Thomas is in trouble. Otherwise he would be here." He saw everyone's unease and added, "Is there anything we can do to help him?"

"I don't think so." Kessa stepped in front of the heroes. Average Torth might dismiss her as a figurehead, but she wanted the Twins to understand who she was. She was in charge of penitents and renegades. They needed to see that she was their overseer.

"I'm inclined to trust you," Kessa admitted. "But I have more questions."

She shifted her focus from Mondoyo to Serette. Until Kessa could speak to the stoic-faced girl Twin, she would not fully understand this duo. She was curious to learn more.

"I want to hear Serette's side of the story," Kessa said. "And I want to hear it in her own words."

CHAPTER 8

STONE-COLD ENVY

Silence stretched out.

One could learn a lot from body language, but Kessa could not even guess what Serette was thinking or feeling. The girl's face remained stony.

Kessa sighed. She didn't want answers filtered through a proxy, but she did need to satisfy her curiosity. "Serette, are you willing to allow Mondoyo to speak for you?"

Serette gave a single, subtle nod.

"All right." Kessa gestured for Mondoyo to float back within telepathy range of his partner, but Garrett interrupted.

"Hold on." The old man stepped forward. "Before we move on to Serette, I want to know how the hell these two fooled the Torth Majority and escaped from a bunch of nuclear warheads aimed their way."

Kessa allowed the question. The answer was probably complicated, so she might have saved it for later, but she was curious.

"Well?" she asked Mondoyo. "Answer that, please."

In Torth fashion, the Twins seemed to reach an instantaneous unspoken decision.

"I got lucky," Mondoyo said. "Zai was stationed aboard my ship."

"And you persuaded her to go renegade with you?" Garrett's tone was dry with sarcasm. "Was it easy?"

"Oh, not really." Mondoyo laughed in a self-conscious way. "It took me weeks to persuade her. I had three round-the-clock guardians, and I didn't even try it with the other two. I knew they would never be convinced. So I had to, uh, kill them."

He made killing Servants of All sound like a mundane chore.

"I sensed deep-seated doubts buried in Zai's subconsciousness," Mondoyo said. "I took a chance and wove little hints into her daily routines. Just subtle little clues, hinting that if she wanted to truly be in charge of her own destiny, she might find a way with me. I had to let the idea occur to her on her own."

Kessa made a mental note about Mondoyo's skill set. He might be more socially savvy than Thomas.

"When I judged she was ready," Mondoyo said, oblivious to Kessa's assessment, "I presented her with my desperate plan."

"But that was a huge risk." Garrett sounded somewhat admiring. He liked bravery. "She could have gone into the Megacosm and told everyone that you were about to go renegade."

"Uh, no." Mondoyo gave a humorless laugh. "I overclocked my perceptions. If she had decided to ascend? In that nanosecond, I was prepared to trigger a hidden laser that was tracking the back of her head. It would have liquefied her brain before she could emit a death scream in the Megacosm."

Kessa's beak fell open.

"I like contingency plans." Mondoyo looked ashamed. "Sorry."

"Right. Right." Garrett seemed to struggle not to show his own reaction. "Makes sense. So you had Zai deliver insanity gas to your minders on the missile ship?"

"Exactly," Mondoyo said. "I made sure it filtered through their ventilation system during a time window when I was supposed to be asleep."

Kessa wondered how many Torth Mondoyo had killed that way.

And slaves. Had any slaves died as collateral damage? Kessa wasn't sure she wanted to learn the body count. The Twins might be very useful as allies, but they were ruthless.

"So I get how you escaped," Garrett said. "But what I really want to know is how you communicated with your partner? You two were torn apart." He used his hands for emphasis. "How could you message each other without using the Megacosm?"

"Mostly," Mondoyo said, "we didn't."

Garrett arched a questioning eyebrow.

"I didn't need to tell Serette where I was going." Mondoyo shot his partner a fond look. "She knows me. She can anticipate just about anything that I would do."

The girl Twin exhibited no warmth. She studied Kessa from afar, her eyes too knowledgeable and ancient.

"I didn't mind giving Serette time to figure out a way to escape," Mondoyo said. "It gave me a chance to chat with my slaves. I wanted to know them better. And of course, I also wanted them to get comfortable with the concept of me being a penitent instead of their owner."

Social savviness, indeed. Mondoyo had probably guessed that Kessa would question his newly freed slaves before anything else. He had purposely shown up with a bunch of people eager to vouch for him.

Pragmatic.

But also human, Kessa thought. Wasn't that what friends were for? Mondoyo was basically saying that he had made friends.

"I aided Serette through proxy deliveries," Mondoyo said. "No one else could have solved the encryption on my messages. It was enough for her to reprogram the warheads aimed at her lab vessel."

Garrett gave a nod and stepped back. He looked thoughtful.

"All right." Kessa indicated that the Twins should float closer together. "Mondoyo, I am ready to hear from Serette. Please act as her voice."

Mondoyo scooted his hoverchair close to Serette. He looked gratified.

Serette continued to look like an aloof Torth.

"Serette." Kessa hesitated and decided to start with her least important question, just to satisfy her own personal curiosity. "What does your name mean? Why did you choose it?"

Mondoyo bowed his head. When he spoke, it was very strange, because Serette mouthed the words. Mondoyo's voice went higher in pitch. He sounded colder as well.

"Serette is the goddess of wisdom among the yinn cloud people. Their cosmology places knowledge at the apex of power. It suited me."

Penitent Torth were supposed to be humble. Kessa disapproved of them taking the names of gods. This was not an acceptable penitent attitude. The whole point was to get Torth to quit thinking of themselves as godlike beings.

"What about you?" Kessa shifted her focus to the boy Twin, disparaging. "Is Mondoyo also the name of a superior being?"

He looked embarrassed. "I named myself after a legendary runaway slave. The original Mondoyo stole knowledge from the gods and brought it to his people, the volcanic nussians of Husharai, so they could thrive." He gave an apologetic shrug. "I know it's grandiose. I just wanted to match Serette's theme. She usually shows me the right path. We work best when we're on the same, uh, wavelength."

As Kessa studied how the Twins floated next to each other, she saw their mutual comfort. They were like a mated pair.

"Okay." Kessa focused on the girl Twin. "Why did you come here, Serette? Tell me why you decided to leave the Torth."

She expected an answer similar to those of Zai and Mondoyo. Serette probably wanted the freedom to feel emotions and to make true friends.

Instead, the girl Twin's reply was a shock.

"I did not wish to leave the Torth Empire." Serette's lips moved in sync with Mondoyo's cold partner tone. "I am a Torth."

The troops straightened, on alert. Ariock looked stormy, Evenjos looked deadly, and Kessa bitterly wished that Thomas was present. No doubt he would have picked up on implications that everyone else missed. He would have said something to calm the mood down.

Mondoyo cleared his throat. "Serette has very good reasons for leaving," he assured everyone, using his friendly tone of voice. "I came here for the freedom to feel emotions. But Serette came here for the freedom to explore science. She wants intellectual freedom."

He gazed at Serette with an unmistakable expression: adoration.

Serette nodded, and Mondoyo spoke in that creepy altered pitch. "This is Serette speaking. I had everything I wanted, as a Torth of Indigo-Blue Rank. I was content. Until." Her weak hands curled into fists. "The Majority began to remove tools that I need. They took away my colleague." She glanced toward Mondoyo. "They aimed nuclear warheads at my lab. They threatened to end my experiments."

There was no anger in Serette's face or her proxy voice. Nevertheless, Kessa imagined a volcano of suppressed rage. This was a supergenius who had a logical, practical, and fully Torth reason to hate the Torth Empire.

"I used to think Mondoyo was crazy for wanting to leave," Serette-by-proxy went on. "I asked him, in private—before the Majority tore us apart—to reconsider. Many times. But. It was I who began to reconsider, when the Majority put me in a prison vessel. And forced me to work on a project I had lost interest in. At gunpoint."

The troops looked captivated. Perhaps they also heard Serette's unspoken thirst for vengeance.

"Still," Serette said through Mondoyo's voice, "I would not betray the Majority. Then Mondoyo vanished. And I knew where he would go. I thought of him working with the Conqueror. Inventing things. Living to adulthood. Working in taboo fields of science. They might do anything. They had more freedom than any supergenius in history. And I was stuck." Serette indicated her frail, concave chest. "Dying."

Her conclusion was inevitable.

"The Torth pretend to value knowledge," Serette-by-proxy said. "Instead, they destroy it. They pretend to value scientists. But they shackle us. I was never free among them. They don't value supergeniuses. They give us early promotions, but their gifts are appeasements. So we won't complain. They would have used me. Then killed me. Because my knowledge, and my work, is nothing to them."

Mondoyo's voice smoothed out, becoming his original tone.

He said, "Serette belongs here. I know she's not a conventional penitent, and she may have trouble adapting, but she is willing to learn. I promise."

Kessa had heard enough to make a decision. "Freedomland welcomes you, Mondoyo and Serette."

CHAPTER 9

OULU

Thomas figured he might regret going to Earth. Someone might guess he was here.

And it wasn't his world. Not really. Being born and raised in New England did not make him human. He wasn't entitled to any of the rights or freedoms humans had.

But he was fortunate to be one of the Torth who could go unnoticed in a human crowd. He had inherited a bland appearance, courtesy of having two Servants of All for parents. Evenjos's regenerative healing had brought that out.

He walked down a street in Oulu, Finland, hands in his pockets.

One hand manipulated the remote that controlled his leg braces. No one heard the quiet whirring sounds. People gave him casual glances and friendly nods. They saw a fourteen-year-old who walked with a stiff gait.

An everyday, normal, typical fourteen-year-old boy.

No one thought he was exceptional or bizarre.

That in itself was an exhilarating and amazing experience—a state of existence Thomas had thought he would never attain.

When passersby greeted him, he greeted them back in the local native language. No one looked at him twice. People did not suspect that he was reading their minds. The locals did not automatically assume that he was evil, or too powerful, or a threat to the galaxy. Or even handicapped.

They looked at his clothes and thought that maybe he was a bit scruffy.

They thought he was a poor kid playing hooky from school.

They saw the way he walked and assumed he might be recovering from an accident. Or maybe he had a touch of cerebral palsy.

A few of the people he passed thought he could use a good meal. They wanted to feed him.

Their blithe charity made him want to weep.

It was a shock every time, even once he learned to expect it. Earth wasn't his ancestral homeworld, but it just might be the one populated planet in the universe where he could settle into pleasant anonymity.

As Thomas passed picturesque buildings and iron fences and decent human beings, he wondered where he truly belonged. At the forefront of a galactic war? He supposed that he did have a moral obligation to liberate all the slaves in the galaxy . . . except . . .

Did he?

The savior complex was Ariock's thing. Not his.

He was a Torth, and Torth did collectively need to atone for their millennia of tyranny. He knew that he ought to atone. But should he do that by zombifying prisoners and using his victims to massacre millions of combatants? Was galactic conquest a good path to personal redemption?

Or might he choose a gentler way?

His crimes as a Yellow Rank were relatively minor in comparison to most of his brethren's. Perhaps he did not have to atone endlessly. And atonement could take many forms, couldn't it?

He might live a life of meager kindnesses instead of grand gestures.

He might transform himself into an unremarkable, humble, and kindhearted teenage human. It would be the existence he would have had, if he had been born with human genetics instead of a monstrous Torth legacy. He could work on erasing his abhorrent Torth traits rather than striving to be a hero and always falling short.

Why not try it?

Thomas located a school by reading people's minds. The kids were having an indoor and outdoor lunch and recess period, since the weather was warm enough. Some of them were his age.

He let himself in through a chain-link gate.

"I'm new," he said in Finnish, taking a seat next to a couple of boys who looked geeky enough to be welcoming of a stranger.

"Oh." The boys made room for Thomas. "Hey."

Thomas could not help but overhear their thoughts, and he gleaned that these boys had been talking about geek stuff.

"What do you think of my Millennium Falcon?" one of them asked Thomas. He held up a miniature spaceship, hand-painted in shades of gray.

The plastic toy looked sleek and fanciful, like a cross between a flying saucer and a rocket. It did not remotely resemble an actual streamship or starship. A real interstellar vessel would not have windows. Those were unconscionable points of weakness.

But it was just a toy. It was based on fiction. Why should Thomas care if its design was implausible?

"Isn't it cool?" the toy owner's friend said.

The boys exuded eagerness. They wanted to meet someone who shared their passion.

"Awesome!" Thomas said, and they beamed.

He felt like a liar.

He hadn't said anything untrue, but he was being untrue to his emotions. A cool toy would be a scientifically accurate one.

The boys kept talking. Their conversation hinted that Thomas was welcome to join in, since he had signaled that he shared their fandom. They gave him friendly looks.

But Thomas could not look at spaceships, even plastic approximations, without thinking of the life he had shed. How many freed slaves and Alashani warriors had died during his absence so far? Had the Torth attacked in some new way?

When he considered what Ariock and Vy and Cherise might be dealing with right now . . .

Well.

He didn't want to think about all that.

He stood abruptly. He might try living as a normal human, but a schoolyard playground wasn't quite right for him. There was no common ground. He had never been as innocent as these teenagers. It felt like too much of a stretch to pretend to be like them.

Anyhow, he disliked a modern mythos about spacefarers whose crews included slaves, even if those slaves were robots, apparently programmed to be affable and servile.

"Where are you going?" one of the boys called, emanating hurt bewilderment.

Thomas realized that he had unintentionally insulted the pair of welcoming kids. He was used to interfacing with people who accommodated his quirks.

"Oh. Sorry." Thomas walked stiffly back to their table with an apologetic look. "I have to leave. But I wanted to tell you, I'm from outer space, and the best interstellar ships are bulky, not aerodynamic. They get slammed with pebbles and particles moving at many thousands of kilometers per hour." He pounded a fist into his palm to demonstrate. "They can take it. Because they're protected by overlapping hoods of ultradense ionized tungsten. Materials science is the future." He gave a nod toward one of the boys. That one had an aptitude, he sensed. "You might want to look into the field of polymer engineering."

The boys gaped.

With one last apologetic, friendly smile, Thomas turned and picked his way across the schoolyard.

He was just about to slip through the chain-link gate when he sensed a teenage girl sizing him up. She wore all black. Black lipstick, Wiccan pendant, heavy mascara. Her dyed black hair showed blond roots.

Thomas sensed that the girl liked his somber expression, and the fact that his eyes hinted that he had seen things. Adult things.

"Sneak in, sneak out?" The goth girl walked her fingers.

Against his better judgment, Thomas paused. "I'm just here for a day."

The girl sauntered up to him. "Only one day?" She stood very close, violating local conventions of personal space. Her scent was fruity and waxy. "Well, then," she said. "I'll shortcut the introductions. I am Jana. I'll just test you out."

She kissed him.

It was a full-mouth kiss, sudden and impossible to predict.

Thomas shoved aside his various reasons to jerk back. All those reasons were tied up with zombies and Torth and zombified Torth and other stuff that was irrelevant to his new beginning.

He pretended to be the person whom Jana believed him to be.

Cynical thanks to bad luck. Not cynical because of a superhuman brain stuffed with millions of lifetimes of absorbed knowledge.

Newly powerful in the way of a teenage boy growing into manly strength. Not a severely disabled boy who had gone through ultra-unique and powerful regeneration healing.

Life experiences on par with hers.

Fourteen years rather than one hundred and forty million years.

Thomas effortlessly zeroed in on her home life: a dysfunctional family. Flirtations with boys who might give her a place to escape to. Jana yearned to get out of her stagnant neighborhood and to do something remarkable.

Thomas could like Jana, and even respect her. He wanted to rescue her.

He pulled away.

If he befriended Jana, or asked her out on a date—even if they both agreed to live in the present, and to ask no questions—he would sense her wondering. And if he took her on another date? And another? Intrigue would wither and eventually die. Once that happened, she would need answers.

"I'm not who you think I am," he confessed.

??? Questions bloomed inside her mind.

Thomas sensed all the things she wanted to know. Who did he think she thought he was? Why did he walk stiffly? Why was he in this schoolyard for one day only? Who were his parents?

Parents. He didn't want to think about that topic.

He was here to escape the truth. But deceit wasn't his thing.

Since he refused to lie, he supposed that put human relationships out of his league. He would be unable to even accomplish a platonic friendship. Never mind coworkers or passing acquaintances. It was all impossible. He could not befriend people unless he could be totally honest with them. So he ought to give up on being human.

Unless . . .

"I have to go," he told Jana.

He felt her self-esteem crumple. She began second-guessing the way she had kissed him and her whole approach.

Thomas gently took her by the shoulders. "I'm a traveler from outer space." He gazed into her hazel eyes. "I can see into people's souls, and I see that you're capable of having a future that everyone here will envy. Take singing lessons. Your voice can lead you to fame."

She looked dazzled.

Thomas gave her a kiss that satisfied them both.

Then he left, resisting an urge to help her, or to rescue her. He had known Jana for three minutes. Ordinary people would never consider that enough time for any kind of meaningful relationship.

It shouldn't count.

As soon as he rounded the corner at the end of the block, he used his modified tablet to order a rideshare service. He would hack into the bank account of a crime ring. That would give him plenty of stolen funds, enough to buy a plane ticket to somewhere more suitable for him to embark on a journey of personal atonement.

CHAPTER 10

TO FRIEND A FOE

"Premier Boryuchal tells me that you refuse to train with telepathy gas." Ariock walked along a row of proud warriors.

He didn't want to be a disciplinarian. He wanted to inspire hope, not resentment. But although these warriors wore the lightweight space armor that Thomas's lab had designed, they were being obstinate about certain things.

"If you intend to kill Torth," Ariock said, pacing the other way, "you need to adapt to the weapons they use. That's what I've been doing."

He indicated his own armor. His galaxy plates were modified for space combat and gas combat, with air tanks that connected to a high-tech helmet. He'd retracted the faceplate.

One of the warriors grunted in a sullen way. He tugged at the air tank on his back, emphasizing his discomfort with the equipment.

Another warrior muttered, "Why are we even bothering? The Hero Fleet is better equipped to kill Torth than we are."

That was actually true.

The threat of gases—inhibitor, telepathy, and insanity gas—had rendered urban combat too dangerous. Now, when Ariock wanted to liberate a city, he damaged its supply chain. His mismatched collection of streamships and shuttles acted as a blockade. The best pilots in the Hero Fleet were gaining notoriety, able to defeat Torth in aerial combat. The Hero Fleet could ensure that Torth populations were unable to count on rescuers.

Kessa's spies were the other half of that equation. They spread information and secret weapons, empowering local slaves to overthrow their own masters.

"Warriors can still make a difference in battle." Ariock regarded them, frustrated. "Besides, you live in the free cities. We have to be prepared for anything."

The last thing he wanted was to lose more warriors. Didn't they understand how important combat training was—for their own survival, if nothing else? Otherwise they would simply become targets for the Torth.

"I am ready for combat," a warrior said in a steely rasp.

Ariock looked toward that one. She was taller than the others, and she stood apart from the rest. She had black hair with a white streak.

Zai. The renegade Servant of All.

Ariock tried to hide his unease. Kessa's lieutenants had evaluated Zai using telepathy gas, multiple times. They swore she was legit. Zai wanted to kill her own kind. She was trustworthy.

And yet . . .

She was a Torth.

Zai stepped out of the line and boldly spoke for herself. "The shani warriors refuse to spar with me," she said. "They won't go near me. They fear me."

She took another ominous step toward Ariock.

He stepped back and shielded himself.

It was embarrassing, how much he feared this one individual. But he didn't want her to get within telepathy range. She was too intense. She could disable him with a pain seizure if she got close enough. What if she was angling for an opportunity to stab him?

"I chose this." Zai indicated her custom-fitted space armor, which was black and purple, like any warrior's armor. "If you want me to help fight the Torth Empire? That is your choice."

Zai looked bravely defiant, as much as any soldier.

Ariock began to feel like a hypocritical fool. Why was Zai among the warriors, if not to serve as one of them? Why had Ariock bothered to ensure that she wore battle gear instead of rags?

He wished he had time to personally train Zai. These days, his schedule was a mess of mass-teleportation, space warfare, and miraculous feats no one else could perform. He was always aiming at one target or another.

Or maybe he was making excuses to avoid Zai.

What would Thomas have advised? Ariock missed his friend's wisdom. Thomas almost certainly would have welcomed Zai, unless he detected nefarious motives buried inside her mind.

Thomas alone had been the voice of reason when Ariock fell for the Death Architect's trap. And afterward? Thomas had offered forgiveness to Ariock, even solace.

"If you want to talk," Thomas had said, *"about your dreams, or anything—"*

"You have work to do," Garrett had interrupted. *"Leave Ariock alone."*

Thomas had obeyed, floating away. But he had given Ariock a look of concern and said, *"You know where to find me."*

Ariock had been too ashamed, too self-loathing, to seek more advice from Thomas. But looking back now, he knew that Thomas was a true friend.

Ariock needed to honor that.

He needed to respect Thomas's wish for Torth allies.

"I do want you in combat against the Torth," Ariock said to Zai, decisive. "If the warriors refuse to work with you? Then I will."

The warriors looked shocked.

"Messiah?" Premier Boryuchal sounded unnerved. "That is unnecessary. I can, uh, mandate sparring sessions. I wasn't strict enough. You really don't have to . . ."

He clearly wanted to say that the messiah should not put himself at risk. He just didn't want to make it obvious.

"I'll take over her training." Ariock let his power shield dissipate. "I never should have dumped this responsibility on you or anyone else. I can see that the Alashani are not comfortable working with a renegade telepath. But I am."

The premier looked embarrassed. He sputtered, searching for excuses.

"Follow me," Ariock told Zai.

He infused his body with extra strength and leaped to a rooftop three stories up.

No one wanted a stray sky croc to bother them, so rooftops were a good place for Yeresunsa sparring sessions, or for being alone. Only a few buildings were crowned by rooftop gardens or terraces. Most were bare.

Ariock turned and saw that Zai was having trouble. She had fallen short and now she clung to a balcony. From there, she somersaulted up, then determinedly climbed the stone face of the building.

Ariock leaned down and offered her an armored hand.

Zai grabbed his hand and let him haul her onto the flat roof.

They faced each other. Ariock backed out of her range quickly, unsure how fast she could soak up secrets. Surely not as fast as Thomas?

Low-hanging clouds sailed across the morning sky.

"So," Ariock said, "you spent almost a week among the Alashani, but you didn't learn how to infuse your body with extra strength and speed?"

Zai took a moment to respond. Once she had caught her breath, she admitted, "No."

The Alashani must have shunned Zai, preventing her from getting within telepathy range. Still. Thomas and Garrett would not have let that stop them from learning.

"You didn't sneak around?" Ariock asked. "I'm sure you could have gotten within range of someone."

"I wished to be seen as a friend," Zai said. "Not as an intrusive enemy. I did not wish to cause offense or make people uneasy."

Ariock studied her, wondering if she had visited Earth. Had she ever playacted as a human?

Most of the Dovanack family had been killed by someone like her.

"I visited Earth once." Zai seemed to guess at his unspoken suspicion. She removed her helmet, shaking out her hair. "I was stationed in the nation of India, since my features align somewhat with that human ethnicity." The white streak in her hair was vibrant against her black locks. "I never harmed any humans." She held Ariock's gaze. "Some Torth want to dominate the people they see as inferior species, I think because they secretly fear they are an inferior species themselves. They are driven to prove their superiority. I was never one of those."

Ariock reassessed Zai. She wasn't a creepy automaton. She might really be an ally.

Zai broke her gaze away, looking downcast. "When I was a Servant of All, I did not stray from what I was told to do. I wholly embraced the spirit of what it means to serve All. But that is exactly why I came here." She looked up, desperate. "I no longer wish to serve All."

She did seem genuine.

"This is a place of freedom." Ariock gestured at the urban sprawl. "For me, also. I was a prisoner inside myself, even before the Torth ripped me away from safety and tried to torture me to death."

Every Torth in the galaxy knew who the Giant was and where he came from. Even so, Zai nodded, looking grateful for what he had shared.

"Let me see what you can do," Ariock said.

Zai looked worried.

"I promise, I won't react with deadly force," Ariock reassured her. "Unless you actually try to kill me."

"I will not," Zai assured him in her raspy voice. "It would be futile even if I wanted to. Both you and the Imp—I mean, Garrett—appear and vanish unpredictably."

Ariock shifted his weight, unnerved by her open admission that she had studied his self-defense skills.

"I can teleport," Zai said. "Although I only have enough strength to do it once. If I use it up now, I will be useless for a few days."

"And you can read minds." As Ariock considered the possibilities, he realized that Zai was almost like a second version of Garrett.

Or better.

Zai was intimately familiar with the enemy leadership. She could select targets for assassination, teleport behind a dangerous Rosy or Servant, and choke them with razor wire. Or, if their armor was too thick for razor wire? She might slice off their head with an ionic blade.

Blaster gloves were too unreliable when facing off against high-ranked Torth. A disruption field could jam a weapon and prevent it from firing.

There was no point in filling up the Mirror Prison when Thomas wasn't around to zombify prisoners. These days, the most important tactic in any battle was to slaughter the most dangerous Torth in the battle zone. That tended to be a guessing game. The Torth had grown savvy about their optics. Sometimes Garrett was able to fish information out of the Megacosm, and if he managed to select and kill the local leader, the whole battle ended faster. Fewer soldiers died.

Zai could do that.

"Can you item-teleport?" Ariock asked.

"Yes," Zai said. "But I cannot teleport across interstellar distances, as you can." Her tone held a hint of yearning. "I would like to learn."

Thomas would have surmised her potential long before now. Ariock wished he could have consulted with Thomas instead of proving himself to be an inattentive and rather inferior tactician.

"If I dart in and out of your range of telepathy," Ariock said, "do you soak up all my secrets? How much do you gain of what I know?"

He was trusting her word.

"Not much," Zai said. "I am not a supergenius. Most Torth gain an impression of emotions and surface thoughts within a few seconds. If I was to delve into your secrets? That would be a mind probe, which would require much of my focus. I could not fight and probe at the same time."

That matched Ariock's memories of being a gladiator and what Vy had told him of being a slave.

"Is the Conqueror . . ." Zai hesitated, as if unsure. "Is Thomas going to come back?"

Everyone had noticed Ariock's missteps in battle planning. More and more people were begging for Thomas's return. Ariock had assured the war council that Thomas would never abandon the war, and he believed that, most of the time.

Yet the days kept passing.

"Of course." Ariock forced himself to sound certain.

Zai waited, probably hoping for an actual explanation for the Conqueror's absence.

Ariock cleared his throat. "Uh, let's try a bit of light sparring. I really do want to gain a sense of your fighting style."

Zai took a battle-ready stance. She looked as flattered as an Alashani who was given the chance to spar one-on-one with the messiah.

"While Thomas is away," Zai said with delicacy, "you may find the Twins capable of filling in for him."

Ariock wanted to avoid going anywhere near the Twins.

Then again, his avoidance of Zai had been a mistake, hadn't it? He could use more wisdom. Garrett's advice wasn't enough. Perhaps he would risk a meeting with the odd pair of renegade supergeniuses.

"Right," Ariock said brusquely, making his tone all about military duty. "How about this? I don't want you in my range a whole lot, so let's mock up a situation where you have to protect that urn over there." He pointed to a decorative urn. "I'll attack the urn. You defend it."

Zai offered a terse smile. She had the plastic-like skin of a Torth, unused to smiles or frowns. Even so, the expression did something nice. She looked human.

And pretty.

Agh. Ariock tried to axe that from his mind. Why did Zai have to have such athletic poise, like Vy? Why were their names so similar, phonetically?

Would Vy ever accept naked intimacy with her gigantic ogre of a boyfriend?

Did Vy want to just be friends? Was she too timid to say so? How many more nights could Ariock sleep with her cuddled next to him, or on top of him, without going mad from yearning?

Ariock forked a bit of lightning at the urn. Zai slammed it away with a searing thermal current.

The urn did not last through a second round. Next, Ariock had them practice on a crenellated railing. And then on a flower bed. Soon they were laughing and taking turns defending inanimate objects from each other's friendly, silly attacks.

CHAPTER 11

DHAKA

"Foreigner! Scram. Get out of my way."

The speaker was an old curmudgeon who resented Thomas and other street children in the slum. Their filthy nests blocked the walkways. The curmudgeon had concluded that Thomas must be the unwanted son of a Russian criminal or someone equally despicable. Why else would a foreign kid scrounge for work alongside homeless orphans? He must be stupid, to have run away in a slum in Bangladesh. Or perhaps he was a troublemaker, purposely sold into slavery by his family.

Thomas jogged down the narrow staircase before the old man could throw a bucket of urine over him.

He had to grip the rusty railing and covertly work his leg braces using the remote hidden up his sleeve. After a week spent on his feet, collecting plastic bottles and selling flowers at bus stations, he was able to walk without powered assistance from his hidden braces. But he still had trouble with stairs and uneven ground.

He stumbled into a stinking alleyway. This place was familiar to him, and so was the tired orphan boy who waited for him to show up. The boy carried an extra-large plastic bag for gathering trash.

They did not exchange words.

They did not need to. Thomas acted like he did not understand more than a few words of Bengali. In Dhaka, no one expected a foreigner to be eloquent or to know the language at all. That was one reason why Thomas had chosen this place. He could be honest when no one expected him to explain himself.

Abhaga sensed that they were kindred spirits, even without words.

They were both doing penance.

They were penitents for the same reason, too. They were both paying for the crime of existing when no one wanted them to exist.

Thomas had chosen this slum as a fitting location where he might serve his penance, whereas Abhaga had less freedom of choice. But otherwise, Thomas had learned that he and Abhaga had a lot in common. Both of them had been forsaken by biological parents who could not, or would not, care for children. Both of them struggled to eat and sleep in a universe that did not respect them. They had been judged unworthy of love before they were even born. They were both survivors, despite odds that were stacked against them. Both felt an enormous burden of shame from transgressions and aggressions they had committed in order to survive, no matter how necessary those actions had seemed at the time.

And they each seethed with directionless anger at the unfairness and injustice all around them.

Thomas sensed it in Abhaga, of course.

And Abhaga had taken one look into Thomas's eyes, and he had seen the same.

That made them friends. They didn't need to speak the same tongue or share a similar background.

Thomas followed Abhaga through trash-filled streets. They each scooped up discarded plastic bottles and dumped them into the bag, dodging colorful hand-pulled rickshaws and men wearing patterned sarongs or loose-fitting Western clothes.

It was the same every day. Street kids like Abhaga did not attend school. They had no official names, no birth certificates. They hid from authorities, because they understood that corrupt orphanages meant they were likely to become victims of abuse or slavery. Girls tended to disappear from the streets, snatched by nefarious organizations. Boys were less valued by the snatchers, but although many boys remained "free" to work for street bosses, few of them pondered their own futures.

Thomas ached by the time they hauled the full bag to the trash hole where Abhaga's boss lived. Thomas stayed hidden around a corner while Abhaga got paid his usual meager fee, plus another empty bag to fill.

Abhaga bought a hot lunch at an alley bazaar. They sat on the edge of a mud puddle and shared the meal.

It wasn't enough food for two boys going through puberty. Thomas was grateful to receive a few morsels of bhel puri.

He had given away his hacked tablet when he'd first arrived in Dhaka, and any international banks were outside the slums, so he could not easily access funds. He wanted his penance to be authentic. Otherwise it would not count.

For over a week now, he had shared the deadly risks that his friend braved. Uncaring drivers. Disease. Sadistic people looking for a weak victim. Any of those common dangers, plus dozens more, might get either of them killed. Abhaga was used to this life, and he had shown Thomas the kindness of guiding him through it.

Lunch ended. They trekked along a filthy waterway, collecting more plastic trash.

Thomas did not have the stamina to keep up with Abhaga all day. He tried. But by the time sunset tinged the clouds, glimpsed between grimy alleyways packed with old wires and desiccated signage, he limped. It was a struggle to limp back to where they slept.

"You are not built for this life, foreigner," Abhaga said, leaning back against the trash bag he used as a cushion. He had no idea that Thomas could understand his words. He spoke mostly to show companionship. "I don't know why I help you. Snatchers look at you like meat to sell. And because of that, they look at me, also."

Thomas clasped the boy's forearm. It was a sign of gratitude.

Abhaga settled down to sleep. Thomas sensed kindness in his mind.

Companionship meant a lot to this boy, who had absolutely no one he dared count on. Abhaga was taking risks, giving up precious food and vital safety, because he cared. He was desperate for someone who needed him.

And vice versa.

Thomas lay awake while his friend slept, huddled under a pile of newspapers and trash to keep the drizzle off.

He had come to Bangladesh in order to serve a penance. He'd wanted to suffer as a human orphan, as if he'd been born with decent human genetics instead of terrible Torth tendencies and powers. But he had expected to serve alone. He had come to a country where he could avoid questions, so that he could be effortlessly honest.

This bond was unexpected and frighteningly powerful.

Thomas felt as protective of Abhaga as he used to feel about Cherise. There was no distance between their suffering. There was no gulf full of misunderstandings. Thomas and Abhaga were not slave and Torth, or prince and pauper, or supergenius and illiterate child.

They were cursed souls together.

Thomas listened to the sound of rain on corrugated roofs, and the voices of a family in one of the broken-windowed tenements.

He began to reexamine his notions about penance.

Abhaga was not a bad person. Despite whatever unfortunate people he came from, despite the fact that he had stolen petty cash and food at times, the streetwise orphan was very clearly a victim of circumstance.

Yet Abhaga would never acknowledge himself as a helpless victim.

The street kid reasoned that he must somehow deserve all the rot and indifference that surrounded him. He believed himself to be worthless. He despised himself.

That was healthier than raging at the injustices of his existence and screaming at every slight like a madman, in the way of some homeless drug addicts. That much rage led straight to death. Any street kid could see it.

Am I doing the same thing as Abhaga? Thomas tossed and turned. *Am I blaming myself because I am afraid to be angry? Do I deserve penance at all?*

Maybe he was not tainted or evil, the way everyone thought. Maybe he was wrong about that.

He began to feel angry at people.

Garrett.

Ariock.

Evenjos.

The entire Alashani nation.

Millions of freed slaves.

Millions of penitents.

All the Torth in the universe.

Stupid humans.

The Death Architect.

Even people like Kessa and Varktezo and Vy and Cherise and the Pink Screwdriver.

He was sick of people. He hated people.

And that really scared him.

The next day, he trudged after Abhaga, sore and brooding. He was no longer sure he belonged in a slum, picking up garbage, because of something like original sin. He had not chosen his genetics. He had not chosen his parents.

All he had ever done was try to help. And to survive.

In return, he was feared. He was treated like a nasty, unsightly, defective, disposable tool.

Thomas kept missing plastic bottles. Abhaga shot him concerned looks.

"You have made me late," Abhaga fretted when he finally hauled the bag to the trash hole. He presented the collection to his boss.

It wasn't enough. Instead of payment, the boss yelled at Abhaga.

"I will do better." Abhaga scampered away. "I am so sorry, boss."

He jogged away, and Thomas followed like a guilty shadow. His slowness had cost them both a much-needed meal. He needed to try and set aside his anger, at least for the remainder of today.

Four tough-looking teenagers stepped out of an alleyway.

"You sick?" one of the boys asked Abhaga in mock sympathy.

They must have overheard the boss. They sensed weakness, like sharks detecting the blood of injured prey.

"Or in love?" another cooed, staring straight at Thomas. "You think the foreigner will protect you? You think he has rich parents?"

It was obvious to anyone with eyes that Thomas was living on the streets. He wore a hat that only partially hid his grimy face. Not all foreigners had money and power. He was clearly a victim, not a ransom.

Abhaga shot Thomas a terrified, helpless look. *Run!* that look said.

One of the teenagers grabbed Abhaga and hustled him toward a decrepit doorway. Another seized Thomas. The proximity made their intentions obvious to a mind reader. There was an underground market for sex slaves. These snatchers had been used for sex when they were young, unable to defend themselves, and they curried favor with a crime boss by recruiting others like themselves. Boys like Abhaga could be coerced into just about anything. He had no one to protect him.

So they thought.

If Thomas had been in a penitent mood, he would have accepted this attack as something he and his friend deserved. He might have waited for a calm opportunity in which he might quietly escape with Abhaga.

Instead?

He was sick of injustice. Abhaga did not deserve to be attacked or disrespected or treated like garbage. Nor did Thomas.

He reached into the mind of the nearest attacker and drilled down to his core.

He hesitated. These teenagers used to be victims. Perhaps sympathy was called for?

Nah.

Thomas wrenched the thug's core with ferocious savagery.

The thug became an empty echo of Thomas's will. His mind was broken beyond repair. He could not choose to blink, to swallow, or to do anything except receive instruction.

"Protect me and my friend," Thomas commanded. "And survive." He had to say it all out loud, in Bengali, since his victim was not a mind reader.

The command overrode every remnant motive and goal inside the zombie's mind.

Screams of pain and a flurry of movement followed.

The zombie mercilessly grabbed another snatcher's wrist and twisted. There was a sickening snap. The teenagers fought each other, trying to subdue their brainwashed friend, unable to guess what was wrong with him. Passersby rushed to see what the problem was.

The zombie, of course, fought like his life depended on victory and nothing else in the universe mattered.

Thomas ducked under a thrown punch. "Let me and my friend escape," he commanded. "Do not obey any commands from your street gang. Prevent your gang from chasing me or my friend."

It was cruel to abandon the zombie, but Thomas figured the zombie was doomed anyway. They died within weeks even with the best hospice care.

Thomas gestured for the awestruck and suspicious Abhaga to follow him.

"You speak Bengali?" Abhaga said in a hurt tone. "What did you do back there?"

Thomas pushed his legs to maximum speed. He had to focus on jogging while not slipping in mud.

He led Abhaga several alleys away. Once he judged they were safe, he stopped in an alley clogged with parked rickshaws. He faced his bewildered friend.

"What happened back there?" Abhaga asked. "Why did you pretend to not know our language?"

Thomas would never spew lies. It was time to say goodbye, time to quit this experimental penance. He was done atoning for his existence.

Yet he could not quite walk away carefree. Abhaga was the one person in his life who had shown him nonjudgmental kindness.

"Come with me," Thomas said.

A trek on foot to an international bank could take all day, so instead, Thomas walked the crowded streets until he sensed an opportunity.

"Badrul," he said, speaking the name of a man whom he kept pace with. "Badrul Badsha, I am speaking on behalf of a student you failed to pay."

The man turned to him, startled.

"That student has ties to the mafia," Thomas said to the teacher who moonlighted as the co-owner of a center for outsourced labor. "You have a habit of big promises followed by lies. You steal wages, and many people know. Someone powerful is angry."

The corrupt teacher searched the street for any sign of hidden thugs.

"You have one chance to make it right." Thomas offered a significant look full of threats. "I am here to give you your chance."

The man decided to play ignorant. "I don't know you." He walked faster.

"Bad choice." Thomas began to melt into the crowd.

The man had a change of heart. He followed Thomas through an outdoor aisle between tunics for sale. "Can we talk elsewhere?"

"I'm not going anywhere alone with you," Thomas said.

"Which student?" the man demanded. "I can guarantee it was all lies."

Thomas had absorbed the names of many dozens of students whom this teacher had hired, acting as a benevolent boss until he allegedly ran out of funds, letting them go without pay while he hired another batch of workers from another class.

"I'm not going to tell you," Thomas said.

The man huffed. "I did not do what that student said. But I don't want trouble." He pulled out his wallet and thrust out a wad of banknotes.

Thomas pocketed the money and walked away without another word.

"Wait!" the corrupt teacher hurried after him. "Is that enough?"

"You'd better hope it is," Thomas said.

The man was so scared, he took out the rest of his money and gave it to Thomas. "That's all I have."

Thomas took the cash and walked away, leaving the corrupt man to stand in the street and ponder the calamity he might have brought upon himself.

Abhaga had judiciously watched from the sidelines. He rejoined Thomas, gawking at the pocket where the money had disappeared. "Are you a jinn?"

The mythological jinn had powers that went beyond human senses. "I suppose I am," Thomas said, since no unaided human could sense telepathy.

"Really?" Abhaga began to ask a lot more questions.

Thomas paid a rickshaw pedaler to take them to a more luxurious neighborhood. On the ride, he deflected questions, but he answered one.

"I can grant wishes," Thomas admitted in Bengali. "Yes. I know what is in your heart, and I can transport you to a lush land full of welcoming people. They will care about you."

Suspicion warred with disbelief and yearning in Abhaga. There was always a catch with jinn. Thomas's words sounded like a lure, like something a kidnapper would say.

Thomas went into greater detail. He had glimpsed his friend's mind, daydreaming while he picked up plastic trash.

Abhaga often imagined himself afloat on a raft, with a powerful current ferrying him to a bountiful land full of joyous, welcoming people. In his best dreams, he owned his own boat, and it had a colorful canopy with tassels. He traveled through a land where people missed him and were glad that he had found his way home.

"That place exists." Thomas tried to impart his sincerity. "I come from there. But it is very foreign. More foreign than anything you have seen, even in movies. The people are alien. But they will welcome you, and treat you with kindness and respect."

Thomas suspected a lot of Alashani maidens would do more than welcome a virile human male into their enclaves. Rumors were spreading about the power potential of human hybridization. Albino war heroes whispered about having babies with humans.

Lucky Abhaga.

"Why are you not there, then?" Abhaga asked, scrutinizing Thomas while the pedaler rang his bell and wove around pedestrians. "Why did you leave?"

"I was born to the wrong people," Thomas admitted. "You would be celebrated in Freedomland. Not me. I left because I was unwelcome."

He was the equivalent of an orphaned trash picker. So were all the penitent Torth. They waded through muck, eyes downcast, apologizing and being ashamed of who they were.

How many of them truly needed to atone?

Many of them did, perhaps.

But not Thomas.

He was done saving ungrateful people, done with apologizing for who and what he was. He wasn't going to tiptoe around the war council ever again. He refused to serve penance for the crime of being born.

Forget Freedomland.

Forget the war.

Oh, and the Torth? Let them stagnate. He had wanted to save the Megacosm, and that still seemed like a worthwhile goal—but how could he save knowledge if the owners of that knowledge threw it away like trash? If they refused to join his side . . . ?

Well. They had made their choice.

He did not have to feel guilty or obligated to save them.

He was done.

"So even if I choose to believe your promises and go to your foreign land," Abhaga said, "you will leave me alone there? You will not stay?"

A lump formed in Thomas's throat. But there was no way around the truth. "I am unwelcome in Freedomland," he reiterated. "I have not found where I belong. All I can do is keep searching."

Bitter abandonment stabbed through his friend. Abhaga wondered how rich and powerful Thomas was, if he could simply breeze away from these muddy slums or from wherever he felt trapped.

Tears welled in Thomas's eyes. The feeling was sharp and unexpected, and he tried to hide his guilt, to blink away the emotion.

Then he gave up. He was done hiding who he was.

"You're right about me," Thomas said. "I can breeze away. But I promise, only my body breezes away. Not my mind. Not my heart." He wiped away his tears. "When I first came here, many people saw me begging and struggling, and only you helped me. That matters. That is everything. You are my friend. Nothing will change that."

Abhaga was too hurt to trust himself with words. *A real friend would not dump me somewhere like I am trash*, he thought, unaware that Thomas was reading his mind.

"Stop here," Thomas told the rickshaw pedaler. He had spotted an international bank with an ATM.

He led Abhaga through a glass door. He made a substantial cash withdrawal of illegally obtained funds from a hacked account. He added that wad of banknotes to the remainder from the corrupt teacher and handed it all to his friend.

"What is this for?" Abhaga made no move to take the money.

"I have the power to grant wishes," Thomas said. "But you deserve better than abandonment from me. So." He offered the banknotes. "Take this as a promise, not a gift. My leaving is not forever. I will return."

Abhaga stared at him with deep mistrust.

Thomas considered offering more promises. He could set Abhaga up with a good life partner, or a career that entailed respect and wealth, and so forth. He really could grant wishes.

But.

But the Torth Empire might soon make a mockery of every human's hopes and dreams. If the prophecies of Ah Jun were legit, then the war against the galactic oppressors would fail without Thomas and his supposed wisdom.

It was best not to overpromise.

Best not to pretend he was a hero or any kind of purely benevolent force. He was done striving for that impossible goal.

Thomas put the banknotes on a ledge. "I came to Dhaka to punish myself. Your friendship changed my path. I want to contemplate my future path, but I must do it alone."

He would take an airplane to northern Russia, then hike into the taiga forest and uncover his camouflaged streamship.

Then? A hot launch into the frigid void of space.

The galaxy was infinite from an individual's perspective. Thomas could park himself on any number of lonely planets and become a hermit. It would be easy. In quietude, without injustice and bullies around, his own shame and rage would eventually die down.

Once he was ready to let go of everything.

He would do a trial run first.

"This money will tide you over until I return." Thomas clasped Abhaga's arm to reinforce their friendship. "I am sorry that I am not a good friend." He was a bad friend to many. "I will return, but only to repay your goodwill as best as I am able."

He walked away, proving to himself, once again, that he was not human.

Abhaga called after him. "Are you going to trick someone else?"

"No," Thomas said. "I will go where the only voice is wind."

CHAPTER 12

GREETING GREATNESS

Kessa shaded her eyes to watch the sky croc circle the academy. It landed with practiced grace on the Dragon Tower and crawled inside. Azhdarchidae was left alone to roost, waiting for Thomas.

I miss him, too, Kessa thought to the distant animal.

She made her way into the science annex. People greeted her with surprised reverence. She asked for Varktezo, and soon they were in a closed office with a spectacular view of the city.

"How are you these days?" Kessa sat across from the adolescent.

Varktezo adjusted his goggles over his brow ridges. Despite his white lab coat, he looked rumpled and harried.

"Oh, I'm fine." Varktezo said it in a way that made her question sound ludicrous. "Other than the fact that we're facing certain death without Thomas."

Kessa clicked her beak. Just how demoralized were the lab technicians?

"I've got a battalion of shy assistants trying to wrangle shani warriors into clinical trials," Varktezo went on. "None will volunteer because they don't trust anything the Twins have invented. And guess what? The Twins are not as easy to work with as Thomas, plus everyone is afraid to even talk to them. So my own assistants won't vouch for them. Oh, and half the technicians are fooling around with telepathy gas at work, so they're forgetting to leave written messages. And the people I assign to keep them organized keep failing, and I feel like no one truly wants to help."

He compressed his beak and looked stern.

Then he accidentally broke his somber mood by sipping a neon-orange energy drink.

"I'm sorry." Kessa wondered if she should have asked someone else to work with the Twins. Varktezo had seemed eager for the job when she'd asked him, but then again, he tended to be eager no matter what. "If you don't think you can oversee the Twins, I—"

"No, no!" Varktezo cut her off. "I like the Twins. I want to continue working with them."

She cocked her head, inviting further explanation.

"They're just different from Thomas, that's all," Varktezo said. "They take getting used to. They're weird and creepy. But brilliant!"

"Have they provided boons?" Kessa asked, probing.

"Oh, yes," Varktezo said. "They've greatly improved our communications network. Have you noticed that there's no longer any lag in intergalactic live streams? They explained that although time is relative, there is a quantum matrix of 'now' that exists as a . . ." He saw that he was losing her interest and switched topics. "And our targeting systems are perfected, thanks to the Twins. We won't have to send as many pilots into danger. They've keyed up—"

"What about immunity to the gases?" Kessa broke in.

Varktezo took a deep breath, as if bracing himself.

"I'm not a molecular biochemist," he said. "But they've made great progress. Our lab had been homing in on a particular set of ribosomes for several kilohours, trying to identify how they influence the neural gamma waves, because that's what determines the intensity of an individual's sphere of . . ." He saw Kessa's impatience and cut to the chase. "Anyway. Bam!" He pounded his hands together. "They solved it in two hours. That's all it took them."

Kessa wondered if she understood correctly. "Okay. This was a project you and Thomas have been working on for a few, er, kilohours?" She stopped herself from saying "blinks of Morja." Every cosmic body had a different rotation and orbit, which made months impossible to correlate across planets. The Freedomland academy had developed a universal way to measure time. One kilohour was actually a bit less than a month on Umdalkdul and Reject-20, and it was more than a month on Earth and Nuss, but it was roughly a month.

"Right," Varktezo confirmed. "We would have gotten it eventually, but we're not in synergy like the Twins."

"Synergy?"

"It's hard to explain," Varktezo said. "If you ask the Twins, they'll make it sound like they just accidentally happen to have a wider baseline of knowledge than anyone else, because of their age and their mutations. But it's definitely more than that. They're pulling from here and here and here and here." Varktezo made grabbing motions at different spots in the air. "And they test those things against each other and integrate everything that makes sense. I don't actually understand how they work. But it's intimidating to watch." He shrugged. "To be honest, if I was the Torth Empire, I would be terrified."

That was heartening to hear.

"Predictive models indicate that their version of immunity will work," Varktezo said. "Oh, and guess what? They casually invented a temporary version of the inhibitor. Has anyone told you about that?"

Kessa had heard a rumor. "Go on."

"It's a patch." Varktezo mimed sticking something onto his neck. "Just a skin patch, like a little bandage. You put it on and it inhibits your powers. Peel it off and you're a full Yeresunsa again." He chuckled. "The Bringer of Hope was super interested. He asked us to manufacture a bunch of them, custom-sized for him. I imagine it would be very useful in scouting Torth-dominated planets!"

"Hmm." Kessa imagined it would be useful in a variety of situations. "But they're still working on immunity?"

"They're getting close." Varktezo threw his hands wide. "Why don't you just talk to them yourself?"

"I will," Kessa said. "First, I want your uncensored opinion. Do you have any reservations about them?"

She took Varktezo's report the same way she interviewed any of her lieutenants. She tried to get a sense of whether the Twins were capable of friendship. That was her goal. She listened, not only to Varktezo's praise for his new underling colleagues, but also to his inflections and body language.

"I'm ready to meet them," Kessa said.

"Great!"

Varktezo led her toward a large underground laboratory in the basement levels of the academy. This was the Twins' home, where they slept and ate and worked, safe from the eyes of the Torth Empire.

"I posted a schedule of caretakers for them." Varktezo indicated a bulletin board with photos of ummins and govki pinned in a certain order. "But the helpers are begrudging. I have to keep firing and hiring new ones."

"I will send you a work pool of reliable caretakers." Kessa knew she had overlooked that detail. The Twins were as physically disabled as Thomas used to be.

At least their health was no longer deteriorating. Thomas had had the foresight to prepare a welcome kit for any renegade supergeniuses who might join him, with research library passwords plus several hundred vials of NAI-13. Each Twin took a daily injection.

Unfortunately, the medicine could not undo neuromuscular damage. The girl Twin was in particularly poor health.

Kessa followed Varktezo through a vault door. Soon she stood on a wraparound balcony, peering down at the circular workspace below.

The Twins floated at opposite workstations, back-to-back. They sat in close proximity. Their movements complemented each other in strange ways, hinting that they were of one mind.

The girl Twin used a robotic arm to drop some kind of liquid into a mysterious machine. The boy Twin paused in the middle of entering data, like he was listening. When the boy Twin resumed typing, the girl Twin completed her action with more surety.

"They're like that all the time." Varktezo kept his voice down. "They don't need to talk to each other."

Kessa descended the ramp. "May I interrupt your work for a few minutes?" She did not want to seem ungrateful or rude, since this pair of renegades had already gifted her people with scientific leaps.

Both Twins swiveled to face her, one on either side.

"Sure," Mondoyo said.

Kessa boosted herself onto a countertop so she could face them at eye level. Her distance might seem like paranoia, but she was entrusted with sensitive military secrets, after all.

"First of all," Kessa said, "thank you for your scientific help. You should have received thanks from Ariock and everyone on the war council."

Serette gave an imperious nod.

Mondoyo looked embarrassed. "We haven't done much yet. It would be really helpful if we could match ideas with Thomas. I'm sure if he were here, we would be able to present immunity to the inhibitor by now."

That was a heavy hint. Like everyone in the galaxy, the Twins wanted to know when Thomas would return.

It was a perilous topic. Anything Kessa said might give the Twins a hint that Thomas's reputation was disgraced, and what conclusions might they draw from that? How welcome would they feel, as renegade supergeniuses themselves?

She didn't want to stir that stew.

"I would like to know what obstacles you face," Kessa said, "in terms of rectifying the gaseous weapons you invented. Are there any resources you need?" She gestured around the lab. "Anything that would make it easier for you to invent immunity?"

"No." Mondoyo shook his head.

Serette glared at him.

"Okay," Mondoyo said in a relenting tone. "We understand that regeneration healing is a lot to ask for. Maybe too much?"

It was too much. Kessa had already raised the topic during a private council meeting with the heroes. The few remaining Alashani healers lacked the raw strength and stamina, and Ariock, Evenjos, and Garrett were too busy mitigating constant disasters to take a week off to give intensive regeneration healing.

Two weeks, in actuality. Each Twin would need it.

"But," Mondoyo went on, "neither of us is in great health. Especially Serette." He had no idea that Kessa had already advocated for this request. "We're very grateful for the supply of NAI-13. That helps a little. But would the heroes be willing to schedule a week in order to gift Serette with a future?"

Kessa wished there was another solution. Improvements to the medicine, perhaps?

"I am sorry," she said truthfully. "The heroes are unwilling, for now. I think they would change their minds if our side of the war gains an easier way to defeat Torth troops. That would relieve the pressure on them and free up their time."

Mondoyo and Serette nodded. They understood the unspoken pressure.

"We are working on immunity to the inhibitor." Mondoyo studied Kessa with a piercing Blue Rank gaze. "But when we do invent it . . . we want to be sure you understand the implications."

When. Not if.

That sounded very promising. Kessa hid her surge of hope. "Yes," she said. "I know it will make Yeresunsa mostly invincible." The Alashani war heroes would become even harder to deal with.

"It will change the course of civilizations," Mondoyo said in the colder, higher tone of Serette. "When Rosies and Servants no longer have to capitulate to the Majority, most of them will go rogue."

That was hard to imagine.

"It will break the Megacosm," Mondoyo said in his normal, friendly tone. "So it will send a lot of Torth fleeing here, to Thomas's side. Are you prepared for that?"

Break the Megacosm.

Right.

Kessa doubted the Twins could accomplish what she and Thomas could not. True, her people were unequipped to handle a massive influx of Torth allies. That was painfully obvious. But it wasn't worth worrying about. If the Torth Empire burst at the seams and died? Ha, a few growing pains in the free cities would be insignificant in comparison to the galactic victory celebrations.

"Thank you." Kessa slid off the counter and brushed off her tunic. "I have heard you need Yeresunsa volunteers for clinical trials. I will make sure you gain some."

"We appreciate that." Mondoyo looked shy. "All we really want is for Thomas to return. From what we've gathered, he's gone on a sabbatical, or a holiday? Or something?"

His probing tone sounded innocent. But Kessa suspected the Twins had guessed the truth by now.

"If anyone can get a message to him," Mondoyo said, "I really think he would want to know that we're here."

Kessa wished it were that easy. She hid her sadness. "If I can pass along your message," she said, "I will."

She began to walk toward the spiral ramp to leave.

"So," Mondoyo said in the colder, higher-pitched tone of Serette. "He ran away."

Kessa paused and turned back, meeting the accusatory stare of the girl Twin.

"We don't know," Kessa admitted.

Mondoyo looked abashed. "We're just worried. The people of this scientific establishment have treated us very kindly, and we're comfortable. But . . ." He cringed, as if afraid to go on.

"Please," Kessa invited. "What is it?"

"I did not quite expect so much isolation," Mondoyo said, his tone ashamed. "I detect a lot of mistrust, and it is not entirely because of what we did. It is because of what we are. Penitents." He included Serette and himself in his gesture. "We thought Thomas was bridging the gap between renegade Torth and liberated slaves? But it is plain that many people have a moral problem with Thomas. They're afraid of him. So they're afraid of us." He swallowed.

Then he added in Serette's tone of voice, "People in your city have tried to murder him."

Kessa felt an unfamiliar sense of shame about her own people. She nodded, acknowledging the truth of it. "The Majority of Torth sometimes make unwise decisions, rooted in fear. It is the same with former slaves. We have our own majority, I suppose."

Mondoyo studied her. "You do not follow your majority?"

Kessa shook her head. "Never. Not even when I was a slave."

"Thomas worked closely with you," Mondoyo observed. "He trusted you."

Kessa thought of Thomas agreeing to answer any question she asked, any time. She thought of their private meals together. "He did."

"Then I will trust you," Mondoyo said impulsively. "So I will tell you this: Thomas should be everyone's top priority. You will not win this war without him."

Kessa raised her brow ridges. Mondoyo had not said anything she had not thought herself. But it was rare to hear it stated so irrefutably.

"Sorry." Mondoyo hunched his shoulders in shame. "I should not presume to tell you your job."

"You have never met Thomas in person," Kessa said. "What makes you so certain?"

Mondoyo gaped, as if she had said something nonsensical. Then he looked chagrined. "You're right," he said to Serette, presumably for Kessa's benefit. "She asked a scientific question." He focused on Kessa. "Thomas keeps figuring out things no one else has ever figured out. From your perspective, it must look normal? But I think a mind like his only comes along once in a thousand generations. Everything he's accomplished is incredible." Mondoyo gestured around.

"He has done a lot," Kessa agreed.

"I really want to meet him!" Mondoyo said. "I want to learn how, exactly, he outwitted the Upward Governess. And the Death Architect! He could have tied her in knots if Ariock hadn't fallen for her bait!"

The boy Twin seemed unaware that he just insulted the messiah and de facto ruler of the free galaxy. He kept praising Thomas in an excited rush.

"He outwitted the Torth Majority not just once, but multiple times. He's set up a situation where he might actually topple the Torth Empire! And what resources did he have to start with? Nothing! He had absolutely nothing! He didn't even own a slave!"

Kessa supposed that was a fair assessment.

"He was raised by primitives!" Mondoyo said in Serette's higher pitch. Then he looked mortified, and he quickly said, "Um, we mean humans. Sorry. We don't mean to be insulting. It's just, um, they have a different level of technology."

Kessa had little patience for euphemisms. "Yes."

"He cured his own illness," Mondoyo said in a haughty Serette tone of voice. "Even before he wrangled healing from ultrapowerful Yeresunsa, using ancient and long-forgotten knowledge, he invented a way to live to adulthood. He pioneered new paths into taboo sciences."

Kessa nodded, acknowledging the truth of that.

"Anyone who wants to kill him is an idiot!" Mondoyo said.

Serette nodded.

"He just runs right over obstacles," Mondoyo went on. "He doesn't let anything stop him." His face was flushed. "Do you realize how amazing that is?"

Kessa made a guess. "You came here to meet Thomas?"

Mondoyo dipped his head and raised his shoulders in defense. "Yes," he admitted. "We value freedom, and that's why we're here. But . . ." He shrugged helplessly. "We really, really want to meet the Conqueror."

Kessa missed Thomas more than ever. He ought to be here.

"I'm sure, with his help," Mondoyo said, "we would conquer the Torth Empire right away, and probably do a lot more good. We just need to meet him."

"Well," Kessa said, "if you have any insights about where Thomas might have gone? Please tell me."

"Earth," Mondoyo said promptly.

He sounded so certain, Kessa gave him a demanding look.

"We don't know for sure," Mondoyo admitted. "But given the facts we do know? We've calculated greater than seventy percent odds that he went to his planet of birth. For closure."

Kessa figured she would share that conjecture with Ariock.

"He likely avoided his home region," Mondoyo added in the higher-pitched tone of Serette. "And he can blend in easily with humans. He likely made himself difficult to find."

"Thank you." Kessa nodded to the Twins, making sure she included the silent one. "You've been very helpful."

"If you want him back," Mondoyo said in the high, cold voice of Serette, "then you must change the hatred against him."

That was obvious, at least to Kessa. But why did the girl Twin make it sound like it was Kessa's personal responsibility?

"Do you have any suggestions?" Kessa dared to ask.

The Twins exchanged a quick glance that was fraught with unspoken meaning.

"It is within your power," Mondoyo said in the arrogant voice of his partner.

That must be wrong. Kessa was just an administrator, not someone who changed the course of history. An elderly ummin could not adjust the hearts and minds of billions of people. It was an impossible task for any one person to accomplish.

Wasn't it?

Then again, defeating the Torth Empire was supposed to be impossible, yet Thomas had opened up the possibility.

He had done that alone. He had laid the groundwork even when everyone doubted him, while he was in a dungeon pit, and while he was a Yellow Rank, isolated and weak among the most powerful rulers of the galaxy.

"I will think on it." Kessa tapped her beak, reevaluating her current approach to redeeming the best of the penitents.

Wasn't Thomas a shining example?

He was a full-blooded Torth. Kessa had wrongly considered him human and therefore better than a penitent.

And that was a major mistake.

Thomas was a penitent. He was one who had atoned. He was a redeemed penitent.

Yet more than half of society was making the same mistake Kessa had made. They did not believe redemption was possible for a Torth.

They did not understand what criteria had been met. They had not heard. They had not seen. They did not know. They celebrated military victories but not moral victories. They would not accept redemption for penitents unless the potentiality of it—the reality—was made unavoidably obvious.

It was easy to overlook ideals and moral triumphs during the day-to-day operations of a galactic war. Much of what Kessa did was reaction rather than action. The remaining heroes were doing the same thing, reacting on the fly, not planning ahead.

But Thomas planned.

That was why his victories challenged the galactic rulers.

Kessa walked away, her mind and heart full of ideas. Moral celebrations, she thought, were even more important than military triumphs.

CHAPTER 13

DEFENDER OF THE MEEK

"Ariock?"

Garrett's distant voice was tinny and minuscule. It came through an earpiece, and it had to filter through Ariock's vastly expanded awareness.

Ariock began the process of consolidating and compacting himself. Part of him was clouds. Part of him was marsh water. He was air, he was grass, he was mud, he was the living limbs of trees.

He withdrew and withdrew some more.

"Are you done over there?" Garrett asked. "Can I have a word in private?"

Ariock was not done. The brine-soaked wetlands were littered with debris from his tornadoes and waterspouts, but the Torth fleet continued to pound his Hero Fleet.

At least the local Torth were uncoordinated. They had no leader. Zai had teleported next to the Torth in charge and beheaded him with an ionic-bladed scimitar. The Torth never saw her coming.

She was fast becoming Ariock's favorite warrior.

"Where are you?" Ariock asked. He figured Garrett was in the nearest secured free city. The old codger insisted on being on the same planet as Ariock, even when he wasn't slated for battle. He had spent the past few days ghosting around on Earth in search of Thomas.

"TriSolstice City," came the distant voice.

Sure enough.

"I'm near the mayoral lounge." Garrett sounded tired. "In the tallest tower near the spaceport."

If Garrett's powers were drained from clairvoyance, then his life spark would not stand out as a vivid blaze. Ariock might need to ghost around to find his exact location.

"See you in five to ten minutes." Ariock slogged across spongy ground. Mud sucked at his armored boots up to his calves. After being a titan who encompassed miles of air and terrain, his armor felt too heavy, his body too small.

The Torth of Mixed Marsh MetroHub were cut off from any possibility of aid. Their supplies and vehicles belonged to Ariock now, and their slaves were in full rebellion. They were conquered. Their military ranks just hadn't fully admitted it yet.

People jumped in surprise when Ariock appeared in the makeshift headquarters inside a city spire. He was used to surprise. In some ways, his near-unlimited raw power was embarrassing. Frequent teleportation was like flaunting immense wealth, like arriving in a private jet.

"Do you have the conquest in hand?" Ariock asked the pilot commandant. "I need to leave for a bit."

"The city is ours, Bringer of Hope." The ummin hopped onto the rim of a morph fountain so he could face Ariock without needing to crane his head all the way back. "We couldn't have done it without you."

Ariock doubted that. It would have all gone wrong if Zai, plus a contingent of three warriors, had not rounded up every Rosy Rank in the city. The Hero Fleet was doing everything else. All Ariock had to do was act intimidating.

Well, perhaps he had prevented a few Torth from escaping.

"All the Torth are on the inhibitor?" Ariock wanted to make sure.

"They are." The commandant looked proud. "I have specialists scanning them with telepathy gas right now. They'll sort out which ones are truly dangerous."

Ariock could not help but marvel at how much things had changed. A few months ago, he never would have imagined ummins using telepathy in order to evaluate captive Torth. They were filling a role that used to be solely Thomas's job, determining which Torth might become loyal penitents and which hid nefarious powers.

"Most of the Torth here surrendered even before their slaves rebelled!" the commandant said. "Isn't that remarkable? The kneelers are becoming more common."

"It is remarkable," Ariock agreed.

His forces were winning battles again, even without Thomas's genius plans. That was something to celebrate.

But Ariock knew it wouldn't last. He kept having that recurring nightmare about the Death Architect and her bomb. She was out there. Scheming.

And the Torth Empire still owned ninety million planets, most of the habitable galaxy.

Maybe Garrett had good news to share? Perhaps he had found some hint of where Thomas might be hiding?

"Keep up the good work," Ariock told the commandant. "And thank you."

With that, he ghosted several hundred miles, across hummocks and islands and waterways that reflected the three moons of Umdalkdul. There was TriSolstice City, glittering like a jewel in the night. Ariock found the mayoral lounge. He flitted through adjacent rooms as fast as an eye blink.

Garrett sat alone in a Zen-like meditation lounge with shallow canals and rock gardens and subdued lights.

Ariock avoided the shimmers of water. Anything reflective messed with clairvoyance. Even his armor was burnished, so he would not be too big a target for Torth assassins.

He had to focus high up, next to a sandstone wall. He pulled his body through to that location and fell heavily to the stone floor.

"Finally!" Garrett clasped his silvery staff. He looked like a delighted old wizard.

"What's the news?" Ariock asked.

"I found the boy!" Garrett said excitedly. "Kessa was right. He's on Earth."

Ariock instantly forgot all his worries. Everything else seemed insignificant. "You found Thomas?" He kept his tone low, aware that his deep, rumbling voice could carry through walls.

"Yep. I caught sight of him in Mongolia, if you can believe it."

"Mongolia?" Ariock wondered if Garrett could be mistaken. Thomas had no ties to anyone on the Asian continent, as far as Vy knew.

That was why Ariock had only scanned New England. He had spent several nights ghosting in and out of the homes, schools, restaurants, malls, parks, ski lodges, lakes, and other locations that Vy had said Thomas had visited. Ariock had thoroughly explored the Dovanack mansion, which now looked like a haunted fortress, home to mice and bats.

He'd found no hints.

That was when he'd brought Garrett in on the search. The old man had the raw power, skill, and inclination to ghost in circles across Earth while Ariock teleported fleets and won battles.

"Are you sure?" Ariock asked. Garrett wouldn't joke about something as important as this. Would he?

Garrett snorted. "Well, I wasn't sure at first. The boy's dressed like a native tribesman. I had to scan three times before I confirmed it was really him."

"Okay." Ariock still felt skeptical, but he was also excited. He missed talking with his friend. Plus, he really wanted to make sure Thomas was all right. "Where is he, exactly? Wait. You didn't bother him, did you?"

"No," Garrett said. "I think you're right about that. He's more likely to listen to a friend than to me."

That was good.

"Show me where he is, on a globe," Ariock commanded.

"I'm not so good at holographic illusions," Garrett said, but he concentrated. A pipe appeared out of thin air. Once it was lit, he blew smoke.

The smoke took shape into a foggy white approximation of Earth.

The globe turned, showing Asia. Bubbly protrusions indicated mountains. Flat sweeps hinted at desert regions. Smoke curled around the hinted outlines of lakes and oceans.

Garrett used the pipestem to point at an empty slash. "That's Lake Baikal."

"Is that where Thomas is?"

"No," Garrett said. "It's just the nearest landmark. The boy's more than five hundred miles to the south and east." He wagged his pipe, and mist swirled into a knot around a nondescript location on the globe. "The middle of nowhere."

Ariock tried to memorize the map. "Okay. Is he near a town? Are there any other landmarks?"

"Well, there's the Khentii mountain range," Garrett said in a dry tone. "But he's not on a pilgrimage to the sacred tomb of Genghis Khan or anything like that. He's about fifty miles from there, just roaming the wilderness by himself."

Ariock wondered if he should be wary of any threats to his friend. Might there be dangerous Torth on Earth? Was that why Thomas was in such an unpredictable location?

As Ariock thought about it, he realized that Earth was likely rife with Servants of All. Some powerful rogues might fake being an American or a Brazilian or a Turkish citizen, rather than getting ordered into deadly battle at the behest of the Torth Majority—or getting consigned to the Mirror Prison and turned into zombies.

"Weird, right?" Garrett said.

Ariock didn't think that anything was necessarily strange for Thomas. "I might need a few hours to assess his situation before I go to him."

"Definitely," Garrett said. "But, uh, I might have tipped the boy off."

Ariock should have expected as much. Thomas was just about impossible to sneak up on. Still. "How?" he asked.

"My sphere of influence is not insignificant," Garrett said.

"You were there?" Ariock narrowed his eyes. He had commanded Garrett to stay away from Thomas should he successfully find him.

"How do you think I could find him?" Garrett said defensively. "I had to scan eight billion humans, and the quickest way was to assess their life sparks. Don't worry. I didn't let him see me. There was no contact."

Ariock tried to relax.

"Earth is crawling with intense life sparks, by the way," Garrett said.

That confirmed it. Hundreds or even thousands of Torth military ranks were creeping around Ariock's homeworld. They were blending in with humans, perhaps even murdering them. Or breeding with them? Ugh. It was almost enough to give Ariock a mission, except he did not want to accidentally spark a Yeresunsa battle on Earth.

"The boy's keeping himself somewhat drained of power," Garrett said, "so his sphere of influence is very low-key. Very hard to detect. Mostly, he blends in with the local wildlife. I mean herds of cattle. Horses. Goats. Wild gazelles."

Ariock studied Garrett anew. No wonder his great-grandfather was exhausted. He must have visited Earth repeatedly, searching for that proverbial needle in a haystack.

"It's a miracle I found him at all," Garrett admitted. "It was just lucky timing. I happened to scan that region in the predawn hours, when his powers must have replenished a little bit, after sleep. He stood out slightly. Very slightly."

"Ah," Ariock said. It seemed Thomas really did not want to be found.

If the Torth on Earth were busily scanning for ultrapowerful life sparks . . . ? Ariock's sphere would wash out all others on the planet. That would be a dead give-away that he had arrived—and that he cared about Earth.

"I'll have to wear the new inhibitor patch when I go," Ariock realized.

"Did you actually test it on yourself?" Garrett asked with disapproval. He probably thought the Twins had weaponized the patches in some traitorous way.

"Of course." Ariock had tried out one of the stickers, and it had suppressed his powers. When he peeled it off, he regained his full power instantly rather than having to wait three days. It worked like magic.

"You'll need to be extra cautious." A dark undertone in Garrett's voice hinted at misgivings. "The Torth might detect you in the moments before you slap the in-hibitor patch on, so you can't spend too long enjoying a wilderness sabbatical. Just grab the boy and leave."

Ariock gave his great-grandfather an annoyed look. Thomas was not a slave. He needed to be persuaded to return, not browbeaten.

Garrett sucked on his pipe. He seemed to be holding in a lot of possible criti-cisms or warnings. The fact that he was quiet . . .

Well, that made his intentions obvious.

"I don't want you to spy on me," Ariock warned, "while I'm on Earth."

Garrett gave him a defiant stare. "I won't—"

"Whatever conversation I have with Thomas," Ariock said firmly, "it's private. I don't want you listening in."

Garrett's brows knitted in a deep frown. "Ariock, you're going into enemy territory without your powers. I hope you realize that Earth is a danger zone right now. There are a zillion Torth champions who would love to—"

"I'll have a supercom," Ariock broke in. "In case of emergency. But I don't want you there in any way, shape, or form."

Garrett looked pained. "Don't you think you might need backup?"

Maybe. But Thomas needed safety more than Ariock did, and he wouldn't feel safe if Garrett was spying.

"I wouldn't interrupt, I promise," Garrett said. "I'd be out of sight, out of mind. But I need to protect you. You're my great-grandson."

"No." Ariock considered pleading with Garrett to respect his privacy, but he was sick of pleading for his great-grandfather to be reasonable. Garrett ought to know that eavesdropping was disrespectful.

Wasn't that how Garrett's relationship with his daughter had soured? The old man had kept spying on Rose, ostensibly to keep her safe. His overprotectiveness had backfired. Rose had learned to mistrust and then even hate her father.

Yet Garrett continued to believe that his methods were the best. He saw himself as a guru, a wizard, a mentor, when he was actually a screwup.

Perhaps he was just too corrupted by power?

"You're right." Garrett seemed to shrink. "You are absolutely right. I won't spy on you."

Ariock felt guilty. He stood within Garrett's telepathy range, and he had forgotten to censor his thoughts.

Oh well.

In truth, he hated the need to revise and edit his own thoughts. That was one of the main problems he had with telepathy gas. The stuff was humiliating. With mind reading, it was far too easy to offend someone, or humiliate someone, by accident. Was it any wonder the Megacosm had turned toxic over the eons?

"Sorry." Ariock did regret his unintentional insults. "But I think there's good reason for you not to eavesdrop on my visit to Thomas. I need you to protect our lands while I'm gone. You should be focused on Freedomland and the rest of our cities."

Garrett's face creased in a rueful smile. "All right. You can count on me."

"Thank you." Ariock gently laid a hand on Garrett's shoulder. "And thanks for finding him. And everything. You took on a lot of burdens while I . . ." It was difficult to admit. "While I wallowed in guilt and self-pity."

Garrett gave a short laugh. "You're a Dovanack. That's what we do."

Ariock offered a tentative smile. "And we're protectors." That was why Garrett worried for him.

"We are." Garrett smiled up at him. "I know you'll bring the boy back, safe and well."

CHAPTER 14

HUMANITARIAN

"Don't read my mind," Vy said. "And hold still."

She felt a twinge of fear, kneeling so close to someone who could torture her to death with a thought. At least, she thought Zai could do that. Zai used to be a silent slave master not so long ago.

But Ariock trusted this renegade. That counted for a lot.

Vy washed the poorly stitched wound on Zai's upper arm. An ionic blade had sliced through her tungsten armor, all the way down to bone. Zai was lucky not to lose her whole arm. She might still have lost it if she hadn't sought out Vy. Somebody else had closed the wound with a messy touch.

A penitent, no doubt.

Torth without the Megacosm were . . . well . . . primitive. In the Torth Empire, specialist Blue Ranks had mostly done plastic surgery, not battle triage, and they had relied on robotic precision tools plus a lot of collective knowledge. Only a few of them remembered any superficial medical procedures.

A former Blue or Green Rank must have remembered enough about medicine to sew this wound closed, but not enough to incorporate hygiene, or to use absorbable sutures. They hadn't even used silk or nylon. It was some kind of industrial-grade plastic monofilament.

"I'll need to remove these amateur stitches." Vy positioned the arm so that the wound would not gape or tear. "Sorry. It will hurt. I'll use surgical glue and healing foam on you afterward."

"Go ahead," Zai said.

Vy carefully clipped and tugged the stitchwork out. She tried not to feel like a slave grooming her owner. It was all too easy to imagine Zai probing her mind, learning secrets about Earth, humans, or the Bringer of Hope.

"I am not interested in your secrets," Zai said. "I would not harm you in any way. I promise."

Vy just had to trust that this renegade was a true renegade.

"I am simply admiring this field hospital," Zai said.

Medics tended military pilots and newly liberated slaves, bustling beneath floating chandeliers that reflected on enormous glass walls and sky domes. This used to be the Torth equivalent of a yacht club. Bioluminescent vines decorated the waterfront. Sleek-looking submersibles floated next to clean white docks.

People shot mistrustful looks toward Zai. Many had learned to recognize Vy as a medic from paradise.

"I probably shouldn't have come here," Zai said.

"You should have come here first," Vy argued, spritzing the cleaned wound with healing foam. "This is where warriors come for triage."

Zai made a noncommittal sound, and Vy realized that someone had probably pressured the renegade to seek her out. A fellow mind reader?

A lot of newly collared penitents might be injured just as badly as Zai, or worse. Vy would have to double-check to make sure enough medical supplies went to the penitent quarters. Conquests tended to be violent. Former slaves rose up against their former masters, and there was intergenerational rage.

"Okay. All done." Vy added a bandage around the sealed wound for extra shielding. "Don't do anything strenuous for a couple of days. You can remove the bandage tomorrow. Ask that clerk over there for a topical gel that will minimize scarring. If she gives you trouble? Tell her the Lady of Paradise sent you. Or come back and tell me."

"Thank you." Zai looked demure. She stood and walked in the indicated direction.

"Angel." Someone pointed at Vy.

Vy washed her hands and face in a busy public restroom. The industrial metal piping proved that this was actually a co-opted slave zone, with toilet stalls divided by hastily erected privacy screens. It would be improved in future weeks. Freshly conquered cities always needed some rebuilding and improvements.

Everyone was glad to be winning again.

Vy made her rounds, checking on patients with shrapnel cuts or missing fingers from blasts. Medics greeted her with respect. Many had watched her training videos.

She blinked in surprise when a couple of albino shani warriors approached her, decked out in full black-and-purple armor with mantles. Neither looked injured.

"Paradise must have been quite a wondrous place," one of the warriors said, "to produce someone as kind as you." He offered Vy a clean hand towel. "I was just wondering if I can be of service? I have a modicum of healing skill."

"Oh!" Vy reassessed the warrior. "That would be welcome."

"I am actually helping, as well." The other warrior jostled closer. "My aunt is a well-to-do merchant. I've paid ten ummins to fetch things for your field hospital here."

"Oh." Vy looked from one warrior to the other. Had her bloodstained uniform magically transformed into a ballgown? "Well, um, thank you."

She tried to walk on. The two albinos flanked her. They were shorter than her, like most cave people.

"Hair that glows like candlelit copper." The rich warrior gave Vy a worshipful look. "Skin as unblemished as a newborn mushroom. You are beautiful, Lady Vy."

The healer warrior tsked. "He is clearly seeking to buy favors from you. I am here only to help."

"To bask in her radiance, you mean," the other said.

Vy stopped short. Had someone dared these two Alashani to hit on her?

She was a known friend of *rekvehs*, plus she was ungainly and tall. Everyone knew she was in a serious relationship with their messiah. Until now, no Alashani man had ever tried to befriend her.

"If you wish to be helpful," Vy said pointedly, "there is a severely injured pilot over there." She gestured. "I am busy, good warriors. Have a pleasant evening."

She stepped around them.

Behind her, she overheard the healer growl at the rich one. "Agh, why couldn't you have waited to take your own turn?"

The rich one made a haughty sound. "How many warriors has your family produced? None, except for you. You're a lucky charm. Face the truth! You would father powerless babies, even with her."

Vy gaped at the insinuation.

"Well, she'd rather have someone powerful in her bed," the healer snapped back. "Instead of a weakling like you."

Vy whirled around and glared at them.

"I'm hardly weak!" the rich one was saying. "And I'd be much better at showing her a good time."

"Why would she care about superficial tassels and fine dining? She's—"

"More than a breeder!" the rich one puffed up. "Have you forgotten that she comes from paradise? You're not even fit to wash her feet."

"And you're a moron with a tiny—"

Vy hurled the towel down. "I'm not interested in your shriveled mushrooms."

That got their attention. The men gaped at her use of the euphemism for a certain male body part.

"Whatever you've heard about humans and powers? It's wrong." Vy told the lie with as much sincerity as she could muster. She needed to give these cretins a piece of her mind, and never mind who overheard. Human beings were not a breeding program. This was a lesson these Alashani had better learn fast.

Although the evidence was, unfortunately, hard to deny.

The Dovanack family proved it. Four generations of Dovanacks had grown more powerful with every successive generation as they interbred with humans. Thomas had seemed to be an exception to the hybrid rule—until everybody learned that his biological parents were both Torth. He wasn't a hybrid.

The albino men blushed. Then their eyes widened, and they fled.

Vy huffed. Cowards. She wasn't going to do anything as undignified as chase them, although her bionic leg might enable her to catch up easily. She wondered if Cherise had to deal with similar . . .

Everybody in the vicinity was bowing and kneeling.

"Messiah," some murmured.

"Bringer of Hope," others said.

Vy turned, grinning. No wonder the cretins had fled. Ariock towered over the crowd, as big as a nussian even though he wore simple woolens. He strode toward her.

"Vy," he said, his deep voice resonant. "Mind if I . . . oh." He saw the bloodstains on her loose pants and tunic. "You're not hurt, are you?"

He healed her even as she said, "It's not my blood."

Vy shivered from the refreshing sensation. Her various aches and sore spots vanished. She felt energized, like she was just starting her day, although she was hungry.

"I'm not the one who needs healing around here." Vy playfully smacked his chest, knowing it didn't hurt him.

She expected Ariock to look guilty. Instead, he said, "Can I steal you away?"

Vy knew without having to ask he had something important to tell her. Ariock would not interrupt her work otherwise, or ignore hundreds of injured soldiers who could use healing.

And it was secret news. Ariock was acting jovial, masking something.

"Of course." Vy matched his casualness.

Ariock gently placed his huge hands on Vy's shoulders. "Is everything good here?"

"It is." Vy was glad he was finally learning that he could not take care of everyone. The Hero Fleet was important, and so were field hospitals. Ariock was right to let the medics do their jobs without patronizing interference.

Plus, he could not be everywhere at once. He could only heal one person at a time, and his time and power were better spent on mass-teleportation and other major endeavors.

Warping elsewhere was familiar to her by now. The busy atmosphere of the triage center vanished. In its place? Profound silence.

And sunlight.

Vy stood on a mountaintop with Ariock. Clouds drifted below them. A greenish tint to the sky, plus the luminous daytime moons, let her know they were still on the planet Umdalkdul. A distant forest was shades of blue, as lumpy as brambles.

Vy felt Ariock's protective bubble of atmosphere dissipate. The air became fresher, and coldness seeped in.

A crisp breeze stirred the loose wisps of hair around her braid. It was refreshing after the hospital, with its odors of blood and medicine and hygienic salves.

Ariock magically made a thermal blanket appear. He draped it over Vy's shoulders.

"Thanks." Vy gave a little laugh as she wrapped the blanket around herself. Ariock was a hero in all the best ways. "You showed up just in time."

"Oh?" The wind sharpened, and Ariock gazed down at her with concern. "Wait. Were those warriors bothering you?"

Ariock's shadow engulfed her, although he was oblivious to that, as usual. Vy had glimpsed him in storm mode earlier. Mountainous clouds had tracked the approximation of his head and shoulders and upper body. The immensity had flashed with superbolts of lightning, an explosion of clouds aglow from a sun that had already set beyond the watery horizon.

It had been easy for that storm to reach dripping arms across miles and swat Torth fleets into the stinking marsh.

Ariock looked human now. He was being gentle. But Vy was not going to erase the immense Ariock-shaped thunderhead from her memory. He had no clue that Vy had seen him how his enemies saw him.

"No, they were no problem," Vy said breezily. "I was just surprised. They want to breed with humans." She tried to laugh.

Ariock did not look amused. The air pressure dropped.

"It's nothing I can't handle," Vy assured him. She hugged him, wanting kindhearted Ariock instead of angry Ariock. "Just hold me?"

He softened. Soon he was seated on the ground, and Vy got comfortable on his lap. She preferred it when he wore soft clothes like this.

"So, what's up?" she asked.

Ariock leaned back on his hands. "Garrett located Thomas."

Vy's mouth fell open. When Ariock had given up the search on Earth, she'd assumed her guess had been wrong.

"You were right," Ariock said. "He's on Earth."

"Yay!" Vy hugged Ariock. She wanted to dance with joy.

Thomas had been gone forever, it seemed. It had actually been a little more than one month, but so much had changed in that time. Their side of the war had floundered and then found some tentative footing. They had gained the Twins. They had organized a decent fleet.

But anyone at the top knew the Torth Empire still owned far too many resources.

The Torth had countless dreadnoughts and swarmships. They had millions of Rosy Ranks. They had quadrillions of kamikaze slaves. If Ariock spread himself any thinner, Torth armadas would overwhelm his territories and reconquer a planet or two.

"That's great news!" Vy said with enthusiasm.

Ariock sounded pained. "I don't think he wants to be found."

"Oh." Vy supposed that if Thomas wanted to return, he would have done so. "You're trying to decide how to approach him?"

Ariock nodded. "What do you suggest?"

"Hmm." Vy was almost tempted to tell Ariock to item-teleport Thomas without his permission. But that wasn't the right way to handle anybody on their side, let alone Thomas.

She just wanted to speak to her foster brother. She wanted to apologize to him and check to make sure he was all right. She wanted to know why he had left.

Should they send an emissary? Someone friendly and not intimidating? Someone whom Thomas was definitely fond of?

Vy imagined Varktezo wandering the streets of Afton. The chief lab technician would exclaim about clever human habitations and everything else about paradise.

Or what about Kessa? Thomas respected her, and her reaction to human societies might be amusing.

Then Vy imagined humans reacting to ummins. Nope. That was a bad idea, especially if Thomas was someplace like New York City.

Anyhow, Thomas might correctly assume that their choice of a friendly emissary was pandering or manipulative. He might just be offended.

His friendships were difficult to gauge. Azhdarchidae might be the only being he'd be unequivocally happy to see, and a huge sky croc would not blend in on Earth at all.

The Twins? They might be a good choice, but Vy didn't want to remove them from their laboratory bunker. Earth might be dangerous ground, with the whole Torth Empire bent on hunting them.

Besides, there was no guarantee of mutual respect. Might their meeting with Thomas turn into the equivalent of a volatile chemical reaction? That could be bad. The Twins outnumbered Thomas.

Ariock broke into her thoughts. "I want to talk to him face-to-face."

Vy gazed up at Ariock's concerned expression.

"I think I owe him that," Ariock said. "If he ran away, it's at least partly due to me."

Vy realized that she shared just as much guilt. She had not stopped any Alashani from screaming, *Down with rekvehs!* She had failed to shield her foster brother.

They all had.

"Just don't bring Garrett," she said.

Ariock chuckled in a bitter way. "Don't worry. I'm not that stupid."

He was so self-aware, so conscionable, Vy impulsively reached up and kissed him. She loved this man. Ariock was a good person, despite a zillion odds, despite all the power-related reasons why he shouldn't be.

Ariock blushed.

"When I go to Earth," he said, ". . . would you come with me, to protect me?"

Vy studied him. She wasn't exactly strong enough to protect the strongest person in existence.

"The Torth will be alert for my sphere of influence," Ariock explained. "And there are a lot of Torth hiding on Earth right now. So I'll have to temporarily lose my powers."

He opened his palm and showed her a round sticker.

"Oh!" Vy recognized the skin patch, which he must have obtained after his most recent visit to the Twins. "Does it actually work?"

"It seems to," Ariock said.

So. He meant to be powerless when he talked to Thomas. He would be purposely making himself vulnerable, possibly for the first time ever.

He respected Thomas enough to do that.

While the rest of the war council bickered about how Thomas was a traitor, Ariock was going to set aside his own stress and talk to Thomas like a human being. He would risk his own safety in order to communicate with Thomas on equal footing, on neutral ground.

Vy nestled closer. Ariock's stature suited him. It took rare strength to risk a galactic-size reputation along with personal security and self-worth.

"Of course I'll come with you," she said. "And protect you."

CHAPTER 15

MERE MORTALS

Vy still had trouble believing it. "Mongolia?"

"He's in these hills." Ariock began to hike, laden with camping gear. "Garrett said he moves around a lot, and he's impossible to pinpoint. But we'll find him. Or he'll find us."

Vy hurried to catch up. Like Ariock, she wore hiking attire, although she carried a lot less on her back and shoulders. Her bionic leg helped to propel her over gravelly scree and uneven grass.

Slow-moving, puffy clouds dotted the sky. There were so many individual clouds, they could be mistaken for a herd crossing the crystal-blue expanse.

And the hills! Vy gazed at ibex grazing on a distant slope.

Locusts whined in the grass. Butterflies alighted on wildflowers. A cold breeze swept down from the distant snow-capped peaks.

They hiked along a ridge, occasionally dipping into valleys. Vy wasn't too worried about being seen. Even if some nomadic tribesmen happened to spot Ariock from a distance, there were no yurts or vehicles, no trees or bushes. His size would not be apparent. Vy was so bundled up in warm clothes, she might be mistaken for a child next to him, perhaps.

Even if a witness did spread rumors about a Goliath roaming these steppes, Ariock would be gone by the time more people rode out to investigate.

And there was no one.

Vy saw gazelles. As they hiked, an eagle soared past, close enough for its streamlined beak and eyes to be visible.

She wasn't particularly worried about Torth, either. Ariock had a habit of flickering to Earth. He did it unpredictably, and always for a few seconds—just long enough to teleport NAI-13 or other unique items back home to Freedomland. Such flickers must alarm the Torth who prowled Earth, but this time would not seem any different.

The Torth had no idea that Ariock had fully teleported to Mongolia and slapped a temporary inhibitor patch onto his neck.

They would not guess that he was powerless and vulnerable, trudging out in the open. As far as the Torth Empire knew? Ariock was enjoying a day of rest and relaxation in Freedomland. If they happened to scan this area, Ariock would register the same as any large animal, like a yak.

Also, Garrett scanned the Megacosm on a regular basis. He would surely use the supercom to alert Ariock if an emergency occurred.

They explored more hills. More valleys. At one point, a fox trotted boldly across their path.

Ariock's boots left Bigfoot-like impressions, flattening grass and earth. He was laden like a pack animal. They could have wasted a lot of time hunting for brackish ponds or rare creeks, but instead, six gallons of water were buckled against Ariock's chest and back. He carried bedrolls and more.

He never paused for a rest break.

Vy's authentic leg ached from walking all morning and past noon. She wasn't sure if she could match Ariock's endurance forever.

She pondered the mystery of Thomas. Why had he run away?

It seemed uncharacteristic. Thomas held on to his principles even when he suffered abuse. He had obeyed Garrett without complaint. He'd saved the Alashani even after they'd kept him in a dungeon pit.

Had something major shifted in his heart?

Guided by his interior moral code, Thomas saved people and entire civilizations. If Thomas had discarded his guiding principles . . .

That was too terrifying to imagine.

Their shadows grew long.

"What if he went somewhere else?" Vy wondered, struggling to catch up with Ariock. "Maybe he got tired of the scenery."

Ariock gazed at the panorama. He seemed to admire all that he saw. "I think he's here."

It did look like a place Thomas would like, Vy inwardly admitted.

And Ariock, too. He seemed refreshed. Perhaps he identified with Thomas's urge to escape the grind of battles and war councils. Anyone who went solo in this area must be trying to get away from people.

Vy adjusted the bandanna holding back her braids. "If he's here, maybe he's hiding from us."

"Maybe," Ariock admitted. "But I'm not ready to give up."

Vy accepted that. "Good," she said.

Shallow runnels divided the land. She scanned the shadowy areas, wondering if Thomas was watching them.

In a gully that led to more hills, Vy cupped her hands and yelled. "Thomas?"

Ariock's voice was louder, stronger, deeper. "THOMAS?" he boomed across the valley.

A couple of rabbits jumped away.

By mutual unspoken agreement, they shouted into a gully every so often. The only way they'd find Thomas was by chance. Maybe, if they were lucky, he'd set up hidden sensor equipment behind rocks or under grass?

What would Kessa say about this trek? Kessa dreamed of visiting paradise and meeting more humans. If she was here? *Earth seems very empty.* Kessa would probably make a polite observation along those lines, hiding her disillusionment.

Yet parts of Earth were overpopulated. There were major cities. Thomas could have traveled to a pristine reject planet if all he'd wanted was a scenic getaway.

Why choose Earth?

He must have a reason. A human reason, because what else did this planet have to offer over the best uninhabited reject worlds?

Was he visiting someone in particular? Did he even know anyone in northern Asia?

Or was he striving to understand human nature?

If he wanted to understand humans, then he had not given up on himself. Although he had learned that neither of his parents were human, he might still yearn to participate in a culture that valued emotions and creativity and freedom.

If so, then Vy felt hope. He had not run away forever.

The first stars were visible when Ariock eased off his pack. "I guess we'll make camp and search again tomorrow."

Vy didn't argue. She plopped onto a bundle of blankets and rested.

In addition to all the water and bedrolls, Ariock had brought gear that humankind had not yet invented. Ultrasonic bug traps would allow them to sleep comfortably out in the open. Auto-recharging devices leeched energy from the planet's magnetosphere. Even so, it looked like a lot of work to erect a perimeter with sensors and auto-netting.

"Want help?" Vy asked, although the idea of standing and moving again made her want to groan with pain.

"No, you rest." Ariock stretched, then pressed a hand against his lower back. "Ow. So this is what a muscle ache feels like?"

Vy laughed. Ariock had suffused his body with Yeresunsa power all his life, not even realizing it. He had that much excess power. No wonder it didn't occur to him to take rest breaks.

"Honestly," Ariock said, grinning, "I'm glad for a whole day without responsibilities. It's like I'm just . . ." He searched for the right word and laughed at the irony. "Normal."

A second later, predictably, he looked ashamed.

Vy spoke before he could apologize. "It's good to be normal." She admired his strong silhouette as he set up a fire pit. "Although I don't think that describes you."

Ariock smiled as he gathered dry clumps of grass for fuel.

"You're good at this," Vy observed. "It's like you've gone camping without powers before."

"I have," Ariock said, to her surprise. "My dad used to take me on wilderness trips." He used a lighter to get a small fire going. "We camped in North Dakota once, which is kind of like this area."

"Oh." Vy rested her head in one hand.

She guessed Ariock missed his parents as much as she missed her mother. Inside the ten-foot-tall galactic conqueror, there was a normal boy.

"We don't get a choice for dinner." Ariock unwrapped sausages, a meal they both liked, from a sustained frozen packet. He began roasting them on a rotisserie fork.

Night was beginning to engulf the land. Just one familiar old moon.

A freezing wind ruffled Vy's bandanna and made her nose run. As the temperature dropped, she huddled deep inside the blankets. "Mmm," she said, commenting on the smell.

"If we don't find Thomas by the end of tomorrow," Ariock said, "then I guess we'll have to go back. I can't take too many days off in a row."

Because cities would burn. Millions of people could die while Ariock was absent.

He sounded neutral, but Vy could tell that he was managing guilt and disappointment. Ariock never took failure well.

"Well, I'm glad we got some time off," Vy said. "And I'm glad to be here with you."

They ate warm, delicious food. Ariock served her, so she didn't need to unwind herself from the thermal gear.

Afterward, they chatted. They fantasized about decorating their own yurt. That morphed into idealistic lonely retreats. Would Ariock build a Fortress of Solitude? Only if it was a springtime version, with Vy's choice of flowers.

"How about a jungle pond?" Vy said in a teasing tone. "I could bathe there."

Ariock blushed. They both remembered a time when he had glimpsed her breasts, right after their escape from the city of slaves. He had stared at her as if enchanted.

A lonely howl resounded across the land.

Another distant wolf joined the call, and more. Vy could not judge how far away the animals were. Their wails were eerie. She snuggled close to Ariock, appreciating his mass. He shielded her from the wind.

"They won't bother us." Ariock scooped up the remains of their meal and locked the scraps inside a sealed container. "If they do, I'll have to rip off my inhibitor patch."

"Or?" Vy patted her prosthetic. "I could shoot them and protect you."

Ariock laughed in appreciation.

The nocturnal howling ended after a while. Vy and Ariock both agreed that they needed sleep. They settled on their bedrolls, bundled up.

It was so cold.

"Is this supposed to be summer?" Vy murmured. She kept track of the Earth calendar, but maybe she had miscalculated.

Ariock moved. He pulled his bedroll next to hers and lay on his side, shielding her from the wind. He pulled her into his arms.

Vy scrunched closer.

Enfolded in his embrace, she felt warm and safe. She was in a foreign land. It was strange to have no busy agenda, no immediate duties weighing on her mind. There were so many stars above . . .

It was nice to be taken care of.

Vy smiled. She usually draped her arm across Ariock's massive chest, not the other way around. She was always ready to wake him up if things started to float. There was always some wariness in the back of her mind, whenever she was this close with him.

But not right now.

"I keep trying to connect to the air, to make the wind die down," Ariock confessed. "It's weird that I can't."

"Mmm. You're warm." Vy snuggled against his stomach. She liked the pullover he wore, so much softer than armor. "I can sleep like this. Are you comfy?"

He stirred. "I'm afraid I'll accidentally hurt you with my arm spikes."

Vy gave him a playful kick. "You've never worried about that before," she pointed out.

The iron spikes embedded in each of Ariock's forearms were blunted. Really, they were only dangerous when used with violent strength. His tailor modified his custom-sized shirts to accommodate the disfigurement the Torth Empire had left him with.

"I should file them down," he said.

"No." Vy touched one of the spikes on its blunt edge. "You won these."

The Torth had embedded iron loops into Ariock's radius and ulna bones so they could chain him up. Ariock had since sculpted and refashioned the crude iron into something subtle that helped him kill Torth.

"They're like a collar scar," Vy went on. "I don't want you to hide any part of yourself."

Ariock gazed at Vy with tenderness. "You're beautiful."

Vy laughed, aware that her braids were coming apart and she hadn't showered. Poor Ariock just didn't know that other women existed. Women who wore makeup and who tightened their butts by wearing high heels.

She hoped he never caught on.

"You're pretty cute yourself," she teased. It was true. Ariock looked super comfortable, his face illuminated by starlight.

She wasn't sure which one of them began to remove the layers of blankets and clothing between them. Vy probably started it. But Ariock joined in.

They became like one body under the stars.

Nothing floated. No lightning webbed the sky, and there were no earthquakes. The wind continued to blow. All it brought was the scent of wildflowers.

Ariock had superhuman size, but so what? The differential between them was no greater than that of some ordinary couples on Earth.

They were two humans. Mere mortals.

The Twins had unknowingly—or perhaps knowingly?—invented a miracle for Vy and Ariock.

It hardly mattered that the benefit was temporary. It was even better that way. Vy would never want Ariock robbed of his powers, which suited him so well. Majestic strength was part of who he was, as surely as she had a bionic leg.

She was closer to him than she'd ever been, under the stars. She felt his love for her. It did not need to be spoken. It was obvious and unquestionable.

Afterward, she slept in his embrace.

CHAPTER 16

AN END

Vy stretched and yawned. The sky was a cerulean baby blue swept with dramatic gold-tinged clouds.

She disentangled herself from Ariock's arm, using the iron spike as a handle. Her cheeks heated with a pleasurable remembrance of last night.

Dew melted where the morning sun shone. She frowned at the campfire as she redid her braids. How was it still crackling? Hadn't the flames sputtered to embers last night?

A stranger sat on a low rock by the campfire.

Vy squeaked in surprise.

He wore a round cap trimmed in fur, a striped wool kaftan, and fur-trimmed leggings. A large bird perched on his gloved and padded forearm. The eagle was at least the size of the stranger's torso. Its bronze feathers were fluffed to ward off the morning chill, but its golden eyes tracked every move Vy made.

She took a closer look at the stranger's face. "Thomas?"

Vy struggled to comprehend. He looked different. Tanned, and also more confident or something. She was so used to seeing Thomas in a white lab coat or in drab woolens, floating in a dark corner, her mind wanted to argue with this whole situation.

"Freedom empanadas." Thomas held up an unmarked frozen food package that clearly came from Ariock's gear. "Are these stuffed with cliff hopper meat?"

Vy rubbed sleep from her eyes. "Uh, I think so." Cliff hoppers were indigenous to Reject-20 and easy to farm. Their meat tasted like chicken.

"Mind if I share your breakfast?" Thomas asked. "I'll do the cooking."

He no longer sounded childish. His voice had deepened to an adolescent timbre.

"Sure," Vy said.

The eagle flapped a bit, then settled, as Thomas balanced thawing empanadas on rotisserie forks. He rested the forks against rocks, perfectly balanced.

Vy felt like she was watching a different person, not the foster brother she used to take care of. He moved so easily. Maybe he was relying on his powers? That would explain the campfire, anyway.

He must be draining himself constantly in order to go unnoticed by Torth agents on Earth.

Ariock stirred awake and sat up. He followed Vy's gaze to Thomas. "Hey."

"Hi, Ariock," Thomas said.

As if nothing was awkward. As if this was just a normal outing.

The air seemed fraught with unvoiced caution. Ariock and Thomas had a lot to say to each other, and they must be afraid of driving the other away.

"Want any water?" Ariock asked.

"I'm good," Thomas said. "I have a canteen."

Ariock gathered the blankets and relocated himself next to Vy at the campfire. Thomas made no complaint about the fact that they both sat beyond his telepathy range. He seemed content to not read their minds. He looked comfortable, cross-legged with his eagle, letting the empanadas cook.

"You look well," Ariock said.

"So do you," Thomas said. "It's good to see you two. It's weird—I didn't sense your sphere of influence at all." He looked at Ariock quizzically. "And I figured it would take at least another week for you to find me."

Ariock looked like he was about to brag about the temporary inhibitor patch. But then he heard the implication in Thomas's words. "You knew we would come here?"

"I figured you would search." Thomas stroked his eagle's head. The bird's eyes went half-lidded in pleasure. "And you're tenacious. Heh. Or rather, Garrett is tenacious. He must have searched tirelessly for weeks." He glanced up at the clouds, as if to acknowledge an invisible listener. "I guess he's here, too. Hey, Garrett."

"I told him to stay away." Ariock sounded defensive.

"Uh-huh." Thomas sounded skeptical.

That was fair. Garrett tended to lie, and he might even lie to Ariock. If Garrett was invisibly here, eavesdropping on their conversation, none of them would know it. Mind readers could not detect disembodied minds unless the clairvoyant ghost was right on top of them.

"Well, anyway," Thomas said, "I'm glad for your visit. It's nice to see you."

Vy faced her foster brother across heat-bent air. When would one of them break the ice and talk about something important?

This felt similar to the first time they had ever met. Vy had been there, in the sky room, when Ariock was afraid to move, afraid to accidentally foreground his size in front of strangers. And her foster brother had gone ahead and blurted Ariock's fears out loud. But he had also shared his own secret, his own deep vulnerability, to put the giant at ease.

Vy didn't want to scare Thomas away now. She searched for a nonthreatening conversation opener.

"You made a new friend." She gestured to the eagle.

"Yep." Thomas smiled with fondness. "I have an affinity with animals." He smoothed the bird's feathers. "I've trained her to be my extra eyes and report back to me. That's how I found you."

"Oh." Vy privately doubted Thomas had effortlessly trained a full-grown eagle in a matter of days. He might have jump-started that training with his power of suggestion.

"You're not using surveillance drones?" Ariock asked.

"Nope," Thomas said. "I didn't bring any alien tech. I wanted to see how little I needed to get by alone."

Vy nearly asked him why. She stopped herself, because it might come out like an accusation.

She couldn't think of a tactful way to broach the topic of his abandonment. She settled for the simplest and purest truth. "I missed you."

Thomas's smile was wan.

And bitter.

"Everyone misses you." Ariock's deep voice startled a jerboa into racing away. "Especially me."

Thomas did not look fond or pleased. His expression was cagey.

The eagle fluffed up as it watched the fleeing rodent. Thomas made a throwing gesture, and the eagle launched, flapping toward the jerboa.

Thomas painstakingly stood. He carried the hot empanadas away from the fire. His walking had improved so much, Vy was no longer sure if he wore leg braces under his pants or not.

He placed the breakfast on a rock, like an offering. "This is yours," he told Ariock and Vy. "So you don't need to come into my range."

Did he think they were afraid of him?

Just because they'd learned that his biological parents were both Torth?

"I'm not afraid of having you reading my mind," Ariock said, while Vy went to fetch the meal.

"I know." Thomas went back to the fire and sat on his rock. "I'd just rather avoid overhearing your stress." He nodded toward a clump of grass. "Mice are plenty of complexity for me to absorb right now. I don't need to add any more."

Was that a hint that he'd really needed this vacation?

Or was he telling them that he resented his most recent task of absorbing over a million penitent minds within a few days?

"Thomas . . ." Ariock hesitated. "I'm sorry for all that's happened."

Vy handed Ariock two empanadas and gave him an encouraging look. She sat down and nibbled a corner of her meal. Thomas was already digging into his.

Ariock went on. "I don't care about your parentage. I don't consider you a Torth."

Thomas gave him a flat look. "You should care."

Was that anger? Vy couldn't quite read his expression.

"I just mean that I'm not defining you by your biological parents." Ariock thought for a moment. "As far as I'm concerned, you're human in all the ways that matter."

Thomas regarded Ariock from across the fire. The position of his head made Vy think that he was disparaging.

"I'm still your friend." Ariock set aside his breakfast. He was trying hard. "So are Vy, and Kessa, and a lot of other people."

"Mm-hm." Thomas ate his breakfast and said nothing else. His reaction was so neutral, it could have turned the sky gray.

"We all miss you." Ariock did not quite plead for Thomas to return, but the note of despair was obvious. They needed the Wisdom of prophecy in order to win the war.

"I'm sure you do." Thomas finished off the empanada with relish. "Well, I think it's kind of you to come all the way out here, while your troops are left hanging, just to tell me how much you miss me. That's nice. I appreciate the effort." He dusted off his hands. "But I'm not coming back."

Ariock looked as if he'd been attacked.

Vy felt shocked, too. Was this her foster brother? The Thomas she knew would never just up and quit. Not when so many people needed him.

"Eat your breakfast," Thomas said invitingly. "Before my eagle steals an empanada."

Ariock looked like he was searching for the right words.

Vy felt like she was witnessing an armistice between two nations. Ariock was good, and he was right. Meanwhile, Thomas was her rescuer as well as her foster brother. Surely they could come to a mutual understanding?

"Thomas." Vy leaned forward. "We know you've been treated unfairly. We talked about it a lot after you left. Ariock is making major changes."

Ariock nodded, giving her a grateful look. "That's right. People won't be allowed to hold angry rallies against *rekvehs* anymore. I've tolerated the undergrounders more than enough. We'll make sure no one attacks you."

"That's a nice sentiment." Thomas's tone was uncaring. "But it's pointless."

Ariock stared at him.

"If you stomp down on the undergrounders with laws, and enforcement for those laws," Thomas explained, "you'll come across like a tyrant and a brute. They'll trust you less. And they'll hate me as much as ever."

Ariock frowned, as if stumped by a difficult problem.

Vy inwardly thought that Thomas might be right. The hatred against mind readers had very deep roots. People would try to assassinate Thomas no matter what laws existed, no matter how well they were enforced.

But why was Thomas letting that stop him?

The undergrounders schemed against an evil that only existed in their imaginations. Flen preached against an illusion. Surely Thomas knew that? He had never let haters or bullies stand in his way before.

"I'll protect you," Ariock said. "I promise. I'll make sure you're safe."

"I don't care." Thomas gazed at the dancing flames of the campfire, perhaps using his powers to refuel it. "I didn't run away from haters, Ariock. That's not why I'm here. I came to Earth to atone."

To atone?

Vy surreptitiously studied her foster brother, trying to guess at the guilt weighing on his soul. Did he still hate himself for sentencing Ariock to death? Or for torturing Cherise? He had done those things in order to survive and to escape. Plus, he had made up for his wrongs. What additional absolution was he looking for?

"You saw my confrontation with my father?" Thomas asked. "Did Garrett show it to you with telepathy gas?"

Ariock hesitated, then gave an embarrassed nod.

Vy nodded, too. She was never going to be able to forget the shock of experiencing the Megacosm in that way.

"Then you know how the Torth Empire experienced it," Thomas said. "You felt, thirdhand, how much guilt he carried for fathering me."

That was true. It wasn't the key takeaway Vy had focused on, and Garrett had not seemed to care much about it, either. But yes. The Somehow Nexus had felt a lot of guilt as he'd blasted himself to death.

Thomas had witnessed that suicide firsthand. A child should not have to absorb that much torment, especially from a parent.

"Most Torth feel guilt," Thomas said. "I feel it, too. I came to Earth to find out if there was any path to redemption for me. I thought maybe I could earn enough salvation to approximate feeling like a human being instead of a monster."

Vy wanted to hug him. Why did the best people in the universe need to be so self-hating? She wanted to assure him that he was human in every way that mattered.

Instead, she stayed on her side of the campfire. Thomas seemed to want personal space.

"But I began to question why I was atoning," Thomas went on. "Was it for the sins of my parents? Because they paid. They paid for what they did."

Vy did not question that.

"Or was it the things I did as a Yellow Rank?" Thomas asked. "But I made up for those. As best I could, anyway."

"You have nothing to atone for," Ariock said. Vy nodded in agreement.

"Garrett would say otherwise," Thomas pointed out. "Lots of people would say otherwise."

"They don't count," Ariock said.

"Kessa," Thomas said. "She counts."

Vy could not imagine Kessa condemning Thomas as a sinner, or anything like that. She began to say so.

"I meet all the criteria for being a penitent Torth," Thomas said. "That's what I am. According to the laws of our society—the laws I set up, with Kessa, and with your help—I am a penitent."

Vy wanted to reject his Torth identity like it was poison. She was willing to pretend he was fully human. Heck, she had never even suspected that he was an alien when they'd lived in the Hollander home. That must count for a lot.

"You're not a Torth," she said, pleading for him to understand.

Thomas faced her over the campfire. "But that's exactly what I am."

She tried to think of another angle. How could she convince him to reject his supposed Torth-ness? If she could do it, surely he could, too?

"Growing up," Thomas said, "I observed the people around me like they were alien life forms. I never belonged. And later, when the Torth enfolded me into the Megacosm? I felt like I was home."

Vy didn't want to hear that.

"I never fit in with humans," Thomas said. "I tried." He gestured at the vista around them. "I came here, to Earth, to try one last time. I went to a high school in Finland. But there's nothing left in me that's childlike enough to mesh with kids. Then I went to a city in Bangladesh, to be a foreign stranger. It didn't work. I couldn't keep up the charade."

Vy stared at him. Her heart was breaking. It sounded like he really had tried.

"When I believed that I had one alien parent and one human," Thomas said, "I wondered why my supposedly human father left so little impression on my genes. Now I know. I don't have anything human in me."

Vy wondered why he kept insisting on reminding them of that painful fact. Why was he making such a point about being inhuman, nothing but a rotten Torth?

"So you're genetically a Torth." Ariock said that forcefully, no doubt as pained as Vy felt. "Fine." He blew out a breath, as if to dismiss the confession. "That doesn't mean you're bad! All that really matters is the way you were raised. So, you see? You're as human as I am."

Thomas shook his head without shame or pride. "That's not all that matters."

"Your genetic heritage doesn't change anything," Ariock insisted.

"It changes everything." Thomas sat there, implacable, unruffled. "It matters to everyone. Including me."

Ariock looked uncomfortable, having been called out on his polite fib. "Okay." He hunched and admitted the unpleasant truth. "Yeah, maybe it changes a few things. But it doesn't mean you should quit fighting the Torth Empire! They're in the wrong. You know that."

Vy watched her foster brother, certain that Ariock's arguments must have made some impact. Surely he knew that Ariock was right?

"The empire is terrible," Thomas agreed. "But the Torth are my people."

Vy had a sinking feeling.

"And guess what?" Thomas said. "I'm not ashamed."

Vy winced. Surely Thomas could not be proud of . . . well . . . his Torth heritage?

Ariock looked like he was struggling with what to say.

"Don't worry," Thomas said, seeing their appalled looks. "I'm not planning to join the Torth Empire. I would never do that."

Vy tried to calm down. Of course her foster brother was not evil. How could she even consider that?

"But," Thomas went on, "I won't fight them, either."

That was almost as bad.

Vy stared at her foster brother, betrayed. Was he really okay with just stepping aside to let doom happen?

This was not the friend and brother she loved. It couldn't be. After all the plans he had set in motion, after all the wonders he had accomplished, after all they had suffered in order to beat a galactic empire that no one had been able to challenge until now . . . he wanted to just quit and . . . agh!

Would he let the Torth win?

Ariock looked so upset, the sky ought to be filled with storm clouds rather than sunny. "You're not evil. I don't believe that."

Thomas gave Ariock a pitying look. "Very few Torth fit the human definition of evil. They collectively don't deserve what we've been doing to them."

Vy remembered her time as a slave, fearing death every time she walked the indoor boulevards. The omnipresent threat had been ordinary, commonplace Yellow Ranks. Their flippant murder of innocent slaves certainly seemed evil to her.

Even unripe Torth children, those still on baby farms, had enough influence over their one or two occasional adult orbiters to get their personal slaves killed.

There were no innocents among the Torth. Not when the collective made all the decisions.

Did Thomas not see that?

"It's not your fault that I'm here," Thomas said to both of them. "My problem isn't you, or anyone else. It's here." He touched his own chest. "I've always felt torn between two civilizations. I just got torn apart. I can't continue to rob Torth of free will like I've been doing. I can't live with destroying the Torth people. I know the empire is horrible, and it should be taken down, but I cannot be the one to do it." He slumped, and he sounded broken. "They are my people."

"Garrett could say the same thing." Ariock's voice was rough. "But he isn't abandoning us."

"Garrett isn't a Torth," Thomas said. "He's a hybrid, and it's obvious. He has an Alashani temper. He is Alashani in his heart."

True.

"I was willing to decimate the Torth when I believed I wasn't really one of them." Thomas looked ashamed. "But now I can't. There is no difference between me and the penitents. Absolutely none."

Vy forced herself to look at Thomas, to see what he was urging them to see.

The truth.

He was not human. Not at all. He wore human garb right now, but he was a Torth—and not in a minor way that could be downplayed and whispered about. No. He was wholly Torth.

"The Torth system is evil," Thomas said. "But not the Torth people."

"But the people make the system." Vy could hardly believe that she needed to point out such an obvious fact. "They built it. They maintain it. They vote for all the evil laws."

"That's how I justified punishing them." Thomas acknowledged her with his ancient eyes. "I told myself that every individual Torth is culpable, at least to some degree, including myself. Anyone who participated in the system is automatically guilty. That's why I came here to do penance."

Vy swallowed the arguments she had been preparing. Thomas sounded like he had given the matter more thought than she had.

"I met another orphan here on Earth," Thomas said, "in a similar situation. He was cast aside by parents who couldn't raise him. He struggles to prove his value to a society that doesn't care. Neither of us chose our parents. We did not choose to be born into this world, or this culture. So what are we guilty of? Original sin? Is that what the penitents have to atone for? Is that why they're on their knees?"

Vy doubted there was much common ground between a human orphan and a penitent. Few human orphans were guilty of torturing slaves to death.

Then again . . .

Someone who was truly desperate might resort to acts of violence and depravity. Vy had seen that, as a caretaker of unwanted children herself.

"People do terrible things to survive," Thomas said. "I know you don't like to think of your time as a slave, Vy. But I know your memories. You considered leaving Delia to die. That thought crossed your mind, and if your situation had gotten to a point of utter hopelessness, you would be carrying that guilt around."

He was right.

Vy hated to think of herself as that kind of person. She couldn't even look at Ariock. She didn't want to see his reaction.

"And you, Ariock," Thomas said. "You're fully aware that the beasts you faced in the arena were artificially enraged. The Red Ranks wanted to force you to kill a prison guard, Hithiniesel. They killed her instead when you refused. But what if they'd kept pushing you to do that? Day after day? What if they'd threatened to torture your mom until you did it? Eventually, you would have complied."

Ariock bowed his head.

Vy realized that the Torth Majority had actually managed to push Ariock to that extreme. It had taken them more than a year, but they had gotten the Giant to kill Jinishta and more than a hundred other good warriors.

Thomas did not need to point that out. He had a point. Vy was beginning to see it.

"I survived more intense pressure than either of you can imagine." Thomas got to his feet. "You saw me with the privileges of a Yellow Rank, but inside, I was suffering. I was under the constant threat of death. And despite being a supergenius, even with all the knowledge of the galaxy at my disposal, I could not figure a way out. I was pushed to unimaginable extremes."

Vy had never heard Thomas admit to suffering. This was new.

"Just like every Torth in the Megacosm," Thomas said. "So now I'm a penitent, like the others. But without true, personal reasons to atone? Atonement is meaningless. And without any end in sight, it's pointless."

He made a shrill whistle. The eagle wheeled and flew toward him.

"Migyatel foresaw the tyrant I would become," Thomas said. "It was her final vision. She was right about me."

Vy recalled the traumatic death of the prophet. Migyatel had died from a stroke, and the Alashani population had blamed Thomas. In all the chaos that had ensued—trying to get Thomas's medicine, facing down Jinishta's army, meeting Garrett for the first time, and then major battles and a planetary annihilation—she had forgotten that Thomas must have absorbed Migyatel's final prophetic vision.

That vision had been so overwhelming, so disturbing, it had killed the prophet.

"What did Migyatel see?" Vy asked.

"Zombies," Thomas replied. "Hordes of zombies doing terrible things. Troops that obeyed my commands without question. Torth fearing and worshipping me. Cities burning. And me, a tyrant. I became a Commander of All Living Things. She saw that I could destroy the Torth Empire."

Judging by his bitter tone, he definitely wasn't proud of this. He sounded disgusted.

"I hoped it would never happen," Thomas said. "But it did. And now? I won't be that person. I'm sorry, but my heart isn't in this war. I can't give you the unflagging cooperation you want. I'm not a conqueror."

He held out his padded arm, and the eagle alighted. She flapped to adjust her position.

"I waited for you to find me," Thomas said, "because I wanted to say goodbye."

Vy felt devastated.

"I'm glad I got to see you one last time." Thomas gave them each a nod.

Ariock leaned onto his knees, desperate. "Thomas, we need you." His voice roughened, strained by his admission of vulnerability. "I need you. Please. You know we can't survive without you."

"I'm sorry." Thomas's smile was tense and sad. "Good luck with it all."

He walked away.

CHAPTER 17

THE RETURN OF WISDOM

Ariock searched for something wise to say. He wasn't losing just a friend. Thomas was the only hope for lasting freedom in the galaxy.

But Thomas had clearly thought about his decision, and he wasn't impressed by Ariock's offer to protect him, or even by Ariock's friendship. He had chosen to quit.

Because he didn't believe that the Torth were evil.

Because he refused to conquer them.

No, that wasn't exactly what Thomas had implied. He still disdained the Torth Empire—but not its people.

Instead, he spoke for them. He was giving a voice to all the penitents.

Not just the penitents. He was also speaking for the unconverted masses. The low ranks. The children on baby farms. The silent Majority who obeyed the Death Architect because they were afraid to risk their lives and take a chance on something new. Thomas had spoken on behalf of trillions of mind readers, as if he was their ambassador.

Or their sovereign.

Thomas had presented his argument to the one person in the galaxy who could make a major change to laws and reevaluate what the Torth were and how they should be treated.

Ariock stood. "We never should have been making zombies."

His voice carried over the campfire and the plains.

Thomas stopped.

"We can't destroy the empire without Torth allies," Ariock acknowledged. "And I've been mishandling them. They need to become equals in our society. There needs to be a way for that to happen. You're right."

It was a strange truth to admit. Ariock had been so focused on regaining Thomas's help, he had overlooked his own recent positive experiences with renegade Torth allies. Zai and the Twins were incredibly helpful. They were so much more than slave labor.

If penitents were doomed to castigation forever, without a path to redemption, then there would be no more warriors like Zai, no more military scientists like the Twins. Torth renegades would never join Ariock and his forces on a galactic scale.

That needed to change.

Thomas studied Ariock from afar, searching. Maybe he wasn't sure whether he could trust the friend who had ignored his advice. Ariock, like everyone else, had relegated the penitents to the status of inferiors.

Distrust was fair here. Ariock did not pressure him.

"Your invitations in the Megacosm paid off," Vy said. "You were right when you said the Twins would join us. They did."

Thomas looked surprised and interested.

Ariock's heartbeat quickened with hope. Vy had said the perfect thing. "That's right," Ariock said. "They invented a temporary inhibitor." He indicated the patch stuck to the nape of his neck. "So I can go undetected. It works like a miracle."

"Really?" Thomas looked intrigued. "Hm. Well, that is unexpected. And kind of cool."

Judging by his caution, he might think the Twins were being mistreated or coerced.

That wasn't too far off from the truth, Ariock realized with shame. Evenjos had nearly murdered the Twins. Many citizens of Freedomland wished the *rekveh* scientists were dead. They had to be protected in a secret bunker with guards at the door. If there was even a rumor that their remorse was an act, they likely wouldn't survive past a day or two.

Ariock winced in shame. Violence against children was something that Torth did. It shouldn't be such a strong possibility on his side.

The realization made him think more seriously about what Thomas had said. Hatred against penitents would not magically die down. And it was a major obstacle. It could not be swept under a rug, or dismissed and ignored. People such as the Twins, and Thomas, needed a path to prove their value. Otherwise . . . well, why should they value Ariock's brand of freedom?

"They really want to meet you," Vy told Thomas. "They think of you as a hero."

Ariock nodded supportively. "They're residing in your lab complex," he said, just to make it clear that the Twins were not shackled in a dungeon. "They've been a huge help. They implied they can work miracles if they ever get a chance to hash over their ideas with you."

Thomas looked cautious, like he wasn't sure he believed this reversal.

After a moment, he came back to the campfire. He sat.

"I'm concerned," Thomas said, "not only about renegades who decide to help you destroy the Torth Empire, but about Torth people in general." He gazed at the flames. "I'm not cut out to mete out death and destruction to them on a huge scale. I'm not like you, Ariock."

Ouch.

But it was a valid point. Ariock stared into the flames, reflecting on how a less violent future might play out.

"I'm done slaughtering my own people," Thomas said. "And I can't keep defending the people who hate penitents like me."

He was right, Ariock realized. Their side of the war—the good guys—really needed to start respecting Torth as people.

People like Zai.

And the Twins.

Because they were not the enemy. And they were not lesser allies. They were outstandingly helpful.

They were, in fact, refugees.

Ariock felt chagrin at his own stupidity. Refugees like Zai and the Twins deserved protection in exactly the same way as the liberated slaves. To deny them full rights was wrong. And cruel.

Why had it taken him this long to consciously realize it?

Well, he supposed an unmitigated flood of Torth overrunning Freedomland might have a negative impact, even if they were all refugees and allies. Telepathy made them naturally insular.

A balance would need to be found.

Sociological experts such as Thomas and Kessa would need to figure out how former slaves and former Torth could integrate nicely without destroying each other.

"We're going to make changes." Ariock stood, wind whipping him. He walked around the campfire, toward Thomas. "I don't blame you if you don't believe me. But please read my mind?"

He towered over Thomas. Looming was rude, but he wasn't going to sit, uninvited. Not after the way he had mistreated his friend.

Thomas studied him. The eagle cocked her head and assessed Ariock with golden eyes.

"I don't know how well Torth refugees can meld with our culture of freedom," Ariock admitted. "But we need to try. I'm going to put a stop to the whole prison and slave labor system."

"Adjust it," Vy suggested. "It's fair to take prisoners in war. There are still enemy Torth."

Ariock was glad she had articulated that worry.

"The Torth Megacosm is toxic," Thomas agreed. "That whole system needs to be dismantled. It ruins good people, twisting them into monsters." He sounded like he was speaking from personal experience.

"But as individuals," Vy said, "the Torth are like any other people. Some are terrible. Some are great."

Ariock had watched enough human media to understand that no group was a monolith. Vy was an angel, but that was because of the mother who had raised her, and the company she kept, and the experiences that shaped her. It was not because she was born human.

"It's the people around us who unlock our potential," Thomas said. "One way or the other. It's the society we're in."

Thomas looked up at Ariock, for the first time in a long time, with respect. He looked like he was seeing a hero.

"It's the friends we have," Thomas said.

Ariock welcomed his friend's scrutiny. Maybe Thomas was probing his mind, but that was okay. The Wisdom of prophecy needed to be respected and even honored— not as a cretinous ally with a blighted heritage, but as a sovereign in his own right.

Because that was who he was.

"I'm not a sovereign," Thomas said. "Maybe the Upward Governess could have been that, but not me. I'm not cut out for it."

Ariock snorted. "Neither am I." Was Thomas oblivious to the fact that he had literally led people to freedom multiple times? "If I can lead armies," Ariock said, "then you can guide the Torth to a better future." He laughed. "Who else could we trust for that? Not Garrett."

Thomas looked thoughtful, perhaps mulling over the possibility of advocating for Torth penitents.

"You're already their leader," Vy added. "You're the reason any Torth would join us."

Ariock gazed down at Thomas, willing him to see the possibilities. The future did not have to be grim or full of hate. A bridge between former slaves and former Torth was still possible.

Maybe it was a lot to ask, for Thomas to give them all yet another chance?

But couldn't he at least agree to meet the Twins for a few minutes?

"Agh." Thomas looked away. "Go back to your side of the fire, Ariock. I'm getting a crick in my neck."

Ariock stepped back.

Then he stopped. Had he expressed how much he wanted to change things? Should he praise Zai for how vital she was to their victories?

Or maybe he should mention his visit to the Great Mwagru. The seer had probed his self-sabotaging fears and helped him to realize that the zombies were a terrible moral conflict. That was why Ariock dreamed of death.

Redemption for Torth should have been his top priority all along. Not city-by-city conquests. Not space battles. In the savagery of war, he had fallen off his original trajectory and failed to course-correct. Garrett and many other people on the war council had completely lost sight of the goal.

"I'll return," Thomas said.

Ariock bounced on his toes in delight.

"But only," Thomas said in a warning tone, "if you hold to what you said. Individual Torth should atone for their misdeeds, but there's got to be an end to it. They're not guilty of being born and raised the way they were."

"Of course." Ariock beamed. His smile was huge.

"That goes for me as well." Thomas's tone was still a warning. "I need the same liberty as you."

Ariock nodded.

Thomas gave him a stern look. "So you'll prevent Garrett from chaining me up, or imprisoning me, or humiliating me in public."

"Garrett will be reasonable," Ariock said. The old man was devoted to the prophecies. He knew how much they needed the Wisdom.

"Have I ever been wrong about Garrett before?" Thomas asked.

Ariock wanted to defend his great-grandfather, but he closed his mouth. Thomas was hardly ever wrong about anything.

"To Garrett," Thomas said, "every Torth is his murderous father. How well do you think he'll tolerate armies of Torth who aren't mentally enslaved? And me, actively leading and promoting them?"

That was a valid point.

Wisdom implied at least some trust. Without the same rights as free people, Thomas was just a stooge. He was the fool of someone else. That was a problem. How could he act as the Wisdom of prophecy while he was enslaved to Garrett?

Ariock went back to his side of the fire, lowered himself next to Vy, and folded his legs. He wasn't going to have an important discussion with his friends while looming over them.

"I didn't think I'd need to deal with Garrett for this long," Thomas admitted in a wry tone. "No offense, Ariock, but I figured he was destined to die. He takes stupid risks every day."

Ariock smiled at the banter. But he acknowledged Thomas's concerns with a nod. "I'll act as a buffer between you and Garrett."

He should have been better at that all along. He just hadn't respected Thomas enough.

"I need your promise," Thomas said.

Ariock thought about it. Thomas was asking to be a sovereign instead of the equivalent of a torturer. It would be a paradigm shift. Garrett and a lot of other people wouldn't like it.

"I promise," Ariock said. "No one on our side will undermine you again. Not while I'm watching."

There was that look from Thomas again. Respect. Warmth.

Vy looked from one to the other. She looked proud of them.

Ariock felt like a hero.

Soon he would need to return to the war, along with Thomas, but the crackling campfire was relaxing. Vy and Thomas looked cozy. There was something appealing about the wide-open landscape and the fresh air that swept off the distant mountains.

Ariock was about to suggest that they camp out for the rest of the day when his wristwatch buzzed.

That was an emergency signal.

"Lovely timing," Thomas said.

He had directed Ariock to construct superluminal relays, including one embedded on the dark side of Earth's moon. The system was rudimentary. It was just enough for a signal to reach Earth. This particular beacon would only go off if a major metropolis was under attack.

"I was hoping we could enjoy the rest of the day." Thomas squinted toward the horizon, as if imprinting the scene on his infallible memory.

The vast silence, and the crackle of flames, invited stillness. This was not a place for crises or hustle and bustle. This was a place of no expectation.

Yet Ariock felt millions or even billions of unheard screams.

He sensed the threat to his people almost as keenly as if he was a mind reader. He had to rescue people. So he climbed to his feet. "There's a galactic war."

"Yeah, yeah." Thomas rocked forward, standing up. "Okay." His eagle fluttered her wings to keep her balance. "I have some loose ends to tie up here on Earth, but they can wait."

"Like a hidden streamship?" Vy guessed.

"Yep," Thomas admitted. "And someone I made a promise to. I'll have to come back later, just for a short time."

"No problem." Ariock was curious, but he would ask about Thomas's adventures on Earth when there wasn't a crisis. "Do you want to bring your eagle?" He prepared to encompass his friends and supplies within his awareness.

"No," Thomas said. "I'd rather not rip her away from everything familiar."

Ariock thought of his sky room, which used to be his entire world. The Torth had wrenched him away from everything familiar. It had been traumatic.

Let the eagle soar through her stress-free future. That was fair. Animals probably wouldn't even notice if Torth took over Earth.

"I hope you don't mind if I give her a small parting gift?" Thomas gestured with his free hand, and a rabbit hopped out from a clump of grass.

The eagle hopped off Thomas's arm and snatched the prey in her talons. She took off with the snack, winging toward the hills.

"Did you just . . . ?" Vy trailed off. She looked sickened. "You just brainwashed that rabbit, didn't you?"

"I feel bad about it." Thomas peeled off his padded glove. "I praise my eagle friend every time she catches prey without my help. But I, uh, wanted a way to befriend an eagle."

Ariock nodded to himself, inwardly relieved that Thomas had not brainwashed the pet that had perched on his arm. Knowing Thomas, he probably only targeted prey that was plentiful and not endangered or nursing babies.

"He's living off the land." Ariock gently put a hand on Vy's shoulder. "It's no different from what the tribespeople out here do."

"Right." Vy sounded mollified. She must realize that Azhdarchidae hunted in much the same way.

Thomas focused on the campfire and the flames died. Wisps of smoke rose from blackened clumps of grass.

He must enjoy his independence. It probably felt especially sweet after a lifetime of being dependent on caretakers. He could probe an eagle's mind, or peer through the eyes of a mouse, and gain a good sense about the lay of the land.

"Ready?" Ariock reached for the inhibitor patch on his neck. The longer he was absent from the war, the worse things could get.

"Fascinating. An inhibitor patch?" A curious, hungry look entered Thomas's eyes. "I assume the Twins researched how it affects your glymphatic system? Never mind, don't answer that. I'll meet them and ask."

Ariock exchanged a happy, excited look with Vy.

"Ready," Vy said.

"I'm ready," Thomas said resolutely. "Remember, this is contingent on how you treat penitents and other Torth."

Ariock tore off the patch. Within seconds, the edges of his awareness grew. And so did his confidence that together with Thomas, he was capable of transforming the Torth people while also freeing the entire galaxy.

His determination manifested as wind. The clouds sailed faster. Butterflies rose high into the sky. The song of crickets fell into rhythm with his breathing.

Ariock closed his eyes and tuned out the expectant faces of Vy and Thomas. He reached through the stratosphere and into deep space. Soon he was speeding, disembodied, toward his home city on the planet Reject-20.

PART THREE

"The universe doesn't care about your power, your gumption, your beauty, or your intelligence. None of that matters if you want to win the cosmic game of evolution. You just need luck. Or knowledge of the future."

—Unyat

CHAPTER 1

WITH THUNDER

Galactic distances were negligible to Ariock. The cosmic route from Earth to Reject-20 was as traceable as the lines on the palm of his hand. All was dark, cold emptiness, except for the fierce luminosity of stars and their orbiting satellites. Ariock wished he had enough time to explore the fertile spheres. Instead, he hurtled, disembodied, past stars and planets, until he arrived at . . .

A fiery apocalypse.

Black smoke choked Freedomland. Military shuttles dropped toward the coastal city or chased one another over its stratosphere, shooting missiles.

The Torth should not be able to swarm in so close.

They must have teleported into the spaceport and taken control of it. Ariock inwardly cursed himself. He never should have left Garrett in charge for so long. Where was the old man? Where was Evenjos? Was Kessa safe?

And why hadn't Ariock received more than a single crisis signal?

The Torth must be wrecking his superluminal communications network.

Some vestigial part of Ariock's disembodied mind remembered Vy and Thomas. He needed to protect his beloved city, but he ought to seek advice before he went charging in. So instead of rushing to rescue people, the way he wanted to, he snapped back to his body in Mongolia.

He opened his eyes to sunlit grass and a blue sky. Butterflies flittered off wildflowers.

"Freedomland is being invaded by Torth," Ariock told them.

Vy gasped. Thomas stepped close enough to scan Ariock's mind. He paused for a second, which seemed to be enough time for him to weigh various options.

"I need to be on-site," Thomas said decisively. "Teleport me to the Twins' bunker."

Ariock began to suggest that Thomas would be safer on a planet that wasn't under invasion. Perhaps he ought to just stay on Earth for a bit longer?

"You can't leave me and Vy unprotected." Thomas spoke before Ariock could say a word. "If any Torth scan your mind? They'll learn we're on Earth, and they'll get to us before we can hike to my hidden spaceship in Siberia."

Ariock clenched his jaw, hating the logic. It seemed wrong to bring a child into a war zone.

But he had learned that ignoring Thomas's advice led to disasters, such as the Alashani underground being flooded or a hundred warriors getting slaughtered.

Enough of that.

Thomas might not have time to explain the intricacies of his plan, or whatever inferences he had gleaned, but he knew what he was doing.

"The Twins' bunker includes workstations that can hack into city controls and major weapons," Thomas said. "The Torth may think they've taken control, but I have solo override access to everything. They're not used to an individual who can take that much control. And my return won't be common knowledge yet. That will give us a huge advantage."

Thomas might be able to wallop a lot of Torth with all that technology at his fingertips. Ariock felt a bit of relief. He would not be the only warrior in this fight.

"One more thing," Thomas said. "If the Twins are anywhere nearby, don't appear to them in person. It's a bad idea to startle them. Don't pop into existence right next to them."

Ariock wasn't sure he wanted to think too hard about what that warning implied. Were the Twins on guard against enemy teleporters? Were they ready to defend themselves with a gaseous weapon?

"All right." Ariock drew a breath, steeling himself for danger. He encompassed his friends and gear within his awareness.

Soon he was ghosting through fire, smoke, launchpads, bedrock, and a vestibule hidden well beneath the academy. Overlapped chrome plates shielded the warren of underground bunkers that Ariock had carved out of granite. His perceptions slid helplessly off the chrome plating.

Fortunately, he had connected the bunker to the academy by an underground passageway. One had to know where to look.

Ariock appeared in the secret passageway with a clap of thunder. He brought fresh air from Mongolia along with his friends and gear. The displaced air caused a sudden pressure change and a mini shock wave.

Booming sounds came from above. Bombs, missiles, or blaster cannons.

"Don't leave just yet, Ariock," Thomas warned. "Let me suss out what's happening."

He led the way to the vault door of the bunker and tapped a keypad. The door retracted.

Inside the round room, ummins, govki, and other aliens gaped. The area was packed with lab technicians who had sought the nearest bomb shelter. There might be some students in the mix, too. Weak light filtered through the slitted sky shafts, wan and red.

"Thomas?" Kessa stood among them, gawking with disbelief. "Ariock?"

Thomas offered a nod of acknowledgment. "Hey, Kessa."

He walked through the crowd, as if his walking presence was completely normal. His colorful Mongolian woolens added to the strangeness.

Ariock ducked under the vault door. He had sized most rooms in his city to accommodate every species, including nussians, but he had purposely made bunker doors low. A bottleneck could be defensible against Torth invaders.

Clusters of workstations filled half the floorspace. Scattered people were clearly trying to bring the system online. The Twins floated in their own nook, and they stopped to stare at Thomas. They looked like children glimpsing a legendary hero.

Thomas didn't spare them a glance. He crossed the musty-smelling bunker, walking past off-line monitors that were dark and dead. He seemed to choose a workstation at random. He flipped on its backup power supply and took a seat.

"The Torth have appropriated our own transports and major weapons." Thomas opened and scanned menus on the holographic projection dashboard. "My guess is that they've enlisted help from the local penitent population."

Ariock frowned, trying to figure out how this invasion was possible. The lone shuttles that had slowly been invading his solar system had been too isolated to pose a unified threat.

"It's possible the Torth have figured out galactic teleportation." Thomas said that with casual nonchalance, as if it did not entail a cataclysm. "Maybe they've learned how to link and boost each other's power."

This was worse than a disaster.

If Torth champions could hopscotch from one planet to another, millions of powerful combatants would pop into Ariock's centralized stronghold without warning. This was an apocalypse.

And how many penitents had they enlisted? Thousands?

The Torth Empire must have detected Ariock's long absence and decided that now was their best chance to attack. They were all about striking while Ariock's people were undefended.

He should have killed all the space lurkers, as Garrett had suggested.

He should never take a vacation ever again.

Vy looked sick with hopelessness.

"It's not as bad as it seems." Thomas gave them a reassuring glance, and somehow, Ariock felt a little less despairing. If Thomas thought there was a probability for victory, then there was a good chance.

"It looks like the Torth did destroy our supercom network." Thomas scrolled through a minimalist menu. "And the planetary network as well."

"Yup." That was Varktezo. "We can't get our defenses online." The ummin had risen to his feet, having been hidden behind another cluster of workstations. "I guess they must have missed one relay satellite, otherwise you would not have received the emergency broadcast."

Ariock could imagine that. His relay satellites were strung throughout the solar system, orbiting planets or masked as part of asteroids. The Torth attackers might well have missed one or two. Or perhaps a kneeler had thwarted them.

But in an emergency, wouldn't Garrett have broken his promise about staying far away? The old man should have visited Ariock and Thomas in person to alert them.

Unless he was overwhelmed with fending off the unexpected invasion.

A journey to Earth would deplete one-fifth of Garrett's raw power. He would not risk that if he was embattled. Or incapacitated.

Or dead.

How many hours had Garrett been fighting?

Ariock decided to berate himself later. He needed to save people. Everything else had to wait.

"Ariock," Thomas said before Ariock could run out the door. "I need your help to repair the communications satellites." He used his own holographic power to display different hardware parts. "You'll put these together. Here and here." He animated the diagram, demonstrating. "With luck, the Torth won't notice the repairs until it's too late for them."

Ariock wasn't sure why the planetary network should be a top priority, but he decided not to question it. "All right."

"It's not just for personal communication," Thomas said. "It's machine to machine. This will enable me to control all our missile launchers. Not to mention the transports and shuttles, which I can fly as drones."

"Got it." Ariock expanded his awareness upward. He extended himself through the stratosphere and into orbital space, pinging back and forth due to the speed of orbiting objects. He was a pro at finding satellites.

He wished he was saving people, but instead, he allowed Thomas to walk him through the repairs step by step. He used his powers to fuse machine parts together in orbital space.

"It's online," Thomas said with satisfaction after running a test via his workstation. His fingers sped through holographic menus.

Workstations and lights throughout the bunker powered on. The immense wall monitors flickered and began to display different views of the city, obscured by smoke and ash. Flames licked at cliffside buildings.

A recorded voice played from multiple speakers. She spoke two words in the slave tongue: "System online."

Ariock's supercom vibrated.

"Ignore your queue of emergency notifications," Thomas told Ariock. His fingers flew, and on the monitors, blaster cannons seemed to come alive and swivel toward airborne targets. "You'll need to item-teleport vulnerable people to our underground bunkers. Save as many people as you can."

That was what Ariock wanted to hear.

"Don't get near any Torth," Thomas warned. "Wear your galaxy space armor as a precaution, but even with your visor sealed, even with air tanks, they might have invented new ways to sabotage the tungsten alloy. Also, telepathy gas is a dark energy matrix. No armor can protect you from that."

Something had taken Garrett and Evenjos out of the battle. Telepathy gas? Or was it some unholy combination of that, plus inhibitor gas and insanity gas? Or was it something new?

The unknown threats made Ariock feel on edge, like his blood was boiling and freezing at the same time. He only dared use his powers from afar. That compounded the risks. Big actions such as earthquakes and tornadoes always carried a risk of hurting his own people.

Vy gripped him and pulled him into a fierce hug. "Stay safe."

She kissed him.

"You too," Ariock said fervently.

This wasn't his nightmare, he reassured himself. He didn't want to abandon Vy during a dangerous time, but some instinct told him that this bunker was the safest place she could be.

He jogged toward the exit. Since he could not teleport through chrome-plated walls or ceilings, he had to enter and leave this place the same way everyone else did, through the vault door.

"Call me if there's an emergency," he called over his shoulder.

At least emergency calls could get through now that he'd repaired the main satellites. This invasion must have been extra terrifying due to the obliteration of communications. That explained why so many people were stranded aboveground, in shops or apartments or classrooms.

And it was so easy for the Torth to learn things when they were on the ground, wreaking havoc.

As soon as Ariock was away from the mirror trap of the bunker, he stretched his awareness to his armory. He held out his arms and item-teleported the defensive outfit onto his body. Once the joints and visor were sealed, he arrowed his awareness upward.

The smoke from fires and explosions had created particle thunderheads.

Ariock teleported himself inside an immense cloud. Encased in armor, he could ignore frigid temperatures and icy dust. All he cared about was finding survivors.

He found them. Life sparks filled his city, in closets or in locked rooms.

The glow of Evenjos was sedate rather than a fierce thrum. She hid under the ocean, no doubt afraid to reveal herself, since inhibitor gas could end her life. Ariock imagined her as kelp, caught helplessly in ocean froth. She must be in a pathetic mood.

Yet her diminished status hinted that she had actually risked her life to protect the city. Ariock saw telltale signs as he inhabited buildings and streets. The wreckage here did have a border.

Evenjos must have expanded into a monstrosity and shielded the city from aerial bombardment.

In fact, she had ferried thousands of people—mostly shani—to a rocky island. She must be shielding them there, and she had probably healed countless injuries. Nothing else would deplete her so much.

The life sparks could not tell Ariock anything more. If Garrett had any power left, he was indistinguishable from the thousands of Rosies and Servants who were marauding through the streets and slaughtering innocent people.

It was time to be a hero.

Ariock rocketed up high, into the stratosphere. Then he let himself go into free fall.

While his body plunged through the mass of smoke clouds, he went into a clairvoyant trance. It was unnerving, letting his body fall while utterly vulnerable, but it wasn't his first time. Enemy transports tended to avoid smoke and turbulence. He estimated that he had at least a full minute before his body encountered any region of risk. That was plenty of time for a practiced teleporter like himself to get things done.

He ghosted through the academy.

He glided in and out of halls and secret passageways faster than an eye blink. Although he did not find Garrett or Cherise, he did encounter classrooms full of cowering people.

He entered one for a split second without bringing his body all the way through. The moment in which even a hair on his head entered the classroom gave him enough of a mental edge to widen his awareness and encompass all the people and desks and chairs in the vicinity. He did not waste time on rounding up the people. He simply scooped it all up within his awareness, desks and people alike, and then he deposited them all into the secret tunnel.

The surprised people would get the idea and find their way into the safe bunker. Done.

Ariock's consciousness slammed back inside his free-falling body. He fought vertigo and reversed his fall.

He supposed he could have stowed himself somewhere less dynamic, but would a random basement truly be any safer than the clouds in motion?

He didn't think so. Like Thomas had said, there were the gaseous weapons to consider. The Torth must have suffused most of the city with telepathy gas and worse.

They would set traps for Ariock. They knew that he would return.

The sky was a pastel emptiness, banded with stripes from the gas giant that neighbored Reject-20. It was so huge, and Ariock was so good at defying gravity, he nearly tricked his brain into believing that the largest void was below him instead of overhead. He rocketed through this windy region of the stratosphere—and abandoned his body again.

He ghosted, uncaring about his helplessly falling body. He located more people who needed saving.

He blinked through classrooms, lab rooms, warehouse closets, and more. He scooped up a hundred people here, a hundred there, and exported them to safety. He teleported each group in a rapid series, as intensive as a gamer in the zone.

The Torth Empire would not murder all his people. Not if he could stop them.

CHAPTER 2
TRANSGRESSIVE THOUGHTS

THE TORTH EMPIRE WILL PREVAIL!

The Pink Screwdriver sneaked behind Lieutenant Yolpeen's townhouse and cowered against the ivy-covered wall. She dared not shelter in her cubbyhole or any place where she might be easily found.

The Conqueror will never return.

The Giant is gone.

The remaining enemies are outmatched by those of Us who can leap across interstellar distances.

Kill those uppity runaways!

How dare they enslave (superior beings) Torth!

Traitorous penitents marauded through the streets. They tore down signs and stole weapons, having been liberated. They vandalized shops at the behest of their whispering orbiters. Some of them even did it without qualms.

You no longer have to obey slaves.

You are free.

JOIN US!

(or die)

The summons thundered inside her brain. The Torth Majority was inside her head.

Well, it wasn't quite the whole Majority. A measly rotation of one to three orbiters peered through her eyes. These were bored low ranks who wanted to vicariously experience the invaded enemy city through hapless penitents. They did not care who she was or who she used to be. They were just using her as a pair of eyes and ears.

But her temporary orbiters had their own orbiters, who had their own, and so forth. They were a thread of the vast cobweb that comprised the Torth Majority. The Pink Screwdriver could hear the Majority, attenuated and distant, yet thunderously powerful all the same.

Blast that nussian!

Yes!

Throw a grenade into that doorway!

The Pink Screwdriver dropped out of the Megacosm with her jaw clenched.

How could so many of her fellow penitents be selfish idiots? Did they really want to wreck all the painstaking care that Kessa had put into their rehabilitation? Was it worthwhile to trash the homes and shops of decent people?

How forgiving would Kessa be once she learned that a bunch of penitents had shot and killed innocent bystanders?

How would the Conqueror react if he ever returned?

The Pink Screwdriver knew she ought to ascend into the Megacosm and reinvite her audience. That was survival. If the Conqueror was truly gone forever, then pleasing the Torth Majority was likely her only chance to survive.

Instead, she bitterly hoped that every Torth in this invasion would fail to notice her absence.

She did not actually enjoy having orbiters anymore. It felt dangerous. It was also weirdly embarrassing. Ever since she had stopped repressing her emotions, events in her life felt more visceral, more significant. She didn't want every mind reader in the galaxy judging the way she experienced things.

A handful of incurious peepers was all right. The Pink Screwdriver had needed to hear the news, and that was the price of hearing it.

But enough was enough. Her personal secrets had surpassed a critical mass, and she would not invite thousands of voyeurs to comb through her recent transgressions.

She had experimented with pleasuring her own body, like she was an animal.

She fantasized about cuddling with the Conqueror.

And also with a fellow penitent who called himself Jake. And not just with those young men, but also with certain Alashani war heroes. And maidens. And even with humans. She had all sorts of beastly thoughts.

And even weirder? She observed sisters holding hands, and friends laughing over frozen treats, and mothers with their children, and seeing those bonds tugged a different sort of primal desire inside her.

She kept wondering what it would be like to reject her Torth identity forever. Could she truly become a person? A singular person, disconnected from any audience, without any greater purpose? Was that possible for someone like her?

Those thoughts bounced around the vast absence left by the Megacosm.

Perhaps her mental transgressions were meager, but they were many, and they were persistent. Her savagery would earn her execution.

So she hid from the executioners and the vandals and everyone else. She was reduced to being an animal in survival mode. If she were a Yeresunsa, she probably would have set the whole yard on fire by accident out of sheer terror. All she could do was hope that none of the invaders would pop out of thin air within sight of her.

Someone ducked through the tropical plants in a neighboring backyard.

The Pink Screwdriver nearly fled. But the figure went still, and she recognized *(the Fluid Obloquy)* Jake.

Everything about Jake was sharp and angular. He had a sharp nose, pronounced collarbones, and hair that fell in a precise way. Not that his outward appearance mattered. The Pink Screwdriver was still Torth enough to value someone's mind over their body. Jake, formerly known as the Fluid Obloquy, had a gentle and caring soul, combined with formidable mental acuity. She marveled that so few people were attracted to him. He was quite unique.

He saw her.

She leaned against the wall, grateful that it was him and not one of the marauding traitors. Jake smiled at her posture of repose. Like her, he was one of the penitents who freely used his face to express his thoughts.

Jake made his way toward her, stepping over flowers and shrubbery.

The Pink Screwdriver wasn't sure if meeting now was a good idea. Should they risk caressing each other, or acting like fools, while the city was under an invasion?

They were beginning to take privacy for granted, and that was stupid. This strange penitent existence might turn out to be a mere blip in their total life-spans. They could not afford to be unguarded. The Conqueror *(Thomas)* had abandoned his people. Including them.

A whistling sound came from above.

The Pink Screwdriver looked up just in time to see a fiery explosion and a rainfall of burning debris. A transport had just blown up.

A smashing sound came from the street. Metal screeched against metal.

Was that a hovercart crash?

The Pink Screwdriver climbed the ladder to the rooftop garden, taking a risk to gain a view. By the top, she was breathing hard. She prepared to duck behind an urn.

But the vista held her captivated.

Missiles angled toward every transport in the smoky sky. There was another fiery collision. And another.

The remaining transports jerked upward, or else they dove, trying to escape death.

It was no use. Even if they did not encounter a missile, they were blasted by one of the cannons that protected the city's airspace.

Jake had followed her. He reached for her hand.

"I thought the Torth took those weapons off-line?" she said, gazing at fiery explosions in the air. Like many penitents, she had gotten into the habit of speech.

The Conqueror, Jake thought. *He must have returned to protect Us.*

Flower petals floated upward, caught in heat updrafts.

The Pink Screwdriver accepted Jake's hand. The touch helped to quell her desire to ascend into the Megacosm. She wanted to share this moment with someone.

I'm afraid to ascend also, Jake silently let her know. *I do not think I can be a Torth again.*

At least she wasn't alone.

Neither of them was alone. The Pink Screwdriver saw other penitents hiding in backyards, or in windows, or rooftop gardens. They gaped at the sudden destruction of the Torth fleet.

Even the traitorous penitents began to hide, darting into cubbyholes or under bushes. Aerial drones were targeting individual Servants and Rosies with stunning precision. Those military ranks used their powers to hurl fireballs at the mechanized attackers, but they were unused to fighting robots . . . or mechanical drones controlled by a supergenius.

Some of them might have escaped. But many were too slow, or too drained, to be effective against the onslaught.

The Pink Screwdriver held Jake's hand and admired the Conqueror's handiwork.

She would thank him in person, if he ever deigned to see her again.

Yet, at the same time, she understood that today had nearly been a loss. What if the Conqueror had not returned? Then she and Jake might well be forced back into the Torth Empire. The Majority would have them executed for their transgressions.

This day was a victory. But what about tomorrow?

What about a year from now? Or a decade?

The Torth Empire owned every planet in the galaxy. They owned the stars, the temporal streams, the fleets.

The Conqueror *(Thomas)* had wrenched another prize out of their grasp. He had pulled off another miracle. But there were cities on Nuss that had changed hands multiple times, conquered and reconquered and then reconquered again.

Jake squeezed her hand, acknowledging her worries. *We are only flotsam, helplessly riding each wave,* he thought. *We do not control the fate of the galaxy.*

He seemed untroubled by that truth. Power had never sat comfortably on his shoulders. Jake had been relieved to stop believing himself to be a god.

Perhaps the Pink Screwdriver ought to feel the same way.

She did not. Powerlessness made her feel like she was embedded in the Torth Majority, carried along by other people's votes. Why did she have so little control over the collective decisions around her? Could she possibly change anything?

This war might last her entire life and beyond. Every win and every loss would bring fear. Could she exist like that, worrying over the implications of faraway news?

"Look," Jake breathed, his voice emphasizing *(!!!!!)* shock. "Are you seeing what I'm seeing?"

The Pink Screwdriver followed his gaze.

Then she knew that she had to ascend, no matter the risks. She could not believe what was happening. The Megacosm was the only way she might comprehend the strangeness taking place down below, in the streets of Freedomland.

CHAPTER 3

CONQUEST

Kessa could not quit the grin that stretched her beak. Fears had weighed heavily on her ever since Thomas disappeared, and now she felt so light she could almost float.

Minutes earlier, the city—and the whole galaxy, it seemed—had been doomed. The Lady of Sorrow had transformed into a monster and batted away shuttles and bombs all night, but the Torth had eventually driven her away, either with the triple gaseous threats or with their relentless attacks. Evenjos had evacuated along with most of the shani warriors.

Rumors swirled about Garrett. It was said that both he and Zai fought valiantly and protected thousands of people, but the rumors had died down. Maybe one or both of them had fallen. The war palace was in another part of the city and communications were broken. No one knew if they survived.

Kessa had feared that even if Ariock returned, he would blunder straight into a Torth trap.

Instead?

Kessa laughed from the joy of seeing Thomas healthy and well. She could hardly wait to hear about how the Bringer of Hope had persuaded the Wisdom to return.

But the story needed to wait for a safer time. The bunker trembled from distant shock waves, causing equipment to rattle. Dust sifted off the ceiling.

"Look!" someone shouted.

The lab's other occupants pointed at the live-stream views high up on the wall. As Kessa watched, a streamship angled toward a shuttle and collided with it in the upper atmosphere. Electricity swept outward as the larger streamship continued on its way with a shuttle-size dent in its hull. The collision created a visible shock wave.

In another monitor, a swarm of robotic drones flew toward armored Torth like predators hunting prey. One drone slammed into a Torth's head. That Torth fell.

Other Torth invaders ran. Drones chased each and every one, like intelligent bullets.

"That should teach the Torth to mess with us!" someone yelled.

Missiles launched. They targeted aerial transports. Each missile hit its target, no matter how the transports swerved and rolled.

Kessa gawked at the carnage.

In every view, invaders tried to flee on hovercarts or hoverbikes. Thomas must have spent a lot of time building a defense system, because remote drones intercepted them, blasting them from above.

Kessa had never seen Torth weaponry do that.

Well, that made sense. The Torth Empire was all about harmony and cooperation. Torth did not shoot each other on a large scale. The Majority had ensured that no single citizen had the technological power that Thomas was now displaying.

He must have broken dozens of ancient Torth laws.

"Thomas is doing it!" someone yelled. "He's saving us!"

People watched the monitors as if invested in a contest, waiting to see a winner. The cheers crescendoed every time a Torth invader ran or died. Lab technicians bounced on their toes, too overcome with happiness to act like dignified professionals.

Kessa was surprised when her secretary, Yanyashta, impulsively hugged her.

She laughed and hugged back. Freedom might be a tiny point of light inside the vast darkness that was the Torth Empire, but it would not be extinguished. Not today.

Thomas seemed oblivious to all the celebrations. His hands raced through holographic menus, selecting commands and setting variables.

Yanyashta hissed and jerked away. One of the Twins was approaching.

"We can help to make this a more complete victory, I think." Mondoyo's eyes sparkled with what looked like joy. "Will you hear our suggestion?"

Penitents, in Kessa's experience, rarely showed emotion. Mondoyo was the exception to the rule. Every time she spoke with the pudgy supergenius, he seemed to be trying to make up for lost time.

"Yes?" Kessa invited.

"While Thomas slaughters the invaders," Mondoyo said, "will you allow Serette and me to remind all Torth in the Megacosm that they are welcome to find refuge in Freedomland?"

Kessa tightened her beak. Penitents were not permitted to ascend into the Megacosm. That was one of her rules. "If I allowed that," she said, stressing her refusal, "the Torth would be able to see through your eyes, figure out where you're hiding, and bomb us to death. So no."

She figured that would send Mondoyo away. He avoided confrontations.

But he lingered, almost rudely close.

Kessa stepped back, trying to give him a hint. He should not enter within range to read her mind.

"We calculated the risk-to-reward ratio," Mondoyo said. "And the odds are very favorable for us. There is only a two percent risk that any Torth can get past our cascades of mental trivia and dredge up sensitive military intelligence. The Death Architect is our biggest concern, and her schedule indicates that she will be asleep right now. Together, Serette and I are swifter thinkers than she is. We can leave before she probes our minds."

Kessa shook her head. Thomas had already invited Torth renegades to join him. He had begged. He had pleaded for the entire Torth Empire to switch sides. It hadn't worked. Why try the same futile gambit again? The Twins had shown up only after he'd quit trying.

"Do not ascend," Kessa ordered.

Mondoyo looked so frustrated, Kessa wondered if he could read her mind despite the respectful distance between them. She took another step back.

"I know you think it's futile," Mondoyo said. "But Thomas did not fail. He persuaded the Upward Governess right away. And me. And, I believe, millions more."

Millions. And more.

Kessa frowned. Surely more than three renegades would have made the perilous journey to Freedomland if Thomas's pleas had worked at all?

Thomas himself had all but admitted failure. She had seen defeat in his slumped shoulders as he'd zombified lines of captive Torth. She had heard defeat in his refusals to meet her for dinner. He had stopped believing it was possible.

"Many Torth are opportunistic," Mondoyo said. "They're afraid to leave the empire." He indicated the monitors, where blasters targeted and destroyed armored Torth. "Right now, the Conqueror is giving them good reason to be afraid to stay."

Kessa saw a cornered Torth shoot down a drone. Moments later, a nussian tackled him.

"The Majority will be teetering right now," Mondoyo said, "due to the sudden reversal of this battle. A lot of Torth only want a logical reason to switch sides. This would be a well-timed message." He spread his hands. "Once they see how well we're treated? And how easily Thomas can win? I think our message will be enticing, particularly to other supergeniuses."

That was a good argument.

Kessa wondered if she was being fooled.

"Hold on." She walked briskly to Thomas.

Part of her feared that he would ignore her, or worse, get up and leave. She could not gauge why he had left or whether he could afford a minor interruption.

"Thomas?" Kessa decided to keep her request succinct. "The Twins wish to try and persuade more Torth to join us. I want to trust them, but I would like your opinion."

Thomas glanced at her from the corner of one purple eye. "I've been known to be wrong when it comes to matters of trust."

She didn't know how to respond to that.

Thomas scrolled, tapped, tapped and scrolled. Holographic tools blinked in and out of existence as he made quick selections. "I think you're a better judge of character. It's your call."

Kessa blinked.

"Sorry." Thomas sounded distracted. "Let's catch up later? I'm enacting a remote takeover of the enemy-controlled transports."

Kessa left him to his work. She crossed the floor, back toward Mondoyo. Serette had joined him, floating by his side. One Twin awaited Kessa's decision with a friendly, amiable expression. The other one looked sour and annoyed.

"How do you plan to persuade the Torth?" Kessa asked the Twins bluntly. "What arguments will you use?"

"We don't look like much," Mondoyo said humbly. "But in the Megacosm? Supergeniuses command a lot of respect."

Kessa had heard that. The Upward Governess had been elected to serve the Majority as the de facto ruler of the galaxy for a brief time. Now the Death Architect seemed to be filling that role. Supergeniuses did have an outsize influence.

She nodded for him to go on.

"Four of the best have joined Thomas's side," Mondoyo said.

Was he counting Thomas? Kessa wondered.

"We like being here," Mondoyo said. "Other Torth will, too. They don't have to remain trapped in a dying empire that gives them fewer rights than slaves. We can point that out."

Serette nodded.

Kessa perched on a desk and assessed the Twins. Perhaps two humble penitents with twinned minds might actually succeed where the Conqueror had failed?

"Thomas did not fail," Mondoyo said.

Kessa scooted back. Had she accidentally sat too close to him, within range?

"Sorry." Mondoyo looked embarrassed, and he floated backward a bit. Serette did the same, perfectly in sync with him. "I was just reading your face, not your thoughts. Anyway, we believe that Thomas primed the Torth Majority to go for an alternative lifestyle. All they need right now is a little tiny push."

On the monitors, grenades flew.

Wildfires died.

Torth died.

"Just a bit of extra persuasion," Mondoyo said.

Perhaps, with the right timing . . .

"All right," Kessa decided. "Go ahead."

She hoped she was not making a galaxy-size mistake.

But Thomas seemed to trust her. So did the Twins.

The two supergeniuses bowed their heads in unison. They closed their eyes, perhaps to minimize the chance of any foreign Torth peering through their perceptions.

Kessa watched them.

The Twins did not show any hint of emotion or expression. The Megacosm tended to have that effect. It sucked up attention.

"Holy sand vipers!" someone exclaimed.

"Are you seeing what I'm seeing?" a technician asked. She sounded like she was pleading.

Varktezo gawked at the monitors, wide-eyed with disbelief.

Kessa glanced in that direction . . . and she slid off the desk, standing, because she had to stand to take in the impossibility taking place on multiple screens.

The Torth had quit defending themselves, or setting buildings on fire, or murdering innocent people.

Instead, Torth were kneeling.

Some appeared to inject themselves with inhibitor, then go prostrate on the ground. But other Torth shot their kneeling comrades in the back! Or they hurled balls of fire.

They clashed, more serious than any Alashani duelers.

Torth were fighting Torth.

Soldiers stood back and watched while their targets killed each other.

Kessa tore her gaze away from the insanity displayed via live stream, wondering if the Twins had anything to do with this.

Mondoyo and Serette opened their eyes in unison. One seemed triumphant, one regretful.

"The Torth Empire," Mondoyo reported, "is in civil war."

Kessa tried to comprehend what that meant. Were Torth-versus-Torth battles taking place throughout the entire galaxy? Not just here?

Thomas's mouth fell open. He looked as if he was experiencing something new and incredible for the first time ever.

"The Megacosm," Mondoyo said into the silence, "is breaking."

CHAPTER 4

THE TWINS SYMPHONY

The Sterling Strop was honored to be in charge of this historic battle.

No one had expected the Giant to return to his home base, much less with the Conqueror, but for all practical purposes, they were constrained. They were unwilling to damage their own territory, nor would they expose themselves to the triple gas. The Conqueror hid in a bunker. The Giant hid in clouds. Even the Shapeshifter and the Imposter were gone, hiding away. The enemies were nothing but cowards.

So the Torth Empire had to prevail here.

Nobody could thwart the gods. A lot of Torth believed that. Therefore, it was a good bet.

A drone buzzed past a nearby Rosy Rank and decapitated him with a blast.

Oof. Someone had illegally programmed local machines to obey a governance key.

A blaster cannon fired, taking down a Torth-controlled transport. The Sterling Strop glimpsed more carnage in his mental news feed. Explosions thundered as Torth-piloted transports were shot down.

Blood-soaked pain and mayhem bloomed in the Megacosm, shared and re-shared by millions of distant voyeurs.

The Conqueror (that criminal) must be in control.

Shouldn't We surrender?

Shouldn't We teleport away?

His orbiters churned with doubt. *You are outmatched,* many of them whispered inside his mind.

You did well (you almost took over the Conqueror's stronghold!),

but you cannot defeat the Conqueror.

Abort this mission, the Torth Majority urged the Sterling Strop.

Leave.

You (and your champion peers) are too important for Us to lose.

That was probably good advice.

Yet it was tentative, a suggestion rather than a command from the Majority. A strong minority of Torth wanted the Sterling Strop to proceed.

And he was not ready to give up and flee.

The Sterling Strop swaggered through the oceanside city beneath its gas-giant sky. Runaway slaves hid from him or fled. No doubt they were ashamed of their own inferior, servile nature. They were no threat at all.

Mere vandalism had put a dent in the Conqueror's forces. It was plain to see. The enemies were a menace in news feeds, but up close? They were truly nothing but a band of runaway slaves. Almost all their equipment and supplies were stolen from the Torth Empire.

The Sterling Strop was worthy of the scimitar sheathed on his armored back. He knew it. That was why the Majority had elected him to lead this battle. The Death Architect had commissioned fewer than five hundred of these precious, uniquely engineered ionic blades, and they were only granted to the most powerful champions in the Torth military. The Sterling Strop was in the same league as the disgraced Former Commander.

Except he would do better than she ever had. He was smarter, more determined, and he had youthful vigor. Many Torth knew that he would make a solid Commander of All Living—

!!!!!!!!!!!!!!!!

!?!?!!?!!?!?!?

The Megacosm swirled with shocked perplexity.

The Sterling Strop halted in his steps. He reprioritized his attention, immersing himself fully in the Megacosm.

The Twins!?!?!?!

Torth on various worlds and space stations prodded their comrades. Ever more Torth joined the Megacosm, jolted awake by excited neighbors.

Everyone was powerfully curious about why the Twins had dared to ascend into the Megacosm. What did they wish to share?

Have they (the Twins) ransacked the secret laboratories of the Conqueror?

Are the Twins actually returning to Us?

With useful military secrets?

Yay!

The Sterling Strop went into orbit around the girl Twin's mind, and then the boy Twin, skating past both, carried along by the Majority. His invasion of Freedomland might amount to just another lost battle. Defeats had a predictable outcome now: captured Rosies and Servants would be turned into zombified minions.

So he craved good news, or at least solid new information.

???????????????????

Once the audience was huge and thunderous—not just billions, but trillions—the Twins began to impart their message.

The freedom lovers, the girl Twin thought.

Those whom you have wrongly labeled as enemies, the boy Twin clarified.

Are creators—

—not destroyers.

The huge minds of the Twins were like mirrored gas giants, one with an optimistic tilt and one with a pessimistic rolling rotation. Both shone with sincerity.

The freedom lovers are authors, artists, explorers,

guided and inspired by a polymath (Thomas the Conqueror).

The Twins plainly believed the propaganda they were spouting.

Had they been hopelessly spoiled by forbidden pleasures? It seemed that the enemies—maybe not the Conqueror, since he'd been absent, but Kessa the Wise?—had turned them into pliable pets.

How tawdry, the Majority whispered.

Yet the largest minds in the Megacosm sharpened with interest. The Geodesic Flux, the Rind Topographer, and even a few immature supergeniuses . . . all of those who were awake immediately screened their reactions behind random trivia.

Their embarrassment was obvious. They were clearly hiding illegal emotions and thoughts.

The Sterling Strop glared into the distance, down a ramp and into a plaza where runaway slaves gawked at the explosion-filled sky. He drew his scimitar just so he could hold a weapon. Champions such as himself ought to execute the empire's remaining supergeniuses before they could betray civilization.

Instead of answering all the derogatory criticism aimed their way, the Twins shared their firsthand experiences as penitents. They replayed quiet mornings in each other's company. They had an ease of working that they had never known before, without fear or impediments.

They enjoyed strange and intriguing conversations with a runaway slave, Varktezo. His wacky ideas had them both thinking more creatively than they ever had before.

They'd had a conversation with Kessa the Wise. That runaway actually regarded them with friendly respect instead of despising them, as might be expected.

And there was music.

The boy Twin played a symphony inside his mind. It did not come from any runaway slave or any primitive civilization. He had composed the music himself.

He had concretized his symphony in reality using a synthetic audio compilation program, which the girl Twin had written herself.

!!!!!!!!!!!!!!!!!!!!!!!!!!!!!?

The Majority recoiled. Music was forbidden.

This was not a small faux pas. This was not contained to one neighborhood in some minor city. Trillions of Torth, throughout the galaxy, were exposed to the melody.

And it stirred illegal emotions, which many Torth would rather not experience. Yet they all shared it.

Hope.

Ephemeral wistfulness.

Sublime happiness.

Exploration.

Wonderment.

Adventure.

Camaraderie.

Discovery.

Stop, the Majority begged the boy Twin.

STOP.

STOP STOP STOP STOP!!!

Despite their protestations, a large minority of Torth must yearn for more of the music—because they kept listening.

The Sterling Strop was one of those. He rarely used tranquility meshes, but he was familiar with their mood-suppressing effects. Music did the opposite. It was more like a suggestion rather than an imposition, but it did enhance his mood.

Imagery unfolded throughout the Megacosm, inspired or evoked by the music.

Every emotion had so much variation. So much nuance. Far from being primitive grunts or bestial whistling, music seemed infinitely textured. Was it a new frontier?

An unexplored frontier?

The girl Twin added an undercurrent of additional music, uplifted by the back-drop of her partner's auditory symphony. *Emotions are a branch of cognitive science.* The girl Twin addressed the entire Torth Majority. *That which You, in Your infinite ignorance, eschew as illegal—forbidden—is actually the path to creativity, innovation, and enlightenment.*

Scientists throughout the Torth Empire exchanged comments, debating the merits of her supposition.

Could it be that emotions are a branch (an unexplored branch) of My field of expertise? a renowned neuroscientist wondered.

Could be, a bitter supergenius commented. *The Torth Majority forbids so many sciences. (Bioengineering) (Artificial intelligence) (Superluminal research) Why not emotions, too?*

And music, the governor of a major hub city chimed in.

I think the Twins have proven it, a brave anthropologist concluded. *There is a lot more to learn about love and friendship than anyone wants to admit.*

More Torth agreed. Not just supergeniuses, not just scientists, not just high ranks, but also their admirers.

Billions of admirers.

The Sterling Strop recoiled from the debates, yet opinions flowed all around him, even from his own orbiters.

There is nuance to emotions that We (neuroscientists) fail to acknowledge.

> *We (Torth) are entirely too focused on a narrow subset of emotions (fear and hatred).*

> *Why not love?*

> *Why does the Torth Empire outlaw so many good things?*

> *Shouldn't the Majority reconsider their restrictive laws?*

A well-respected Indigo-Blue Rank radiated anger. *I don't want to live the rest of My life in obeisance to stupid, meaningless, constrictive laws.*

Other scientists rallied to him. *Yeah!*

I'm sick of constraints!

> *Me too!*

The mental simulation of music coming from the Twins gained a strident under-tone, as if to underscore the shifting mood of the Megacosm. A subversive counter-opinion whispered just beneath the Majority's *STOP* protestations, so manifold that it was impossible to repress or ignore.

We (Torth) ought to reconsider ancient laws.

> *Reconsider what is forbidden.*

> *Reconsider.*

A quandary shook the Megacosm.

The Sterling Strop experienced it as if the universe was wrenching apart. The Megacosm was as infinite as space, but it had become so riddled with doubts, its cohesion was in jeopardy.

The Majority—the eternal, omnipotent Majority—writhed, as if it might cleave into two separate halves.

??? !!! ??? !!! ??? !!!

> *!!!! ???? !!!! ???? !!!! ????*

Amid the chaos, one of the elder supergeniuses, a twelve-year-old known as the Rind Topographer, drew an audience by renouncing her godhood.

Tell the Conqueror, she urged the Twins. *I am done being an idiot (a Torth). I surrender. I beg the Conqueror to save Me!*

!!

Even as her treachery shocked the Majority, hundreds of her orbiters followed suit. *Save Us.*

We quit being Torth.

WE ARE PENITENTS!!!

They bowed to their slaves.

They peeled off their blaster gloves and either tossed them down a garbage chute or handed them to a slave.

They spoke out loud, many with rusty, whispery voices that had not been used since infancy. "I am no longer Torth. I am penitent."

The anguish of the Majority worsened. Indecision gripped the Megacosm, causing seizures everywhere.

!!!! ???? !!!! !!!! ???? !!!!

STOP! Half the Majority interjected what they believed was reason and rationality into madness. The forbidden sciences were forbidden for good reasons. Emotions were degrading and dangerous. Civilization needed to reject nonsense.

A mature supergenius, the Geodesic Flux, mentally threw down all those arguments. *The difference between right and wrong is obvious (to Me),* he thought. *I am tired of pretending otherwise (to survive). I loathe self-deception. Enough of it! I am joining My better colleagues (the pioneers) (the Conqueror and the Upward Governess and the Twins and the Rind Topographer and even the Colossal Failure), even if it means My death.*

He spoke out loud to his nearest slaves, who looked disbelieving and confused. "The Torth Empire has wronged you. I no longer want to be a Torth."

His orbiters followed suit.

Tens of millions of Torth, on various cities on various planets, abased themselves before their slaves.

Loyal Torth rushed to stop their traitorous neighbors. Blasts and death screams resounded throughout the Megacosm. Minds winked out, either to escape the mental chaos or because they had been shot to death.

!!!!!!!!!!!!!!!!!!!!!

!!!!!!!! ( ) !!!!!!!!!!!!! ( ) !!!!!!!!!

!!!!!!!!!!! ( ) !!!!!!!!!!!!!!!!! ( ) !!!!!!!!!!!!!!!!!!!!

The Sterling Strop barely realized that he had fallen to his knees. He'd dropped his scimitar and put his hands over his head, trying to shield his naked mind.

But it was futile.

The Majority was no longer paying attention to him or to his little battle. He was nothing. He was a leaf in a storm, a pebble orbiting a gas giant. He didn't matter at all.

All modesty was gone. Millions of Torth conveyed the stray thoughts of penitents and deviants, since no one was certain about laws or propriety any longer. Many Torth were no longer even sure if they wanted to be Torth.

A few million glommed onto the mind of some random penitent known as the Pink Screwdriver, because she offered prohibited notions.

I've enjoyed all kinds of forbidden pleasures. The Pink Screwdriver milked the anticipation. The way she shamelessly manipulated her audience into begging for more, she might as well be a primitive storyteller, tugging at people's savage emotions.

???????????????????

Billions of Torth piled into orbit around her.

I had sex, the Pink Screwdriver finally revealed.

!!!

Her audience demanded details. Was sex as disgusting as primitives made it look? Was sex actually fun? Or was it just as exhausting as exercise?

It was spectacular. There were fireworks at the end, inside and outside. The Pink Screwdriver replayed a memory.

A visceral, emotion-laden memory, rife with sweat and obscene intimacy, and a shuddering orgasm, on top of a shockingly recognizable person.

THE CONQUEROR?????????!!!????????

The Sterling Strop leaned over and vomited. He banged his forehead against the ground and didn't care about the humiliating pose. A bilious spew erupted out of his mouth.

He couldn't stop himself from soaking up the vicarious memory of sex with the Conqueror.

She had liked it.

No, he shouldn't.

He couldn't handle this.

That monstrous, smug, bony little supergenius looked healthier than ever. He even felt *(ughhh)* healthy.

So it's not all bad, the Pink Screwdriver concluded.

Extra shock waves slammed through the Megacosm after that disgustingly *(sexy)* shameless penitent dropped out.

*!!!!!!!!!! * !!!!!!!!!!!! * !!!!!!!!!!!!!! * !!!!!!!!!!!!!!!!!!!!!!!!! * !!!!!!!!!!!!!!!!!!!!!*

*!!!!!!!!!! * !!!!!!!!!!!! * !!!!!!!!!!!!!! * !!!!!!!!!!!!!!!!!!!!!!!!!!!!!!!!!!!!! * !!!!!!!!!!*

*!!!!!!!!!! * !!!!!!!!!!!!!!!!!!!!! * !!!!!!!!!!!!! * !!!!!!!!!!!!!!!!! * !!!!!!!!!!!!!!!!!!!!!!!!*

A bunch of Torth backed away. A minority quorum formed, in distant settlements and on faraway starships.

We won't bow before someone as uncouth as the Conqueror, thousands of disparate groups agreed.

We will not be enslaved by his runaway slave minions.

Nor will We obey the constricting Majority.

Farewell, suckers!

We are ON OUR OWN!

And they quit listening to reason.

Twenty thousand Torth on NovaView Orbital went rogue. They ejected unwanted audience members and severed themselves from the Megacosm. Only a few individuals on that starship continued to allow outsiders into their minds.

Isolated scientific stations and explorers likewise supported the anarchical madness. They had no desire to murder penitents, or to become penitents. They dropped out of the Megacosm as if godhood itself was toxic.

*!!! * !!!! * !!! ( ) !! * !!!!!! * !! ( ) !!!!! * !!!!! ( ) !!!!! * !!!!!!!! * ( ) * !!!!!!!! *

The Sterling Strop heard explosions and screaming in the distance.

His cohorts were being slaughtered by drones and by runaways. Yet he could not wrench himself away from the Megacosm. The sounds of mayhem in his vicinity were meaningless imitations of a much more significant battle taking place in the minds and hearts of every wakeful Torth.

The Megacosm was full of wannabe penitents.

Far from begging for a rescue, these new penitents bragged about friendships they planned to make and families they wanted to have.

!

  !

    !

     !

      !

       !

The Sterling Strop peeled off his blaster glove, curled inward, and wept.

Civilization felt like a twisted parody of itself. Smart discourse was gone. Insightful discussion threads no longer existed. Anyone who quested for knowledge—who sought recordings or facts—fell off a metaphorical cliff.

There were no facts.

There was no verifiable history.

The pillars of knowledge were vanishing, and all the discussions and fields of study they used to support . . . all that was in ruins.

Anyone who asked questions about love or friendship or art or speech or music was shot.

Anyone who made inquiries about certain branches of cognitive science was likely to get shot.

How could anyone champion a Majority that no longer existed?

The Sterling Strop might as well declare himself a penitent and kneel to former slaves. Maybe the Conqueror would have mercy and allow him to become a soldier instead of turning him into a mindless zombie?

Maybe there was a future somewhere in the galaxy.

He wept.

CHAPTER 5

CHOSEN BY GODS

The bone-cutter knife glistened on a public display shelf, as if begging for a hero to steal it. Its blade had an opalescent sheen. Its edge threw off multicolored refractions, hinting at precision. Even the hilt was lovely, a carving of ummin hands clasped over an oblong egg.

Aeyong thought the hilt looked like an ummin fertility symbol, although she could not guess why uncaring Torth would collect such things. Yet they did. The knife gleamed amid an array of beautiful knickknacks.

Aeyong trudged past the public display shelf every work shift. She pretended not to notice the knife. Other slaves likewise pretended not to see it.

Perhaps they really didn't notice?

Few slaves fantasized as much as Aeyong. She had posed careful questions to her bunk mates and neighbors, and most of them refused to discuss the idea of running away, even if it was purely hypothetical.

Aeyong supposed they were all full-time liars. They told themselves that they were content with servitude and indoor living.

She hated their insincerity.

She hated Torth even more.

Her owner was a fat Green Rank who hoarded lacy, frilly things, as well as gemstone-encrusted things. She entered his suite with her usual sigh of resignation.

Her job, every shift, consisted of gently wiping filigree and lightly dusting lacework. She used a handheld vacuum to clean delicate carpets. She scrubbed lattice stonework with a tiny squeegee, getting the dust out of each little hole. Every fifth and sixth day, she had to clean the undersides of decorative sills. Every tenth and eleventh day, she soaped and wiped the big windows.

It was her responsibility to keep track of the cleaning schedule. If she messed up, her owner would punish her. He would even tell her why.

Thanks to her fastidious owner, Aeyong was dogmatic about tracking the passage of days. She swapped duties with her coworkers sometimes, but she never forgot the schedule. A third mistake might send her back to the slave auction block. She might end up with a more sadistic owner. Or worse. If no owner claimed her, she would join the hordes of sad, expendable, unowned slaves.

She wrung out a washcloth and soaped it up again.

Beyond the window, it was an overcast day in this nameless city. Aeyong wished it would rain. She yearned for a break from the sunlit view and all the things her owner seemed to enjoy. She loathed the way he ate morsels that made her beak water from their enticing fresh-baked aromas. She had to pretend that Torth foods were poisonous for ummins. Otherwise drool might escape her beak.

Aeyong retreated into her imagination.

In her mind, she wielded that glistening blade.

That blade could kill Torth with one stab. It could even slice holes in walls or windows. It could slice off slave collars. It was magical. And in Aeyong's imagination, she knew how to use it.

Her best friend refused to believe that freedom was possible. Aeyong didn't care. She cut away his slave collar and shouted for him to follow her. She was a runaway!

She led a group of freed slaves outside.

She ran through fields of golden flowers and gossamer ferns. She and her friends existed without Torth, without suffering, without fear. The only problems they—

Someone gasped.

It wasn't Aeyong. Nor was it any of her coworkers, since it wasn't their turn to endure their owner. They worked in other rooms.

She turned around, half wondering if her imagination was still in control. Surely her owner would not gasp? That made no sense. Nothing could startle a Torth. The gods never made sounds of shock or surprise.

The Green Rank dropped his half-bitten pastry. It rolled on the floor.

Aeyong suppressed a sigh. She would have to clean away the crumbs. But, well, maybe she would be able to surreptitiously eat the remains of the morsel? Her owner looked flabbergasted. He seemed too preoccupied to notice a minor transgression right now.

She cautiously picked up the morsel.

Her best friend feared that she would die young, condemned for having such an active imagination, and for taking too many risks with her thoughts. Time was proving him wrong. Aeyong had earned fine wrinkles around her eyes. She wasn't entirely sure that was a good thing.

"I am sorry," a whispery, raspy voice said.

Aeyong looked up in disbelief at the Green Rank. Had he actually spoken words that were not a command?

His green eyes met her gaze.

This must be a cruel prank. Torth never saw their slaves. Aeyong knew she ought to cower in submission, or return to her duties. She should not allow a Torth to bait her into a painful punishment.

Instead, she glared at her owner. Was he so sated and bored that he wanted to toy with her emotions?

She refused to respect that sort of behavior. The Torth could call themselves gods, but really, what made them any different from predators that toyed with prey?

Oh no. Aeyong was supposed to be meek and submissive. If she couldn't handle that basic law . . .

She tried to remind herself that life was worth living.

The Green Rank reached into his robes and pulled out his blaster glove.

Aeyong popped the morsel into her beak and chewed fast. If these were her final moments of existence, then she intended to savor as much as she could. Let her owner feel offended. She hoped his offense was so great, it caused him pain or humiliation.

Were such emotions even possible for a Torth? Probably not.

Her owner did not don the glove. Instead, he offered it to Aeyong.

Aeyong stared in disbelief, the sugary taste still sweet on her tongue. This was a mind game. Slaves were not allowed to touch weapons. Everyone knew that. Even ignorant children on slave farms knew that.

Or had she lost her grip on reality? Was she poisoned by hope, as everyone warned her might happen?

A blaster glove was a superior weapon to a bone-cutter knife. It was the weapon of the gods. And here was a god, apparently choosing her to wield it.

Her owner slid off his cushioned seat and fell onto his knees. He bowed to Aeyong, as if she was the god and he was the slave.

"I am not a Torth anymore," he said in his raspy, underused voice. "I will obey you, as a penitent."

He looked serious.

Aeyong took a step back, unsure whether she should grab the blaster glove and flee, or simply flee. This must be a trap.

A crashing sound came from another room. Someone screamed in terror. Could that be her coworker?

A wet blast followed, and the scream choked off.

Her Green Rank owner hurriedly donned his blaster glove, apparently forgetting that he had just offered to give it away. Aeyong jumped backward.

But her owner did not aim at her. Instead, he stood and faced the doorway. He looked more expressive than usual. There was fear on his countenance. And determination.

Two wild-eyed Torth barged into the relaxation room.

Soothing lights played on their skin and shimmering robes. Yet these were not the calm, stately gods that Aeyong was familiar with. Their robes were spattered with blood. Each wore a blaster glove. They aimed at the Green Rank.

He aimed back.

Silent blasts tore through the room.

Before Aeyong even had time to prepare for what was happening, the shots hit their targets in wet explosions.

There was no time to run or hide. Aeyong stood next to her owner as he fell, his torso a bloody mess.

Another blast tore him apart.

One of the yellow-eyed intruders fell, bleeding from a gaping wound. The other one approached, glaring at Aeyong or her owner, or maybe both of them.

Footsteps. Running. Someone light and fleet-footed was coming.

The attacker half turned toward the doorway. He was blown backward, blasted into blood-soaked pulp.

Aeyong stared in utter disbelief. A slave—an ummin like herself—had actually run up and killed that surviving Torth! And he had used a forbidden weapon, a blaster glove!

"The Torth have gone mad," the other ummin yelled.

Everyone had gone mad, as far as Aeyong was concerned.

The other ummin gestured toward her owner, who lay gasping and dying in a pool of his own blood. "Take his glove. It's your weapon now."

Aeyong knelt next to her owner, disbelieving.

"Take it," her owner rasped. "The future is in your hands." His gloved hand twitched. "Aeyong."

All life left his green eyes.

So gods could die as easily as slaves. The myths were right.

Aeyong had not guessed her owner even knew her name. It seemed unbelievable that a Torth would care to learn the name of a slave.

Or that he would be shot to death by fellow gods.

Or that he would kneel before Aeyong, and apologize, and offer her a god's weapon, right after she had gobbled his fallen pastry in front of him.

She heard distant shouts and distant blasts.

"Take your glove and follow me!" The other ummin took off running, apparently eager to face more mayhem.

Aeyong pulled the glove off her dead owner's hand. She could have disdained his corpse, maybe spat on it, but she wondered if he had been possessed by some decent god just before his death. If there was a better god who cared about slaves, she would revere that one.

The glove fit her hand poorly. There was an extra finger hole, since it was designed for Torth.

She studied the geometric symbols on the back of the glove. She had seen Torth touch those to make the gloves work.

She aimed at a piece of furniture and tapped symbols.

After a bit of practice, she learned how the weapon worked.

Other slaves would refuse this blessing. They were invested in the pretense that servitude was healthy and that freedom was a toxic fantasy. That was how they stayed sane.

Aeyong thought they might need to adjust their way of thinking.

Maybe the crazed ummin with the blaster glove was actually sane.

Maybe normal slaves were the crazy ones.

The blaster glove was big and loose on Aeyong's hand. She plucked an adjustable bracelet from among her owner's many treasures and used it to seal the glove in place. Now it would not fall off by accident. No one could rip it away with casual ease.

She stepped out of the gemstone-encrusted suite and toward a future that used to exist only in her wildest fantasies.

CHAPTER 6

CRACKED 'COSM

Garrett lay in a pool of his own blood, struggling to think through excruciating pain.

He shouldn't have dared to leave the bunker. He had tried to escort a few nussians to safety, but he should have known better. His crooked leg meant he hobbled slower than a walking pace. He couldn't run. Not after he'd stupidly lost his powers.

A grenade had killed one of those nussians. The explosion had left Garrett and the other two nussians injured. Garrett wasn't sure what had impaled his lower back, but it had pierced his armor, and probably his liver and right kidney as well.

Wrong place. Wrong time.

Yet somehow, Garrett was not dead meat. He had managed to crawl into an abandoned kitchenware shop. That was all he could do. With the supercom network down, there was no way to call for help. With his powers inhibited, Evenjos could not easily locate him. All he could do was suffer and hope—

His supercom vibrated.

Garrett flipped on the holographic menu projection. Never mind if the soft glow put him in danger. How was the network back online?

People had sent him pings. Zai. Kessa.

Ariock.

He chose Evenjos.

"What's the news?" he asked as a ghostly holograph of her head coalesced in the shadows between hanging pans.

"I thought you might know?" Evenjos's voice was reduced, channeled through the wristwatch device. "What made the Torth suddenly attack each other? Oh, and Ariock is back. I sense his presence. We can only hope he brought Thomas."

A fresh wave of agony swept through Garrett. He grimaced. Sweat rolled down his cheeks. He might actually prefer getting decapitated to this pain.

"Where are you?" Evenjos sounded urgent.

"Third Street between Stream and Victory." Garrett groaned in pain. "Kitchenware shop."

Seconds later, a sparkling white gown appeared, filled out by the shapely body Evenjos preferred to default to. She ended the call and knelt even as her lush, lilac-colored hair was still coalescing. Starlight glitter suffused the air where she appeared, like fairy dust, sparked from the stirrings of her power.

Evenjos folded her wings and spread her hands in the air above Garrett's injury. The pain receded.

Garrett felt his internal organs knitting back together and other repairs taking place. He had been in shock. He had been close to passing out from blood loss. Death would have ensued within minutes. That had been a fatal injury, he realized.

Now?

It felt like a new day. The devastating injury might as well have happened a month ago.

Garrett sat up straighter. He was thirsty and ravenous from the aftereffects of healing.

He gingerly touched his midsection. Nothing wrong.

He laid his head back against the wall so he could admire the wonderful goddess who had healed him. Never mind Ariock's criticisms about her. Her healing power was overwhelming and undeniable, and anyone who found themselves the subject of her care should feel divinely blessed.

He had known that a century ago, when he was seventeen years old, back when she had offered him her power so he could break free from the Isolatorium.

"What is happening in the Megacosm?" Evenjos extended one arm toward a rack of water bottles for sale. She used her powers to float one to Garrett.

Garrett grabbed the water and gulped it down. That helped ease his nausea and hunger a bit. "I suppose I should find out."

He assumed his great-grandson's return was the reason Evenjos felt safe enough to flit around. Judging by her most recent memories, the invaders no longer seemed interested in vandalism or murder. Many of them bent over and vomited. Or they crashed transports. Or they wept.

Others shot the weeping ones in the back.

Still others turned their blaster gloves on themselves.

Something major was happening.

Garrett closed his eyes, blocking out distractions. He ascended into the Megacosm.

*!!!! * !!!!! * !!!!!! * !!!!!!!! * ( ) * !!!!!!!! * ( ) * !!!!!!!!!!!!!!!!!!!!!!!!!!!!!!!!!!!*

An armada surrounded the planet known as Bountiful—one of the wealthiest planets in the galaxy. Torth aboard dreadnoughts aimed comet-class missiles at *(the traitors!) (the insane deviants!)* cities full of mind readers who had decided to bow down and submit themselves to the Conqueror.

Innumerable Torth were surrendering to him.

To the boy.

Entire hub megalopolises full of Torth wanted to join the boy. Right now.

Every Torth on the FlatRing Station declared themselves penitent. They surrendered their weapons to their slaves and knelt in supplication. *Conqueror, protect Us*, they begged.

Because the Megacosm hardly existed anymore.

It was a fractured mess, a heaving avalanche of lost knowledge and unanswered questions. Just being there made Garrett queasy. It was enough to make a lifelong Torth vomit. There were choruses of agreement, but they were in conflict with opposing choruses. There was no obvious Majority.

The Torth Empire was at war with itself.

"Holy calamities." Garrett couldn't think of adequate curses or proper reactions. MoonGarden, Parity, Vagary, Ringworld, Yoft, Endless . . . more than seven hundred hub planets were exploding in violence. At least half the Torth-owned galaxy seemed to have severed itself, eager to join the Conqueror. Millions.

Billions.

Trillions.

Stunned, Garrett dropped out of the Megacosm.

Evenjos gave him a questioning look.

Garrett reached for her hand, and she gave it to him. He clasped it. He wanted someone who understood what this moment meant. It didn't feel real. He didn't quite believe it.

She picked up his emotions. She gazed into his eyes.

"The Torth Empire," Garrett said, his mouth dry, his throat thick with gravitas. "It's falling apart."

Evenjos looked young with disbelieving curiosity. Her eyes were large. She emitted (???) demands for clarification.

"We've got to go to the boy. He's here. In Freedomland." Garrett tried to ghost, but he couldn't achieve the clairvoyant trance since he had breathed inhibitor gas.

Evenjos began to remind him that the supercom network was online. Garrett didn't wait for her to finish explaining. He saw Thomas in his list of contacts and immediately called.

No reply.

Garrett growled. The boy was supposed to prioritize Garrett's calls, but perhaps he was too busy to notice the vibration signal?

He was too busy defeating the Torth Empire.

Garrett wanted to demand confirmation and clarification from someone who understood what was going on. Was this really happening? How? He impatiently selected Kessa from his list of top contacts.

Kessa's holograph took shape. There were sounds of celebration in the background. "Garrett? I am glad you're all right."

"Where are you?" Garrett asked. "Where's the boy?"

Kessa smiled. "Thomas is with me. We're in the research bunker, beneath—"

Garrett ended the call and struggled to get to his feet. He wanted to run, to fly, but without his powers, even simple actions were nearly impossible. He was geriatric.

"Here." Evenjos used her powers to give Garrett his silver staff.

He leaned on it, grateful.

Evenjos's power washed over Garrett, this time cleansing his skin and armor. He felt renewed. Even without a mirror, he knew that his beard and hair were a pristine snow white, and his black armor shone.

"I'll get us there fast." Evenjos scooped him up, handling him as easily as if he was a child. Her current form was slender and dainty, yet she had the physical strength of a nussian.

He was grateful to know a goddess.

She carried him outside and spread her wings. They soared over a city that looked quiet and peaceful from the sky. There were moving figures on rooftops or balconies, here and there. The streets were empty except for dead Torth.

Within minutes, they landed at an unobtrusive outbuilding in the academy complex. Evenjos used her powers to open the locked door. She carried Garrett down ramps and into a secret passageway, breezing through the tunnel faster than a hovercart.

They encountered a crowd.

It seemed a lot of people wanted to meet Thomas and Kessa. People were feverishly congratulating each other, or reporting the various ways in which they believed the Torth Empire had fallen.

"They say the entire Megacosm collapsed!"

"What about the Death Architect and their other supergeniuses?"

"Are you saying the Torth no longer have an empire?"

"A whole bunch of them declared themselves to be penitents!"

"Some went rogue, also."

"They're going to start their own spin-off empires?"

Garrett wanted to be set down. Evenjos read his mind and put him on his feet.

Together, they made their way toward the vault door to the bunker. Garrett sensed *(???)* a thirst for information. These people were itching to interrogate the first mind reader they saw.

"Is it true?" someone shouted. "Is the Torth Empire defeated?"

Thunder cracked, and a scent of ozone filled the tunnel. Ariock dropped out of thin air and landed on his feet.

"Bringer of Hope!" people cheered.

"Ariock!"

Ariock straightened to his full height, towering over everyone else. He had found enough time to put on his formidable space armor, with the galaxy embossed on his chest plate. His shoulders gave him the shape of a thunderhead.

"Is it true?" he asked Garrett. "What's happening in the Megacosm?"

"The Torth Empire," Garrett said, "is fractured into bits." He couldn't help but smile, because the victory was his as much as it was anyone's. He was the Will of Ah Jun's prophecies. He was the igniter, the one who started it all. "The Torth are no longer united under a single ideology. They don't have a clear Majority." He grinned savagely. "And I don't think they ever will again."

People whooped.

"For real?" Ariock's beaming smile was as rare and joyous as a planet-rise reflected on the ocean.

"It's real." Garrett limped through the vault door, entering a crowded space. "Well, let's go see the boy."

People moved aside, respectfully clearing an aisle for Garrett, Evenjos, and Ariock.

Thomas was at the center of a lot of speculation. He stood without any apparent leg braces, happily talking to lab assistants. When had he grown inches taller than Varktezo? When had he begun to look so healthy?

Garrett swallowed a feeling that seemed enormous and overwhelming.

Maybe it was his pride. He didn't want to admit that he might have made a mistake or two about Thomas. A misjudgment.

Eh. Maybe a lot of them.

Evenjos prodded him. She sensed Garrett's surface thoughts, and she wanted him to put aside his pride and . . . well . . . give the boy his due.

"Thomas," Garrett said.

Thomas looked at him. He had never heard Garrett use his name.

Well, if this wasn't cause for praise, then nothing was. Did it really matter that Thomas was a full-blooded Torth? Did it matter that he had nameless parents? He had just destroyed the evil galactic empire.

He was a damned hero.

Garrett dared to limp even closer, so that their ranges of telepathy overlapped. He allowed himself to bask in the incomprehensible complexity that was Thomas's mind. This was the brain of a miracle worker. Garrett had expected this war to draw out over centuries. Somehow, Thomas had found a shortcut. He had done the impossible and caused the Torth Empire to collapse from within!

Thomas had promised that millions of Torth would willingly join their side. Garrett had failed to believe him.

"You did it," Garrett admitted.

His vision blurred with tears. When he had first put together the book of prophecies, it had all seemed so improbable.

Everyone around them fell silent. Some wanted to hear what the mind readers would say, since only Garrett and Thomas had the ability to peer into the Megacosm and report on what was happening in the Torth Empire.

"We won," Garrett said.

The crowd fluttered with relief and joy.

"The war is over?" Kessa asked, grinning with the shared triumph, but also with a hint of disbelief. She turned to Thomas. Everybody did.

Thomas met the expectant gazes with a satisfied grin.

That was answer enough. Thomas would not look that happy unless he had a good reason to.

All of a sudden, the bunker crowd lost its decorum. Everyone was celebrating. People bumped fists. They screamed with victory and began to pour fizzing drinks for each other. Some of them danced jigs.

"IT'S OVER!"

"THE TORTH EMPIRE IS BROKEN!"

"WE WON!"

People were dancing, jumping, embracing, sharing grins and love.

Garrett ascended into the Megacosm, just in case there were any existential threats he had missed. Someone must have woken the Death Architect. Shouldn't he pay attention to the last scraps of major news in the cataclysm? She might find loyalists, even with the empire collapsing.

!!!!!!!

News pinged between Torth who were interested in forbidden pleasures. Apparently, a penitent had shared her sexual exploits.

One of her adventures was bedding the Conqueror.

!

Garrett dropped out of the Megacosm and struggled not to gape at Thomas. He tried to scan the boy, seeking an explanation, but he might as well examine the inner workings of some ludicrously complex machinery. Any answers he sought were buried inside constantly shifting cascades of data.

Thomas avoided his gaze.

"Really?" Garrett spoke out loud to underscore his consternation. A supergenius ought to know better than to let his guard down around a potential enemy. Someone like the Pink Screwdriver could strangle a boy to death before anyone could stop her! Or what if she had turned out to be a sleeper agent? She could have weaseled Thomas's military secrets out of him, then disseminated that information to the Torth Empire. Garrett wanted to yell at the kid.

But he didn't. Thomas was a damned hero. Never mind whatever shenanigans he'd gotten up to, never mind what risks he'd taken. It had turned out all right.

Ariock saw their silent exchange. "Is there a threat?" he asked.

"No," Thomas said.

Garrett cleared his throat. "Nope." He squeezed Evenjos's hand and decided to let the dalliance go unremarked upon. The Conqueror deserved a chance for love, even if it was with a . . . a . . .

Well. With a Torth.

"The Megacosm is factionalizing." Thomas spoke past Garrett, to Ariock. "Their unity is dissolving. Most of the factions are harmless to us. There might be a few that we have to worry about. I think a cult will gather around the Death Architect, and that might cause us problems. But otherwise?" He shook his head, a grin on his face. "The Torth Empire is collapsing. It won't rise again. Not like it was."

Celebration broke out anew. People cheered.

Ariock made a fist of victory and then drew Vy into a hug. Then Kessa. He reached for Garrett as well. Evenjos joined the group hug, and soon they were all laughing.

"We've gained more cities and planets than we can handle," Thomas said. "So we'll have to handle them somehow."

Ariock hesitated, then threw his arms around Thomas in a gentle hug.

Thomas pushed him away, laughing. "I didn't do much. Really. This victory wouldn't have been what it was without Mondoyo and Serette." He beckoned to the Twins. "Hey! Come over here and join us."

The Twins hovered in their own pocket of space. They looked uncertain as they floated closer.

People stepped out of their range. Kessa and Varktezo did not. They studied the Twins with fresh respect.

"A symphony?" Thomas's eyes sparkled with admiration. He leaned over and gave Mondoyo and Serette each a fist bump. "We should translate that to an audio recording sometime, so people can listen with their ears as well as with their minds."

The Twins looked shy but pleased. Mondoyo seemed happy to return the fist bump, as if he had been raised in American culture instead of on a Vazzan baby farm.

"I'm so glad to meet you." Thomas sounded like he meant it.

"I can't believe you're actually here! In person!" Mondoyo sounded like a kid visiting Disneyland. Even Serette was flushed with excitement.

Garrett folded his arms. These three children acted as if they were enjoying a schoolyard recess instead of an impossible-to-pull-off miracle that was already changing galactic history. Why did supergeniuses have to be so casual? So unpretentious? If they were smug elitists, then at least he could justify the intimidation he felt in the presence of their gargantuan minds.

Judging by the way they were nodding silently to each other and gazing adoringly into each other's eyes, they were conducting a mutually respectful discourse. They could condense a lengthy scientific treatise into nanoseconds.

Or maybe they were hammering out details of how to defeat and destroy the Death Architect?

Or how to rule the galaxy as a trio?

Or all of that, at the same time?

Garrett cleared his throat, aiming to interrupt their silent schemes. "So. What're our next steps, Thomas?"

CHAPTER 7

BRAIN DRAIN

The Climbing Storm sucked her thumb.

She knew that was wrong, against the rules of the baby farm where she lived. If anyone saw her bizarre comfort-seeking behavior, she would fail to graduate to adulthood. Adults tended to forgive supergeniuses like her, but it was best not to take risks or cross lines.

Getting chopped up for organ donations seemed like a faraway danger right now, though. There were scarier things.

She hid inside the blocky playground labyrinth, in a dark recess for slaves. There was hardly any light. It felt safer than her own bedroom, where anyone might barge in and find her.

She hoped Nuzzy, her slave, would remain silent.

The Climbing Storm had told Nuzzy to carry her here, since she could not walk or crawl very well. Nuzzy was a grown-up govki. He was good, but like all slaves, he missed a lot of information and he had no idea what was going on. His furry body cushioned her, wrapped around her, soft and comforting.

She trembled. She could feel Nuzzy's heartbeat and smell his fear. He was afraid because she was afraid.

She took a risk and peeked in on the Megacosm again.

The chaos was worse. Throughout the empire, Torth shot their comrades in the back or the head. Torth threw grenades at their rogue neighbors. All the while, that symphony played in the background—the one orchestrated by the Twins.

You traitors (you so-called penitents) don't deserve to live!

!!!

Wrong! Get off Our planet!

!!!

No! We claim this planet for the Conqueror!

All hail the Conqueror!

The Megacosm heaved and tossed like a dying god, fracturing and cracking along fault lines that few people had even noticed until now.

Many of the new penitents—the ones who wanted to worship the Conqueror— believed they must surrender their weapons and obey their slaves. But that seemed like madness to the Climbing Storm. She wasn't that stupid, and she was only four years old. Anyone who threw away their weapons became vulnerable.

Fools! Can't you see the Twins fell for propaganda?

The Conqueror just wants more Torth slaves!

The arguments back and forth made the Climbing Storm wonder if she ought to attempt to form an actual opinion on her own.

But she was too young for that.

It was hard to make evaluations without guidance from adults or older kids. The Climbing Storm was curious about the Conqueror, but she doubted that such a mature and accomplished supergenius would value her. She was unripe. Everyone knew that supergeniuses younger than six years old were essentially worthless.

Unlike able-bodied people, she genuinely relied on slaves to survive. Would the Conqueror assign slaves to her? Or "friends," or whatever he called slaves over on his side?

Probably not.

The Climbing Storm really didn't want to make a mistake that would ruin her life forever, or get her killed. She sucked her thumb and hoped the Majority would reemerge from the madness and show her what to think.

Amid the violence and losses, a boulder of sanity arose.

In normal times, a thirteen-year-old child with a penchant for torture would not have been so esteemed. Everyone agreed on that fact. But the Death Architect was the eldest surviving supergenius who remained loyal to the Torth Empire. She had dealt serious damage to the enemies.

It was about time she showed up.

HELP US!

  SAVE US!

Billions of minds flocked into orbit around the tranquil behemoth of a mind, desperate for solutions to this cataclysmic eruption of battles storming across the galaxy. The Climbing Storm went with them. She wanted rational answers and safety as much as anyone.

The Twins bowed out of the Megacosm, unwilling to directly challenge the elected leader of a galactic civilization. They feared the Death Architect's ability to probe their minds and learn their exact locations. Their symphony faded as hundreds of millions of penitents likewise dropped out.

Whew. That calmed things down a bit.

The Climbing Storm dared to hope that the Megacosm would eventually settle into its normal state.

Although, in truth, it had felt rotten for a long while. The Climbing Storm was very immature, but even so, she outshined most adults in the field of philology. She estimated that the Megacosm had begun to feel like an unstable teeter-totter around the time when the Colossal Failure had killed himself. The loss of a maturing supergenius always made a dent in universal knowledge. The Megacosm had seemed to become more porous.

The holes had increased and gotten larger when the Majority assassinated the Upward Governess.

No one had treated that as a cause for alarm. Scientists regretted the loss of such an industrious supergenius, but . . . well, traitors deserved death. Besides, the Upward Governess had suffered from multiple physical maladies. Everyone expected her to die. There were always new baby supergeniuses to replace the elders who blinked out of existence.

The Climbing Storm had crawled along obscure nodes at the time, soaking up research. She had concluded that the Megacosm was cohesive enough. Things were fine.

But the Conqueror kept spreading his message about emotional freedoms, eroding the confidence of countless Torth. His mental invitations and his imaginary hugs had stirred up a lot of furtive secrecy. Many Torth must harbor secret doubts about the war, or about the enemies, which they did not want their colleagues or neighbors to find out about.

The Climbing Storm had noted when it became commonplace for high ranks to avoid the Megacosm. That was historically abnormal. Some of the highest ranks were only sharing half of their daily wake cycles with their orbiters. That was miserly.

They offered solid excuses. The Death Architect and other supergeniuses purported to be hard at work on inventing new weapons. Governors and other petty leaders claimed they were worn out from offering constant reassurances to the Torth Majority.

And then the boy Twin had vanished and gone renegade.

And then the girl Twin.

Now? Other supergeniuses were surrendering to the Conqueror. They left, and avalanches of knowledge fell away. Every aspect of collective knowledge seemed rotten to the core, held in untrustworthy minds that might turn rogue at any moment.

HELP US! the remainder of the Majority roared. It was a plea, but they were so distraught and so numerous, their plea came across like a demand. There were billions.

SAVE US!

GUIDE US!

SOLVE THIS!

The Death Architect was an exemplary example of godlike calm. Her tranquility drew people the way a black hole drew matter. Billions more Torth joined the orbiters around her, trembling. *Please (please) please (please) PLEASE HELP US???*

The Death Architect gave a quiet exhalation. Her rejection of love and friendship and slave emotions made her the epitome of peaceful logic.

Oh, My constituents (orbiters), she thought without any pity or care. *Don't You see? We (the great and mighty Torth Empire) are stronger (better off) without the whiny dead weight of traitors, rogues, barbarians, and slave sympathizers.*

Many of her orbiters recoiled in shock.

!!!!!!!!!?!!!!!!!!!!!?!!!!!!!!!!!!!!!!!!

( ) ( ) ( ) ( ) !!!

*!!!!!!!!!!!!! * ( ) * !!!!!!!!!!!!!!*

The Climbing Storm sucked on her thumb harder. Her eyes widened even though there was nothing to see inside this darkened slave closet.

KILL ALL TRAITORS!

** ( ) * ( ) * ( ) ** ( ) * ( ) * ( ) * ( ) * ( ) * ( ) * ( ) * ( ) **

Death screams filled the Megacosm.

Too many Torth figured the Death Architect was their best possible leader, despite—or because of—her uncaring attitude. Surely she would invent a superior weapon? Surely she would pull all the vast resources of the empire into a victorious configuration?

The death cultists shot their colleagues and neighbors without qualms. They wanted a strong and united empire. They would do anything to get that. Their murderous determination sounded like ferocious, bestial snarling.

*!!!! * ( ) * !!!!*
*!!!!!! * ( ) * !!!!!!*
*!!!!! * ( ) * !!!!!*
*!!!!!! * ( ) * !!!!!*
*!!!!!! * ( ) * !!!!!*
*!!!!! * ( ) * !!!!!*
*!!!! * ( ) * !!!!!*

Yet many other Torth—billions, in fact—were horrified by the bloodshed.

This was not a small, localized rebellion. Nearly a quarter of the wakeful Torth Empire now declared themselves to be kneelers, interested in joining the Conqueror.

And 3 percent were inclined to go rogue.

On Tzogratzar, citizens sealed themselves inside the forums of various cities. Other citizens tried to blast the doors open. Still others sabotaged those efforts.

On Permadrift Orbital, all the citizens bowed to their slaves and declared themselves penitents. Only one refused. He locked himself in a bath closet.

In a city on Hoosf, children blasted their way out of a baby farm, intent on aiding one faction or another.

!!!!!!!
!!!!!!!!!
!!!!!
!!!!!!!!!

Mobs chased down traitors. Even more death screams filled the Megacosm.

Others encountered resistance in the form of slaves armed with blaster gloves.

What did the Death Architect have to say about the fresh waves of kneelers, penitents, and rogues?

Kill them, she thought with a mental shrug.

*!!!!!!!!!!! * ( ) * !!!!!!!!!!!!!!*

Being a Torth isn't worth it, a supergenius known as the Spin Overture announced to her own audience of many thousands of orbiters. *I quit. Conqueror, rescue Me!*

That sent her orbiters into a frenzy of *????* and *!!!!!!!!!!*

You elected Death, the Rind Topographer let the Majority know. *Isn't it obvious which side of this war values creativity and ideas and life, and which side is ruled by stagnation, regression, and death?*

The roiling, ailing Majority rose up all around her.

In agreement.

** ! * ! * ! * ! * ! * ! * ! * ! * ! * ! * ! **

Their minds met, joining in an immense choral wave that washed away all dissenters.

WE CHOOSE.

WE SURRENDER.

CONQUEROR, SAVE US!

WE ARE PENITENTS!!

And the Death Architect?

She remained tranquil, as if civilization was not crumbling. *We (Torth) ought to preemptively kill all the remaining supergeniuses except for Me,* she decided. *The others cannot be trusted.*

Her chorus of orbiters agreed.

The Climbing Storm gasped out loud. Alarm flooded her, so much that she automatically dropped out of the Megacosm.

Her blaster glove was in the compartment of her hoverchair, back in her bedroom. She had no way to defend herself. A measly weapon wouldn't save her anyway, if her entire baby farm decided to gang up and kill her. She couldn't fend off a mob of murderous children and adolescents.

She hated being below the Megacosm. It made her feel sunken and trapped inside her own unloved body.

She turned and buried her face into Nuzzy's fur, much to the slave's shock and surprise.

Hugs were definitely illegal. No child ever hugged a slave. It meant death.

Yet Nuzzy tolerated it because he was good. The Climbing Storm was glad for something—someone—she could count on. She was no longer sure about anything else. She had no idea what was illegal anymore, or what would get her killed, or save her.

Well, that wasn't quite so.

She had absorbed replays of the Conqueror whenever he entered the Megacosm. He claimed that he would welcome anyone, even if they were weak. Even if they were scared.

Maybe he would actually value an unripe child supergenius, after all?

But he was busy right now. He was conducting a battle, killing the Torth who had invaded his city. And before that, he had been absent from the Megacosm for many wake cycles.

But perhaps some of his penitent friends, like that weird Pink Screwdriver, would hear a specific cry in the Megacosm and convey a message to him?

The Climbing Storm threw herself wholly into the Megacosm, blaring the location of her baby farm. *I SURRENDER! I RENOUNCE EVERYTHING! CONQUEROR? SAVE ME!*

She was only one more kneeler, one more newly converted penitent. There were trillions. Her cry would have been lost in the chaos, dismissed and ignored because of her immature status, except for the fact that she had the rare supergenius mutation.

!!!

Kill the Climbing Storm! many Torth chorused. *Kill all supergenius traitors!*

They mentally tugged for the attention of children on her baby farm. *Find her. Kill her.*

Far away, on another planet, the Geodesic Flux choked, suffocating. Someone had invaded his bedroom and was strangling him.

The Rind Topographer begged for a rescue. Her pleas evaporated into meaningless echoes as a blade sliced her neck wide open.

*!!!!!!!!!!!!!!!!!! * ( ) * !!!!!!!!!!!!!!!!!!!!!!!*

Other supergeniuses emitted shocked death screams. The Stalled Proofer. The Stemmer Linguist. The Neurobioticist. The Spin Overture. The Mechanized Meeter. They left afterimages of coppery surprise and regrets.

*! * ( ) * !*

*!!!!! * ( ) * !!!!!*

*!!!!!!!!!!!!!!!!!! * ( ) * !!!!!!!!!!!!!!!!!!*
** ( ) * !!!!!!!*

Half of the Megacosm seemed to cave in and collapse, like a continental plate slipping, except far worse. It was cosmic. It was like an accretion disk sucked into a supermassive black hole.

Scientific groups moaned that they were set back by centuries.

History groups screamed that they had lost millennia worth of information, not backed up anywhere.

Every discipline, from military armaments to astronavigation to nutrition and medicine to childcare, and more . . . they felt a drain.

Every Torth in the empire felt it. Too much knowledge was gone. The mental landscape became pockmarked with craters.

!!!!!!!!!! ( ) !!!
*!!!!!!!!!!!!!!!! * ( ) * !!!!!!!!! ( ) !!!!!!!!!!!!!!! * ( ) * !!!!*
*!!!!! ( ) !!!!! ( ) !!!!!! * ( ) * !!! ( ) !!!!!!!!! ( ) !!!!!!!!!!!! ( ) !!!!!!!!!!*

The Climbing Storm mentally turned this way and that, searching for any of her esteemed knowledge mates who might have survived.

Her own bedroom was being ransacked. She was the only supergenius who had preemptively hidden from her guardians and peers.

Of course, she had not foreseen this calamity. Only someone with a precognitive power could have foreseen this. She had only hidden because she'd felt scared, and she had been too ashamed to let anyone notice the slavish emotion roiling inside her.

FIND HER.

Footsteps shook her hiding place. Adolescents tore through her baby farm, searching.

Nuzzy curled around her. He understood that she was terrified, and that pathetic fact seemed enough to make him sympathetic, even without understanding why.

Just as a forest grows healthier by shedding dead leaves, the Death Architect thought while she orchestrated her cultists, *We (the Torth Empire) shall grow healthier by shedding Our weak-minded deviants. Only true Torth have any value.*

The Death Architect understood how fast supergeniuses could react. Her sudden and offhand command to kill supergeniuses had ensured that there was very little time for warnings or rescues.

She had planned this.

Or she had anticipated the opportunity, anyway.

The Climbing Storm couldn't guess how or why, but she understood that the Death Architect had groomed Torth to trust and respect her. The Death Architect never, ever disagreed with the Majority. She catered to their every whim. Thusly the masses were conditioned to obey her with very little self-examination or skepticism. That was why so many Torth clung to her now, worshipping her as if she was an actual god.

But couldn't they tell that a decimation of the Torth population was not strength?

It was not an improvement. Anyone with a brain ought to understand that.

The Upward Governess had certainly understood that. So did the Conqueror.

*!!!!!! * ( ) * !!!!!!*

*!!!!!! * ( ) * !!!!!!!!*
*!!!!!! * ( ) * !!!!!!*
*!!!!!!!! * ( ) * !!!!!!!!*

In cities across the galaxy, anyone with a teleportation power vanished. Perhaps they were going to murder any surviving supergeniuses, such as the Climbing Storm? Or had they gone to kneel before the Conqueror?

Let cowards flee, the Death Architect crooned. *We (true Torth) do not need feeble slave emotions. We are above that.*

The Death Architect might tell herself that all this destruction was a benefit, and her constituents might believe it . . . but the Torth Empire had been truly mighty, with 38.2 trillion citizens. Whatever was left after today, it would not be comparable. Not even close.

Who needs traitors? Orbiters echoed the Death Architect's opinions with fervency.

Shoot penitents!

Take out the trash!

Get rid of the riffraff!

Bomb the slave sympathizers!

Kill kill KILL!!!!

They mentally cavorted around the enormous mind of their patron—while in the physical realm, they shot anyone who questioned the order.

This time of chaos will end, the Death Architect assured those of her cultists who harbored reservations, smoothing away their worries. *We (the true Torth) will end up more pure. The Torth civilization will be stronger and better than ever.*

Knowledge flushed away in the absence of supergeniuses and scientists, leaving massive sinkholes.

Billions of minds rejected godhood.

If the Climbing Storm had recognized what was at stake earlier, she would have begged the Conqueror to rescue her when he was actually present and listening. It seemed blatantly obvious now that the Majority had never truly valued supergeniuses or knowledge. Her orbiters claimed to worship facts and truth and logic above all else. Torth prided themselves on that. But now they were okay with murdering supergeniuses?

They were tossing knowledge away like it was garbage.

They used to have such a nearly infinite supply of knowledge, they had taken it for granted.

The Conqueror was different.

He never would have sanctioned the murder of supergeniuses. He went so far as to teach runaway slaves how to be scientists, because he valued every mind, no matter whose mind it was.

The Torth Majority, on the other hand, had voted to destroy the populations of baby farms on a whim.

The Climbing Storm should have been clued in when those baby farm massacres had happened on the moons of Umdalkdul. The Death Architect had justified that decision, claiming that she wanted to prevent the Conqueror from finding soft and easy targets for his conversion methods. She had killed assets—thousands of adolescents, children, toddlers, babies, and fetuses—before the Giant could show up to claim them.

Few Torth had questioned the massacres at the time.

But they had been wrong.

Today, the Conqueror was gaining billions of penitents without infiltrating a single baby farm.

And the Megacosm was a fractured mess. There was no longer any definitive Majority. There was no clear path to success.

Save Me, Conqueror, the Climbing Storm begged.

But the Conqueror wasn't in the Megacosm.

Where did all the knowledge go? many Torth thrummed, feeling their way through the chaos that the Megacosm had become.

Where are the answers?

THIS IS WRONG.

STOP.

WE NEED SUPERGENIUSES.

The Climbing Storm was amazed that she was not wholly alone. Self-proclaimed penitents urged the children on her local baby farm to *RISE UP* and *DEFEND HER.*

Some of them actually wanted to.

Children donned their blaster gloves. Some hid. Some shot at aggressors.

!!!! * ( ) * !!!!!!!

!!!!!!!! * ( ) * !!!!!!!!!

Even some of the death cultists wondered, *Is it necessary to kill toddler super-geniuses?*

The babies can't possibly pose any threat, can they?

They are useless.

Why should We kill the unripe ones?

Baby supergeniuses are future assets, the Death Architect informed her constituents. *We ought not give the enemies any chance of stealing valuable (minds) resources for future use. Kill them.*

Her cultists trusted her and believed her.

Seismic waves lashed the already chaotic Megacosm. Everyone sensed a garrote choking off the breath of one toddler.

!!!!!! * ( ) * !!!!!!!!!!!

A blast destroyed another.

!!!!!!!!!!! * ( ) * !!!!!!!!!!!!!

And the last one, the youngest baby.

!!!!!!!!!!!!!!!!! * ( ) * !!!!!!!!!!!!!!!!!

The Climbing Storm wrapped her twig-thin arms around herself and buried her forehead in Nuzzy's fur. She couldn't stop herself from weeping. She felt every death almost as if it was her own.

Yet she clung to the Megacosm, searching for any sign of stability, any glimpse of normalcy. Most of all, she scanned for any sign of salvation.

It was all coming apart.

It fractured into insanity.

!!

!!

!!

!!
!!
!!
!!
!!
!!
!!!. . . . .
. . . .
. . . .
. . . .
. . . .
. . . .
. . . .
. . . .
. . . .
. . . .
. . . .
. . . .
. . . .

DRAGON ARMOR

Five colony starships.

Fifty-five comet-class battleships.

Hundreds of dreadnoughts.

Millions of streamships.

Countless spaceports, orbital stations, and industrial colonies. Billions of urban areas.

Nine trillion newly penitent refugee Torth.

Seventeen thousand penitents who had powers, like Zai.

A quadrillion newly freed people who were eager and willing to be enfolded into Kessa's amalgamated protectorates.

And counting.

Ariock was bombarded with estimates that were impossible for him to imagine. He was minuscule next to the freed galaxy. It was humbling. Even with his cosmic level of raw power, he had never ghosted to more than a fraction of all known inhabited worlds. There were entire galactic arms he had never visited. There were sapient species whom he had yet to meet a single member of. He had not even lived as many subjective years as most of his new subjects, if they could be called that.

Was he their ruler? Their protector? He didn't even know.

"So what do we do?" Ariock said, interrupting Garrett's victory tallies. "How do we handle all this?"

He looked past Garrett, past Evenjos, past Vy, past the Twins, past Kessa and Varktezo. Thomas stood at the far end of the makeshift conference table, which was actually a countertop with the lab equipment cleared off it.

Thomas pulled off his colorful round cap. He leaned on the countertop in his shirtsleeves. One arm was encased in a control sleeve that glowed with power displays.

His answer was simple and majestic. "We show them how to live in our new empire."

Our empire.

A galaxy.

To rule.

Ariock tried to process all that. He was glad to be seated, even though he sat on the burnished floor, since he had not teleported his meteorite throne or any other extra-large chair into the bunker. His space armor was flexible enough. And sitting, he was just about as tall as people who were standing.

No one suggested relocating to the war room. Everyone in the research bunker was still stunned, still processing their victory over the old galactic empire.

"How can we communicate with trillions of newly freed slaves?" Kessa asked. "That seems like an obstacle."

"Quadrillions," Thomas corrected. "It will be multiple quadrillions before the end of today."

Kessa was clearly trying to grapple with the scale of their newborn empire. She had a very salient point, Ariock realized. Their supercom network only reached three worlds. Four, if one counted Earth. Mind readers could communicate instantly between any world, but his own people could not.

"Without guidance from us," Garrett realized, "they'll all go rogue."

"We cannot possibly hold a galactic empire together," Evenjos agreed.

Thomas had an answer. "We'll need to visit a lot of hub planets within upcoming weeks and years."

Ariock resigned himself to a busy future with lots of teleportation.

"Before that," Thomas said, "Kessa and her lieutenants will select mouthpieces from among the newly converted penitents in all the major cities." He pulled up an office chair and sat. "We'll have some basic tenets for them to pass along to their local mayors and leaders. A constitution, if you will."

"A galactic constitution?" Garrett considered it. "How can we enforce it? What's to prevent the planets from tossing it away and going rogue at the first opportunity?"

Ariock nodded. People needed mutual understanding. That was crucial to something as hegemonic as an empire. If different provinces could not even communicate in a timely way . . . ? Without functional justice, without law enforcement, there was no empire.

Thomas seemed about to answer, but Kessa spoke first. "There is a promise implicit in what we have done."

Garrett looked ready to argue.

"And we can make more promises." Kessa looked around the conference table, especially at Ariock. "We will unite the planets. Not only with superluminal relay stations—I understand that it will take lifetimes to manufacture and implement so many—but with songs. And stories. And with art."

Varktezo frowned in puzzlement. "How can you distribute art if you are relying on penitents as the only means of communication?"

Ariock inwardly agreed. Mind readers were not renowned for their singing and storytelling skills. Plus, he could imagine some penitents backsliding, trying to establish their own mini-tyrannies. It was inevitable. Telepathy gave them a natural advantage over other people, and they would try to exploit that again and again.

"I am talking about art that is inescapably grand," Kessa said. "And art that can last for eons. Like the Stratower." She gestured overhead, implying the city above them. "Ariock and Thomas have already made a start. They created the academy. And the war palace. Those are impressive buildings."

But they could do better.

Kessa did not have to say it. They could build even more magnificent, imposing, awe-inspiring edifices.

Ariock straightened, armor creaking, and never mind how much room he took up. Kessa had a point. She was absolutely right.

There was room in this galaxy for never-seen-before wonders.

Thomas seemed inspired as well. "I see what you mean," he said to Kessa. "We can build space stations and commemorative monoliths and academies of such artistry and grandeur that not even the most elitist Torth can deny their architectural superiority." He seemed to admire something that only he could see. He was probably imagining something hyperrealistic. "We would build things that are entirely new, that don't look derivative of the Torth Empire at all."

The Twins shared a look of incredulous amazement.

Kessa nodded happily. "Former slaves all have a shared culture, as well as a shared history. We speak the same language. And there will be a promise of an intergalactic communications network to come."

It might work.

Ariock felt as if he was seeing the outline of something that dwarfed him to insignificance. There was a future after the downfall of the Torth Empire. It was real. It was on its way.

It just might need some help being born.

"The philosophy of Gwat might aid in unification," Mondoyo said, ducking his head in embarrassment. "I would humbly suggest that you spread that, along with the new constitution and whatever else."

Adherents of Gwat tended to be less judgmental than other people. Ariock supposed the penitents would like that. If everyone followed Gwat, penitents would be welcomed rather than ridiculed.

"These ideas merit discussion," Evenjos said, peering grandly around at the assembled leaders as if she was still an empress. "But shan't we deal with emergencies right now?"

On monitors around the room, Torth kicked their weapons toward freedom soldiers or knelt before them. Fires guttered in a rainy drizzle that Ariock had instigated a while ago. People cautiously emerged from bomb shelters and explored damaged shops or apartments.

Ariock wondered what mayhem was tearing through Torth-ruled metropolises while his city recovered. Just how many disasters was he oblivious to right now?

"Oh, that reminds me," Garrett said. "Thomas? I forged a suit of space armor for you."

Thomas looked surprised.

"As a gift," Garrett said sheepishly. "I was saving it for when you returned. Now I think it's not quite enough of an apology. But it's a start. I'd be honored if you wear it while we cement our reign or whatever. I'd rather you be as protected as possible."

"I'm interested," Thomas said, and Ariock silently agreed.

Ariock wore the equivalent of a custom-fitted starship hull, except it was plated to be flexible. His great-grandfather had taught him how to reshape the hardiest materials in the known universe. Ionic tungsten was marginally stronger than the colloidal crystal armor worn by Torth champions and shani warriors.

"I would teleport it here," Garrett said, "but I'm on the inhibitor. Ariock? You'll find it in our shared cache."

"Can't ghost from here," Ariock said, climbing to his feet.

The others followed him out of the bunker. Happy technicians moved out of the way, bowing with respect or shouting out praise for the Teacher and other heroes.

The passageway was barely large enough for their group. Ariock's head nearly brushed the ceiling.

While Thomas removed his tribal accoutrements, Ariock followed Garrett's precise directions. He item-teleported the custom-tailored armor onto his friend.

Soon Thomas wore overlapping plates that mimicked the scales of a sky croc. The iridescent, reflective scales were designed to confuse lesser clairvoyants. Thomas would be a difficult target for Torth champions to home in on. There were also air tanks, a badass helmet, and streamlined golden accents.

"This is perfect." Thomas looked down at himself. He gleamed like a hero out of a tale.

This was who he really was, Ariock thought. A legend.

"Dragon armor," Thomas said.

"When you twist minds," Evenjos said with approval, "you should seal the face-plate. The remaining scattered Torth will tremble when they know you are coming for them."

All three supergeniuses looked unamused.

Ariock spoke, aware that no one could ignore his deep voice. "The remaining Torth will join our military. Either that or we'll hunt them. No more zombies."

Thomas nodded with fierce pride. "I'm done twisting minds."

The Twins exchanged glances of relief and joy.

"But . . ." Garrett looked as if he was reevaluating his grasp on reality. Even Kessa looked shocked.

"It's a new universe," Vy said.

"We'll transform the Mirror Prison into something else," Ariock promised. He thought of Zai. "Maybe a barracks for our atoning champions."

Varktezo had a wry twist on his beak.

"For now—are there any major disasters that I can mitigate?" Ariock looked forward to acting as a hero instead of as a butcher. "Does anyone in the galaxy need my help?"

CHAPTER 9

TO RESCUE KNOWLEDGE

Ariock didn't want to keep taking up so much space inside the crowded passageway. With his raw strength, he could do a lot of good by himself. "Point me in a direction," he offered.

Thomas, Garrett, and the Twins closed their eyes, no doubt scanning the Megacosm. They would find where the most lives were endangered amid the cosmic upheaval.

"Ooh." Garrett winced. "They're murdering knowledge."

The Twins opened their artificially blue eyes. Judging by their grave expressions, there was at least one major disaster going on.

Even Thomas looked as if he'd been mentally attacked. "I should have anticipated this." The self-blame in his voice was as sharp as a blade. "The supergeniuses are dead."

Ariock gaped. Shouldn't the Torth Majority respect their own thought leaders enough to refrain from assassinating them?

"There's one we might save." Thomas focused on one of the mirrored walls and projected a galactic disk on it. "Ariock? We'll have to act fast."

Ariock paid attention as the holographic galaxy zoomed in. All the superclusters, nebulas, and other celestial structures along the route were new to him. He struggled to internalize the cosmic landmarks. If only he had a photographic memory.

"Be careful." Garrett leaned on his staff for support, emphasizing his state of depletion. "Some Torth will expect a hero or two to show up to save this girl, and the dregs are not all idiots. The Death Architect is still out there."

So. The Death Architect had survived the massacre of supergeniuses.

"She orchestrated this tragedy." Mondoyo sounded regretful. "I'm sure she'll rile up some of her orbiters to become her loyal cult members."

"And she can't be assassinated," Garrett added. "Her address is a secret. Apparently she lives on some unknown asteroid, tended to by slaves. Maybe robots."

A chill washed through Ariock. The Death Architect dwelled on an asteroid, just like in his recurring nightmare, the one where Vy was taken from him.

Whatever. The war was over! They had won. Dreams were just manifestations of stress and other emotions. It was time to let go of his fears.

Thomas rotated his projection, zooming in on a serene-looking planet. "Ariock? This is where we're going."

The holographic planet rotated. Clouds faded to invisibility, revealing oceans and continents.

"Firmament," Thomas named it.

More zooming in. An alien mountain range. An urban sprawl in its midst. And inside that metropolis? An underground facility.

Thomas's holograph zoomed in to the facility. Judging by the waterslides and monkey bars, this was a playground for children. It was a baby farm.

And beneath the playground? Crawl spaces for slaves.

A little girl shivered in a crawl space, in the dark, clinging to a furry govki.

But this child was not an adolescent like the Twins or like Thomas. She was very small.

Ariock frowned with fresh disgust for the Torth militants. What depraved idiots wanted to assassinate a toddler?

"Have you memorized the cosmic route?" Thomas said urgently.

"Uh . . ."

"Never mind," Thomas broke in. "I'll go with you. Let's start with this." He projected a route to a nebula. "We'll teleport in stages."

Kessa sounded worried. "You should not take risks, Thomas. We only just regained you."

"I'm wearing this nifty new armor. I'll be safe." Thomas sealed his faceplate.

His holograph remained, an insistent sign.

"This won't take more than a few minutes." Ariock wrapped Thomas into his awareness. He wished he could reassure everyone, including himself, that he would never get outsmarted by the Death Architect again. But it did seem dangerous to enter an unstable situation where he had to protect Thomas, himself, and the toddler supergenius, all at the same time.

He just had to trust Thomas to handle any surprises.

Ariock sealed his faceplate and sent himself out across space. He pulled himself and Thomas to the correct nebula.

Another holographic route appeared, colorfully aglow against the backdrop of space. Thomas was directing him again. There was no supercom coverage out here, but heroes and battle leaders had local radio transmitters built into their helmets. Thomas's voice came through, tinny and slightly electronic.

After a few turnarounds and points of confusion, plus patient refreshers from Thomas, Ariock found his way to the correct planet and then the correct baby farm.

It was chaos inside.

Adolescent Torth combatants fled from Ariock's sudden gargantuan presence. One of the nearest preteens aimed an unhesitant blast at Thomas's head.

By now, everyone in the Megacosm knew that Ariock required a second to reorient himself after he teleported. He relied on his galaxy armor to protect him in that second of vulnerability. So it was with Thomas and his new dragon armor. The deadly blast split and fizzled out around Thomas's helmet.

The preteen ran.

Ariock used his powers to bend metal, narrowing the bars of a geometric climbing dome until it formed a pen. That would serve as a cage.

He found no joy in using his powers to jail the would-be assassin. The kid was too young to be evil.

"Round up the problems while I go to her." Thomas's voice crackled in Ariock's helmet.

While Thomas wriggled into a carpeted tunnel sized for children, Ariock scanned the playground for life sparks. He grimaced at bloody footprints on the floor. Had all these kids turned into monsters?

They looked like human children.

But they had no emotion in their eyes, and some of them wore adult weapons.

Ariock let most of them stay hidden. He only used his powers to strip off their blaster gloves. If they had entered this playground armed, he teleported them into the makeshift pen. That should keep them out of trouble for a few minutes.

But they would climb out as soon as the Giant quit watching them, for sure.

Then what?

Ariock wondered if these murderous children would obediently wait for a quorum of adult Torth to tell them what to do next. Young Torth throughout the galaxy must be in the same uncertain situation. They would need to choose whom to follow.

If they didn't go rogue, they might choose the Death Architect.

Or the Conqueror.

If they chose the latter, their former comrades would want to kill them. If they chose the former, they would have to evade liberated slaves and penitents.

So it was for all Torth. Entire cities and spaceships must be rioting. The quadrillions of newly liberated slaves were not safe, either. Many would have to shoot die-hard Torth in order to claim their freedom. There must be billions of innocent people caught up in calamities that were not of their own making.

Ariock wished he could rescue everyone.

"It's okay."

Thomas's voice was gentle. Ariock wasn't sure he had ever heard such a tone from his friend.

"You're safe now," Thomas said.

It was impossible for a lifelong Torth to sound so kind. Anyone who heard the Conqueror speak out loud would know he was not sadistic.

Thomas reemerged from the carpeted tunnel, crawling in his dragon armor. He stood, then turned and offered his hand to help a tawny govki emerge. A disabled toddler lay in a carrier on the govki's furry back.

The govki helped her to sit up. The girl's eyes were round with wonderment, shiny with the vestiges of tears.

"This is the Climbing Storm," Thomas said. "And Nuzzy."

Ariock gave a nod, aware that they could not hear him with his faceplate sealed. Nuzzy was one lucky govki. Instead of dealing with the violent mayhem on Firmament, she or he would get teleported directly to Freedomland, along with the sole surviving underage supergenius.

"We're ready," Thomas said.

Ariock enveloped his passengers within his awareness. He rocketed across the galaxy, disembodied.

Soon they were home.

CHAPTER 10

TO NOTHING

Since the Teacher was elsewhere in the galaxy, Varktezo looked to the other mind readers for clues about what might be happening. Garrett, Serette, and Mondoyo wore expressions like gods watching a cosmic event.

Could they be persuaded to share what they saw in the Megacosm?

In fact, they ought to share. They were penitents, or the equivalent of penitents.

"I want to see the Torth Empire collapse," Varktezo announced.

The nearest lab technicians looked startled and worried, but a few clicked their beaks in agreement.

"Where do you keep the telepathy gas emitters?" Kessa asked.

"Upstairs!" Varktezo considered using his wristwatch to call on an assistant, but the city was recovering from the invasion, and it would be rude to ask someone to drop what they were doing in order to fetch the devices.

Varktezo darted past the hubbub and rushed up ramps. Invaders had ransacked the research annex, but a few rooms were undisturbed. He was able to gather several emitters.

Done, Varktezo sped back down the ramps.

He nearly smashed into the back of an armored leg. The air smelled of ozone.

"Excuse me." Varktezo squeezed past the Bringer of Hope, who was an overwhelmingly large presence in the passageway.

The Teacher still wore his gleaming black dragon armor. He'd retracted his visor. A shocked-looking govki stood next to him, cradling a hatchling Torth—a Torthling?—in his uppermost pair of arms. The slave's collar glowed in active mode.

"You succeeded?" Varktezo guessed.

Ummins and other onlookers padded into the tunnel. The mirrored walls made the crowd look bigger than it was.

The newly arrived govki looked so stunned, he might drop the Torthling he was holding. She looked almost as entranced by the technicians and other free people, her eyes round and dark.

"Welcome to Freedomland," Varktezo said.

"I am a penitent." The Torthling had a tiny, squeaky voice. "I surrender." She gummed the words, as if her teeth were too few or too small.

Kessa stepped out of the crowd. "You can hand the little one to someone else, if you wish," she said to the govki. "You are no longer a slave."

"Right, Nuzzy!" the Torthling said urgently. "Torth are not in charge here. My name . . ." She hesitated, then seemed to reach a decision. "My name is Nea."

The flustered govki held on to Nea, even though another govki reached out, offering to hold her.

"Welcome to Freedomland, Nuzzy," Kessa said with warmth. "And Nea."

Varktezo studied the immature supergenius with curiosity. Nea was disabled, like the Twins. Her limbs were bony and underdeveloped. Those eyes, though. She had the bright curiosity of a hatchling, yet also more knowledge than any child should have. That was creepy.

He looked forward to getting to know her better.

"There's a problem on Saytsay Lal," Garrett said gruffly. "They've slaughtered a few million kneelers and they're activating nukes."

"I am near depletion," Evenjos said with regret.

"I'll go alone," Ariock said with magnificent stoicism. His faceplate was retracted, revealing his determined expression. "Just show me where it is."

"Your supercom won't work there," Garrett warned. "But I'll watch over you in the Megacosm. And—"

"We'll find trustworthy allies on-site to help you," the Teacher finished.

That was actually possible, Varktezo realized. Billions of Torth throughout the galaxy had surrendered to the Teacher.

Galactic routes were always complex, with dozens of zoom-ins. While the Teacher showed the Bringer of Hope the way, Varktezo placed emitters around the bunker. "This place will soon be inundated with telepathy gas," he warned various technicians. "Anyone who is uncomfortable with telepathy should leave."

Dozens of people exited.

Varktezo overheard them offering to give Nuzzy a tour of Freedomland. Nea wanted to go, too. Most of the crowd exited to visit shopping centers and fun neighborhoods.

Ariock vanished with a thunderclap and a scent of ozone.

"I want to watch him, too." Vy gave the Teacher, Garrett, and the Twins an insistent look, urging them inside the bunker.

"I'll pass." The Teacher nearly tripped in his haste to jog the other way. "I'll be upstairs in my lab if anyone needs me."

"Thomas?" Garrett called. "You should stay. When Ariock returns, he might need another cosmic route."

"Then send him upstairs!" the Teacher hollered over his shoulder.

Varktezo hoped the Twins would be brave enough to share their minds with nontelepaths. He gestured to the open vault door.

"Are you sure you want to share minds with me and Serette?" Mondoyo sounded skeptical.

A few more stragglers rushed away.

Not Varktezo. He shrugged. "Sure, why not?"

The Twins exchanged looks, but they seemed to agree that it was a decent idea. They floated inside.

Garrett sank into a cushioned chair. Kessa had the mildly curious look she often wore. Vy also lounged in a chair, no doubt eager to watch her boyfriend slaughter Torth. Evenjos was present as well, her slender hands clasped together in her lap.

"Ready?" Varktezo asked the room.

No one objected.

Varktezo rushed around, dialing the emitters into active mode. Garrett closed his eyes. He was probably already soaring through the Megacosm, seeking glimpses of his great-grandson.

Varktezo headed toward an empty chair, eager to . . . to . . .

Oh no.

He was treading on oceans of thought instead of the burnished floor. The bunker vanished from his senses, subsumed by war.

Millions of wars.

A cosmic infinity of wars.

Torth aggressed on Torth in more locations than Varktezo could process. Death cultists ran through hallways, shooting every kneeler they came across. Nussian bodyguards were commanded to barrel through forums and kill everyone in sight. Liberated guards did the opposite, saving everyone in sight. The monsters in prison arenas were set free to rampage. Newly converted penitents did whatever they could to give newly freed slaves a fighting chance to survive. Others grappled with death cultists or rogue maniacs for control of governance tablets, or they tried to barricade themselves inside governance lounges.

Individuals took over cities. Life support systems. Guided missiles.

Violence was the main theme, but there was even more going on.

Torth minds whipped from one terrified mob to the next, seeking stability, seeking anything that resembled the Megacosm they knew and trusted. Any location where penitents or death cultists won a decisive victory became solid hummocks in the collapsing swamp.

But these were hardly unified. Their cooperation was tenuous and fleeting. And the more self-aware they were of the galactic scope of the problem, the more apart they grew.

There was no hope of reunification. Every mind reader had to make life-or-death decisions, and those had to be specific to their own cohort or habitat. An airship with the air being sucked out of it had different problems than a baby farm dominated by death cultists.

So individuals splintered away from the Megacosm.

They splintered again and again.

Varktezo flailed. He was carried along by thoughts not his own, sensations foreign and painful, and utter chaos.

There he is.

The grandfatherly mental voice was like a buoy on a storm-tossed sea. Varktezo knew this mind! It was his teacher! Not the Teacher—not Thomas—but it was *(Garrett) (Jonathan Stead)* the one who taught telepathy lessons.

Something familiar.

Varktezo wanted to seize Garrett's mind and cling to it. Minds were metaphysical, yet somehow, he did stay with Garrett's mind, following it. Orbiting it. They moved in a certain direction, toward a specific battle zone.

A titan of steel, stone, and storm clouds grabbed a launching streamship full of death cultists.

Ariock?

Well, this was the Bringer of Hope the way Torth saw him, not the way friends saw him. The Giant wasn't holding back. He had fully manifested as a titan, with thunderhead shoulders and eyes that glowed with lightning. The stormbringer moved with the violent energy of a tornado.

Varktezo watched in open-beaked awe as Ariock smashed the ship onto a steel plaza. Hundreds of cultists screamed without words.

*!!!!!!!!!! * ( ) * !!!!!!! * ( ) * !!!! * ( ) * ! * ( ) * ! * ( ) * !*

Their lives winked out within a second.

Elsewhere, other minds cheered.

!!!!!!!!!!!! ∧ ∧ !!!! ∧ ∧ !!!!!!!!!! ∧ ∧ !!!!!!!!!!!!!!!!!!! ∧ ∧ !!!!!!!!!!!!!!

The Bringer of Hope must not be worried about accidentally hurting his own people. At all. Varktezo had never seen him like this, towering and savage.

Garrett's mind warmed with pride. *That's my boy*, he thought, referring to the titan who was even now seizing a second ship full of enemies.

Varktezo gathered that the ships had been launching toward a space-based military factory. They had plotted to hammer the planet Saytsay Lal with nuclear missiles. Presumably, they wanted to throw themselves on the mercy of the Death Architect. They were trying to impress her, to prove their worthiness as "true Torth."

Some (misguided) Torth still have faith in Our uncaring colleague, Mondoyo explained without words. *Even now.*

Fools, Serette put in.

The minds of the Twins moved like a never-ending figure-eight whirlwind, an infinity symbol that was also a Möbius loop and twinned whirlpools of data and a diatomic molecule and a binary star system. Varktezo felt like someone glimpsing a galactic disk through scudding clouds. They were beyond overwhelming.

Intellectually, Varktezo knew that Serette and Mondoyo were adolescent children who relied on regular injections of a medicine manufactured by humans. They had fatal congenital illnesses. He knew they worked in a lab and obeyed his directives. They were technically under his command.

But they were also a galaxy.

Together, they contained the empire.

As foreign Torth cried to the Twins for help, one conveyed the data, one processed it, one collated it into decision trees, one did checksums, one spun a final answer, the other edited it, and then they responded together.

There was no cessation to their thoughts. They never rested, never mentally blinked, never wondered. They absorbed the thrashing Megacosm and becalmed many of the minds they observed.

SAVE US? countless Torth begged. They mentally reached upward toward the great binary mega-mind.

PLEASE

PLEASE

PLEASE???

The Twins made no promises, as the Conqueror and the Death Architect were known to do. They were just taking it all in so that the event would be recorded. Mondoyo believed that such a recording would have historical value, whereas Serette wanted to harvest rare scientific knowledge before it died. They were not here to rescue anyone, or to condemn anyone.

Save yourselves, Serette suggested.

Kneel before your former slaves, Mondoyo suggested.

Side with the one whom many of you call Conqueror.

The opposing side is death.

Varktezo mentally recoiled from their huge, chilly, binary mind. He was glad not to be a Torth right now.

A much smaller mind—Garrett—offered to show him around. Garrett might be impressive when he was teaching telepathy lessons, but now? Varktezo was suddenly aware that in most ways, Garrett Dovanack was ordinary.

He wasn't even that old. There were quite a lot of Torth who were older.

He was well traveled, but so were a lot of Torth.

He was a powerful sorcerer, but he wasn't the only Yeresunsa in the galaxy. Far from it.

Ah, but I chose the right side of this war before anyone else, Garrett thought with satisfaction. He soared over the minds of countless newly converted penitents who cried for guidance or who just wanted to shout praise for the hero whom they used to think of as the Imposter.

Jonathan Stead, many thought.

The first renegade.

The best of Us.

Garrett grinned. Varktezo felt it more than he saw it.

In that alien city on Saytsay Lal, the storm titan dissipated and fell apart as Ariock downsized. Varktezo saw the Bringer of Hope vanish through the shifting perceptions of kneelers who watched from a nearby building with glass domes.

A vault door rolled open and ozone wafted past Varktezo. The sound and smell felt a bit more real than the war-torn points of view that saturated his vision. It felt unfiltered and firsthand.

"Where—" Ariock began to say.

"Thomas is upstairs in his lab," Garrett interrupted. Every word resonated with telepathy. "Go talk to him about where to go next."

Ariock's point of view felt big. He was taller than everyone, but excessive in other ways, too. Keyed up. Alive. Increasingly overwhelmed.

We don't want to overwhelm him (the Giant) (the Bringer of Hope) (the Son of Storms), the godlike mind of Mondoyo thought.

Serette's godlike mind agreed. *With all that we know.*

Ariock left in a hurry. The door rolled shut faster than usual.

Varktezo wondered if he should feel intimidated, like everyone else. He sensed that Evenjos, Kessa, Vy, and the few remaining lab technicians were near a breaking point. The nonstop bombardment of war experiences was getting to be too much for them. There were only so many times they could watch Torth get blasted to death, stabbed, rammed with spikes, run over by hovercarts, trampled to death, kicked out of towers, or sucked out of airlocks and into space. They were also experiencing the points of view of children and elders and kneelers, hiding or struggling to make survival plans or wresting weapons away from enemies. It was a lot. It was across countless worlds and in alien landscapes. Varktezo's colleagues wanted to take a breather.

Yet he liked omniscience.

He liked the Megacosm.

This is a broken Megacosm, Serette corrected him.

It is not as We knew it, Mondoyo agreed.

? Since Varktezo was their overseer, he demanded a fuller explanation.

So the Twins showed him.

Varktezo sensed their gentle guidance, like towering clouds holding him aloft so he could have a fuller view of the upheaval spreading to infinity in all directions.

Those knots, Serette pointed out.

Those gaps, Mondoyo pointed out.

The violence has not peaked yet—

—because not all Torth are yet awake.

At any given moment of present time, approximately one-fourth of the empire is collectively asleep.

They are waking up now—

—to chaos.

Varktezo felt it. Trailing populations of Torth piled onto the already astronomical numbers of penitents and rogues and refugees and opportunists and cultists. Each of those groups was composed of subgroups. The subgroups had cliques and factions. The collective was a fractured mess of sprawling chaos.

Even as he watched, they broke apart even more.

And the Death Architect? Serette wondered. *Is she taking defeat with her usual aplomb?*

The Twins sought the massive mind of the Death Architect. Only a few thousand orbiters were currently paying attention to her, which made her seem as harmless as a distant storm on the horizon. She might as well be in a corner.

Let's get a better view, Mondoyo suggested.

The Twins zoomed in closer. Varktezo sensed that it used to be very easy to navigate the Megacosm. Now? It was entirely impossible for ordinary mind readers. Many factions barely clung together by a thread: one single mind. Some were entirely disconnected from each other. The Twins had to gingerly hop from one unstable minicosm to the next.

And in between each minicosm . . .

There was silence.

Vast silence, as unending as space-time.

It is coming undone, Serette explained with sadness. *All of it.*

The Twins guided Varktezo through knots of chaos, past stray thoughts hurled at them and their ummin satellite. Many Torth struggled to comprehend why their civilization was undergoing collapse. They had not paid attention to politics or faraway war fronts. Or they had just woken up.

The Twins brushed off pleas for salvation or random questions. They specifically sought "true Torth," otherwise known as death cultists. Those were Torth with unshakable faith in the Death Architect.

How could they still trust her?

The mental voice of their leader muttered across gossamer threads, from one mind to another. *I will fix all problems. I am germinating a Solution.*

The Death Architect didn't actually care about the mayhem or any of her loyalists. Varktezo sensed her dispassionate attitude. The only reason she was in the Megacosm at all right now was so she could tally her losses and take stock.

Soon she would be left without an empire to command.

Her attitude is not due to circumstances, Mondoyo gently explained.

She has always been perfectly emotionless, Serette agreed.

Varktezo marveled that anyone would worship such an uncaring being.

Then again, as he thought about it, plenty of slaves and shani worshipped deities who offered just as little. His own parents—one dead, one given a place of honor in Freedomland—used to offer aromatic incense or pretty stones to the sand spirits. Varktezo used to wonder why they honored spirits who chose not to intervene in people's misery.

Why were the spirits so aloof? It was because they worked in "mysterious ways" that no mere slave could comprehend.

That was what adults told hatchlings like Varktezo.

They also told him that he should stop demanding to know the unknowable. He was supposed to trust that the intentions of the gods were good.

That nonanswer had comforted his fellow hatchlings. Not him.

Perhaps some Torth were like those hatchlings, trusting that the mysterious ways of the Death Architect were intrinsically, unquestionably benign. They assumed their own lesser minds could never comprehend her gargantuan consciousness. They assumed she must be aligned with their best interests.

Perhaps her bland disinterest could actually be seen as proof that the civilizational collapse was just a blip, an historical aberration that she would soon correct?

She did have a track record of success. She was self-assured. She might have grand plans. It made sense that some Torth would trust in all that.

Well, Varktezo didn't trust her.

They hit another pocket of silent nothingness. In contrast to all the action, all the pleas and worship and plans and war-zone mayhem, it was jarring.

Varktezo sensed the Twins questing for other minds—any other minds. They were reaching, twisting, seeking.

There was no one else.

Serette found another minicosm, and the Twins zoomed there, to acrid smoke and people dying aboard a wrecked space vessel. There was no way to help them, so the Twins moved on. Back to nothingness.

Then another minicosm. This one was a city where newly converted penitents were trying to establish law and order while the local slaves thought everything was topsy-turvy.

The Twins followed a tenuous thread to another colony, where former slaves were armed and in charge. But that minicosm was losing cohesion.

It wobbled and vanished like a soap bubble.

Back to the overwhelming nothingness.

The early beginnings of the Megacosm must have been sparse like this, Mondoyo mentally remarked inside the vast nothingness.

Indeed, Serette mentally chorused. *When it first formed, there would have been a lot of nothingness to overcome.*

It probably required constant mental discipline, Mondoyo elaborated.

Serette agreed. *They would have had to train themselves to seek during every waking hour.*

It probably felt unnatural to the early Torth, at first.

*But the network of minds accreted, like space dust accreting into a planet,
until it became eternal.*

Boundless.

Endless.

And now it is coming to an end.

Varktezo appreciated their sad commentary on the collapse of their civilization. He was actually grateful for the companionship of their binary mind. If he were alone in this vast nothingness with just his own mind, or even with companions such as Garrett or Kessa, he would feel crazy, small and lost. The Twins were a mobile galaxy. They contained multitudes, even if it was all refined and condensed inside two personalities.

They even cooperated like Torth. They were in sync. They could seek and find minicosms about a hundred times faster than an ordinary mind.

And they loved each other. A lot.

Varktezo sensed that, too, and it enhanced his sense of security with them. The Twins would never let each other down. Trust was rock-solid to them. They had mutually agreed to guide Varktezo, so there was no faltering. That was what they did.

He traveled with them long after Kessa and everyone else had left the bunker.

He watched the Torth Megacosm evaporate into asteroids, into puddles, into dust, and finally . . . into nothing.

CHAPTER 11

SISTERS

Nine hundred illustrious albinos sat in the grand marble atrium of the war palace. They wore purple mantles over their ornate robes.

"Um." Vy stood in front of the huge galaxy throne, clearing her throat. "Thank you all for coming."

Yanyashta squeezed Vy's arm in a reassuring manner.

Vy wished Ariock could address this powerful crowd of Yeresunsa. He would have done so with ease. Instead, he was rushing around the galaxy, putting out fires in the wake of the Megacosm's collapse. Garrett and Evenjos were helping, too, teleporting ambassadors and dignitaries from planet to planet. Linked, that duo was nearly as capable as Ariock. But there was so much to be done. Every hub planet in the known universe needed law and order and some semblance of civilization. They wanted superluminal communications satellites. They wanted hope. Otherwise, the planets might just descend into barbarism.

Yanyashta spoke, her voice amplified by a lapel mic. "As you have all heard by now, we had a momentous victory. The Torth Empire is in collapse."

That ought to be cause for cheering. The collapse had occurred several days ago, but it was really an ongoing event.

A few warriors grinned and pumped their fists. Others looked dour.

Vy saw Yanyashta was getting increasingly nervous. The liaison secretary was used to dealing with military mayors and other dignitaries, but facing so many of her own brethren seemed to challenge her. She had grown up in cave cities where warriors were the pinnacle of society.

Vy forced herself to speak. "This means your military service is no longer mandatory."

That should be a relief.

"We have set up a pension for all war heroes," Vy went on, her voice amplified. "Ariock values every one of you. This victory would never have happened without you. He knows that. So he, and all of us, want you and your families to live comfortably."

Many warriors looked appeased. Whew. That was good.

Now came the hard part.

"Um . . ." Vy cleared her throat. "Also, Ariock will grant special rewards and fair payment to anyone who pledges to continue their military service for another year. There are still the dregs of the Torth Empire out there, causing problems."

Some of the warriors looked thoughtful. Not Flen. He was one of the premiers in the front row, complete with a fancy brooch holding his mantle in place, and he glowered.

"What kind of special rewards?" someone shouted.

Vy had given a lot of thought to the matter. "For example," she said, "you could ask for your own cave system on any planet of your choice. Uh, except for Earth." She wanted to minimize the risk of a generation of hybrid superbabies. "Or you could get your own luxury streamship." She thought that would be pretty cool, although the technophobic shani would probably disagree.

"Could I meet a human?" a female premier called out.

Vy thought of Abhaga, an orphan whom Ariock had teleported to Freedomland at Thomas's behest. The poor human was now stashed inside the Dragon Tower for his own safety.

Another premier laughed. "Everyone wants to date a nice, tall augmenter."

Vy forced a grin. "Earth is off-limits. That may change in the future, but, uh, well, you could ask for your own custom-built personal villa. How about that?"

The warriors seemed unappeased.

"Or you could request a mayoral appointment," Vy suggested. That would entail its own set of responsibilities. "Anyway, the requests are up to you. Ariock and his team will either grant you what you want or tell you to ask for something else."

Vy sneaked a glance toward Cherise. Her foster sister sat amid a sea of albinos, in the side gallery reserved for family members.

"Do you have any questions?" Vy asked.

That was a trigger. Voices suddenly competed to be heard, echoing off marble pillars. It reminded Vy of press conferences.

"Why won't you let us mingle with humans?"

"Yes. We need to rebuild our population. What is the problem with your people?"

"And why do you feel the need to bribe us?" Flen's shout twisted with contempt. "It's because you want us to work alongside *rekvehs*, as if they are trustworthy warriors. They are evil!"

There it was. The hatred.

Vy tried to feel sympathy for Flen. She definitely felt it for his family. She remembered Flen's sister, a flamboyant and cheerful young woman, and she hoped that albino had not suffered before she died.

An unlikely hope.

By now, Flen might have heard that his loved ones had died in torturous scientific experiments. Rumors were crossing social boundaries. Penitents and former slaves were beginning to befriend each other, and they talked. Everyone knew the secret location of the Death Architect's lair had never entered common knowledge, so it remained impossible to rescue the enslaved albinos who had been shipped there.

"Kessa works with penitents." Yanyashta put her hands on her hips. "I don't see her crying about it."

"I work with Zai," a premier shouted defiantly.

"Some of them don't even talk out loud!" someone else yelled.

Others shouted in solidarity. "Some of them act like Torth!"

"You can't expect us to trust our lives to slimy *rekvehs*!"

Rekveh. Vy was getting really sick of that word. Couldn't the fully trustworthy penitents be called telepathic citizens or something? Kessa must be mulling over a new term for them. As Thomas had pointed out, they should not be expected to atone forever.

Something had to change.

Vy stepped forward. She wasn't really afraid, or so she told herself. Her upgraded prosthetic leg hid gas emitters as well as blasters. She wore a dress with a slit so she could inhibit their powers and do a few roundhouse kicks if she had to.

"Ariock entrusts his life to a mind reader." Her proud voice filled the atrium, and people quieted. "And so do I. Before we left our homeworld of Earth—before we even knew that Torth or slaves existed—Thomas was a member of my family."

The Alashani were actually listening. Perhaps they were stunned by her daring admission.

"Thomas is my brother," Vy said. "My foster brother—because humans don't leave babies to die just because they can read minds. My mother, Elaine Hollander, took him in. I'm proud of her for it."

Some of the war heroes looked outraged that Vy dared challenge their notion of who was good and who was evil. Flen and others began to leave.

These were the idiots who wanted to breed with humans so they could raise superbabies.

How dare they.

Vy had their attention for now, and she decided to let loose. She was going to say things she had wanted to say to the Alashani ever since she'd met them.

"Thomas saved his own life when no one else would, or could." Vy remembered late nights he had spent working. "He saved me from slavery." Vy touched her neck, where the slave collar had once been. "And Kessa. And he saved your people from a planet that was flooded and dying in an apocalypse. He didn't have to do any of that! He could have left the disaster zone that was your world without creating a gigantic colony starship. We didn't have to ferry millions of refugees away from the apocalypse. Thomas's starship saved you. It was one hundred percent his idea. It was his engineering, his creation, his concept. He was the one who saved all of you."

The Alashani ought to be reminded of that often. Like every day.

"And now?" Vy went on. "I don't know how many quadrillions of former slaves are free because of him. He destroyed a cancerous empire that kept your people underground and in the dark."

Someone began to shout a protest. "But it was—"

"Ariock didn't start this war or mastermind any of it," Vy cut in, furious. "I know Ariock is the galactic hero that everybody sees. He's your messiah. He is the storm. But Ariock himself would tell you, if you would deign to listen, that he isn't the main hero of this conquest." She opened her palms, pleading for them to acknowledge the truth. "It's Thomas."

Some of the Alashani looked thoughtful, or troubled. Maybe Vy had managed to reach a few hearts and minds?

Vy caught sight of Cherise in the side gallery. Was that a look of guilt? If so, good. It was about time.

"I've known Thomas for longer than anyone else in this part of the galaxy," Vy said. "I knew him before he was the messiah's *rekveh*, before he was the Wisdom of prophecy, before he was the Conqueror, before he was anything except a disabled child. And I can tell you, he's a good person at heart. He always has been. That's who he is."

She hoped Cherise heard that. Somehow, it felt far easier to say it in public than it was in private, to her foster sister's face. This way, it wasn't a personal attack.

"Thomas knows that both of his biological parents were Torth." Vy turned to address the side gallery as well as the warriors. "That pains him. But he stepped up and fought the evil empire anyway. He didn't let family honor become an excuse to stand back and let injustice happen. That's what most Torth do—they tell themselves they are in the right family, the right clan, and therefore they are always in the right. They let horrendous things happen because of their own rigid self-righteousness. Thomas isn't like that."

Vy paused, allowing her audience time to ponder that statement.

Then, just to make sure they understood the parallels, she added, "Thomas isn't like you. He's better. He would never put his own race or genetics on a pedestal. He doesn't think as narrowly as a Torth. Or an Alashani."

Albinos recoiled as if she'd slapped them.

Yet they did not leave. The warriors did not attack Vy. They seemed to remember she was their Lady of Paradise, beloved of their messiah, and quite a few of them seemed to be reevaluating their own self-righteousness.

Yanyashta was wide-eyed. She clearly had not expected the turn this speech had taken. Vy was supposed to bestow rewards upon these war heroes, not deliver an angry rant.

Vy realized, now, that she wasn't the right person for this job. Maybe Cherise was?

"The Torth Empire is still a threat on some planets." Vy cleared her throat, eager to exit before the warriors could form a mob. "If any of you are brave enough to fight real enemies instead of bullying penitents who are already defeated, please see Yanyashta. The rest of you can go and hide."

With that, Vy was done. She switched off her lapel mic.

"Sorry," she whispered to Yanyashta.

Then she hurried away. She wasn't going to hang around answering questions—or being accused of colluding with an evil *rekveh*, or falling for Torth propaganda.

She didn't know how Ariock kept his patience with the Alashani warriors.

"Vy?" Cherise hurried to catch up.

Vy did not slow down. If Cherise wanted to offer empty platitudes, she could wait until Vy was in a better mood.

"Can we talk?" Cherise asked. "Somewhere private?"

Vy glanced at her foster sister, trying to judge how serious her request was. "I'm heading to my office," she said. "We can talk there."

If Cherise planned to make excuses for Flen and his buddies, Vy would actually kick her out. She was fed up with the undergrounders and their supporters.

Behind them, Yanyashta fielded questions and complaints. Vy was grateful, impressed by Kessa's secretary.

She navigated ramps and corridors in the immense war palace, passing people who were wrapped up in their own business. The palace was busier than ever. Thomas and Ariock had retrofitted several halls to include major holographic displays that showed live streams from other worlds. There were new domes and spires atop the building, too. The war palace was becoming a nexus of administrative activity.

The pretty afternoon sky soothed Vy somewhat. Once inside her office, she strode to the glass doors that led to her balcony. The ocean sparkled on the horizon, tranquil and colorful, reflecting the banded gas giant in the sky.

"I know I lost my temper back there," Vy admitted. She pulled two balcony chairs together. "I'm not a fan of the Alashani attitude, and it showed."

She half expected Cherise to start an argument.

Instead, her foster sister sat in one of the chairs, prim and uncomfortable.

Vy sat next to her. "What's on your mind?"

The city sprawled below them. Creatures soared in the distance, like seagull-iguana hybrids.

"How is Thomas these days?" Cherise asked.

As if that was a normal question.

Vy scrutinized her. Cherise had not asked about Thomas's health or well-being in at least a year. Her questions about Thomas usually had an ulterior motive.

"Well," Vy said, "he's great. He has awesome new armor that Garrett forged for him."

Cherise looked amazed. "He's getting along with Garrett now?"

"Kind of," Vy said. "He gets along with most people."

"Why does he need armor?" Cherise asked.

"Just in case." Vy met Cherise's curiosity with a defensive glare. "He's your foster brother, too. You've missed out on a lot."

Cherise looked nonplussed.

"He made a friend from Earth," Vy went on, wondering if she could rattle Cherise's composure. "A street kid from Bangladesh. His name is Abhaga."

Cherise's eyes widened with wonderment and surprise.

"Apparently Thomas owed him a favor or something," Vy said. "Abhaga is set up in the Dragon Tower with tutors to teach him the slave tongue. Maybe you could help with that?"

Cherise looked intrigued.

"Please don't repeat that," Vy said pointedly. "Abhaga is overwhelmed with culture shock. He doesn't need a bunch of albinos gawking at him or trying to have his babies. So don't tell Flen or anyone else. Okay?"

"Um, okay." Cherise blushed, realizing the implications. "I won't," she agreed.

"There's lots of other news," Vy said. She thought about Nea, the toddler supergenius, and Thomas's rapport with the Twins. She could tell Cherise about Thomas's many projects: his commemorative edifices on various worlds, and his superluminal relays, which would eventually connect planets with real-time communications. Vy might even mention that Thomas credited Cherise for inspiring his architectural designs.

Instead, she said nothing.

She was getting tired of acting as the intermediary between her foster siblings. She wished Cherise and Thomas would just talk to each other like they used to do.

"So . . ." Cherise seemed to melt a little bit. "He really defeated the Torth Empire? How? I mean, I've heard the news reports, but . . ." She trailed off, hinting that she wanted a firsthand account.

"Through friendship and kindness." Vy studied her foster sister and wondered if it would be patronizing to point out the obvious: Cherise could ask Thomas directly. All she had to do was step up and request a meeting.

Vy decided to test out the question. "You could ask him yourself."

Cherise looked troubled.

Vy sighed and gazed at the city, feeling torn between her foster siblings. Cherise had lacked so much of love and loyalty growing up, it made sense that she clung to what Flen gave her. It was sad, but understandable.

As for Thomas? He seemed to have all but forgotten his once-strong bond with Cherise.

Maybe that was for the best.

"I've used telepathy gas," Cherise blurted.

"Oh?" Vy peered at her foster sister, surprised. Telepathy gas was banned in the Alashani quarter.

"In secret," Cherise clarified. "I wanted to find out how Thomas perceives things. At least, that was my excuse the first time."

Vy stared at her. "You did it more than once?"

Telepathy gas was popular at parties. A lot of people had tried it at least once, but Vy never would have suspected Cherise. This was almost as weird as finding out that an Alashani was huffing the stuff.

"So," Cherise said, "I'm learning a lot about how other people think. And what they think."

"Huh." Vy wondered if Cherise had absorbed the common opinions about Flen and his undergrounders. A lot more people were feeling friendly toward Thomas these days. Quadrillions of slaves had been freed. Families and loved ones through-out the known universe were being reunited, and it mattered a lot.

"Have you used it?" Cherise asked shyly.

"A couple of times." Vy felt queasy when she remembered having been in the mental presence of the Twins. That was too much. Far too much. "But I find it overwhelming. Ariock hates it, too. I guess it's an acquired taste thing? Neither of us really wants to put in a lot of practice hours."

Cherise nodded in acceptance.

They sat in companionable silence for a while, watching the ocean shimmer. Perhaps Cherise was dancing around a topic, working up the nerve to get there?

"I want to visit Thomas."

Vy actually clapped. Finally!

This was cause for celebration, almost as much as victory over the Torth Em-pire. This was a milestone. It would lead to happiness, she felt sure, or at least to some resolution and closure between her estranged foster siblings.

She leaped off her chair and hugged Cherise, laughing with delight. "Oh my God!"

Cherise seemed startled by Vy's reaction. "Uh, how should I make an appoint-ment? Does he have a receptionist?"

"The whole research annex has a reception desk," Vy said. "But never mind that! Let me arrange a meeting so you won't need to do it in public." She sat back down. "I'm sure Thomas would be willing to meet you outside the city." It would be easy to charter a private yacht or something, if Ariock was too busy to teleport his friends around.

"No." Cherise looked resolute as she shook her head. "I'm done being quiet about my feelings." She leaned over and clasped both of Vy's hands. "I'm going to dump Flen."

CHAPTER 12

VICTIM OF A VICTIM

Friendly mind readers.

What an obscene lie.

Flen shot a glare toward the so-called Mirror Barracks as he trudged past Penitentiary Boulevard. The so-called heroes had rebranded the prison, transforming it into a safe haven for villainous scumbags with Yeresunsa powers. They wanted to encourage the Zai types to feel safe. They wanted them to mingle with upstanding Alashani.

What a joke.

Anyone with an ounce of good sense would seal the Torth Yeresunsa inside those underground barracks and let them die.

Flen went around to the back of the Martyr Street Emporium. Few people knew that Councilor Yarl owned this business through one of his mercantile brokers. Docks lined the back alley. The security team of albinos nodded in recognition. One of them picked up a gift-wrapped box and handed it to Flen. "Your gift, Premier."

"Thanks." Flen tucked the delivery under his arm and walked away. The box was heavy, but he infused his body with a bit of extra strength to make the carrying easier. Anyone who saw him would probably assume he was bringing a gift home for his betrothed.

If only secrecy wasn't a necessity. But Thomas had more people under his thrall than ever.

When news reports announced that both of Thomas's parents were Torth—meaning that he was not a hybrid angel from paradise, but a full-blooded Torth—well, that should have been conclusive evidence of Thomas's nature. He was a Torth. How could there be any room left for doubt? Flen had actually dared to hope that even Ariock would turn against the *rekveh* who pulled his strings.

But the *rekveh* was too smart.

According to the latest news reports, Thomas had singlehandedly destroyed the Torth Empire. The public actually praised him as a once-in-a-millennium hero.

Flen wasn't sure if he could believe any of the propaganda spouting from every radio station and so many mouths. Were slaves really in charge of Torth cities throughout the galaxy? Had the Megacosm really collapsed?

Flen had not seen any of that firsthand.

Torth were joining Thomas. That much was true. That creepy reformed Servant of All, Zai, had only been the first of many. They were overrunning Freedomland. One could hardly walk down the street without encountering a silent, sauntering Torth.

Flen carried the heavy box to the garage beneath his building. He opened his storage locker, placed it inside, and tore off the gift wrap. He added the precious smuggled item to the rest of his collection.

Gas emitters.

Dozens of them.

There were also egg-shaped grenades, weapons that were very difficult to procure. They could only be purchased on the black market. Flen reached out to touch one of the dangerous weapons. Soon. Killing a supergenius mind reader would not be easy, and it would require perfect timing and a lot of luck. But Flen was a veteran at killing Torth. He had good friends who were equally skilled.

And that damnable *rekveh* was flush with victory and overconfidence.

It was possible.

It would work.

And when it was done? The city would finally wake from its spell, and the Alashani nation would be free to go its own way. They could find a beautiful dark cave and exist the way they used to.

Alashani were not meant to endure breezes. Or wind. They were not meant to see sunlight.

Flen sealed his secret storage locker. He climbed the ramps to his apartment and unlocked the door. When he entered, he nearly tripped over a petite hovercart floating a few inches above the floor.

Ugh.

How many times did Flen have to remind his silly human fiancée that Torth technology was evil? A Torth could seize control of such vehicles and operate them remotely. Thomas might be using this one right now to listen, to record, to spy. Torth used everything and everyone.

Two packed suitcases weighed the vehicle down.

Flen found Cherise in the bedroom, packing more suitcases with her clothing. A stab of betrayal ran through his core body.

"What are you doing?" he asked, stunned.

Although he knew.

Cherise glanced at him with her iridescent amber-orange eyes. Her very gaze was Torth technology. She used to have fascinating dark eyes, as fathomless as cave pools, but she had opted for lens implants to correct her myopia, replacing her glass spectacles. She had done that without even discussing it with him, as if his opinion was meaningless. That had led to a major argument.

What was it with her and secrets? Why couldn't she ever discuss things like a decent person?

"I'm not happy here," Cherise said. "In this relationship."

She continued to wad up clothing and push it into her luggage, as if that was more important than having an adult conversation.

"So you're not even going to discuss it." Flen felt like punching something. Not the stone wall. That would only break his fist. "You're just going to run away? Like a coward?"

Cherise stared at him for a moment.

Then she relented, as he had guessed she might. "We have fundamental differences, Flen. You think my friends are evil. I can't—"

He interrupted her lie. "I think your friends are innocent." He emphasized that. "They can't help being suckered in by a demon who knows every truth and desire inside their minds. No one can resist that. The only reason you and I are safe, and sane, is because we're far from his control."

Cherise held a robe on her lap, as if it was a comforter. "Thomas isn't evil. He never was. I misjudged him. And I want to . . ." She hesitated.

Flen stared at her, silently daring her to complete what he feared would be an unholy sentence.

". . . and I want to be his friend again," Cherise said.

Flen stared at her.

He knew he had been losing Cherise. He had seen and heard signs that she was being warped by the propaganda that pervaded this city. But he had struggled to ignore those signs, because he understood that Cherise had a kind heart as well as a depth of hidden potential.

Nobody else seemed aware of how exceptional she was. Not only was she a ludicrously talented artist, not only was she gorgeous and graceful; she was also a full-blooded human, with all the magical genetics that entailed.

She had the potential to carry an ultrapowerful Yeresunsa in her womb.

With her, Flen could father a messiah. The true messiah.

He needed her.

Not only because of her power as a future mother, but also because of who she was. Cherise had held Flen in the wounded days after his family was taken away by Torth, when his world was destroyed. She had comforted him every night. Her long hair had caressed his face like cool water. Her angelic fingers had stroked his skin.

And now she wanted to forsake him?

The orb lights flickered. The hearth flared.

Flen tried to get a grip on his reeling emotions. Emotional anguish was never a good thing for a Yeresunsa. He summoned all his training. He took a deep breath and forced himself to imagine water trickling over smooth stones. Calm.

Perhaps this wasn't a fully intentional betrayal?

The end of the war brought a lot of changes. Perhaps Cherise merely felt stifled by the fact that Flen was suddenly around every day and she didn't know how to cope with that?

The growing population of penitent Torth made everyone uneasy. Flen was supposed to protect his wife-to-be. Maybe he was not doing a good enough job?

"If you feel you need a break from me," Flen said, meting out his words, "I understand. I apologize for any offense I have caused."

Cherise looked wary. She watched him out of the corner of her eye as she packed more clothes.

"If you are actually going to visit the *rekveh* . . ." Flen stopped. He could hardly believe Cherise would be so stupid. Everyone knew what Thomas was capable of. If Cherise got within telepathy range of him? She could lose her opinions, her personality, everything that made her a good person.

She could be turned into a puppet, like Ariock. Or worse. She could be reduced to a zombie.

"Are you not worried about the absolute power he wields?" Flen begged to know. He just wanted to protect her.

Cherise softened. "I am, a bit," she admitted. "But he hasn't driven Vy away yet. Or Kessa. They're not afraid of him."

"They're brainwashed." That seemed obvious to Flen.

Cherise shook her head. "No. I . . ." She swallowed, and Flen saw her fearful reluctance to talk.

Then she straightened and faced him.

"I've been reading Varktezo's mind," Cherise said.

Flen gaped.

"That's right." Cherise latched one suitcase, then the other. "I've been going to telepathy raves. I read minds there."

Flen's mouth hung open. How could Cherise go around reading minds? Didn't she realize how that made her look?

Like a Torth!

She kept speaking. "Varktezo isn't brainwashed. He genuinely cares about Thomas, and he isn't afraid to hang out with him. There's no fakery there. Oh, and no mindlessness."

She lifted both suitcases, one in each hand, and carried them toward the cargo cart.

Flen hurried to block Cherise from the door. He could not figure out how she'd gotten so thoroughly fooled by the *rekveh*, but she must be mistaken about the ummin laboratory assistant. Monsters like Thomas did not have genuine friends. It was impossible. There must be another explanation.

What if Cherise was already brainwashed?

Had she secretly met with the *rekveh* while Flen was on military duty or otherwise busy? When had she been duped?

Flen balled his hands into fists and resisted an urge to punch the door frame. Why did Cherise have to be so gullible? So vulnerable to propaganda?

"You have good reasons to hate Torth." Cherise looked as if she wanted to caress Flen's shoulder, but she saw how tense he was, and she drew her hand back. "But I feel like I'm losing my mind by listening to you. Because you're wrong."

She pushed the luggage cart out of the suite.

Her soft contempt twisted inside Flen like knives.

She was beyond salvation, beyond reason. She was a stooge. And clearly, she wanted to run to her master.

To report something?

Just how many undergrounder secrets did she know?

Flen had not told her about his stockpile of weapons, but she might have asked innocent questions while he was oblivious. She could have weaseled information out of Flen when he was half-asleep. Or when he was lying in her arms after he'd expended his energy and man-seed on her. After she'd gotten everything she wanted.

Flen finally allowed his anger to have an outlet. He infused his arm with supernatural strength and slammed his fist into the door frame so hard, it formed cracks. He punched the wall again. Rocks rained down.

Albino heads poked out of doors to see what the commotion was about.

"You were a slave long enough to know better than this!" Flen yelled. "You can't trust him!"

Cherise left the luggage cart in the hallway and fled.

"Cherise! Come back!" Flen felt as if he was losing something enormous. Somehow, her betrayal hurt even worse than when he'd learned that his family was dead. This felt different. It almost felt preventable, even though it surely wasn't.

"Cherise!" Flen fell to his knees, crying. He stared at the cart she'd left behind.

The *rekveh* would probably send a minion to gather her luggage. She wasn't coming back.

It wasn't fair. Flen was the victim of a victim. That insidious, smug little Torth named Thomas was to blame.

"Cherise."

CHAPTER 13

DEEP THOUGHTS INTERRUPTED

Astronomical complexities spun through the lab, perceivable only to mind readers. Methodologies, heuristics, radical equations, and mental diagrams whipped back and forth between Mondoyo and Serette, their layered ideas processed faster than any computer.

Thomas was the maestro conducting their orchestra. He shaped their thoughts with enhancements, teardowns, and alterations.

He had never dared to imagine that innovation could happen this fast.

Serette and Mondoyo didn't need words, spoken or written. Words would have slowed everything down painfully. But they replaced some of Thomas's best theories with solid science. Together with Thomas, their enmeshed brains formed an ultra-super-ternary mind. It was all just . . .

Well. It was indistinguishable from magic.

The door alert chimed.

? ?

Thomas was surprised by how late it had gotten and how tired he was. Evening clouds had sailed in. He had spent all day sitting in this sunny lab, inventing an entirely new branch of neuroscience. They were on the verge of finalizing a breakthrough. Soon, Evenjos would have nothing to fear. Soon, Ariock would be utterly invincible in battle. Remnant groups of Torth would melt away, unable to compete, unable to reverse engineer the immunity pills, since they had largely driven away their own scientists.

Nothing could stop the heroes. The conquest of the Torth Empire would become irreversible.

Incredible. Thomas could imagine the mental voice of his chief lab assistant, almost as if Varktezo was orbiting his mind. Heh.

Thomas stood. It still felt unnatural to stand instead of rotating his hoverchair. *I will take this as my cue to get going (appointment with Ariock).*

I need a break as well

Thank You for spending time with Us

It was My pleasure

Later

See You

Parting thoughts flashed within a millisecond as the ternary mind broke apart. Thomas understood the Twins' wordless expressions, laced with subtext and nuance that carried loads of data. He understood, for instance, that they respected and valued his mind, just as he admired the Twins more than he could ever express verbally.

He walked toward the door. He didn't really care who had rung the chime to visit. It was past time for him to leave. He should eat dinner before he went on a scheduled outing to build monuments with Ariock.

He supposed he was just desperate for ways to take his mind off the loss of the Megacosm.

Over the past few days, Thomas had worked his way around to seeing the loss as a net positive. The old Megacosm, despite its glorious cosmic harmony, had been a forest choking off sunlight. Its lushness had poisoned anything new that might grow in its stead. The thicket had been beautiful and intricate and worthy in its own right, but it had also been repressive and dark, suppressing new ideas, new innovations, and new ways to exist cooperatively.

It had had to go.

But the loss was still painful.

Serette and Mondoyo grieved for the Megacosm as much as Thomas, and more. Mondoyo took microsecond-long mental breaks. Serette hyperfocused. That was how they mourned.

They also missed their colleagues more than Thomas did. None of them had met their intellectual peers in person, but that hardly mattered. Mondoyo and Serette had absorbed public and a few intimate life experiences directly from their fellow ripe supergeniuses. Thanks to his close working relationship with the Twins, Thomas now carried the Rind Topographer, the Geodesic Flux, the Spin Overture, and others inside his soul, as much as he carried the Upward Governess.

So many dead and gone.

Supergeniuses were now the equivalent of a critically endangered species. Thomas was painfully aware of how few survived. He wasn't a victim, per se, but he was . . . well, maybe he was a little bit more lonely.

At least he had saved Nea.

At least he could keep Serette and Mondoyo protected.

He was aware that a rogue faction of Torth had managed to smuggle a presentient infant out of a baby farm. No one knew the baby's whereabouts, gender, or whether it was still alive, but it was rumored to be a supergenius. Thomas could hardly navigate the cosmic remnants of high telepathy. There were millions of mini-cosms.

The cosmic grandeur was gone. The galactic harmonies were gone.

They were just a bunch of isolated cults.

Thomas walked past Varktezo. His chief lab assistant sat at a workstation, engrossed in holographic displays. He wore a turtleneck tunic, the latest fashion for ummins. His new girlfriend, Ounzong, must have bought that for him. It made him look sharp.

Ooh, thanks! Varktezo emanated friendly gratitude.

Thomas stopped in his tracks. He glared.

(Oops!) Varktezo was full of intrusive *(sorry, Teacher!)* knowledge.

Thomas had not even noticed Varktezo turning on the emitters. That was the thing about telepathy gas—it was insidious. It had no smell, no taste, no texture, and three telepaths enjoying an intense scientific mind meld could not even detect it.

"How many times have I asked you to not use telepathy gas around me or the Twins?" Thomas said. "It's rude."

But it's so wonderful (useful)! Varktezo argued. *I just want (a chance for equality) to listen in on your ternary Mind.*

The stuff was a hazard as well as rude. Telepathy gas reflected Thomas's mind control power right back at him. If he tried to zombify someone? He would wreck his own mind. If any enemy Torth were smart enough to be able to locate Thomas right now, they could teleport here, and he would be unable to twist their minds, unable to defend himself.

Varktezo wasn't even worried. *It's like viewing a sunset watching a symphony hearing an ocean,* he thought in a stream. *I want to participate!*

Thomas sighed.

He remembered his first impression of the Upward Governess. She had seemed like a goddess of knowledge, dazzling and incredible and impossible to ignore. That was, more or less, how he appeared to Varktezo right now.

He hated it.

"Please stop." Thomas had already begged Varktezo, more than once, to quit using telepathy gas around supergeniuses. Would he have to make it a fireable offense?

!!! Please, Teacher, I meant no offense. I just learn so much this way!!!

Did spying really count as learning? Varktezo was a voyeur. He basked in the cascade of excess experiences. Lots of lab assistants would have done the same if they'd had access to the right equipment plus knowledge of how to use it, but that didn't make it all right.

None of us needs orbiters, Thomas replied without using his voice or opening his mouth.

I'm not your orbiter. Varktezo was indignant. *I'm just listening in.*

Thomas silently pointed out that "listening in" meant eavesdropping, which meant voyeuristic spying, which was exactly what orbiters did. Ergo, Varktezo was an orbiter.

Thomas sensed faint traces of amusement from all the way across the room. He should not be able to overhear the Twins' moods at all from this distance. Ugh. Telepathy gas spread everything too far. It was nasty, like fog.

"Please turn off the emitters," Thomas said. "And never use them again when you're around me. I mean it."

Varktezo mentally grumbled. He got up and ambled toward one of the triangular emitters, but he dawdled. He didn't want to lose his fount of knowledge.

Losing knowledge hurt so much.

Thomas understood that. He didn't think he would ever get over the destruction of the Megacosm. He would grow old yearning for it. Trillions of mind readers would miss it forever, and they would sadly tell their kids and their grandkids and their great-grandchildren about the galactic marvel that used to exist.

But homogeneous groupthink was dangerous.

The Megacosm should never be allowed to arise again, even as a ghost of its former glory.

Thomas thought that Ariock should outlaw telepathy gas. They needed to eradicate the stuff from existence. It had too many dangerous implications.

Eradicate it?! Varktezo glared at Thomas. *Oh, so you want to ensure that only natural-born telepaths get to hog all the advantages? Forever?*

The door chime sounded again. Thomas ignored it, shaken by what Varktezo had thought.

Was he subconsciously being elitist? Was he trying to ensure that Torth remained in power? He could see how Varktezo read the situation that way.

But really, he just didn't want to facilitate the formation of cults of personality.

Thomas shot his thoughts to Varktezo in one lightning-quick pulse. *There is a reason we still punish mind readers (penitents) if they mentally link up in a group of ten or greater.*

Kessa had the right idea, trying to prevent minicosms from forming. It was already too easy for disgruntled penitents to ally without ever meeting, via a temporary minicosm. That was sure to happen again and again. Telepathy gas raves were just as bad, enabling people to turn into mobs.

You (and Kessa) are trying to stop an avalanche, Varktezo thought. *You are trying to stop the weather.*

Maybe.

Well, Thomas had a friend who could literally stop the weather. Whenever he and Ariock teamed up, nothing was impossible. Together, they would figure out a way to discourage people from forming dominant-group mobs.

He hurried toward the door. Perhaps the visitor would be Ariock?

Or Kessa. Now that Thomas's fling with the Pink Screwdriver was working its way through the rumor mills, his friends were hearing about it. He expected Kessa, Vy, or maybe even Evenjos to drop by soon.

What would they advise?

Should he dare to see the Pink Screwdriver again? Did he even want to?

Thomas tapped the door opener, so preoccupied that he did not give himself a chance to scan who was on the other side. The Pink Screwdriver was loads of fun, and she was ultrahot. The problem was she apparently didn't value privacy nearly as much as he—

!

Cherise.

! !

Thomas stumbled backward and tripped over his own feet. Someone caught him and steadied him. Varktezo.

Blood rose in Thomas's cheeks before he could even think about why, or how to stop the painful blush. Here was Cherise, more radiant than he had ever seen her, wrapped in a vermilion cardigan, with turquoise and silver in her hair. Her amber eyes were piercing and sharp. Not only did she see Thomas; she saw his soul.

His naked mind.

His massive, abnormal, freakish mind, on full display in all its crazy weirdness.

Oh, and he'd been thinking about screwing the Pink Screwdriver.

Cherise had absorbed that whole thing. Because the room was full of telepathy gas.

Why did she have to surprise visit him right now? Thomas fervently wished he hadn't answered the door so impulsively. He wished he hadn't opened it at all.

Cherise turned and ran.

Thomas clung to the door frame. His ineptitude was obvious. He was no good for someone as wholesome as Cherise. He didn't deserve her. He deserved screwups, former Torth like himself, who could blunder along with him.

? Varktezo clicked his beak in consternation. *Don't you (Teacher) believe that nothing is impossible?*

Thomas hesitated. If he chased Cherise, he would be a monster chasing an innocent victim.

In what universe did he imagine it was possible for an emotionally nubile human and an emotionally stunted Torth to get together? He was infantile compared with Cherise. And anyhow, she could definitely outrun him. Thomas had built up some adolescent strength, but he was no athlete.

"Oh, just go after her!" Mondoyo said out loud.

Serette's mental voice was thoughtful, as if bogged down by intense calculations. Emotional nuances were still a deep mystery to her. *She'll be waiting, I guess? Does she want an apology? I'm not sure why.*

Mondoyo began to explain.

Meanwhile, Varktezo gave Thomas a friendly shove. "Stop being an idiot. Go after her!"

Full of doubts, Thomas jogged down the corridor.

CHAPTER 14

SEEN

Cherise swished through the Plaza of Welcome, its multitiered ramps fronted by cultivated ivy. She felt stupid for imagining Thomas would actually greet her as a guest in the inner sanctum of his laboratory complex. Of course he had moved on, just like she had. Of course he had a girlfriend.

A Torth girlfriend!

No one was supposed to know that he was . . . wow, doing activities . . . with a penitent.

One who looked sort of like Cherise. Wow.

But never mind that. There was more to him than that stab of a secret. Cherise had actually looked forward to experiencing Thomas telepathically. She had expected to perceive him the way Varktezo did: as a friendly Teacher. He would contain a lot of knowledge for sure, but it would be knowledge that was kind.

Instead? Thomas might as well contain the galactic Megacosm.

There was no end to his knowledge that she could detect. He was a cosmos. Was there even a personality buried in all that? One might as well attempt to find a single human inside a galaxy. He was an amalgamation, not even a person at all.

"It's a sum-is-greater-than-the-parts situation," Thomas said. "I'm not buried beneath knowledge. I am the knowledge."

Cherise turned.

Thomas stood on an electric scooter on the walkway a tier above her. He still looked like the boy she used to love, despite a zillion changes.

All right, he wasn't remotely the same. He could stand and walk. His voice was deeper. He was older and definitely wiser. Yet part of him remained a kid.

The one who had shielded her from bullies, whether at home or in school.

The one who used to coach her in algebra.

The one who used to keep her up late most nights, commenting on her thoughts, reminding her that she had value.

The one who had literally talked her out of suicide.

"I do want to see you." Thomas zoomed around the turn and onto her level. He stepped off the scooter. "Sorry for chasing you away. I didn't intend that. At all."

Then why had he inwardly cursed upon seeing her? Thomas acted nice now that he'd had time to calculate a response, but Cherise could not trust that. She had experienced firsthand the dismay he'd felt upon seeing her. It even made sense. She had witnessed the towering cosmic storm that was his mind. How could anyone be forgiving and compassionate with countless millions of Torth personalities occluding their judgment?

Cherise began to pull back.

"What I felt, when I saw you, was aimed at myself." Thomas gently gripped her hand, a signal that he wasn't ready to let her go. "It was a mix of disgust and shame, directed inward. I didn't want you to catch sight of my naked mind."

His excuse seemed unlikely. What did he have to feel ashamed of? Clearly, he shared his innermost thoughts with other people. Varktezo had been in that room. Heck, Thomas probably enjoyed overwhelming people with his titanic mind. No doubt he did it to Ariock and Kessa and Garrett and all his friends at the top of society.

He only wanted to exclude Cherise.

Why? Was he ashamed of his fling with the *(ugh, that name-title)* Pink Screwdriver? So what? He was single and he was the Conqueror. He had every right to have a *(!!!)* secret Torth girlfriend.

Cherise let Thomas keep his grip on her hand. She searched his eyes, wondering if a meager nontelepath like herself could detect dishonesty in a supergenius. Was he lying? Did he secretly hope that she would leave?

"That's not how I feel." Thomas seemed breathless, as if he couldn't find the right words. "I'm not excluding you. I actually don't let anyone read my mind." He seemed to realize he'd been caught hanging out in a room full of telepathy gas with his buddies. "Uh, unless I can't help it."

Was he implying that the Twins and Varktezo had coerced him into being in that room? Was he their prisoner?

"No," Thomas said, frustrated. "It's natural, working with the Twins. And I like working with them. But I asked Varktezo not to turn on the telepathy gas. He did it anyway." Thomas's tone became wry. "He's hard to stop."

"So." Cherise put her hands on her hips, wondering if she was reading the situation correctly. "Only mind readers get to read your mind. They're natural. But no one else? Because it's just not natural?"

"Um . . ." Thomas seemed to realize he had just excused himself into a corner.

"So, the Pink Screwdriver gets the special privilege of reading your mind," Cherise said pointedly. "She's allowed to have a secret language with you. Because that's natural and cool."

Thomas blushed. Hard. No doubt he had let the Pink Screwdriver read his mind a lot.

"You only want people who are fun to read your mind," Cherise said, restating what he had implied. "Not Kessa. Not Ariock. Not Vy. Not any of the heroes who helped you win the war. Only mind readers get a direct line to your thoughts?"

It seemed she had guessed correctly. Thomas gulped and took a step back.

"And the rest of us, the plebeians, just have to guess?" Cherise concluded.

He didn't deny it.

Cherise rolled her eyes. Thomas was a hero—and he thought he was superior to everyone else. He figured mind readers were inherently better than nontelepaths, entitled to more stuff, and why? Because of a power they'd been bioengineered to be born with?

Well. If Cherise had assessed him correctly, then she had better steer clear.

She had just left Flen because she was done with his smug Alashani superiority complex. She wasn't going to leap into a relationship like that ever again. If Thomas wanted to ensure that mind readers were always on top? Then this was the last time they would face each other. She would rather stay solo and lonely than become a stooge for a self-important leader with elitist notions.

She did not need boons from a boy whom everybody revered as a Conqueror, or the Wisdom of ancient prophecy. He must think quite a lot of himself.

She began to say goodbye.

"Wait." Thomas sounded pleading. He actually got down on his knees.

That got Cherise's attention. She had not expected this able-bodied, Conqueror version of Thomas to be capable of humility.

"You're right," Thomas said.

She braced herself for a punch line. She wasn't sure she knew Thomas at all anymore, and she suspected this might turn into a cruel jab at her expense.

"You're right," he said again. "It's hypocritical of me to invite only mind readers into my mind and exclude my friends. I was thinking big-picture. I want to prevent anything like the Torth Empire from arising again. But a ban on telepathy gas would only lead to inequality and set us up for tyranny and hatred." He paused. "I'm wrong. I'm wrong about it. Varktezo tried to tell me. I just didn't listen to him. So thank you for making me see the truth."

Cherise did not hide her skepticism. Had the inequality aspect really just occurred to him? Since when did Thomas fail to think of everything important?

"I can be fallible," Thomas said dryly. "I have super intelligence, not super wisdom. And also, uh . . ." The guilt was back. "I actually don't want close friends reading my mind. That's the truth. There's a lot to judge."

Considering how red his cheeks were, that might be the unvarnished truth.

"Mind readers all have guilt in common," Thomas said. "Serette and Mondoyo invented weapons that got countless people killed. They used to own slaves. They're guilty. Same with the Pink Screwdriver. All penitents know how that side of the equation goes. They understand it. That's why I'm more comfortable letting them see who I am. They're not going to judge me."

Guilt.

Cherise saw that in his face. She could not read his mind right now, in this open courtyard, but honesty was his trademark. She believed him.

"I share guilt with all penitents." Thomas shook his head. "I don't want to subject you, or anyone else who isn't a penitent, to that."

He felt immense guilt?

About what? About being a Torth?

"Of course I feel guilty for being a Torth!" Thomas painstakingly got to his feet. Facing each other, they were the same height. "I abused you, Cherise. I treated you like disposable trash because the audience inside my head told me to. What thinking, feeling person wouldn't feel guilty about that?"

He was being genuine. Cherise saw that. He was ashamed of something awful he had done for survival, something he had done to rescue his foster sisters, and Ariock, and Kessa, and others.

Was it possible to be too ashamed to apologize?

Was it possible to beat oneself up without ever saying a word out loud?

Cherise thought of her own baby sister, the one she had failed to protect when she'd been too busy trying to survive her mother's abusive neglect.

If there was such a thing as an afterlife, then Cherise would have a chance to tell Glitzy that she was sorry for being a failure of an older sister. Until then? Cherise would keep carrying her internal guilt. She would always know that she had failed, even though other people forgave her, even though she'd had valid excuses.

She reached across the distance between herself and Thomas.

She took his hands in hers. Those hands felt warm and familiar, despite all the changes.

Thomas looked into her eyes and said, "I'm sorry." His voice was a gentle whisper. "I'm sorry that I hurt you."

She saw kindness there. The same kindness Thomas had always had.

He had refused to apologize for more than a year, but it was not because he hated her. Nor was it because he felt superior to her. It was because he had never forgiven himself.

"You saved me," Cherise admitted. "More than once." She squeezed his hands. It was as if the distance between them no longer mattered. Cherise wanted it gone.

She wrapped Thomas in a fierce embrace.

She felt his arms go around her.

"You saved me, too," Thomas said. "More than once."

"I'm sorry," Cherise mumbled into his shoulder, for all the wrong assumptions she had made about him. "I've heard the crap the undergrounders say about you. You don't deserve any of it."

She had thought she was an expert in betrayal. She had to revise everything she thought she knew, because she now realized that Thomas had betrayed himself even more than he had betrayed her trust. He had let the Torth Majority pressure him. Just once. But once was more than enough.

That self-betrayal might have actually given him the courage and determination he needed to escape the Torth Empire.

"Exactly," Thomas confessed. "When the Torth forced me to betray you, I knew I had to escape at any cost, even if it meant my life, even if it ended up getting you and Vy killed. Garrett has tried to take credit for that escape. He sent me nightmares. That did help. But the moment when the Torth forced me to torture you . . . ? That killed me inside. I wouldn't have survived much longer as a legit Torth. That was what truly lit a fire inside me." He put a fist over his heart. "Here."

Cherise clasped his fist. She had completely misjudged him.

It seemed unforgivable. She had assumed Thomas was like her cruel mother. Or like a typical Torth, ruthless and single-minded and determined to be right, even if he had to step on friends to become a force to be reckoned with. Garrett was like that.

Flen was like that.

But not Thomas. He was different.

"You see me," Thomas said with fondness. "You really do."

They gazed at each other. Cherise wanted to get reacquainted with him, since there were so many changes.

"There's nothing to forgive." Thomas brushed a lock of her hair away from her cheek, past her shoulder. "You strayed from the path of Gwat for a time. I've strayed from the path, too. Telepathy has its dangers, but I shouldn't ban the use of telepathy gas. Not if I actually value a chance at equality for everyone." He shook his head, seemingly disgusted by his own folly. "You pointed out—"

"STEP AWAY FROM CHERISE, YOU *REKVEH!*" Flen's voice ripped across the Plaza of Welcome, boosted by power.

CHAPTER 15

HER CHOICE

Cherise jumped as rocks exploded near her head.

A spear haft clattered down along with debris and torn ivy. The head of the spear was gone, taken by the explosion. A grenade? Attached to a thrown spear?

Flen must have hurled the grenade in the way he was most familiar with.

To kill her?

No, not her. Cherise saw Thomas had jumped or fallen backward. He sat on the ground a distance away. Dust from the explosion covered his shirt and vest. Dust sifted off his hair.

While Cherise marveled at how stupid Flen was—attacking Thomas? In public? Oh, and shouting a warning first?—an egg-shaped canister clattered onto the flagstones between Thomas's feet.

It was emitting pink gas from both ends.

The inhibitor trail led upward past Thomas's face. He would have to hold his breath to keep his powers. Cherise expected him to use thermal currents to shield himself, but instead, he threw himself across the walkway. He landed against decorative shrubbery that formed a barrier atop the next ledge.

More grenades exploded in the place where Thomas had been a second before. They'd been hurled from the tier above.

Cherise did not waste time trying to identify Flen's cohort. In order to save Thomas, she'd shield him with her body. She threw herself over him.

Let the undergrounders try to blast their supposed enemy apart with grenades now.

She remembered Flen lighting candles to honor the memory of his sister, his mother, his father. He had mourned his family's chambermaids as well. And also quite a number of his warrior friends. Guresh, Yavin, Shassatel, Tavish, Orla. All he had left of them were memories. He knew loss. If nothing else, Flen valued the sanctity of life—as long as it was shani, or shani-adjacent. There were lines he would not cross.

"GET OUT OF THE WAY, CHERISE!" Flen's amplified voice boomed off decorative stones and bushes.

She hugged Thomas tighter. He was an angular but not-so-fragile mass beneath her. She felt the leg braces hidden by his pants. They were forehead to forehead, with Cherise on top.

When they were kids living in New Hampshire, she had hardly let herself imagine that a position like this was possible.

"Help will come," Thomas said in a quiet voice that only Cherise could hear.

What did that mean? Had Thomas sent an emergency alert?

These days, emergencies only happened to strangers on faraway planets. No one would expect a crisis in the heart of Freedomland.

"MOVE APART!" Flen hollered. "OR YOU BOTH DIE!"

Thomas pushed Cherise, trying to move her away. "I can't protect us," he whispered fiercely. "I breathed inhibitor poison."

Well. Crap.

Cherise refused to let Thomas go. She trapped him between her arms. As long as she covered him with her body, he would be safe.

"Don't shoot yet." Flen sounded annoyed. He was closer, his voice no longer amplified.

Cherise turned. The walkway was a miasma of pink fog. Beyond that, above the fog, three armored shani balanced on the wall. They were veiled in the old style of their warrior culture, so their faces were hidden.

The one in the center unwrapped his veil.

Cherise would have recognized Flen even if his face had remained covered. She knew his custom-fitted armor, which was unique, embossed with artistic flourishes she had designed.

He stared down at her and Thomas with contemptuous hatred.

"I don't want to harm you, Cherise." Flen's tone was harsh with pain and blame. "Is this truly your choice?"

Her choice.

Deep down, Flen must understand Cherise had purposely chosen Thomas over him. Yet he yearned for her to give him some cue that she was brainwashed.

He wanted her to be possessed. Brainless. Nothing but a helpless doll.

Like what her ma had tried to turn her into.

Flen wanted that for her, too.

Cherise let out a sound of anguish. She used to stay up nights with Flen, combing her fingers through his hair. She had held him while he wept for his stolen family and dead world. She had been so grateful for the way he made her feel special, buying her gifts and calling her his angel. She had followed him as far as she could while staying true to her own morality, and then farther.

Flen had reminded her that she was more than an unloved orphan. She had loved him for that.

But her ma had also had moments of kindness.

"I have a blaster glove." Thomas wriggled beneath her, trying to pull the weapon from his vest's inner pocket. "If we can lure them closer . . ."

He trailed off, probably realizing how futile that was. Flen wasn't stupid enough to get that close. He remained high up on the wall, with grenade-tipped spears ready to throw. The warriors flanking him each drew spears as well.

"I'll spook him," Thomas whispered.

Cherise knew Thomas could psychologically freak anyone out if he put his mind to it. He might even play media that would mislead or trick Flen. But she thought she had a better idea.

She rolled to face Flen, putting Thomas behind her back. He didn't advise her to try something else. So this was a good idea.

"Flen?" Cherise raised her arm, blocking any easy trajectory to Thomas. "Flen, I just found out I'm pregnant with your child."

Flen's luminous eyes burned with intensity.

Cherise held her hands over her flat stomach, as if to protect something growing inside there.

"Halt!" Flen commanded his warriors.

They lowered their spears. Between their veils, Cherise saw their pale lavender eyes, full of doubt—plus envy. Everyone knew the rumors about human hybridization. It was common knowledge throughout the city, thanks to telepathy raves. There were Alashani who openly demanded that humans should join the free galaxy. Cherise had even caught penitent laborers assessing her from afar.

Every penitent or shani wanted a human girlfriend or boyfriend.

"Your baby is inside me." Cherise caressed her stomach, protecting an imagined treasure. "Please, don't shoot?"

"Get away from the *rekveh*!" Flen sounded more anguished than ever.

Thomas spoke in a very low whisper, hidden behind her. "Tell him you've had dreams that you carry the messiah."

Thomas must have probed her mind.

But he was right. Cherise knew what such a claim would do to Flen's psychology. Flen yearned for a family. He yearned for a true messiah for his idealized underground Alashani nation.

There were people hurrying along plaza ramps toward them. Rescuers, perhaps?

"I've had dreams, Flen," Cherise called. "I've wondered what they meant. But now I think I know." She hesitated, stalling for time.

The undergrounder warriors noticed the interlopers. They readied their spears.

Cherise went for impact. She shouted as if a powerful admission had been torn out of her. "I think our baby will have powers!"

One of the other warriors swore. "She's under evil influence." He prepared to throw his spears.

"Don't harm her, Emstachor!" Flen snapped.

"You said we must act quickly!"

"Right?" the other warrior agreed. "We agreed to ignore whatever trickery the *rekveh* tries. You yourself predicted that it would use Cherise as a shield. Remember?"

Flen looked miserable. It was strange to see him armored and in battle mode, yet he was clearly hesitant. "What if she carries the unborn true messiah?"

The two warriors exchanged disgusted looks across Flen.

Two nussians galloped on all fours toward them.

Cherise cradled her stomach. "I've seen our son with a corona around his head, flying above the Alashani nation. He is destined to be a leader!"

"You gave the *rekveh* time." The third warrior was annoyed. "Now is our only chance to kill it. Your girlfriend is in the way? I'm sorry." He hurled three spears in quick succession.

Cherise rolled to shove Thomas out of the path of impact. But she knew she wasn't fast enough.

A riderless scooter flew over the walkway, cartwheeling end over end. It intercepted the spears. All three weapons slammed into the scooter, and their grenade tips exploded.

The fiery conflagration fell toward Cherise. It was slightly off course, thanks to the thrown scooter. A nussian had hurled the small electric vehicle.

"Yanalthram?" Thomas said with disbelief, recognizing their nussian rescuer.

Flen's undergrounders hurled their spears in a fury. But people were shooting at the shani all of a sudden, and the rattled shani failed to infuse their spears with superhuman speed.

Cherise decided not to wait for them to make another attempt. She and Thomas were near the ledge, and the hedgerow beneath them should cushion a fall. The angle of the wall would then act as a shield. Cherise wrapped Thomas in a protective hug and carried him with her.

They plummeted.

Instead of landing in bushes, strong arms caught them. Cherise had not expected this rescue, and she was so surprised, she exclaimed.

Then she was laughing in recognition. Wasn't this nussian one of her nicest students? "Quiryeskul?"

Quiryeskul snorted a greeting. "Varktezo announced a campus-wide alert. He asked everyone to defend you two."

That explained why the Plaza of Welcome was growing crowded with students and soldiers, and even a few shani warriors. Almost everyone was armed. The undergrounders would not be able to escape. Not easily.

"How did he know?" Cherise imagined Varktezo standing in front of surveillance cameras. That was a bit creepy. Did the chief lab assistant have a habit of spying on Thomas?

"He received an alert from the Alashani quarter," Quiryeskul explained.

Thomas smiled. "Daindlor."

Before Cherise could ask for clarification, her perceptions ran off and multiplied. She was seeing double. Triple. She felt phantom sensations.

And she became aware of infinite godlike knowledge.

Quiryeskul fell into a nussian crouch, overwhelmed. She released Cherise and Thomas and backed away, trembling. No wonder. The mental glory that was Thomas could not be denied. It would be like denying gravity or air or sunshine. Impossible. Thomas looked disappointed, and he looked young and also a bit frail, but those were merely superficial facts that floated atop the majestically complex masterpiece of his ever-churning thoughts.

He was not human.

Anyone who glimpsed his mind knew that immediately.

It was undeniable.

His guilt was also undeniable, acrid and overpowering. What was he so guilty about this time?

Cherise had partied with enough telepathy-crazed students to know how to follow a strong emotion down to a personal event memory. She looked.

Apparently, Thomas had a hidden conjecture about how Varktezo had learned that his Teacher was in trouble. Thomas had briefly, guiltily, touched minds with Serette and Mondoyo.

They did that every so often, no matter where they were in the universe.

Mind readers mentally harmonized with like-minded individuals whenever they mentally stretched in the right direction. Few Torth were like-minded anymore—but Thomas, Mondoyo, and Serette were. The Twins were a binary mind, and whenever Thomas joined them, they bonded into a ternary mind.

All three of them liked that.

They did it as often as they dared. Their triad was not nearly as solid or as wondrous as the Megacosm, but it was the best substitute anyone could create. So when Thomas was attacked, his first instinct was to mentally reach out for his friends Serette and Mondoyo.

He was ashamed of that.

He had used privilege. He and the Twins had broken Kessa's law. Penitents were not supposed to ascend.

"Oh stop." Cherise pulled Thomas into a hug. "You were under attack. Exceptions can be made."

The Twins had possibly alerted Varktezo even before Daindlor called. Therefore, they might ultimately be responsible for saving Thomas. They might be monsters, but they were also heroes.

Like Thomas.

Don't forget your part in saving me, Thomas thought, clinging to Cherise.

"DIE, *REKVEH*!" A spear slammed into the ground nearby.

Seconds later, Flen fell off the towering, ivy-covered wall. He had been tackled by a nussian. They both fell, the nussian landing heavily, Flen twisting like a cat at the last moment to land on his feet. Flen bounced up and drew his two last spears with a murderous look in his eyes.

Cherise shoved Thomas behind her. Never mind the galactic enormity that was Thomas's mind. That mind was incongruously encapsulated inside the mortal body of a cute adolescent boy, the one she had always had a crush on. And he was still lightweight enough for her to push.

! !

Flen rushed at Thomas with his spears. He must have lost his powers as well as his reason. He was all *(die) (die)* and *(hate)* and *(how dare he) (that freak alien mind!) (what a monster)* and *(protect her) (mother of my soon-to-be-born miracle)*.

Cherise was grateful that she wasn't actually pregnant. She wanted no family with this lout. She never wanted to bind herself to someone so unhinged.

Flen skidded to a halt.

He gaped at her.

Oops.

Cherise backed up, arms spread to protect her favorite freak mind reader. Her cheeks heated. Being caught in a blatant lie felt shameful, even though she had done it solely to protect Thomas.

Lying made her feel like a bad person. Like maybe Flen was right about her flaws.

Was she stupid and weak-willed?

Silent understanding emanated from Thomas. He knew all about unwarranted shame. But . . .

He respected her. He thought she was a good person anyway.

In fact, gratuitous shame and guilt and remorse gave them common ground.

Perhaps those feelings were what separated heroes from villains?

Yeah. Cherise smiled.

Thomas smiled.

Flen transformed from perplexity to outrage. In this telepathy gas zone, he felt the naked rapport Cherise and Thomas had with each other. His lips drew back in a snarl that could have matched that of a wild cannibalistic zoved. He went so red, he was nearly purple.

He charged with both spears held in readiness to impale both the *rekveh* and the *(wrong) (contemptuous) (stupid) (traitorous)* human.

Cherise sensed Thomas doing mental calculations. He guided Cherise with the slightest pressure of two fingers, preparing her to sidestep at a crucial instant. He readied his blaster glove.

In the end, though, Thomas and Cherise didn't have to do anything.

A force swept Flen off his feet. His spears magically ripped out of his grip. Screaming in rage, he flipped end over end, then got pinned against the ivy-covered wall.

He screamed incoherently. With his powers, he would have broken out of the power hold, but he was impotent.

Cherise looked around for Ariock. The colossal messiah was nowhere to be seen.

But she did recognize three shani at a distance. Instead of helmets and armor, they wore street woolens. They must have been interrupted in a normal day's activities. Only their purple mantles showed their status.

Haz. Nulshta. And an old man, Daindlor.

The first two were Flen's longtime friends. Haz and Nulshta had been drifting apart from him, especially since the deaths of Orla and Jinishta. Flen had grumbled that they were jealous of his promotion to premier. Cherise suspected they refused to join the undergrounder movement.

"Why are you wearing your armor, Flen?" Haz said, stalking closer to his childhood friend. "You didn't sign up to continue your military service."

Nulshta approached Cherise and Thomas. "Are you all right?" She stopped as she entered the telepathy zone. Her eyes widened.

It's all right, Cherise told Nulshta without words or voice. *Thank you for saving us.*

Thomas wordlessly echoed Cherise. His mental gratitude might as well have been a chorus of thousands. His mind towered in a way that would make an army look insignificant.

Nulshta trembled, gaze fixed on Thomas. She took an intimidated step back. Then another.

Daindlor hurried to join Haz. He stopped short as he entered the telepathy zone and rotated his shocked gaze toward Thomas.

"Let's get out of the zone." Thomas guided Cherise away, waving as if to dissipate smoke.

Meanwhile, Haz stripped Flen of his weapons. He must be ignoring all the telepathic input in order to snap glowing circlets around Flen's wrists. Cuffs. Those were used to track and identify criminals.

Flen's burning gaze fixed on Cherise.

She hung in the telepathy zone for a moment longer, even after Thomas vacated the area. She might as well be alone with Flen, mind to mind with him.

Haz stepped back uncertainly. He kept a power grip on Flen, to prevent him from attacking like a wild zoved. Haz's mind was all apologies. He thought that he should have done more to mitigate Flen's toxic tendencies.

Cherise laid a hand on Haz's shoulder, letting him know he had done nothing wrong. If Haz had earned shame for being so forgiving of Flen, then so had she.

Coward. Flen wanted to hurt Cherise. *Traitor. Weak-willed woman. Perpetual victim. Stooge.*

Cherise gazed at her ex-fiancé. But she did not see him. Instead, she remembered his friendly sister. She had met his sweet mother, with her understated sense of humor. She had only met Flen's father once, briefly, but she tried to summon a mental image of that illustrious councilman, as well.

They deserved to be well remembered.

Instead, Flen was desecrating them. They were survived by a deluded, self-absorbed, criminal brat. That was their legacy.

Who cares about them?! They're dead! I'm the one who's alive! Flen snarled, wordless, but his impulsive response to Cherise's thoughts was plain to anybody within the telepathy zone.

Haz gaped. Nulshta groaned.

They saw, now, that Flen had quit mourning his family. He used their terrible deaths as a justification for his own Torth hatred.

At least some of his grief was a sham.

Your family was light-years better than my biological mother, Cherise silently let him know. *They loved you. As did I.* She turned her back on Flen. *They deserved better. As did I.*

"I will honor their memory," she said out loud.

And she walked away, toward Thomas.

CHAPTER 16

BETWEEN HOME AND AFAR

Her daughter would be twenty-four, if she was alive.

Elaine Hollander lit a candle.

She sat on her creaky bed and watched the flame, bright against the greenery outside her bedroom window. Violet might be alive. There was torment in not knowing. Elaine had things to do tonight. Laundry needed to be put away. Homework and chores needed oversight. Her youngest wards needed dinner and routine care.

But it was Thursday evening. Every Thursday, Elaine took time to honor the memory of her funny, smart, and sweet Vy.

She mourned her foster children Cherise Chavez and Thomas Hill, also. They had all gone missing together on a Thursday night, two winters ago. Elaine wanted to remember them equally. But she had known her redheaded daughter by far the longest. The ache of that loss never went away.

Elaine had given birth to Violet. She had held little Vy in her arms as a baby. She had nursed her, watched her toddle around, and helped her grow to be a vibrant and gorgeous young woman who had so much to offer the world.

Vy had disappeared without a trace.

Search parties had combed Afton and the surrounding towns, searching for Elaine's red van with its handicapped license plate. They had driven up and down obscure roads and looked at abandoned cars in towing yards. Police had searched cell phone records, but according to pings, their phones had traveled north and then seemingly vanished into thin air. Satellite searches were unhelpful, perhaps because the region was thick with forests. Tree cover obscured a lot of things.

The van remained missing. So did Thomas, Cherise, and Vy.

They're alive somewhere, Elaine tried to assure herself, gazing at the steady flame while the forest outside darkened behind it.

She just could not imagine any explanation for their disappearance.

Could they have been somehow abducted by human traffickers? Thomas might be valued by some nefarious organization, despite his special needs and the expense of caring for him. But what about Cherise and Vy? Surely a slavery organization would rather target girls who were easier to mistake for someone else? Cherise, with her mixed ethnicity, had unusual features. Vy was six feet tall with naturally auburn eyelashes and eyebrows.

More saliently—photos of them had circulated on nationwide news programs. Newscasters had exclaimed over their background as foster siblings and their mysterious vanishing in the middle of a snowy night. They should be recognizable to a lot of people.

The van might have gone over a cliff.

Perhaps it was buried under a rockslide or underbrush, or in some forgotten bog or pond. Someday, someone would find it.

Someday, Elaine would get closure.

For now, she kept tormenting herself with stupid ideas that her sweet Vy was alive and calling out for her. Her throat tightened involuntarily. Despite her candle ritual, she was bereft. In moments like this, her joy was gone.

A black marble rolled along the base of the candle tin.

As Elaine examined the mysterious marble, which was flecked with mica, it began to glow. It projected a holograph upward.

Elaine stared in disbelief at the semitransparent apparition, glowing against the dusk outside the window. It couldn't actually be Thomas. Although the holograph only displayed his head and upper torso, this looked like an able-bodied version of her fosterling. His spine was unbent, his shoulders even. And he was a teenager.

Thomas would be fourteen now, nearing fifteen.

"Thomas?" Elaine allowed herself to sound uncertain, like a crazy old lady, since she was, in fact, questioning her own sanity. This could be a vivid hallucination. Maybe she had literally lost her marbles.

"Hi, Mom," the holograph said.

The voice had a tinny quality, coming from a tiny speaker somewhere in the marble. It was the awkward voice of a teenage boy instead of a child. Yet Elaine gasped and clapped her hands over her mouth to hold in a scream of shock and unexamined emotions. A stranger would not call her Mom.

"We had reasons for not contacting you until now," Thomas said. "Safety reasons. If we had tried to reach out before, it would have resulted in death for a lot of people. But the ordeal is over, and you're safe, and so are we. Vy is here. And Cherise also."

Vy's voice came from the marble. "Mom! I love you. I've missed you so much." Vy!

Elaine cried. She had to stuff her joy and her bliss inside so she could experience more. A holographic version of Vy stepped into view behind and above Thomas. She looked like a queen, with her hair shining in artful coils around her head.

Her voice was all Vy, and all sincerity. "I miss you more than anything."

Elaine tried to embrace her daughter. Her hands went through the apparition. It was an illusion.

The holographic Thomas went on. "There are still a few risks involved with a visit. But we figured it's time."

Vy nodded emphatically.

"If you'd like to see Vy in person," the holographic Thomas said, "then please clear your schedule for midnight. You should be in your bedroom at that time, with the door locked. Be dressed for travel. We can have you back home by morning."

Elaine pressed her hands against her teeth, seeking reassuring solidity instead of the softness of lips, unable to stop a sound from seeping out. Yearning. Was this reality?

"See you at midnight, then?" the holographic Vy asked.

Elaine squeaked. She hoped they understood that she was agreeing.

"Sorry for all the heartache." Thomas paused, looking guilty. "You didn't deserve two years of grief. We really do miss you. You're the best mother any of us could have hoped for."

The holograph vanished.

Elaine immediately stood and tried to make the marble activate again. She rolled it around and tested it on a variety of surfaces.

No matter what she tried, the marble behaved like an ordinary marble now. It had no buttons or hidden latches. It did not project anything. She would be unable to prove to anyone else that she had actually seen Thomas and Vy, alive and well.

Maybe that was intentional?

If there were risks involved in a visit, then Thomas and Vy might not want her sharing the news. Did they expect Elaine to act like nothing was different?

The rest of the evening passed in a blur. Elaine could not focus on cooking or anything else. She resorted to asking for help.

"Please watch the kids?" she begged her eldest ward, the one who attended the local community college. "I'm not feeling up to anything tonight. I'm sorry. I need to lie down."

She must seem feverish, because Marissa agreed without protest.

As the hours ticked toward midnight, Elaine alternately sat or paced her bedroom. She used her phone to do internet searches about marbles. She learned about marble racing, but nothing about holographic messages. She searched her room for any other weirdnesses. Nothing. She laid out different choices of clothing. She made sure her door was locked.

How could anyone visit her inside a locked room?

She opened her window, but it was on the second floor, facing the driveway, and it had a screen. Neighbors would notice if someone climbed a ladder to sneak in or out.

She dressed in a stylish autumn outfit, layered with a cardigan. It seemed ridiculous to wear her nicest jewelry, like she was going to attend a dinner party, but why not?

During the final minutes, Elaine simply sat on her bed and stared from her clock to the open window and back again.

She halfway believed a fairy tale was coming her way. The other half of her felt certain she was completely delusional.

The clock ticked to midnight.

Elaine held her breath, ears attuned to the slightest sound.

A breeze rustled some papers.

There was a sigh of windblown leaves outside. Nothing else.

. . . Until her ears popped.

Suddenly, Elaine was no longer sitting on her bed. She was no longer surrounded by the scent of vanilla candles and fecund summer growth and her wool quilt. Instead, bands of unseen power seemed to hold her upright in midair.

She was in a palatial hall with a reflective chrome floor.

Elegant sconces lit glossy walls between mica-flecked pillars. It smelled of warm minerals.

Elaine's soft shoes touched the floor. She realized that she should stand. As soon as she had her balance, the unseen power that had wrapped around her body let go.

She shuddered, running her hands down her torso. That was so weird.

"Mom?"

Elaine turned and saw her daughter.

In reality! In person!

"How are you?" Vy smiled with warmth and enfolded Elaine in a huge hug.

Elaine hugged back. She just wanted to celebrate, but her daughter was saying all kinds of strange nonsense. She claimed that teleportation was disorienting. What did that mean?

"I want to explain everything," Vy said apologetically. "But that would take more than a few hours."

Elaine laughed. She held her eldest daughter, her only biological child, in a tight embrace. Vy clutched her back. Maybe they had both felt destroyed. Now they were whole.

"I've thought about you so much," Vy said after a moment. "I felt horrible about the way we left you. That was my fault. Sneaking away. If I had any clue about where it would take me? I would have said something."

"Shh." Elaine patted Vy's back, wanting to comfort her.

At last, they stepped apart.

Elaine studied Vy, perplexed. What was her daughter wearing? It looked classy and elegant, but it wasn't from any recognizable culture. There were a lot of precious metals and rich pastels.

"You look like you went to a land of Far Away." Elaine kept her tone light and joking. "And they made you their queen."

Vy did not burst out laughing, or offer an explanation for her regal hairdo and clothes. "Ah. Well." She sounded embarrassed.

"It's okay, you don't owe me an explanation." Elaine realized that her joke must have sounded like passive-aggressive nagging for answers. "Not right now. I just want to see you." She stepped back.

"We can sit down." Vy gestured behind Elaine.

There was a huge and artful sofa that Elaine had failed to notice. She allowed her daughter to lead her to the seat. They sat together.

Elaine searched the cavernous hall. No one else was present.

"Where is Thomas?" she asked. "And Cherise?"

"Thomas sort of has a job," Vy said. "He figured it would be best for you to meet him and Cherise on a future visit. Otherwise you'll get overwhelmed."

Elaine accepted that, although she thought Thomas was underestimating her capacity for handling weirdness.

Except for one thing that Vy had implied. "A future visit? Uh . . ." She clasped Vy's hands. "Aren't you coming home?"

Vy shook her head.

Elaine's heart tore a little bit. It was not nearly as painful as the sorrow of the last two years, but it still hurt.

"Why?" she asked her daughter.

Vy adjusted herself on the couch, facing her mother with earnestness. "I've thought about it a million times. I want to visit you, of course. But . . ." She hesitated, clearly searching for the most kindhearted wording.

"You've made a life here," Elaine realized.

It wasn't such a shock. Not after the news that Vy, Cherise, and Thomas were alive and well. Elaine wondered if anything could ever truly shock her again after tonight.

Deep down, she had long guessed that Vy was destined to go her own way. Vy was a helpful daughter. She understood her own worth as a caretaker for disabled kids. But she had a wild streak, didn't she? Vy got excited by wacky adventures. She liked to explore abandoned mills and derelict churches. She wanted to chase storms.

"Tell me all about it." Elaine made herself comfortable on the couch. Knowing that Vy was happily alive in a foreign land was a lot different from imagining Vy to be a moldering skeleton. Anything else would be easy to bear, in comparison.

Vy looked like she was having trouble choosing where to begin her story. She was happy here, that was plain, but she had a lot of news to share.

"Actually," Elaine revised, "tell me about the new someone in your life."

Vy looked surprised. "How did you know?"

"Most people won't leave everything for just a new job," Elaine said. "Or just for a change of scenery. They might tell you that's why they're doing it, but usually there's a person at the other end. Or a major passion. People move for love."

Vy nodded with a happy, silly grin. "It's love."

Elaine rested her cheek in her hand, happy for her daughter. "Okay. So tell me about this person. Can I meet him?"

Vy's grin faltered.

"Or her?" Elaine guessed.

"He's very unusual," Vy said.

Elaine shrugged that caveat away. "I work with unusual people. And so have you." She thought of Thomas. Was Vy dating someone who was visibly disabled? That wasn't something to be shy and embarrassed about. Vy ought to know better.

"Um." Vy hesitated. "Most of what I might tell you would sound like I'm lying. My boyfriend is unusual across multiple spectrums." She brightened. "Uh, but I can tell you why he's right for me."

Elaine looked forward to that.

"He's kind." Vy tapped a finger, demarcating a trait. "He's considerate of every-one, no matter who they are." She tapped another finger. "He's a real hero. Like you, Mom! He saves people."

Elaine smiled in fond gratitude.

Vy unfolded another finger. "He's humble. He has all kinds of reasons not to be. But even though he wields a lot of power, he holds on to his humility. Oh!" She held up her thumb. "And he's human. I mean, in all the best ways."

That sounded a little ominous. Elaine tried to hold on to her smile. Was Vy planning to marry a manipulative billionaire or something?

Vy held out her thumb, displaying all five digits. "And he's basically a giant spacefaring wizard galactic emperor with more power than Superman."

Elaine busted out laughing. Vy had the best sense of humor.

Vy smiled weakly and waited until her mother stopped laughing. "I love him, Mom. I don't even know if that's healthy, since I don't know about his future, long term."

"What do you mean?" Elaine thought about Thomas's disability. "Are you afraid he'll die?"

Vy made an evasive shrug. "It's possible. He takes risks. That's part of who he is, but yeah, he isn't a stable, nine-to-five type of guy. We'll never have a white picket fence and a standard . . . well, a standard anything."

Elaine put her hand on Vy's arm. "When I was dating your father," she said, "I thought we were stable together. I thought we'd have forever."

Vy was listening. Her father had died young. Unexpected leukemia had stolen him away.

"Man plans and God laughs," Elaine said, quoting a proverb. "If you love this guy? Then I'm not sure you should take decades of future planning into account. You never know what the future is. All we can do is live our best lives, based on who we are right now."

Vy grinned. "I love that advice."

Elaine grinned back, hiding her worries. Doctors had predicted that Thomas wouldn't live to adulthood. How was he doing? Had Vy hooked up with someone with a similar prognosis?

"Well," Elaine said, "when can I meet this boyfriend of yours?"

Vy looked embarrassed. "I thought we would save that for a future visit."

Was Vy ashamed of her chosen man? Or was she afraid of how the secret "he's human" boyfriend would treat her mother?

Either way, it was a bad sign. One should not feel ashamed of their loved ones, or afraid of them. Vy, of all people, ought to know that. Anyone who cared for children from abusive homes ought to know that.

"Uh, or . . ." Vy saw Elaine's sharp concern. "Do you think you're up to handling a major shock?"

Wasn't learning that her daughter was alive a major shock?

Vy looked cautious and expectant.

Elaine laughed and nodded. "Of course. I can handle anything." Any fresh shocks would seem minor in comparison. She didn't even understand how she had arrived in this palace.

"Cool." Vy smiled. "I would love for you to meet Ariock." Her grin turned to a serious expression. "Um, you should know he is literally a giant. He is ten feet tall."

Elaine stared at Vy, waiting for the joke's conclusion.

Vy stared back. She looked serious.

Hmm. So her boyfriend was tall. That exact size had to be a ludicrous exaggeration, but there might be a kernel of truth in it. Elaine internally recalibrated her expectations. Perhaps Vy was embarrassed that she had spent her life around small, weak children and had then gone for the exact opposite in her love life?

"It's fine." Elaine squeezed her daughter's hand. "You can love a man of any size, so long as he treats you well."

Vy looked relieved. She giggled a little bit and tapped a tiny device pinned to her stylish collar. "Ariock?"

A deep voice came through the device. "How's your visit going?"

"Great, and Mom can hear you."

"Oh, hello, Mrs. Hollander."

Elaine leaned closer. "Uh, hi. Ariock?"

"Mom is ready to meet you," Vy said. "Are you busy?"

The voice of Ariock sounded amused, with a touch of being honored. "Not at all. I'd love to meet her. Should I enter through the doorway?"

"Please," Vy said. "Any time you're ready!"

She gave her mother a reassuring smile.

Elaine searched for a doorway in the palatial room. Sure enough, there was a massive entrance at the far end of the hall, framed in black marble. How else would one get inside this room?

Teleportation?

Nah. That was fantasy fiction. There must be a reasonable . . .

The arrival of the boyfriend derailed Elaine's thoughts. He ducked under the marble lintel.

He had to duck.

Even from this distance, Elaine saw that the entryway was suited for a palace or a cathedral. No one should need to duck under a doorway that was likely ten feet tall.

And he wore very impressive armor.

His armor was obsidian, with flecks of mica or diamonds embedded on his massive chest plate in a spiraled cluster. The mica trailed over his huge shoulders and biceps, implying the trailing arms of a galactic spiral. And the joints were well engineered. Nothing creaked, but there was no disguising the heaviness of his foot-falls. This man was a titan. He was a whole new definition of tank.

As he came closer, Elaine began to crane her head back.

Ariock was larger than reality should allow for.

"Sorry about my outfit." Ariock patted his chest self-consciously. His voice was big and deep. "I'm between official tasks, and this is how I usually appear in public."

"Oh." As Elaine's lips came together, she realized that she'd been gaping at Ariock in astonished shock.

How embarrassing.

"Yeah, Mom, Ariock is kind of like a one-man army," Vy said. "He protects Earth and a whole lot of other planets."

"Planets?" Elaine was no longer sure whether Vy was joking or not.

"Come sit," Vy invited Ariock. "You're looming otherwise."

The plush sofa was oversize, but it wasn't that oversize. Elaine realized that this titan would have to sit on the floor.

Ariock gestured briefly, and a huge stone armchair popped into existence be-hind him. It even had cushions.

Ariock sat.

Without even looking.

As if it was normal. As if titanic furniture magically appeared for all galactic giants who were extremely unlikely to exist.

"Mom," Vy said, snapping her fingers in front of Elaine's face, distracting her from the improbable Ariock in his improbable chair. "Mom. Are you okay?"

Elaine swallowed. She had assumed Ariock would be the size of a pro wres-tler. Giants did not exist. Magic did not exist. Her mind felt like it was melting or unraveling. Either this was a new sort of reality or it was a cruelly vivid halluci-nation.

She reached into her pocket. She still had the marble. At least that felt real.

"You're safe, Mom." Vy hugged Elaine. "I promise."

"I could go," Ariock said.

"No," Vy told him sternly. "She'll get over it. Please stay. She asked to meet you."

Ariock settled comfortably in his custom-sized armchair.

"I had trouble adjusting to the galaxy and other stuff, too," Vy told her mother. "I know it's a lot to wrap your head around." She turned to Ariock. "I think she just needs a moment."

Ariock turned a curious gaze toward Elaine. "Well, she raised you, so I figured she can't be too easy to shock."

Vy giggled.

Somehow, that exchange made everything click inside Elaine's mind. This was reality. Regardless of what this titan looked like, regardless of what he was capable of, her daughter was happy in his company.

Why should anything else matter?

"So, young man." Elaine clasped her hands on her knee. She allowed herself to see the youthful good humor on Ariock's face. "How long have you been dating Vy?"

MEETING MOM

Elaine's mind reeled from shock. She felt like she was on shaky ground despite the plush couch she sat on with Vy. *Was this grand marble hall located on an alien planet? Was that why gravity felt slightly different? Or was her imagination running wild?*

She wanted to know a lot more about this gigantic galactic-armored mystery man her daughter had chosen. But she would start small with meager, safe questions.

"Maybe a year?" Ariock answered when Elaine asked how long he and Vy had been dating.

"About a year and a half," Vy ventured.

"Yeah," Ariock said warmly. "That sounds right."

"Hmm." Elaine kept her tone respectful and polite. "So, do you have any family, Ariock? Brothers or sisters? "

He shook his head.

"He's an only child," Vy responded.

"Vy met my mother," Ariock said. "But she's unfortunately deceased."

"Oh." Elaine heard the pain in his voice. "I'm sorry to hear that. "This titan's mother must have died within the last two years if Vy had met her.

"Ariock does have a . . ." Vy paused, then seemed to edit what she had wanted to say. "An ancestor who's alive. But I think we should save that meeting for a future visit. Garrett can be overwhelming."

Elaine pictured a colossus even larger than Ariock. "Sure," she faintly agreed. Did Ariock come from an alien race of titans?

He did not speak like a foreigner. His diction and use of language was very New England.

"How did you two meet?" Elaine asked. That should have been an innocuous, safe question.

They exchanged concerned looks.

"We met the night we were abducted," Vy said. "When we disappeared. Thomas was told to go to a mansion in the woods. It turned out to be where Ariock and his mother lived. We found out later that the aliens wanted to collect us in one place, far from any witnesses, so they could abduct us. They specifically wanted Thomas and Ariock."

That implied a long story. A rabbit hole.

Elaine decided to avoid it for now. She wasn't mentally ready to learn about aliens.

"Can we get you something to drink?" Vy touched her mother's arm. "There's a sweet beverage I think you might like." She turned to Ariock. "Can you get nectar for the three of us? And maybe spike it with some brandy?"

Ariock remained seated in his gigantic armchair. He extended one big hand as if to present something.

A chilled canister suddenly appeared on the burnished chrome floor. Condensation smoke rose off it. A stack of thermos cups sat next to it.

"Is he a magician?" Elaine tried to sound casual, but her voice refused to cooperate.

"Pretty much." Vy leaned over and poured the liquid into a mug. She handed it to Elaine.

Elaine wrapped her hands around the drink. "He just, er, makes things appear?"

"It's more complicated than it looks," Ariock said, apparently deciding that he owed her a proper explanation. "I have to psychically leave my body and travel to the place where the thing is, then wrap my mind around it. Then I have to relocate the focal point of the object to my corporeal existence." He saw her lack of comprehension and waved dismissively. "It's all very scientific."

Vy seemed to think he had made a joke. She grinned broadly and poured a cup for herself.

"It took me a lot of practice," Ariock added.

"Yeah, like a whole day," Vy said sarcastically.

"At least a week," Ariock corrected with good humor. "Maybe a few months to get really good at it." He leaned down and poured a cup for himself. The mug in his hands might as well be a dollhouse teacup. He assessed it, shrugged, and drank the contents in one swallow.

Elaine sampled the beverage.

Tastiness exploded on her tongue. She stared at the liquid, wondering what sort of miraculous concoction could taste so good.

"What is this?" she asked.

"It's specially formulated to taste good to humanlike beings," Vy said. "Without any side effects or negative health impacts." She reconsidered. "Unless you drink it way too much."

"Oh." Elaine had hoped she might be able to find it in a grocery store but supposed that was unlikely.

"How are things at home?" Vy asked. "How's Marissa? And Jordan? And little Gigi?"

Elaine heard her daughter's eagerness to reconnect. So she spoke about mundane life for a while and updated Vy on how her foster siblings were faring. One had graduated and gotten a remote job. One had reunited with her birth mother. One had limped around on crutches after a soccer accident. One had been placed in the household of his aunt. One had stopped needing diapers. A lot had changed in two years.

Probably not nearly as much as the changes Vy, Thomas, and Cherise had undergone.

"I'm not going to just talk about me the whole time," Elaine said after a while, though both Vy and Ariock had been listening with fascination.

Elaine considered how to ask some of the more pertinent questions she had. There was no polite way to bring up compatibility. Finally, she just asked Ariock bluntly. "Are you an alien?"

He looked embarrassed.

"Sort of." Vy answered for him. "And sort of not. The answer is complicated, Mom. He's right for me, though."

Elaine faced her. "Is he a different species?"

Vy thought about it.

She seemed to come to a decision. "He's as human as I am."

Elaine threw away caution. Never mind rudeness. "Then why," she asked, "is he so big?"

Vy was getting defensive. Elaine could see her anger.

Ariock leaned forward, his voice gentle. "I have a nonhuman great-grandfather."

Ah.

Except that didn't explain much. Elaine began to ask how a titan and a human could make a baby.

Ariock seemed to see her concern, and he spoke before she could ask. "There are three human-related species that we know of. I'm a hybrid of all three. Hybrids have extra powers, and they can have unexpected traits." He gestured to himself. "Some Torth are bioengineered for heavy gravity environments. I inherited a mutation of that, and thanks to the hybrid wild card factor, it manifested as superstrength plus runaway gigantism."

"Oh." Vy looked at him.

Ariock shrugged. "That's how Thomas explained it. I asked him."

"Oh." Vy seemed speculative.

"He told me I'll never stop growing." Ariock leaned back in his armchair, looking morose. "Unless I can convince Evenjos to do some kind of super high-stakes, never-done-before brain operation."

"Really?" Vy perked up, looking hopeful.

Elaine studied her daughter. No wonder she was worried about Ariock's future—or rather her future with him.

"It would be risky," Ariock said. "So we'd have to wait until all the emergencies and attacks die down."

"Right," Vy said. "Of course."

Elaine realized that she was overthinking the physical differences between Vy and her boyfriend. Maybe they would marry; maybe their children would inherit strange qualities. Or maybe they would never have children. So what? This was who her daughter wanted to be with. He seemed like a good person.

"What are the other species like?" Elaine asked.

Vy took Elaine's empty mug and put it aside. "There are lots of sapients. Some look human. Some really don't. Some have powers." She included Ariock in her gesture. "We've discussed introducing Earth to them, or vice versa."

Elaine was silent, absorbing.

Aliens on Earth?

Humans mixing with humanoids?

What would happen to her world?

Vy squeezed her mother's hands. "I think that's enough for one visit."

"Bu . . ." Elaine wanted to stammer and cry at the same time.

"I just want you to know we're not the oddest couple possible." Vy aimed a fond look toward her gigantic armored boyfriend. "There are quadrillions of incredible people in the galaxy. Also? Take a look."

Vy stretched out one leg, pulled up her skirt, and revealed a contraption around her thigh that looked like science fiction.

She tapped her lower leg. It made a hollow sound.

"It's a prosthetic," Vy said.

Elaine gaped in wonderment. Part of her reeled at the thought of some horrific accident where her athletic daughter had lost a leg. But this prosthetic looked like a natural leg. It even moved like one.

Such a marvel could change the lives of amputees everywhere.

"I need to know where you got that," Elaine said.

Vy smiled. "There's a lab. I'll show you around on a future visit. Thomas would love to see you."

For the first time since their visit began, Elaine felt herself relax with happy acceptance. She had not lost her daughter or anyone else. Thomas must have found a place where he fit in. Cherise too, she presumed.

She might have to mentally adjust to a lot of new paradigms. But no doubt Vy had done the same.

Elaine turned to the galaxy-armored titan. "It was wonderful to meet you, Ariock."

"Same." He seemed happy to meet the person who had raised Vy.

Elaine held out a hand, wanting someone to lift her off the plush couch. Ariock leaned forward to help.

"I hope to see more of you," she said. "You'll have to tell me the story of that armor. And how you became Earth's protector."

He beamed.

So did Vy. This joy was all Elaine had ever wanted. She had her family—whole at last.

CHAPTER 17

FORSAKING ALL

The Serendipitous Day arrived in Freedomland when it was warm and sunny.

He teleported into one of the city parks, a flowery crown atop one of the urban hills. He took a moment to surveil the greenery and the garden paths, as if sharing the scene with thousands of orbiters inside his head.

That was just old habit. No one else shared his thoughts. The Megacosm was shattered into a million shards.

The Serendipitous Day had considered joining one of the rogue minicosms, or founding his own. Should he join the death cultists? Should he captain his own splinter cult? Should he kneel and become a penitent?

After many days of weighing pros and cons, and sampling each option, he had finally chosen his fate. This strange new metropolis, Freedomland, had ironically become a seat of magnificent galactic power. This was the place to be.

The Serendipitous Day wore a woolen cloak over his skintight white armor, disguising his former status as a Servant of All. He had been careful to reprogram his eye color before leaving the battleship he used to captain. Now, instead of blank white eyes, his eyes were *(purple)* the naked color.

He shoved his hands into the pockets of his cloak and slouched, like a human or a shani. He made his way down a crowded boulevard.

Although he had never visited Freedomland in person before today, he could map its famous landmarks. The tropical mountains and the banded gas giant in the sky were familiar. He had vicariously experienced this city plenty of times, through fellow Servants of All and through the eyes of penitent spies, before the Megacosm collapsed.

Slaves *(no, not slaves, they are people)* of various species filled the streets, strolling or shopping.

As the Serendipitous Day squeezed past crowds, he sensed many of these people expected him to act a certain way. They wanted him to be servile *(no, not servile, friendly)*.

It felt unnatural. It went against all his instincts and lifelong training.

He nodded to slaves *(people)* who glanced at him. He broadened his cheeks in the human expression of a smile. It caused his face to ache. His facial muscles were unused to such treatment.

He wanted to spend a leisurely time exploring this enemy *(no, not enemy)* city before officially enslaving himself to the Conqueror. But pretending to be a penitent was more exhausting than he had anticipated. It felt like wearing a mask. Should he reply to that nussian who had greeted him in the slave tongue? Should he try to set that crying govki child at ease? What was he expected to do? Every minor interaction, even an exchange of glances, required social decisions that he felt unprepared to make.

He would undoubtedly feel more at ease among his own kind.

So he cut his leisurely exploration short and went straight to the Mirror Barracks.

A pair of nussian sentries let him through the open gate. He entered a chrome lobby, its reflective walls a defense against any Rosy or Servant of All *(like himself)* who might wish to teleport inside and wreak havoc.

He searched for penitents, but all he saw were slave species. Nussians guarded every tunnel entrance. Unlike guards under Torth rules, these nussians squatted, at ease. They played games. None spoke, yet they seemed to communicate without words.

"Let me stop you." A motherly nussian intercepted the Serendipitous Day. "I never forget a face. You're new, aren't you?"

The Serendipitous Day was unsure how to respond. Questions were unnecessary in mental exchanges. Should he agree that he was new? Wouldn't that be an insult to her intelligence, to state a fact so obvious that she had already deduced it for herself?

He searched for someone who could read minds. He didn't want to deal with an inquisitive nussian.

"What is your name?" the nussian asked.

At least that was an easy one to answer. "I am the Serendipitous Day."

His name-title conferred great respect in the Megacosm. At least, it used to. Lesser ranks could not earn such fortunate-sounding monikers.

The nussian gave him a bland look. "Is that the name you wish to be known as, as a penitent?"

The Serendipitous Day hesitated.

He knew, even without probing this nussian's mind, that names were a signal that a former Torth was ready to move on and discard Torth societal values. Alashani warriors felt more comfortable fighting alongside Zai rather than the Shrewd Awareness.

Or Opal.

Or Bob.

"I am . . . uh . . ." The Serendipitous Day trailed off.

He had assumed the enemies *(the freed slaves)* would vote on a new name for him, the way Torth voted on name-titles. He had never imagined he would be asked *(allowed)* to choose his own.

He wanted it to mean something, if it was actually going to belong to him.

It felt like too weighty a decision for one individual to make. Shouldn't names be decided by committee?

"Think on it." The nussian led him to a cabinet. "I assume you want to join us?"

"Yes," the Serendipitous Day said. "I will fight for the Conqueror."

"You will fight for Kessa," the nussian said, correcting him. She handed him a package. "Here's your mantle and cuffs."

The Serendipitous Day knew, even before opening the package, what it contained. In all the lands protected by the Conqueror, warriors with powers had to wear garments in public that marked them as Yeresunsa. For albinos, the garment was a purple mantle that draped over their shoulders. The penitent version was the same thing, except in black instead of purple. Penitent warriors also wore cuffs that wrapped around their forearms, like gauntlets. People could see at a glance that they were beholden to the so-called heroes.

It wasn't so different from having white eyes.

The nussian sucked in her breath as the Serendipitous Day removed his traveling cloak. She knew what white armor meant. "Ah, you were a Servant of All?"

He nodded, donning the black gauntlets.

"We haven't seen anyone new since yesterday," the nussian said. "For a while, we were receiving hundreds every day."

The Serendipitous Day wondered why this nussian wanted to chitchat with a former Servant of All. Did she imagine that she had anything in common with someone who used to own hundreds of slaves and bodyguards? Someone who used to command the governors of major metropolises? Someone who had been the admiral of a space fleet?

They had absolutely nothing in common.

Maybe she was an idiot.

Perhaps all former slaves had grandiose notions about themselves? How pathetic. Anyone with an iota of sense could figure out who was really in charge in this new empire of heroes, and it was not the nussians or the ummins.

He would learn nothing from a mere minion. He looked beyond her, toward the nearest tunnel. Surely his fellow mind readers would coach him in how to behave here?

"Acknowledge my question, please." The nussian's demeanor lost some friendliness. She seemed to know what he had been thinking.

The Serendipitous Day looked at her. How could a stupid nussian possibly be so sure she knew what he'd been . . . ?

!!!

He became aware that this nussian was actually hearing his thoughts.

The lobby was full of telepathy gas!

That explained why no one else was speaking out loud. These nussians were *(so weird!)* mind readers! He should have realized it right away. It was just so unexpected, so unnatural, and he had to navigate all kinds of culture shock. This was just . . .

The Serendipitous Day backed away, unsure if he could find the ends of the telepathy gas zone. The so-called gas was undetectable to natural mind readers like himself. It wasn't even a gas. It was a dark energy matrix of some sort.

"No," Sulmunaul said. "Stay."

That was her name. He absorbed it. This intake clerk was not an empty-headed minion, but a lieutenant of Kessa's. He should have guessed as much. How did the Conqueror ensure loyalty from his penitent troops? He had subordinates probe their minds. He had lieutenants do it.

It would be supremely stupid to offend a lieutenant who was probing his mind.

The Serendipitous Day halted. If he failed to pass this weird exam, then he might be rejected. Scary. Would they kill him? Or worse: Zombify him?

"You don't need to worry about negative consequences quite yet." Sulmunaul emanated reassurance. "A lot of newcomers react the way you did. The process of becoming human is a long one. No one expects you to transform overnight."

That was slightly reassuring.

"I do want you to answer a few questions, though," Sulmunaul said gently. "You don't have to say anything out loud. I don't need you to fake being human. This is a stressful transition for you, and everyone here will understand that."

He sensed her honesty. She was used to working with former Torth.

A tension left his shoulders and back. The Serendipitous Day had not even realized how afraid he had been. He never would have guessed that a few meager words—words!—from a former slave would set him at ease.

Her words worked like magic. It was even better than the effects of a tranquility mesh. How was that possible?

"Yes." Sulmunaul acknowledged his amazement. "So, what brought you here?"

Telepathy gas put them on equal ground.

That equality was extremely weird to the Serendipitous Day. He was unused to gazing upward into the broad orange face of a nussian and considering her to be a person rather than a possession. He had been wrong to think of her as a minion. Someone—Kessa?—was trusting the judgment of this lieutenant. And the Conqueror was trusting Kessa's judgment.

There was an unseen network of mutual trust and respect going on here between former slaves and former Torth. That seemed unthinkable, but this nussian lieutenant was proof.

The Serendipitous Day swallowed. What had brought him here? That wasn't the sort of question a Torth would ask. It was so imprecise, so generally broad. There were so many possible answers.

Sulmunaul mentally acknowledged that it was a broad question. Yet she was curious. She wanted his reasons.

The Serendipitous Day thought back to the Day of Collapse. When the Megacosm had fractured, his fellow Servants had vanished, either going rogue or joining the enemies. He had eyed the planet Earth.

It had been close. He could have used one of his armada's small shuttles to get there in less than a day.

Once on Earth? He could have assumed a false human identity. Servants of All had been doing such things for millennia. His features looked vaguely Asiatic. He could have gone to China, or to the United States, or to some smaller country, and taken a few weeks to absorb the local language. As a mind reader, he could easily determine who wanted what. Survival would be easy among the native primitives. He could thrive there.

Like a garbage eater preening atop of a heap of trash.

He would have always been yearning for the stars. And for power. He had passed numerous tests and distinguished himself on many levels to become the admiral of a space armada. Was he just going to throw away all his hard-won prestige?

Maybe the Torth Empire would recover.

Or maybe a smart faction would form out of the rubble and reassert galactic dominance.

He had waited for that. He had bided his time aboard his massive ship while his crew abandoned him. He had relaxed in his private suite, swinging in and out of various minicosms, seeking some champion, or some organization, that might be worth following.

But none were impressive.

Rogue cults tended to run out of ammunition and food supplies long before they could achieve whatever foolhardy goal they wanted to achieve. Most rogue Torth were actually starving right now, unable to scavenge enough food to meet basic minimum daily nutritional requirements.

Without knowledge, Torth were nothing.

All their collective knowledge had been inside the Megacosm. That was gone. Without that, individual Torth were reduced to tribes, to polities, to bickering factions. That made them easy pickings for the newly armed and liberated slaves of the new empire, or the Protectorate, as people were calling it.

The only Torth faction that held any promise was the Death Architect and her cult of followers.

She was a ray of hope for many Torth. Her promises were as great and mighty as the Torth Empire used to be. She kept reassuring her occasional orbiters that the Torth Empire would win. In fact, she promised that any Torth who joined her would reap power beyond anything imaginable. She was preparing to strike a death blow to the enemies. Her cultists believed that they were destined to found a second Torth Empire. It was inevitable! The future Torth Empire would be even better than the first!

What tempting promises.

The Serendipitous Day had believed her for a short while. He had been prepared to fight and die at her behest, to help establish a better version of the Torth Empire. But . . .

??? Sulmunaul leaned forward, eager to catch his reasons for exiting the death cult.

It is not that I disbelieved the Death Architect, he admitted. *She truly believes her own assurances. And I respect her intelligence. But . . . well, I observed her leadership style.*

The Death Architect was sadistic. She sent her loyal cultists into enemy zones without the slightest regard for their safety. She never took their individual needs or wants into account.

And she never revealed so much as a hint of her secret schemes.

She claimed that secrecy was paramount, or else the Conqueror would win. Maybe that was true. But it engendered a situation where only one Torth in that cult had eyes and ears and a brain, and it was her. Everyone else was as blindly ignorant as slaves.

Rosy Ranks flew into battles for her, expecting to win liberated slave-held cities. Instead, they died by the thousands. Why? Just to seize control of a handful of obscure factories and old scientific research facilities on worthless asteroids?

The Death Architect directed her cultists here and there without any explanation or apparent purpose. When her cultists were slaughtered by enemies, she reacted without remorse, without so much as an insincere note of regret. She deemed every command to be "necessary." Why? No one knew. She had a grand plan. Her secrets would eventually lead to victory, and that was all anyone needed to know.

Her promises weren't enough for Me, the Serendipitous Day silently confessed.

Besides, the Death Architect was sickly, not someone that a self-respecting Servant of All would ever consider obeying in civilized times.

That was when he'd begun to think that a life in exile on Earth wouldn't be so bad. Except Earth was no longer a playground for sexually deviant Servants of All. The Conqueror had ties to that planet. He would rid it of all Torth.

Where else could a rogue Servant of All go?

The Serendipitous Day had never considered himself a kneeler. He had no wish to enslave himself to the enemies who had destroyed everything he valued. And yet . . .

He could not help but compare the secretive, reckless leadership exhibited by the Death Architect to the much looser and respectful leadership shown by the Conqueror.

Mind readers who fought for the Conqueror went into battle fully informed. They were told whom to target and why. Penitent warriors were even allowed leeway to make their own choices in the heat of battle. If they chose to aid a fallen compatriot instead of killing a target, for instance, they could be lauded instead of punished.

Penitent warriors might live a poor lifestyle compared with their peers in the remnants of the Torth Empire. They owned no slaves.

Yet they seemed happier overall and more content with their lives.

The Serendipitous Day had wanted to understand why. How could anyone who felt the shame and guilt of atonement possibly be content with their own existence?

So he had studied them from afar. He had analyzed them.

And he had concluded that it had something to do with their wider array of options in life.

Between battles, penitent warriors did more than simply consume food while receiving a chorus of praise or judgment. They touched each other. They experienced music or poetry. They had enlightening conversations with aliens. They expressed creative or innovative impulses, regardless of what rank they used to be.

Nobody told them not to. In fact, their human impulses were encouraged.

That was interesting.

A week ago, the Serendipitous Day would have rejected the very idea of bowing and kneeling before the Conqueror's minions. He would have shot Kessa if he'd had the opportunity. Yet now . . . ?

He suspected that all his vaunted Torth values might actually be flawed.

The very foundations of civilization had been flawed. The whole thing had broken, hadn't it? The Megacosm had cracked and spilled trillions of citizens into the abyss of loneliness or into enemy territory.

It was time to try the other side.

"You've come to the right place." Sulmunaul wrapped one big arm around his shoulders. She guided him toward a tunnel that led to penitent bunk rooms. "We're glad to have you."

The Serendipitous Day wanted to shake off her arm as too friendly, too slavish. He wanted to ignore her words as irrelevancies.

Instead, he found that her silly pleasantries mattered to him, somehow. So did her friendly warmth.

None of it should matter. None of it should affect him at all. Yet it did.

It mattered a lot.

Maybe it wouldn't be so bad to be here, to serve Kessa as a penitent warrior?

Maybe he would take a next step in his career and become something more than a Servant of All.

CHAPTER 18

INVINCIBLE

Evenjos floated on a warm air current above a populated peninsula of one of the galaxy's hub planets. She had loosened her corporeal form to become widespread water vapor. Anyone who looked up would see only clouds.

It was undignified, to be nothing but dust or foam or water vapor. Evenjos would have preferred to sleep next to Garrett, or perhaps to relax alone on a patio with a glass of liquor. But ever since her resurrection, she had learned new abilities—and new limitations. She could achieve nonsentient forms, and she could avoid drunkenness, if she wished. But she was also fragile in a very particular way.

She would die if she slept like a mortal being.

She would die if she got inhibited or fully depleted.

So whenever she felt tired, worn down from lending her strength to Garrett or from healing countless people, she felt a memory of entombment, like an icy breath on her neck. That was her cue to take a break from whatever she was doing. She dared not let anyone reach her during these times. Instead of sleeping, she floated and allowed her mind to drift in a dreamlike state, resting in the way of a dolphin or a fish.

Her depleted feeling ebbed after a while.

When she judged herself strong enough to wreck cities or flood canyons, she regathered herself and slowly coalesced into the winged empress form that was most comfortable for her. She yawned and stretched. Some mortal habits never quite left her. She did not need to yawn or even breathe, yet her spectral mind refused to relinquish the semblance of autonomic processes.

She circled above the land. It was simple to locate the life spark that was likely Garrett's. He glowed like a beacon to her Yeresunsa senses.

Evenjos poured through the air ducts of an impressive skyscraper, then regathered herself inside the huge, glassy bedchamber at the pinnacle. Garrett was dressed, groomed, and reading a book—a modern book from Earth, not the book of prophecies—as he finished eating a bowl of oatmeal.

He sensed her before he saw her, of course.

"I kept your supercom safe." He pushed her earpiece across the breakfast table.

"Thank you." Evenjos primly took her earpiece. She hoped she hadn't kept Garrett waiting for an inordinate amount of time. How long had she rested? Three hours? Twelve hours? She had no idea what the average day-night cycle was on this world. It had been daylight when she'd gone into cloud form, and a night cycle had passed, and now it was daylight again.

"We need to take a break from matters on Tzogratzar." Garrett laid his book aside. "Thomas wants us back home for a meeting."

"Thomas?" Evenjos had never heard of Thomas making a commanding request like that. The heroes were free to interfere anywhere in the galaxy, however they saw fit. Even if Thomas wanted to enact an important new policy, he would not take credit for it. He would normally let Ariock lead anything military. Kessa led anything civil or societal.

"I don't know what he wants," Garrett admitted. "But I'm guessing it's important."

Evenjos checked her voicemail. Sure enough, there was a prearranged meeting time and place, and it had been set up by Thomas.

There was no hint about the topic. The meeting was to be held in a cozy room inside the laboratory complex, not the war palace. It seemed this was a private matter, not something Thomas wanted to present to the public or to the war council.

"How much time do we have?" Evenjos tried to quell her uneasiness. Whatever secret news Thomas wanted to tell them, it couldn't be bad. Surely not. The Torth Empire was defeated, dead, and stomped on.

Maybe this was just a lighthearted, friendly get-together?

"You're right on time." Garrett pushed away his breakfast and stood. "The meeting is about to start. Ready to go?"

"I . . . I guess." Evenjos studied Garrett, hoping he had a hunch as to whether they were heading into happiness or a storm.

It couldn't be devastating news, could it? If the Megacosm had reconstituted, Garrett surely would have noticed and told her.

Garrett clasped her hands. "The Megacosm is dead. So is the Torth Empire. Come on. Maybe this is good news."

That was possible. Thomas did deliver good news every once in a while, didn't he? Like the supercom network. That had made all sorts of things possible.

"All right." Evenjos leaned very close to Garrett. "Do we have a delegation that we need to bring to Freedomland? Or any supplies?"

"Not this time."

Evenjos was secretly pleased. She enjoyed boosting Garrett's raw strength to her own level, to empower him to mass-teleport, but conserving her power was also good. It meant she could last longer before her next rest period. She liked being alert and among people. Resting was too much like . . . well . . . like the worst torment she had ever endured.

She embraced Garrett.

Not only did she embrace him; she bodily merged with him. She spread herself under his garments. She encased him in a veil of dust so light and airy, his skin and his white hair and beard appeared to sparkle.

Her wings were lightweight enough for him to teleport with, so she left those out, whole and folded along his shoulders. Now he looked like a weathered angel.

Ready? Garrett asked in a wordless thought.

Ready, she confirmed, headless and voiceless.

Garrett's mind vanished from her senses. That was the clairvoyant trance.

A second later, they were on a different world.

Gravity was different, atmospheric pressure was different, the lighting was different, the scents and ambient sounds were different, but Evenjos was used to the sudden reality shift of teleportation by now. She regathered herself and took shape as her empress self, still riding Garrett around the shoulders just because it was fun.

"Get a room, you two," Ariock said.

Evenjos kissed Garrett's ear defiantly. Then she hopped off.

The room had several workstations, but they were dark. There were also comfy beanbags and plush hoverchairs, the sort used as office furniture. Kessa sat in one. Varktezo sat in another. Thomas floated at the head of the room in his own hoverchair.

And the Twins floated within his range.

Evenjos frowned at the mass murderers. The childish duo looked harmless and disabled, of course. The girl had a tube across her face, plugging her nostrils. A mechanical breathing aid? The boy perpetually sagged to one side. His roundness helped prop him upright, along with support from his molded backrest.

People made a lot of exceptions for the Twins, but allowing them to sit in on a secret meeting between heroes seemed too lenient, even for Thomas. Kessa ought to raise her brow ridges at their presence here. According to her own laws, penitents must be kept away from sensitive military information.

"We have news," Thomas said, "that you've waited a long time for." He swept the room with his gaze, including Ariock, Evenjos, and Garrett. "It will potentially change . . . uh, well. It could change the galaxy and the way society functions in a massive way."

Again?

Evenjos exchanged a glance with Ariock, and she saw her own worry reflected there.

Garrett sat on a sofa, and Evenjos sat next to him. Ariock took a seat on one of the beanbags sized for extra-large people. They all faced Thomas and his extra-bold statement.

The boy could have used a few more cushions to prop himself up. In another context, he would have looked ridiculous, like an adolescent sitting in a grown-up's chair, taking himself too seriously. But this was Thomas. It was impossible to think of him as a normal teenager.

Thomas presented a round tin container on his lap. He twisted the lid off and showed them what lay inside.

Pills.

A few dozen round, chalky tablets, easy for a person to chew and swallow, did not seem like a miracle on the same level as collapsing the Megacosm. Evenjos exchanged skeptical looks with Garrett. This was no supercom network, no brilliant war strategy.

"This," Thomas announced, "is immunity to the inhibitor."

Evenjos leaned forward. She leaned farther and farther, eyes wide and mouth agape, ogling the pills that could make her functionally immortal.

No one would be able to slay her.

Ariock and Garrett exchanged a glance. Their eyes were alight as if they had just won the war all over again.

Because that was what this meant. Winning.

Winning forever, repeatedly, without fear. The last dregs of the Torth Empire would recede like shadows before a bright spotlight.

Insanity gas was so hard to manufacture and to deliver, the broken Torth Empire seemed incapable of using it in battle anymore. Telepathy gas might still confound Ariock, but he could rely on soldiers who were practiced at using it. If the inhibitor was no longer a threat . . . ?

Ariock and all the warriors would be unstoppable.

Thomas spoke in a tone of apology. "I know this is a case of too much, too late," he said, "instead of too little, too late." He closed the tin. "That's why I invited you here as a small group. I want to discuss the ramifications before we make any policy decisions about how to distribute this."

"Ramifications?" Ariock paused.

Evenjos forced herself to remain restrained, to sit and think. She tried to think of what dire consequences Thomas imagined.

She looked around. The shani warriors were conspicuously excluded from this extremely beneficial announcement. The entire war council was absent.

"This," Thomas said, holding up the tin full of immunity tablets, "paves a path for Yeresunsa to become unstoppable." He gave Evenjos a look fraught with meaning. "The way they were before the Torth rose to power."

Oh.

Evenjos wanted to defend her own imperial era as utopian. But she had lived in this era for long enough to absorb some of its moral sensibilities. Her reign had been flawed. Not just her reign, but the entire system that she had inherited, and which had been in place for centuries before her birth.

Yeresunsa in her era had lived like gods. Of course they saw their own privilege as fair, just, moral, and the very pinnacle of civilization.

Torth during the Torth era would have said the same things.

Things were different for slaves and for peasants. They had seen those respective eras as tyrannies, and they were correct.

"If we make this public knowledge," Thomas continued, "then all Yeresunsa will want immunity to the inhibitor. The shani are used to revering their Yeresunsa, so it wouldn't be a huge change for them. But for the rest of the free galaxy? It's an ugly paradigm shift. Penitent warriors would become invincible. How long will they be content to atone and obey Kessa's lieutenants?"

Garrett looked grim. No doubt he was able to imagine the worst of former Torth.

"So you want us to keep it a secret?" Ariock asked.

"For now." Thomas shrugged. "It's what I recommend."

"What do you mean, 'for now'?" Garrett sounded suspicious. "Until when?"

Thomas looked like he was about to reply, but instead, he gave Varktezo an encouraging look.

The ummin lab assistant stepped forward. "Until we develop the bioscience to engineer Yeresunsa powers in ummins and other sapients."

Evenjos's jaw dropped.

Ariock looked just as stunned.

"It's just a matter of time," Thomas said blandly, as if Unyat's ultimate dream was an easy future achievement.

Evenjos stared at him.

"I know scientists who are doing active research on bioengineered powers," Varktezo said. "I don't know if they'll get anywhere. But Thomas thinks it's achievable."

Thomas nodded.

Garrett tried, and failed, to speak. Evenjos felt the same way.

"Level the playing field," Ariock said, his tone warm with approval. "Just like telepathy gas has done. It's a good idea."

Thomas smiled.

"So, about these immunity pills." Ariock gave the tin a speculative look. Apparently he was done contemplating the apocalyptic idea of everyone in the galaxy gaining bioengineered powers. "Does immunity override the inhibitor patch, if I'm wearing one?"

"It does," Thomas told him.

Ariock looked less than thrilled. Evenjos realized that he would have to juggle what he wanted on any given day: battle, or sex with Vy. He would not easily be able to have both.

"How long does one pill last?" Garrett asked.

"This generic prototype will give you four to six hours of protection," Thomas said. "You should take it before a battle, and you can expect it to wear off afterward." He gave Ariock a look. "You'd need two pills to achieve the same effect. Ideally, we will formulate a custom-tailored version for each Yeresunsa." He gave the Twins a fond look. "Or rather, Mondoyo and Serette will move forward with that research. This was largely their innovation."

"No." Mondoyo blushed. "You did most of the creative work."

"Hardly," Thomas said. "It would have taken me at least an extra decade to figure it out on my own." He spoke to Ariock. "They helped me unlock several key areas of neuroscience."

That explained why the Twins were here. They already knew about the miracle of immunity. They had helped invent it.

Garrett stood and held out his hand. "May I?"

Thomas handed him the tin.

Garrett held up one tablet and inspected it closely. He was probably probing its composition with his awareness.

"Will it work on Evenjos?" Garrett asked.

"The Evenjos version, in particular, might take some finagling to get right." Thomas looked toward her. "The Twins have great ideas about how to test it without risking your life, if you'll provide a small sample of your dust."

Evenjos hesitated.

"Do you trust me?" Thomas asked her.

She understood the subtext. If she trusted Thomas to be her friend—and she did—then she ought to trust his friends, the Twins.

But her hesitation wasn't about trust.

Evenjos stared at the purplish tablet Garrett held between his thumb and forefinger. She might not even need scientific experimentation to learn how the pill was supposed to affect Yeresunsa. She could delve Garrett or Ariock while they dosed up. As an expert on physiology, Evenjos would learn which chemicals blocked the inhibitor.

She would also, in all likelihood, learn how to simulate the effects of both the inhibitor and immunity to it.

She would become, in effect, a god of gods.

She would learn the secrets of how to shut down stormbringers such as Ariock, as well as how to make herself or other Yeresunsa invincible in battle.

Evenjos met Thomas's gaze. And she saw his knowledge. He had already made his peace with everything that she was just now realizing.

"I trust you," Thomas said kindly.

That was almost too much to bear.

Evenjos backed away. Garrett watched her with concern, not understanding how lonely immortality and power could truly be. Maybe she would be able to explain, someday. Maybe such incisive power would matter someday, in a future where anyone at all could become a god.

But for now?

"I am happy for my friends," Evenjos said carefully. "Ariock and Garrett. But I am not ready for this much immortality."

"Are you sure?" Garrett sounded wounded, as if he could not believe her decision.

"I am content as I am," Evenjos said.

"But," Garrett said, "you're mortal. Technically."

"So are you." Evenjos trailed a hand down his weathered, wrinkled face. Longevity pills could only prolong his life so far. Rejuvenation healing would give him another century. Maybe more. But if Garrett had a finite amount of time left to live . . .

Well.

Maybe she would try to follow him past the death barrier, once his life expired. She would cross the river and see where souls ultimately went.

She would skip the next rearrangement of the future galactic civilization.

Garrett stared at her with a mixture of fear and admiration.

CHAPTER 19

DISGRACED

The Former Commander of All Living Things—
—is far too grand a name-title for such an undeserving piece of ruination.
What should We call her instead?
The Worst Failure?
The Apocalypse Pawn?
The Unelectable? (Because elections no longer exist thanks to her.)

The Former Commander trudged through a chaotic crowd, winding past hover-carts laden with cargo, all heading toward the cracked and damaged spaceport on Grapeland Island. She wasn't sure which was worse: ignominy or utter desolation. She had sampled both.

After the Day of Collapse, she had spent a few weeks aboard her own luxury streamship with no one except a few starving slaves for company. But her store of food and drinks was finite. She would eventually run out.

So she had docked at an abandoned space station. The Torth had fled and left a lot of food behind, but they had also left a lot of slaves. Those unowned slaves were a grubby, unruly mob. She could have gassed them to kill them all, but to what end? She would still be alone.

A Torth alone was nothing. Torth needed to be part of a collective. Otherwise? They weren't people. They might as well be slaves.

With that realization, the Former Commander had scanned for promising minicosms.

Grapeland Island had been a good choice—for a day. But it turned out that having Torth in charge of a city was not enough to ensure safety. The local minicosm was tenuous and riddled with the petty concerns of individuals.

Without access to a galaxy's worth of knowledge, without instant cooperation, Torth could not achieve greatness. Torth no longer controlled supply chains. They did not own all the manufacturing plants. And so all the remaining Torth were reliant on dwindling stores of food and ammunition.

And they had to guard those supplies themselves, using surveillance systems or even their own weapons. Even the most pampered of slaves might turn traitor.

Data marbles kept appearing in slave zones, in secret. The Giant and the Imposter might be responsible for some of that campaign, but there was a whisper network among the very slaves themselves. Information dissemination was a rampant and increasingly widespread problem. No matter how strictly slaves were controlled, they found ways to gossip. They talked about freedom as a reality instead of just a myth. They repeated stories of Kessa the Wise.

The Former Commander walked creakily past a group of Red and Brown Ranks. She sensed contempt radiating from their minds.

How about if We call her the Apostate of All Ruination?

How about the Doom of the Galaxy?

One of the Red Ranks idly considered shooting her in the back. But he was more interested in survival as he directed a nussian work crew to load crates of nonperishable foods onto a convoy of hovercarts.

StayYoung City was only nine hundred miles away, and the Giant was there right now, in person. The locals here on Grapeland Island were rattled. According to whispers from the StayYoung minicosm, the Giant was unbeatable.

He might actually have immunity to the inhibitor.

Even without that unfair advantage, the enemies were unstoppable. Whenever they showed up with military force, more than half of a local Torth population would instantly kneel. Defiance meant death. The enemies no longer wished to police their penitents. Their message was clear: join us or die.

It was time to abandon all major cities.

The Former Commander saw an extra hoverbike abandoned by the roadside. She was a skilled rider, and she could use it to speed past cargo carts, to get to the spaceport faster.

But she wasn't sure how many pedestrians would tolerate her flashing past them, self-important.

She no longer wore a mantle of office. No white shroud, no twisting shoulder horns. She had left it aboard her luxury streamship. Yet she still had the sinewy limbs of someone who was mechanically enhanced. The curved scimitar strapped to her side was a champion's weapon, and although her armor was dented and stained, it was white. On top of that, her hollow cheeks and papery skin made her recognizable. She probably had the most infamous face of any living person in the known universe, aside from the Conqueror.

Look. The Ruined Commander moves like she is arthritic.

Maybe she ran out of painkillers?

The Worst Commander? Hmm.

How about if We call her the Disgrace?

I like it. Simple and to the point.

What a Disgrace of a leader.

How did she manage to live to such an old age?

A committee of local Torth in the Grapeland Island minicosm held a vote. To them, the Former Commander of All Living Things became the Disgrace. They ratified her name-title within seconds.

It was not nearly as grand as a vote should be. *Because the Disgrace ruined life as We know it.* Torth passersby glared at her.

The Disgrace would have liked to defend herself, but there was no denying the fact that her reign had been apocalyptic. She ought to be strung up in the Isolatorium and tortured to death for making so many wrong choices.

Too bad the Isolatorium was destroyed and gone.

She replayed her worst mistake over and over: the moment when she had dismissed the feral boy as a nonthreat.

She had been warned. The Upward Governess had told her that the Betrayer could cause unprecedented problems for the Torth Empire. But she had blithely dismissed those warnings. She had thought that no individual could bring the galactic empire to its knees. A mere child? Especially one with a severe physical disability?

He had seemed so powerless.

Instead, the Betrayer had become a burrowing parasite, eating away at the core strengths of the Torth Empire. He had pecked at the trunk until it was hollowed and ready to break at the slightest touch.

And then he had transformed into the Conqueror.

Even if the Megacosm reconstituted itself, even if Torth civilization could somehow reemerge and reassert its dominance, future generations would be traumatized by this war. The Conqueror had changed everything.

Wouldn't a better leader have killed the feral child right away?

The Disgrace had actually wanted to have him killed, even before he became Yellow Thomas. But what sane leader would ignore the most respected scientists in the galaxy plus her own constituents? The top ranks—the Servants of All who secretly ran civilization—had welcomed Yellow Thomas. If she had dared to execute him, then her own secret cabal would have condemned her as a traitorous failure.

So she had let him live.

The Disgrace was not sure what a more competent Commander of All Living Things would have done in her stead.

You were in charge. A fat Yellow Rank narrowed his eyes at her. *We (the Majority) elected you (the Disgrace) to make well-considered choices for All of Us. You should have done so even if those choices were personally hard. You should have put the fate of the glorious empire ahead of your own selfish fears and desires.*

The Disgrace trudged onward. She supposed she had been selfish, to allow the feral child to live. She should have paid more attention to the threat and less to her own personal concerns.

It was ironic that she had still outlived so many of her more cautious peers.

No individual should be permitted to be as wrong as she had been and live.

Perhaps she should go and sweep trash for the pleasure of enemy runaways? She could kneel before the minions of the Conqueror. An ignoble death as a groveling penitent might be the fate she deserved.

Or, a passerby silently commented to her, *you could join forces with the wisest individual in the universe. That's where I'm headed.*

The Disgrace stopped to stare at the Torth who had made the offer. He was a preadolescent with dirty clothes and unkempt hair.

Do you have a problem with how I look? The boy child stared defiantly into her milky-white eyes.

His black irises signified no rank. He was technically not even a person. He was just a potentiality who had yet to pass his Adulthood Exam.

Ugh. Whoever was in charge of the Grapeland baby farm must have released all the unripened individuals into the adult population. It seemed the babies were being permitted to fend for themselves, since no one could guarantee their care and safety anymore.

The same situation must be pervasive in many cities. Helpless infants and fetuses were probably abandoned, left to die and rot. Meanwhile, the mobile children probably had to fight for table scraps and other necessities.

No self-respecting Torth would share meals or other limited items with a bunch of nonpeople who had not yet passed their Adulthood Exams. How many worthless children were running around, stealing from adults?

I have a right to exist. The child was defensive. *I would have passed the Adulthood Exam, if one was given to me. I am a Torth (a person) as much as you are. I miss the Megacosm as much as you do.*

He turned away, scanning the local minicosm for a pilot who might be willing to let him hitch a ride to the Araya Moon Belt.

No one ever respects kids, he thought. And she sensed irony beneath his frustration. This adolescent child thought that the Disgrace, of all people, ought to recognize how capable kids could be. She had been outmatched by a kid.

He was right.

The Disgrace fell into step beside the adolescent, putting aside her notions of who counted as a person. An entire generation of prepubescent Torth was going to grow up without rules, without discipline, and without proper exams to weed out the duds.

Roaming children like this boy child would build the future, whether or not older generations of Torth approved of them.

As she limped into the damaged spaceport, she opened her bottle of painkillers and swallowed one. She was a mess of stress-related ailments. It was reckless to waste her dwindling supply of pills, since she had no idea if she would ever obtain more, but, well, caution was not in her nature.

Ships roared off launchpads. Down on the lower levels, hovercarts squeezed past each other, laden with cargo.

It was just another planetary evacuation.

Again.

The adolescent scanned the scene and located a passenger streamship. Torth heading toward that ship emanated hope. They were not just fleeing the planet Bountiful. They had somewhere specific to go.

The Death Architect will save Us, they chorused.

She's as smart as the Conqueror.

She promised to restart civilization.

None of these death cultists knew exactly where the Death Architect had hidden herself. She might be on any one of fifty thousand asteroids. A search would likely be fatal, thanks to all the decoys, mirror chambers, and death traps the little girl had set up on her asteroids.

Nevertheless, the Death Architect was still able to issue cryptic commands to her most ardent followers.

Millions of her cultists floated near temporal stream gateways in deep space, awaiting the right moment to jump to wherever she commanded them to go. Many hurtled past space rocks in unpredictable, patternless trajectories. That way, no one could easily attack them.

Why?

They waited for something. Who could guess what? The Death Architect wasn't giving any hints.

The adolescent hurried toward the death cultist ship, but the Disgrace hesitated. She scanned the bustling spaceport. Perhaps some other faction would allow her to join them?

Might she still command enough vestiges of respect to get herself invited in with a rogue survivor cult? That way, she might end up on some outpost or colony starship full of survivors, where she could . . .

Die of old age?

She would die in exile, in an isolated fragment of a dying society, among people who blamed her for their many losses.

She would die without any social influence.

Alone.

Like she was no longer a person at all.

She put her skeletal hands on the jutting bones of her hips. Did she really want to settle for fading away? Did she truly wish to die in obscurity?

She felt as if she had been born to please crowds. If she discarded that core part of her identity, then what was left?

A streamship pilot saw her and slammed a mental gate down. He would not allow the Disgrace to join his small band of rogue survivors.

The Disgrace wondered how justified the blame was. Sure, she had caused the Torth Empire to collapse, but she hadn't been alone, had she?

Shouldn't others bear some responsibility?

For instance, how about her predecessor in office? That previous Commander of All Living Things had wrongly assumed that Jonathan Stead was a corpse. His arrogant mistake had directly led to the flourishing of the Dovanack family and the existence of the Giant.

The Somehow Nexus had also made a grave error in judgment when he'd illegally inseminated a fellow Servant of All. What a criminal. He had illegally brainwashed his secret romantic partner, wiping away her memory of sex. That selfish, careless act had created an embryo that grew into the Conqueror.

What about the Swift Killer? What if that impulsive freak had not revealed her powers to the public? If she'd had some actual self-control, then maybe the Servants of All as an institution could have retained their authority and their dignity. Then the Conqueror never would have gained enough leverage to make a wager with the Torth Empire.

The Upward Governess had also made a poor decision, recommending that the Majority give the Adulthood Exam to a feral supergenius who had been raised by humans. Oops.

And what about the various generations full of individuals who had elected and promoted those fools?

The Torth Majority itself had welcomed Yellow Thomas. The masses had voted to allow him to determine the execution of the Giant.

They had elected the Disgrace.

They had elected her predecessor in office.

How far back did the mistakes go?

The Disgrace wondered if the Torth Empire had actually doomed itself.

Civilization had broken apart at a touch. An intimate touch, but still. Just a touch. Wasn't that a sign of deep internal rot?

It must have been rotting for centuries, perhaps for millennia.

By the time the Conqueror showed up with his "join Me" invitations, perhaps the whole empire had already rotted away to nothing but a weak husk, ready to topple.

Hundreds of Torth walked up ramps, into ships. More loaded cargo into holds. The Disgrace looked from ship to ship and tried to figure out where she ought to flee next. Was there any hope anywhere in the galaxy?

The Death Architect needs champions. That came from the adolescent boy, who watched her from afar. *Are you sure you don't want to join Us (so-called death cultists)?*

The Disgrace recalled her one private visit to the Death Architect. For a moment, she could smell battlebeasts and feel their drool. Her stomach flipped. She never wanted to see that little girl again.

And yet . . .

Somebody did need to remake the Torth Empire without all the rot and corruption.

Civilization needed a fresh start, without all the hard-packed grime from multiple generations of poor decisions.

The Disgrace hesitated, unwilling to be at the mercy of a child, no matter how smart.

Then she touched her scimitar and reminded herself that she could teleport away in an emergency. She could kill the Death Architect if she had to.

What was life without a risk or two?

She strode toward the death cult ship. If civilization was going to have a future, it needed to start somewhere.

CHAPTER 20

THE POWER OF

Ariock glanced at Thomas's holographic guidelines as he whittled a mecca out of a mountain.

He extruded verandas of lacework stone, courtyard plazas, halls within halls, and observatories that defied gravity. Whenever he leveled off a balcony or incorporated the agate beauty of the bedrock, Thomas wordlessly adjusted his blueprints.

This was magic.

It wasn't war. It wasn't killing.

The act of carving monumental buildings could be dismissed as frippery when compared with freeing the galaxy from slavery. Yet this act filled Ariock with more pride than any battle had ever given him.

He was leaving a legacy of grandeur.

His academic complexes, his museums, his courts of justice would be gazed upon with awe and reverence for generations to come. His colossal structures, carved from bedrock or diamond-hard crystals, would outlast the dregs of the fallen Torth Empire. They might stand for eons.

He was a creator.

He didn't have to settle for being a destroyer.

He could do this all day, every day. And so he had rescheduled military ceremonies and victory parades. Establishing foundations in major urban areas was more impressive than any parade, anyway.

The liberated planets needed some shared pride. Otherwise, they would begin to drift apart and make war upon each other.

And Kessa was giving them a shared purpose: the pursuit of knowledge. If she instated the Code of Gwat as a religion, well, that was fine as far as Ariock was concerned.

He extruded another colonnade on the new immensity. Mer nerctan dignitaries raised and lowered their heads in approval. Once Ariock and Thomas finished, the local populace would add crystal glass panes, accent lighting, docking bays, statuettes, and furnishings. Request Academy would become wholly theirs.

Ariock stepped back to admire his handiwork. From this distance, the newly extruded monolithic structure looked as delicate as gingerbread, but it was sandstone and jasper and tourmaline. He had reinforced the balconies with ionic tungsten struts.

"That's enough for me." Thomas sounded winded. "I'm done for today."

Ariock still felt energized, but he nodded, glad to switch gears. He knew whom he'd be spending his time with next.

He hoped Vy wasn't busy.

"How do I look?" Ariock tugged the hem of his charcoal-gray fabric shirt, hoping that it still fit in a flattering way. Every few months, he needed to add an extra inch or two of fabric to all his clothing, or ask his tailor to do so. He wished he could command his own body to stop growing.

"Vy will approve," Thomas said.

That was good.

Ariock observed a polite ceremony with the dignitaries, dedicating the newly built academy to the people of Request City. He felt awkward among strange aliens. Even when he was friendly, trying to set people at ease, he might as well be an incarnation of clouds or starlight. Even when he wore understated civilian clothes, he didn't have the same humble appearance as Kessa.

He accepted profuse gratitude from the military mayor, and he made sure the mayor included Thomas.

Finally it was time to leave. Ariock teleported back to Reject-20.

"Good luck," Thomas said, making himself at home in the cozy lab he shared with the Twins.

"Do you think she'll like the ring?" Ariock asked.

"No spoilers," Thomas said. "Go ask her!"

Ariock left Thomas in the research annex of the Freedomland academy and teleported to his own palatial suite. He used his powers to comb his hair and exfoliate his skin until he shone with health. He selected one of his ready-made travel packets. The patch would inhibit his powers temporarily, and the chalky tablet would give him immunity to the inhibitor. He was more likely to need one rather than the other. He tucked the packet into his clothes—along with a small velvet box.

Then he crossed the hallway and knocked on the entrance to Vy's suite.

Vy looked casual when she opened the door. Her thick red hair was in a simple braid. She always seemed to expect a normal-size friend and had to crane her head back.

"Are you in the mood for a romantic getaway?" Ariock asked.

Vy smiled. He loved the way she looked, sly and innocent at the same time. Sexy.

Their dates were always private. Neither of them wanted to be mobbed by awestruck aliens, so Ariock liked to take her to uniquely beautiful natural vistas.

"What's the best setting you can imagine?" Ariock asked her. "Mountains? An island? A rainforest waterfall? Today is special."

Vy giggled. She leaped up, and Ariock caught her in one arm. "What makes today special?"

"I'll tell you when we get there," Ariock said. "Where are we going?"

Vy laughed. "How about somewhere with an awesome view and perfect weather?"

That was easy. Ariock already had a destination in mind, on a planet known as Saintly. The mountains were far more prominent than any range on Earth, yet their slopes could be balmy. He teleported to a scenic outcrop with Vy in his arms.

"This is incredible!" Vy grinned at the landscape of deep gorges and sheer cliffs.

Ariock set her down. He spread a cushy blanket for their comfort.

"Why is today special?" Vy asked.

Ariock hesitated. In his imagination, this moment was supposed to be casual and momentous at the same time, but now he wasn't sure he could pull that off.

And he wasn't all that sure of her reaction, either.

Vy raised one red eyebrow at him.

Ariock realized he was tongue-tied. This was a big moment. A huge moment. One stupid mistake might cost him his entire future with Vy.

Was he rushing things? Was he pressuring her? Ariock swallowed and tried to regain some semblance of confidence, but it was futile. What made him believe he could come across like a potential husband?

He wasn't even close to being husband material. He was a freak. He went around slaughtering Torth every evening before dinner. There could be militant outbreaks for the rest of his life, and he would always be called in to handle them. He could not offer a peaceful married life.

Wasn't he arrogant, to be so certain that he was worthy of her love?

He should have sought romantic advice. A counselor might have wisely advised him to not even try this.

Vy slid both of her hands up Ariock's shirt, reaching up toward his chest. "Your heart is racing," she said with concern.

Ariock got down on one knee.

Vy looked baffled. Then her eyes widened with sudden understanding.

"I want to ask you something," Ariock said. For better or worse, he had gotten himself into this predicament. He needed to follow through before Vy concluded that he was having a medical episode.

She looked worried. That didn't bode well. She wasn't expecting this at all.

"Violet Hollander . . ." Ariock drew out the tiny velvet box and opened it, displaying the delicate ring. It resembled a halo, its platinum filigree suggesting a lacework of fine branches, each curled around a tiny diamond.

Her eyes went even wider.

"Will you marry me?" Ariock dared to ask.

Why would anyone sane want to marry a monster who caused storms whenever he was upset? He was trembling. He had probably just doomed their relationship.

Vy gasped and burst into joyful, happy tears. "Yes!" She threw her arms around Ariock's thick neck. "Yes!"

He was so surprised, he nearly forgot to be gentle when he hugged her back. He laughed against her shoulder.

She was laughing, too, with delight. "Are you sure you want to marry me?"

"Why wouldn't I?" he asked.

"I mean, I'm just a plain Earth girl." She sounded serious, as if revealing an embarrassing fact.

"You're not plain." He ran her braid through his fingers. Sometimes he wondered how she could be so oblivious to her own worth. She had a habit of false modesty.

Something made a rapid clicking sound behind them.

Vy turned and laughed with surprise. "We have an audience."

A large nest perched inside a craggy cleft. A critter sat within, watching them with interest. It could have been a cousin to griffins.

"Oops," Ariock said, mortified that he had failed to scout the area. The griffin-like baby animal had enough size that its parents might prove threatening. "I'd relocate it," he said, "but I think it would be easier for us to relocate."

"No. It's fine." Vy stopped Ariock before he could gather up the blanket. "I don't mind a bit of danger."

"Really?" If Ariock had to fend off a creature attack, that would ruin the mood. Vy would see his brutish side, and then she might reconsider the idea of marrying him.

"This needs to be refitted," Vy said, trying to twist the ring onto her finger.

Ariock embraced the platinum with his powers and stretched it until the ring slid comfortably onto her finger. "How about now?"

Vy admired it on her hand, delighted.

"I designed it myself," Ariock admitted. "With advice from Thomas."

"It's perfect." Vy pulled him toward the blanket.

Soon they were kissing. Vy draped herself onto his lap. "Always being a hero," she whispered. "I don't know how I got you. I'm the luckiest woman in the universe."

Ariock began to heat up from her caresses and kisses. Sunlight beat down on them, warming the air. He struggled heroically against carnal urges, but his awareness jumped out. Pebbles began to float.

"Hold on," Vy said, as Ariock said, "Just a minute."

Vy rolled partway off him. She reached into her discarded sundress and pulled out an inhibitor patch in plastic wrap.

Ariock laughed. He held up his own travel packet, showing her an identical patch.

He let Vy paste her patch onto his neck. As soon it was all the way on, his expanded awareness curled up. Pebbles fell. The mountains around him were safe and proud, and he became fearless in a way that had nothing to do with battles.

"Now then." Vy perched on his chest, face-to-face with him. "You're not going to cause an avalanche or whatever, right?"

She was so self-satisfied, lying on him. So cute.

Ariock could have gazed into her eyes forever. Whenever he was with Vy, the problems of the galaxy seemed irrelevant. Here, he was not a cargo carrier, or a stooge for Garrett, or muscle for Thomas, or a messiah figure for quadrillions of slaves. He was beholden to only one person.

An endless future spread out like the vista around them, sparkling and seemingly infinite.

Yet a shadow of his recurring nightmare made itself known.

Not only did his dream self fail to protect Vy, but he failed everyone. Even himself. He woke up every morning feeling as if he had died.

What was wrong with him? Why couldn't he just enjoy this moment? Why not revel in the fact that he was engaged to the most amazing woman in the universe?

When Ariock had consulted a seer, the Great Mwagru, he had realized his own stupid fear of losing the people he loved. He feared losing Vy, just as he had lost his father and his mother, and such a loss was unthinkable. It would shatter him.

He loved her so much, it was scary.

The dark side of him wanted to stash her in some secret haven that only he had access to.

Vy's smile said she supported any decision he made. She was there for him, no matter what.

Ariock had needed to see that. Her smile made his nightmare fade to meaningless nonsense.

And a better explanation for his apprehension came to him. Other warriors welcomed invincibility, since the crumbling Torth Empire still had a few loyal Servants of All and Rosies. Oh, and nuclear weapons. Lots of those. But Ariock defeated such threats with relative ease. He was so overpowered, well, of course he was afraid to lose his power for a short time!

He feared his own excessive power and he also feared being totally powerless. What else was new?

"Let's throw aside our fears," Vy said in a tender voice. She gently kissed Ariock. "Take off your clothes."

All his energy that had gone into air and stone was concentrated within his body. He was not even close to being a storm god. He was wholly human. But he was an extremely energetic human.

When Vy moved, wriggling, touching, and kissing, Ariock quit protesting and responded in kind.

CHAPTER 21

IMPARTIAL

The first time Kessa watched a movie was in Cherise's humanities class.

Cherise and Vy had talked up the experience, but Kessa privately did not expect much. She figured it would be five or ten humans reenacting some drama from their provincial history, with exaggerated gestures and a lot of overdramatic effort. So Kessa had sat in the back of the classroom with her arms folded, expecting a recorded theater troupe performance.

Instead . . .

Her beak fell open at the story. It was about power and family and grievance and justice and vengeance. Any sapient who had lived under Torth rule could identify with the thematic underpinnings.

And the value and effort put into the production! It was like peering through a window into another world, another time. The movie transported everyone who watched it. In some ways, it was even better than sharing a memory through telepathy gas. It was more coherent, easier to follow, and more emotionally gripping. It was art on a grander scale than Kessa had ever experienced.

It seemed to her that many artists, musicians, actors, and writers must have cooperated to create the masterpiece. She did not know if Rome was a real place, or if humans truly enslaved each other or fought as gladiators before an audience, but she was ready to believe it.

"Will you let me borrow your library of movies?" Kessa had asked Cherise later. "I wish to study humanities on my own."

"Sure." Cherise seemed to reconsider. "Uh, some of the media might not make sense to you." Her tone became light and joking. "Also, be careful not to get addicted. Some humans spend their whole lives watching TV and not doing much else."

Kessa took the warning seriously. She understood the temptation to escape day-to-day mundanities by falling into other people's stories. That had been a temptation in the slave Tunnels, too. Her mate, Cozu, had been so enamored of heroic tales, he had imagined himself as a heroic runaway.

Cozu was not the only slave who had died in an attempt to stand out and be his own hero.

Once Kessa obtained a curated bunch of Earth media from Cherise, she was careful to mete it out. She watched one movie every other day.

But she believed that these glimpses of human life helped her become more effective at her job. She found herself looking at penitents in strange new contexts. That sullen one over there—might he imagine himself to be an unjustly convicted prisoner? And that woman on that roofing crew, she looked like the sympathetic main character in the colorful animated adventure Kessa had just watched.

It wasn't that Kessa had lacked the imagination to equate penitents to humans. It was that until recently, they had seemed far too many steps away from becoming respectable and kindhearted people like Vy or Cherise. Or like Kessa herself, for that matter.

Penitents never laughed or joked. They did not sing. They did not repeat stories or even gossip out loud.

How could such emotionally damaged beings ever integrate into larger society? It seemed like an insurmountable challenge.

Kessa experimented. She played episodes of TV shows or screened films for a preselected group of penitents, those who truly strove to act human. Stories that addressed emotional trauma, in particular, affected the group. Characters such as Spock and Data were a lot like penitents struggling to become human. They grappled with emotions often regarded as tough or dangerous. Similar motifs were addressed with superhero characters, such as the Hulk, Wolverine, and Batman. There were even emotionally repressed romantic characters, such as the Phantom of the Opera, and in children's stories, such as Pinocchio.

Maybe there really was no significant moral difference between humans and their genetic cousins the Torth?

Perhaps the same moral baseline was shared for all sapients, including ummins. Even animals were not exempt from emotional bonding and conditioning.

Kessa thought about that while she walked the halls of the research annex, on her way to check on the Twins. One should refrain from rushing to judge others. That was a core tenet of Gwat. One should avoid making moral judgments without total and complete knowledge of the context and the circumstances.

Didn't that imply an absolute morality shared by all sapients?

The surviving Torth were no longer smug with excess knowledge. In fact, their stunted social skills made them inferior to other people, in a way. Reports from Kessa's lieutenants indicated as much.

Still deep in thought, Kessa entered the workroom of the Twins. She closed the door quietly and trotted down the metal ramp toward their workstations.

Thank goodness there was no telepathy gas here. Varktezo might think absorbing the thoughts of supergeniuses was fun, but he also enjoyed visualizing abstract algebraic structures. His notion of fun was far from typical.

The Twins worked side by side, their backs to Kessa. They waited until she was close before they simultaneously quit manipulating menus and rotated their hoverchairs to face her. Their facial features were quite different from each other—round and dark versus distorted and pale—but they were identically bland.

They should have acknowledged Kessa's presence as soon as they heard the door open. Penitents were expected to show deference toward her.

"What are you working on?" Kessa sat on a desk, putting herself at eye level with the Twins.

Serette wheezed. Clear tubes ran up her nose, connected to a ventilation system on the back of her hoverchair.

"Oh, we are reverse engineering temporal streams." Mondoyo indicated his workstation.

Kessa gazed at incomprehensible layers of holographic data. She supposed a more controlled temporal stream network could benefit the free galaxy. Maybe it would allow for easier commerce? It would facilitate the spread of knowledge. People across the galaxy would be connected, as once only Torth had been connected . . .

Hmm.

Or it might lead to a repeat of calamitous mistakes.

"Uh." Mondoyo seemed nervous. He was too far away to read Kessa's mind, but he had probably read her facial expression. "If we can improve galactic transportation, it should help you to administer the new galactic empire without help from Ariock and other teleporters. You'd be able to visit faraway planets with ease."

That was potentially valuable. Kessa kept hearing disturbing reports from faraway planets, like Othko and Quintessence. There were places where penitent Torth got outright massacred.

And there were places where liberated slaves were trying to revert to Torth rule. Those regressive idiots believed that life had been safer and more predictable with Torth in charge. Ugh.

Mondoyo cleared his throat. "Uh, we have a favor to ask."

That put Kessa on edge. The Twins had not earned the sort of redemption Thomas had earned, as far as the public was concerned. So far, their inventions only benefited the most powerful people in existence. Ariock, especially, used a temporary inhibitor patch whenever he wanted intimacy with Vy. He was likewise happy to slaughter death cultists without risking the inhibitor.

Would an improved temporal stream network change the balance? Perhaps the benefits would outweigh the destructiveness of their gaseous weapons.

"Serette is dying," Mondoyo said.

Serette lowered her gaze, as if suffering a fatal illness was a faux pas.

"We have a supply of NAI-13," Mondoyo assured Kessa. "We're extremely grateful to Ariock and Thomas for giving us that. Neither of us would have lasted this long without it. But . . ." He shrugged uncomfortably. "Serette is very old for a supergenius who hasn't gone through regeneration healing. Her lungs and heart aren't working properly. We've tried everything that's medically feasible, but she needs, uh . . ."

Kessa remained quiet, allowing Mondoyo the dignity and discomfort of making the request.

"Regeneration healing would save her life." Mondoyo's voice cracked. "Like what Thomas had."

The Twins might not be mated in a sexual or traditional way, but their love was undeniable. It humanized them.

If regeneration were a small, cheaply feasible procedure, Kessa would not have hesitated. If she could wave her hand and heal both Serette and Mondoyo, she would have done so.

But she recalled the intense week surrounding Thomas's regeneration healing. It had begun with a massive relocation to a reject planet so the heroes could prepare, storing their raw strength. They had all needed to be at peak performance. Then there were three days of suffering for Thomas. That lengthy process had nearly depleted the Strength, the Transformation, and the Will. It had left them vulnerable and open to attack, including more than a day of recovery afterward. It had derailed all their other important efforts and work.

There were fewer risks from the Torth Empire now, but cultists would certainly take advantage of the heroes' absence. Millions of people would suffer or die while just one of the Twins underwent that kind of healing.

And what about the other Twin? Serette would insist on the same treatment for her partner.

"We understand this is an enormous ask." Mondoyo looked guilty. "Thomas will not be able to persuade the general public. Serette needs an advocate who has everyone's respect." He gave Kessa a look that was fraught with hope. "It should come from the person who wields the ultimate authority over penitents."

So they had just been waiting for Kessa to visit.

"Please?" Mondoyo gave Serette a loving glance. "I will do anything to save her."

Kessa shifted uncomfortably with her own authority. It felt like too much. She was not a hero of prophecy.

Serette had never shown human empathy. Her aloofness had nothing to do with her lack of a tongue. Mondoyo was warm and empathetic enough to prove an obvious contrast. Serette was all about pure science—and purity in general. She did not interact with former slaves. Not even Varktezo.

Would the public tolerate a week of deadly mayhem for the sake of giving Serette a precious gift?

The newly freed galaxy was full of unsung heroes. They all deserved lifesaving measures for themselves and their loved ones. But not even Ariock or Evenjos had the bandwidth to heal everyone. It was necessary to be choosy.

Was Serette enough of a hero?

Was she redeemed enough to be on the same level as Thomas?

Kessa knew the answer.

The vast majority of people would take one look at Serette and see an entitled Blue Rank, a mass murderer. They would remember the insanity gas massacre.

Yet Serette and Mondoyo were actual heroes. They deserved to be acknowledged for the good things they had done and were doing. Serette ought to undergo a partial healing, if that was possible.

Or perhaps the research team under Varktezo could pioneer something? New medical technology might benefit common people as well as privileged supergeniuses. That would be a lot more palatable to the public.

"I will consider what options are available." Kessa slid off the desk and walked away, unwilling to endure the gazes of ultrasmart children.

She was beginning to understand why heroes like Thomas and Ariock were burdened with guilt. The hardest decisions impacted fellow heroes, unsung or otherwise. Their choices rippled into the future like waves, upsetting the balance of what was to come in order to perfect the setup for the next pivotal event.

Every major choice was haunting.

SUPERVILLAIN

Life is good, Ariock thought.

He was self-aware enough to know that this much existential contentment was warranted and long overdue for him. He lay on a blanket beneath a deep night sky peppered with stars, hands folded, more relaxed than he had felt since armored Torth had busted into his sky room.

Vy lay next to him, peaceful and satisfied, her loose hair surrounding her naked body in waves.

They fit together.

A tight fit, but they both seemed to enjoy that. Ariock doubted he could be any happier. He was going to get married! He had a future with Vy as his wife! It wasn't subject to the whims of an evil galactic empire.

There were no more barriers. The Torth Empire was in retreat.

Die-hard Torth were leaving every major urban region, piling into their beat-up starships and flying toward remote outposts that could support life. They were giving up. The future could only be brighter and more happy than—

His wristwatch pinged with the private channel sound.

Ariock tapped it to show that he was listening.

"Ariock." Garrett's gruff voice crackled over the supercom, relayed from sketchy satellites. "Meet me in the war room ASAP. We have a problematic situation."

"Got it." Ariock sighed. The old man was usually realistic about threat assessment, so there was probably something awful happening, somewhere in the universe, that only Ariock could handle.

Vy cuddled up. "No rest for the galactic hero," she said teasingly.

Ariock understood that she was not making fun of his life. Vy just had so much faith in him, she could not imagine him letting people down. No doubt she figured he would slay any threats and be home in time for dinner.

Ariock kissed her forehead. "I'll be back in time for lunch. Ready to go home?"

Vy nodded sleepily.

Ariock teleported them to his bedroom suite in Freedomland. He left Vy on the huge bed and searched for more of his specially formulated immunity tablets, simultaneously using his powers to dress himself. Immunity was more necessary than armor. He never went into a dangerous situation without extra tablets. He found the container on a shelf and pocketed it.

Fully armored, he decided to skip a leisurely walk. He teleported directly to the lobby outside the war room.

Kessa looked startled. She smiled in relief when she saw the sudden arrival was Ariock. "I guess I am on time." She stepped off her hoverbike.

Ariock led the way inside. Garrett and Evenjos sat side by side at a vast table of burnished meteorite.

Kessa took a seat. "Where is everyone else?"

"This is a secret meeting." Garrett wore a grim look. He rested one gnarled hand on the tabletop. "We're going to start by bringing you two up to speed."

Ariock sat in the throne-like chair reserved for him. "Where's Thomas?"

"On his way," Garrett said. "He's the one who called this meeting. He asked me to fill you in."

"Okay." Ariock item-teleported a water pitcher and cups. He splashed the pitcher full of pure water from his favorite mountain stream, then used his powers to simultaneously pour cups for everyone present.

"Thank you." Kessa pulled her cup closer.

Evenjos gave her own cup a dismissive look. She did not need nourishment. Ariock felt some chagrin, remembering that she was essentially undead.

"All right." Garrett stood, implying that this was an official report. "A few weeks ago, the Death Architect seized one of our superluminal nodes. That was no big deal. Or so I thought at the time."

Rogue Torth grabbed anything they could get their hands on. Mostly, they stole weapons and food. Communications satellites? Well, Ariock supposed the loss of the Megacosm had crippled Torth everywhere. It was no surprise that the death cultists wanted radios and supercoms and whatnot.

But so what? What could the remnant dregs of the Torth Empire possibly learn from eavesdropping on random people?

"You're making the same wrong assumption I made," Garrett said with a pitying look toward Ariock. "Unfortunately, they didn't steal it for use as a spy device. Or not solely, anyway. The Death Architect wanted to reverse engineer Thomas's communications technology. And that's what she did."

Ariock tried to think through the implications. What would an enemy super-genius do with superluminal communications technology?

He was stumped. Phone calls weren't going to replace the Megacosm. Movie streaming was a poor substitute for what Torth could already do with their minds.

"You should know this, Ariock," Garrett said in a barely tolerant way. "What can the internet do that Torth cannot do?"

Ariock didn't like to feel like an idiot. He drained his water cup, hiding his annoyance. The old man had probably learned whatever he knew from Thomas.

"Computerized automation!" Garrett spread his hands as if that explained everything. "She's gained the ability to synchronously link up devices across the galaxy."

Kessa gasped. She must have grasped the implication, and it horrified her.

"That means," Garrett went on for Ariock's benefit, "she can rig bombs to simultaneously explode. She doesn't have to rely on her followers. She doesn't need her death cultists at all. She has sole control over drones near every hub planet!"

"Are you sure?" Ariock wondered if a disaster had already occurred. "How do you know?"

"We know very little." Garrett emphasized the last two words, as if ignorance was personally offensive. "But I pieced together some stray thoughts from a minicosm, and I got worried. Her cultists are talking about artificial gravity grids and degenerate matter. Also extremal combinatorics. We surmise that they want to use temporal streams as leverage for payloads. I hardly know the baseline science behind what she's asked her cultists to do. They hardly know, either."

"Okay." Ariock did feel vaguely stupid. He should have foreseen terrorism from the death cult. But he was unable to imagine whatever terrible threat Garrett seemed to fear.

"So this morning," Garrett said, "I visited Thomas and reported everything I've overheard."

"Okay," Ariock said, his tone encouraging. "And . . . ?"

"And now we are more than worried," Evenjos put in. "We are terrified."

Ariock still felt slow. He was missing something. If the Death Architect had rigged a disaster, wouldn't she have already set it off? What was delaying her?

"For all we know, she's rigging it right now to go off at the press of her little finger!" Garrett mashed the air with his finger, miming the savage press of a button.

Thomas's voice came from the doorway. "I'll fill you in. Brace yourselves. It's complicated."

He floated into the war room on his newly minted smoky-gray hoverchair, flanked by the Twins on their own hoverchairs. Although Thomas could walk nowadays, hoverchairs and hoverbikes were a way to traverse large areas at a pace that was faster than a brisk walk.

Thomas parked at the table, and the Twins glided to a stop behind him. Ariock poured water for the trio of supergeniuses.

"Serette and Mondoyo are going to be vital to helping stop this threat," Thomas explained. "So I took the liberty of inviting them."

The Twins looked a lot less healthy than Thomas did. The girl Twin wore breathing tubes and wheezed with every breath.

Ariock began to get up, to heal the child. Evenjos beat him to it. She broke apart and reformed in a standing position, whereby she poured healing energy into the ailing girl.

It had little effect.

Evenjos returned to her seat, looking disappointed. Ariock could not add anything beneficial on top of her efforts, so he remained where he was. No healing or medical intervention would save a supergenius in a death spiral. The girl Twin needed regeneration healing.

Perhaps Ariock should have spent time on Serette rather than fooling around with Vy? Agh. He had so much trouble juggling his schedule.

Thomas ignored the byplay. He used his power to project a holograph above the huge table. Miniature solar systems hung in midair, replete with planets, space stations, dreadnoughts, and the flecks of streamships. They all moved in sedate, aquatic trajectories.

"We have evidence that the Death Architect had her cultists bury nuclear bombs in urban centers," Thomas said without preamble. "She accomplished this before our people fully took over certain hubs, such as Permafrost City. She would have had the foresight."

His holograph lit up with hundreds of target markers.

Were those urban centers? In danger?

"They'll be remotely activated," Thomas said. "I doubt their transceivers are superluminal, since she presumably buried them before she gained that technology. But she now has the technology to create intermediary transponders. She can have those positioned close enough to each bomb to trigger its activation sequence."

The holograph gained a secondary set of lights, red and threatening. Each transponder targeted a hidden bomb.

Ariock noted that the transponders could be hidden anywhere at random. They were in deserts, forests, underwater. One of them showed up on an orbital satellite.

"And then," Thomas said, "boom."

Holographic cities exploded in rapid blooms.

The casualties would be devastating.

"How long do we have?" Ariock leaned forward.

"No idea." Thomas made the admission as if it pained him. "We've already found four bombs and deactivated them, thanks to Kessa."

Kessa looked bashful. "I had nothing to do with it. The first bomb was discovered by a local on Paleoterra. Each city has its own investigators. They are doing what they can."

"You've coordinated the search," Thomas told her. "And we're grateful for that."

It seemed they had already discussed this threat and taken care of it. Ariock shifted in his chair, wondering why he had been invited to this meeting. He might be able to ghost around and detect fissile materials, but that would be a long, slow process, compared with what teams of searchers could accomplish.

Besides, he was not the only person who could ghost. Plenty of penitent warriors would be willing to find the bombs and deactivate them.

Ariock considered changing the topic. Kessa might be thrilled to hear about Ariock's engagement to Vy! Perhaps the happy news would get Thomas out of his pessimistic mood?

Thomas gave Ariock a look that seemed heavy with portent. "Unfortunately," he said, "I have reason to believe that these metro bombs are a casual side project for the Death Architect. I suspect she's doing it only as a means of distraction. She doesn't want us to guess her real purpose."

That was ominous.

"Judging from what Garrett picked up from her cultists," Thomas said, "I believe she is planning something much, much worse."

Worse?

Ariock stared at Thomas blankly, unable to imagine anything worse than nuclear bombs hidden beneath neighborhoods and nurseries on hundreds of planets and rigged to explode simultaneously at the touch of a button by a sociopathic supergenius.

Maybe Thomas was trying to be funny? Was this his idea of a joke?

Thomas cleared his throat. "It seems she's directed her cultists to take control of a quantum spin foam research station. They've also taken an experimental collider, and we have evidence that they've constructed copies. And they're cannibalizing gravitational gridworks, which means they're likely creating ultracold neutrons, or containment for degenerate matter or hyperons."

None of that meant anything to Ariock.

"They're manufacturing black holes, in other words." Garrett sounded as if he was explaining elementary math to a child.

"That's one theory." Thomas shot Garrett an annoyed look before focusing on Ariock again. "Their activity suggests that they are theoretically capable of star lifting. That means they can generate a ring current around a star and collect plasma, and turn the results into homogeneous cold catalyzed nuclear matter. That's the stuff inside neutron stars."

Ariock sighed, tapping his fingers on the tabletop. His telepathic friends had already discussed this threat before he'd even woken up this morning. Of course they had. And they didn't need things explained to them. Ariock was just their big, dumb helper, the one who was always a few steps behind.

They probably didn't even want Ariock in a strategy meeting. That was why they hadn't invited him until now.

"Dumb it down, please," Ariock said curtly. "What do you need me to do?"

"Sorry." Thomas looked guilty. "I'm making inferences based on what scant evidence we've been able to glean."

"She doesn't want us to figure out what she's doing," Garrett said. "She hasn't even enlightened her loyal cultists. They're making their own guesses, albeit not too dissimilar from ours."

"I need more information," Ariock said.

"Okay," Thomas said. "She has the means to destroy a solar system. That won't be totally devastating if it's localized to one system. But we have a wrinkle: the temporal stream network."

Thomas's holograph became a glowing web of galactic fuzz, like a flattened dandelion head ready to blow apart. It vaguely approximated a spiral disk.

"Temporal streams are a great gift to our galaxy," Thomas said. "They were constructed by ancient aliens, and to this day, no one knows how to create new ones. But that gift is also a back door to terrible destruction."

Ariock supposed that must be the case for all great gifts. It was certainly true for Yeresunsa powers.

"Temporal streams can deliver us across light-years instantly," Thomas said. "But by that same token, they can also spread destruction faster than light speed."

Ariock didn't like where this explanation was heading.

"So, for instance," Thomas said, "if the Death Architect is able to catapult degenerate matter into two ends of a temporal stream, each payload will feed mass to the other. To give you some idea of the forces involved: One teaspoon of degenerate matter is heavy enough to pull this planet out of its orbit. Drop a teaspoon of that stuff, and instead of it falling, the planet will rise to meet it."

Ariock considered his own strength.

He might be able to shift the ultradense payloads off course. He could only do one at a time, however. What if he had to deal with several at once?

Each payload would weigh more than a planet, possibly more than a star.

Did his strength have a limit?

"They would destabilize into black holes," Thomas went on. "Black holes that grow continuously in a relativistic loop." His holograph zoomed in on one piece of fuzz. It began to strobe, as if crisscrossed by fast moving shadows. "Each would very quickly grow supermassive. They'd merge together and overwhelm the whole temporal stream network."

His diagram morphed into the galaxy.

An explosion seared through one tendril of one of the spiral arms. Countless stars went dark.

Ariock hoped Thomas would use plain language sooner rather than later. He shook his head, indicating how lost he felt. He hadn't even had breakfast yet.

"It would explode outward," Thomas said, "ripping through multiple solar systems within a matter of hours, simultaneously in the quantum meshwork of 'now.'"

The galactic map grew blotchy. Stars died in clusters.

"She can automatically extrapolate the calculations needed to hit key solar systems," Thomas went on. "And she can hit them using superluminal relays now, without anyone needing to be on-site."

"The destruction would grow into a blight on our galaxy," Garrett said.

"And it could become unstoppable," Thomas said glumly. "Unfortunately, we're only guessing as to the exact nature of her doomsday device. It might not be a supermassive black hole. Instead, the payloads might induce zero-time quantum tunneling, which converts a metastable Higgs field into a decaying false vacuum. That would cause all matter around every temporal stream to vaporize, and the destruction would rapidly expand."

Thomas threw his hands wide, and holographic stars vanished in flashes of light.

"Or she's creating chain reactions that engender blobs of dark energy," Thomas said, "to overwhelm gravity and other forces. The dark energy would accelerate the expansion of space to the point of creating a localized Big Rip. That's the catastrophic end state of unlimited expansion."

His holograph exploded in a vaporizing light display.

Then it vanished.

Everything was gone.

"Another possibility is a Q-ball storm," Thomas said. "Or a strangelet storm. Any of those paths would cascade into a calamity that wipes out all the habitats and worlds in our galaxy." He stated it plainly: "She's plotting to destroy as much of the universe as she can."

PART FOUR

"One of them is Wisdom. One of them is Strength. One is Will, and one is Transformation. Without them, I see no Glory."

—forgotten fragment from the prophecies of Ah Jun

PERFECT STILLNESS

The Death Architect gazed at the frigid depths of outer space.

To those who were ignorant, space was nothingness. Her asteroid was so distant from any star, its rocky surface resembled the barest hint of a shadow. It blended with the emptiness beyond.

The temporal stream was likewise invisible.

She had programmed a glowing fringe in her display to suggest the drifting rift in the fabric of space-time, coded to resemble something like an aurora borealis. That gave her the ability to track its motions. The universe was in motion. Galactic arms and globular clusters and solar systems all had their own motion, and there was cosmic radiation to consider, as well as the spin and pull effects of gravity, mass, and velocity. If one wanted to use a temporal stream, one needed to pinpoint its ever-changing location in all dimensions, with accuracy down to the nanosecond. One needed to enter at an exact trajectory and within a specific range of velocities if one wanted to reemerge in the correct place. Otherwise? Those who failed suffered immediate and crushing nonexistence.

She had readied all the mathematical formulas needed to target this nearby temporal stream. She had to adjust her calculations as the cosmic radiation and deep space medium changed.

The Death Architect is great.

The Death Architect is mighty.

The Death Architect is the best (the best) THE BEST.

Distant melodies sang inside her head. She had never needed the affirmations of idiots, yet her loyalists praised her. They reached out to anyone who shared their devotion.

And they attracted more idiots.

Many Torth yearned for civilization *(the Megacosm)*. They refused to join the Conqueror as kneeling penitents. They survived in small bands, or in large survivalist groups, and they wanted their old, comfortable lives back.

The Death Architect has plans!

The Death Architect is wiser than the Conqueror!

The Death Architect is guaranteed to win!

Some rogues refused to join that chorus. Some Torth refused to take orders from a pubescent child, no matter how smart she was. Others simply disliked the Death Architect. They thought she was too secretive. Some preferred to place their trust in thought leaders who habitually revealed their ideas. Several million followed the Clement Serpent, a Servant of All who had rallied a lot of survivors on Tenth Ocean. More than ten million followed the Null Distraint, adding ships to her rogue armada.

But most survivors were tired of running.

Every time they scanned for fellow survivors, they sensed that the cult of the Death Architect was bigger and stronger than the last time they had checked. Her worshippers swirled with certainty.

She is not marred by anger, fear,
> *love, friendship,*
>> *or other slave concerns!*
>>> *She is perfection incarnate!*

Various rogues wondered if they dared resist such a smart leader. What if they would miss the opportunity of a lifetime?

So they joined the death cult.

In duos or trios, in tens or even in thousands, they joined her faction. Distant Torth clicked into orbit around strong minds who, in turn, orbited the massive mind of the Death Architect. Every day, every hour, brought more.

And at last, they no longer felt like a loose collection of skeptical individuals. They were a constant thrum that never slept. They shared a unified purpose.

They were a nation.

They were becoming greater than a minicosm. They were her Necrocosm.

Move that magnetic rocket nozzle to here, the Death Architect directed one skeletal branch. *Destroy that streamship*, she directed another twig. *Do not give the enemies a chance to get suspicious.*

She had eighty million hands and eyes.

She inhabited hundreds of hub solar systems.

She was a sentient version of the galaxy, more aware of the cosmos than anyone who had ever existed before her. She tracked death launchers on a superluminal network. She oversaw factories of killer drone swarms that would serve her whims. She made it her purpose to study astrophysics and celestial forces as no one else had ever legally been permitted to do, until now.

Relativity didn't matter. The limitations of time and space and distance were mere inconveniences. Just as with the reconstituted Necrocosm, all her death launchers were tied together in a quantum matrix of now. They would shoot their payloads at the exact same instant, no matter where they were in the galaxy.

DEATH TO THE ENEMIES! her orbiters sang as they followed her myriad of murky instructions.

> *We trust you, Great Mind!*
> *When will You strike down the Conqueror and his forces?*

The Death Architect wished she could allow some displeasure to dribble out of her mind. Her orbiters should never question her or speculate about her purpose. The small-minded fools ought to know better.

But she felt nothing.

Anyway, the future was preordained. She had ordained it.

Soon.

That was all she gave them.

Then she dipped out of her frail and newborn Necrocosm in order to think freely.

Her nemesis, the Conqueror, was crippled by his slavish fondness for people. Cherise. Varktezo. Kessa. The boy Twin. The girl Twin. The Climbing Storm. The Pink Screwdriver. The Shrewd Awareness. Azhdarchidae. Abhaga. The Shapeshifter.

The Giant. And so many other idiots. The supposedly victorious supergenius was collecting quite a harem of obligations.

He would never unshackle himself from all those obligations.

He was like a rich Blue Rank weighed down by too many jewels and slaves. Ownership could become a burden. Even if the Conqueror deduced the Death Architect's ultimate plan, his so-called friends would slow his thoughts and deeds. They would give him too many excessive variables to consider.

And his time would run out.

The Death Architect took a moment to appreciate the spartan minimalism of her lair. She'd had the foresight to reinforce abandoned rigs and stations with black tungsten hulls, and to further protect them with mirrors and traps. This small fortress used to be a mining rig. Its water recycler was inefficient. There were few lights. No air fresheners. No luxuries. The quarters were cramped.

But from afar, this defunct rig was nearly impossible to spot, hidden within the dark crevice of an asteroid. It floated in a vast field of similar rocks.

Not a single other sapient knew about this lair—other than the Former Commander, who knew better than to reveal the location to anyone else. Whenever the Death Architect wanted a shipment of supplies, she used the superluminal coms she had reverse engineered to deliver an encrypted map to one of her many worshipful pilots. Once the pilot delivered cargo to the intake receptacle of her hideaway, she released her battlebeasts into that airlock so they could hunt and kill and eat the pilot. The Necrocosm was too fragile to endure death screams, let alone to probe the secrets of a dying mind.

She would do it again for her next shipment.

The Conqueror wasn't going to find her.

Battlebeasts gnawed on bones in the corner cell. They had already eaten the last of the experimental albinos.

Ugly noises did not irritate the Death Architect. Although she would never admit it in public, she did not actually comprehend the difference between ugliness and prettiness, or good versus bad. Why tag raw data with value judgments? Weren't judgments inherently worthless?

Data was neither bad nor good. It just existed.

And everything was just data.

She provided for her battlebeasts by feeding them cargo pilots and the remains of scientific experiments. That was expedient. But they were hungry again, so she needed to order another delivery.

Unless she decided to end the universe right now?

The Death Architect lowered her eyelids and fixed her gaze upon the faraway temporal stream. She stopped breathing. She went perfectly still.

Biometric sensors measured the dilation of her pupils and the expansion and contraction of her chest. That data was conveyed, through superluminal relays, to the death launchers.

One second.

Two seconds.

Three seconds.

Sleep would not set off the chain reactions meant to destroy all of creation. But perfect stillness would. Deathly stillness. When she died, everything in the universe would be unmade. Everything and everyone would follow her into death.

Four seconds.

Five.

Six.

Seven.

Eight . . .

The Death Architect purposely shifted her gaze and lost her stillness.

It was tempting to wait out the ten seconds to end it all right now, but she was not quite ready. Not yet. Her killer drones were nowhere near delivery. Her death launchers were not all fully rigged or properly tested.

Anything less than perfection would open up a possibility that the Giant could flicker across the galaxy and stop the ultradense payloads.

She still had a little more work to do.

The Death Architect ascended into her Necrocosm, where millions of minds swirled around hers, fawning, eager to help her achieve perfection on a project they were unable to comprehend.

Soon, she assured her multitudes. *Soon You will All know what I am working on.*

CHAPTER 2

DOOMSDAY COUNTDOWN

Destroy the universe?

Ariock wanted to reject that cartoonish nonsense. The Death Architect was a heartless alien, sure, but this went beyond destructiveness. It was stupid, mindless craziness.

He hoped it was a joke. He hoped he had misunderstood.

"You understood correctly." Thomas hunched his narrow shoulders, as if the incomprehensible threat was his fault. "I'm guessing she enacted this plan by reverse engineering our superluminal communications network. Our technology is the key she needed to make this work."

He said *we* and *our*, but Ariock heard his guilt. Thomas had invented the technology.

He blamed himself.

"Are you absolutely sure about this?" Evenjos asked Thomas in a pained voice.

"Right." Kessa seemed eager to pinpoint hope. "You say that you have scant evidence. Is there any chance that your interpretation is wrong?"

Thomas shook his head. "She's taking every step I would take if I was going to destroy everything in existence."

Everyone seated around the table stared at Thomas. The fact that he actually could kill the universe . . . Just how often had he contemplated supervillainy?

"She has particle colliders," Thomas said. "And Hawking radiation suppressors. The type of equipment she's stealing suggests she's creating containment for something substantial. More substantial than stabilized micro–black hole grids."

Mondoyo leaned sideways, speaking from slightly behind Thomas. "Due to the war, supergeniuses have become free to work on anything. It's the first time in history we've been mentally free like this. And it's been this way for over a year."

Ariock suppressed his unnerved reaction. Kessa, Evenjos, and Garrett exchanged glances. They all knew that the Torth Majority had forbidden its own citizens from inventing weapons of mass destruction.

But now?

The Death Architect had no constraints. She was free to do whatever she felt like doing.

"Not only that," Mondoyo said in the higher-pitched voice that meant Serette was speaking through him, "but the Torth Majority told us to invent weapons of mass destruction. They specifically commanded us to do so."

"Exactly," Thomas said grimly. "The Death Architect has been given a free pass to ponder ways to murder people. There's no consortium of scientists who will vote against her or tell her no. She murdered the other supergeniuses. There's no one left on her side who can act as a voice of dissent. There's no more Torth Majority to question what she's doing. Or rather, her cultists have united into a new sort of Torth Majority. They have a Necrocosm, and it's one hundred percent obedient to her."

Ariock had blithely disregarded the Death Architect as a low-key background threat.

Now he realized that she was the main threat. The Torth Empire at the height of its power was hardly as deadly as that little girl—or rather, she was a product of the Torth Empire at its height. Why had he forgotten that?

Well, he knew why. She was a child. A disabled little girl.

Ariock no longer saw the Twins as monsters, having visited them a few times. He could not fear Nea, the four-year-old. He had ceased to fear supergeniuses. Rebuilding galactic infrastructure had seemed more important than dealing with the last surviving Torth threat.

That was horrifically shortsighted.

"No one has even guessed what she's up to," Thomas went on, "except for us." He indicated himself and the Twins.

Ariock stared at the place where the holograph had visually vaporized.

Would he end up alone and dying as a failure in a black void of utter nothingness?

Like in his recurring nightmare?

"Why?" Ariock asked the obvious question, because he felt lost. "Why is she doing this?" He could barely grasp the situation. "Why does she want to destroy the universe?"

"That child has been a sociopathic murderer since she was a toddler," Garrett said. "The Majority should never have let her off a baby farm."

"I don't know her well." Thomas sounded pained. "But I've visited her mind, and I think it's safe to say she doesn't fear death. Or anything. She's not sentimental. She won't care. It's likely she arrived at this idea based on some chain of logic."

Thomas was never wrong.

"She has no survival instinct," Evenjos said in a tone of realization.

"That is correct," Mondoyo said. "She had an excuse to live—for scientific curiosity—but she may be chasing an idea that overrides that. We know her well." He glanced toward his ailing partner to include her. "We've had concerns ever since she successfully plotted to murder the Upward Governess."

"I thought that one was murdered by the Swift Killer?" Ariock said, remembering his failure to protect the brave supergenius.

Thomas and Mondoyo both shook their heads.

"Who do you think whispered in the Swift Killer's mind?" Garrett asked.

Ariock supposed he must have known that.

He just didn't want to imagine an enemy who looked so sweet and innocent. He had seen holographic representations of the Death Architect. She wore bows in her hair.

Yet that sweet-looking child had defeated him, a galactic hero with near-infinite strength.

And hadn't she also tricked Thomas, in a way?

"She murdered all our colleagues," Mondoyo reminded everyone. "She exploited the fears of the Majority."

Indeed, the Death Architect had lured other supergeniuses into death traps.

"Without emotions," Mondoyo said, "what purpose is there to life? The Torth are not truly emotionless. They only pretend. They wear tranquility meshes and suppress their inner truths. But the Death Architect is one of the rarities who actually lacks emotions, as far as we can tell." He seemed to receive an extra thought from Serette, and he nodded toward her. "Right, except for scientific curiosity. She does have that."

Ariock struggled to maintain a good mood, but a sense of desolation engulfed him, as if he was dreaming rather than being awake. Inside his imagination, Vy tumbled away into darkness, screaming for him.

He couldn't save her.

Failure.

Misery.

The end of all things.

"So what do we need to look for?" Garrett asked with a confused frown. "I guess you're saying she can contain black holes. So does she have a rig somewhere that we can destroy?"

"She has the means to mine neutron stars," Thomas said. "But we don't know where she's mining." He projected a holograph of tumbling asteroids and glowing hints of temporal streams, all in motion. "With her colliders, she can contain degenerate matter. I would recommend that we destroy those, but by now she'll have made duplicate facilities, hidden from us."

"She can do that?" Garrett asked.

"She has millions of worshippers," Thomas said. "And robots, possibly. The laws are gone. She can invent or manufacture whatever she wants."

"The entire galaxy is her lab," Mondoyo said.

Ariock felt hope slipping away.

He could detect life sparks within a solar system, if he spent days of focused concentration. But it would take him eons to scan the whole galaxy in search of nefarious activity. He had failed to detect every enemy ship within his own personal solar system, where Freedomland was located. Ghosting had its limits.

"Can we shut down the temporal streams?" Kessa asked.

That was an excellent idea.

But Thomas shook his head sorrowfully. "No. Serette and Mondoyo are providing paradigms that might allow us to deconstruct the meshwork of now, but please understand, this is very theoretical quantum physics. No one knows how temporal streams work. Not even the Death Architect."

Mondoyo spoke up. "She doesn't have to. She's using them as-is."

Thomas nodded. "We're all starting from scratch, since the Torth Empire outlawed this research. In twenty-four thousand years, no one ever figured out how to divert temporal streams, or how to create new ones, or shut them off. We'd like to solve this. But there are no precedents. And time isn't on our side."

"So what should we look for?" Garrett asked. "Are we going to just scan the Araya Moon Belt for the umpteenth time and hope that this time her lair jumps out at us?"

The Death Architect lived on some unknown asteroid, shielded by mirror traps. Finding her seemed impossible. But if they could ascertain her general vicinity . . .

Well.

Ariock figured he could probably destroy a solar system. He could crush the planets, one by one.

Innocent people lived on Tuthwa and in Permafrost City and other cities in the Araya Moon Belt, but maybe they could evacuate before he obliterated moons. Asteroids. Planets. Whatever it took.

The emptied cup in his hand bulged over his fingers. He had subconsciously enhanced his strength and crushed the metal.

The high windows darkened. Ariock's mood was making the clouds thick and ominous. Dust motes floated throughout the war room, buoyed by the excess tendrils of Ariock's extended awareness.

Everyone gave him a look. Some were judgmental, some were sympathetic. The pity was worse.

Ariock struggled to pull himself together. He was such a psychological mess. He felt like a battered gladiator psyching himself up before his next fight.

"Unfortunately," Thomas said, "I would assume she has fail-safes in place. If she wants to destroy the universe, she'll have automated the whole process. Including the trigger. I would bet that her doomsday is set to trigger upon her death."

Garrett swore.

Evenjos echoed him.

Ariock felt like a doomed idiot. Why was his first impulse mindless destruction? The Death Architect probably wanted him to come charging in like a blundering bull. She had manipulated him that way before.

She kept outsmarting him.

And everyone knew it.

"Are you saying we're doomed?" Garrett threw his hands up in exasperation. "There's no possible way for us to find her facilities before she detonates everything?"

Thomas replied in a bleak tone. "There's a way."

"One way," Kessa said.

Everyone looked toward her.

Kessa blinked, as if surprised they hadn't all thought of it already. "Thomas must brainwash the Death Architect into telling us where to find the trigger. He needs access to her mind."

Thomas nodded. "Correct."

But that circled back to the original problem. They needed to find the Death Architect.

Except instead of killing her, they had to either take her prisoner or else bring Thomas to her lair.

"We have to take that abhorrent child alive," Garrett said in a tone of disgusted realization. "We have no choice."

Thomas nodded.

Garrett swore again.

"Why can't we use her cultists?" Evenjos looked from Garrett to Thomas. "Abduct them. Brainwash them. Then let them go with secret orders to find the little girl and report her location to us!"

If not for the dire situation, Ariock would have been impressed by Evenjos's flexible thinking, as well as her willingness to rely on Thomas's evil power. She used to fear his brainwashing more than anything.

"I'm willing to try that," Thomas said, although he sounded unwilling. "But her followers—"

"They're clueless," Garrett said in a hopeless tone. "She surrounds herself with battlebeasts and slaves. Maybe robots. None of her followers know where she is."

"And she'll expect us to try anything to find her," Mondoyo added. "She'll take precautions."

The universe was running out of time.

Ariock felt it as surely as if he watched an hourglass or a clock. The entirety of the universe was on a countdown timer. The people who sat at this table were the only ones between doomsday and salvation.

"It's not entirely hopeless," Thomas said. "Kessa has been making inroads in the search."

Kessa looked surprised to be called out, but she readily explained. "Our network of spies and smugglers never stopped searching for the Death Architect. They have reported suspicious confiscations. It is known that the Death Architect experiments on humanoid subjects. She used a lot of Alashani for her scientific tests."

Ariock straightened. This sounded morbid, but it also might lead to hope.

"We need to implant superluminal trackers into people," Thomas said. "Especially in Alashani who live outside Freedomland."

Like Flen.

"It's invasive," Thomas admitted with a guilty look. "I know. But I think it's a wise precaution at this point." He gestured around the table. "And we all need tracker implants. I'll have one, too."

Evenjos looked skeptical. A tracker wouldn't work with her unique body unless she made a conscious effort to carry it at all times.

Ariock wanted to say that they would find another way. A better way.

"Anyone who might run into her cultists should be trackable," Thomas said. "That includes everyone here. One of us might even serve as bait, if we come up with a plan to lure her. She might take a risk if she thinks she'll get to run experiments on an actual hero of prophecy."

Garrett chuckled in a morbid way.

"Right. Okay." Ariock made himself sound normal, but on the inside, he was all too aware that he was no match for a supergenius.

His brain was merely human. Fallible. Weak and mushy.

The Death Architect had already beaten him. Twice.

His future was blackness and death.

The end of all things.

No. Ariock refused to let that become the future. Wasn't it nothing but a stress dream?

Garrett had once told Ariock that he might have a touch of a seer ability.

But that just meant having hunches. If Ariock could actually dream the future—what a ridiculous notion!—then he would have dreamed about quite a lot of things before they happened. Surely he would have foreseen the Torth showing up in his sky room? Oh, and the death of his father? And of his mother?

A fragment from a past nightmare flashed through his mind. A heap of corpses. He was their killer, and he was shocked to see that his mother was one of the corpses, severed in half by a twisted piece of metal.

A chill ran through Ariock. Hadn't he actually dreamed his mother's death while she was still alive?

Trauma could mess with memories.

Anyway, he had dreamed all kinds of horrors when he was a gladiator, thanks to that mesh helmet. Maybe it was just a coincidence.

Everyone, particularly the mind readers, gave Ariock looks of sympathy. Thomas looked like he wanted to say something.

Ariock felt like an overgrown child. Did he need soothing? He was the Strength. He needed to be strong.

He took a deep breath and forced himself to be a functioning hero. "I'm fine," he said. "I'll wear a tracking implant or whatever you need. And I'll get rid of any rigs or bombs. Just point me in the right direction."

CHAPTER 3

TRIPLED

Thomas felt guilty for ignoring Cherise. But he was ignoring all people who wanted to check on his well-being, plus Azhdarchidae. He even felt guilty for taking naps.

He no longer allowed himself to get full sleep cycles. There was no time. Whenever he began making erroneous assumptions due to fatigue, he excused himself for the sake of his coworkers. They did likewise. Thomas, Serette, and Mondoyo had learned to work together as a ternary mind. If one of them malfunctioned, it became a drag on the other two.

For efficiency, they had synced up their schedules. They had a regular nap time.

As soon as nap time was over, Thomas stretched, sipped caffeinated nectar and ate some macronutrients, then stood and walked across the lab to rejoin the other two recently woken supergeniuses.

They were visualizing ultracomplex mathematical modules. One of those representations might be the key to disrupting superluminal transmissions. If Kessa's agents could not find the Death Architect, if Ariock and Garrett failed to find her hidden colliders and smart missile launchers—and so far, all efforts had failed—then their best hope of stopping doomsday was to disrupt the triggering transmission.

Thomas sat in the hoverchair reserved for him, facing his peers.

Serette and Mondoyo were fatigued. Instead of updating Thomas on mathematical modules, they sent a different sort of update.

We have tried to impact the Necrocosm.

They will not heed Us.

Maybe Your influence will be the deciding factor?

Thomas ascended, seeking faraway minds who might be willing to orbit his mind and vice versa. He sensed many disjointed harmonies. Most of the rogue nations never invited the Conqueror into their minds. They rejected him.

But the death cultists were different.

Like an orchestral score, they had achieved a greater presence than the sum of their parts. They formed their own malevolent glow, like a newborn star. They tugged his attention as surely as the tug of gravity.

The Death Architect is restoring civilization!

We are here!

We are harmonious!

WE ARE THE TORTH EMPIRE!

Thomas sighed. Their unified trust in their leader made them feel strong, powerful, and safe. But it was an illusion.

She wants to destroy the universe, he informed the death cultists.

Individual minds recoiled. His evidence against the Death Architect was too complex for most of the cultists to understand, let alone accept. They figured the Conqueror was just stirring up more trouble. They refused to let him steal what little dignity they had left.

They would not listen.

Ah well.

Thomas dropped out of the Necrocosm. He wasn't sure if converting the death cultists to his side of the war would even make much of a difference. The Death Architect was working with automation.

He took charge, leading the way forward. Serette and Mondoyo were both more knowledgeable than Thomas, but they were afraid to lead. They wanted to avoid blame for any catastrophic lapses in judgment.

Not only that, Serette thought. *You (Conqueror) are a better innovator than Mondoyo or I.* Her partner was creative, but she thought that the Conqueror was even more so.

Thomas paused his latest mathematical visualization and studied Serette with biometric scrutiny. *You're distracted.*

Simply breathing was a struggle for her. That compromised her processing speed. Ventilator tubes filled her nostrils, and a machine helped her lungs to fill and empty.

Serette did receive regular healings from shani these days, as well as regular doses of NAI-13 and medical care. She would have been dead weeks ago if not for those measures.

You (Serette) ought to be in hospice care. Thomas hated to bring it up so bluntly. Her ailments were exactly what would have killed him if he had never received regeneration healing from his heroic friends. She was one month older than he was.

No. Serette's thoughts were vehement. *I'm not ready to retire.*

She kept downplaying how much she was struggling.

Mondoyo reached for Serette's hand and held it.

Thomas might have insisted that Mondoyo let his partner retire so the two of them could focus on stopping doomsday for the entire universe. That would be logical and rational and practical. Instead . . .

Well, Serette was not the only one whose mind was faltering.

Mondoyo was also heavily distracted, fearful every time Serette struggled to get enough oxygen or her heart skipped a beat. Mondoyo served as their high-functioning calculator, but his heart wasn't in the game. He was operating well below peak efficiency.

Thomas let his mathematical holograph dissipate and put his entire focus on this matter. After all, here was a problem that he might actually be able to solve.

He activated his wristwatch and selected Evenjos from his short list of contacts.

"Please visit me right away," he said as soon as Evenjos answered. "In the mathematics lab."

No, Serette thought as Thomas ended the call. *We (those of Us who oppose the Death Architect) cannot afford to lose so many days just for me. I understand that. I agree with it. This work is too important to interrupt for a week.*

Mondoyo gently squeezed his partner's hand. *We need you, Serette. The universe needs you (I need you).*

I can survive for another week (probably), Serette thought.

She was being wildly optimistic. Her condition was terrible, heading toward critical. Even with state-of-the-art medical intervention, she was unlikely to live out the week.

Evenjos poured into the lab as a dust ribbon. She took on her default goddess shape, then arched one purple eyebrow at Thomas in a questioning look.

Mondoyo and Serette looked impressed. They were never sure how much authority Thomas wielded, and it seemed they had not expected the Lady of Sorrow to respond so willingly.

Thomas pointed to Serette. "If my friend dies, she can't work. We're trying to stop an accelerated Big Bang that will end all of creation. I realize that you have very important duties, but how about if we get on the same page with priorities? Serette needs regeneration healing. This should be your utmost priority."

Evenjos's wings drooped.

Thomas scanned her mind and fished out the obstacle. Garrett.

Agh.

He tapped his wristwatch and selected the old man's icon from the menu. "I need you in my mathematics lab," he said. "Right now."

Please stop, Serette begged without words. *There is no need to interrupt the work of heroes just for me. This disruption is both futile and unnecessary.*

Mondoyo silently disagreed with his partner.

Garrett entered the mirrored room, grumbling and leaning on his staff, followed by the smell of ozone. He pressed one hand to the small of his back. He probably had one of his common backaches. "What's wrong?"

Thomas pointed to Serette. "If my coworkers die, then my efficacy will be reduced by sixty-seven percent. That's unacceptable. Regeneration healing for Serette needs to be your top priority, above everything else."

Garrett huffed in a way that Thomas really disliked. What he said was even more despicable. "Only one of them is dying. The other one is in relatively good health."

Thomas began to argue that Serette's death would negatively impact Mondoyo.

"You interrupted me for this?" Garrett glared at Thomas. "Millions of sapients could die because I left in the middle of defusing a bomb. I realize that you are a very important person. I get your complaint. But Evenjos, Ariock, Kessa, and I have already discussed this. If we drop everything to heal one of your team members—a penitent, I might add—that means certain death for literally billions of people. And it might be worse. You know why. The Death Architect has to be our top priority right now." He stamped down his staff for emphasis. "We. Have. No. Choice."

Thomas briefly imagined setting Garrett on fire.

But while that would be cathartic, Thomas believed in the prophecies of Ah Jun. There was too much evidence to dismiss the ancient collection of reproduced paintings. And Garrett was the Will. He was the driving force, the instigator, the catalyst, and perhaps he was also the ender—the hero who would keep the other heroes on track to the final victory.

Maybe.

If only the old man would allow someone else—someone smart—to look at that ancient book.

"We are truly sorry." Evenjos emanated sincerity. "Serette, I owe you and Mondoyo an enormous debt. I want to heal you. If I could heal you with my own strength, I would."

But she could only do it with aid from Garrett and Ariock.

Unless . . .

"There are other powerful individuals." Thomas thought of humans as augmenters. Everyone suspected that humans could boost Yeresunsa, but so far, Vy was unable to augment Ariock's raw power. Cherise had tried linking with Flen. There was some missing component, perhaps a trick to making it work.

"What about the penitent warriors?" Thomas asked. "We have millions of them on our side now. Gather enough of them together and have them link, and they might approximate Ariock's raw power."

Evenjos exchanged surprised looks with Garrett.

"That's actually a good idea," Garrett admitted.

Mondoyo radiated hope. He gazed at Thomas as if he was the answer to all problems.

"Can I speak with you in private for a moment?" Garrett beckoned to Thomas.

Privacy was a farce among telepaths. It seemed Garrett wanted to avoid an immediate reaction from Serette or Mondoyo about something.

Thomas pushed himself to his feet.

He followed Garrett to a far corner of the room. Once they were beyond the telepathy range of everyone else, Garrett sent a thought, encoded in the radiance of honesty.

The Twins are not in the final prophecies, he let Thomas know. *I think they have already served their role. It must have been their symphony that destroyed the Megacosm (maybe also immunity to the inhibitor). We no longer need them.*

How mercenary.

Thomas leaned closer, trying to catch glimpses of secret prophetic paintings. He caught shadowy hints. Was there a painting that resembled Vy, kneeling by a tunnel that led to outer space? And a suggestion of a painted version of Thomas floating in outer space?

GET OUT OF MY MIND. Garrett leaped back, holding his staff out as a barrier.

Thomas glared.

"The bottom line," Garrett said out loud, still scurrying backward, "is that no one is getting special favors right now. Evenjos could heal my arthritis without any power boosts from me or Ariock. She could fix this leg." He indicated his crooked leg. "And my back. Don't you think I would like that? But I asked her not to. You know why?"

Thomas did.

"Because her power is best spent on more important tasks right now!" Garrett pounded his staff down, emphasizing his point. "Thanks to immunity, she is able to wade into enemy territory and destroy rigs and other equipment. That is more important than fixing bodies or even saving lives. We need to stop the end of the universe!"

Thomas took a step closer to Garrett. He had to look up at the old man, but he knew that his posture was threatening. "If you want to make excuses for being a jerk?" he said. "Fine. But since doomsday is right around the corner, it's past time for you to share your clues. Show me the book!"

Garrett held up a hand. A force field hardened in the air, shielding him.

Wow. Was he that afraid?

"I have good reasons for holding back," Garrett said in the holy tone of a sage.

"Like what?"

"If I tell you, it all goes to hell."

A deflection. How predictable. Garrett might even be lying.

Heat waves began to bend the air.

"Get control of yourself." Garrett sounded disgusted. "I have to get back to saving lives. Maybe you can think about doing the same?" He walked toward the door. "Oh, and please resist the urge to bother Ariock about this. He has enough on his plate." Garrett waited for the door to slide open and threw one last glare toward Thomas. "In fact? Leave Ariock alone. That's an order."

With that, Garrett was gone.

Thomas knew it was useless to chase someone who had the power to teleport. He nearly tried anyway.

He was so sick of taking orders from Garrett. He didn't want to mindlessly obey. He wasn't a cultist, like those idiotic followers of the Death Architect. Nor was he a child.

Maybe Serette was actually necessary, contrary to what Garrett believed?

The old man might have overlooked something vital. He likely had no clue how to interpret the final prophecies. He was probably keeping secrets for no other reason than that he was terrified of losing his vaunted authority. His damned pride might doom the entire universe.

Surely Wisdom was superior to Will?

Thomas didn't mind being subordinate to a naturally competent leader, like Ariock. But a bully like Garrett? It was intolerable.

"Um?" Evenjos backed toward the door. "I am so sorry, Thomas. I would help, but . . ." She spread her wings and began to disintegrate. "Sorry."

Thomas realized that he had actually scared Evenjos away. Fiery sparks lit the air around him. He was that furious.

He forced himself to retract his awareness. It was disturbingly easy to lose control of Yeresunsa powers. What a stupid magic system. It shouldn't be tied to emotions. Who had designed it?

Still fuming, Thomas walked back toward his coworkers.

Serette's chest rose and fell in wheezing rasps. That was her normal breathing nowadays. She was already visualizing formulas, businesslike.

Mondoyo was simply sad.

I doubt I am the key to saving the universe, Serette assured her partner. *A week-long disruption of our work would be insane. It could be all the Death Architect needs to win.*

Anguish spiked off Mondoyo. His emotions were as huge and frightening as tectonic plates.

Thomas glared sternly at Serette. He hated how factual she was. But deep down . . . Well.

Deep down, he knew Serette and Garrett were right. Regeneration healing would put Serette and Evenjos out of commission for a week. Their absence would impact Mondoyo, Garrett, Ariock, and Thomas himself.

It was too much.

Serette might be vital to saving the universe, but more likely, saving her life would cascade into the end of all things.

It wasn't fair.

"Let's get back to work." Thomas took his seat.

The three of them struggled heroically to focus on ultrafast mathematical processing in pursuit of superluminal jamming. But even while Thomas fretted about his dying friend and about how to stop doomsday, another part of his mind worked on yet another problem.

The book of prophecies lingered in the back of his thoughts.

His argument with Garrett was not over. If he was going to thwart the Death Architect, then he absolutely needed to see that book.

CHAPTER 4

PROPHETIC

Ariock hesitated outside the mathematics lab. He didn't know why Thomas had invited him for a chat, and he felt guilty as he knocked on the door frame. Everyone knew better than to interrupt the trio of supergeniuses.

A moment later, the door slid open.

"Come in," Thomas said.

Ariock ducked through the entrance, painfully aware that he was supposed to be storming death cult space stations right now. He should have refused a friendly visit.

Then again, Thomas shouldn't casually take a break, either.

They both needed to stop doomsday, not hang out.

Burnished copper plates reflected orb lamps and tall strips of overcast daylight. An intricate holograph showed mathematical complexities, although most of the workstations were turned off. No one else occupied the vast room.

"Serette and Mondoyo are taking a break." Thomas lounged in a cushioned chair. "They needed sleep. Speaking of which, I know you're not sleeping as much as you should. I wanted to catch up with you about your nightmares."

Ariock paused, ashamed. Rain clouds followed him everywhere these days. He wished his moods weren't so obvious to everyone in the city. "I don't want to interrupt your work."

Thomas leaned forward and clasped his hands, the pose of a psychologist. "You're my friend," he said. "I'm never going to be dismissive of your concerns, especially because you're not as dumb as you keep thinking you are. You're one of the smartest people I know. If something is bothering you, then I'm guessing it's important. So please, have a seat." He gestured to a companion seat within his range of telepathy. "I want to hear it."

That was generous.

Ariock eased himself into the beanbag chair next to Thomas. It could accommodate most species, but the seat was too close to the ground for him to do anything but stretch out his long legs. He leaned against the wall and braced himself for his friend's disappointment.

"My nightmares haven't stopped," Ariock admitted.

Thomas gave him a troubled look.

"I saw a spiritualist, like you suggested to Vy," Ariock said. "It helped for a while. But . . . I don't know. I guess I'm under a lot of stress."

He waited for Thomas to agree.

The boy said nothing.

Ariock tried to break the awkward silence. "I'm sure you also have nightmares about being a terrible failure and the Death Architect winning. Right?" He tried to lighten the mood by laughing.

"No," Thomas said. "I don't dream much."

"Oh."

"You have this dream every time you fall asleep?" Thomas sounded concerned. "The same dream?"

"Uh, yes." Ariock felt like a patient sitting next to a psychologist.

But he didn't want to give anyone reasons to be concerned for his mental health. He was supposed to be the Strength. That meant he shouldn't shatter under pressure.

"How long has this been going on?" Thomas asked. He must know the answer already, but he was humoring his friend.

Ariock obliged him. "A few months."

"And it's the same nightmare every single time you fall asleep? Is the frequency increasing?"

Ariock didn't want to admit that he was afraid to fall asleep. "It was a few times per week, at first." He tried to shrug away the dreamlike miasma of despair that clung to him. "But ever since we found out about the Death Architect? Yeah." He was so tired. "It's all the time."

Thomas looked like he was the one who needed reassuring.

"I've talked to people," Ariock said. "For advice. Like, Vy. She took me to that spiritualist, a seer named the Great Mwagru. We had an excellent talk." Ariock shifted, ashamed of how needy he was. Wasn't he just wasting Thomas's valuable time with a rather trite problem? "And I mentioned it to Garrett." After all, it was impossible to keep major secrets from the mind reader he worked next to every day.

Thomas's gaze sharpened. "What did Garrett say?"

"Well, he said it's stress." Ariock was feeling more and more ashamed. "He said the prophecies make it clear that we're destined to win."

Thomas looked upset.

Ariock felt humiliated, having listed a bunch of people who had already reassured him. He must seem so needy. His face burned. "I'm sorry." He began to get up. "I know that I'm not helping anyone by having stress nightmares. I get that. I just . . ." He was so embarrassed. "I just thought that maybe you'd have some advice? To make it stop."

"Sit down," Thomas said.

Ariock sat back down.

"Your recurring nightmare isn't due to stress," Thomas said.

Ariock's mood elevated. Was there an actual diagnosis for him? Was there a cure for whatever was causing the recurring nightmare?

"You're dreaming the future," Thomas said. "You have a low-magnitude prophetic power."

Ariock assumed that was a joke. He waited for the punch line.

"No one ever told you." Thomas sounded serious. "But a lot of people know. Your mom knew. She told Vy and Cherise that you had a prophetic nightmare before your father died. You warned your family to not take that flight."

Ariock's mind leaped back in time to fire and acrid smoke. He had tried to carry his father, but he'd been too young. Big for his age, but not strong enough. And he remembered a feeling that it had all happened before. He'd had a dreamlike feeling that he had already lived the disaster.

Or dreamed it.

"No."

Ariock stared at Thomas, silently urging his friend to tell him that this was an elaborate, twisted joke. It had to be a mind game that Thomas was playing. That would be preferable to . . .

Death.

Devastation.

The nightmare sent tendrils of fear into Ariock's waking life, hinting that all his successes were pointless and a waste of time. It felt like the end of all things.

Thomas looked furious. "You're predicting a future catastrophe. And nobody bothered to tell you."

Ariock felt shaken and betrayed. "Are you serious?"

"Of course," Thomas sounded bitter. "I've been asked to keep quiet about your prophetic dreams. But I can't keep doing that in good conscience."

Ariock wondered what sort of backstabbing ally would demand that his friend keep silent about such catastrophic news. Was it Garrett?

He could picture the old man making it an order. Garrett probably justified it by telling himself that he was protecting his great-grandson.

Protecting him from the truth.

Shielding him from reality.

What an arrogant, self-entitled jerk.

"I find your nightmare to be beyond alarming," Thomas went on. "You're dreaming a prophecy that predicts the death of my foster sister."

Every time Ariock awoke with Vy next to him, he felt as if everything was all right. She was everything. But if the nightmare was prophetic . . .

Was she going to cease to exist?

Was there anything he could possibly do to prevent that?

"Your dream is something we all need to take very seriously," Thomas was saying. "It might signify the death of the universe. It's a disturbingly strong hint that Ah Jun's prophecies are not a guarantee of success, like Garrett believes. In fact, it's a major clue that Garrett is wrong. And an idiot."

Ariock was still struggling with the diagnosis. He had no room in his mind for anything else.

He had predicted his mother's death. He had tried to dismiss that nightmare as a mismatched memory, a disrupted sense of time caused by trauma. But he was wrong.

That had actually been a prophetic dream.

Just like his prophetic dream foretelling his father's death.

He had buried his sense of déjà vu, but Thomas's words unlocked the whole ordeal. He remembered now. He had screamed at his parents. He had thrown their luggage, trying to make a mess, trying to get them to stay home. His mother had listened. But not his father.

As for the Torth abduction? Ariock had suffered disturbing dreams for weeks leading up to it.

Some disquieted part of his soul had tried to blanket his heart and make him forget. But hadn't he paced the sky room constantly, certain that a terrible storm was on its way?

Prophetic nightmares.

Those terrible dreams were a stark contrast to his good dreams. Sometimes he dreamed about soaring over beautiful terrain with Vy. He dreamed about Vy having powers.

But apparently only his bad dreams came true.

Helpless despair and rage coursed through Ariock. It was such a volatile mixture of feelings that he wasn't sure what to do about it. The sky outside darkened, echoing his mood. He couldn't help it. He wasn't even sure he cared.

Why should he care about anything, if the universe was predestined to end in a few days?

Why should he even bother to try?

Fiery tendrils whirled in front of Ariock. Thomas was speaking, standing, snapping his fingers, trying to regain Ariock's attention.

As if conversations mattered. As if anything mattered.

"What?" Ariock said.

"Talk to Garrett." Thomas's tone was as dark and stormy as Ariock had ever heard it get. "You need to demand to see the book of prophecies."

The prophecies of Ah Jun!

Ariock abruptly stood, seizing on that ray of hope. Even if he had some feeble form of prophecy, he was nowhere near as talented as Migyatel had been. And Ah Jun had been an oracle. Her paintings must supersede anything that Ariock or any other prophet dreamed.

If Ah Jun had predicted victory, like Garrett claimed, then Ariock's nightmarish prediction might be insignificant.

But he had to see. He had to know whether Ah Jun had predicted if his bride would survive.

He had to know the real truth, not just the spin that Garrett put on it.

He had to make Garrett show him the damned book.

No more whining excuses. No more secrets. Garrett owed him the plain truth—especially since he had looked directly at Ariock and lied! He had told Ariock that his nightmare meant nothing!

"Does Garrett know that my dreams forecast the future?" Ariock asked, just to make sure. Deep down, he knew that Garrett must know. Garrett was a damned mind reader. He had spent his whole life spying on his own family.

"You bet," Thomas said.

Ariock clenched his fists, so furious that lightning rippled up his arms. It was time to confront Garrett Olmstead Dovanack. Him and his arrogant initials. Him and his patronizing lies.

A small hand touched his arm. Ariock looked down.

"I want to be there," Thomas said,

CHAPTER 5
HERO

Ariock would not confront Garrett alone. He summoned the heroes of prophecy, but he did not explain the purpose of the meeting. They would have to wait for him to show up. And first?

He stopped at Vy's office.

Vy interrupted herself in the middle of a conversation with Cherise and several other people. She knew that Ariock never barged in like this.

"Can I talk with you?" Ariock asked. "Sorry to interrupt."

"Uh, sure." Vy apologized to her guests. They shot curious looks toward Ariock and Vy, but none dared to demand an explanation. They let Vy exit with Ariock.

"Mind if we talk in my home suite?" Ariock asked, and he barely waited for Vy to nod.

Once they were alone, he sat on the oversize couch so he wouldn't tower over Vy. She liked to snuggle whenever they were alone together, but she sensed the seriousness of his mood, so she did not plop down onto his lap. Instead, she took a dignified seat on the normal-size rocking chair.

"I need to know something." Ariock broached the subject without preamble. "My dreams predict the future. Did you . . ."

He saw her lack of surprise, her pained look of guilt. The answer was plain on her face.

He asked anyway. "Did you know that I have a prophetic ability? Because *I* didn't know."

Vy hunched with shame.

She had known.

The whole time.

Ariock had casually told Vy about his recurring nightmare that he couldn't save her, and she had known that his dreams predicted the future, yet she had pretended to be emotionally serene. For months. Such devastating news would make anyone quake with fear, yet if Vy wept, she did not do it where Ariock might see.

Instead, she'd held him. And comforted him.

She probably sneaked back to her own suite so she could cry alone.

That blew Ariock's mind even as it hurt his heart. Didn't Vy trust him? Was she afraid to be honest with her fiancé? Was he so unpredictably dangerous that she felt she had to coddle him?

Vy stood and went to him. "Delia asked us to keep the secret from you."

His deceased mother?

"She made us promise," Vy said.

Ariock could not imagine why.

"She was protecting you," Vy said, as if that explained things.

What had his mom wanted to protect him from? The truth? Himself?

"She didn't want you to blame yourself," Vy explained gently. "For, uh, for failing to save your father." She brushed his cheek. "Because his death wasn't your fault. You were just a little kid. You did everything you could. But you were a child."

A lump rose in Ariock's throat. There was a phantom smell of fiery electrical smoke.

He had failed. His mother had carried that knowledge ever since it happened. And she had let Ariock forget.

Will had been a hero that day. He had bravely manifested his powers as he died, just to save Ariock.

And Ariock had the nerve to call himself a hero. Like a delusional fool.

Well, all right, he had earned some heroic status. He was the leader of a galactic empire, after all. And although he had failed to save his father and his mother, Garrett Dovanack shared some of that blame. The old man had also failed.

Vy climbed onto the couch next to Ariock and put her arms around him. "I thought about telling you, multiple times," she admitted. "But I didn't want to add to your burdens."

That hurt. Vy was supposed to trust him.

"I didn't see the point in making you aware." Vy swallowed, and Ariock realized anew that she was facing her own mortality. Yet she'd pretended to be happy to share a future together with him. She had celebrated his marriage proposal. All the while, she had carried this terrible knowledge alone.

Just how emotionally delicate did she think he was?

Well. Perhaps she was right. Ariock supposed he did have a savior complex.

He gently pulled Vy onto his lap. He held her. It felt good to give her some degree of comfort, to remind her that she didn't have to face doom alone, or necessarily face doom at all. They were in this together.

Vy clutched him.

For the first time in months, Ariock felt as steady as a rock and as invincible as the galaxy itself. At last, thanks to Thomas, he understood the implications of his nightmare. That meant he no longer had to question his own instincts or his own sanity. He knew exactly what his feeling of foreboding was.

Knowing made all the difference.

"You don't have to protect me anymore," Ariock told Vy. "I'm sorry that you thought you had to carry that burden for both of us. But it's not yours alone."

Vy relaxed into his embrace and gazed at him with wonder.

"I've been sheltered all my life," Ariock admitted. "I had a magical great-grandfather looking out for me, making sure the Torth didn't touch me until I was old enough for self-defense. I had a dad who taught me to enjoy life. And a mom who made sure I never had to face any hardships unless I wanted to face them. And a supergenius friend who's wise enough to guide me in the right direction. And you, the best person in my life, to remind me that I'm human, and that humans are important."

Vy grinned weakly, but she seemed pleased.

"A lot of stars aligned to create me." Ariock was building up to a point, and he knew it was important. "I've been manipulated onto a heroic journey. I'm the

Strength, according to a prophecy that's older than the Torth Empire. My path was laid out thousands of years ago. And I had the best people to guide me every step of the way."

Vy stroked the fuzz on his cheek. "That's not fair. You did a lot of it yourself."

"I had a ton of help." He needed to make that plain, not only to Vy, but to himself. "I was forged by you and other people in my life. But . . ."

If he was going to fully grow into his role as the Strength, then he could not afford the overprotection of his loved ones. He was their shield and their protector. Not the other way around.

"I don't want to be shielded from anything," Ariock said. "An effective weapon has to face hardships. I need to be allowed to face this, unsupported."

Vy studied him with love and hope. "Do you believe you can change the future?" Her gaze turned inward, no doubt toward her own predicted death. "I don't see what you can do."

"I'm not accepting it as inevitable." Ariock stood.

How many times had he faced certain defeat? More times than he could count. When the Torth had defeated him in the dead city, he should have died from the fatal wound in his chest. Instead, he had used the last of his strength to shove Torth off the ruined tower. When the Stratower fell, he should have been crushed. Instead, he had thrown the biggest building in the galaxy at a Torth armada, and then he had teamed up with Thomas to create a colony starship and rescue a planetary population.

"I've defeated certain doom before," Ariock said. "I can do it again. Never mind my nightmares. Never mind Garrett's interpretations. Ah Jun was the most powerful prophet who ever lived. She was an oracle. I need to see what she foresaw, and I need to see it firsthand. And then? I'll come up with a plan."

Vy looked at Ariock like he was a true hero.

"Actually—" Ariock grinned. "I'll let Thomas come up with the plan."

That had them both laughing, and the dark clouds over the city dissipated.

CHAPTER 6

HOPELESS

The courtyard atrium overlooked the ocean ports of the city. Garrett, seated on a plinth and looking relaxed, smoked a pipe. Evenjos stood next to him, regal and radiant. They probably expected a simple update about the ongoing sabotage and dismantling of the death cult.

Ariock sat on a marble bench across from them, beyond their telepathy ranges. He had left Vy behind, since this would be a tense confrontation. He didn't want Vy in the middle of a heated argument between powerful Yeresunsa.

They didn't have to wait long for Thomas. Without his hoverchair, dressed in ordinary street clothes and a sun hat, Thomas looked deceptively unremarkable. Just a teenage boy.

"All right, we're all here," Garrett said as Thomas sat on a plinth. "What's the update?"

"Great-grandfather." Ariock addressed the old man with cold formality. "I've been having a recurring dream. You told me to ignore it."

Garrett raised a bushy eyebrow, inviting further explanation.

"But," Ariock went on, "I've learned that my dreams are prophetic."

Evenjos looked shocked. Garrett swore, but he didn't seem entirely surprised. He used his staff to lever himself to his feet, shooting a narrow-eyed glare at Thomas that promised revenge.

"You knew." Ariock did not conceal how much that hurt. His closest family member had not trusted him with the truth.

"Your dream is not a certainty," Garrett said hurriedly. "The prophecies show us winning. We're on the right path, according to Ah Jun, and she was an oracle. Your dream is vague. It doesn't really count as prophecy."

Ariock wanted to believe that. He wanted to put his faith in the prophecies of Ah Jun and trust that everything would turn out all right.

But Ah Jun had died a thousand generations ago.

Had her prophecies even included Vy?

Thomas stared hard at Garrett. "Why don't you show Ariock the book so he can confirm that for himself?"

Garrett's stare became ferocious. "Certain knowledge is dangerous."

Ariock tried to hold on to his good feeling. But whom was Garrett trying to protect? His extremely overprotected great-grandson?

Garrett had devoted his entire life to shielding his heir. He had given Ariock a massive inheritance, plus all the protection that superpowers and a fortress could provide. He kept making sure that Ariock was safe and loved and cared for. Oh, and clueless. Garrett wanted his great-grandson to be painfully ignorant so he could blindly stumble his way along the hero's journey that Garrett had carefully plotted and laid out for his feet.

That much coddling led to backfires.

If Ariock had been allowed to forge his own path, then perhaps he wouldn't fall to pieces whenever he met with disappointment. His mother might have entrusted him with hard facts and treated him like a man—an adult—instead of a big, scary child. She would have told Ariock that she was dying from cancer. She would have told Ariock that he had foretold his father's death.

His fiancée, too, would have shared her deepest fears with Ariock, instead of protecting him from his own overreactions.

Ariock was done being manipulated by a paternalistic mind reader. His deep voice was so strong, the ground trembled. "Show me the book."

"It's not worth seeing." Garrett scrambled onto the marble plinth that supported the colonnade. That did not make him tall enough to meet Ariock at eye level, but he tried. "The future can be hard to face. Let me tell you something."

Ariock prepared to override a pointless lecture.

"Not everyone can handle iffy news with courage and grace." Garrett made a fist and thumped his chest. "I'm destined to die. Ah Jun painted my decapitation. That's my future."

Ariock winced at that unexpected confession. It was hard to believe. Garrett was so full of grit and vitality, he seemed eternal.

Evenjos gripped Garrett's hand, her gaze filled with love.

And sorrowful resignation.

She knew.

Thomas, too, looked as if this was old news.

Ariock recalled offhand comments from his other friends—Vy and even Kessa—implying that they wouldn't need to put up with Garrett forever.

And he realized that everyone else had known.

Everyone except for him.

Maybe no one trusted Ariock. Or maybe they just didn't want to share knowledge with their mentally slow sidekick? Maybe it was too much effort to elucidate to a nontelepath? Ariock supposed he should have tried telepathy gas more than once.

"I don't know when it will happen," Garrett was saying. "Or who will slice my head off. I have no idea." He looked slightly harried, as if he half expected someone in the atrium to do it. "But that ending is coming for me. I've had to make my peace with it. Now, do you think you could do the same?"

Ariock thought carefully about his answer.

He could handle death in battle. That was what being a protector meant. He wasn't as emotionally fragile as Garrett seemed to assume.

Apparently his thought process was too slow, because Garrett interrupted it. "Strength is strength. But strength isn't wisdom. And it isn't strength of will."

His insult was plain.

"I'm not saying you're a coward," Garrett hastened to explain. "I'm talking about our roles. Ah Jun foresaw that you would be the embodiment of Strength. And I'm the embodiment of Will." He thumped his chest again. "I can handle anything if it ensures our victory. But you're not me. You want to see the future? What if a glimpse of the prophecies sends you into a spiral of self-hatred and despair?"

Ouch.

"Because that's your pattern," Garrett said.

The old man had a point. Ariock wanted to defend his own fortitude, but when he thought of Vy tumbling into outer space, soundlessly screaming, sucked toward oblivion faster than he could reach her . . .

That was a future he would reject no matter what.

Maybe he couldn't handle hard truths if they were too painful? Maybe he did need to be kept ignorant for his own safety?

"In my experience," Thomas said, "knowledge is always better than ignorance."

Garrett glared at the teenage supergenius.

"And I have more lived experience than anyone else alive except for Serette and Mondoyo," Thomas said, underscoring the validity of his point. "No one should gatekeep knowledge. That's what Torth do. That's how the Death Architect operates."

Garrett puffed up his chest, affronted. "I'm not the Death Architect."

"You're keeping us in the dark," Thomas said. "Needlessly."

"You want a road map of your next step?" Garrett smoked his pipe. "I can tell you the panel I saw. It's Wisdom triumphing over Death with the three of us backing him up. Torth throughout the galaxy fall to their knees."

Thomas looked thoughtful.

Not shaken, not shocked, but thoughtful. It seemed Thomas had already considered that implied future. He had the mental tools to figure it out. He just hadn't bothered to talk it over or share it with the rest of them.

Then again, Evenjos didn't look shocked, either.

Garrett must have shared that future prediction with her. Vocal discussion was unnecessary for mind readers.

Only Ariock was excluded.

He was their sidekick, shielded from potent truths and important conversations, shepherded and manipulated. It seemed the mind readers discussed a lot of things before calling Ariock into certain meetings. They told him only as much raw truth as they thought he could handle.

"You see, this is the problem with loving a commoner." Evenjos gave Ariock a condescending stare. "I warned you. Now you are obsessed with protecting the poor, delicate girl." She drew closer to Garrett, draping an arm over his shoulders and gazing at Ariock with self-righteous judgment. "If anything will lead to disaster, it will be that."

Whatever the future was, Evenjos probably knew it. Garrett must have told her.

And Thomas must suspect it.

All three of them had watched Ariock struggle with his recurring nightmare. They had let him suffer with uncertainty for months. They all knew or strongly suspected that Vy was fated to die, and they hadn't spoken a word about it.

Not out loud, anyway.

Thomas had the excuse of a promise made to Delia Dovanack, but she was dead. He could have said something sooner. Instead, he had waited for an opportune moment to finally enlighten his supposed friend.

All three of these mind readers had absorbed Ariock's greatest fear—losing Vy—yet even now, they still refused to tell him whether it was inevitable or not.

They all probably knew the answer.

But they didn't really care about Vy. Not the way Ariock cared. They might want to save the universe, but Vy was expendable.

And they did not trust Ariock to handle that well.

They did not respect him.

At all.

Calmness came over Ariock. He didn't feel outraged at all. He was tired of battles and fighting and war. He only wondered why he kept striving to win the respect of fellow heroes who secretly castigated him as a hopeless fool.

Why should he obey allies who did not trust him enough to let him make important decisions?

He wasn't actually one of the four heroes. That was obvious.

Perhaps the whole story of the four heroes was just a lie designed to pacify him. Even though Ah Jun had depicted the Strength in paintings, he was barely a participant. He was always missing vital information. He was blindfolded and deafened and chronically ignorant. The true heroes were Wisdom, Will, and Transformation.

Ariock stood and walked away.

He didn't belong among the people who made actual plans and actual decisions. He shouldn't have been allowed to call a meeting in the first place.

"Don't go!" Thomas sounded alarmed. "We need you. We can't save the universe without you!"

"You are important," Evenjos said.

"You're the heart of our team," Garrett called. "Ariock. Wait."

A force field of hardened air appeared in front of Ariock, blocking his exit. That must be Garrett's doing.

"We can come to an agreement," Garrett said raggedly. "I'll show you the next prophetic pivot. How about that? Just please don't quit!"

How magnanimous.

"How about if you show us all the prophecies?" Thomas challenged Garrett.

Ariock turned around, aware that the problem wasn't just Garrett. All three of the mind readers were secretive.

Ah Jun had painted them as equals with Strength, not his superiors. The prophet Migyatel had described them as his advisers. She had made it sound like they would become his support team. So perhaps prophets could be wrong.

Or maybe the future was not set in stone. Maybe people had to make certain things happen.

"I want to be an equal with the rest of you," Ariock said.

They looked as if he was speaking gibberish.

Evenjos shook her head, at a loss. Garrett pretended not to have any idea what Ariock was talking about.

Thomas, at least, was honest. He looked guilty.

"No more secrets." Ariock emphasized each word. "If you can't trust me with facts? Then I'm not your equal. If you don't respect me? Then it's clear you don't respect anyone who isn't a mind reader."

That truth seemed to hit home. They all began to look guilty.

"Either we work together as equals, or we don't work together at all." Ariock would quit a team that was built on lies and mistrust. "Evenjos?" He looked at her.

"You lied to me, manipulated me, and tricked me, all because you thought you knew what was best for my love life. That proves what you really think of me."

Evenjos could not deny it. She looked down in shame.

Ariock shifted his gaze to Garrett. "You've manipulated me for most of my life. And recently, you pretended that my deepest fear meant nothing. You lied to my face. You've been withholding a major and vital secret from me, apparently because you will never trust my judgment."

Garrett looked ashamed.

"I don't know whether you're right or wrong," Ariock admitted. "But if you don't give me the chance to prove myself? Then you've ensured that I will never be someone worthy of trust."

"I suppose you have a point," Garrett mumbled.

Ariock wasn't done. "I do not accept your judgment of me. You don't get to decide who I am." He turned to the teenage boy. "Thomas, I believe you've never told a direct lie. But you're a social engineer."

Thomas looked unimpressed by the accusation.

"You manipulated me into this confrontation," Ariock said, "so you'd get to see the final prophetic paintings."

Thomas acknowledged that with a bold nod.

"That's understandable," Ariock said. "But are we friends to you? Or pawns?" He didn't need to hear the answer. Instead, he gave everyone a stern look. "Let's trust each other. Now. Either you trust me with the major secrets you're hiding, or this ends. I need partners who get that I'm one of them."

CHAPTER 7

THE PACT OF STRENGTH

These were proud heroes. They weren't going to share vital secrets with someone whom they regarded as weak-minded. So Ariock waited for Garrett, Evenjos, and Thomas to reject his ultimatum. He expected it.

"You're right." To Ariock's surprise, Garrett eased himself down on the plinth. "I haven't been trusting you. Maybe that's a mistake." He glared around the courtyard, including Thomas and Evenjos in his gaze. "I'll reveal my secrets provided they reveal theirs."

Thomas looked burdened.

"No," Evenjos said, alarmed. "I do not think that is a good idea."

Interesting. So the mind readers did not even trust one another. They were all hoarding secrets, perhaps important secrets, at a time when the universe needed them to work together more than ever before.

They weren't a team.

Were they even friends?

Ariock sat across from Garrett, making himself comfortable. "I'd like us all to trust one another," he said. "I would go ahead and tell you about my prophetic dreams, except . . ." He gave them each a pointed look. "Oh, well, you already know everything about me."

They couldn't deny it.

"Who wants to go next?" Ariock asked.

"I'll go last." Garrett sounded chummy, as if some critical problem had been solved and now they were just a bunch of friends hanging out.

Ariock gave him an unfriendly stare.

"My secrets are a doozy." Garrett spread his hands apologetically. "I'd rather save the mind blowing for the end of the meeting, just in case it ruins the mood and makes you all hate me."

Ariock hoped that was hyperbole.

Thomas and Evenjos sized each other up, clearly daring the other to go first.

"I do have a secret," Thomas admitted. "But it's pointless to tell you in this context. It's no big deal. It's not worthy of discussion."

"Tell us anyway," Garrett demanded.

Thomas looked toward Evenjos, as if hoping for a rescue.

"My secret is irrelevant." Evenjos stepped back. "It will not help us. It has nothing to do with our current situation."

Their demurrals piqued Ariock's curiosity. He saw Garrett's gaze sharpen, and he knew that his great-grandfather also wanted to know what unimportant secrets Evenjos and Thomas considered to be worth guarding.

"It's worth sharing," Ariock said, "even if you think it's irrelevant. This is about sharing vulnerability with each other. I've already done that, involuntarily, with all of you." He gestured invitingly. "I'll do my best to keep an open mind. I just want fairness. You know every major secret I've ever kept. For instance, I'm sure you know that I got engaged to Vy."

"Congratulations." Garrett did not attempt to sound surprised.

Evenjos and Thomas politely echoed the sentiment.

"I knew," Thomas admitted.

Of course they all knew. Ariock and Vy had told no one. They had agreed that it was premature to celebrate any kind of future while the Death Architect was still at large.

"You're good people." Ariock looked at Thomas and then Evenjos. "Whatever secrets you're keeping, I doubt it will alter my basic opinion of you. I just think some equality will make us a stronger team." He considered Kessa's work with penitents and added, "Telepathy gas has equalized the field, a bit, between mind readers and non–mind readers. Do you want me to use it?" He shrugged. "I kind of hate the stuff, but if you'd rather share your secrets with me that way, I'll do it."

"That's not necessary." Thomas sat on a marble step. "I'll tell you what I've kept hidden, provided that Evenjos and Garrett also share their secrets at this same meeting."

Evenjos tightened her lips. But she nodded, and took a seat on a step facing Thomas. "I can do that." She turned to Ariock. "You won't like my secret, though. It won't help you."

Ariock wasn't sure Evenjos had any clue what he would or wouldn't like.

"Agreed." Garrett looked around at them, and said, "This is a prophetic pivot point."

Thomas looked interested. "This? Right now?"

"Yup." Garrett puffed on his pipe. "I believe this is the Pact of Strength." His round gesture included the courtyard and the four heroes who faced each other.

Thomas wore his rarest look: surprise.

"So let's go ahead," Garrett urged. "What's your secret, Thomas?"

Thomas eyed Ariock with caution. "Are you sure you want to hear something that will lower your opinion of me?"

Ariock recalled another time when Thomas had been this reluctant to reveal a self-incriminating secret. Ariock had insisted until Thomas painstakingly told his tale about the Gotte couple, the foster parents whom he had killed by accident.

Thomas had been so ashamed. So self-hating.

But after he had shared that terrible secret from his past? He had begun to lose some of his long pent-up mistrust of himself. He had begun to loosen up, and to consider that he might be human after all. He had accepted the side of himself that made mistakes.

Not only that, but Ariock had learned a lot about Thomas from that revelation. He had begun to see the boy as a potential friend instead of as an unstable ally. He had recognized Thomas's self-hatred and identified with it.

Cherise, too, had begun to lose some of her antagonism toward Thomas. And Vy. And the ummins from Duin. They had learned that their Teacher was capable of shame and humility, which made him less like a Torth and more like them. That opened up a path for friendships.

"All right." Thomas seemed to be paying attention to what was going on inside Ariock's mind. "Maybe you have a point." He took a deep breath, as if bracing against an attack. "I guess I can go first."

Ariock nodded with encouragement.

"But I'm warning you," Thomas said. "It's not a good secret."

Ariock did his own internal bracing for bad news. "Go ahead."

Thomas removed his sun hat, allowing a better view of his eyes. "I'm more Torth than you realize. I've never been good with emotions. I yearn for tranquility meshes. I don't like being around groups of people. Acting friendly is always an act for me. It's an effort. I'm most content when I'm alone and at work."

Anyone who visited Thomas on a regular basis was familiar with his brusque manner and his occasionally brutal honesty. Thomas didn't do fun. He always held himself apart from other people.

None of this seemed like news to Ariock. He waited for a big reveal.

"So I don't have the heart and soul of a hero." Thomas seemed frustrated, like he was giving a lecture to an obtuse group of students. "I've been given power. But I should never be trusted with power." He emphasized that. "I put on a good face and pretend that I'm mostly harmless and that everyone should trust me. But where does that lead?" He looked at Evenjos. "You know where it leads."

This must be a reference to the mind readers who had imprisoned Evenjos and went on to found the early beginnings of the Torth Empire. Unyat. And Audavian. Both of those monsters had pretended to be friendly during their rise to power.

Ariock recalled the story as told by Evenjos. Audavian had begun his life as a Formula freak child in a slum who had won a scholarship or something to a Yere-sunsa academy for royalty. He had charmed everyone there.

And the original Unyat? The first supergenius in existence had begun as a hedge doctor for peasant serfs. He had become a folk hero. Perhaps he had even believed his own message of granting equality for all people.

Thomas might be like Unyat and Audavian in superficial ways. But Ariock doubted he was anywhere near as monstrous.

"What's your secret, Thomas?" Ariock prompted.

"That's it." Thomas hunched his shoulders with shame.

Ariock couldn't believe it. He wanted to make sure. "That's it? Your big secret is that you don't trust yourself?"

"Yes," Thomas said.

"You're wrong." Ariock blurted it out. "Of all of us, I trust you with power the most."

Thomas stared at him. "I'm not wrong."

That sounded final.

Ariock supposed he understood. He didn't quite trust himself with power, either. He wouldn't get intimate with Vy unless he was wearing an inhibitor patch. That was just common sense.

"So what should we do?" Garrett sounded nonplussed as he stared at Thomas. "Lock you up in a cage and trot you out when needed?"

Ariock shot his great-grandfather a warning look. At least he hadn't said "pit."

"Maybe that's a good idea," Thomas said.

He sounded completely serious.

"That's ridiculous," Ariock said.

"You're being awfully dismissive," Thomas said. "A supergenius telepath is telling you, beyond doubt, that he should not be trusted with a ton of power."

Ariock recognized an off-kilter self-assessment when he heard one. But Thomas seemed overly invested in an untrustworthy image of himself, so Ariock played along. He nodded and managed not to roll his eyes.

"You'll need my help to deal with the Death Architect," Thomas said, his voice wooden and emotionless. "But afterward? I think you may want to reconsider locking me up. Or you should put me on some kind of permanent version of the inhibitor."

Garrett looked thoughtful.

Ariock tried not to groan in disgust. "Thank you, Thomas," he said. "Let's move on."

CHAPTER 8

MERRIMENT

Evenjos looked at the heroes of this era—all men whom she had begun to love. Thomas. Ariock. And especially Garrett.

She wanted their respect. She wanted to keep her secret shame well hidden.

"What's your secret, Evenjos?" Ariock asked.

Evenjos smoothed a lock of her curly purple hair over her shoulder. She wanted to do her part in defeating the death cultists who were remnants of the Torth Empire. If she was going to set things right in the universe and make true reparations for all the wrongs she had caused, then she needed to learn the final prophecies of Ah Jun. That meant honoring the pact she had made here.

Some things were more important than her pride.

"I am directly responsible for the rise of the Torth Empire." Evenjos hung her head, unwilling to meet their gazes. "I never told you."

She had their attention.

"I made myself sound like a hapless empress who got caught off guard by events beyond my control," Evenjos confessed. "But that was not the case. I was close—very close—to the man who was directly below Audavian in the House of Telepathy. I was there for everything he did."

She felt the sharpness of Garrett's focus.

Garrett would never be so rude as to probe. He was as gallant as anyone from this era could be. But he was also a third-magnitude telepath, and he'd spent enough time with Evenjos to suspect her secret. He probably couldn't wait to hear the sordid details.

"My lover's name was Elome." It felt strange to utter that name out loud after so many millennia. Evenjos wished she could ensure that Elome was forgotten forever. Instead, here she was, talking about him. It was like bringing a piece of him back to life.

"Elome was a third-magnitude telepath," Evenjos explained. "Except he was actually fourth magnitude. He kept that fact hidden. He wore a third-magnitude sigil, which tricked everyone into believing that was his limit. He fooled me into believing it."

"Fourth-magnitude telepathy?" Ariock was clearly struggling with the archaic terminology. "Is that mind-twisting?"

"It is brainwashing," Evenjos corrected. "Light mind-twisting."

"So you were a victim," Garrett said.

How kind. Garrett laid out an easy route for Evenjos to escape blame.

Evenjos shook her head. "I could tell truth from lies." Sorrow weighed heavily inside her until her default body felt ready to spill apart into rivulets of water. "I should have easily sensed what Elome was doing to my mind. Instead, I was blinded by the glow of treasures and merriment."

Ariock looked embarrassed on her behalf.

"I was the most powerful person of my era," Evenjos said. "I could have sent Elome away with a word. That was my responsibility."

Garrett went to Evenjos and hooked an arm around her winged shoulders. She nearly flinched away, expecting a mind probe.

But he only held her. His proximity was a warm comfort. "It wasn't your fault," he said.

Except it obviously was.

"It sounds like Elome tricked everyone around you," Thomas said. "Not just you. He must have manipulated everyone in your royal court."

"I suppose so." Evenjos had not given a thought to Elome's lesser victims, although she doubted that Elome would have brainwashed every chambermaid in the palace. He would have only altered the memories of a few key people to keep them from reporting his secret communications.

"Plus," Thomas said, "Elome was acting on the directives of Audavian, who was, in turn, following advice from Unyat. In some ways, you were a victim of a victim."

"That does not excuse my role in what happened." Evenjos folded her wings close around her body, wanting to hide from Garrett's sympathetic gaze. She understood that Thomas and Garrett were trying to downplay her role, to make her less guilty. They were good friends. But leaders should not be excused for egregious mistakes.

As the goddess-empress of her planet, she could not claim ignorance nor helplessness. She could not be forgiven.

"I was their pawn." Evenjos closed her eyes and forced herself to confess the most humiliating parts. "Elome was my consort. He slept in my bedchamber. I was with him for fifty years, with all the happiness you can expect from a pairing that lasted that long."

Was it her imagination, or did Garrett deflate?

She had not expected the old man to be capable of jealousy. He claimed that he had no room in his heart for love. He was fond of her, and that was all.

"Elome used my power," Evenjos confessed. "When he linked with me—and linking is consensual, that is the nature of how it works—he boosted himself to fourth magnitude. He must have been trained by Audavian in the illegal arts. So he whispered in my ear, and he changed my mind. And I . . ." She had to catch her breath, she was so ashamed. "I let him."

"No, you didn't," Garrett said firmly.

"I don't think so." Ariock sounded less certain. He must realize that in the same situation, he would also blame himself.

That was correct behavior. The strongest person in any partnership dynamic should always be the one to shoulder all the responsibility. Ariock understood that.

"May I?" Thomas stood, hesitant.

Clearly, he wanted permission to absorb her long-dead past. Perhaps he would spy on her intimate fun times with Elome. Perhaps he would look further back and find her other shame—her commoner lover.

But why not?

There was nothing left to hide. Evenjos doubted that her lesser secrets mattered, now that her friends knew what a self-absorbed tool she had been.

She nodded.

Thomas stepped into Evenjos's range and sat next to her.

He was quiet for a few moments. His eyes were active, though. Evenjos could feel him rooting through her entire life. He was learning three hundred years' worth of royal meetings, banquets and balls, press conferences, alien dignitaries, Yeresunsa councils, and everything she had done in private to amuse herself.

Garrett looked alarmed. "Is this really a good idea?" He raised an arm, and Evenjos knew he would use his powers to seize Thomas and drag him away.

"I'm done." Thomas held up his hands in a warding-off gesture. "You are not to blame." He clasped Evenjos's arm. "Elome would have fooled most people. He did, in fact, fool everyone you knew. I think you missed a few clues, but they were minor and easy to overlook. Most people would have done exactly the same things you did."

If anyone else had tried to assuage her guilt with such claims, Evenjos would have dismissed them. But coming from Thomas the truth-teller? Her vision blurred with tears of relief and gratitude.

She had to get ahold of her emotions. Otherwise she might literally fall to pieces and become a puddle on the floor of the courtyard.

"Your people would have been doomed even if you had figured out Elome," Thomas said. "And in a worse way. Audavian would have had you assassinated so he could install a more obedient puppet emperor on the Crystal Throne."

Evenjos supposed that made sense.

"The great war between Torth and Yeresunsa would have happened sooner," Thomas went on. "And the predecessors of the Alashani would have had less time to prepare for life underground. The Alashani might never have existed if you had accused Elome and forced a reckoning. That means Garrett would never have been born, and Ariock never would have existed. My biological mother wouldn't have had a mission to assassinate the Dovanacks, so she wouldn't have stayed on Earth long enough to abandon me there and give me a chance to grow up. None of us would be here."

Evenjos gaped. Those second-order effects had never occurred to her.

"You've been blaming yourself way too much," Thomas said. "For years."

Not just years. Millennia.

A new revelation hit Evenjos with the weight of concrete. She had been so used to being alone at the pinnacle of every major decision, she had simply become unable to accept being a hapless pawn. Victimhood was unnatural to her. So she had rejected it as impossible. No matter what anyone else said, no matter what her own instincts said, she had decided that she was not a victim.

But Thomas saw the truth. He cut straight through her self-delusion.

Evenjos leaned against his narrow chest and sobbed.

Thomas put his arms around her, emanating a mixture of embarrassed sympathy and awkward teenage mortification. "It wasn't your fault." He patted her winged back.

Garrett sat on her other side. "It was never your fault."

"In fact," Thomas said, "your love for Elome might have planted the seeds for the downfall of the Torth Empire. Elome was the epitome of a closeted rogue agent. He probably loved you in secret. And his secret emotions were likely an inspiration for later Servants of All, who had their secret cabal. That culture of deep secrecy planted mistrust among mind readers. It laid the fault lines for a fractured Megacosm."

Thomas forgave her.

They all did.

Elome, Audavian, and Unyat had unleashed havoc upon the galaxy. They had ushered in a dark age that led to countless deaths and widespread slavery. But maybe Evenjos was not to blame at all. She had been a fool, deafened by laughter, yet she had also been an innocent person of her era. Everyone in her court had been just as misled.

Garrett held his arms open, and there was love there. Not mere fondness. Garrett accepted her, including her strengths, her flaws, even her hidden weaknesses.

Evenjos pulled away from Thomas to lean into Garrett's less awkward and stronger embrace. His scent was comfort. His warmth was all that she had lost, given back to her.

Ariock enfolded all three of them in a huge hug.

That was silly enough to make Evenjos laugh. Soon Garrett and Ariock, and then even Thomas, were laughing as well.

CHAPTER 9

THE FINAL PROPHECY

After the group hug, everyone took their respective seats and turned toward Garrett. The expectation was palpable. Thomas had to clasp his hands to keep from rubbing them together. This was it. Finally, the knowledge he most needed, the facts he never should have had to wait so long for.

"All right." Garrett held out his hand, and a heavy tome fell out of thin air. A podium also appeared. Garrett set the prophecies down and pages magically turned.

"Here's what I've been keeping secret," Garrett said. "Don't say I didn't warn you."

Thomas came forward to stand near the book for a better view. Evenjos and Ariock did the same.

The book settled into an open position near its end.

The two-page spread depicted the courtyard in which they now stood. It showed the four heroes with Ariock presiding over them.

"The Pact of Strength," Garrett said, pointing to the archaic script.

"I guess that's now," Ariock said.

Thomas's skin crawled as he considered how ancient the original mural had been. Ah Jun had truly seen much and very far. Her feverish paint strokes proved that she had felt her visions viscerally. He was almost glad he could not meet the oracle. If any one mind could overwhelm his capacity to absorb, it would be hers. Unyat must have lived in terror of meeting her.

Garrett used his powers to gently turn a page. The following spread was all text written in the curling script.

"Most of this text is commentary," Garrett explained. "It's the blathering of scholars trying to make sense of relics they cannot comprehend. I've learned to pretty much skip anything that isn't the words or paintings of Ah Jun herself."

He turned another page. More alien script.

Ah Jun had had disciples. They, in turn, had had disciples, and they strove to preserve every painting, poem, and prediction from the oracle. Her cult had eventually decayed as they suffered extreme hardships over multiple generations. They had melted into the Alashani underground, who maintained a tradition of preserving sacred relics and chanting prayers.

A few eccentric Torth, too, had tried to preserve their empire's origins. Although the Torth collectively forgot who Ah Jun and Audavian and Evenjos used to be, some historians bartered shreds of the ancient past. Garrett had masqueraded as a Torth Blue Rank in order to gain as many valuable relics as he could get his hands on. He'd also stolen sacred relics from the Alashani, which he, unlike the Torth, had access to. Garrett was probably as capable and dedicated as any disciple of Ah Jun had ever been.

"The Return of Strength," Garrett translated, showing a page with text that curled around a painting with the recognizable brushstrokes of Ah Jun.

In the painted panel, Thomas and Vy shoved a reluctant-looking Ariock forward.

"No idea what that's about," Garrett confessed. "It's a minor prophecy, not a full-page spread." He turned another page.

Thomas casually took a step back, to be absolutely sure he was out of Garrett's range. He had just glimpsed a small panel that showed a boy with apparent dominion over the galactic disk. It looked like his secret, half-formed plan about brainwashers was unnervingly real as a future possibility.

But Garrett kept turning pages. Thomas had sensed the old man's focused mood before he'd exited his range. There was a major revelation coming up.

Something bad.

"What's that?" Ariock pointed.

Garrett stopped, letting them see a wall of text around a painted panel: a little girl with ribbons in her hair. Her eyes were closed, but a third eye was wide-open upon her forehead. The cosmos surrounded her.

"It says, 'Death Steals Certainty.'" Garrett read from the painted inscription. "I've never been able to figure it out. I mean, obviously it's the Death Architect. But what's she doing?"

Thomas sensed that his friends were mystified. But he had enough background knowledge to hypothesize. In the time of Unyat, a third eye signified the intracorporeal powers: telepathy, prophecy, clairvoyance, or healing.

Since all Torth were mind readers, a panel about telepathy would not be remarkable enough to include in the prophecies. Clairvoyance, too, was pretty common among Torth. And the Torth had gradually bred healing out of their gene pool. The Death Architect likely did not have that power.

That left prophecy.

For the first time since viewing the book, Thomas felt rattled. If the Death Architect was stealing certainty, that seemed to hint that she had access to knowledge that the heroes lacked. If she could foretell the future . . .

"Oh." Thomas said in a shaky voice. "This explains a lot."

"What do you mean?" Garrett looked at him, surprised. He clearly had not expected to learn anything new about the prophecies.

"The Death Architect is two years younger than me and the Twins," Thomas explained. "She hardly pays attention to psychology or sociology, yet despite her blind spots and her youthfulness, she keeps besting us. She's always a few steps ahead of us. It's as if she's incredibly lucky." He gestured to the book. "Which would make sense, if she can see the future."

Garrett swore. "Holy crap. Are you saying she's a prophet?"

"I think that makes sense," Thomas said.

Evenjos sagged. Ariock swore.

"Is she a full-fledged prophet?" Evenjos asked. "Or just a seer?"

"I don't know." For all Thomas knew, the Death Architect was an oracle. That would make her unbeatable.

"Does she know about Ah Jun?" Ariock asked.

"I don't see how she could," Garrett said. "The Torth do have copies of the prophetic paintings in obscure collections and such, but there's no way any of them would understand the significance. They never learned . . ." He trailed off.

Thomas understood why Garrett's face had gone grave. The Torth Empire had not known much about prophets—until they began to enslave innocent Alashani.

The Death Architect could have absorbed information about Migyatel and other prophets from her recent torture victims.

"Crap," Thomas said. If his nemesis could foresee every major prophetic pivot, she would figure out countermeasures.

"At least we know now," Ariock said.

"Right." Thomas tried to sound confident.

Garrett looked begrudgingly thoughtful. After decades of studying the prophecies in secret and alone, he had never expected to gain new insights. "I'll go on." He reverently turned page after page.

There were more cryptic paintings between commentary script. An asteroid field. Kessa presiding over a huge crowd. An artistic rendering that might depict an event horizon.

And then a full-page panel.

Thomas was surprised to see that this important event showed none of the established heroes. Instead, it showed Vy. The painted version of his foster sister was glowing and surrounded by stars. Her eyes were closed, as if in bliss. She looked powerful.

Ariock leaned closer. "What's happening there?"

"The inscription is 'The Disgrace of Death,'" Garrett said. "Your guess is as good as mine."

Thomas began to cogitate guesses.

Ariock sounded worried. "She shouldn't be alone."

Garrett allowed them all to study the painting for a while longer. Finally, Ariock made a conductor's gesture, and Garrett turned the page.

More alien script. Then a two-page spread of Thomas and Ariock, both armored for battle, and a monstrous holographic map of the galaxy between them.

"Wisdom and Strength," Garrett read.

He kept going. They were running out of pages. A solar storm. Evenjos and Vy together, both flowing into a backdrop of stars. "Glory and Certainty," Thomas read.

And then a panel of Garrett losing his head.

In the painting, Garrett's bearded face was upside down, decapitated. His neck spurted blood.

"Always a pleasure to see that one," Garrett muttered with sarcasm.

Thomas translated the unexpected caption out loud. "The Sacrifice of Will."

"But who is sacrificing me?" Garrett asked pedantically.

Ariock reached over to squeeze his shoulder.

"Yeah, yeah." Garrett shrugged off his concern. "Thank you for your early condolences. Are you sure you want to keep going? Because the ending isn't perfect."

"Show me." Ariock's voice was deep and merciless. "I need to see."

Garrett sighed in resignation. He paged slowly past blocks of textual commentary. The Dragon Tower in twilight. And then Vy . . .

This panel depicted Vy tumbling through space without a spacesuit. She looked like she might be freezing to death.

Anguish roared off Ariock. Clouds coalesced over the mountains, gathering for a deluge.

Thomas reached up and laid a comforting hand on Ariock's thick arm. But he hated this painting almost as much as the big guy did. Couldn't anyone prevent this event from happening?

"This doesn't mean anything definite." Garrett paused on that page. "Ah Jun painted all kinds of visions. These small panels don't necessarily come true. They're just approximations. They're not pivotal events, in the grand scheme of things. They don't have to be accurate."

But it wasn't really a small panel. It covered an entire page. Ah Jun had captured Ariock's recurring nightmare with feverish perfection.

"Wait, let me read the caption," Evenjos said.

Thomas had soaked up the archaic alphabet from her mind. "It's 'The Loss of Certainty,'" he said out loud, for Ariock's benefit.

It did not explicitly mention death. That was something.

Garrett glanced at the sky. "If it storms, I'm relocating indoors. I won't let the pages get wet. They're delicate."

Thomas sensed Ariock struggling to put aside his emotions for long enough to see the whole book. He wanted to see something hopeful.

The next page showed Ariock, nude but tastefully twisted to hide genitalia, floating in space and surrounded by beads of glowing water and stars. He looked like he was bathing in stars. Weird.

"The Glory of Strength?" Thomas translated, mystified.

Garrett turned to the final page of the book of prophecies.

The final two-page spread was dark and dreary. It was a crater and stars. A slender figure stood in the crater. Thomas recognized the black dragon armor Garrett had made for him, and his own physique.

It was a painting of himself.

The inscription was ominous. *The Lone Survivor.*

"This is known as the prophecy of the lone survivor." Garrett's heavy mood implied that this was what he had dreaded to reveal. "According to the commentary of Ah Jun's disciples, four heroes will go into darkness to defeat Death. Only one hero will return from that final battle."

Thomas felt as if he'd been knocked back. Was he going to lose Ariock and Vy? Garrett and Evenjos? None of that seemed fair. And even if that miserable fate was preordained, shouldn't the lone survivor be someone better than an antisocial Torth? Someone like Ariock?

Something was wrong.

Thomas refused to accept that final prophecy. Ah Jun had purposely made her paintings misleading. The inscriptions were often closer to the real truth than the picture. The lone survivor might not actually be pictured here. Maybe Thomas was confronting a ghost who would be resurrected. Maybe . . . well, it couldn't be exactly what it seemed to be.

Evenjos bowed her head. "I do not accept this fate readily," she said. "But in a way, it is a comfort. If I am to end, then I want it to be in saving the whole universe." She reached for Garrett's hand. "I only wish Ah Jun could have respected me enough to paint my final moment, as she painted yours."

Exactly. Ah Jun had painted Garrett's death, but nothing for Ariock or Evenjos or even Vy? That was telling. They might survive in some way.

"She seems to have left out all kinds of details," Garrett admitted. "It's enough to make me wonder if I've misinterpreted the whole thing."

The sky was darker than ever. The emotions roiling off Ariock were intense enough to make the mind readers within his range watch him nervously. He stared at the final spread as if it had wounded him.

"I'm sorry," Garrett said.

Ariock glared. He looked betrayed.

"I've had time to make peace with my fate," Garrett said. "I'm sorry that I had to hit you with it this way. I understand you'll need some time to—"

"You lied to me." Ariock backed away.

Garrett spread his hands. "I once asked you if you were okay with doing whatever it took to defeat the Torth Empire. You said you were on board."

"But what about Vy?" Ariock clenched his massive fists. "My nightmare is going to come true. Isn't it? You said it wouldn't."

"We don't know." Garrett spoke with uncharacteristic sympathy.

"The prophecy could be misleading." Thomas hoped he was being realistic. "We're not seeing any painted deaths, except for Garrett's. To me, that means Vy's death is far from certain."

Ariock shook his head and Thomas sensed the spiral of his thoughts. Ariock hated his own helplessness.

"The prophecy of the lone survivor only refers to the four heroes," Garrett said. "Maybe Vy will survive? We simply don't know."

"But *I* won't survive." Ariock took another step away. "Even if she does. She'll be alone."

"We don't know that." Thomas felt as if he was still grappling with shock himself. He could hardly imagine a future where he would be the only hero in existence. Thomas Hill: the smartest person in the galaxy and the most powerful person in the galaxy, with a healthy body and no challenges and what might be an infinite future ahead of him.

What sort of existence was that?

He'd have no peers. He'd be just as alone and weird as he used to be when he was a child in foster care, except with a very dangerous and tempting amount of power. It wasn't right.

But if that was the cost of saving the universe?

Well. If someone needed to pay the ultimate price and make the ultimate sacrifice, that might as well be three of the heroes of prophecy—and the fourth who survived. This was their duty. Thomas would be the lone survivor, if that was what was required.

Ariock walked away. "I need to think about this."

Garrett reached out, then gave up. "Take some time. But come back. You're the hero we need."

"We are here for you," Evenjos added.

Ariock stepped off a ledge and soared away faster than a transport. He vanished into the billowing storm clouds.

"Drat." Garrett flipped the book closed.

"I need to think, too." Thomas shoved his hands into his pockets and walked away. No one tried to stop him from leaving.

CHAPTER 10

SHIRK

"But if we tell humankind . . ." Vy trailed off, interrupting herself.

She and Cherise and Abhaga were seated in a loose circle on a veranda, where they had a view of ocean and mountains. The sudden sweep of clouds alarmed her. Storms rolled in from the mountains sometimes, but never this fast. Not under natural circumstances.

Vy stood.

"What?" Abhaga had an endearing accent.

"Her boyfriend's in a bad mood," Cherise explained. "He influences the weather."

Abhaga accepted that without so much as a raised eyebrow. After approximately three months, he had learned enough of the common slave tongue to be conversational. He was still learning who his friend Thomas was and what the alien universe was like. Vy guessed that Abhaga had experienced enough culture shock to last several lifetimes. She could relate.

Vy tapped her wristwatch to activate the menu, but she wasn't sure if she should interrupt Ariock. He had gone to confront Garrett about the book of prophecies, and whatever he had learned, it seemed to be giving him an outsize reaction. He might be furious. Or terrified.

Vy scrolled to another icon, then hesitated, unwilling to interrupt Thomas, either.

"Vy."

Ariock's deep voice had a way of vibrating in her bones. He alighted next to her. The veranda creaked under his weight, grout cracking between tiles.

He was upset, but he was doing a good job of hiding it. Vy noticed telltale signs that strangers would overlook. His deep-set eyes were more intense than usual. His immense shoulders were rounded in a more protective way.

Cherise and Abhaga backed away, giving them room. Abhaga's eyes were wide. He had seen Ariock a few times, but rarely this close.

"What's wrong?" Vy wanted to stroke the fuzz on Ariock's face, but although she was six feet tall, she would have to stretch to reach that high. She touched his chest instead.

"Nothing." Ariock sounded like he was enduring high pressure. "I was thinking of getting away for a little while. Can you join me?"

Something was definitely wrong. Ariock wouldn't shirk his duties. The Death Architect and her cultists were still out there doing terrible things, which meant Ariock had bombs and space rigs to find and destroy.

Lightning flashed across the clouds.

"Uh, sure." Vy offered an apologetic smile to Cherise and Abhaga. "Would you mind continuing the conversation without me?"

"We'll save it for another day." Cherise's tone reassured Vy that they would not make any major decisions about the fate of Earth. Not without Vy's input.

The scene vanished. One moment Vy was experiencing an afternoon with her friends, the next, she was in a twilit forest. Ozone hung in the air, its scent sharper than usual. Animals slunk past alien trees, blending into the leafy gloom. Ariock's arrival must have unsettled them. They resembled walking stick bugs the size of deer, complete with doeish eyes.

Vy imagined the skies were clearing up over Freedomland. Ariock had brought his stormy mood here, wherever here was. She nearly asked. The gravity didn't feel like Reject-20. The plants and animals were obviously not Earthly. Maybe this was Parity or Verdantia or one of the other habitable hub planets.

"What's wrong?" Vy asked.

"I just wanted to get away." Ariock looked sad. He scooped her up in one arm, the way he did when he wanted her close.

Vy leaned her head against his massive chest and wrapped her arms around him. She wanted to help him grapple with whatever he'd learned about the future.

"What would you think about having our wedding right here and now?" Ariock asked.

Vy wondered if he was joking. "I want friends to be there. And maybe a somewhat traditional ceremony? With witnesses who aren't just weird alien bug deer?" She playfully walked her fingers across his chest, trying to take the sting out of her rebuke. "I can tell you learned something bad."

She hesitated, not quite wanting to learn the truth. If she was doomed to die soon, with no way to avoid it, she didn't want the gory details. She just wanted to enjoy what little time she had left.

"I'm not sure I'll survive." Ariock leaned against an alien tree, backed by gloom.

Chills rippled over Vy. She clutched him tighter. Her own ending was hard enough to swallow, but she had never imagined death for Ariock. He was too strong. Too unstoppable. Nothing should be able to defeat him.

It didn't make sense. It wasn't fair.

Ariock kissed her. "We don't have to go through with the preplanned future. We could stop here. Abandon the war. Let the universe do its thing without us."

Oh, that was tempting.

Vy gripped his head and held him away so he would stop kissing her and tempting her. "But the universe needs you. Doesn't it?"

"I don't care." Ariock kissed her again.

"Everyone in the universe will die unless you follow the prophecies," Vy pointed out. "You can't quit."

Ariock held her against the tree trunk, supporting her on a branch. "I've already saved the universe. Is it so bad if I miss one final battle?"

Vy enjoyed the feel of his big hands on her body. She thought she should remind him of his duty yet again, but did he need reminders? Ariock always did what was required. She was pretty sure he would face death to save the universe.

For now, he was taking what pleasure he could while aware that doom was hanging over his head. Was that so bad?

Vy wanted the same. She wanted him alive. She wanted what they had to never end.

The sky rumbled as Ariock kissed Vy. A light rain misted the air. Ariock made his clothes vanish, and Vy began to undress, but she hesitated. Her man was in a dangerous mood. He looked naked and strong in the twilight beneath the trees, like a god of the woods.

Ariock pressed an inhibitor patch to his neck.

The air seemed to lose pressure and relax. Mist evaporated. A critter tentatively chirruped, and another one answered. Vy hadn't even realized how much tension he had been contributing to the atmosphere until it was gone.

Ariock still looked divine, but there was a subtle difference now, something that Vy could hardly discern. He looked a little bit vulnerable.

He was human.

Vy pulled off her clothes and invited him closer. They fell into each other's arms. Although the brooding atmosphere was gone, they created their own steam.

GALAVERSE

Thomas sat cross-legged in his newly constructed shrine to real-time information.

The main interior of galaverse hall was larger than any cathedral or throne room. It accommodated endless ghostly holographic news feeds. Images streamed between soaring pillars, showing Sediment City on Yoft, Lambent City on Tenth Ocean, SilenceSphere Orbital, CurlVents MetroHub on Toishifel, and hundreds more.

Ariock had even mounted camera marbles at a spot along the Dovanack driveway, just for fun. The three-dimensional projection showed no people, just trees and an occasional wild turkey or deer. The feed bounced across interstellar relay stations to reach Freedomland, the nominal capital of the galaxy.

Few people could handle the information overload in this hall. For Thomas, it was a place of quiet meditation where he could experience a ghostly simulacrum of the Megacosm. He sat on the quietly rotating hoverdisk of the central dais, taking in wonders.

Evenjos was decimating a Torth stronghold on Parity. Fayfer and her many pilots were harrying the remains of a Torth space fleet toward the JourneyEnd Orbital, where defeated Torth had no choice but to kneel in submission and become penitents. Weptolyso was training an army on Algyp, teaching the savage nussians there to adhere to a new justice system. They might attempt to retrain battlebeasts as service animals, but that was a project for the future.

Garrett was on Hretshu, showing his gratitude to victorious freedom fighters by healing fatal injuries. It was strange to see Garrett healing people instead of wreaking havoc, but the collapse of the Torth Empire had brought out his kinder side.

Nethroko was consolidating friendly forces on Nuss. The liberated population of that planet had elected him to be consul of Nuss, and the war council and Kessa's lieutenants had both agreed, ratifying that decision. If the new galactic empire was going to last more than a few years, it would need wise decision-makers at the top of society.

Pung had not volunteered for the job of consul of Umdalkdul, but the war council unanimously agreed that the heroic smuggler who had traveled with Kessa and Ariock since their earliest adventures would be the most reputable and honorable representative possible. So Pung was reluctantly acting as a consul there, with eager help from Councilor Deschuba and his family.

Thomas flipped through live feeds from Enera, Paleoterra, SilverVeil Colony, the Yins, Lateral City, Glukgorba, and more. He didn't see any hint of an existential threat to the universe.

But the Death Architect operated in a communications abyss. She was outside of his many territories, unseen by his people or his drones.

The irony was visceral. Slaves used to operate in the few caves that Torth could not surveil or did not know about. Now? Only the most dangerous of Torth were driven into hiding, operating with the same degree of secrecy.

Thomas closed his eyes and reached outward with his mind. He sought any mind who might sense him and draw him in, wanting his attention or a shared exchange. Just in case.

Static.

Radio silence.

Where once there had been mental palaces and oceans and universes, now there was nothing.

Because of him.

Thomas tried not to weep. They weren't literally gone, he knew. Not really. Some factional Torth groups still shared their thoughts, and he could even join some threads, if he tuned into the right mental frequency, so to speak.

But any Torth in the universe would recognize his gargantuan mind. They would need to trust the Conqueror, or have curiosity about his thoughts, in order to invite him into whatever minicosm they had created. The Death Architect and her cultists were not interested. Neither were the various fundamentalist sects of Torth remnants.

Thomas searched. And he searched. But he was as lonely as he used to be on Earth, before he had learned of the existence of other sapient species.

When he imagined how much cosmic knowledge his decisions had obliterated . . . how many lives his decisions had ended . . . cities burned, spaceships blown up, torture enacted . . . oh, how could anyone respect him? How could anyone regard him as anything other than a monster?

"Is this a simulation of what the Megacosm feels like?" Cherise asked.

Thomas opened his eyes. She stood before him in a fiery sundress. As the dais rotated, she climbed up onto it, joining him.

"It's overwhelming," she said.

"Not to me," Thomas admitted. "This is a small sliver of what's happening in the universe. It's silent and peaceful and far away, not at all like the Megacosm used to be."

It was relaxing. That was one upside to this poor replacement for real-time galactic knowledge. The Megacosm had been many things, but rarely had it been relaxing. Not for him, anyway.

Cherise took a seat next to him. No fear. No guardedness. Thomas sensed that she spent a lot of time with Vy and Abhaga these days, and they saw him as a hero. Since Cherise used telepathy gas to facilitate Abhaga's language learning, she was picking up on the common appreciation for Thomas, as well as Bengali and other knowledge from the street orphan.

Cherise now felt guilty that she had judged Thomas so wrongly.

"I haven't defeated every threat." Thomas thought about the ominous prophecy of the lone survivor. He was glad that Cherise could not read his mind. There were hints that Vy would suffocate in outer space, and Ariock and Evenjos did not seem to have any preordained resolution to their respective stories. Ah Jun had not painted their endings.

Cherise was not shown, either. She might live, she might die, but Ah Jun had not seemed to count her as important enough to include.

"I don't think you can count me as a hero," Thomas warned Cherise. "We still need to defeat the Death Architect. I don't know what will come of that."

Cherise remembered that her foster sister had departed with Ariock in a stormy mood. All their teasing talk about weddings and mixed marriages between humans and shani had ended abruptly. Vy and Ariock had not returned since yesterday.

"What happened between you and Ariock?" Cherise dared to ask. "Where is he?"

"We're still on good terms," Thomas said, although he wasn't entirely certain about that.

"Where did he go?" Cherise asked.

"He needed some time off," Thomas said.

Cherise gave him a very skeptical look. Armies were stranded, in need of mass-teleportation. Ariock had been impossible to communicate with for more than a full day.

Thomas didn't want to toy with her or mislead her. So he took a moment to evaluate how much he should reveal.

He settled on the full truth. He might not have trusted anyone else with it, but Cherise understood all that was at stake.

"Garrett showed us the final prophecies," Thomas said. "According to Ah Jun, only one of the four heroes will return after the final battle with the Death Architect."

Cherise immediately grasped the implications. In the back of her mind, she imagined a painting of Ariock standing alone. He was Strength personified. If anyone survived, she assumed it would be him. Not Transformation. Not Wisdom.

She gave Thomas a look of profound sympathy.

"The painting," Thomas said, "was of me. Alone."

"You?" Cherise studied him, gauging how serious he was.

"Me," Thomas affirmed. "Ariock took it hard."

"Oh no."

"But all of Ah Jun's prophetic paintings are misleading," Thomas hurried to add. "Maybe the death of the other heroes is metaphorical. She really left it open to interpretation. I don't think we can know what that painting means until it happens."

Even as he spoke, his voice faltered. He desperately wanted to believe his own words.

Death was so final.

The prophecy was specifically labeled as the lone survivor. The lone survivor of what? Of an apocalypse? Of death? Or of something else?

There was a glimmer of hope there. Thomas felt sure of it.

Ah Jun had been a genius of causality in the same way Thomas was a genius of neuroscience. Her prophetic paintings might be mystically vague in order to make interpretation tough for the Death Architect. Hm. Perhaps the hopeful glimmer was only apparent to someone with enough empathetic intelligence to read between the lines. It was a gift from across the eons.

"Is Ariock coming back?" Cherise asked, her tone as somber as the question warranted.

Thomas decided not to offer reassurances. Once again, he decided to test Cherise, to see if she could handle the truth.

"Ariock has been plagued by a recurring nightmare," Thomas said. "I don't normally make it my business to reveal other people's secrets. But Vy knows, and I believe she would want you to know at this point. Delia entrusted both of you with the secret of Ariock's precognitive power."

Cherise looked unsurprised that Thomas had known that.

"The book of prophecies confirmed Ariock's biggest fear," Thomas said. "He understands, now, that his dreams are prophetic. He thinks he's going to lose Vy."

"Lose her?" Cherise asked worriedly. "How?"

"The prophecies are not totally clear," Thomas said.

"Death?" Cherise guessed, watching his face.

"That is the implication," Thomas admitted.

Shock and sorrow radiated off Cherise.

"If I can save her, I will," Thomas said. "But I'm also focused on trying to stop the Death Architect from destroying the universe. She has a doomsday device, and she'll use it, unless I can figure out where and when."

Most people would have been overwhelmed by all the dire news. Cherise seemed to know Thomas well enough to believe in and trust him.

"You'll stop her," Cherise said. "You'll save the universe."

"I have an idea of how to begin," Thomas admitted. "But I'm hesitant."

"Why?"

"Because." Thomas wondered how to describe his own moral uncertainty. "I'm problematic."

Cherise was listening.

"I destroyed a civilization," Thomas said, struggling to explain. "Sure, the Torth Empire had to go. We all know that. But when my biological father faced me and shot himself in the head, he blamed himself for causing my birth, thereby setting up a path toward the destruction of the most majestic and utopian empire in the history of the known universe. And I can never forget. He blamed me for ending his civilization. And he was absolutely right."

Cherise nodded, as if Thomas had said exactly what she expected him to say. "Do you care about Kessa?" she asked. "And Varktezo?"

"Of course."

"What about Nea?" she asked. "And the Twins?"

"Of course." Thomas understood her point. He had saved many Torth refugees. He had liberated slaves, including people he valued quite a lot.

"And me?" Cherise said. "And Vy? And Ariock?"

"I know the Torth Empire had to go," Thomas reiterated, although her questions did make him feel better about it.

"But even though you saved a lot of people," Cherise said, incisive, "you still think you should have saved more."

That was it. Exactly. Cherise had pinpointed the main factor driving his internal mess of guilt. She had done it without even reading his mind.

"Yes," he admitted.

He thought of the supergeniuses who had been murdered—the ones he would never get to meet in person, as well as the one who had mentored him. They were a mere baryonic halo around a galaxy of guilt.

"When the Torth took you and Vy as hostages," Thomas said, "my quest to find the Lady of Sorrow took us through the Isolatorium. While I was there, I saw a little girl. A Torth girl. She was being tortured to death. Probably for the crime of helping slaves."

He was never going to forget that child prisoner. He still saw her forsaken look in his dreams.

"I didn't save her," Thomas said. "And she is only one of many nameless victims. No one would take risks to rescue Torth children, or even spare a thought for them."

"You did, though," Cherise said. "You saved Nea."

"I saved a fraction of Torth children," Thomas said. "Not most of them. The Torth Homeworld got destroyed because of events instigated by me, and that little girl I saw died in the wreckage. Countless cities burned because of me. And more will burn before the year is over."

He expected Cherise to reason with him, to say that he had done more good than harm, and that his heart was in the right place. That was what Vy would say. It was what Varktezo and other friends would say.

As if good intentions were the most important thing.

"I set a galactic collapse in motion," Thomas explained. "I've been trying to guide the fallout, but it's a chaotic mess, with rocks falling every which way." He indicated the live streams throughout galaverse hall. "All I can do is watch while some people suffer who don't deserve it."

The Torth Empire had arisen because a scientist named Unyat had wanted to end suffering and inequality on his planet. Oops. Good intentions did not always lead to good outcomes. Thomas had done a nice thing by liberating slaves, but he didn't want to sow the seeds for some future atrocity.

He was trying his best. But he wasn't an oracle. He had blind spots.

"I ended the Megacosm," Thomas said with all the mournfulness that statement deserved. "I ended eons' worth of knowledge. I killed it."

Cherise snuggled against him and kissed his cheek.

Thomas blinked in surprise.

"You're right," Cherise said. "You're a really despicable person. You destroyed knowledge. You let children die."

He was surprised by how readily Cherise accepted his darkness.

"You've tortured slaves," she went on. "You've removed people's free will and caused them to suffer horrible deaths."

How could she stand him?

She sidled closer. "But you're also a wonderful person." Their lips were almost touching. Her breath warmed his face. "You're complicated."

She knew his flaws. She had spent years analyzing his flaws, mulling them over, one by one.

Even so, she had decided to accept him.

Her face was close. Right there.

A long-buried remnant of Thomas seemed to wake up and shake off a dusting of snow. Cherise kissed him with her full lips.

Her kiss was sweetness itself. Part of him had waited all his life for this kiss.

Another part of him yearned for something better.

He wanted to meld with thirty trillion souls.

His mind was complex enough to simulate a minicosm, and it craved someone of even greater complexity. Not even a fellow lonely supergenius could have fulfilled his psychophysical and sociological needs. He wanted a Megacosm.

He let the kiss end. It was sweet, but it was merely human.

CHAPTER 12

MERCIFUL

Thomas stood at the head of the war room. He had called this council, and now he faced skepticism.

Ariock's absence was noticeable, his throne-like chair empty. The group of heroes felt diminished. The fancy chairs were all pushed away from the massive table, except for the seats occupied by Kessa and Cherise. They sat across from each other, looking mystified by the lack of councilors and battle leaders.

Garrett appeared with a pop of air and a scent of ozone. He was in full battle armor and too irked to take a seat. "This had better be about Ariock. Where is he?"

Evenjos separated from Garrett. At first she was smoke, but she solidified and shook out her purple hair.

"I know how to defeat the remnants of the Torth Empire," Thomas told them.

He expected a positive reaction. Maybe some fanfare?

Instead, Garrett folded his arms. "Torth are already defeated. I need to be out there, helping our stranded armies."

Ariock's absence meant all the scheduled mass-teleportations throughout the galaxy were halted. There was chaos.

"Billions of people need healing," Evenjos added, taking a seat next to Kessa. Her gentle tone was not accusatory. "There are terrorists who are using Ariock's absence to attack our people."

"We have literally trillions of fires to put out," Garrett growled. "So what is this really about?"

Thomas wondered if his outfit made him too easy to dismiss. He wore the plain woolens of a shani day laborer. Hey, it was comfortable, plus he had pockets to rest his hands in. He disliked brocaded formalwear.

"I mean," Thomas said, seeking a path toward clarification, "I know how we can stop the death cult and their terror attacks."

That got their attention.

"We can end the Necrocosm," Thomas said, "for good. We can destroy all the Death Architect's resources and force her to halt her plans."

Garrett's anger simmered down. "Really?"

Thomas nodded.

"How?" Kessa asked.

"All righty." Garrett took a seat as readily as a pupil. "You have my attention."

Thomas took a deep breath. Once he lit this fire, it would burn across the galaxy and supercharge everything. There would be no way to snuff it out.

And he knew that he would have regrets. He would feel the aftermath for the rest of his life, no matter how long or short that life was.

He yearned to discuss his daring plan with Serette and Mondoyo. But the Twins had their own personal concern looming large. Serette was bedridden and Mondoyo was worried sick about her.

So Thomas had thought about it alone all night. For a supergenius, that was equivalent to agonizing over a decision for multiple years. Finally, he had decided to do what Ah Jun had hinted at in one of the small panels. He was fated to dominate the galaxy.

"I'll need your help." Thomas clasped his hands behind his back and began to pace. "The Torth have a high percentage of brainwashers among them. Five to eight percent, I estimate."

Cherise looked shocked. Garrett blanched.

"That shouldn't be a surprise." Thomas waved dismissively. "We always knew mind control wasn't unique to just one Torth." He gestured to himself. "Telepathy is foundational to the Torth Empire, and mind control is just a high magnitude of telepathy. Lots of Torth have the potential. But it's locked away. The power is dormant inside them."

Evenjos tapped her jawline, looking thoughtful. "It makes sense. Extracorporeal powers are easy to discover on one's own, but intracorporeal powers are another matter. Those require some sort of psychological awakening."

"Thomas's father had that awakening," Kessa pointed out.

"It won't be common," Thomas assured his friends. "If there were a lot of Torth who could brainwash each other, that would have entered common knowledge in the Death Architect's Necrocosm. Garrett would have learned about it."

He did not explain that such a power was far more useful when wielded with utter secrecy. His biological father had wisely kept his brainwashing power a secret.

"Is this just conjecture on your part?" Garrett looked suspicious. "How did you come up with that estimate of five to eight percent?"

"I've detected the potential locked away inside a lot of Torth," Thomas admitted. "When I was searching for the hidden danger who turned out to be my biological father, I began to notice that some Torth had extra influence over others. It was extremely subtle. I never would have noticed, except for the fact that I was absorbing tens of thousands of minds in rapid sequence, and they were in a telepathy gas zone. That turned their thoughts into an ambient atmosphere instead of constrained to the four-yard radius. I noticed that their moods had an effect on other people's moods. And none of them were aware of it. I was the only one who noticed."

Kessa looked pained, as if she was reevaluating everything in her life. She must be concerned about her lieutenants, wondering how many might be in danger. What if meek penitents could subtly brainwash their overseers?

Garrett swore. "Well, this is disastrous." He jumped to his feet, pacing with furious fear. "Is there any easy way to tell which ones are dangerous? What do we do? Kill them?"

Thomas raised his voice, wanting to stop Garrett from spiraling into a fear-fueled rampage. "They're useful. We're going to make use of them."

Garrett stopped and stared with incomprehension.

"Allow me to explain." Thomas forced himself to be patient. If only Ariock were here to take control of the meeting.

"Go on," Evenjos said.

Thomas gave her a grateful nod. He began to pace in slow, measured strides, not because he felt restless, but because movement was a method of commanding attention. When he was in motion, people were more likely to listen to what he was saying.

"We have a bunch of clueless brainwashers," Thomas said. "If we act fast, and in a holistic manner, we can, uh, change the minds of all the unrepentant, hardcore enemies in one fell swoop."

Only Kessa seemed to comprehend what Thomas was driving at. Her eyes widened.

"Step one," Thomas said. "We prep the enemy Torth populations. We distribute telepathy gas and our own brainwashers, plus boosters in the form of Yeresunsa warriors."

"Hold on." Garrett scrunched up his face as if confronting a difficult puzzle. "Are you saying what I think you're saying?"

"Probably," Thomas admitted. He wasn't proud to reveal his plan. He had spent all night trying to justify it on a moral level.

Nevertheless, he went on. "Step two: We make an announcement in the Necrocosm, something that gets the enemy Torth riled up. Step three: I ascend into the Necrocosm to drill down and lightly brainwash the brainwashers. We form a mesh network that converts all the enemy Torth."

In the final analysis, Thomas had figured that Torth who wanted to rob former slaves of freedom did not deserve total freedom themselves.

Still, he worried that he might have misinterpreted that equation. Morality was so slippery, so difficult to evaluate.

"You can brainwash people through the Necrocosm?" Garrett asked with a frown of uneasiness.

Thomas nodded. "I zombified a Servant of All that way back when the Torth invaded my lab with the pink inhibitor gas. The caveat is, it has to be consensual. They have to let me into their minds. That means I'll have to do it ultrafast, before they realize what I'm up to. That's why this meeting is secret." He gestured around.

"You want to trigger a mass conversion." Cherise's gaze seemed to drill into Thomas's soul. "You're going to brainwash the brainwashers, then use them like tools."

Shocked silence. Everyone was staring at Thomas as if he had sprouted horns.

"Yes." Thomas hoped his plan wasn't diabolical. "If my estimates are correct, there are enough brainwashers to go around, boosted by telepathy gas and Yeresunsa, to convert just about every death cultist into a penitent."

No one jumped up to decry his plan, at least.

"I can only brainwash a limited number of people in one go," Thomas went on, explaining. "And since I'll be doing it through the Necrocosm, the death cultists will have a chance to go on high alert and reject me. That means I need to set up a chain reaction that keeps going even after I stop."

"And it does have to be light brainwashing," Evenjos said in a tone of realization. "Because anything more entails permanent brain damage. Then the brainwashers could not use their power on anyone else."

Thomas nodded. "Correct."

"Light brainwashing," Garrett stated flatly. "Can you do that?"

"Yeah," Thomas said.

Garrett's suddenly guarded expression revealed what he thought about that. Evenjos also gave Thomas a sharp, assessing look.

"I've experimented on animals." Thomas tried to shrug away his embarrassment. Why was this so shameful? "I've lightly brainwashed snails and crickets. Things like that."

Kessa gave him a probing look.

Cherise asked him flatly, "Have you ever done it to a person?"

"No!" Thomas said. "Of course not." He softened his tone, reminding himself that wrong assumptions about him were typical. He did have a lot of nefarious power. He did come across as creepy sometimes. People would jump to conclusions.

"When I was stuck in a dungeon pit," Thomas said, "I brainwashed a cave slug. That was the first time. Since then, I've learned more. Light brainwashing wears off after a few hours. It's not permanent. There's no lasting brain damage. It's, uh . . ." He searched for the best way to describe it. "A subtle effect."

Evenjos nodded in recognition. For a wonder, she didn't look judgmental. "In my time, fourth-magnitude telepaths would illegally help drug addicts to quit their addictions. Or they would influence people to get out of bad habits. Mostly, people pretended not to notice if a black-market telepath was operating in their neighborhood. They did more good than harm."

"Really?" Garrett looked amazed.

"On balance." Evenjos gave him a look of frustration. "Of course, I was betrayed and stabbed in the back by a fourth-magnitude telepath, so I do not have a wonderful view of them."

"It's barely even brainwashing," Thomas said. "I would call it suggesting." He saw their uneasiness and couldn't help but add, in a creepily suggestive tone, "Don't you agree?"

Garrett gave him a withering look.

"We should be against robbing people of their free will," Cherise said.

A guilty blush crept up Thomas's face. He had invited Cherise to this secret meeting because he wanted to gauge her reaction. She had a better moral compass than his own. Now he wondered if he was suggesting an atrocity without even being cognizant of what it was.

"But," Cherise said, "this isn't that."

Thomas felt lighter.

"These aren't the Torth who passively sat around until their empire fell apart," Cherise said. "These are the ones who actively go around murdering innocent people. They're terrorizing former slaves. So I think it's fair to temporarily brainwash them to get them to stop."

"Yes," Kessa put in. "We have to defend ourselves."

Thomas was relieved that both Cherise and Kessa were in agreement. He was taking the right course of action.

"What will stop the converted Torth from reverting to their evil ways?" Evenjos asked. "Surely we cannot trust them after the light brainwashing wears off."

"We can," Kessa said, politely disagreeing with the former goddess-empress. "Right now, we are managing more than twenty-eight trillion penitents. They are not all happy to be where they are." Her lieutenants were all expert peacekeepers by now. "But they obey our laws because they have nowhere else to go. Once Thomas destroys the Necrocosm? It will be the same for the newest wave of converts."

"Using power to change their minds, temporarily, is no different than using any weapon during a war." Cherise gave Thomas a look of respect. "They'll still be themselves. They'll become our prisoners, but they'll have the same chance to work toward redemption that any penitent has."

She pulled a dog-eared origami lion out of her pocket and placed it on the table.

Thomas recognized it. He had folded that little gift for her on another planet, more than a million lifetimes ago.

"It's a kinder fate than most of them deserve," Cherise said.

CHAPTER 13
KILLING STROKE

"Does the Death Architect know your plan?" Kessa asked, her tone somber. "How much of the future does she foresee?"

"All I can do is blindly guess," Thomas said.

If only he could peer into the Death Architect's labyrinthian thoughts. What misapprehensions was she operating under? Was there any way to change her mind?

Everybody made wrong assumptions. Supergeniuses were no exception. Sure, supergeniuses were more cognizant of epistemological pitfalls, since they were able to compare and contrast so many lifetimes of absorbed knowledge, but the Death Architect must have a few critical flaws in her reasoning. Those flaws had led her to want to destroy the universe.

Thomas just didn't know her well enough to be certain of what she misapprehended.

"I don't think she's an oracle," Thomas ventured. "That's a fifth-magnitude power, extremely rare. I doubt she sees a comprehensive tree of possibilities. It's more likely she can see her own future, which gives her the power to make her own luck."

"Great," Garrett muttered with sarcasm.

"She has limits," Thomas assured the old man. "Even if she foresees my plan, she left herself wide-open to this attack." Prompted by looks of interest around the table, he went on, explaining, "she has zero interest in getting to know her own people. So she has no clue which of them is capable of brainwashing, whereas I can very quickly identify our own fourth- and fifth-magnitude telepaths—and hers, too."

"You already know who they are," Kessa said. "Don't you?"

It wasn't a question. Kessa was savvy, and she had politely called Thomas out. He couldn't help but admire her gumption.

"Yes," Thomas admitted. "I won't share that knowledge until the last minute, of course. We don't want to give enemies a chance to prepare."

"Can you brainwash the Death Architect through the Necrocosm?" Garrett asked with hope.

"I'll try," Thomas said doubtfully.

"Even if she slips away," Kessa said, "this is a brilliant attack. She will lose all her minions."

Except for the drones and robots.

"Yes," Thomas said. "She'll have nothing left except for whatever processes she already set up to be controlled from her lair. I hope her losses will prevent her from being able to trigger doomsday."

Garrett had run out of complaints. He smiled wickedly, probably imagining the little girl stranded in whatever dark lair she had made for herself, unable to call for help. "I like it." He leaned back and made a cigar appear. "She might spout a warning to her cultists, but they won't heed it. She's too uncaring. Her commands lack emotional impact." He gave a smug nod and puffed on his cigar.

"Exactly," Thomas said.

"Then let's get started," Garrett said, fully on board now. "What do you need?"

Thomas hesitated. He had already calculated the number of fourth-magnitude telepaths he would need to quickly brainwash.

"I will require a substantial power boost," he explained. There was no way around that. "I'll need to link with Ariock for his raw power. And you two, Garrett and Evenjos. We'll also enlist as many warriors as we can rope into helping us out."

Evenjos looked disturbed. Her gaze darted to Garrett. "This is something we should discuss further."

"Nah, I get it." Garrett chomped on his cigar. "Even if it's a chain reaction, the boy will have to take on some ungodly number by himself. He's the only one who can identify the brainwashers. He needs to convert them all in a very short window of time, before the Death Architect can get a major warning going in the Necrocosm." He gave Thomas a speculative look. "How many? And how fast?"

"At least a million," Thomas said. "Within a minute."

Even with immense borrowed power, Thomas wasn't sure he could reach across the galaxy and crawl through so many minds, leaving fresh tracks and changes. He had never attempted anything like it before. He had experimented with directing swarms of alien bugs, but that was a much smaller scale. Bugs had much simpler minds.

He might fail.

But he had to try. He wanted to rob the Death Architect of all her resources.

"There you go," Garrett told Evenjos. "The boy has stamina, but not like that. We can't risk him running out of power in the middle of this rapid-fire brainwashing. Otherwise the Death Architect will gain enough time to have them assassinated."

Kessa looked like she was doing mental recalculations.

"It will spark a mass conversion event," Thomas reiterated. "My million will get it started, but there will be at least two trillion operative brainwashers once it gets underway. My message of peaceful surrender will roll through the entire Torth population in a matter of minutes."

"Two trillion?" Kessa's eyes widened. "That is more than the number of death cultists."

"It's five to eight percent of all Torth," Thomas explained. "The brainwashers. They, in turn, will spread the surrender to the rest of the galactic Torth population, no matter what side they're on. All thirty-eight trillion Torth will receive the mental impulse to surrender to me."

Cherise gawked. So did Kessa.

"I see." Evenjos's purple eyes were alight with excitement. "The surrender impulse will affect all Torth, but it won't matter to the ones who are already on our side."

"Exactly," Thomas confirmed. "The mental impulse is harmless and wears off after ten or fifteen minutes. It will only make a difference for the ones who need to be converted. They'll kneel, hand their weapons to their slaves, and they'll divulge their locations and secrets to me and Kessa's operatives. When it wears off, they'll be penitents wearing collars."

"They can't go back," Kessa agreed.

"Can't they form the Necrocosm again?" Cherise asked.

"They may try," Kessa said, "but it takes much cooperation. My lieutenants are vigilant for signs of it. They use telepathy gas to scan new arrivals as well as work crews."

"This is actually brilliant," Garrett admitted, his tone begrudging. "There may be a few isolated cases who escape the mass surrender, if they happen to be alone and nowhere near any of our brainwashers or telepathy gas zones or armed forces. But it will be the barest fraction of a fraction."

Thomas suppressed a twinge of sorrow.

He pretended that he wanted nothing more than to wipe out the last vestiges of his mother and father's universe. He did want to end tyranny—but he would miss the Megacosm, now and forever.

He would even miss the Necrocosm.

That loss was a price Garrett seemed able to shrug off. Everyone seemed okay with it. Everyone except Thomas.

"The remnants won't even be populous enough to fuel a minicosm," Garrett said excitedly. "They'll be utterly defeated, unable to serve the Death Architect. The masses who surrender will take all their tablets, spaceships, weapons, food, and all that."

Thomas nodded.

"Logistics." Garrett rapped the table, calling attention to the concept of a checklist. "We need to prerelease telepathy gas in enemy territories, forums and boulevards and other public places with crowds."

"Yes," Thomas said. "Mind readers can't easily detect it. They won't know the suggestive impulse is about to ripple through their cities if we're careful not to set up too early."

"Will you speed walk all our brainwashers through the use of their power for the first time?" Garrett studied Thomas, quizzical. "What if they refuse?"

"Most penitents will follow my lead." Thomas didn't want to admit how many of them outright worshipped their Conqueror. "Those who are loyal to me will, uh, brainwash the ones who resist."

"Of course." Garrett snorted a dry laugh.

"The telepathy gas will work as extra insurance in that regard," Kessa realized. "Not only will it spread the suggestion widely, but it will ensure that the brainwashers have their own mental suggestion reflected back on them. They will be converted if they were not loyal to Thomas already."

Evenjos looked stunned by the scope of the plan.

Kessa stood, as if inspired and restless. "You need to maximize the number of death cultists who are in the Necrocosm when you strike."

"Yes," Thomas said.

There were many preparations to make. Their military forces needed to be prepared to take advantage of a sudden collapse of the Torth Necrocosm. Thomas wanted a specific time for the mass conversion. He would secretly enlist the help of certain fourth-magnitude penitents. He also wanted to secretly recruit Yeresunsa who were willing to link with those penitents, to boost their raw strength.

"How will you rally the death cultists?" Kessa asked.

"I have ideas," Thomas said. "For instance, I can promise to spill a major secret."

"Ha," Garrett said. "Tell them you're going to teach them the secret of how to brainwash! Little do they know, you're corralling them into a situation where they will never be allowed to use that power again."

"Or," Cherise said, "you could reveal which Torth are the secret brainwashers. That would send the Necrocosm into a panic, wouldn't it? They'll all be getting ready to shoot their neighbors."

"That would do it." Thomas liked the idea.

"I think now we know why the secret cabal of Servants of All wanted you," Garrett said, amused. "This explains it."

Thomas had figured that out more than a year ago. The secret cabal had wanted their own weaponized version of Audavian.

"But they had brainwashers among them all along," Evenjos argued. "They could have used them instead of Thomas."

"They had no clue," Thomas said. His own biological father had possessed Audavian's power, but instead of using it for the betterment of all Servants of All, he had kept it secret. He had hoarded it for his own private use.

In contrast, Thomas's brainwashing power had been common knowledge right from the start. The Upward Governess had dug out his worst experiences in foster care and showed them to the whole Torth Majority.

"Ah," Evenjos said. "I suppose secrecy around that power makes sense. Audavian was pulled down by his own constituents once they realized he was brainwashing his allies."

"It is possible some Torth do know they can brainwash or twist minds," Thomas admitted. His biological father had been an example of that. "But it's a lot of pressure to sneak around in an empire full of mind readers. They may feel relief to have it out in the open."

"Did the secret cabal of Servants expect that you would change the minds of all 38.2 trillion Torth?" Kessa studied Thomas.

"They would have urged me to use my power judiciously," Thomas said, "on select individuals who were major social influencers."

"The Torth couldn't have boosted his power to the level needed to brainwash the entire Megacosm," Garrett said. "They don't know about linking." His forehead furrowed as he took another look at Thomas. "You need Ariock."

That was undeniable.

"Do you know where he is?" Garrett's gaze drilled into Thomas.

Thomas felt like a traitor. Ariock and Vy hadn't been gone for long. Just three days. Thomas had spent more than a month alone in various human places on Earth, picking trash in Dhaka and hiking around Mongolia.

"Ariock is still wearing his superluminal tracker," Thomas admitted. "Like all of us."

Garrett stood. "He might remove it."

"Let's give him one more day," Thomas said.

CHAPTER 14

PRESSURIZED STRENGTH

Ariock lay in a lush meadow even more colorful than a cartoon rainbow. A breeze riffled alien trees that looked like cotton candy. Every flower on this planet had crystal centers.

Vy petted the friendly little indigenous animals that nestled up to her. She looked content.

But instead of enjoying this remote alien paradise, Ariock couldn't stop thinking about the countless sapients who were suffering while he took a leave of absence. Was he being heartless and selfish? He gazed up at the daylight moons.

Go back! his inner moral compass shouted. *You've taken more than enough time off. Save the universe!*

Instead, he cuddled closer to Vy. They had devoted the last few days to simple, hedonistic pleasures, making up for years of tension. The relief was almost as good as the sex.

He didn't want it to end.

He didn't want Vy, or himself, to make the ultimate sacrifice. Why not camp in various wildernesses until the universe ended?

A popping sound caused Vy to jump and scamper under the blanket. The air smelled of ozone.

Ariock sat up, more saddened than startled. He had not removed the tracker stuck inside the pocket of his pants, which were crumpled on the ground nearby. Vy had one, too. He had considered getting rid of them, but he had decided to remain reachable. Maybe Thomas or Kessa would talk him into returning to civilization and doing his duty.

He almost regretted that now.

Ariock used his powers to levitate clothing. He and Vy were dressed within seconds.

He heard Evenjos sigh wistfully. Garrett spoke in a gruff voice. "It's up to you, Thomas."

With that, Garrett and Evenjos vanished. Ariock sensed their overwhelming double life spark depart, and Thomas stood there alone.

"I came up with a way to defeat the Death Architect," Thomas said. "But I'll need your help."

Of course. Not a surprise.

Ariock picked himself up and stood, towering over Thomas. He had worn an inhibitor patch every day for the past four days. Now he peeled it off, and the sky began to darken with clouds.

Anyone else would have been intimidated. Not Thomas. He wasn't fully grown, yet he had a way of looking formidable, even when dressed in understated clothes.

"This can't wait any longer," Thomas said. "I'm sorry. But we need you if we're going to save the universe."

It must be easy for the lone survivor to face the final battle. Thomas was guaranteed to survive. Vy would tumble into space, Garrett would be decapitated, and Ariock's fate wasn't mentioned at all. Only Thomas would emerge unscathed.

"I know we're asking a lot," Thomas said. "It's more than anyone should have to face."

No one else could do it, though.

Vy looked pained. But even she was nodding.

Ariock tried to agree. He tried to say that he would heroically sally forth and do anything that was required. But the words stuck in his throat.

There was a difference between bravery in the face of death and resignation to death. He always fought for survival, for freedom, for winning. Never for death.

Vy grasped his arm. "We're blessed," she said. "We've had everything. A lifetime crammed into a few years."

It didn't feel like a lifetime at all to Ariock. It felt like a beginning without a middle or an ending. He wanted a lot more life.

When he considered diving back into the struggle to save the universe, the despair of his nightmare rose up like bile inside his mind.

Fate was bigger than he was. Destiny had been orchestrated for him, not just by Garrett, but over millennia and a thousand generations, starting with an oracle who had known every pivotal event in his life. Ariock was supposed to bravely rush to meet it.

But instead of accepting a heroic death as his fate, he wanted to knock it aside and defeat it.

"What if I leave the heroics to the lone survivor?" Ariock said stiffly.

He could seize Vy and teleport away right now. It would be easy.

"Then you'd only get to enjoy yourself for a few days or weeks longer," Thomas said calmly. "Because you'd be letting the Death Architect win."

"Ariock." Vy grabbed his arm, and he got the hint. Whenever Vy grabbed him, it meant she had something significant to say. He had better listen.

He knelt to face her at eye level.

"You and I are not the only people in love." Vy grasped Ariock's face. "You started this journey by caring about people you've never met. That's one of the reasons I love you. You recognize the worth of other people. It never mattered to you whether they were born without the same advantages you have, or whether you know their life story or not. Well." She gestured. "There are a zillion people who have as much right to live as we do. They deserve a future as much as we do."

Ariock imagined alien families—and human families, too, for that matter—who expected to continue living. A thousand generations had suffered. Their descendants had finally won freedom, and if that was snatched away from them on the whim of a sociopathic Torth, wasn't that a sick joke? He couldn't let that happen.

Even if it meant leaving his fiancée to die in the black void of space?

"Garrett commanded me to brainwash you," Thomas said, as if he was remarking on the cloudy weather.

Ariock felt an unfurling sense of infinity at the edge of his bodily awareness. Maybe it was fate. Maybe it was his own potential stature, fully rested and more titanic than a hypergiant star. He could assume the gravity of this solar system. He could fight.

He just didn't want to fight a good friend.

"Garrett insisted that I make you return by any means necessary," Thomas said. "That's what he said. 'Ariock needs to be at the final battle, no matter what it takes.'"

Ariock got to his feet, sizing up the supergenius. Thomas would not actually zombify him. Would he?

"You're not going to . . ." Vy looked incredibly uneasy.

"No," Thomas said. "Of course not."

Ariock wanted to believe him.

"I won't take away your free will," Thomas said. "Even if that means dooming the universe. You're my friend. You might become my brother-in-law. As far as I'm concerned, your fate is entirely your own."

Ariock remained tense. He knew Thomas never told lies, but sometimes the boy did bend the truth. Sometimes he was ruthless.

Thomas backed away, beyond telepathy range. "I leave it up to you."

There was a time when Ariock would have risked this heroic death without hesitation. He used to take serious risks to protect Vy, Cherise, Kessa, and Thomas, even when he'd barely known who they were. All he had known was that they were more worthwhile than himself.

He no longer felt that way.

But he also remembered vowing that he would never become as callous as elders like Garrett and Evenjos. Was he still as vulnerable—as human—as he had been back then?

There were so many people in the galaxy, a webwork of interconnected loved ones. That network was more precious than the Megacosm. It was the whole point of existence. Vy was willing to die for all those strangers. She was willing, because strangers could become friends.

Vy had once been a stranger in Ariock's home. He had once been a stranger to her.

"I am with you," Vy told Ariock in a whisper. "Come what may."

Trust glowed in her eyes. She trusted Ariock to save the universe. She trusted him to figure out a way to escape the final prophecy and save everyone.

That was bravery.

Ariock let his awareness unfurl for a moment, cosmic in scope, yet he was also human in all the important ways. There was more to being human than humility. It was in the small moments. Touches. Laughter about silly things that didn't matter. The vulnerability that came with having a body that had various flaws.

Love.

Maybe that was eternal, even if his body died.

"I, uh, could make it easier for you," Thomas said, shy and hesitant. "Only if I have your permission, of course."

"What do you mean?" Ariock demanded.

"In the long-gone era of Evenjos," Thomas said, "there were, uh, black-market telepaths who used a very mild form of brainwashing. They helped addicts kick their addictions and warriors face battle without fear. The power of suggestion wears off. It's temporary. There are no long-term side effects."

Ariock nearly condemned Thomas for keeping such a sinister secret. But then again, he understood why Thomas was always downplaying his powers.

Those who knew Thomas knew he would never hurt friends on purpose. Everyone else was too terrified of him to be his friend.

"You can make Ariock forget his nightmare?" Vy asked.

"I can," Thomas said. "Temporarily. And only with his permission."

"It won't damage him?" Vy asked.

"No." Thomas shook his head. "The effect will wear off after a day."

Wasn't a daring hero better than a reluctant one?

Ariock knew that in battle, he was at peak performance only when he stopped caring about collateral damage. He was at his most unstoppable when he didn't have worries.

"Do it," he told Thomas.

The boy looked surprised.

Ariock knelt. "It's the only way I'm going to be able to do this. Erase my worries for a day. I give you my permission." He swallowed his fears, and added the truth. "I trust you."

Thomas had risked a lot by coming here alone and admitting that he could have brainwashed Ariock. That was a show of trust and respect. He deserved the same. This was what friendship was.

Thomas solemnly stepped forward. He held a hand out and touched Ariock's forehead.

Ariock felt his fears ease away.

The threat to Vy wasn't a certainty. It was a nightmare without context. It was a vague hint from a moldy book.

It was nothing.

CHAPTER 15

INTO THE NECROCOSM

The galaverse hall was decked out for the biggest victory celebration yet.

Bioluminescent vines and flowers accented hundreds of slender pillars, with semitransparent battles playing between them. There was beauty even in faraway violence. It was a feast for Cherise's eyes. The real-time news feeds filled slots from the crystal floor all the way up to the holographic ceiling, where a smattering of stars gave the impression of infinite space.

"Just a few minutes left." Vy sat next to Cherise, eyeing the elongated hourglass that dominated the central dais. Glowing, multihued sand fell through the column's waist in a steady trickle.

The heroes of prophecy did not need to ride in on lions or radiate sunlight. They only waved to the crowd. Dignitaries and battle leaders cheered as Thomas strode up the main aisle, followed by Garrett, Evenjos, and Ariock.

"They look best when they're not wearing battle armor," Vy said with a proud smile.

"Yeah." Cherise prepared her sketching pens. A blank page waited on her lap.

She didn't know how her foster sister could be so sublimely happy while a prophesied doom hung over her head. Apparently, Ariock had had a recurring nightmare hinting that Vy might suffocate in outer space.

And the lone survivor would be Thomas.

There was no way to escape or defy a predicted future. The public did not yet know what was in store, but if they knew, Cherise wondered if they would be so cheerful.

"There's nowhere to sit," Garrett grumped.

"It will only take a few minutes," Thomas assured him.

Cherise began to draw the heroes as they arranged themselves on the dais.

She was no oracle, but she understood the importance of artistically capturing momentous events. When Thomas destroyed the last vestiges of the Torth Megacosm—the Necrocosm—she wanted to render that moment onto paper. She could give it more emotional impact than a photograph would provide.

"Thomas," Evenjos said. "Can I ask you to leave us for a minute? I wish to say something to the others."

"He'll just absorb the conversation the instant he comes back," Garrett said dryly.

"Pretty much," Thomas admitted, walking away.

"I know," Evenjos said. "I just want a minute without him listening."

Thomas left without protest. He faded from sight behind veils of holographic cities on alien worlds.

Cherise could not help but contrast his behavior to that of other Yeresunsa she knew. Flen would have said something bitter and resentful before exiting. He would have taken the exclusion as a personal insult.

Thomas rarely seemed offended.

Well, it was probably easy to be benevolent and easygoing when you were the most powerful authority in the galaxy.

Maybe it wasn't such a good thing that Thomas habitually bottled up his feelings. Cherise raised her eyes to a news feed where grim-faced albinos hurled lightning at Torth Red Ranks. The view was too far away to make out individual faces, but judging by the urban moonscape, it could be Permafrost City. That was where Flen was exiled to.

He was at his best when slaughtering Torth.

What would he do without war to keep him occupied? Hopefully he would find a way to replace his justifiable rage.

Cherise shifted her focus to the three heroes standing in front of the glowing hourglass, illuminated by clusters of spotlights. She layered in the details of Evenjos's tiara and wings.

"We are about to give Thomas enough power to take over the galaxy," Evenjos said, leaning close to Garrett and Ariock so she could speak in a tone of confidentiality. "Are you both sure this is the wisest course of action?"

"Now isn't the time to back out," Garrett said. "We're committed."

"We still have time." Evenjos indicated the towering hourglass.

"It's not that much power," Ariock said.

Evenjos gave him a look that begged to know what universe he was in.

"I mean," Ariock said, "my sphere of influence encompasses a solar system, so together, we aren't giving him much more than that."

"He is going to brainwash billions or trillions of mind readers," Evenjos said. "With powers. He could usurp us in an instant."

Cherise supposed that was a legitimate concern. Still, Evenjos's skepticism reminded her of Mrs. Hollander, as well as scientists and other adults from their life on Earth.

She exchanged glances with Vy. Her foster sister rolled her eyes, and Cherise smiled. They were both familiar with wrong doubts about Thomas.

"Once we are linked with him," Evenjos went on, "none of our possible self-defenses will work. He will be in total control, and he can twist our minds faster than we can possibly react. Do you realize that?"

"You're being unfair," Ariock rumbled. "Do you honestly think—"

"I like him, too," Evenjos cut in with fierce defensiveness. "I trust him. I consider him my friend."

Ariock closed his mouth. He looked confused.

"But . . ." Evenjos bit at her lip, as if ashamed. "I also liked and trusted Elome."

Cherise had been prepared to defend Thomas. Instead, she felt herself sympathizing with the former goddess-empress.

Trust could be broken. Friendships could curdle. Those who ought to be the best people sometimes turned out to be the worst. That was a truth. Not everyone knew it, not everyone learned it, but those who did never forgot.

Cherise had done her best to put aside her bitter memory of yellow-eyed Thomas tormenting her. She understood that he had done it to save her life. His reasons were good. But that act had levered a rift between them, and other friendships had grown in that rift. Cherise still felt Flen's caresses. She still saw his caring smile in her mind.

Judging by Thomas's occasional melancholy, he also yearned for someone else. The Pink Screwdriver? Or the Upward Governess?

Cherise didn't begrudge him for his unspoken yearnings. There was an undeniable chemistry that existed between telepaths, particularly telepathic supergeniuses. Who else was like them?

Not Cherise.

She loved Thomas. Part of her would always love him, but she wasn't sure she could embrace the power differential between herself and him the way Vy did with Ariock. There was no inhibitor for mental gigantism. Even if some procedure could reduce Thomas's brain to a normal level of intelligence, Cherise didn't actually want that. She would never excoriate the brilliance that made him who he was.

"It is possible he could even brainwash us by accident," Evenjos was saying. "We are going to loan him more power than any mind controller has ever wielded before. We don't know what that will do."

The Dovanacks exchanged uneasy looks. Everyone knew that Thomas's power was no laughing matter.

"I don't see what choice we have," Garrett said. "It's not like we have better ideas."

"That's exactly it," Evenjos said. "We are under time pressure." She indicated the hourglass. The sand had almost run out. "I am not saying Thomas engineered these circumstances. Or rather, he did, but I hope not with nefarious intentions. I believe he is our friend." She shivered. "I only wish we had more time to weigh the implications."

Garrett hugged her.

Evenjos leaned into his embrace, clutching him. "I'm scared."

It was a compelling image. Despite their godlike powers, despite their invincibility, Cherise had learned that they would not have eternity together. Garrett was doomed, according to an ancient prophecy. Evenjos probably knew it, too.

Cherise glanced at Vy. She wanted to include her foster sister in the heroic image.

The hectic messengers in the hall skidded to a halt so they could watch the final moments of the hourglass. The same must be happening in council rooms throughout the galaxy. Planetary consuls and military mayors had been briefed on what to expect. Soon they would bear witness to the end of one galactic empire and the birth of a new one.

How many people trusted Thomas to do what he'd promised?

A surprising number, Cherise guessed. She talked with former slaves every day. They lived in an age of miracles. Nothing surprised them. So what if a Torth girl could magically explode the galaxy? A liberated gladiator with infinite strength was sure to triumph, because a long-dead oracle said so. Why worry?

Thomas emerged from a cascade of holographs. "It's getting close to time."

"We trust you," Ariock said in a tone of reassurance.

Thomas smiled in his young but ancient way. He must have absorbed the fact that Evenjos feared he would turn into a galactic megalomaniac, but he didn't look offended as he went to stand between his friends.

He was the same boy Cherise had met in the Hollander home years ago.

"I wish we could help with the power boost," Vy said wistfully, watching the heroes clasp each other's arms. "Humans are supposed to be amplifiers, but it's like our power is locked away."

Cherise had tried to link with Flen and boost his Yeresunsa powers. Vy had admittedly tried to do the same with Ariock. They'd failed. If there was a way to unleash the power of humans, it had yet to be discovered.

Maybe humans were only valuable as breeders.

Cherise inwardly resolved to remain single, if that was the case. She wanted to be valued for her art above all else.

Thomas would understand.

The air began to sparkle. Dust floated, caught in eddies of excess power. Loose parts of Cherise's clothing billowed, levitated by the magic radiating from her friends.

Judging by Thomas's distant gaze, he had ascended into the Necrocosm.

EXPONENTIAL

TORTH! Thomas thought, making his attention-seeking boldly public.

The dregs of Torth civilization tuned into his massive mind like moths attracted to moonlight, like flowers opening to the sun. *Why is the Conqueror clamoring for attention?* many wondered.

Has He come to gloat?

Or will He beg for Us to join Him, as usual?

Bah!

Go away, Conqueror!

None of Us are stupid enough to kneel before Your minions!

We are TRUE TORTH!

Thomas smiled joylessly. They probably deserved this.

His own biological father had been like these fanatics, loyal to a fault. What a misguided tragedy. The Somehow Nexus was beyond salvation, dead, but most of these cultists could be saved.

Thomas hid his true goal beneath cascades of mundane trivia.

He told the death cultists, *I AM WILLING TO FORGIVE YOUR TERRORIST ATTACKS AND MURDERS OF MY PEOPLE.* Meanwhile, he surreptitiously collated each pinhead of a mind. He privately categorized every individual, figuring out whom to target. *BUT I NEED YOUR UNDIVIDED ATTENTION. I WILL ONLY COMMUNICATE THIS ONCE.*

Intense interest needled Thomas. ?????????????????????????????????

More and more Torth piled into his mind. Part of Thomas marveled at their individuality. There was beauty in the patterns of the masses. They mimicked the invisible yet elegant mathematics that comprised the material universe.

YOU WILL NEVER GET A SECOND CHANCE, he warned the fractal crowds, analyzing individuals while they poked their neighbors or awakened their sleeping comrades.

He waited until their collective curiosity boiled at a feverish pitch. Then he stoked it higher.

SOME OF YOU HAVE A POWER TO BRAINWASH, he let them know. *I (AND I ALONE) KNOW WHICH ONES AMONG YOU HOLD THAT INCREDIBLE POWER.*

Stunned disbelief. ?!?!?!?!?!?!?!?

The Necrocosm stuttered. Death cultists all but tripped over each other's minds in their eagerness to orbit the Conqueror and learn what secrets he was about to reveal.

One lone voice protested.

She would have been lost amid the waves of eager anticipation, except that her mind was enormous enough to rival that of the Conqueror. The sheer weight of her thoughts tugged at his millions of orbiters, dividing their attention.

REJECT HIM, the Death Architect warned. *SHUT YOUR MINDS TO HIM. HE SEEKS TO DESTROY (ME) US.*

The Conqueror rejected her accusation. *I AM HERE TO HEAL THE DIVIDE BETWEEN ALL TORTH.* He mentally opened imaginary arms that were large enough to engulf millions of wayward souls. *WHY NOT TAKE A VOTE LIKE CIVILIZED PEOPLE? DO YOU COLLECTIVELY WISH TO LET A SINGLE INDIVIDUAL DECIDE WHAT IS BEST FOR ALL?*

The Majority swirled. Voting seemed like a peacetime luxury.

But they remembered peace. They did yearn for harmonious decision-making. That was how things ought to be.

WHO WISHES TO LEARN HOW TO USE YOUR DORMANT MENTAL POWERS? Thomas wondered, barely aware as Ariock and his other heroic friends took hold of him. *COME. YOU MAY ALL TAKE A LESSON FROM ME.*

NO! the Death Architect roared. *REJECT HIM! YOU MUST REJECT HIM!*

But she offered no alternative lure. She gave no explanation.

Some of the death cultists were curious enough to inspect the Conqueror's mood. They discovered honesty. Mind readers could not lie to each other in the Necrocosm.

I WILL NOT KEEP YOU IN THE DARK. Thomas welcomed all seekers of knowledge. Unlike the Death Architect, he wished to inform them of what they were capable of. *I WILL SHARE. I WELCOME ALL.*

Some of the most die-hard death cultists felt torn.

Most, however, checked in with others, eager to hold a vote the way they used to, back when the Torth Empire had been mighty and wholly united. They did not appreciate how secretive the Death Architect was. She ordered people around like a tyrant, never offering rewards. That wasn't the Torth way.

The Conqueror might be a dangerous tyrant, but at least he embodied something of the old Torth spirit. He wanted to share.

HE WILL SHARE POISON! the Death Architect insisted. *I KNOW WHAT IS BEST FOR ALL OF YOU. WORSHIP ME OR YOU WILL BE ENSLAVED!*

Thomas let her rant. Her passion was only a pale imitation of true emotions. She was faking her concern, and everyone knew it.

Her nonstop tranquility used to be attractive, back when the Megacosm had sought stability. But the masses were burned out on her brand of stability. They wanted a leader who truly cared about them.

I CARE ABOUT EACH AND EVERY ONE OF YOU, Thomas assured them.

It was nothing but the truth. He was able to acknowledge the personal and unique merits of every influential Torth within his audience, and they truly appreciated that much individual attention. They felt seen.

The Death Architect did not groom individuals for leadership, the way the Servants of All used to do. The Death Architect never offered promotions or rewards. She did not shower her upper ranks with trust.

LET ME SHOW YOU THE SECRET. Thomas urged each high rank to rally their favorite orbiters, who rallied still more.

They came to him in droves. They swarmed him, eagerly attentive, knowing that he never lied.

IT'S A TRAP! the Death Architect warned.

But her warning failed to grab attention the way a blared alarm or a mental scream would have done. Only a few Torth heeded her and dropped out of the Necrocosm.

The rest rushed into orbit around the mind of the Conqueror.

You are a brainwasher. So are you. Thomas began to point them out.

Their comrades and neighbors stiffened, wary of anyone who held nefarious personal power. They checked their blaster gloves, just in case they might have to shoot in self-defense. They had not quite expected the Conqueror to point out actual brainwashers. They had just wanted some generalized instructions.

And you (and you) andyouandyouanyoayuyuyuyuyuyuyuyu. Thomas sped up the identifications.

Meanwhile, in the corporeal world, he squeezed the hands of his friends.

This was how sharing ought to be. Not casual, but intimate. His friends held him . . .

. . . and gave him more power than he could imagine.

There was a difference between absorbed experiences and firsthand experiences. Now Thomas felt the difference between knowing Ariock's strength and having Ariock's strength. Waves of power charged him up until he trembled. Tears leaked from his glowing, hot eyes. For the first time in his life, he knew with utter certainty that he had not been born to ascend to godhood. This was too much power.

The last remnants of the boy he used to be vaporized. Innocence and vulnerability fell away. He was all-knowing. All-seeing. All-powerful. Almighty.

The sudden wariness from Evenjos and Garrett seemed utterly insignificant.

Thomas directed a surge of power into the orbiters he had secretly chosen as his ideal vessels. He no longer had to hold their attention, because he had become undeniable. He was truth itself. He gripped their minds and powered right past their reservations and straight into their cores.

MINE.

He inhabited a fractal of Torth. He seized a thousand minds at once.

MY VASSALS.

He pressed his will upon their minds and forced them to absorb his expertise on brainwashing. *LEARN.* And so they did. Within an instant, they learned how to invade other minds, how to drill into their core, how to gently massage other people's moods and emotions until they were receptive to unthinkable ideas. They learned how to pressure others with a subtle trickle of power.

Now for the mass twist.

SPREAD SURRENDER.

His chosen vassals became extensions of his will. They were so overwhelmed with their new knowledge and power and duty, they had no room to examine it. Unable to fight his power of suggestion, they immediately reached out and made power-induced suggestions to their neighbors and comrades.

Surrender to the Conqueror.

Kneel.

Submit.

That message rippled and spread throughout the Necrocosm, leaping from the vessels to their orbiters, from the epicenter to the outer reaches.

The Conqueror seized another fractal, another thousand minds, and did it again, all within a microsecond, too fast for the Majority of death cultists to register what was happening. And again.

Some distant part of himself, still in touch with the vessel that contained his mortal brain, noted warmth tricking toward his mouth. A nosebleed. Another distant part of him worried about an aneurysm or a stroke. He wielded the power of a god, but his body was too fragile, unused to so much power.

Torth combatants tried to run. They tried to escape. But telepathy gas filled the forums and the plazas and the space stations where they ruled. That had been set up beforehand by subversive slaves. The death cultists had been blissfully unaware of it—until now.

Anyone within the vicinity of a brainwasher could not outrun the message.

Rosy Ranks and Servants of All became unwilling battery packs. Brainwashing vassals mentally instructed them to come close, to link, to offer up their own raw strength.

They joined hands.

They boosted the signal.

YOU ARE CONQUERED. The Conqueror conveyed pure truth. He rode the crest of unimaginable power while peering through a million pairs of eyes and understanding a million alien souls. *KNEEL.*

His vassals knelt.

GIVE AWAY YOUR WEAPONS.

Torth raiders went from attack mode to willing surrender. Battles faltered on many thousands of planets. Death cultists bowed down, and aliens shot many of them before realizing that their enemies had dropped to their knees and stripped off their blaster gloves.

CEDE CONTROL. SURRENDER TO MY PEOPLE.

Monolithic space rigs spun out of control as their operators ceased to carry out precise orders.

A Torth dreadnought gave up and was bombed into oblivion.

Neutron star stations shut down. The kneelers aboard those rigs no longer wanted to cause trouble for their new lord, the Conqueror.

Transports crashed. Some of the wrecks burst into flames.

Weptolyso's soldiers were striking hard and fast everywhere. Squadrons accidentally assassinated Torth champions who had suddenly knelt and surrendered.

The Conqueror attempted to seize the hugely complex mind of the Death Architect, but she was wily. She dropped out of the dying Necrocosm in that millisecond, preserving her own free will.

So the Death Architect wasn't around to see the final gasps of her civilization. She did not experience Torth brainwashers altering the minds of their neighbors and orbiters en masse. She did not see her carefully constructed machinery crash and burn.

She was not around when the final iteration of the Necrocosm collapsed into nothingness.

But the Conqueror experienced it.

Brainwashed converts dropped out of various mental audiences, aware that conspiracy—a mental language—was against the law of the civilization which they had just embraced. The few remaining surviving cultists dropped out as well, unwilling to risk being brainwashed. Veteran penitents knew better than to ascend. Not when any alien could use telepathy gas to see what they were learning or pondering.

The last echoes of thought faded away.

The Conqueror listened to an eerie, empty, echoing quietude more profound than any silence he had ever known.

Holographs displayed celebrations. A few isolated Torth continued to fight, but they looked confused and terrified, their access to knowledge cut off, their comrades missing.

They gave up. They had to.

Soldiers collared them.

Alien civilians emerged, whooping in triumph. Soldiers jumped off hoverbikes and grabbed each other with the joy of unexpected victory. Mer nerctan populations swayed their bony heads in sync. Crowds of nussians leaped up and down, causing buildings to shake. Ummins shot streamers into the air or set off their versions of fireworks.

The Conqueror could not hear the celebrations. The hall was silent, the holographic displays lacking audio.

Tears streamed down his cheeks along with a trickle of blood from his nosebleed. He let go of his friends. He shoved them away.

The Necrocosm would never reemerge. The Megacosm was gone forever. The few defiant Torth who survived today were too few and too fragile to form the basis of a civilization. They dared not mentally gather. Not when Thomas and trillions of penitents might be listening at any time. They were dregs.

And they were done.

Superluminal transmissions would replace the purpose the Megacosm had served. But Thomas knew that his satellite network was a poor substitute for the grandeur he had destroyed.

He had killed an immensity.

Not just people. Not just their individuated wisdom. He had killed their collective knowledge.

Thomas listened. He held his mind open for seconds that stretched like eons. He longed to hear someone else even as he dreaded it.

Nothing.

The vast stretches of space between stars were devoid of thoughts.

It was all deadness.

PART FIVE

"The Torth Empire never understood the concept of a soul. It's an elusive concept. There is no fixed set of properties, no standard for comparison, yet the word does have meaning. A soul has the capacity for love and friendship and an ability to sympathize, plus their own individuality. So it defies definition, even in the language of pure imagination."

—Cherise Chavez

COMMANDER ONE

She had once led all living Torth in existence, and thus had commanded all living things.

Now she stared into a black void.

Space was as desolate as what remained of the galactic empire she used to rule. Her planets. Her armadas. The slaves her people had owned. All were gone.

Even the audience in her head was gone, leaving the disgraced Commander utterly alone and adrift in the escape pod she had used to flee the cataclysm.

She had been aboard a mining rig when it happened. A fellow Servant of All known as the Ever Rascal had suddenly clasped hands with an unranked adolescent. It turned out the adolescent had a terrible power to brainwash everyone in the vicinity. Boosted by the Ever Rascal's power, that adolescent had . . .

Well.

The disgraced Commander had fled from all the suddenly docile kneelers, throwing desperate Torth out of her way so she could take the last escape pod and keep her free will.

Now all she had left was the supremacy of being a Torth. She still had her own personal freedom.

That was something.

She retracted her faceplate, allowing herself to breathe slightly more freely inside the narrow confines of the escape pod. She was free, but she was a corpse. Her bones knew it. The endless silence inside her head confirmed it.

She touched one of the horns of her mantle of office. She had teleported to the city where her political detractors had stored the mantle, and now she wore it again. The Majority had expected to bestow it upon the next Commander they elected, but that was a bygone era. There would be no future Commanders of All Living Things.

She was the last.

The disgraced Commander studied her hands, encased in skintight armored gloves. At one hundred and eighty-eight years old, she was a lanky skeleton, frail and feeble despite many biomimetic enhancements. This escape pod lacked food, it lacked slaves, and there was no way to navigate to the nearest temporal stream.

Like all Torth, she relied on the Megacosm for cosmic maps. The Megacosm was her support system, her emergency backup, her everything.

Without the Megacosm or the Necrocosm? She was no more consequential than a speck of dust.

She supposed she could teleport somewhere. Might she retire to a wilderness planet and live the remainder of her life in miserable seclusion?

No doubt there were former Servants of All copulating with humans on Earth right now, attempting to leave some sort of personal legacy in the form of hybrid offspring. They had lost their audiences and any chance of being remembered for eternity. Their offspring might be powerful enough to wield some sort of influence over the native savages.

But they would not be Torth.

The disgraced Commander was too old to be a gamete donor, anyway. She could not bear children, even if she were willing to endure such a humiliating and disgusting activity. All she could do on Earth was die.

She had no wish to end her life where savages might laugh at her corpse or bury her in a dirty hole.

There was only one seminoble ending for her, a superior being who used to rule the galaxy.

The manual switch to open the airlock was bright and obvious. It seemed to whisper that she was a disgrace. She ought to die. That button filled in for all the mental voices she no longer heard.

She hesitated, reflecting upon the many, many things she should have done differently.

The Conqueror. She should have killed him back when he was weak and she was powerful. That was a frequent lament in her mind, since it was her single biggest point of failure. The Giant as well.

But her more recent failures were just as terrible.

Yeresunsa could boost their powers through linking. Why hadn't that ever occurred to her? Why hadn't she ever thought to experiment with intimate connections, no matter how alien intimacy was?

The Conqueror had not hesitated to use the dark magic of friendship in order to destroy her civilization.

He had linked with his friends and then brainwashed her colleagues. Fellow Servants of All had suddenly turned against their peers and low ranks. They might still be rushing through cities and stations and outposts, brainwashing any Torth they came across. A wave of meek imperatives—*surrender*—had crashed through the remnants of the Torth population like a supernova. There had been no way to stop it.

But there had been a way to prevent it.

The disgraced Commander should have had all Yeresunsa killed shortly after the cabal revealed itself. The Majority, in its collective wisdom, had known that Yeresunsa were problematic. They had voted to execute all Servants of All.

Rightly so.

But instead of agreeing to lie down and die, the disgraced Commander had foolishly insisted on becoming a champion. She had allowed her own selfish desire for self-preservation to take priority, even above the preservation of Torth civilization. She and her fellow Servants of All had postponed their own executions and influenced the Majority to let them live for a while longer.

Now those same Servants of All had just destroyed the free will of almost all the surviving superior beings in the galaxy.

They had become weaponized minions of the Conqueror.

The disgraced Commander should have guessed he would try something like this. She had been shortsighted.

She waited for the audience in her head to concur. But no one cared. The cold, thoughtless universe had no judgment to offer.

She would die alone.

That was terrible. But at the same time, oddly, she felt more free than she ever had before. She did not need to worry about feedback the next time she ascended, because she would never ascend again. She did not have to consider what other Torth thought. Instead of catering to the Majority . . .

Well. She supposed she *was* the Majority now.

She could vote for anything.

If she elected herself Commander of All Living Things? Then that was the will of the current Majority. She would be the Commander.

She was the Commander again.

No one voted against her.

The Commander bent over in the confined space and strapped her scimitar to her armored back. Perhaps she would pay the Conqueror a visit. Should she try to kill him for all the destruction he had wrought?

She gave it a quick vote. Yes.

Or . . .

She had another suggestion. She could use her champion's weapon to chop the head off the abhorrent little girl who had given it to her.

The Commander instinctively tried to ascend, to share her reaction. The wretched Death Architect must have made some catastrophically wrong calculations! So much for her sunny promises to destroy the enemies!

But there was nowhere to ascend to. No Megacosm, no Necrocosm, no orbiters, no other minds.

Well, she was tempted to kill the Death Architect anyway. After all, she still remembered the convoluted route to that obscure asteroid in the Araya Moon Belt. She might very well be the only surviving person in existence who actually knew how to visit that gloomy lair.

Nah.

The lair was laced with deadly traps, and anyhow, without the Necrocosm, the child was entombed. It wasn't the Isolatorium, but it was the next best thing. The Death Architect's cataclysmic failure had earned her a drawn-out death amid her battlebeasts. That was justice.

The Commander sealed her faceplate. Invulnerability was always a good idea when one went into enemy territory, and the whole galaxy was now enemy territory. She would teleport to Freedomland and see whom she might assassinate.

A message light blinked in the corner of the navigation display.

The Commander frowned at the transmission signal, disbelieving. The Death Architect had enabled ship-to-ship messages, but there were no more Torth left. Were there? The nearest vessel, that mining station, was now full of brainwashed converts who obeyed the Conqueror.

Might this message be a relay from him? Some last cruel jab?

Or . . .

The Death Architect had relied on the Necrocosm to direct her loyalists. Now that that was wiped out . . .

Might this message come all the way from the Araya Moon Belt?

The Commander opened her faceplate and activated the message to play it.

It coalesced in a holographic projection, bright against the blackness of space. A womanly figure took shape. To the Commander, any visage so fresh-faced might as well belong to a child, although this person was physically mature. Her braided red hair was recognizable.

It was the silly human with an enhanced leg, the one whom the Giant was emotionally bonded to.

As the Commander watched, the holograph of the lover suffered a gruesome attack. Something sliced through her neck. Her head came off.

The blood was crudely animated, since it was just a graphical simulation wrought by a single imagination, rather than a detailed transference powered by many hundreds of collective minds.

Another crude holograph took shape. The Giant. The simulated version of him looked overwrought and horrified.

The holographs faded away.

That was the entirety of the message.

The Commander replayed it. Torth used crude glyphs in the absence of a telepathic connection, but this was more sophisticated. It was like pure imagination transformed into a visual representation. Someone with impressive technological skill had concocted it.

She guessed the Death Architect must have sent this message to every ship, shuttle, and station within her technological purview.

But why?

The Commander compressed her thin lips and forced herself to think.

Clearly, the Death Architect had been working on some grand scheme before her nemesis obliterated the Necrocosm. She had kept her loyalists busy with all kinds of mysterious tasks. They had worked in factories for gravitational carpeting. They had drilled wells into neutron stars to extract astronomically dangerous degenerate matter.

In fact, the bombings and other attacks upon enemy troops had almost seemed like a sideshow.

I will destroy the enemies, the Death Architect had promised.

She had radiated confidence.

Was she still confident of victory even now, entombed on her asteroid? Was the Death Architect capable of destroying the Conqueror and reconstituting the actual Megacosm? Was that possible?

The Commander found herself yearning. She kept trying to ascend, to learn more, but the galaxy was lonely and silent.

Perhaps the Death Architect wanted to enrage the Giant, as she had done before, to make him go charging blindly into a trap? Could he get sucked into an artificially created black hole? Was that what the Death Architect had been constructing?

The Commander had never studied astrophysics. She wasn't sure if anything could defeat the seemingly invincible Giant. But the Death Architect had outsmarted him before.

It seemed possible.

Other isolated survivors like herself would receive this message. But how many of them could teleport?

And how many would dare to teleport directly into the Giant's stronghold and risk attacking his most beloved companion? Especially since the Conqueror must be monitoring Torth equipment, using his minions to watch and listen. He would certainly warn the Giant.

The Commander knew that she was very likely the only person willing and capable of carrying out this mission. It might get her killed—but it might restore the Torth Empire to its glorious heights.

She was the Majority.

She held a quick vote and verified that, yes, she was critical to restoring civilization. She mattered.

She represented All.

She adjusted her scimitar, put herself into a clairvoyant trance, and zoomed to Reject-20, the planet of Freedomland. It might take a while to locate the one-legged human. The Commander might need to stalk her prey, ghosting repeatedly until she found the human alone and apart from her ultrapowerful protector.

But the Commander was old enough to hunt with patience.

She was no longer just the disgraced Commander. She was also the Majority. She *(We)* had a lot to live up to.

She *(We)* dared not fail the Torth Empire again. Not ever again.

CHAPTER 2

RICHER THAN ARIOCK

Vy walked around the sitting room, switching on telepathy gas emitters. She felt awkward, turning on telepathy gas when she was alone in a room, but members of her practice team would show up at any minute. Huchanu, Maerlo, Yishbaka, and Fru. They were mostly strangers to each other.

That was ideal. If Vy was going to share her mind, including intimate details of her life . . . well, she certainly wasn't going to do it in front of Ariock! Some thoughts between a couple ought to remain secret. Otherwise, where was the fun?

Vy's practice team hardly comprehended human biology. They wouldn't judge her.

Now that the room was prepared, Vy made it cozier. She added another glowing orb to the windowsill. Her mom would approve of the glow, the mineral fragrances, and other touches that added warmth.

Her thoughts began to feel echoey. That was the telepathy gas, reflecting her own mind back upon her.

It ought to make her feel extra safe. As Thomas had put it, *"Rogue Torth can't attack you with a pain seizure or twist your mind as long as you're on telepathy gas. You should use it frequently, until we can verify that all the remaining death cultists have given up or surrendered."*

As long as Vy was in a telepathy zone, she was—in theory—on equal footing with an average mind reader. And she was armed with inhibitor microdarts. Her prosthetic leg contained all kinds of weapons against Yeresunsa and other attackers.

And more than one superluminal tracker.

Ariock had insisted on that. He wouldn't let Vy out of his sight unless she was trackable, capable in a fight, and among friends. He had even suggested importing the Hollander family. Since she spent most nights cuddled with Ariock in his huge bed, her suite went unused. She could loan it to a friend.

A mournful chorus echoed from the streets below.

Vy stepped onto the open-air balcony and gazed down at the singing performers who led the funerary procession. As the Torth Empire had died, so had one of its last supergeniuses. Serette had breathed her last breath as the Necrocosm collapsed for the final time.

The deceased supergenius had more mourners than might be expected. Ariock, Thomas, Kessa, and Varktezo walked beside the bier, the place of honor for close family members. Lanterns swung from yokes across their shoulders.

Unfortunately, most of the other mourners seemed insincere. Thousands of aliens trailed the bier, all dressed up and proud to participate in a public spectacle. Vy wondered how many of them took note of Mondoyo's absence, and what they thought about it.

She gazed across the deepening dusk to where the academy blended with cliffs. The Dragon Tower was an obvious silhouette, with only a few lit windows. Mondoyo was in one of those rooms.

Alone.

Vy worried about him. Gossip never stopped, but she didn't think there was anything nefarious in Mondoyo's request to skip Serette's funerary procession. He had apparently asked to be left alone to mourn.

"If we are to avoid becoming Torth ourselves," Kessa had said during the last council meeting, *"we must stop branding people as inferiors in a way that can never be changed."*

Vy had agreed. Ariock had agreed.

"But how do we accomplish that?" Cherise had asked. *"A badge? That will only call attention to what they are. You can't change people's minds that easily."*

That was true. Anyone familiar with the penitents could see they had a long road ahead of them if they were ever going to be respectable members of society. Zai was an outstanding warrior, but it was hard to imagine anyone other than Ariock allowing her to command troops. Who would feel comfortable obeying a former Torth? Mondoyo was an elder supergenius, but if he floated down a street by himself, people were likely to throw garbage at him and ask where his overseer or lieutenant was.

"You're right," Kessa had acknowledged to Cherise and the rest of the council. *"But language is a direct path to people's hearts and minds. Just as we influenced people to stop thinking of mind readers as godlike Torth and to instead think of them as penitents, in atonement for their cruelties, so we should do again, for the redeemed ones."*

"What word could we use?" Vy had been mystified. She could not imagine a word with that much power.

"Humans." Kessa had looked at her. *"The redeemed penitents are humans."*

Vy kept mulling that over in the back of her mind.

There was an enormous difference between Torth and humans. Still, she automatically accepted certain mind readers as human, at least on a provisional basis. Thomas was human. It didn't matter that neither of his parents had been human. He was, and always would be, her brother.

Hadn't Mondoyo earned a similar status?

Vy thought of the heroic deeds Mondoyo had done to prove his worth. He had defied the Torth Majority and risked his life to join Thomas, bringing liberated slaves and Zai with him. He had influenced Serette to join him as well.

Thanks to Mondoyo and Serette, Vy and Ariock were able to have an intimate love life. The Twins had created the inhibitor patches that Ariock used every time he and Vy were alone together.

And immunity to the inhibitor had saved countless lives. The Twins were the reason why so many warriors survived today.

The Twins had broken the Torth Megacosm with a mental symphony.

And Mondoyo had done even more. He had invented improvements to military technology, empowering soldiers to defeat Torth in multiple battles. Mondoyo had personally dispensed real-time tactical advice during a few battles. According to rumors, he had actually predicted several Torth attacks, thereby saving entire city populations.

Who knew what other miracles Mondoyo would go on to invent or pioneer after he received regeneration healing?

He has earned human status, Vy knew. Her own thoughts echoed the sentiment back to her, buoyed by telepathy gas.

Not all humans would adopt Mondoyo, Vy supposed. But she would be honored to include such a hero as a member of the human race, and even as a member of her family. Could she adopt him as her brother?

Not everyone had a loving family. Vy supposed that in one way, she was rich beyond measure.

She had been rich in this way even before becoming a galactic princess. She had been born rich, even more so than Ariock. She was wealthier than the richest Torth.

And she was only just now realizing it.

She had endured hardships, but there was always someone protecting her, cherishing her, giving her a prosthetic leg, showing concern for her well-being. Not everyone had that. And she'd had it all her life.

She wanted to share some of her wealth. She decided that she would offer to adopt Mondoyo. The poor kid was so alone.

Someone knocked on the big, ornate door. Ah, her practice team was beginning to arrive.

Vy hurried to cross the room—but a skeletal wraith in dirty white armor materialized in front of her.

!!!

Vy stepped back, not believing her eyes. Had her brain regurgitated a horrific fragment from her own memory banks? Was this a hallucinatory side effect of using telepathy gas? Was it possible to get a bad batch of the stuff?

But the smell was real.

Ozone, which meant teleportation. Plus an elderly smell that reminded Vy of a nursing home.

The Commander of All Living Things was so enhanced, she no longer looked quite human. Instead, she fell into an uncanny valley of human resemblance, all sinew and armored carapace. She wore her mantle of office. Twisting horns swept off her bony shoulders, supporting a shroud-like cape. The height of her mantle, combined with her space boots, made her tower over Vy.

And those empty eyes! She looked like a zombie, except she was aware.

Vy reflexively brought up her knee to release a spray of inhibitor darts from her prosthetic. The latest generation of darts was designed to seek bare skin instead of armor. If that didn't work, Vy could release a pink cloud of inhibitor gas.

But she was already too late.

The Commander moved with superhuman agility, somersaulting out of harm's way and rolling behind Vy. She wielded a scimitar that could slice through armor, flesh, and bone with equal ease. She definitely planned to slice open *(the girl with the enhanced leg)* Vy. And once she killed the redhead? She would behead her and hide with the severed head until she recovered enough raw strength to teleport across the galaxy.

To the Death Architect's lair.

The Commander knew where the secret lair was!

Vy tumbled into a somersault, receiving a surprised *!!!* reaction from the Commander instead of a fatal blade injury. Telepathy gas made every impulse as clear as day.

Telepathy gas! The Commander had not expected that. *That stuff never should have been invented.*

No one else knew where the Death Architect resided. Not even Thomas could learn that. Vy tugged on her blaster glove and whirled to aim at the Commander's legs instead of her head. Doomsday was still a possibility unless Thomas confronted the Death Architect in person. He alone could twist her mind and force her to neutralize her universe-ending chain reaction.

!!!

The Commander stared at Vy with blank white eyes. Although she had the neutral expression of a corpse, she radiated emotion. Shock. Dismay. And a very stunned feeling of betrayal.

She had trusted the Death Architect.

Maybe not entirely, but a little bit. Enough to obey the little girl's holographic message to assassinate Vy. As a death cultist, she had anticipated death to the enemies, not death to everything and everyone in existence.

Not death to All.

Vy sensed the Commander tighten her grip on her scimitar, but her focus had shifted off Vy. She wanted to end this fight and hide so she could recover enough raw power to ghost across the galaxy. She wanted to escape.

No, Vy thought. She sprayed inhibitor darts at the Commander's long, bony face.

The Commander whirled away, radiating anger and uncertainty and fear.

An insistent knock sounded at the door. "Lady Vy?" a confident student called from the other side. "We're here! Should we just come in?"

Vy tuned out her concern for her practice team. There was too much at stake. This was a matter of universal importance.

As Thomas had explained it, the Death Architect almost certainly had a dead man's switch set up. The universe could go boom the instant she died. Absolutely no one should approach the dangerous supergenius except for Thomas.

Vy needed to detain the Commander and try to fish out the location of the Death Architect.

She dug into the woman's mind, searching for a cosmic route.

NO! The Commander was unused to having her inner self accessed by a mere (*human*) primitive. Yet she was also grappling with her own deteriorating certainties. Would the Death Architect actually destroy everything in existence? Weren't there safeguards?

Well, no. The Commander remembered that laws were gone, science was gone, and the Majority was reduced to just her. A scheming supergenius could do whatever she wished without worrying about judgment.

Vy sprayed more inhibitor darts, all the while scanning her enemy's thoughts. She examined runnels of determination. When she found one concerning the Death Architect, she traced that runnel deeper, past resentment, past murderous intentions, down to its bedrock of facts.

Mind probes were advanced telepathy. Vy was only a novice. She was painfully aware of her own inexperience, yet she had practiced enough to theorize how this might be done.

She drilled past facts she already knew, seeking more.

The cosmic route was too complex, with too many steps to remember in a glance. Vy would need to study the route in order to learn it.

No time. She tried to shower her enemy with inhibitor darts.

How (rude) dare you! The Commander dived behind a sofa. She would have vanished out of range if they were both Torth.

But they were not.

This was a roomful of telepathy gas, and their minds remained wide-open to each other.

The door opened.

Someone gasped.

Vy sensed a flood of worried thoughts and a flurry of motion. Her teammates were grabbing weapons.

Aware that she only had milliseconds before her attacker would get shot, Vy invaded the Commander's mind with all her determination and strength. She drilled down, seeking any key to the Death Architect's lair.

She connected with a core and—

!! /

/ !!

Air exploded out of Vy's lungs.

CHAPTER 3
LINKED

Excruciating pain robbed Vy of any ability to draw breath. There was no air. Her saliva bubbled. Her mouth burned with frost. She saw a rocky landscape in the starry darkness of space even as her vision clouded.

Space.

This wasn't the telepathy practice room. Judging by her plummeting sensation, she was in microgravity, which meant the rocks beneath her were not part of a planet at all. This was an asteroid.

Items from her practice room floated away from her. A glowing orb lamp. A rug. Some plush all-species chairs.

A terrified ummin.

Vy recognized Huchanu as one of her telepathy practice teammates. He was drifting away, beak open in a soundless scream, reaching out in futility. Frost blistered his exposed gray skin. His hand worked a blaster glove that might be frozen or jammed.

The Commander seized Vy by the arm and hauled her downward.

Vy wore two superluminal trackers, and she'd stored extra trackers inside her prosthetic leg. Thomas should be able to locate her. But how long would it take?

Cosmic phenomena might interfere with superluminal signals. Thomas would theoretically receive an alert across light-years, if it worked, and then convey the specifics to Ariock.

The Commander towed Vy inside the yawning chasm of an airlock. Chrome walls gave them smeary reflections in the dim starlight.

A gate overhead began to slide closed.

Some metal alloys could block superluminal tracking signals. Vy forced her hand past her skirt, tapping on her prosthetic with numb fingers. The compartment opened. Tiny metal cubes—trackers—floated out.

Vy couldn't be sure if she'd grabbed one tracker, or all three, or none. Her body was a blaze of pain. She made a tossing motion overhead and hoped that her frozen hand had let go.

Something tumbled into space. Vy could hardly see through the fog of her frozen eyeballs. She hoped she had sent a tracker away, like a wish. The tiny device might tumble for eons and never deliver. It was tenuous.

The gate slammed shut without a sound.

Vy descended through a soundless vacuum, as lightweight as a bubble, tugged by the Commander. Down. Into a hellish pit with reflective walls?

Everyone knew that mirrors deterred clairvoyants and teleporters. That might explain why Vy and the Commander had appeared on the asteroid's surface instead of inside this mysterious facility. Did that matter? Vy was losing consciousness, too long without air . . .

An inner gate whooshed open below her.

Vy heard it right after her ears popped. She felt artificial gravity along with a rush of air spewing from vents.

She gasped. She couldn't believe she was still alive, let alone conscious!

Her throat tasted like sour raspberries. Pins and needles took over her skin as she thawed out. Her ears were ringing.

She landed on a grated steel floor along with the Commander.

Gravity was light and gentle here. Despite the long fall, Vy's prosthetic took the brunt of the impact, and she was more or less unharmed.

She stood, ignoring dizziness. She wanted to be alert before the Commander could recover from hypoxia.

The stringy old Torth gasped on the floor. She had failed to seal her faceplate before they teleported.

It seemed they were both here by accident.

Well, it couldn't be entirely an accident. Someone had teleported them here.

Vy backed away from her enemy, moving farther into the gloomy corridor. She could only guess where she was. The Death Architect's lair? That was what she'd been searching for. That was where the Commander had wanted to go.

Vy couldn't be sure what had happened, since her mind was no longer harmoniously entangled with the Commander's. But she could almost piece together what had happened. Back in the sitting room, she had dug into the Commander's memories, seeking a route to the Death Architect's lair. And the Commander had . . .

What? Panicked?

Panic might give someone superhuman strength, but not even Garrett had enough raw strength to teleport with passengers. This was far beyond the scope of power of a single Torth. Only Ariock was strong enough to bring passengers, and he would never do something this cruel and clumsy. Ariock was too well practiced to be responsible for this mess.

Could the Commander have linked with someone extraordinarily powerful?

It must be someone whom she had not expected to boost her strength. She clearly had not intended to bring chairs and other things, like poor Huchanu, dying in the cold void of space.

Thomas had hinted that humans might be power augmenters, as well as breeding stock for ultrapowerful Yeresunsa.

Was this what he meant? Vy realized with shock.

Was *she* the catalyst?

Torth, Alashani, and humans formed a peculiar triangle. Thomas had said they were all related, and that humans were some sort of augmenting factor. In fact, hadn't Thomas invited Vy to join the Yeresunsa when they'd all linked in order to revive Ariock from his depletion coma?

At the time, Vy had thought he was just being inclusive. Now she wondered. Thomas must have suspected something about human power, but he hadn't known how to test it or unlock it.

Telepathy gas is the key, Vy realized.

Thanks to telepathy gas, she had drilled into the Commander's mind, just like a Torth giving someone a mind probe. She had connected with the Commander in a primal way, mind to mind, self to self.

She had linked with the Commander and boosted her raw power to an astronomical level.

In an eerily graceful motion, the Commander stood. Her face was corpselike in the dim glow of recessed light strips.

Vy still wore her blaster glove. She just wasn't sure it would shoot after exposure to space.

Meanwhile, the Commander's space armor included a blaster. In a showdown, the Commander would likely win. She had superhuman reflexes.

The Commander opened her thin-lipped jaw and uttered a syllable in a creaky whisper that sounded dead. "Come."

She beckoned with bony fingers.

As if Vy was her slave.

Vy steeled herself and took aim. She was not, and would never again be, a slave. If the Commander wanted to use her as a battery pack? No. Vy would be willing to link with Thomas or Ariock to enhance their power, but she would never voluntarily link with a Torth.

Vy thumbed the trigger.

A blast roared out and gouged a dent in the chrome wall behind where the Commander had stood. The old Torth had thrown herself aside, and now she was too close, coming at Vy like an alien nightmare.

Pain drilled into Vy's head.

For a moment, all the sickening hatred, terror, and helpless humiliation of slavery returned to Vy. She had to obey. She was nothing.

No.

That was wrong.

She was Lady Vy. She was the daughter of Elaine Hollander, friend to Kessa the Wise, sister of the Conqueror, and bride to Ariock Dovanack. The galaxy turned on her advice.

And she had power.

Her power might be locked away, but she knew it was there, no matter what an idiotic Torth thought about her primitive human heritage.

Vy suffered the pain seizure but followed it to its source. She could not read the Commander's mind. She had no way to navigate other than to blindly feel her way along a path that felt correct after so many practice sessions with telepathy gas.

Ariock avoided practice. He hated the way reading minds felt. But Vy had been taking more and more sessions, in part to better understand penitents, and in part so she could help them adjust to their new lives. If the redeemed penitents were going to be called human, she wanted to be involved.

The pain seizure involved a mental channel. Vy sensed it.

She retraced it to the Commander's mind and drilled in, throwing the pain right back at her.

For a moment, she thought she sensed (*!*) the Commander's shocked surprise.

Vy stood tall as the Commander flinched. That gave her an opening to attack. Vy had heard enough battle lore—and soaked up wartime memories through telepathy gas—to know that snap decisions mattered. So she aimed and thumbed the trigger.

The Commander deflected the blast with her scimitar blade.

The wily old Torth had drawn her durable weapon faster than Vy could track with her eyes. With such superhuman speed, the Commander could slice off Vy's head within a second.

Vy searched for an advantage. Any advantage.

The Commander's mantle made her too tall for the corridor. She had to crouch a bit. Vy knew, from late-night chats with Ariock, that he would wreck a ceiling or knock down walls if he felt too enclosed during a battle. One could not be effective as a fighter if they had to crouch or if they had trouble maneuvering.

That was one problem with size.

Vy backpedaled. She ducked under piping. This corridor had industrial pipes everywhere, although many looked broken or corroded.

The Commander was forced to duck. She came at Vy, but Vy was ready.

She took aim with her gloved palm, as a feint. Then she used her other hand to trigger her false knee.

It blasted a hole in the Commander's shroud.

The Commander hurled her scimitar as though it was a spear. Vy did not know she'd been sliced until her braid loosened, coming undone. The ionic blade had lopped off the ends of her hair.

The scimitar returned into the Commander's waiting grasp.

That was disconcerting. The Commander could have easily decapitated her just now.

One did not need telepathy gas to guess why she wanted Vy alive. The Commander was going to confront the Death Architect, and that was dangerous. She might want to re-tap her newly acquired incredible human power source.

Or she would do what Torth usually did when confronting a greater power: flee. In that case, she would want to bring Vy as a powerful hostage.

Not again. Vy was nobody's slave or hostage or battery pack.

The ground trembled. Vy hardly noticed, since she was busy with her prosthetic. She jerked her knee up, then kicked out. That action sent a spray of inhibitor microdarts toward the Commander. She might miss, but then again, the old Torth still had not raised her helmet's faceplate. Her papery skin was exposed and vulnerable.

The Commander spun, turning her shroud into a shield.

Vy cursed. Maybe she shouldn't try to nullify the sole reason why the Commander wanted her alive. If the Commander lost her powers, that would render Vy useless to her.

They stared at each other across a distance.

The Commander's jaw was set. That was a look of frustration.

The ground trembled like a train was bearing down on them.

Vy leaped to one side—just in time. Three knobby battlebeasts barreled out of the darkness, as fast and as heavy as speeding cars. Their enormous, toothless mouths opened wide, trailing drool. Two more skeletal battlebeasts emerged from the opposite end of the corridor.

No time to figure out attack and defense. Vy began blasting.

She was lucky to have two guns. With her prosthetic in action, none of the beasts could get close enough to snap her up in their jaws.

They tried. Snarling and snapping, they climbed over the body of a dying pack member.

Vy used to marvel that such ridiculous-looking aliens could be so deadly. Battlebeasts resembled toads, naked and usually bloated, without fur or armored skin or clothing. They didn't have claws or spikes. But they were enormous, on the same scale as nussians, and a large portion of their size was their mouths.

This bunch looked particularly lean. Starved?

Vy peered around the heap of toadlike bodies she had blasted to death and saw the Commander still struggling to fend off one last enraged battlebeast. Judging by the blood splatter and the corpses, she had used her scimitar to hold off the rest.

Vy stepped on a beast corpse. Once her knee was propped in the right direction, she fired a cannon blast.

The last battlebeast died.

The Commander stared toward Vy. Her emotionless face was hard to read, but Vy imagined perplexed shock inside her mind. She understood that Vy could have killed her and the battlebeast at the same time.

Mercy was an alien concept for most Torth.

"I want to stop the destruction of the universe," Vy said to the Commander. "Either help me or stay the hell out of my way."

CHAPTER 4

ACROSS THE COSMOS

"Bringer of Hope!"

"We love you!"

People on the sidelines cheered as if this was a victory celebration instead of a funerary procession. The few former Torth who had been permitted to join the crowd paid their respects, touching Serette's funeral casket like they were Alashani honoring a fallen warrior. Very few aliens did the same. Instead, they honored Ariock.

"Son of Storms!"

"Messiah!"

Perhaps Mondoyo's refusal to join this procession wasn't such a mystery. None of these people had known Serette.

Ariock had barely known her, either.

That made him feel guilty. Serette had helped to end the Torth era. Sure, she had invented a terrible way to defeat Ariock—apparently she was the primary mastermind behind insanity gas—but she had atoned. Now Ariock wished he could have talked a few more times with Serette, because she'd gone from villain to hero. She had helped destroy the Megacosm. Ariock had not witnessed her mental symphony, but he had heard about it from Thomas.

"Are you doing okay?" Ariock glanced down at Thomas, who walked next to him and Kessa. "If you need to take a break, everyone will understand."

Thomas had guarded his expression all day. A stranger might assume he was lost in thought, but Ariock knew better. Supergeniuses didn't get lost in thought. Not for more than a few seconds, anyway. That pensive look meant Thomas was struggling with emotions.

With Serette gone, Thomas was the eldest supergenius in existence. Mondoyo was nearly a full year younger than his partner had been. He remained cloistered in the Dragon Tower in order to grieve.

I understand about survivor's guilt, Ariock thought to his friend, skipping the tedium of language.

Thomas looked grateful and a little bit surprised. Maybe he hadn't expected Ariock to identify his problem.

We can blame Ah Jun, Ariock thought. The oracle was the main reason why Ariock and Thomas were still alive while so many of their friends and colleagues and family members were dead around them. Each loss hurt. Each loss was an insult to what should be.

"I'm really worried about Mondoyo," Thomas admitted. "I want to connect with him, but he isn't—Hold on." He stopped walking and frowned at his control sleeve. "This had better not be more political spam."

Ariock's eyes widened as he glimpsed the holograph that played atop Thomas's sleeve. A crude simulacrum of Vy . . . and a sword sliced through her neck!

Her simulated head toppled away. Her headless body was replaced by a crude animation of Ariock, enraged.

The funerary procession came to a halt. Kessa said something to appease the crowd, but Ariock was fully focused on Thomas.

"That's got to be a message from the Death Architect," Thomas said. "It looks like one of our crews picked it up from a shuttle we appropriated. Probably ten minutes ago."

"Where is Vy?" Ariock's awareness spiked out, and he let it unravel across the crowd, across the entire city.

If only Vy's life spark would stand out to him like a beacon. She wasn't powerful. She never registered as anyone special to his Yeresunsa sense. He just couldn't find her this way.

"I'm checking right now." Thomas had access to all the superluminal tracking signals, and he scanned through menus on his sleeve. "Crap." He sounded devastated.

Not just worried. Devastated.

All of Ariock's suppressed fear and rage rose to a boil. He felt as if he was entering battle. The crowd surged away from him as he held out his arms and item-teleported his galaxy armor onto his body. Soon he was bulky with spikes and tungsten plates. His helmet fit snugly in the gorget. He left the faceplate retracted for now.

"She's halfway across the galaxy," Thomas said.

"What?!" Ariock felt sure he had misunderstood. He was too upset to think.

"I don't know how she got there," Thomas admitted. "There's no Necrocosm for me to scan for answers. But her tracking signal is coming from the Araya Moon Belt."

"Show me how to get there," Ariock commanded.

Thomas focused on a cleared space in front of him. Points of light coalesced, forming a galactic map. Ariock studied the highlighted region. He memorized the route as the map zoomed in, ratcheting tighter and tighter. More zooming. More ratcheting.

"Take an immunity pill," Thomas said. He popped a pill into his own mouth.

Ariock had actually forgotten that crucial safety tip. He item-teleported two immunity pills directly into his mouth and swallowed. They should take effect quickly, making him invincible in battle.

"My dragon armor is in the aerie," Thomas said. "Put it on me, please. I'm coming with you."

Ariock never did well when his attention was split, and he didn't want to have to protect Thomas while he also wanted to rescue Vy. But if Thomas believed he needed to be there—

"Bring me," Thomas said in a tone of command.

Ariock decided not to question his friend's judgment. He item-teleported the outfit, hastily stripping off Thomas's brocaded cape and other accoutrements and replacing them with the armor designed and created by Garrett.

Kessa stared at them both with wide-eyed anxiety. Nearby people shouted questions, but Kessa only said, "Be safe. Bring Vy back."

"Tell Evenjos and Garrett," Thomas said. "And tell them to be extra careful. I think this is the Death Architect's lair. She'll have traps. Assume she's smarter than I am. And remember, we cannot kill her without ending the universe."

"I will tell them." Kessa stepped away, already making the call on her control sleeve.

"Ready, Ariock?" Thomas used his projection power to step through the hellishly complicated galactic route one more time. "I can't tell whether Vy is in or outside the asteroid, and I don't know what to expect. Please prioritize caution about all else."

Mirrors blocked clairvoyance. Ariock steeled himself for a mind-numbing search of the faraway asteroid field. He memorized the route as best he could and admitted, "I may need help getting there."

"I know," Thomas said.

Ariock wasted no time, sinking into a clairvoyant trance. He wanted to get there on his first try, but it was like trying to solve a jigsaw puzzle of fog divided into a million pieces. Space was three-dimensional, and every slight rotation in perspective made each view indistinguishable from other celestial regions.

Thomas gave him custom-tailored directions each time he snapped back to his body. Finally, after several dozen attempts, Ariock ghosted across the entire route to the correct asteroid.

"Bring air." Thomas sealed his visor. His voice came through the supercom, tinny and distant. "And force the airlock open. Bring me inside along with you."

Everything about the asteroid looked sinister. Ariock sealed his own visor, then ghosted back to the asteroid. He spent precious seconds finding a smooth door embedded in the frosted rock. It was nearly indistinguishable from the rest of the icy surface.

Once he was sure of it, he teleported his core self across countless star systems, including Thomas and a bubble of air encased in a pressurized shield.

He forced the airlock door open. They descended into utter darkness.

Ariock didn't need to be told how airlocks worked. He used his powers to seal the upper gate before he forced the second gate open. He detected dank but breathable air in the dark corridor beyond. Thomas led the way.

Unlike Thomas, Ariock barely fit in the corridor. He had to hunch, his spiked shoulders scraping each wall.

He tried to ghost, determined to find Vy, but every surface was mirrored. The reflections baffled his disembodied self, and he returned to his body, frustrated and annoyed by the claustrophobic environment.

Thomas opened his visor. Ariock did the same. It was best to conserve their air tanks for when oxygen was needed.

"Expand your awareness," Thomas suggested.

That was such an obvious next step, Ariock felt humiliated for needing the suggestion. He cautiously sent his awareness down the hallway and through walls, searching for life sparks.

Three people. No, four. One of those life sparks blazed. That one had to be a Yeresunsa.

"The strong one is probably our teleporter." Thomas walked down the corridor in the correct direction, having absorbed Ariock's thoughts. "It could be a rogue cultist. Please stay on your guard."

Ariock followed Thomas, ducking and twisting and then even crawling to avoid pipes and wires. He wanted to rip the stuff out of his way, but he didn't want to risk destroying the life-support system.

At least he was light on his feet and knees. Gravity was artificial here, and weaker than it was on most planets.

A child-size shadow skittered through the darkness ahead.

Ariock did not detect a life spark there. Was it a robot? Or a strange reflection in the mirrors?

The shadow came back, floating in a hoverchair. Its eyes were too close together and glowing in a dangerous way.

"It's a trap," Thomas said before Ariock could decide how to react. "I'll disable it. Hold on." He tapped his command sleeve.

Ariock became aware of hissing gas. He was glad that he'd swallowed immunity pills.

"Remember," Thomas said, moving forward again. "If you see the Death Architect, do not kill her. But you'll need to prevent her from moving. Shield her and stop her from using any electronics."

Otherwise the universe would be destroyed.

"Right," Ariock said.

Deep down, though, he knew that he would find Vy, protect her, and save her, no matter what. Thomas had temporarily erased his memory of the nightmare, but it was coming back to him. That terrible desolation. That failure.

He wasn't going to let it come true.

CHAPTER 5

TOUCHED

The Death Architect was troubled when she should have been untroubled.

All was quiet in the background of her mind. She ought to be reveling in the purity of solitude, the freedom to act as she pleased. The Necrocosm was reduced to a mere memory.

But her lair had just been unexpectedly invaded.

According to the surveillance sensors in her facility, two individuals—the one-legged human and the Torth formerly known as the Commander of All Living Things—were rushing toward her.

They were supposed to be dead. The Death Architect had foreseen their deaths, and she had provoked that situation by sending a crude digital message using the Conqueror's supercom technology. The disgraced Commander should have executed the one-legged human and gotten murdered for doing so.

Instead, here they were.

Why? How?

The Death Architect understood machinery and data, but she had a hard time demystifying people and social reactions. Had the Conqueror somehow foiled her perfect ending?

Her finger hesitated over her control sleeve. It would be easy to kill these two intruders, even without her prized battlebeasts. She could use robotic drones to shove them out an airlock. Or . . .

There was mathematical symmetry in the idea of a showdown.

The Death Architect was a deadly device herself. She had transformed herself into the biggest bomb in history. She even had an extra canister of insanity gas hidden inside her robes.

Why not let the intruders end her life? She could make them enraged. Make them stupid.

That way, the Giant's love interest would ironically instigate the heroes' doom. The disgraced Commander would accidentally end the universe after having accidentally ended the Torth Empire.

Ha. It wasn't her exact perfect ending, but the future was already off course. This was just as good.

Soon everything would cease to matter. Matter would cease to exist.

The Death Architect double-checked the status of her remote-controlled swarm transmitters. Thirteen out of her seventeen launchers were online, their payloads heavier than stars and full of destructive potential. That was sufficient to start a chain reaction, upon her own death, that would doom the universe.

Each launcher bore a scimitar sigil. They were hers, through and through. Her minions had obediently followed her instructions. Whenever she had detected a risk that one of the death cultists might go renegade, she had ordered others to assassinate the problem. They had faithfully done so.

She regretted losing them.

The Death Architect still didn't understand how, exactly, the Conqueror had gained total control over most of the galaxy and robbed her of her minions. Although she had managed to outwit him a few times, he was unexpectedly formidable. How had he wrecked the Necrocosm? How much power could he appropriate from demigods such as the Shapeshifter and the Giant? What dark magic enabled him to use their power?

Friendship?

The concept of friendship eluded the Death Architect. Friendship was not like the relationship between a master and a minion. It had something to do with equality, but that made no sense to her. Surely the Conqueror had no peers?

If only the Death Architect could exploit the power of friendship the way her nemesis did. What if she could boost her precognitive power? Then she might see beyond the possibilities that affected her own path. She would know so much more.

She might even gain a power to time travel. That was an alluring idea.

Unfortunately for her, friendship was too abstruse, too alien, for her to run experiments using it. Consensual cooperation was beyond her comprehension. She had reluctantly given up on the possibility of time travel.

All she could do was explore near-future potentialities. She discarded scenarios milliseconds after building them, seeking the most likely combination of events.

Why had the future become so murky after the Necrocosm died?

Why did she have the disquieting impression that the Conqueror might surprise her?

He couldn't possibly find her hidden asteroid. Could he? Even if that one-legged human wore a superluminal tracking device, the signal would be scrambled. The only way the Conqueror could possibly locate this asteroid would be if . . .

Well. If the one-legged human had managed to toss a superluminal tracker into space.

Was that possible?

The Death Architect needed to find out. She instinctively tried to ascend, but there were no distant minds for her to connect with. No one was reaching out. The Necrocosm was gone.

If she could have felt chagrin, she supposed she would have.

Well, there were other ways to harvest information.

The Death Architect snapped her fingers and beckoned to her sole remaining battlebeast. The starved creature slunk to her side. It was well trained.

She reached out her bare hand.

The battlebeast eyed her from its peripheral vision, disbelieving. It had never seen her purposely touch anyone. Indeed, she so rarely touched other living creatures, this seemed like a momentous thing for her to do.

Her pet quivered in anticipation. Battlebeasts slept in piles in their native swampy habitat. They liked being touched.

She stroked his oily, mottled skin. As rapid, far-off footsteps broke the frosty silence, she let her intentions drift, dreamlike. The future of this battlebeast played out inside her mind.

Unsurprisingly, he didn't have much future left. He was going to die within the next few minutes.

But not in a glorious bang of universal annihilation.

?!

The Death Architect's mouth fell open as she experienced an emotion other than scientific curiosity. Shock.

The near future she had just glimpsed was multiple standard deviations beyond her calculated range of plausible scenarios. The odds of *?!* happening were vanishingly small. The Giant should not be here. And the Conqueror himself . . . !

After the initial shock, the Death Architect's flesh goose-bumped in anticipation.

There was no time to analyze prophecy, no time to question the status of her launchers or other equipment. She might still have enough of an advantage to destroy all of existence, but time was of the essence.

She went statue-still in an attempt to trigger doomsday.

Victory must be hers.

CHAPTER 6

ULTRADENSE

Ariock tore open a wall so he could follow Thomas into an industrial room. The vault doors in this place were too small for him.

The former Commander of All Living Things was the source of the intense life spark. Even in space armor, she looked like a skeletal agent of death. She raised her scimitar and sprinted toward a frail silhouette floating in front of window displays.

Ariock had never met the Death Architect in person, but he had seen representations of her, so he recognized her pigtails and frail shoulders. She looked innocent.

And calm. Even with a wicked blade bearing toward her, the little girl did not move. She did not even blink.

Was she paralyzed?

A gaunt battlebeast uncoiled from the shadows and moved in front of the Death Architect, protective. Saliva drooled from its enormous jaw.

Ariock extended his own protection. He shielded the Death Architect with compressed air. At the same time, he was aware of another occupant of this room.

Vy!

Her hair was loose and cut to shoulder length, her clothes rumpled, and she crouched behind a tabletop. But she smiled as if Ariock was the best sight she'd ever seen. She looked unharmed.

Ariock smiled back at her, happy that his visor was retracted. She could see his face.

"Ariock—" Thomas began to speak, but the battlebeast unexpectedly lunged. Ariock could see all the way down its cotton-white throat.

Blasts tore the animal apart in midair. It twisted and exploded in a rainfall of fleshy gore.

Thomas had shot without hesitation. Slimy parts of the monster fell as he continued to rush onward toward the Death Architect. "Ariock, push her toward me. Shield yourself!"

Just in time, Ariock compressed air. A cruelly curved blade whistled downward and almost sliced through his shield. The blade stopped short of his gorget.

The disgraced Commander revealed no hint of disappointment. She whirled away and raised her scimitar again, this time chopping at Thomas.

Her blade met Ariock's shield again.

"Idiot!" Thomas yelled at the Commander. "She's playing dead, that's obviously a trigger!"

Ariock turned to the Death Architect. With her turquoise eyes unfocused and unseeing, she looked anything but playful. She was deathly still, like a creepy doll rather than a person.

He reached out with his powers.

His extended awareness was what saved him. Some hint of danger rippled through the air, and through the floor as well.

Instead of puppeteering the Death Architect, compressing air to force her body to move, Ariock crammed his awareness into every solid material within sight. He became icy iron. He encompassed as much contiguous matter as he could.

Just as a nuclear blast tore the asteroid apart.

It should have caused the station to lose life-support integrity. Ariock forced the habitat to merely shrug instead of shatter. Fault lines formed. Ariock sloughed pressure into the void of space. He was ionic tungsten. He was the outer hull of the station, and he held fast, as immovable as a mountain. He was the Strength of prophecy.

Inside his awareness, items slid loosely. Grates knocked against each other. Pipes broke and vented steam. Stress fractures formed in walls and ceilings.

But mostly, everything remained functional.

Ariock dared to release his awareness from the station, bit by bit, returning some awareness to his human body. He could not exist as overstressed steel forever. Vy needed him. Thomas needed him.

Some unknown liquid leaked and fizzed in a corner. The walls no longer quite met at even angles, and parts of the room had buckled, but at least this was still a viable habitat with life support.

The disgraced Commander was rising to her feet. Vy looked shaken, but she was also rising.

The Death Architect had been thrown from her hoverchair. Her vehicle was dead, its delicate hoverdisk broken. She lay on her stomach, unmoving. One of her baleful eyes stared into a distance that only she could see, partially obscured by one ribbon-tied pigtail. Ariock wasn't sure if she was actually dead this time or still playing dead. Very little could unnerve him these days, but the little girl was too much like a zombie.

The violence had thrown Thomas off his feet.

Ariock joined his friend in three quick steps and knelt. He poured healing energy into Thomas, enough to mend all wounds.

As soon as Thomas was healthy, he leaped to his feet and rushed to his fallen nemesis. He leaned over her like a sky croc about to gorge on a carcass.

He inhaled.

Ariock knew that type of inhale. Thomas sounded like that when he was feasting on the life histories of penitents. He inhaled just before he twisted the minds of zombification victims. That was the inescapable sound of Thomas winning.

Thomas's eyes widened with surprise.

That wasn't such a good sign.

"Ariock, only you can stop the death of the galaxy." Thomas straightened to face him fully. "She already triggered doomsday. The chain reaction is in progress."

Ariock wanted to item-teleport Vy to safety before he did anything else.

"I'll protect Vy." Thomas spoke rapid-fire, underscoring the urgency. "There's no time for anything else. I'm sorry to do this to you, but you can't bring me or anyone with you."

Pain seared Ariock's eyes. He groaned.

When he reflexively closed his eyes, a burning image of the galactic disk glowed against his inner eyelids. Veins threaded the spiral disk. Circles blazed at the ends of various threads, with features titled in neat lettering. ENKLADAD. STATION FURTHER. SHOOF. REJECT-238. OTHKO BELT.

YOU ARE HERE.

There were many others. He couldn't make the image go away.

"I burned a cosmic map onto your retinas," Thomas explained. "It will fade as your eyes heal, and you have fast healing, so you'll need to be quick. Go to each of the thirteen temporal gateways on that map. They're the names I circled. Each one has an ultradense payload heading toward it at speed. You need to deflect those payloads. Make sure they swerve. If they enter the temporal stream network, the universe is in danger of ending."

Ariock blinked. The galactic map hung in the air even with his eyes open, seared into his vision.

"You'll need all your strength," Thomas warned. "And if you aren't fast enough, you'll need to immediately travel to the Centauri system to protect Earth from obliteration. That's where the first supermassive black hole will emerge."

Ariock began to ask if Vy was truly safe. What if the disgraced Commander tried to murder her?

"Vy is fine!" Thomas cried. "Go!"

A clap of thunder sounded. All of a sudden, Garrett was in the room, fully geared for battle. His beard and hair spilled out, bright white against black armor. Metallic wings shone from behind him with golden light. Ariock squinted, his vision overwhelmed with brilliance as well as the galactic star map.

"Evenjos!" Thomas yelled. "Deflect the payload that's headed to the nearest temporal stream! Ariock, skip that one and deflect the other twelve!"

Evenjos must have hitched a ride as Garrett's disembodied passenger. She decoupled from the old man, materializing as a radiant goddess.

She and Garrett clasped hands and began to speak to each other.

"If we can get telepathy gas in here, I can amplify Ariock's power," Vy was saying. "But—"

Thomas shoved Ariock. "Go, go, go!"

He was weeping.

That, more than anything, conveyed the urgency. Thomas did not cry unless he had a very good reason to do so.

The Death Architect remained unmoving on the floor. She was no longer any sort of threat. And surely Thomas, Garrett, and Evenjos could handle the disgraced Commander with her ionic scimitar.

"Protect Vy." Ariock sealed his visor and began to breathe the air from the tanks embedded in his armor. He ghosted across the galaxy to one of the circled targets seared into his vision, the one labeled RAWU.

He teleported into the void of space.

While he hung there, as useless as a space rock, he discarded all his internal brakes and checks to expand as far as possible. He scanned the area for . . .

Well, that swarm of missiles might be the payload.

Soon his core body dwindled to insignificance. Ariock became an immensity larger than a planet, albeit without much mass or density. The cosmic map seared onto his retinas faded to unseen irrelevance. He existed as cosmic radiation and space plasma.

If he were relying purely on visual data, the missile swarm would stymie him. Each missile appeared to be identical and they all traveled at roughly the same velocity, heading in roughly the same direction. There was no visual way to identify the real threat.

But Ariock encompassed the swarm. It became as much a part of him as his own skin. He immediately sensed which of those many missiles was different from the rest. That one missile was ultra, ridiculously, dangerously unstable and . . .

Heavy.

Heavier than a planet.

Heavier than anything Ariock had ever dealt with. Every fiber of his being, including his human body, slid toward the gravitational pull of that ultradense missile.

The swarm snapped into the heavy missile. Its containment must have failed, or ended, and now their mass was added to its already critically packed density. The payload glowed with unknown energy reactions.

A section of space beyond Ariock danced and warped and glowed in anticipation. Ariock knew without needing to be told that he was perceiving the receptive gateway of a temporal stream.

He had to deflect the payload.

Ariock poured all his focus into the ultradense, ultraheavy, malevolently glowing missile. It no longer even resembled a missile. It looked more like a deformed meteor.

He gained its velocity. Its power. And its mass. He hurled all his newfound weight—the weight of a thousand Jupiters—downward.

The meteor dipped.

Its mass was such that the temporal stream sucked toward it, energy arms reaching for an energy goal. Ariock the deadly meteor forced himself farther off course. As he hurtled away from the temporal stream, the gateway fizzled with particles on their way to join his ever-increasing mass.

Ariock the meteor dared not withdraw. Whatever was happening inside his dense mass, it was a runaway chain reaction. He felt its volatile potential. The payload might transform into something like a star. Or a black hole.

Such a devastating cosmic phenomenon would annihilate the nearest solar system, which he assumed was the Rawu system. It would also annihilate his mortal body and end his life. He couldn't allow that.

But Ariock the meteor had no idea what to do. Thomas was too far away to offer advice.

Ariock was matter. He was heat. He was radiation.

So he channeled energy out of the density and into the void of space. He bled mass. He bled velocity. He didn't know how to unpack it all without causing a dangerous explosion, so he left density alone.

Bit by bit, the mass became relatively stable.

It was still an ultradense abomination of a wrecking ball. But it no longer felt like it would twist into something beyond his control. The meteor flew past the temporal gateway, slower and colder than it had been.

He let it go.

Bereft of density, mass, energy, radiation, and heat, he struggled to exist at all. He was hardly aware of who he was.

Bit by bit, he remembered.

He slammed back to his human size, and the shock of downsizing from a cosmic demigod to a mere mortal caused him to curl up, muscles knotted with tension. His own heavy breathing was the only sound in the universe.

Had that exercise taken seconds?

Or had it consumed precious minutes? Was the universe going to end?

Ariock was exhausted, but the cosmic map still glowed on his vision. He wearily exited his body and ghosted across solar systems and nebulae, seeking the next location.

He had eleven more payloads to deflect.

CHAPTER 7

HEROES OF PROPHECY

"Telepathy gas is the key," Vy said, "to power amplification."

She was unsure if her hard-won revelation would damn all of humankind for generations to come, but she had to speak up. The universe needed saving.

"I can make you more powerful in a telepathy zone," Vy explained to the heroes and villains of prophecy. "That's how it works." She indicated the former Commander. "That's how we got here."

They stared at her with calculation in their eyes. Thomas, outfitted in iridescent black scales trimmed in gold. The fallen Death Architect, with dark corkscrews of hair obscuring one eye. Her visible eye was a brilliant turquoise color. The disgraced Commander, dominating the room with her horned mantle and shroud and her gleaming, ultrasharp scimitar. Garrett Dovanack, sturdy in his spiked black-and-purple armor. And the Lady of Sorrow, resplendent with her metallic wings and impractical shining armor.

Thomas spoke with rapid-fire urgency. "Even if Garrett went to fetch emitters, they'd need the right amount of inertia in the void of space to form a matrix, and we don't have time. Evenjos, you need to go alone. Stop the missile. NOW."

Evenjos evaporated into a cloud. But instead of leaving the asteroid, she solidified directly in front of Vy.

"If we share our bodies, my way," Evenjos said, "that may work just as well as a telepathy zone. Will you accept a merge with me?"

Vy knew there was no time to argue, no time to mull it over. Ariock needed to deflect payloads that weighed more than entire planets. He could not afford to spare extra focus just to keep his vulnerable fiancée alive in the voice of space.

Garrett and Thomas were not human at all, so they could not amplify power like she could.

Vy wanted to merge with Ariock, not the self-centered former empress. She wanted to share her power with Ariock. She wanted to give it only to him.

But this was how she could help Ariock stop the doom of the universe. This was the way.

She closed her eyes and nodded.

Evenjos gently intertwined her fingers with Vy's. Moments later, the sensation increased into an electric tingle.

Electricity brushed through her awareness. A feeling of majesty overcame her. Hands no longer held hers, but there were new sensations. Power radiated from her shoulders. Vy knew, without needing to look, that she had wings.

A dead language echoed inside her. Vy nevertheless understood it.

Garrett watched her *(them)* with wide-eyed wonder and perhaps some envy. Even the Death Architect seemed to be staring at her *(them)*.

Vy heard an inner voice that was not her own. *We must go*, Glory urged. And she (*they*) zoomed through the habitat at lightning speed.

Vy felt as if her own body had been hijacked, but she dared not decouple. She (*they*) had a mission.

The airlock was already opening. The former empress apparently had a nuanced understanding of wiring. Glory knew environments in an intimate way, since she explored everything with her body.

Vy feared the void of space, having nearly died in it. But Glory did not hesitate. She blasted upward toward the stars like a superhero. And Vy realized that Glory suffused her flesh and bones. Glory was oxygenating her blood. Her skin felt tight and inflexible, and she knew she was encased in skintight protection.

They were one and the same. She (*they*) remained mostly comfortable.

Glory directed them toward a mutant meteor that looked like doom. White-hot fissures bubbled along its surface.

Glory reached out one of Vy's hands, and an extension of herself shot in that direction.

But the danger (*!!*) was far greater than expected. She (*they*) could have flicked an ordinary meteor away. This meteor sucked her (*them*) in. Its power was undeniable.

It was a god of meteors.

It had strength like Ariock.

We must escape! Glory struggled to pull away.

Vy went with her, since she and Glory shared a body, and she didn't want to separate in outer space. But she wasn't sure if escape was the right thing to do. Shouldn't they knock the meteor off course? That was their job. Thomas had explained it.

If we can escape, Glory thought, grunting with effort, *then we will succeed in yanking it off course.*

Vy understood, then. The meteor had captured them with gravity. That was like an invisible chain. All they had to do was pull it.

All, Glory thought with dark bitterness.

Vy sensed that Glory was well aware of her own limitations. She was strong enough to yank a planet out of its orbit, she might be able to annihilate a moon, but this . . .

This is beyond Me, Glory thought.

The meteor was all deadly weight. It continued on its collision course toward the temporal stream, undeterred, unstoppable. And it pulled Glory and Vy along with it.

The closer they came, the stronger its pull.

We are going to die, Glory realized with anguish.

Vy sensed her certainty. They were going to be flattened like pancakes upon the meteor, and it would become a black hole within seconds. That would be the end of everyone.

It was inevitable.

NO. Vy surged away from the inescapable pull. Thomas believed it was possible. He had told Ariock to deflect twelve meteors as strong as this one.

Ariock always overcame impossible odds.

Thomas was never wrong about things like this.

Vy and Glory would triumph. She *(they)* had to, so she could be reunited with Ariock. She was going to marry him! She wasn't going to let him down.

COME ON, Vy urged wordlessly to Glory.

Glory surged with her.

LET'S GO! Vy urged.

They became one person with one united purpose. Glory alone was unable to escape the meteor. Vy alone would have died for sure. But linked, they were more than a duo. Vy felt cosmic power radiating through every fiber of her being. She was a conductor.

She was a powerhouse.

WE . . . ESCAPE!

There was a tipping point where the immense power of the meteor seemed to slip. After that, it became easier. Glory and Vy soared away. It was still a struggle, and they had to fight for every mile of distance. But the miles passed. The ultra-heavy meteor swung in their wake, no longer carried solely by its own inertia. It was off course.

Glory laughed. Vy laughed.

They were more intimate than two people caught in an embrace. They shared a body, and on some level, Vy knew that was creepy and weird. She didn't like sharing her body in this way.

I do not like this much intimacy with you, either, Glory replied without words.

Vy doubted she would ever do this again, even with Ariock. Sex was fine, but full-on wearing her body like a garment? She wanted to feel cherished and loved, not used. This was kind of sick.

I do not think Ariock could take linkage this far, Glory admitted without words. *He cannot disassemble his own mortal body into molecules and subatomic dust. He is stuck in his unique corporeal shape, just as you are stuck in yours.*

They *(she)* arrowed through the open airlock in the shattered asteroid remnant. The chrome walls reflected a Vy who looked like a winged goddess. She had the face and proportions of Vy, yet she was also beautiful in a flawless, ethereal way.

She wasn't herself.

They *(she)* breezed past the corpses of battlebeasts, all the way back to the control room—where lightning shook the damaged walls.

The disgraced Commander was trying to kill Thomas and Garrett.

CHAPTER 8

KINDNESS

A blast to the face seemed too prosaic a death for a telepathic, prophetic supergenius.

Thomas hesitated to shoot the Death Architect. How many times had bullies tormented him or stopped his wheelchair? His advantages at this point were completely unfair. He was just bigger. Stronger. The small girl could not lift her head. She was too weak to sit up.

Anyway, Thomas wanted to imbibe her secrets before he obliterated her vast mind.

He stepped closer. Technically, he didn't have to undergo the trauma of killing her. He could just leave once he was done inheriting her knowledge. She was doomed no matter what.

Touch Me. The Death Architect emitted her own craving. She had never expected to meet a mental peer up close.

Thomas knelt by the other supergenius, already reveling in her complexities. He sensed her yearning to know his future. She wanted a hint of what had gone wrong, why her prophetic power had failed to guarantee her victory.

Thomas removed one of his gloves and took hold of her clammy little hand, skin to skin. Prophecy required personal contact.

Her mind was a vast webwork of eventualities and externalities and possibilities. It was truly a cosmic wonder.

But it was also a crib of death as large as a black hole.

The Death Architect felt almost nothing. She foresaw an infinity of possibilities for Thomas and his friends, but to her, depression was the same as joy, poverty was the same as prosperity. She rarely comprehended how tugging one meager thread could alter the entire future pattern.

She lacked insight into the grand tapestry of personal interactions.

Ohhh. The Death Architect welcomed his critique, and Thomas sensed a long-buried kernel within her mental layers, a yearning to meet someone whom she could respect as wise. *What was My biggest mistake?*

Thomas was merciful enough to oblige her. *You tried to provoke the future rather than evoke it.*

The Death Architect begged for elucidation. *?* She wanted to be shown the errors she could not discern on her own.

Thomas explained in the language of pure imagination. *The oracle Ah Jun created emotional steering beacons for people,* he thought, *in the form of prayers and paintings. But you (Death Architect) never understood emotions. You did gain a great wealth of influence over people, more than Ah Jun ever had. And you leveraged your influence like a maestro. But in the end, you threw it all away.*

The Death Architect had grown frustrated with decisions that were not her own and mistaken them for brambles in her path instead of the path itself. She had never understood motives. Mutual trust. Friendships. It was all a mystery to her.

Ah Jun, the Death Architect mused. *Aha, you had help from an oracle. That explains My failure.*

She was unused to the intimate company of a fellow supergenius. Thomas sensed her reaching for her control sleeve.

He easily blocked her weak arm and began to fry the internal circuitry of her device.

The Death Architect pressed a hidden button wired on her other hand.

Thomas sensed the unseen trigger without any visual hint. He wasted no time in vaulting backward, escaping the colorless gas that jettisoned out from the bow in her hair. Thomas held his breath, so he did not smell the odor that was akin to stale beer and chlorine.

Was the Death Architect holding her breath, as well? She might enjoy being calm and rational in the center of a melee. Then again, she might be arrogant enough to assume she was impervious to rage, even a chemically induced variety—

"Thomas!" Garrett roared.

Thomas fell into a roll the way Daindlor had trained him. He sensed the disgraced Commander take a swipe.

His panicked leap backward had placed him within her striking range, thanks to her superhuman agility and speed. It seemed the Death Architect had predicted an opportune moment to send her nemesis into danger. There were advantages to her extremely myopic visions of the future. Thomas had been too dazzled by the endless arrays of what was possible.

He seized the core of the Commander's mind.

Before he could twist it, a bolt of lightning threw the Commander out of his range. Garrett chased her.

The two elders danced around each other, ducking behind workstations and using their powers to hurl glass vials and surgical tools. Each moved with deadly grace. Each wore a mantle and armor. The duelers might actually be evenly matched due to the environment. Garrett dared not unleash a full-force storm inside this delicate habitat, while the disgraced Commander dodged like a cat, protected by her colloidal crystal armor.

Ripples of lightning hit the damaged walls. The station shook as electricity crawled along fissures, petering out.

Thomas sealed his gloves. The structural integrity of this habitat was badly weakened from the nuclear detonation earlier. He needed to stop the disgraced Commander once and for all. As for the deadly girl . . .

The Death Architect glared at him with her scheming turquoise eye.

Thomas could not read her mind from this distance, but that look said enough. She had inhaled her own rage gas.

She probably believed herself immune to its effects. But supergeniuses were expert liars, especially to themselves. Thomas knew that all too well. If the Death Architect had any shred of humanity or slave-like emotions, the neurotoxin would cause it to bubble up until she could no longer suppress or ignore it.

Thomas gave her a nod of pity. He had more important matters to tend to. Ice met lightning in a shower of frozen crystals, and the walls groaned alarmingly. He would zombify the Commander, then—

A winged goddess zoomed into the room.

Thomas gawked at his ridiculously overpowered foster sister. He had never seen Vy look this confident, this much like an equal in power to the Bringer of Hope.

She landed effortlessly. Her shortened red hair rippled in a phantom breeze. Her wings seemed bigger than Evenjos usually made them, and her height was statuesque.

Garrett paused to gape.

The disgraced Commander vanished and then materialized directly behind him.

She must have been holding back. It seemed the extra power boost from Vy had given the wily old woman enough raw strength to teleport in quick succession. She was already in midswing, momentum carrying her scimitar toward Garrett's gorget.

Thomas used a thermic stream to propel himself toward the elders faster than Garrett might react to a shout. Even with his perceptions overclocked, he could not orchestrate a holographic scenario fast enough to fool the Commander. A mind twist was the only thing that would stop her.

The room quaked.

All of a sudden, a fierce wind blew. Thomas could only grab a counter as his toes left the ground, tugged by a tornado he was incapable of escaping.

He had plenty of time to see what would happen next. Unfortunately, his own raw strength and his psychophysical reaction time were not on par with his processing speed. He couldn't fight the decompression gale fast enough.

The Commander resembled a skeleton put together at wrong angles. Her ionic blade sliced through Garrett's armor.

It slowed on the far side, red with blood.

Garrett's head slid off his neck.

Vy screamed with the voice of Sorrow. The goddess wrenched herself out of Vy and took her default shape, with purple hair and wings, leaving Vy to stumble into the tornado.

Thomas sensed his foster sister reel from her own fragility. All her imperfections made themselves known, from the unevenly shorn ends of her hair to the cinched tightness where her prosthetic was fastened to her amputated thigh. Vy flailed in the wind.

Meanwhile, Evenjos caught Garrett's head.

"Evenjos!" Thomas yelled in the thunderous wind. "Merge with Vy! Shield her!"

But Evenjos melted into an indistinct shape, no longer the proud deity. This was the version of Sorrow who had visited Thomas in the dungeon pit. She did not hold the asteroid station together. She did not protect Vy. She only cradled Garrett's decapitated head, uninterested in saving anyone but him.

Garrett's headless body tumbled in the faltering gravity. His blood did not spurt. It bubbled. It formed spheres.

Suction lifted everything off the ground. Damaged wall plates tore apart. Shattered glassware dragged across the metal floor, then flew upward.

The Death Architect slammed between industrial pipes in the remainder of the ceiling. The rents gaped wider, forced open by increasing pressure.

Vy clung to the edge of a wrecked wall, her feet pointed toward the vacuum of space. She was unprotected. Her eyes were wide with terror.

"Sorrow!" Thomas yelled, his voice cracking. "Save Vy!" His foster sister would run out of breathable air unless Evenjos merged with her again.

Sorrow curled around Garrett's head, desperately keeping him alive.

And she was horrifically successful. Garrett looked dismayed. The Lady of Sorrow must be forcing his blood to circulate, keeping his head on life support.

Thomas had to seal his visor in order to survive. He was muted, with an hour's worth of air in the tank on his back. The outflow of decompression sounded like thunder even through his helmet.

The disgraced Commander sped upward with purpose, her visor sealed.

She knocked Vy into space.

They both flew away into the void of nothingness. The Commander went in a different direction from Vy, having accomplished the murder she'd intended.

Everything seemed to break. Time. Space. The ground slid away. The walls came undone.

Thomas used his powers to manipulate vapor and heat, creating a jet to propel himself after Vy. He had no means to give her air or to save her life, but if he could keep track of her, then he would at least be able to tell Ariock which way to go.

A spinning asteroid fragment blocked his trajectory.

It was moving fast, and Thomas jerked back and reversed his jet to stabilize his own speed. A mass like that could break his bones even in his dragon armor. It had nearly smashed his outstretched arm.

Everything was a loosening cloud of matter. Useless debris floated past Thomas. Wires. Electronics.

Garrett's decapitated head floated through his range of telepathy. It seemed Evenjos had let her lover go. She must have realized the old man didn't want to exist in limbo, grafted onto a facsimile of a body composed of magical dust, maintained with unending life support.

Finally. Garrett emitted peace as he lost consciousness, his white hair trailing behind in dreamlike motions.

Thomas jetted around chunks of metal and rock, searching for Vy. He spoke into his helmet, activating the supercom. But there was no response from Ariock. No Freedomland. No one. All he heard was static.

After a while, the static cut off. Thomas only heard his own breathing.

And a distant mental whisper.

. . . die . . .

The spiteful thought came to him, carried on a tidal wave of incoherent rage.

. . . die die die.

Thomas found his nemesis floating in the void of space. The Death Architect saw the Conqueror through vision that was blurred by frost, and she insisted she was rational and *I NEVER FEEL EMOTION I AM A FLAWLESS BEING OF PERFECTION UNLIKE YOU.*

Thomas reached out to the enraged supergenius.

He held her hand.

It was not touch. He wore armor, so he could not feel her or vice versa. The Death Architect did not experience any prophecies or see his fate.

But she felt unspoken solace in his grip.

I am rational, she insisted, hating the Conqueror's incomprehensible kindness. *I am emotionless. I am perfect.*

Frost formed on her mouth and nose. She was dying from lack of oxygen while her blood boiled along with her wordless tirade.

As she lost energy, more suppressed feelings swelled inside her, joining her chemically induced rage. Sadness. Yearning. Fear.

Loss, too. No one had ever hugged her. Kindness had been denied her since her birth on a baby farm thirteen years ago. And now that she felt kindness from the Conqueror, she realized it was everything she had ever wanted. Never mind perfection. Never mind victory.

She wanted kindness.

(Is this why I failed?)

No wonder she had robbed others of kindness, desecrating the wealth she had never learned to value. She could have had a better existence. If only.

They both knew it.

The penitent formerly known as the Death Architect gave up and died wishing she had known kindness. Her eyes glazed to an unseeing glacial blue.

Thomas released her to float with other detritus. He twisted alone in the void of space, searching for anyone else.

CHAPTER 9

SAVIOR

Ariock blinked around the galaxy faster than he had ever teleported before.

He allowed nothing to distract him, aware that the cost of failure was everyone he cared about. His galaxy armor solved his mortal concerns, allowing him total focus. He chased locations on Thomas's cosmic map.

It was impossible for him to defuse the ultraheavy meteoric payloads. He couldn't figure out how to do that. The best he could do was use his brute strength to shove the deadly meteors off course. They were still lethal to stars and planets, but at least they would never hit a temporal gateway and balloon in destructive potential.

He figured he would team up with Thomas to do a more thorough job later on, when they had leisure time.

For now, Ariock could only hope that he wasn't knocking the death meteors onto trajectories that would bring them into contact with some delicate ship, station, or inhabited moon or planet.

It was a good thing Thomas had burned Ariock's retinas with painful precision. The cosmic map slowly faded from his vision. His eyes healed, and the map was gone by the time he finished with the tenth payload meteor.

Fortunately, Ariock recalled where to find the eleventh and twelfth payloads. Sveg. Cygot. He could find them.

But he was running low on time.

The doomsday trigger meant that each payload was sent simultaneously, giving Ariock less time to work with. The first few were missile swarms. But his final targets were already supermassive lethal meteors on the verge of becoming black holes.

Ariock saved the Sveg solar system. One left to go.

He threw himself across the galaxy in search of Cygot.

He found devastation. An entire star was destabilized, sucked toward the ever-increasing mass of the meteoric payload. Planets and asteroids followed in its wake. Ariock could sense the temporal gateway, a rift in space-time opening to welcome the deadly mass.

He went titanic.

He sped across the cosmos. He was the size of a star, with all its power.

But all his size, power, and strength weren't enough. Ariock tried to pull the nascent black hole off its deadly course. It pulled him instead.

Ariock leveraged himself away from the lethal pull of intense gravity—just in time. The temporal stream swallowed the payload. It flared with sickly radiance, as if delighted by the destructive poison it now carried.

Ariock was left alone in a void of defeat and failure.

Earth. Hadn't Thomas said something about saving Earth if he failed?

Ariock downsized from a cosmic titan to a puny mortal. As always, the shock of the change left him reeling.

He was getting better at ignoring that, though. Some part of his mortal self remembered that he was, in fact, a giant. He didn't get knocked down easily. He supposed that someday, if he lived long enough, he would be stuck halfway between being a mortal man and being a colossus. He should be grateful to feel small and delicate whenever he had that rare perspective.

He went into a clairvoyant trance and teleported to the outer orbit of his home solar system.

Safely ensconced in his armor, Ariock floated in deep space. He flattened himself into a net across the equivalent of a parsec. He sought—

A temporal stream erupted, splitting open wider than any gateway should.

It vomited destruction.

Ariock's core of a human body gritted its teeth while the cosmic titan version of himself pushed back against an unending storm that wanted to destroy everything in existence. He swept titanic arms of protection over Jupiter and Saturn and their moons and rings. He had to protect the entire solar system.

He could guess why the Death Architect had programmed her doomsday to destroy this supposedly primitive backwater as one of the first targets. She wanted her enemies to grieve. She claimed to lack emotions, but it seemed even the consummate Torth felt no hypocrisy about being vindictive.

The pressure of what spewed from the temporal gateway was becoming too much to bear.

Ariock hammered back at it with all his strength, trying to beat it. He was packing up a black hole. He was containing a quasar.

He was losing strength.

He hated his own uncertainty and weakness. He was barely holding back the storm of destruction, and if he gave up even for a microsecond, that would be the end of humankind.

Ariock gazed at the blue and white sphere that was Planet Earth. At his current size, it was a marble to him. He could reach out and squish it between his cosmic fingers.

Was the temporal stream network delivering death to multiple solar systems right now?

No.

This could not be happening across the whole galaxy. Thomas would not have told him to protect Earth if there was no hope. Ariock must have stopped enough of the payloads to prevent the whole calamitous chain reaction. The Death Architect had tried her best, but she had been unable to outwit Thomas.

And she had better not try again.

Ariock blasted power against the endless void that wanted to swallow every planet in sight. Head down, he barreled into it and forced the void back. He would protect Earth even if it killed him. No excuses. He could not return to Vy with the blood of all humans on his hands.

The barrage was scouring him away.

As he struggled to maintain his solidity and size, he thought of Vy. He had to stay strong for her.

They were getting married.

Family meant something to Vy, just as it did to Ariock. They had a future to-gether. It didn't matter what fate preferred, or what the Death Architect planned, or what obstacles got in their way. Ariock was not going to give up.

Never.

He would not let billions of humans die because he was too weak.

He was the cosmic storm. He was countless space rocks and ice and radiation and power. He was unstoppable. If he wanted to form planets, he could do so. If he wanted to orchestrate orbits, he had that power. He could create or destroy stars. And he could damn well shield any solar system he chose.

"RrrrAAAAAGH!"

Ariock roared, his mouth as wide as the sun. Solar flares snarled and died in concert with his voice.

The barrage of matter curled backward.

He wasn't sure what triggered the obliteration event. Perhaps his assault pushed the nascent black hole into the temporal stream. Maybe it struck the gateway at a certain angle. All he knew for sure was that his struggle ended with an insane im-plosion of space-time.

The temporal gateway folded in on itself and was sucked into oblivion. It van-ished in a star-size burst of radiation.

The whole spectacle probably had astronomers on Earth worried sick—but at least it wasn't going to kill them. Anyway, they had no idea temporal streams existed.

Or used to exist.

The one orbiting this solar system was definitely gone.

Supergeniuses claimed the wormholes were constructed by ancient aliens, and that they were impossible to alter or create or destroy. So much for that.

Ariock went small and nearly threw up in his helmet. He was so tiny! It was one thing to go from a storm titan to his normal size, but it was another thing to downsize from a stature that made the sun look delicate. He needed a few seconds to acclimate to a whole different scale of existence, and then more seconds to read-just to having a heart and blood vessels and lungs.

He wasn't sure he had enough wherewithal left to teleport right now. His body tumbled through space. He felt battered.

Ariock cleared his throat, knowing his voice would activate the supercom em-bedded in his helmet. It would automatically connect to the command channel. "Can anyone hear me?" he said.

Silence.

"Anyone?" Ariock repeated.

The lack of static or any hint of functionality confirmed his suspicion. The superluminal relays were useless without a temporal stream gateway. The supercom network was dead. At least, it was dead in this sector.

Vy.

Surely she was safe among heroes and well protected? What could go wrong?

Ariock closed his eyes and tried to recall the cosmic map. Where was the Araya Moon Belt in relation to Earth? He wanted to go straight to Vy. Anywhere else would waste his raw strength, which was near depletion after so much rapid jour-neying and moving of supermassive objects.

If not for his worry for Vy, Ariock would have rested in his galaxy armor, floating haplessly through space. He had enough air to last an hour or so.

Instead, he stretched across countless light-years. He found the moon belt. Vy must still be in the Death Architect's lair, but the asteroids all looked alike to him. He had no clue which one had an embedded fortress.

He would have to perform a closer inspection once he was on location. He teleported.

And reeled from exhaustion.

Teleportation usually cost him nothing, but he definitely felt weakened. He had the beginnings of a headache. Warriors claimed that this ache was a warning to stop using one's powers.

Ariock did a barrel roll, straining his eyesight to see every dim rock. He unfurled his awareness. Mirrors would confound his clairvoyance, but they had no effect on his actual awareness. If he encompassed every icy rock, he should be able to detect life sparks.

His widened consciousness encountered . . .

Nothing but frozen rocks.

Ariock fought his own frustration. He propelled himself elsewhere in the asteroid belt and tried again. And again.

He tried several more times before he encountered the vast thrum that was Evenjos.

Not that he could pinpoint her center. Evenjos had always been too powerful for that.

He did, however, see debris.

Lab equipment. Pipes. Cratered ruins. Fractured rocks.

A headless corpse dressed in Garrett's armor.

Ariock recalled the prophetic painting, but he had assumed he would be close enough to save Garrett, or at least make an attempt, when the time came. This wasn't fair. There was no closure. He hadn't had a chance to have one last conversation with his great-grandfather.

A broken wall of rock floated aside and revealed another body. This one wore a suit of dragon armor.

"Thomas?" Ariock said.

The boy seemed to be standing upright, space surfing on a fragment of metal floor. There was a crackle of static, and then Thomas's voice came through, tinny and small. "Thanks for stopping doomsday. Supercom network is down. I can't—"

"Where is Vy?" Ariock broke in.

Thomas made a vague gesture in a direction. "That way, maybe? I couldn't save her."

Ariock swore.

"You're dangerously depleted," Thomas said. "Don't teleport until you've rested for thirty minutes. Otherwise we're both—"

Ariock didn't want to hear it. He was well aware of the risks and dangers. He didn't need a smart teenager to stand in for his mother or his father or his great-grandfather or his fiancée.

He just wanted Vy.

He rocketed away in the direction Thomas had indicated, passing more rocks, more debris. Frozen corpses. Battlebeasts. A dead ummin. Ariock cursed whatever calamity had happened while he was gone. He cursed Evenjos for failing to protect Vy. He cursed Thomas for losing Vy.

Most of all, he cursed himself.

He pushed through his headache and stretched his awareness outward, searching for life in the frozen void.

HEART AND SOUL

Cherise lay in a suspended hammock, swaying gently as she twisted her paintbrush this way and that. It was nice to take a break from teaching and immerse herself in the act of creation. Painting had a flow that relaxed her.

This ceiling mural was not her original concept. It was a visual homage to the Twins amid a powerful sky, commissioned by Kessa and visually staged by Muzmudt. Her ummin alumnus lay in his own hammock nearby, suspended high above the galleria floor.

". . . would love to see what the Bringers of Hope and Light are creating." Muzmudt tended to get talkative every time he mixed a new color. "I've heard so many people exclaim that their buildings are more impressive than the best architecture of the Torth."

Cherise supposed that people had begun to call Thomas the Bringer of Light because of his particular powers. Not only could he ignite wildfires, but he could also project holographs.

The liberated galaxy was seeing a renaissance. New forms of art and music were springing up everywhere. Cherise was proud to be part of that, and to know that her friends were also part of it. Thomas could have turned himself into a heavy-handed military dictator. He could have sequestered himself away in order to focus on morally gray science projects, as Varktezo was doing. There were all kinds of rumors about an inhibitor that could destroy a mind reader's ability to overhear thoughts. Many lab technicians spoke openly about pioneering a way for their own species to gain bioengineered powers.

But Thomas wasn't doing any of that.

Instead, he wanted to unify the newly liberated planets with knowledge and art.

Cherise loved that. Thomas might come across as sinister to a lot of people, but his priorities were decent.

"I'll ask Thomas if we can visit his architectural projects sometime." Cherise dipped her paintbrush into her palette, mixing a subtle glow for a hint of sunrise on clouds. She would wait a few days to talk to Thomas. He must want time to mourn Serette.

An emergency klaxon startled her so much, she dropped her paintbrush.

Muzmudt sat up. "What is that?"

Cherise dialed her supercom wristwatch to a news channel.

All she heard was static.

Panicked, she tried other channels. A voice spoke on a local channel. ". . . can't reach any of the heroes."

Muzmudt began to ask a question. Cherise hushed him. All she could think about was the prophecy of the lone survivor, which Thomas had confided to her.

Had the other heroes died? Was he alone?

She sat curled over her wristwatch, listening intently.

"Kessa's lieutenants assure us that this isn't an attack," the news reporter was saying. "No one has died. If you're just tuning in, the superluminal network is down. We can't contact anyone on a different world. The Bringer of Hope is unreachable. So is . . ."

The reporter went on, listing heroes whom Cherise cared deeply about. Her foster sister. Her foster brother.

". . . we advise waiting," the reporter told listeners. "A team under Chief Scientist Varktezo is working on the problem."

Waiting.

That was probably smart advice. There were no more terrorist Torth. The old galactic empire was dead, and this attack, if it was an attack, wouldn't last. Everyone should just sit tight and wait until the network was fixed, or until the heroes—or possibly just one hero, the lone survivor—returned.

Cherise tossed aside her paint-splattered cloth and began to lower her hammock. "Sorry, Muzmudt. I have to go."

He stared down at her with owlish eyes. "But where are you going? What should I do?"

"Finish the mural without me," Cherise called over her shoulder. "I think I might be able to help my friends. I need to go talk to Varktezo."

And Mondoyo, she added in her head but did not quite dare to say out loud.

Their mural was an homage to the Twins, but even now, few people trusted the renegade supergeniuses. They were too reclusive. Memories of the gaseous attacks invented by Serette and Mondoyo were too recent.

"How?" Muzmudt sounded perplexed.

"I'll tell you later." Cherise peeled off her paint-smattered smock, revealing her belted tunic dress and leggings. No time for jewelry. She jogged toward the nearest hovercart.

Her crucial knowledge was already loose in the city. Alashani warriors wanted to marry humans. Atoning Torth champions wanted to try befriending or dating humans. Several warriors and penitents had invited Abhaga to link with them. Some people would always be hungry for more power.

But no one knew how, exactly, humans could unlock their vast potential to augment powers. If Thomas knew, he had not shared the secret with anyone.

Not publicly, anyway.

Cherise suspected that if anyone in the city knew right now, it would be Mondoyo. The secret must be akin to holding the keys to nuclear missiles.

She wove through traffic, searching for Serette's funerary procession. The city population was not quite in panic mode, but people rushed about and shouted, seeking loved ones and asking about bomb shelters.

At least local calls were going through. The supercom network was down, but citywide communications seemed unaffected.

Cherise swiped her wristwatch until she found the icon for Varktezo. Since she was his friend, she expected to get through.

Sure enough, Varktezo's voice piped into her earpiece. "What's up?"

"Humans can boost Yeresunsa powers," Cherise said, steering through a busy intersection. "I don't know how it's done, but it's possible Mondoyo knows."

"Ooh!" Varktezo sounded excited by the idea.

"Maybe if I augment Zai or someone else," Cherise suggested, "they can ghost around the galaxy and find out what happened?"

"That's an excellent idea," Varktezo said. "I'll talk to Mondoyo. Can you head to the Dragon Tower?"

"Sure—"

Varktezo ended the call before Cherise could ask why he wanted to meet in Thomas's residence. Ah well.

She switched direction and entered the academy campus, parking her hovercart at the research annex. One of the docents in the vast lobby gave her a hoverbike and directions, and soon she was speeding through clean white corridors with beautiful views, past scientific laboratories, and receiving curious glances from passersby.

The Dragon Tower was devoid of people. A nussian security guard let her in, then sealed the huge door behind her.

Cherise parked her borrowed hoverbike and crossed the vast lobby of polished meteorite and mirrors. The space was full of impenetrable shadows. If anyone was hidden behind plush divans and spare machine parts, Cherise could not see them.

She thumbed her wristwatch. Moments later, she heard footsteps echoing on the ramp.

"Cherise?" Varktezo called. He stood several stories up the spiral ramp. "Come on up!"

She hurried to join him, wondering if Thomas would ever get an elevator installed. Varktezo led the way upward.

"I can only guess which room Mondoyo is in," Varktezo admitted, stopping at a door. He pushed an accessibility button, and the door slid open, revealing an empty room.

"Um, wouldn't Mondoyo be at the procession?" Cherise asked, trying to be circumspect. Perhaps the overcrowded streets were too much for him to handle? Penitents tended to dislike busy places.

"He did not go," Varktezo said, moving on to another door, opening it, and moving on again. "Thomas gave him a room here so he could mourn in private."

"Oh." Cherise looked at the ummin, wondering if he had also skipped Serette's funeral.

She supposed the entire lab must be frantic to fix the supercom network. Even if Varktezo had been one of the mourners, the emergency must have pulled him away.

"Thanks for taking the time to be here," she said.

"Oh, the tech workers don't need me looking over their shoulders," Varktezo assured her. "I needed an excuse to check on Mondoyo. I should be thanking you."

Cherise had never properly been introduced to the Twins. She had only seen Mondoyo from a distance. As they continued upward, checking every room, Cherise began to feel ashamed. Should she barge in on Mondoyo's grief?

On the other hand . . .

Cherise felt even more concern for Thomas and Vy and Ariock. They might be in trouble. It seemed absurd that such heroes would require a rescue, but, well, Cherise had saved Thomas before. She would not rule out the possibility that he was in grave danger and in need of help.

One of the doors near the top of the tower was semi-opaque sea glass. The room within must have a light on, because the glass glowed dimly.

Varktezo knocked gently with his pointed fingertips.

No response.

Varktezo tried again. "Mondoyo?"

Nothing.

Varktezo waited for a polite length of time. When no response came, he warned in a loud voice, "I am coming in." He pressed the accessibility button, and the door whispered open.

At first, Cherise assumed the room was empty like all the others.

Then she saw a slumped figure in a hoverchair silhouetted by the window. The portly shape of Mondoyo was recognizable. His back was to them. He seemed to be gazing outside.

"Mondoyo?" Varktezo spoke with hesitation.

Mondoyo did not move or speak.

Varktezo trotted into the room. Cherise followed.

"I'm sorry." Varktezo spoke gently. "I should have come to visit you sooner."

The supergenius was quiet and still. He looked like a statue carved from ebony. He could be communicating telepathically with someone far away, but when Cherise walked close enough to catch sight of his face, a chill ran down her spine.

She definitely felt like an unwanted intruder. Mondoyo did not look at her, did not seem to care that she existed. He looked angry.

"She will be missed," Varktezo said.

"Go away." Mondoyo's voice was deadness. It held no emotion whatsoever.

Cherise stepped backward, aware that she was in the presence of a supergenius who was not Thomas. Mondoyo seemed grief-stricken. But he might also be extraordinarily dangerous and preparing to take over the galaxy.

He might even be the reason why all the supercoms were down and the heroes were gone.

Cherise hoped Varktezo would hurry away. Instead, the ummin walked bravely to Mondoyo and wrapped him in a tight embrace.

Cherise expected Mondoyo to do a Torth thing, like torment Varktezo with a pain seizure. He surely wasn't going to—

Cry.

Mondoyo leaned against Varktezo and sobbed. The keening sounds coming from him were rough, almost bestial, but that was what made him sound human. That was how Cherise knew that he was not just sad, but devastated.

Mondoyo could not speak for many minutes. He trembled and sobbed, and Varktezo held him. Tears leaked from the ummin's eyes as well.

Cherise stood in the doorway. She still felt like an intruder, but for a different reason. She hadn't known Serette. This was a grief she could not share.

"I am so sorry." Varktezo sounded like he meant it. He gently let go of Mondoyo, patting the supergenius into place in his hoverchair. "We came here because we're worried about Thomas. I know this is a bad time to ask for any sort of favor. I would not ask, but I am worried that Thomas—"

Mondoyo broke in. "Try telepathy gas." He sniffed, his reddened eyes fixed on Cherise. "We've surmised that telepathy facilitates the link for humans."

The answer was so simple, Cherise felt foolish. She shouldn't need a supergenius to tell her to try something that was all about consensual bonding.

"Thank you," she said wholeheartedly.

Mondoyo turned away. He went back to gazing out the window.

"Thank you, my friend." Varktezo put his hand on Mondoyo's arm. "Are you going to be all right?"

Mondoyo gave a barely perceptible nod.

"I will visit you later," Varktezo said. "Please call me if you need anything. Even if you just want companionship. That is not shameful. I see your pain, and I want to be there for you."

Mondoyo seemed to radiate pain. He said nothing. He did not move. But his lack of response was an answer in itself.

He was not all right.

"I'm sorry, Mondoyo," Cherise said, knowing her words were a pittance.

She had a feeling that Mondoyo was more important than anyone realized, including himself. He shouldn't be left to struggle with emotions that no Torth was equipped to deal with.

Nevertheless, now that she had a plan to find her foster brother and sister and rescue them, she was in a hurry. She followed Varktezo into the ramped corridor and the door slid closed behind them.

The only question was: Whom could Cherise dare entrust with a secret power boost?

She needed someone capable of teleportation. That meant a penitent Torth with powers. Should it be Zai?

As Cherise hurried down the ramp behind Varktezo, she wondered if she was making a terrible blunder. Not every problem could be solved with brute force.

Then she thought about Mondoyo, alone in that empty room.

Mondoyo was devastated by a loss that could have been prevented. He must despise everyone right now. Even so, he had given Cherise the advice she needed, granting her a chance to save Thomas and avoid her own devastating grief. He had done a great kindness.

And he clearly had given up on expecting kindness in return.

A medical research team might have been able to keep Serette alive if they had made that a priority. Heck, a team of Yeresunsa healers could have done so—if they'd teamed up with a human augmenter, such as Abhaga or Cherise.

They wouldn't have needed unfettered access to Evenjos for a week. A supergenius such as Mondoyo could have disseminated the healing knowledge needed.

Instead, Serette was deceased because the authorities—not just the heroes of prophecy, but also Varktezo and Kessa—had collectively deemed their supergenius allies unworthy of a great effort.

Cherise understood that impulse. She had lived with Flen long enough to feel the normalization of hatred against mind readers.

The entire free galaxy was going to be Torthphobic for a long time. Free people would commit injustices against mind readers even when they tried not to, even with decent laws. Freedom did not solve all problems.

"I want to try trusting penitents more," Cherise told Varktezo as they hurried through the tower's lobby. "What's the fastest way for me to contact Zai?"

CHAPTER 11

TO FOLLOW

Evenjos tried to pull herself together. Garrett would have done what needed doing.

She floated in space as the asteroid broke apart, as decompression sucked enemies and allies away from her. She was ice. She was nothingness.

She floated past the immensity of Thomas's mind. He was safe in his dragon armor, at least for an hour or so. But Vy lacked an air tank. Evenjos needed to serve as life support for Vy right now, no matter how much she was hurting, no matter what devastation was tearing her apart.

She would not let Ariock return to loss.

So she expanded her awareness. She looked beyond Thomas. Ariock's sphere of influence normally washed out all life sparks in the vicinity of a solar system, but for now, Evenjos could easily pick out any life that guttered in this void. There were tardigrades. Bacteria. The former Commander might have teleported to another habitat, because she was gone or dead.

Evenjos kept searching and scanning.

Finally, there was a dimming candle within the debris field, a human life.

Evenjos streamed toward the dying woman and enveloped her body, suffusing her. Soon they were linked and melded together. Evenjos conveyed molecules of air into Vy's lungs, giving the mortal a chance to survive. She tried to become a cosm of warmth and air rather than a failure.

The temporal gateway fluctuated. All at once, it flared, emitting a burst of radiation.

Evenjos as Vy stared at the rip in space-time and wondered if this was the end of everything. Maybe the Death Architect had succeeded after all. Maybe Ariock had failed.

The cosmic energy flooded past her and through her.

Her power responded, surging. She had been dust. Now she was supercharged fermions and charm quarks. She was a nexus of power. She might be able to rearrange matter and birth stars. Her focus and her awareness remained the same, but her abilities increased by an unknown magnitude.

A presence whispered in her. It sounded like an echo of the cantankerous brute she loved.

Garrett was saying goodbye.

Sorrow/Glory reached for the ghost of Garrett/Jonathan Stead, refusing to let him leave without her. The gateway between life and death was her realm. During the millennia when she had suffered, tied to mirrors and unable to live or die, she had resonated with people on the cusp with her. She had visited countless dying souls. The rarities who survived remembered her for the rest of their days.

Back then, she had wielded no power. All she could do was watch, helpless, as others escaped the dark solitude that was her existence.

But Sorrow had power now. She was Glory as well as Sorrow.

Glory was eternal.

Glory was invincible.

But none of that was what she wanted!

She grasped the unseen ghost of Jonathan Stead. She willed him to stay in the realm of the living with her. He was a consummate hero. He had acted nobly. He was her touchstone in this brave new future, the only man who understood her, the only person who cared about the person she used to be and would someday become.

But the remnant of Garrett slipped away.

He was gone over the unknown horizon, where all dead souls went.

Even her power had limits. Glory was alone with overwhelming Sorrow.

This was not the first time Evenjos had failed, yet her own unheroic nature was a shock. Her failure was so huge and unavoidable, she wasn't sure she could bear it. She sobbed.

She experimentally tried to pull away.

Sorrow had borne witness to countless departing souls. She wanted to follow the ghost of Jonathan Stead and catch up with him and join him on the far side of the border between life and death. She wanted to go where she had never been able to go before.

That was all she wanted.

But if she unlinked from Vy, she knew it would mean death for the human. They shared one body. Vy's cells were currently suffused with Glory's cosmic dust. Only the prosthetic leg was not part of the merge. That artificial body part remained keyed into Vy's nervous system, responding to Vy's neural impulses.

Even their brain was shared. It was Sorrow, it was Glory, and it was also Vy.

I'm sorry, Vy thought, her mood laced with shame and terrible resignation. Vy wanted a long future with Ariock. She wanted marriage and maybe children and adventures. She hadn't done enough. She hadn't seen enough.

But if Sorrow wanted to give up, Vy understood.

An eruption of anguish tore through Evenjos. As her own self was binary, she knew there was a danger of losing herself if she remained with Vy for too long. She might become an amalgamation of herself and the mortal woman.

And she would eventually lose her memories of Garrett and all that had come before, especially if she was trapped in the realm of the living for thousands of years.

Unless.

Unless she entirely gave up the part of herself that was Glory and went with Sorrow instead.

She could let Vy have Glory.

?!

Vy tried to understand what was happening. She felt half of the goddess tear herself away . . .

. . . and now no one else shared her mind.

Sorrow floated alone in the deadly void of nothingness. She still overheard the thoughts of her former self. Vy felt strange. Every cell of her body was infused with glorious power. She did not need to breathe. She was healthy despite existing in a vacuum, her hair loose and flowing.

Vy had fully become Glory.

Sorrow relinquished the last bits of her powerful, immortal, magical Glory self. She gave all her dust to Vy. For the first time in her millennia of existence, she became truly incorporeal.

She had no containment. No life.

So she was no longer trapped in the realm of the living. She no longer haunted the boundary between life and death.

Sorrow flitted over the horizon, chasing the soul she would rather spend eternity with.

CHAPTER 12

LIGHTBRINGER

The fact that the universe still existed was a sure sign of victory, Kessa thought.

Camera drones hovered nearby as Kessa led Serette's funerary procession to its end, circling a commemorative statue in progress. The banded gas giant washed the walkway in a glow that was both eerie and festive.

Kessa placed her lantern yoke on the bier. Next, she used her control sleeve to set down the floating platform. She wore an enormous headdress, so she could not bow her head too far, but she clasped her hands. She silently wished the deceased supergenius a peaceful journey across the border from the realm of the living to the realm of the dead.

Kessa was the only visible mourner.

Mondoyo remained cloistered in the Dragon Tower. Thomas and Ariock had not returned. Garrett and Evenjos were reportedly missing in action, and Varktezo must be scrambling to fix the supercom network. Even Vy was gone, having vanished along with a hapless ummin. Amid news broadcasts of absent heroes plus a broken network, the procession participants had wanted to check on their loved ones, so Kessa had given them permission to leave.

Freedomland was uneasy tonight.

Military fleets awaited teleportation. Hospitalized veterans languished and prayed for the Lady of Sorrow to heal them. The galaverse hall was useless, bereft of its open news feeds to various planets.

Kessa's control sleeve pinged. She answered the call.

"Kessa?" Varktezo's holographic face materialized. "If you can, meet me in the telepathy room upstairs in the war palace. Mondoyo gave us a clue. I think we can retrieve Thomas and Ariock, or at least give it a good try."

That sounded promising and ominous at the same time. Kessa grabbed a public hoverbike. She had considered halting the funerary procession earlier just so she could beg Mondoyo for advice, but that had seemed too self-serving. She had chosen to honor Mondoyo's dead mate before asking any favors from him.

Apparently Varktezo had fewer qualms. Maybe that was for the best.

Varktezo awaited Kessa in a circular chamber full of telepathy gas, along with Cherise. Both were dressed for the public, like herself, one in a snazzy coat and the other in a colorful belted dress with leggings.

Kessa slowed as she stepped inside. This was the same room Vy had vanished from, with a curved glass wall and luxurious furniture.

Peace, Kessa.

Sorry for the telepathy gas.

Kessa was adept enough to soak up their news right away. According to Garrett via Thomas via Cherise, the last prophetic painting implied one lone survivor *(!!!)*

of the final battle. Only Thomas was likely to return from the remote confrontation that must be happening right now.

Or that had already happened.

Also, Mondoyo was deeply sad. Nevertheless, he had conveyed a theory to Varktezo and Cherise: Telepathy gas was the key to facilitating an augmentation link between a human and a Yeresunsa. The gas should empower Cherise and *(we have invited Zai) (she should be here any minute)* Zai to ghost anywhere in the galaxy and even to teleport with passengers.

Zai would find out what had happened to the heroes.

Kessa walked the perimeter of the room while she waited, solemn as she imagined Mondoyo alone with his grief. There was an injustice there. He was struggling alone.

Just like Thomas had done for much of his life.

Heroes did not deserve that.

If the Twins had figured out the key to gaining power boosts from humans, they could have used that knowledge to enact regeneration healing. All they would have needed were some participants: humans and Yeresunsa willing to donate their time and energy.

All they would have needed were some friends.

Varktezo and Cherise exchanged an uncomfortable and guilt-laden glance, having read Kessa's mind.

I never got to know the Twins, Cherise thought. *Just like I quit trying to get to know Thomas. It's so easy to judge a person by superficial traits, and so hard to look for points of connection.*

I was too absorbed in my work, Varktezo realized. *But I suppose there's always an excuse.*

Kessa overheard his true excuses. Deep down, Serette had made him feel inferior. He hadn't liked her Torth-like silence or the way her gaze seemed to penetrate his soul. Varktezo really did think of Mondoyo as a potential friend . . . but Mondoyo used to spend all his time with Serette, which made the duo seem a bit unapproachable.

The Twins had had no friends in the land of freedom and friendship.

Kessa paced the room, considering ways to help Mondoyo, to show him that he was cared for. She would prioritize that right after—

?

Zai entered the sitting room.

The penitent warrior had a distinctive white streak in her black hair, which was pulled back into a bun. Her black armor had white accents and she wore a short white mantle, demarcating her as separate from her shani warrior peers. She was a former Servant of All.

Zai hesitated, head cocked, as she absorbed all the unspoken tension and intentions in the room. "Aha." Her voice was preceded by her thoughts, giving it the sonorous echo that Kessa was growing used to with telepathy gas. "I am ready."

Cherise and Zai met in the center of the room.

I don't know how this works, Cherise thought. *I have never linked before.*

Me neither, Zai silently admitted.

The human and the former Torth gazed at each other, full of trepidation. They were roughly the same height, with similar skin tones. One looked soft and colorful, the other hard and black and white.

Cautious, Cherise reached out with her hands.

Zai took them.

This was something new, Kessa thought. A meeting of worlds. A meeting of minds. A melding of differences.

Both the human and the penitent began to relax their mental guards. Kessa sensed their openness, their careful revealing of vulnerabilities. Cherise was going to allow a former Torth to use her. She hated that. But Zai recognized the enormous amount of trust and responsibility she was being given, and she feared that she would fall short, or fail in some way. Power was seductive. Power was easy to abuse. As a former Servant of All, she was hyperaware of the dangers of power.

Their fears merged. Their eyes closed.

They linked.

Their minds seemed to vanish while their bodies remained locked upright, and Kessa understood that this was the clairvoyant trance. Zai and Cherise were together, ghosting across the galaxy. They would explore the Araya Moon Belt.

They did not find anyone on their first try.

After a few minutes, Zai and Cherise snapped back into their respective bodies, gasping from the mental strain. They trembled. Neither had ghosted for such a long time before.

Normally, Zai would be depleted after such an effort. But she felt Cherise's power and she was willing to try again.

Cherise was desperate to find her foster sister and brother, fearful that Vy and Thomas were in deep trouble. So she clasped hands with Zai. They went again.

And again.

Kessa exchanged looks of concern with Varktezo. She could sense fading perceptions floating in the dark matrix of diffuse telepathy, so she knew Zai was getting faster and better at exploring the asteroids. But Cherise's raw power must have a limit. How many more tries would they get?

Again.

And again.

On their sixteenth try, a figure encased in scaled armor popped into existence between Cherise and Zai, right in the center of the room. Telepathy gas made his identity unquestionable. This was a mental titan, a god of knowledge, the Wisdom and the Conqueror and the lone survivor.

But his air supply was low.

Thomas collapsed to his knees. He retracted his visor and gasped.

Kessa knelt by him.

Cherise and Zai broke apart, gasping in sync. Their joyful exhaustion soon became individualized, and they fell into each other's arms, hugging and weeping.

Their recent perceptions floated on telepathy. They had witnessed weird cosmic radiation and fluctuations. Warm colors had throbbed across the wreckage in outer space. Amid all the frozen corpses and debris, they had found Thomas, alone.

He added to the wordless exposition once he'd had his fill of fresh air. Kessa gasped with each revelation as Thomas replayed the final battle, using all the glory of total recall.

Doomsday triggered!

Garrett decapitated!

The Death Architect, vanquished!

The Lady of Sorrow, gone!

Vy sucked into space!

And Ariock . . .

Thomas had directed the depleted giant to search for Vy. There were question marks there. Thomas had sensed the final thoughts of Evenjos as her disembodied mind flitted away from the realm of the living. The Lady of Sorrow was dead and gone—but what had happened to her magic dust? Was it dispersed? Or was it with Vy and Ariock?

We searched all over, Cherise thought.

We did not see Ariock or Vy, Zai explained.

Thomas climbed to his feet. He removed his helmet, revealing mussed hair. Although he missed certain people who were gone, he felt sure that Vy and Ariock were still alive. His certainties overwhelmed everyone else's doubts in the telepathy room.

"Don't look for Ariock and Vy," Thomas said. "They're fine." He headed toward the door, assuming that Cherise and Zai would return to the asteroid field. They would probably bring home the remains of Huchanu, the ill-fated ummin, and Garrett Dovanack. Perhaps they would also search for the escaped disaster formerly known as the Commander of All Living Things.

"While you two tie up loose ends," Thomas said, "I want to check on Mondoyo."

Zai's attention sharpened at the mention of her mentor. The boy Twin had introduced her to the idea of freedom for the first time. He had set her on the path to becoming a penitent warrior. "I want to see him, too."

"We can teleport there," Cherise suggested.

To Kessa, it seemed decadent to teleport across the city. They had access to public hovercarts. But Thomas, Zai, and Varktezo were genuinely worried about their friend, so Kessa wordlessly agreed. She wished she'd had time to check in on the boy Twin earlier.

The five of them appeared in front of a softly illuminated door.

Kessa recognized the surroundings. They had teleported to the spiral ramp in the heart of the Dragon Tower. Someone had taken down a couple of mirror panels to allow for ghosting. A breeze came down through the tower top aerie.

"This is Mondoyo's room," Thomas explained. He knocked gently. "Mondoyo?"

No response.

Thomas pressed the accessibility button and the door slid open. "Sorry to disturb you."

Orb lamps lent a soft glow to the high-ceilinged room. Instead of stars or moons, the banded gas giant filled the night sky. People called those bands "the color ranks," as if defeated Torth ranks were lurking overhead, waiting for a chance to reconquer all that they had lost.

But the mob of Torth would never descend. Their era was over.

A stout figure slumped in a hoverchair, resting on the windowsill. His head was buried in his arms.

"Mondoyo?" Kessa went to see if he was awake.

An ominous feeling made her hesitate.

"Oh no." Thomas said softly.

Kessa followed his gaze down to an empty pill bottle on the floor.

Zai came over to help her. Together, they gently lifted Mondoyo's upper body, pushing him upright. The boy's closed eyes were too sunken and dark. His skin was cold, almost claylike.

He wasn't breathing.

"We're too late." Thomas sat against the wall as if he had run out of strength to stand. "I should have . . . someone should have . . ."

He ran out of words.

But Kessa knew what he meant to say. Someone should have been Mondoyo's friend.

Where were the slaves Mondoyo had rescued? They must be in Freedomland somewhere, dating and making careers and adjusting to life in a free society. How often did they think of the person who had risked his life to escape and rescue them?

What about lab assistants? Only Varktezo seemed willing to talk with Mondoyo as if he was a normal person.

But Varktezo was in charge of multiple laboratories and obsessed with his own projects. In some ways, Varktezo was as self-absorbed as an average Torth. It might never have occurred to him that Mondoyo was hurting and in need of friendship.

Most former slaves dismissed penitents as heartless Torth. Cretins such as Mondoyo were not supposed to need emotional support.

Kessa realized she was shaking with a knot of emotions. She was angry at herself as much as anyone else. Mondoyo and Serette should not have felt so alone. This was injustice. The Twins could have advanced galactic technology by an exponential factor. They might have helped to solve all sorts of problems, from the supercom network to breakaway cults. Now they were both gone.

And this was a loss that could have been prevented.

The early Torth used to be downtrodden peasants. They had gained power and then abused that power. As soon as Kessa's people, the liberated slaves, gained power . . .

It was far too easy to become neglectful or abusive.

It was far too easy to forget what power imbalance did.

What would Thomas learn from the way Mondoyo had died alone? Or little Nea, the young supergenius who had survived a massacre of her brethren? She was the only supergenius alive now other than Thomas.

How about the trillions of penitents?

And the countless quadrillions of freed slaves? Would they ignore this injustice?

They would certainly want to.

Kessa seized her tablet and placed it on the windowsill. She triggered a live broadcast, overriding safeguards to make it a public news stream. She faced the camera. Her head and shoulders would appear on news feeds throughout Freedomland.

And she made sure it was recording, so the broadcast could be sent to other planets whenever the supercom network was restored.

"This is Kessatovtalun," she said, using her full name to let everyone know this was an official communication of importance. "I am announcing the official redemption of two penitents. Serette and Mondoyo, formerly known as the Twins, came to us as willing renegades. They have since proven their worth many times over. Their inventions, including immunity to the inhibitor, saved countless billions of lives. Henceforth, they should no longer be considered penitents or Torth. They are fully redeemed. They are . . ." She had to correct herself. "They were humans."

She tried to tamp down the anger in her tone.

"Unfortunately," she went on, "Mondoyo and Serette are deceased. The free galaxy has lost all the future benefits these twinned renegades would have granted us. I want you to know that they died honorably. They had friends, including me."

Kessa stopped herself before she could go on a tirade about how her friends had been neglected. If she wanted to accuse the whole galaxy of being neglectful, she ought to start with herself.

"Serette died from an illness forced upon her by the Torth Empire," Kessa said. "And Mondoyo died from grief over her passing."

That should quell any arguments that the Twins were evil. A demon would not die from grief.

Kessa saw Thomas in her peripheral vision, despondent. She touched her collar scar, reminding all the viewers who tuned in that someone was responsible for her own freedom.

They should know who it was.

Kessa ended the broadcast without another word. She went to the lone survivor and nudged under his arm, offering herself as someone he could lean upon. She was only one frail ummin, but . . .

She wasn't alone.

Cherise joined them. Then Varktezo. Zai.

Nothing needed to be said. They all helped Thomas to stand tall.

Other occupants of the tower must have noticed the commotion, because Nror shyly entered, followed by Abhaga and then Nuzzy. They bowed their heads to the dead figure of Mondoyo. And they turned to help embrace Thomas.

Even without telepathy, Kessa knew they were aware of what Thomas had done. He had reversed the doom of their galaxy. He had refreshed countless planets with freedom and enlightenment. He was one of a kind.

And he was a friend.

"I will make one more official recognition," Kessa said, even though most of the galactic population was oblivious to her words as yet. "Thomas Hill? You have nothing to atone for. I should have honored you long before your latest battle to save us all."

Thomas stared at each friend. He seemed speechless.

"Freedomland will know," Kessa said, "you are a hero. I can think of no one better to usher us into a kinder future. Everyone will know that we are lucky to have Thomas Lightbringer with us."

CHAPTER 13

GLORIOUS VY

Ariock flew between rock fragments amid distant stars.

Out here, he was no Giant, no Bringer of Hope, no messiah. His galaxy armor was a flimsy gesture of defiance against the deathly void of space. He was small.

When he spread his awareness in search of life sparks, all he sensed was the directionless thrum of Evenjos. Her presence washed out any other life sparks that might be in the vicinity. For all Ariock knew, she was mimicking the space dust around him.

He kept searching for Vy.

His fiancée had refused to give up on him when he was in a depletion coma and a bunch of Alashani had given him a funerary procession. She had trusted him when the Torth took her as a hostage. She had stood by him even when he'd accidentally killed Jinishta and a hundred more of his best warriors. Heck, she had eased the passing of his mother.

So Ariock would not give up until he found her.

He used his powers to dodge tumbling ice rocks, ignoring the throb of his warning headache. Spots danced in his vision. He was dangerously close to depletion. He would die if he kept this up.

Still, he examined debris. He looked more closely at any shape that vaguely approximated the size of Vy.

Most people believed that saving the universe was the right thing to do. It was supposed to outweigh a single person's life. Ariock wasn't sure. If this universe lacked Vy, then it was too dreary for him.

Vy?

Ariock figured he must be hallucinating, because he saw her in the distance. But she wasn't frozen and dead, like the corpses in the debris field. Her eyes were so blue they verged on purple. And her expression changed when she saw him. She looked grateful.

How could she be alive?

Ariock floated into her embrace, disbelieving. Was this some sort of heavenly afterlife? Vy was not frosted like the dead battlebeasts.

Her red hair was weightless and billowing and long again, as though it had never been cut.

Evenjos's powerful thrum made life sparks impossible to detect. And now Ariock did not know if this was truly Vy at all. Was the Lady of Sorrow toying with him? Breaking his heart and mind?

I am Vy. Her voice seemed to breathe directly inside his mind. This wasn't coming through a speaker. Her words felt imaginary—actually, telepathic.

And a refreshing sense of well-being swept through Ariock. His vision returned fully as his headache vanished entirely.

He felt energized again.

Had she cured his depletion somehow?

I am imbued, Vy's telepathic voice said, intimate inside his mind. *I am still human enough to amplify your raw strength in power, so I have given you enough to overcome depletion. But I am also, uh, sort of not human. Glory (Evenjos) (Sorrow) merged with me. She left me with her magic dust.*

Ariock dared to hope.

But how could this be Vy? Even if, by some miracle, she was . . .

Well. She was different.

I can't easily explain it, Vy's mental voice admitted. *When my dust suffuses a body (like yours), it has the same effect as telepathy gas. We are linked. Evenjos did the same for me. She saved my life and kept me alive in space. Maybe the radiation burst that came out of the temporal gateway (before it imploded) allowed me to survive when she (left) died?*

Ariock remembered shoving astronomical forces into the temporal stream.

Were all the gateways gone? He must have unwittingly destroyed the entire wormhole network.

"I don't understand." Ariock couldn't easily shake off his skepticism. "Evenjos chose to die?" That didn't sound like the Evenjos he remembered. The Lady of Sorrow might have wanted to die when she was trapped in mirrors, but later on, she had purposely avoided dangerous battles.

She did, Vy's mental voice affirmed. *She wanted to go wherever Garrett went. I think she was curious about death.*

Ariock remembered how insecure Evenjos used to be. Her own actions—or inactions—had condemned her long-ago people and caused the Torth Empire to arise. Evenjos had carried a burden of guilt. She had been trapped in her own private misery, forever atoning.

Just like Thomas.

Like Ariock.

And like Garrett. But around Garrett, Evenjos had been more playful and more self-assured. The old man had awakened something new in her.

Maybe that was why she had followed him.

"What happened?" Ariock asked.

Vy gripped Ariock's armored hands, and she replayed her own memories. Ariock experienced what she had been through. Vy had amplified Evenjos's already prodigious raw power. Together, they had pulled a death comet off course. The Death Architect had triggered a self-destruct sequence for her asteroid laboratory. The former Commander had decapitated Garrett—and escaped.

Evenjos had not been able to save her lover. Instead, she had merged with Vy again, protecting her in outer space.

"Thomas is safe for now," Ariock reported, once he had absorbed all that had happened while he was deflecting death comets. "But I need to teleport him home before he runs out of breathable air."

I will come with you. Vy held him, her mental voice suffusing him with love. *And I will amplify your power.*

"Don't try to replenish me!" Ariock said, alarmed. A lesser Yeresunsa could not revive a greater one from depletion. If Vy tried, they would both end up depleted and dead. He pulled away.

Vy pulled him back. Her strength was a pleasing shock.

I already have, she thought. *Humans can amplify the raw strength of a Yeresunsa through telepathy gas or through, uh, bodily overlap.*

Glorious Vy. Could this really be his fiancée?

Indestructible Vy?

"Is that how we're communicating?" Ariock asked, his deep voice flat inside his helmet. "Bodily overlap? Are you sitting inside my skin pores or something?"

Her mental voice giggled.

Ariock wanted to peel off his armor and hold her, touch her skin. At the same time, he hoped he wasn't inhaling and exhaling dust motes that belonged to Vy's new body. What did his breathing feel like to her?

I feel you, Vy let him know. *But I'd rather touch you like a human, like a person, instead of this way.*

She glitched. She fell apart, then re-coalesced.

Oops. Her thoughts were ashamed. *Truthfully, I am not used to these powers. I mess up every time I start to consciously think about how I look.*

Her hair coiled into braids. Then it loosened again. Vy's mental voice laughed, embarrassed.

I'm glad you're the only person to see me like this, Vy thought. *I don't know how I'll face Cherise. Or my mom. I don't think I can face anyone else until I can (pretend to be normal) control my powers.*

"I get that." Ariock marveled at the demigoddess who would be his wife. She was more perfect than ever. Her skin had a healthy glow, defiant of outer space.

He wanted to touch her indestructible body, to see how it felt.

Touch me, she urged impulsively, without words.

The communicator inside his helmet crackled. "Ariock?" Thomas's faraway voice said. "Can you find Vy?"

"I'm with her."

"Oh, good," Thomas's voice said. "Sorry I lost you for a few minutes. It was the distance. I sped around trying to get within range again, because guess what? You don't have to teleport. We have another way home."

"Nice." Ariock began to undo the clever buckles on his armor. He took it off, plate by plate.

Undressing was a strangely human act. He usually teleported his armor or clothing on and off. At least he remembered how his armor was supposed to be removed.

"Are you okay?" Thomas asked.

"I'm perfect," Ariock said. "Go home without me."

Thomas sounded uncertain. "Uh . . ."

Ariock had slept next to Vy for months without realizing her untapped potential. If he had known, he would have tapped that. He no longer feared accidentally killing her. He didn't have to worry about power depletion, or mistakes in space, or anything.

Vy could amplify his power.

We can augment each other, Vy silently agreed.

"Anyway," Thomas was saying, "Cherise figured out that telepathy gas facilitates linking. She's empowered Zai to teleport with passengers. They're bringing me home, and they can bring you next. Just—"

"Tell them not to come," Ariock said. "I want to be alone with Vy. And we may not return for a long time. You can tell people that."

"Really?"

"See you later, Thomas." Ariock removed his gorget and helmet.

The silence was total.

He was entirely naked in space. This was the prophetic panel of himself bathing in starlight. Shielding himself was so natural, so second nature to him, he remained comfortable.

Vy's clothing vanished, and she fell into his arms.

They joined.

There was no sweat, no discomfort, no dramatically terrifying size differences. Only fun differences.

They were cosmic.

They blazed like radiation.

They were as dynamic as solar flares.

I love you, they said to each other in a language of electric vibrations that felt like words.

They crashed and withdrew and crashed again, building each other up, climaxing, as powerful as a binary star pulled by each other's orbit.

PART SIX

INSURMOUNTABLE

The former Commander of All Living Things wrinkled her nose, unable to ignore the putrid odor of too many unwashed Torth in a damaged, poorly ventilated spaceship. She stepped over legs and arms and torsos.

Help Us? a gray-haired man prayed.

Help? an adolescent fresh off a baby farm echoed.

The individual thoughts of her shipmates did not form a harmonious choir. They were not a magnificent, thunderous melody. Instead, they were disgustingly reedy. They were as basic as individual voices.

She had to remind herself, repeatedly, that these refugees were actually gods who used to own slaves and govern worlds.

Also, they had been savvy enough to avoid the Conqueror's minions. They remained free and ostensibly proud.

Where will We go? An old, white-haired female Blue Rank choked back a sob. A sob.

How was such slavish behavior acceptable to these grungy survivors?

No one wanted to hear crying. They weren't slaves. That was the whole point! The Commander wanted to kick the old woman.

The old Blue Rank glared at her and imagined throwing her out an airlock. Several other Torth refugees agreed with that sentiment. They might have done it, except they knew the Commander could teleport. She would be able to return and she was hard to kill.

Also, they were reliant on her. Someone needed to import supplies.

What about reject planets? another refugee tentatively suggested. He was a smooth-cheeked young Brown Rank, barely old enough to have graduated off a baby farm. *My data marble (which I savvily confiscated before penitents or slaves could steal it) includes a galactic star chart. If We can navigate the temporal streams, I'll bet I can guide Us to a decent wilderness planet.*

The Commander congratulated the young Brown Rank for his foresight and his civilized willingness to help. *However,* she regretfully informed him, *the temporal streams are wrecked.*

That nearly demolished their remaining sense of self-determination.

But, thought an adolescent baby, *I'll bet the Conqueror will fix the problem?*

If he does, a Green Rank thought glumly, *We still cannot use them. I used to be an aspiring starship pilot. The navigation of temporal streams requires calculations from very mathematical minds. We don't have access to such minds here.* He looked around, questioning.

But he was correct. The refugees had not managed to rescue any mathematicians.

Nor do We own one of those calculation machines the Conqueror's minions (freed slaves) are installing in all their vehicles, the Green Rank went on. *What are they called? Computational devices?*

Computers, another refugee corrected him.

The hundreds of refugees slumped in defeat. Without the Megacosm, their ship was doomed to slow travel. They could not get far enough to even have a hope of restarting their lives again.

They hadn't been able to coax any slaves onto this overcrowded military cargo streamship. They'd had to abandon everything they owned. Although their ship's hull was intact, the plumbing system was broken. There were no showers, no running water.

And they were poorly provisioned. All they had to eat were nonperishable staples, and those would only last for a few weeks with austere rationing.

We're doomed, they thought.

The Commander wasn't so sure about that. She could think of a slim possibility for survival. It was just the seed of an idea. But she suspected she was the only hope for these ragtag survivors of civilizational collapse.

They needed her.

They would worship her once they understood her plan. They would acknowledge her as the Commander of All Surviving Torth.

???

All the filthy, sad remaining Torth turned toward her. Many of them still blamed her for the end of galactic civilization. Some were in a mood to kill her. Nevertheless, they were curious—and desperate.

She survived even after the Conqueror bested the Death Architect.

She has faced the Giant in a rage and lived.

She beheaded the Imposter in a duel.

She may have let Us get destroyed, but she is exceptional in some ways.

They all knew the Commander had tumbled, alone and isolated, in space, using her spacesuit jets to evade rock fragments. And she had ghosted. She had used her clairvoyant power again and again until she'd located this group of Torth survivors. Then she had used the last of her raw strength to teleport aboard this ship.

They had let her rest and recover. A few of them did respect her.

How does she propose We survive? They listened with their minds. They tuned into her.

The Commander revealed her hard-won knowledge with triumphant satisfaction. *Humans,* she thought, *contain huge amounts of untapped raw potential. When I link with a human and give them access to My mind (via telepathy gas), I gain tremendous power.*

The Torth refugees exchanged looks. This was, indeed, news.

This means I can gain enough raw power to teleport with passengers, the Commander clarified. *All I need to do is go to Earth and pick up a human.*

She had memorized the galactic route to Earth. She could teleport there, corner a human alone, saturate the area with telepathy gas, then link with that human and bring it onboard their ship. That way, they would gain raw power!

The Torth refugees looked at each other.

Unanimously, they chose to forgive her.

The entire Torth Majority had made mistakes. Some of them hated to acknowledge that, but these ragged survivors were beginning to accept that they might have to take more responsibility than they ever had in their lives.

Commander, they chorused, acknowledging their sole hope.

Commander of All Torth.

We are so glad to have You.

The Commander of All preened in their attention. A few hundred followers wasn't much compared to what she used to command, but here and now, it felt nice. She was glad to no longer be a total disgrace.

One of the refugees plucked at her filthy robes. *I need a bath. We all need more personal grooming space than this overcrowded streamship provides. Where will You (Commander of All) bring Us, once You have gained the excess raw power a human can provide You with?*

The others chorused that question. They all wanted to know the same thing. Where would they ultimately go?

Not Earth. The Conqueror would monitor the homeworld of his birth.

Not any known planet, unless they could find an underground hiding spot that the Conqueror's so-called scientists would never survey.

Maybe the Commander of All could scan for an ancient space station that had been long forgotten by civilization? She could raid the conquered planets for food and supplies. It would be a meager existence, though.

And she was quite old. If anything happened to her, the rest of the Torth refugees might well be stranded.

I have an idea, the Green Rank who was a pilot trainee volunteered.

Everyone turned to him.

Hasn't the Torth Empire sent colony starships to other galaxies? he thought.

Those departed convoys were almost mythical. Hundreds of generations ago, the early Torth Empire had sent exploratory starships to seek out new civilizations beyond the borders of their own galaxy. The populations onboard those enormous colony ships had eventually devolved into emotional cesspools. They'd been too isolated, too far away to be reined in by the Majority.

So they had severed themselves from the Megacosm.

To this day, no one knew their fates. The Majority, in its collective wisdom, had voted to quit sending Torth to foreign galaxies, so no more were sent. Still, those colony starships might be out there. Self-sufficient. Able to support life. Fragments of a magnificent past, akin to miniature worlds unto themselves.

I like that idea, the Commander of All acknowledged. The Conqueror was unlikely to hunt down the ancient departed starships of the early Torth Empire. He had a galaxy to administer.

We have a future! The refugees cheered without sound, without facial expressions.

We have a future!

We have a future!

The Commander of All Torth strutted before her small empire. Her approval rating shot higher. She had to step over limbs, since there wasn't enough room for a clear aisle, but she decided to overlook that inconvenience.

She would restore them to greatness. Sure, no one knew how to find the mythical lost convoys, but her newfound Majority should be capable of solving minor problems such as that. They were motivated. Everyone here wanted to swap their current battered streamship for something better. They would find a colony starship somewhere beyond the outer halo of the galaxy, and once they had that, their collective would have room to grow.

Grow? a Brown Rank looked perplexed. *Did those ancient starships have baby farm equipment, like embryo generators and artificial womb banks?*

The Torth refugees exchanged looks. They had no easy way to collect gametes from healthy donors. Specialized technicians were required to mix donated sperm with donated eggs, and they had no embryo specialists among them.

Realization dawned upon several female Torth who were of a fertile age. *!!!!!!!!!!!!!!!!!!!!!!!!!!*

They recalled a public announcement by a penitent known as the Pink Screwdriver. That act was disgustingly intimate. It was filthy and savage.

And everyone knew that the entire process of gestating a fetus through pregnancy was horrific. It only got worse once the noisy, emotional infant was born. Who would tend babies? Torth offspring were needy, greedy bundles of emotion. Very few Torth knew how to feed and handle infants. That was work for slaves and specialists.

The Commander of All Torth tightened her thin lips. Yes, the challenges were daunting. She admitted that. Enormous amounts of knowledge had been lost when the Megacosm collapsed. This meager population of civilized Torth would need to reinvent a lot of things. Space travel. Hover technology. Transports. Data storage. Medicine. Agricultural engineering. And yes, baby farms.

Life would be rough for a while. But after a few generations—

Generations?

The ragtag population eyed each other.

The Commander of All Torth tried to reassure them. Primitive sex was going to be a necessity, she supposed. But how difficult could it be? Even animals made it work. Maybe these refugees could learn about coitus from the humans she planned to abduct.

She would be with her constituents every step of the way. She would administer their sexual congress. It might be filthy and animalistic, but she would guide them and make sure they remained as aloof and uncaring as possible.

She was ready to mount and conquer the problem. What about the rest of them?

. . .

. . . .

. . . .

The Torth refugees had no room to move apart in the confined room of the spaceship, but they tried.

CHAPTER 2

SECRET MAGIC

Kessa used to wear a frayed rag over her head. Such were the garments of slaves.

Now she straightened with a bejeweled, filigreed headdress balanced over her brow ridges, cushioned on velvet brocade. She caught glimpses of herself in mirrors and other reflective surfaces. Her galactic headdress was half as large as herself, making her look weighed down.

Maybe that was why the peace council had commissioned it to be so large? They didn't want Kessa to escape from all the responsibilities they kept dumping on her.

Ah well. If she quit, who would take her place?

Not Thomas.

He had left a message to the galaxy that he was retired. That seemed to mean he was tired more than once, since no one could reach him.

Kessa detoured through one of the courtyards around the peace palace, formerly known as the war palace. She wished she could speak with Thomas and ask him why he had left a holographic recorded message stating that he was unreachable. That message would have been terrifying a few weeks ago. Thomas did not even say why he was a hermit, or why he would not visit his friends in Freedomland. He was simply gone.

Like Ariock and Vy. Like Garrett and Evenjos. Like Mondoyo and Serette.

Kessa went to see the progress on the memorial she had commissioned. The colossal slab of pink-and-jade marble was beautiful even in its natural state. The faces engraved on it were only partially finished. For now, scaffolding covered the majestic sculpture.

Once the engraver and his apprentices were done, the faces would include Garrett and the Lady of Sorrow. Not Thomas. Not Ariock. This memorial only showed heroes who had died fighting Torth, and Kessa wasn't sure if the Bringer of Hope was alive or not.

Cherise claimed to have received a handwritten letter from Vy, stating that she was vacationing with Ariock. Many people wondered if that was a euphemism for their heroic deaths. After all, the temporal streams remained nonfunctional. If people wanted interstellar transportation, they had to queue up for one of the time windows when Cherise or Abhaga teamed up with Zai or some other trustworthy penitent who was capable of galactic teleportation.

If the Bringer of Hope was alive somewhere, wouldn't he go back to mass-teleporting people on a regular basis? Didn't he have a sense of duty?

Kessa just didn't know.

She sat on a bench and admired the other faces taking shape on her commissioned memorial. Three children would be depicted on the stone. Mondoyo. Serette. And the Upward Governess.

Never mind their critics. As far as Kessa was concerned, certain renegade supergeniuses had proved themselves to be human.

So they would be depicted alongside Jinishta, Orla, Molyt Dazel, and a host of other exceptional people who were now dead. Kessa had even described Cozu, her long-dead mate. He had been a hero, too. He had taught her the importance of fighting for freedom.

"That's him right there." A well-dressed ummin pointed toward the unfinished memorial. His two adolescent companions craned their necks to get a look. "I'm so glad they included him."

Was this ummin actually pointing to the carved face of Mondoyo? Was that possible?

"He never deserved to die alone," the ummin said with sincere regret.

Kessa recognized the speaker then. She had only met him once, and he had been wearing slave rags at the time, awestruck by newfound freedom. Now he was almost an entirely different person.

"Enplyp?" Kessa said, recalling his name.

Enplyp turned, and his eyes widened upon seeing such a famous person. His adolescent companions gaped and then bowed with reverence. They all recognized Kessa. No one else would be crazy enough to wear a gigantic gem-encrusted headdress.

"Oh, Kessa!" Enplyp bowed. "I owe you gratitude as much as I owe Mondoyo."

Kessa stood, waving away the flattery. "I am just pleased that you recognize Mondoyo as a human."

Enplyp lowered his head in shame. "I abandoned him."

Kessa cocked her head, inviting more of an explanation.

"When I first arrived here," Enplyp gestured around, "in Freedomland, I was overwhelmed by all the possibilities. I forgot about Mondoyo and became obsessed with learning how to pilot streamships."

"And you married our mom," one of the adolescents said with a fond giggle.

"You adopted us," the other said in a pedantic tone.

Enplyp hugged them. "I did," he acknowledged. "But I never checked on how Mondoyo was adjusting to life here," he told Kessa. "I told myself he was a Torth supergenius and he could adjust to anything without help from his former slaves."

Kessa nodded with understanding. She had thought similar things about Thomas once.

"I wanted to visit him," Enplyp clarified. "I really did. He was the Torth who removed my slave collar and brought me here. He proved to me that mind readers can have emotions."

All of Mondoyo's former slaves had defended him and trusted him. That was why Kessa had welcomed the Twins, even though Thomas was absent at the time, unable to scan their minds.

"Why didn't you visit him, Dad?" one of the adolescents asked.

Enplyp looked guilty. "I figured I wouldn't be welcome." He gestured at the distant Dragon Tower. "He had important things to do. I didn't think anyone up there would appreciate an interruption from a mundane hovercart driver."

Kessa opened her beak to correct him. Then she reconsidered.

"I think I bear as much guilt as you, Enplyp," Kessa admitted. "You would have been welcome, but I never made that clear. No one invited you. And they should have."

Enplyp began to protest.

"I don't think we are the only former slaves who have made such mistakes," Kessa said.

Enplyp looked thoughtful. Perhaps he or his children would consider talking to some penitent Torth, or trying to befriend them? Kessa hoped so. The penitent rehabilitation program was supposed to outlive her.

She began to make a suggestion, but her control sleeve buzzed with an event reminder.

"I will be in touch with you." Kessa offered a nod of friendship to Enplyp. "But I have somewhere to be."

He and his adopted children looked honored. "Farewell, Kessa the Wise!"

Kessa walked past decorative trees and fountains. When she saw dignitaries head in her direction, she turned another way. She wasn't going to let anyone make her miss her next appointment.

The pendulum grotto was hidden underground, out of sight from the gardens. Kessa descended a ramp into the cool depths of an artificial cave. Here, an enormous pendulum swung past stalagmites, its motions as regular as any clock.

Kessa stared at the stalagmite that she had been told marked the target time.

Soon.

Even now, Kessa had trouble believing the clandestine party invitation she had received. She had made a few discreet inquiries to make sure the signature avatars—Ariock and Vy—were legitimate and not some sick hoax. Apparently, Cherise had received a similar invitation. So had Varktezo, Pung, and Weptolyso. They were each expected to dress up and go to a specific location, at a simultaneous specific time, and . . .

Well, that time was now.

The pendulum knocked against the target stalagmite.

Kessa's stomach dropped with the familiar sensation of teleportation. Ozone crackled around her.

Even though she'd half expected it, she gasped. Did this power come from Cherise linked up with a penitent champion? Or . . . dare she hope? Was it really Ariock? She hadn't seen him in more than a month.

She landed unsteadily on her feet. Subtle differences in the air pressure and gravity told her she was on another planet. Sunlight danced over decorative bridges dripping with flowers in full bloom. Fountains overflowed with pure water, honeyed nectar, or champagne. Banquet tables offered multiple tiers of tempting morsels.

Other people began to appear out of thin air, looking shocked and amazed. Kessa recognized many of them. There was Cherise in a sunset-colored lacework dress. Nethroko and his family. Utavlug Hano! Kessa smiled upon recognizing the herbalist from Duin, her face painted in a ceremonial way.

And Yanyashta! Kessa grinned at her secretary.

A strange-looking albino appeared, with flamboyant flowers all over his costume and hat. Kessa thought she had heard of this guy. Wasn't he known as the Great Mwagru or something like that?

Pung appeared with his friend Gralet. It was fun to see them dressed in such fancy tunics, with hats nearly as elaborate as Kessa's headdress. Nror and Dyoot were well-groomed. Zai was almost unrecognizable in a clingy dress instead of battle armor. Oh, there was Gosmaga. And Choonhulm. Kessa rarely saw them anymore. And . . .

Were those humans?

Kessa blinked at the people who resembled penitents but clearly weren't. They gaped at every alien as if they couldn't believe their own eyes. And their eye colors were not purple or yellow or red or pink. They were the hues Kessa had learned were common among humans: brown, hazel, and blue.

Vy swept out of the crowd. She wore a shimmering white satin gown with a matching cape. A tiara held her hair back. She was stunning.

"Mom!" Vy held out her arms toward the stout human with red hair.

"Oh, sweetie!" The mom fell into Vy's embrace with a joyful laugh. "This is a beautiful setting for your wedding."

Wedding? Kessa grinned. She was pretty sure that word entailed a ritual binding ceremony for human couples.

A shadow briefly blocked the sun.

The humans exclaimed in awe and pointed. Kessa glanced up to see not Ariock, but a sky croc soaring overhead. It wore a passenger harness.

If Azhdarchidae was here, then his trainer must be around!

Kessa scanned the multispecies wedding guests. Most of the humans were gathered around Vy. They had even drawn Cherise, Zai, and Abhaga into their group.

Kessa looked elsewhere. She walked around the natural pavilion, searching for the person who had removed her slave collar.

Thomas was not near the banquet tables, or the flowered trellises, or the rose quartz staging area with its arched bridge.

Councilor Deschuba ambled over with a plate of food. "Peace, Kessa," he greeted her, as if he had been born a slave. "It is like a dream here, is it not? Have you sampled the fine foods?"

"Not yet. Have you seen Thomas?"

The high councilor looked ashamed, perhaps because of the pit incident. "Ah, I believe he's over there." He pointed to a far corner.

Kessa thanked Deschuba and excused herself. She wound past other guests. And finally she saw him, standing apart from everyone else, slouched with his hands in his pockets. He wore a tailored waistcoat and nice boots, but otherwise, his clothes were nondescript. He didn't look like a war hero or a renegade supergenius or a galactic conqueror. He looked unassuming.

Kessa wasn't fooled.

She approached Thomas, cautious. A galaxy was too much for one ummin to rule. She was bound to make mistakes if she had to make every decision in isolation, and although she didn't want to be reliant on him, there was more at stake than her own ego. So many people needed his strategies and ideas.

CHAPTER 3

TITANS

Thomas had only been at this party for a few minutes, and he already missed his mountain cabin on Reject-843, where the only minds he encountered were those of Azhdarchidae and the indigenous wildlife.

Animals did not expect great things of him. Animals did not worship him, or hate him, or have overcomplicated thoughts about him, or snub him for being who he was. Animals were nice.

He tried not to admire Cherise in her vibrant dress. She was too vivacious, too wholesome, and, frankly, too normal to be with a supergenius. Thomas was glad she hadn't seen him yet. With luck, he would officiate this wedding and then ask Ariock to teleport him away before anyone else could talk him into . . . well, anything.

"Thomas, where have you been hiding all these weeks?" a familiar voice asked near his elbow.

He was so absorbed in avoiding Cherise, he had failed to notice the sparkly headdress angling toward him. How embarrassing.

"I'm enjoying my retirement," Thomas told Kessa.

Kessa radiated a sense of hurt, as if she had been abandoned. "I miss you."

Only Kessa would miss him. Thomas suspected that everyone else in the universe had thrown a celebration upon hearing that he was retired and gone forever.

Even Cherise must be relieved, if only on a subconscious level. She was free to date normal men, or normal teenage boys, without feeling a lingering sense of guilt. Thomas simply lacked the fortitude to pretend to be normal. He just couldn't do it. His mind was so far outside the range of normalcy, he might as well inhabit a different galaxy.

Like Mondoyo.

Mondoyo had tried to fit in. He had written music and poetry. He had tried to act like an average lab technician, like a friend, not creepy or weird at all.

It hadn't mattered.

Everyone knew what he was. No one would ever treat a supergenius like an average person. It was impossible.

"You don't need me anymore," Thomas assured Kessa. "You're handling everything just fine." He nodded in approval at her headdress. "I can't think of a better person for the job."

"I did not expect you to walk away from everything," Kessa said. "You and Ariock. There are still penitent uprisings all over the galaxy. They are not all afraid of our space fleets."

Thomas waved that away. "They'll settle down. You've got this."

"There are separatist groups that wish to reinstate the Torth Empire." Kessa stood with her back to the pavilion, ignoring the mingling and laughter of wedding guests. "They find the slightest excuse for bitterness toward our government and then they overreact. There are breakaway militias recruiting people. I am not entirely suited to deal with freed people who now wish to establish their own tyrannical nations."

Thomas nodded, acknowledging the irony of former slaves who wanted to steal other people's liberty. "They'll never become a majority," he assured her. "As long as wise leaders are in charge, they're just gnats. You don't need me or Ariock."

Kessa radiated a bristly feeling. It seemed she could hardly believe his lack of concern. "The peace council can use your advice for many reasons. The superluminal network—"

"Varktezo will make sure it's rebuilt," Thomas cut in. "And you have help from teleporters plus human augmenters. You really don't need me. Or Ariock."

He hoped he was right about that. Some societal problems were difficult even for a supergenius to solve. Telepathy gas, for instance, facilitated linking between humans and Yeresunsa, and it would grow in popularity for that reason alone. Consequences spun through Thomas's mind in an ever-increasing web. Telepathy was a multifaceted problem.

"You took off our collars." Kessa indicated her neck scar. "You gave us access to technology. You handed us the means to learn as fast as gods."

Thomas hadn't done those things alone, yet he did not correct her. She was angling toward a point.

"We are like children," Kessa said, "learning how to run for the first time. You set us loose in a universe that has roads but that also has cliffs and pitfalls. We were starving, and you just unshackled us and gave us an unlimited feast. And now you want to step back and see what mistakes we make?"

That was unfair. Thomas straightened, glaring at her. He had not retired as a way to mock former slaves.

"A civilization that has to rely on a supergenius," he said, "isn't healthy. And it isn't sustainable. You don't need me. At all."

Thomas sensed Kessa knew that. She was not begging him to return to work. She was here because—

"Thomas?" The voice was incredulous. "No way."

"Cherise said it's him." That whisper sounded dubious.

"Nah. It can't be him."

Thomas turned to see his foster family.

Their mental patterns were jarringly human. He had never expected to talk to these particular humans again, although he should have guessed that Vy would invite the whole family.

Mrs. Hollander's astonished gaze traveled down his legs.

"It's really me," Thomas admitted.

The group of humans quieted with shock.

"It was a magical cure, sort of." Thomas wished he had disguised himself just to avoid this awkward reunion with his foster family.

Mrs. Hollander looked amazed. "The aliens can reverse spinal muscular atrophy?"

"Uh, they're making progress on it." He wasn't going to dive into a long explanation about what Evenjos had been capable of doing. She was dead and gone, according to both Vy and Ariock. Anyhow, Thomas had bequeathed a scientific foundation with funding and informational databanks so that Varktezo and other alien scientists could improve upon NAI-13 and other medicines.

Mrs. Hollander surprised Thomas by enfolding him in a hug. He squeaked.

"I'm just so glad you're okay," she said. "I was afraid you were dead."

To Thomas's shock, she radiated sincerity.

He had been nothing but a self-absorbed cretin. He used to figure that his foster mother's care was impersonal. She loved everyone. But now it seemed she had genuinely missed him, and not solely because he had been her personal financial adviser. She had actually missed his personality.

Well. That was mysterious. And surprising.

"Uh . . ." Unsure how to react, Thomas tentatively hugged her back. He had urged Ariock to prioritize saving Earth during the Death Architect's doomsday attack. Maybe this was why. "I'm glad you're safe and well," he said.

The other kids jostled closer, eager to learn about what Thomas had been up to. It seemed they had received tantalizing answers from Cherise.

"Is that really your dragon?" Ramón jabbed a finger skyward.

"He's more like a pterosaur," Thomas said. "His name is Azhdarchidae."

"Did it hurt, when you got healed?" Miranda still had trouble believing it. "That alien over there"—she pointed to Gralet—"says you can read minds. Is that how you always knew what I was thinking?"

Thomas shrugged. He wasn't going to dive into explanations.

Rochelle pushed closer. "Everyone seems kind of in awe of you. They say you freed a lot of slaves? And you took over a galactic empire! Are they serious?"

"It's a long story." Thomas spoke in a bored tone that invited nothing more.

But they kept asking questions.

Kessa waited on the periphery, her beak twisted in frustration. She was too small to elbow humans aside. Someone else engaged her in conversation, and she went with it.

Cherise was also on the periphery, chatting with alien guests. Every once in a while she shot an amused grin at Thomas.

He tried to interpret what was going through her mind. Why had she pointed the Hollander family his way? Was it some sort of vengeance for his abrupt decision to retire?

He had visited her in secret before he left. *I'm not fit to be around people,* he had said.

And Cherise had replied that she was okay with his absence. Hadn't she? *I'll miss you. But do what you need to do.*

She wasn't going to pine away waiting for him to return. Thomas knew Cherise well enough to know that. She had multiple projects, and she would pursue those rather than pursuing any particular person. Her creative drive was one of her most admirable traits.

"Can we move away from Earth, like you did?" one of his foster siblings asked.

"Yeah!" another kid said, excited. "Can we live here?"

It was somewhat nightmarish to imagine these kids each accompanying a shani or penitent warrior, amplifying their powers to demigod levels. The galaxy might end up ruled by Yeresunsa-human duos.

At least Varktezo was working on countermeasures.

"You'll have to ask Vy," Thomas said. "That would be her decision." He figured she was wise enough to understand the implications. After all, she had flirted with Ariock and his immense power for more than a year.

"Why Vy?"

"Where is she?"

A gigantic shadow fell over his foster family.

They all turned, and in that instant, their attention peeled off Thomas and onto Ariock. The ten-foot-tall groom was much more attention-grabbing than any of his wedding guests. Ariock wore a double-breasted sherwani, with a broad belt and galactic embroidery. He didn't need armor to look impressive and imposing.

The kids gaped.

"I'm the groom," Ariock said with a smile. "I'll be marrying your sister."

The gaping kids emanated fearful uncertainty.

"Oh, hi, Ariock!" Mrs. Hollander had clearly met him before. Even so, it took more than a few meetings for anyone to get used to seeing Ariock up close. "Um, everyone, this is Ariock Dovanack."

Vy's voice came from somewhere to Ariock's right. "Yup, I told you about him. This is my husband-to-be!"

The crowd shifted, and there was the radiant bride.

Thomas had not seen Vy up close since the final battle on the asteroid. She looked somehow more . . . unearthly.

Thomas assessed her, wondering what secret she and Ariock were keeping. He had picked up a hint of weirdness from Ariock earlier, when the big guy had teleported Thomas from his retirement wilderness to this wedding planet. But Thomas really didn't want the intimate details of his foster sister's sex life with a giant, so he had purposefully avoided Ariock's thoughts and focused on the behavioral psychology of herd animals instead.

"We're going to have the ceremony soon," Vy told her family. "But I wanted you to meet Ariock first."

She grabbed Ariock's arm and tugged him, forcing him to lower himself to be closer to eye level. Usually, Ariock was oblivious when someone normal-size tugged him, but the two of them must have worked on their unspoken agreements and mutual accommodations. He responded right away.

Her family had plenty of questions for the giant. Some of them were tactless. But Ariock took everything in stride. He explained that he had grown up in New Hampshire, that he had a growth disorder, and that yes, he was an alien-human hybrid, but he considered himself to be as human as Vy.

"We're planning to travel a lot," Ariock said in response to a question. "But we'll visit you on Earth. I promise."

Vy sauntered up to Thomas with two filled champagne glasses. She offered him one.

"Cheers." Vy clinked glasses with Thomas.

"Congratulations on your nuptials." Thomas took a sip of nectar champagne.

"Thanks for being our officiant," Vy said.

"I wouldn't miss it," Thomas said.

Ariock's deep voice was hard to tune out. "I want to be careful about visits to Earth," he was saying. "Humankind will learn about the rest of the universe, but we think that should be a gradual process. I'd rather not attract a media storm."

"Do you think it's right for us to vanish from the public?" Vy asked Thomas. "I mean, Ariock definitely needs time off. But I do feel bad if we leave for some indeterminate amount of time."

Thomas shrugged. "News about the prophecy of the lone survivor leaked out. It must be nice to have most of the universe think you're dead."

He privately puzzled over that prophecy. Try as he might, he didn't understand how the oracle Ah Jun had made such a huge mistake at the very end of her prophetic sequence. Thomas wasn't a lone survivor. So why had Ah Jun misled everyone? Had it been necessary to ensure the exact sequence of events that led to their victory over the Death Architect? Perhaps everyone needed to believe Ariock was doomed so that the Torth also believed it?

"I guess the prophecy was accurate," Vy mused. "Sort of. I did die."

Thomas stared at her.

"And so did Ariock," she said.

Thomas dived into her mind, too curious to stop himself.

Oh.

Wow.

Thomas gaped at Vy, speechless with shock. He had never felt so unsettled.

This wasn't Vy as he remembered her. This was a newly empowered Vy, with the glorious, indestructible body of a goddess. She could morph into a living planet. Or a blade of grass. She could shapeshift into any form. Her augmentation power could boost Ariock's titanic strength to even more astronomical heights.

The couple did not yet know their own limitations and capabilities.

"Aha." Thomas reassessed his foster sister. "I get why you retired now."

Vy nodded. Her thoughts reflected the truth he had already deduced. She wanted to fully master her powers before she dared to live among ordinary people. Ariock also wanted time to grow used to whatever augmented strength Vy gave him.

They were titans.

"We put off the wedding until we felt like we could hold it safely," Vy murmured. "Without me glitching into a diffuse cloud of fog or melting into a literal puddle of goo." She glanced at Ariock, and the giant blushed.

Apparently the puddle-of-goo thing had happened more than once.

Thomas politely focused on a neurobiological analysis of the grazing habits of alien llamas.

"So here we are." Vy grinned. "I practiced a ton."

She probably meant that literally.

"Great." Thomas sipped more champagne. Vy might actually be able to read his mind, since she could create her own telepathic bond with anyone whose body she could suffuse. Except she had to practice separatism. It was a matter of safety. If she casually linked with Ariock or someone like him . . .

She might accidentally boost Ariock to a degree where he was powerful enough to destroy a continent with a sneeze.

"I guess you're not going to settle into a typical married lifestyle?" Thomas said.

"Right." Vy sounded relieved that he understood. "We're not going to become bureaucrats and hold swank dinner parties. I don't think we should be around people for extended periods of time."

That was wise. Their combined power put them on another level. They were beyond Yeresunsa. One minor quarrel, or even just a slip of concentration, and Vy or Ariock could wind up hurting a lot of people.

"If nothing else," Vy went on, "we would become major assassination targets. Everyone close to us would be in danger."

That, too.

People cheered for heroes like Ariock and Evenjos during a war, but the war was over. Nobody liked gross inequality. Power disparity—and all the envy and resentment that entailed—had led to the rise of the Torth Empire.

"Hm." Thomas pretended to be interested in his champagne. "Planning to have any kids?"

"Grr." Vy playfully punched his arm.

Thomas plucked the answer from her mind. She didn't know if her malleable body was capable of pregnancy.

But she and Ariock wanted kids.

And since they were likely immortal and invincible, they had plenty of time to experiment. They were considering employing a surrogate mother.

Thomas sighed. He trusted Vy and he trusted Ariock, but any offspring they had would be a big question mark. A really huge question mark.

"It's time for the ceremony!" Vy squealed.

CHAPTER 4
WISE

Thomas hooked his arm around Vy's and walked her down the aisle between guests. A transparent veil as delicate as dragonfly wings covered her face. Thomas wore a jazzy waistcoat, having rejected shani fashion trends in favor of fashion from his homeworld.

A breeze shifted the hanging wisteria. People watched as if they were participating in an enchanted fairy tale. Many held their breaths while alien flowers sang like a choir.

There were no cameras. Vy had forbidden personal photography, although the couple had set up several capture marbles so the wedding would be holographically recorded.

Ariock waited on the quartz slab of a stage. He stood between two stepped archways, each one draped in decorations. Thanks to those tall stairways, his bride and their officiants would be as visible as he was, boosted in height.

People sighed with emotion as Vy climbed the stairs on the right. Her bridal train trailed behind her.

She stood on the apex. That put her on kissing level with Ariock.

Ariock tenderly folded back her bridal veil, revealing her face.

Thomas climbed the opposite stairs, filing between Elaine Hollander, Pung, and the Great Mwagru. Weptolyso remained on the ground. He didn't need a height boost.

The Great Mwagru seemed tickled and charmed to meet Thomas in person. He even offered a hug. He was the only shani present at the wedding, and he was so unlike his albino brethren, anyone ignorant of aliens would be grievously misled. Thomas was so surprised that he accepted the hug, offering a friendly grin to the flamboyant seer whom he had neglected to meet until now.

"Friends!" Pung's voice was amplified to fill the pavilion. "Today we are here to celebrate the union of our beloved Bringer of Hope with our beloved Lady of Paradise."

The audience was merry. Many guests laughed, having been unsure if the invitations were genuine or some sort of hoax.

"Please keep this event a secret," Pung went on. "Our friends Ariock and Vy are taking a hiatus from their work. I'll tell you, when I first met Vy, I mistook her for an embarrassed Blue Rank . . ." He launched into an entertaining speech.

Each of the masters of ceremonies had their own flair. Thomas felt markedly less appealing than Pung, Weptolyso, Elaine, or the Great Mwagru. When it was his turn to address the audience, he only offered a few dry remarks. Vy was his foster sister. Ariock was like a brother to him. They were both among his earliest and closest friends. What else should he say?

". . . And now," Thomas said, launching into the actual ceremony, "in full view of galactic law, do you, Ariock Dovanack, take Violet Hollander to be your life mate and wife?"

"I do."

Ariock vowed to honor, cherish, and care about his wife, no matter what. Vy read similar vows for her husband. They promised to resist keeping secrets from each other, and they promised to enhance each other's abilities.

Thomas raised his hands and created thermal currents. Flower petals swirled around the couple. "It is my great honor to pronounce you husband and wife."

Delicate vines floated to the couple, laden with flowers. The vines magically braided into bracelets that matched in style and slid onto each of their wrists. Thomas had no idea whether the twined living bracelets were Ariock's doing or Vy's. Perhaps they had each used their powers to braid each other's?

"You may kiss." Thomas grinned, happy about their happiness.

With their height—Vy on the arch, Ariock standing—everyone could see the love in that kiss.

Thomas used his holographic power to add sparkles and floral designs in the air around them. He took some inspiration from the erstwhile gardens of the Upward Governess.

Next, he created fiery flares to summon his well-trained sky croc. Azhdarchidae swooped low and skimmed overhead. He caused a stir in the audience, and Ariock and Vy ended their kiss, laughing.

After the ceremony, the party truly got started.

"The reception will go on for as long as there are guests!" Pung announced to the excited audience. "We have guest cabins for everyone. When you're ready to leave? Simply tell Ariock, Vy, or Cherise that you wish to go home."

Thomas relaxed a bit. He would stay a short time longer, just for the sake of politeness.

He descended to join the mingling guests. People sampled snack foods with origins from all over the galaxy. A playlist of music piped across the pavilion, and Thomas sensed intrigue from the alien listeners. There was dancing. And laughter.

None of it included Thomas.

He made his way toward Ariock. The big guy knew about Thomas's remote cabin in the rugged wilderness of a planet known as Reject-843. Ariock was the one who had transported Thomas there in the first place.

Ariock was happily chatting with Nethroko and other nussian guests. "Hey!" he said, noticing Thomas. "You did great. Welcome to the family!"

"I'm glad to have you as my brother-in-law." Thomas truly meant it, although he was all too cognizant of key differences between them. Ariock did not have to pretend to be human, whereas Thomas felt like he was pretending all the time.

"Hey," Thomas said. "Um, would you mind if I leave the party early?"

Ariock looked perplexed.

"Like, now?" Thomas clarified.

Understanding dawned on Ariock. He excused himself from the other guests and drew Thomas aside. "I was hoping you'd stay a little longer. Don't you want to see the drone show? Varktezo choreographed it."

The show would be impressive, but Thomas wasn't going to tolerate several more hours of pretending to be a well-adjusted human being. Besides, he meant to avoid Kessa and her questions. "Sorry. I'm no good at parties."

"Okay." Ariock radiated disappointment, but he nodded toward the teleportation flat. "Let's go over there so we don't disturb the other guests."

Once they were alone, Ariock knelt to confront Thomas. "Do you know why we decided to retire from public life?"

"I got it from Vy," Thomas confessed. "So, extra congratulations. I guess she has the power to halt your constant growth."

Ariock looked as if that miraculous idea had never occurred to him.

"Once she studies neurobiology for a few years," Thomas amended. "She has a lot of catching up to do, to get to the level of skill that Evenjos had. In the meantime? She can resize herself, so she's not worried if you end up being the size of a starship."

Ariock rolled his eyes. He must be worn out on size jokes.

"Sorry." Thomas didn't want to ruin Ariock's happiness today. "I wish you both a very happy life together. I meant what I said. You're among my best friends. I do consider you both to be family." He nodded upward, indicating Azhdarchidae. "We're ready to go home."

Ariock's mind brewed. Thomas sensed what he was about to ask.

"Why are you avoiding people, Thomas?"

"I'm not," Thomas said. "I'm just tired."

Ariock shook his head. He didn't want vagueness. He and Vy had shared their secret with Thomas and no one else here. Shouldn't that invite mutual trust?

Thomas bit his lower lip, mulling it over. He did owe Ariock the truth. That was fair. That was the Pact of Strength.

"I'm two million years old." Thomas looked away, embarrassed. He hated to outright admit how alien he was. "That's my lived experience. Most of it comes from Torth, from penitents and prisoners and enemy combatants. I'm no longer psychologically healthy, if I ever was."

Ariock's mood became tinged with guilt. He had urged Thomas to absorb a lot of those memories, back when he had worried about an assassin hidden among the penitent population.

"I have no peers." Thomas forced himself to meet Ariock's gaze. "I'm retiring for the same reason as you and Vy. I'm too dangerous to exist in society."

He nearly went on, wanting to specify the dangers he posed to civilization.

But he had said enough. Ariock understood.

The giant straightened, emanating sympathy and insight.

They stood together for a moment, understanding each other.

"Would you mind if I interrupt you two?" Kessa walked up to them.

Thomas hesitated. He needed to explain that he was just on his way out. Once Ariock collected Azhdarchidae for him, he would exit the reception.

Kessa planted her fists on her hips. "Thomas, when I ask you a question, I expect an answer. That is the pact you made with me."

Pacts.

Thomas swallowed. He ought to honor the pact he had made with Kessa, if he was still honoring pacts. He needed to stick to his principles. If he began to disregard pacts—to tell lies—then he would slide down a road to tyranny. That was all too easy for him.

His principles were the only things stopping him from becoming a monstrous tyrant.

"Did I overhear you say you're too dangerous to exist in society?" Kessa sounded disbelieving.

"It's the truth," Thomas said, defensive. Why did so few people take his warnings seriously?

"Oh, I'm dangerously powerful, too," Kessa said. "I can order any penitent to be sentenced to death. I can likely order death for just about any sapient, and my orders would be carried out. I can send armies anywhere. Such is the authority I wield." She gestured to her bejeweled headdress. "This much power is frightening. I can agree with you on that."

Thomas inwardly admitted that she had scored a point. Kessa did wield power.

And she wielded it well. She understood that if she were to quit, the ensuing power vacuum might invite chaos. She was wise that way.

"Unlike you, however," Kessa said, "I trust myself."

Ariock gave Thomas a sympathetic shoulder pat. "She has a point."

Thomas summoned the courage to be vulnerable. "I'm a civilization killer," he explained to both of them. "I shouldn't be involved with centers of power, no matter what benefits I can offer. You cannot trust me with power."

Kessa clicked her beak. "Are you lying to me? Or are you lying to yourself? I cannot tell."

That accusation stung. Thomas pretended to gawk in outrage, but what he actually felt was chagrin.

Kessa had seen past his excuse. That excuse—that he feared power—was his armor, but it wasn't the whole truth.

He wondered if telepathy gas practice sessions had given her a bit of actual telepathy.

"A lot of people trust you at the center of power," Kessa pointed out. "And you know that. I think you are avoiding us for another reason." Her gesture included Cherise and the Hollander family, enjoying themselves at the party. "Is it that you don't want to endure your friends? Are you afraid of disapproval? Or hatred?"

Thomas sensed her wondering if she had lost his trust. She was mournful.

"I didn't leave because of any one person." Thomas had not meant to hurt her. He should have considered how his abrupt retirement would make her feel.

Even so, Kessa had touched on a salient truth.

"Hatred of penitents is a major problem," Thomas admitted. "It will be a challenge for civilization to overcome."

Kessa softened. "I am doing my best. But the collective trauma of generations is being released for the first time in twenty-four thousand years, and it is not easy to shut down the potential for violence. I am doing everything I can."

"I know," Thomas said.

He did know. He had read a lot of minds, so he knew what most former slaves felt for their former masters and owners. No one protected reformed Torth better than Kessa. Penitents had guaranteed rights, a place in society, and a chance at redemption, all thanks to her.

But Kessa's protections had limits.

Not even demigods such as Ariock and Glorious Vy could solve a society-wide problem with such deep roots.

Elaine Hollander approached, clearly wanting to include Thomas and Ariock in the party.

"I believe you could do a lot of good if you returned." Kessa said.

Thomas overheard her inner thoughts, and he realized that she was actually right. His retirement sent a message to all of civilization. It implied that outreach efforts to penitents did not matter. Serette and Mondoyo were dead. Thomas had seemingly fled, so now it looked as if Kessa could not maintain any friendships with mind readers.

He had not intended to hurt intergalactic relations between liberated people and penitents. He had not meant to damage Kessa's reputation.

"Why don't you trust yourself, Thomas Lightbringer?" Kessa removed her gem-encrusted headdress, revealing the brocaded cloth beneath. "I am asking as your friend."

Thomas felt a lump of emotion in his throat. Kessa's lack of headdress was a sign of respect. It meant they were speaking as equals.

Thomas's foster mother hesitated on the periphery of their circle. "Uh, am I interrupting?"

Thomas glanced at Ariock. His brother-in-law immediately grasped his unspoken request and offered a nod. "I'll check on you later." He turned to Elaine with a smile. "Mom. Uh, can I call you Mom?"

She chuckled happily. "Of course! Please do."

"Great." Ariock beamed. "I'd love to get to know the family better, Mom." He escorted her toward the party.

That left Thomas alone on the teleportation flat with Kessa.

"You are a human." Kessa radiated sincerity. "You deserve every honor you have earned. Will you ever let yourself believe that?"

Kessa wasn't asking much from him.

Perhaps he might serve the peace council as a consultant? Like every ten years or so. Remotely. Surely he could handle that?

"Would it help if I release you from the pact I made with you?" Kessa asked.

Friends did favors for each other. Friends also let down their guard around each other. Kessa was willing to make concessions in order to regain the loss of friendship she perceived. She had shared her full name with Thomas. She had removed her headdress in front of him.

He had yet to share as much of himself with her.

It was time.

"I know what I am," Thomas said.

Kessa clicked her beak a few times, prepared to interrupt a litany of self-hatred.

"I'm a superhuman," Thomas said. "I'm smarter than everyone I meet. And I'm a better person than most of them. I'm definitely human in all the ways that matter."

Kessa's beak hung open. She knew all these things, but she had never expected Thomas to admit them out loud. She had not guessed that he was so self-aware.

Thomas gave a single nod of acknowledgment. He knew. He had known who and what he was for a long time.

"Yet . . ." Kessa trailed off, and Thomas sensed her exploring possibilities in her mind. "You don't trust yourself?" She squinted, trying to make sense of his claims.

"I trust myself alone. In a vacuum." Thomas looked across the pavilion, to where Cherise danced with other wedding guests. Orb lanterns glowed as the afternoon light waned.

"You don't trust yourself among other humans?" Kessa looked perplexed. "I don't understand."

Cherise aimed an enigmatic smile toward Thomas.

He looked away. He definitely did not need the augmented power Cherise could give him. He did not need gunpowder for the kinds of explosions he could spark.

"I think that waving extra power under my nose, constantly, would be a terrible idea." Thomas turned back to Kessa. "That is the wisest advice I can give you, my galactic ruler friend."

He had absorbed the memories of a goddess-empress from a bygone era. He had gained memories from two different prophets in their dying moments. He had never met an oracle, but he had the next best thing—an ability to form hypotheses based on multigenerational time frames. He saw patterns that eluded most historians and philosophers.

"I think I see." Kessa stepped back, assessing Thomas anew. "You are Gandalf the wizard."

She had been watching movies from Earth. Thomas smiled.

"You purposely reject power," Kessa said. "Instead of commanding armies and kingdoms, you are choosing to be a humble wanderer."

"That's right." Thomas almost wished he could emphasize the point by making a pipe magically appear.

Eh, that was a Garrett move as well as a Gandalf move. Besides, he didn't want to get addicted to tobacco.

"Well, then." Kessa squared her shoulders. "How about this? You are subject to the needs of the peace council. You are not a galactic authority. I am. You are a humble wanderer who must obey when I call. Is this agreeable?"

Thomas laughed.

Then he thought about it. He wouldn't mind an excuse to keep an apartment in Freedomland. He might be able to handle the temptations of power as long as everyone, even Cherise, grew to believe he was too self-hating, or too unambitious, to ever become a threat.

He would be just a lowly subject of the peace council.

Just a human with limited power.

"How about it?" Kessa probed.

Cherise was dancing with Varktezo. She whirled closer, her black hair swinging, and for a moment, her sparkling gaze connected with Thomas's. He felt something like an electric tingle. It had nothing to do with power and everything to do with chemistry.

Maybe it would be all right to visit Freedomland on a regular basis.

"Give me a humble job title," Thomas told Kessa. "I'll accept a low-key role as your adviser, but don't ever let me make major decisions that enact sweeping changes to society. You are the decision-maker. Not me. Never me."

Kessa grandly placed her headdress back on her head. With that gear, she became a towering figure. She had grown into her role, even more than Thomas had ever dared hope.

"Give my secretary a way to reach you," Kessa commanded. "Assuming you accept a job as my personal adviser?"

"As long as it's part-time." Thomas wasn't sure if Kessa fully understood what sort of adviser she was taking on. A telepathy gas session would expose his frighteningly alien mind. Then, sadly, she might learn to properly fear him.

"Don't worry." Kessa patted his shoulder. "I will not let you rule."

She walked away, into the party, with one last fond look that radiated trust. Thomas sensed her thoughts. Out of all the people Kessa had ever met, she believed Thomas was the one person whom she would entirely trust with galactic power.

Thomas stood alone, pondering the nature of power, and what sort of person he really was.

ACKNOWLEDGMENTS

Thank you so much for coming on this journey with me.

If you enjoyed the Torth series, please recommend it to other readers. Reviews and ratings help everyone. Much appreciation if you review this book on Amazon, Goodreads, or Audible.

Special thanks to my subscribers and former subscribers on Patreon: Nyroe, Wrath, Godlyskeleton, ryan ukeiley, volpol, NoteOfE, G O L I X T H, KarenSampson, John O'Connor, Adil Riggs, Bunny Waffles, Zak Pr, Josh Cothran, Aqua, Pokey Equation, Xavier Lamphere, Ceagle, The Dargon, JC, Tyler Smith, Sparkie, A. Brown, Pietro Simone, JJBlack, Certa, Jason Gross, Isaac Boyles, faisal, Mitchell, Gres, Grosbilljunior, Orion Mitchell, LiraGuitar-, luke, MrNobody, John Hurley, Chikkane, Jonathan Williams, mythic, TurtleOfRainbow, Andrew Webb, Dave The Technician, Gavin Olsen, Scott Southworth, E, Alexandre Ablon, Conor lennon, Adam Moore, bensorme, Naorke, Sherriff kadir, Corella, Dvn, George Waller, Jack, Jackson Ragland, Derrick McDowell, Philldoran, Alric Good, Joel Wells, Jerry, Notlimah, Timecrafter, Ithri Benamara, F M, Frightful6_7, Jason Denzel, Теодор Жечев, Aph, and my parents. Your support means a lot, and it's hugely helpful to my writer lifestyle.

Huge thanks to my readers on Royal Road and Wattpad. Especially commenters: Cjenx, General Peaceful, Shadow of Marethyu, Zombie Unicorne, Miss Nomer, Smoarville, dishtv, EatMoreVegetables, The Lord of The Cookies, Ghosti, sid_cypher, UpsilionEnlightened, Omni-Origin Perfect-Inheritor, Banarok Lionrage, Raszhivyk, Ars404, Mofy, Megapooz, MicahLM2, playr543, Ceilingfanenvy, Whiplash246, V6ct9r, micpanda, IcefireStarfire, biravincent, _mehatepizza_, ShaunKZ, Rhandyabao5, Joey-Jay_Spooner, Marysiak14, SubZero_005, Kafui27, MelissaKimFernandes, AGENT_88, Art3miss777, DeSmiley, ko0025, lisadavis910, and a whole lot more. I appreciate you very much!

I'm grateful to David Gillions, astrophysicist, for his consultation on how a supergenius might end the universe.

Especially, as always, thanks to Adam Robert Thompson, my alpha reader and husband, who is actually Thomas and Ariock combined (minus their flaws, of course)!

And here's a shoutout to some excellent online communities for readers and authors of heroic and power progression fantasy and sci-fi fiction:

Royalroad.com/ (and its many associated Discord servers)

Facebook.com/groups/scifiandfantasybookclub

Facebook.com/groups/LitRPGGroup

Facebook.com/groups/LitRPGsociety/

Facebook.com/groups/LitRPG.books/
Facebook.com/groups/LitRPGReleases
Facebook.com/groups/349808165619256
Reddit.com/r/ProgressionFantasy/

For future books and series, please follow me on social media, or subscribe to my Patreon or infrequent newsletter.
Abbygoldsmith.com/subscribe/
Discord.gg/gDYVXdS2qz
Reddit.com/r/torth/
Patreon.com/abbygoldsmith